Settings for
BETWEEN
ETERNITIES

© A. Karl/J. Kemp 1985

Miles
Roman Miles

N

Nomentum

ROME

Tibur
HADRIAN'S VILLA

Praeneste

Tusculum

Bovillae
DOMITIAN'S VILLA
Lake Albanus

Aricia

Sanctuary of Diana
Lake Nemorensis

Lanuvium

Ardea

Antium

Fregenae

Lucius's Farm

LORIUM

Trajan's Port

SACRED ISLAND

Ostia

River Tiber

River Aro

IMPERIAL GAME PRESERVE

TYRRHENIAN SEA

Forum Appii

Ad Medias

POMPTINE MARSHES

POMPTINE SHIP CANAL

CIRCEII

Tarracina

to Formiae

AURELIA
VIA CLODIA
VIA CASSIA
VIA FLAMINIA
VIA SALARIA
VIA NOMENTANA
VIA TIBURTINA
VIA PRAENESTINA
VIA OSTIENSIS
VIA ARDEATINA
VIA LATINA
VIA APPI
VIA SEVERIANA

Between Eternities

Books by Robert H. Pilpel

CHURCHILL IN AMERICA
TO THE HONOR OF THE FLEET
BETWEEN ETERNITIES

BETWEEN ETERNITIES

Robert H. Pilpel

HARCOURT BRACE JOVANOVICH, PUBLISHERS

SAN DIEGO · NEW YORK · LONDON

Requests for permission to make copies of any part of the work should be mailed to: Permissions, Harcourt Brace Jovanovich, Publishers, Orlando, Florida 32887

Library of Congress Cataloging in Publication Data
Pilpel, Robert H.
    Between eternities.
    1. Rome—History—Empire, 30 B.C.–284 A.D.—Fiction.
2. Marcus Aurelius, Emperor of Rome, 121–180—Fiction.
I. Title.
PS3566.I514B4 1985   813'.54   85–5638
ISBN 0–15–111928–7

Designed by Francesca M. Smith
Printed in the United States of America

First edition
A B C D E

As the earth is a pinpoint in infinite space, so the life of man is a pinpoint in infinite time— a knife-edge between eternities.
—Marcus Aurelius, Meditations

Between Eternities

FROM THE
JOURNAL
of Lucius Aurelius Verus Celer

IN THE YEAR OF THE CITY 933, THE THIRD BEFORE THE NONES OF JULY
[A.D.180, JULY 5TH]

Some threescore years have passed since I emerged from the vast Indifference; I expect that less than threescore days remain before I am swallowed up again. You might think that a man in my position, a man marked for death by the Emperor, would spend his last few months lamenting, or at least trying to rationalize, his imminent extinction. I find, however, to my considerable surprise, that this is not the case with me. Instead, I devote as many daylight hours as can be spared from the needful ordering of my affairs to the delights of composing this journal; and such nighttime hours as go unclaimed by slumber I devote to contemplating . . . not the quantity of my sorrows but the quality of my consolations.

In truth, I sleep very little; my body, sensing perhaps that it need no longer maintain reserves of strength for the future, allows me to expend more energy in thought and action than I accumulate in rest. Three or four hours with Somnus now leaves me more refreshed than six or seven used to when I had years to dispose of. It seems strange that my vitality should be increasing so at this point in my life, and stranger still that I may be more fully alive than I have ever been when it comes time to open my veins. (Assuming, of course, that our First Citizen does not deny me the dignity of ending my life myself.)

There must be a moral to this paradox, for I lived in terror of death all my life—that is, until the events of recent months revealed the likely nature of my passing. This suggests that it wasn't really death I feared at all, but something death stood for in my mind.

What an odd idea!

How could something absolute, like death, stand for something ephemeral? It's like saying that winter symbolizes heavy cloaks.

And yet the evidence is clear. Before my fate was decided, I used to conceive of the world as a forest of deadly perils, any one of which might come crashing down on me as I sought to pick my way among the others. When I came to have a family, the forest grew even darker and the paths of safety much harder to discern. Without warning a fever might take from me my little Camilla, or an unfettered horse trample down my son; a bit of spoiled cheese might harbor some toxin to carry my wife away, or the coarse freedman who disputes my right to tap the spring that runs through both our properties might send a slave some night to set my house afire.

You will agree that "morbid" would serve as an apt description of the man I used to be; but I cannot say even now that my perception of the world was inaccurate. It *is*, in fact, a forest full of perils, where the slightest lapse can yield the cruelest consequences, yet the strictest vigilance cannot shield you from misfortune. Chance will determine the ease of your progress far more than wisdom or diligence, and virtue will protect you from nothing but self-contempt.

This being so, how can I account for my recent descent into vulgar equanimity? If my perception of the world hasn't changed, what has?

Perhaps it's my evaluation of what I perceive.

I remember the night at the Auriga Tavern, near Capua on the Via Appia, when Marcus and I were en route to Athens. We were joined at supper by a most unusual Jew, named Hieronymous. I say he was unusual because he was unconscionably cheerful. He asserted he was a Jew only by birth, and that his true religion was laughter. Of course Marcus pricked up his ears right away at this, and started to pepper the man with questions.

"Is there a life after death?" he asked.

"No!" said Hieronymous. "All dead people are dead; that's one way of distinguishing them from people who are merely asleep." Then he laughed.

"But what I mean," said Marcus patiently, "is, does our essence, our genius, our soul survive the body?"

"I expect you'll find out when you die."

"But I'd like to know now, without dying."

"And you'd like me to tell you?"

"If you know."

"Well, I don't."

"Oh," said Marcus.

"But I have an opinion."

"Yes?"

"My opinion is that it doesn't matter if there's a life after death."

"It doesn't *matter!*"

"No."

"But it's one of the great questions of philosophy; it bears on the meaning of life, the origin of the world, the nature of good and evil. . . ."

"I have an opinion on those issues too."

"Let me guess: they don't matter either."

"Precisely."

"But they must matter."

"Why must they?"

"Because men have always thought about them."

"Men have always thought about moving their bowels too."

"But there's no mystery about moving one's bowels."

"That's a common misconception among the unconstipated."

"But, sir, excuse me," said Marcus, "our conversation serves no purpose if you will not treat it seriously."

"Oh, there you are mistaken, my young nobleman. You are learning a great deal from me, did you but know it."

"What am I learning, sir?"

"You are learning that men who speak the same language and share the same supper may still inhabit different worlds. You are learning that there's a difference between what the world is, on the one hand, and what you make of it, on the other. You wonder about the next life because this life's not enough for you. And this life's not enough for you because you're not living it but thinking about it."

"But thinking is a part of living," Marcus responded.

"Far too large a part in your case. I advise you to try laughing the next time you feel the urge to think."

"What if there's nothing to laugh at?"

"That in itself would be funny."

"What do I do once I've finished laughing?"

"Laugh again, until the urge to think is quite smothered."

"And then?"

"Get on with your existence."

Marcus was silent for a long moment, his brow deeply furrowed. But then his face lit up with exuberance, as it always did when he got to the core of a thought. "You are obviously a very wise man," he said to Hieronymous. "But is it possible that you came by so much wisdom without thinking a very great deal?"

The Jew acknowledged the point with a respectful nod. "I will tell you how much thinking I did," he said. "In the way of my people, I used to be something of a scholar. I studied our holy books, and as a boy no older than you are I was able to debate points of Scripture with the most learned teachers in Caesarea Palaestinae, which is my native city. Now it happened one morning that the most revered of our elders inexplicably went mad. And his madness took a most terrible form. He began the day by slaughtering a pig with an ax in his own courtyard and eating of its raw hams. He then staggered through the streets in his bloody robes shouting, 'God is a fool, God is an ass, God makes love to goats,' and other such blasphemies. When he got to the synagogue, he squatted and defecated in the outer court, then picked up his ordure and carried it into where only the circumcised are permitted. There he proceeded to pelt his fellow elders with pieces of excrement, dancing up and down as he did so and chanting unspeakable curses.

"Well, most revered or not, this fellow had long since forfeited his right to go on living, and the stones were waiting for him when he finally stumbled down the synagogue's steps. But do you know what happened the instant the first stone struck him?"

"No," said Marcus, wide-eyed. "What?"

"There was an earthquake—not a big earthquake, just one very ominous tremor. . . . Everyone naturally thought God's wrath was about to be visited on the city, and in an instant the temple square was empty of everyone but the crazy old man and me. He looked at me, winked, and shambled off in the direction of the mountains. It was the last I ever saw of him—and he was my father. . . . It was then that I started to laugh."

Hieronymous was right, of course. Or say, rather, that I have always agreed with his philosophy. Regrettably, though, my agreement was confined until recently to the region of my mind; in the realm of my heart and spirit I remained, even more than Marcus, firmly of the opinion that there had to be more to life than being alive. Worse still, I resolved never to be satisfied with my existence until that something more, whatever it was, had been savored to the full. I felt, moreover, that once my great goal had been achieved I would be prepared to die. . . . And why *that* paradox never stopped me in my tracks I do not understand to this day.

I do not mean to suggest that these odd notions ever came to me in the guise of coherent thoughts; if they had, it might not have taken me so many years to discard them, insofar as I've managed to. They came to me, instead, in the form of the nagging dissatisfaction with life that afflicts those who accuse their circumstances of the crimes for which their attitudes are to blame.

There were times, however, when my wretchedness grew so acute that life as it was changed from a torment to a refuge, thus giving rise to yet another paradox. For it was only when the clamor of incessant wanting was stilled momentarily by a sense of defeat and despair that I came close to taking the world on its own terms and deriving solace from its simpler joys. It was never long, though, before I again began striving for some vague yet glorious form of fruition, leaving light, breath, and the continual change of the seasons to those incapable of higher things.

And I suppose, on reflection, that my case was not all that unusual. The secrets of life are known to everyone, after all; it's making use of them that proves so very baffling.

FROM THE JOURNAL

2

[JULY 6TH]

I dreamed about my death last night, and awoke in terror. There in the deep stillness before daybreak all my Socratic equanimity deserted me. I went to the window and stood shivering in the warm air while the eastern stars grew pale against the brightening sky. The smell of damp leaves and earth filled my nostrils, and somewhere close by two pewits called to each other, remarking on the sweetness of the morning.

The thought assailed me as I stood there that I was soon to be deprived forever of such sensuous consummations as this, and a great surge of anguish sent tears streaming from my eyes. My mind balked at the speed with which Time was marching me toward oblivion, and the cruel illusions of escape and reprieve again broke loose from the fetters of reason.

But there can *be* no escape, I admonished myself for perhaps the hundredth time, and there's no chance at all of reprieve. The most I can reasonably hope for is a quiet suicide befitting my rank—a warm bath, a few passes with a blade across my wrists, and then a slow, slow yielding to oblivion, made less sorrowful but no less terrifying by the knowledge that my loved ones will succeed to my estate. Of course, given the new Emperor's vindictive nature, I haven't much reason to suppose that such a peaceful demise will be vouchsafed me. Indeed, it wouldn't be at all out of character for him to order me crucified, or disemboweled, or even flung from the Tarpeian Rock, as was done in days of old, with all my estate rendered forfeit and my family condemned to destitution. Ah, if only I hadn't listened to that pair of senators, with all their fine words about how I alone could "avert a disaster for Rome" by making Marcus see that his sole surviving son was unfit to succeed him as emperor. Hadn't Marcus himself once warned me that the only creature more perfidious than a Greek bearing gifts is a politician appealing to your patriotism. And wouldn't even the most abject fool have thought twice before embroiling himself in the lethal business of the Imperial succession. But worse-than-abject fool that I am, I allowed myself to be persuaded. And it won't be long, I reflected as the stars gave way to dawn in the eastern sky, before my folly is cruelly punished.

Despair engulfed my senses as that thought struck home, and soon the soft fragrance and warm promise of the coming day were utterly blotted out. I found myself, eventually, back in bed, with my arms around my Portia and my lips on the nape of her neck. She slept on, beloved woman, calming me with her gentle numen and the feel and the scent of her skin.

I am more placid now, but anxious still. Why, so suddenly, did my composure disintegrate? And will it disintegrate again? Was my air of philosophical detachment merely that—a pose? Am I to spend the time remaining to me in craven prostration, my heart always pounding, my bowels never still? How loathsome, how repugnant is such a prospect! For more terrible to me by far than death is . . . living in abject fear of death.

I seem to have unearthed another paradox.

Consider: it is always the event, death, we fear; it is never the condition, being dead. And that makes perfect sense, for we were dead— or not alive, at any rate—for an eternity before our birth. Now unless this is only a quirk of language, it would seem to follow that what we really fear is the *transition* from life to life's sequel. In other words, it is the ephemeral process of dying that terrifies us, not the eternal consequences of being dead.

Why should this be so?

Not because the process of dying is painful—because the process of living is infinitely more so. And we don't fear to live—at least, not as much as we fear to die.

And not because death is the "great unknown"—because the unknown, whatever its magnitude, is neutral by definition. One cannot fear neutrality—unless, of course, it stands in one's thoughts for something different.

Perhaps it is merely that we are afraid by instinct, like deer or field mice. Perhaps our fear is merely a reflection of our passion to live.

That makes the most sense to me. For death, when I think of it, seems first and foremost an enormous confiscation, a brute arbitrary act, dispossessing me forever of the feelings, thoughts, and senses I delight in.

Yes! There, *there*, lies the source of my distraction—*I am not ready.*

I am not ready.

It seems my "vulgar equanimity" of the past few weeks may have been little more than a refusal to face the facts.

I am not ready.

The question then would seem to be, why am I not ready—or, more urgently in point, how may I attain to readiness? The answer, I suppose,

must be sought in the examples of those who *were* prepared for death—
Marcus, of course, and the men who were his models, his predecessor
Pius foremost among them. I have retrieved all his letters from their
hiding place. Here on top is the first one, the one he wrote me twenty
years ago on the occasion of Pius's death.

Lorium, March, the sixth day before the Ides
M. Aurelius Caesar to his friend Lucius Verus Celer
Greetings.

My dear Lucio,

*These are sad and hectic days for all of us here. Because our loss is a public loss
and our grief a public grief we have little time to mourn or comfort one another. Then,
too, we are still shocked by the suddenness with which death came. Though my master
was halfway through his seventy-fifth year, we had every reason to feel confident that
he would last beyond his eightieth. His mind was sharp and clear, and the day he fell
ill was without omens or portents of any kind.*

*He rose as usual before first light and rode out to check the vines, joke with his
foreman, and consult with his tenants about when to harvest the first vegetables. Returning
to the house, he worked on state business till midday, took lunch with us, had his nap,
and heard petitions till dinnertime. As the family reclined around the table he started to
tell us the new joke the foreman had told him. But, as always, he began laughing so
much in anticipation of the ending—and we with him—that the ending itself, when
he finally got to it, was something of an anticlimax. His color was as good as his
appetite, and he wolfed down a large slab of alpine cheese at the end of the meal.*

*We believe the cheese was bad. Annia and my little Lucilla had had a few nibbles
and then were sick during the night. My master, who had eaten much more, fell violently
ill and began to run a high fever. He could keep nothing down, not even clear broth,
and his fever got steadily worse. Eutychus did everything he could for him, but by
dusk on the Nones it became clear that he had no chance of recovery.*

*Ah, Lucio, I pray that my passing will be marked by half as much dignity as his.
He called me into his room, kissed me, and ordered his prefects to move the golden statue
of Fortune from his night table to my quarters. Then he bade farewell to the family,
one at a time, joking a little with each of the children as they came to kiss him good-
bye and wiping the tears from the women's eyes with his napkin. When at last all of
us were assembled, he commended the Republic to my keeping and in a weary voice
gave the tribune the watchword for the day: "Aequanimitas." Then, turning onto his
side as if to sleep, he died.*

*I must confess, dear Lucio, that my philosophy is not consoling me as I should like
it to in these sad hours. Or perhaps a more accurate statement would be that I am not
deriving as much consolation from my philosophy as I ought to. No matter how*

emphatically my mind insists that my master's passing is just another incident in the life of the world, just another circumstance from which I should draw increased strength and understanding, still my spirit persists in grieving, in regretting the loss of such a man, even in resenting the fated accident that caused his death. After all my studies, dear friend, I find that I've progressed no further than the antechambers of wisdom, and that I am hardly freer of the tyranny of the passions than when I first aspired to the Stoic creed so many fleeting years ago. ("And thank God for that!" I can hear you exclaiming.)

At least part of the problem, Lucio, is that I was unprepared for the weight of responsibility that was fastened on me two nights ago. I don't mean unprepared in the sense of untrained; few men have been as thoroughly tutored in statecraft as I. I mean unprepared in the sense of unready for, or perhaps unequal to. My friend, I do not think you can imagine what it is like suddenly to find yourself the Final Authority in the eyes of your fellow men. I can tell you in all un-Stoic candor, however, that it is an intensely disagreeable experience. It is disagreeable because one finds oneself abruptly transformed into an embodiment of the pernicious notion that such a thing as a Final Authority actually exists, apart from each individual soul. All at once I am become both the exemplar and the captive of mankind's superstitious follies; and though I have been subjected to Imperial deference for barely two days so far, I already detect in myself some stirrings of sympathy for monsters like Caligula and Nero, who broke under the strain. "For if it be true that the Prince serves as a mediator between men and the Gods, then who shall be found to serve as a mediator between the Gods and him?"

It continues to astonish me, Lucio, that I, who was groomed for the principate from puberty onward and who lived at the Emperor's side for over twenty years, should have had such a purblind conception of what it feels like to rule. Perhaps the easy grace with which my master bore his responsibilities misled me as to the weight of them. Perhaps the idea that I would be ruling jointly with Verus deluded me into thinking that my responsibilities could be shared. Now, if nothing else, my eyes are opened. The weight is indescribable, and as to my adoptive brother, you know better than I how little can be entrusted to that guileless and pleasure-loving spirit.

And so it is I, mortal Marcus, who must care for the Roman state in the unwelcome pseudo-divine guise of Imperator Caesar M. Aurelius Antoninus Augustus; and it is because I feel so lost and so ill-suited for my task that I make bold to address you after all this time, despite the pain I caused you and the scars you must still bear.

Lucio, I always flattered myself that dedication and self-discipline would be enough to sustain me in the performance of my duty. But now my duty is hard upon me, and I am trembling at its magnitude—trembling, Lucio, as I write this, and hovering close to despair. I would be ashamed of myself for this frailty if I were to yield to it. But rather than yield to it I am writing to you, because there is nothing about myself I'd be ashamed to have you know.

I need a friend, Lucio—someone who knows me yet wants nothing from me, someone

I can trust with the secret anguish of my heart. Believe me, though more than twenty years have passed since last we spoke, not a month has gone by without my gleaning news of you from one source or another, as perhaps you are aware. As to the reasons for our parting, let me say only that they were *not* what you have every reason to believe they were; and as to what they were in fact, please let me postpone my explanations until such time as we come face to face.

Lucio, I plead with you to have me in your keeping as a friend. May I rely on you to find some other mediator between yourself and the Gods? May I count on you to disregard my titles, pomp, and grandiose estate? Never for one instant over these many years have I ceased thinking of you as Lucius, peer, counselor, and companion. I ask you now to think of me as Marcus, a man in the guise of an emperor, and a man who seeks your help.

And there was my answer:

Dear Marcus,

How strange it feels to write your name down thus, strange because it is an impertinence to address the Emperor in such a fashion, and strange because it's been so long since I've addressed you, in any fashion whatever.

You urge me, Marcus, to disregard your "titles, pomp, and grandiose estate," and you ask me to be your friend.

I cannot.

In the literal sense of "I am unable to," I cannot. I cannot with any degree of natural ease pretend to familiarity with an emperor of Rome. I cannot with any degree of honesty pretend that the love I bore you as a boy of sixteen still survives after more than twenty winters of neglect. And I cannot, even with the best will in the world, pretend to you that the pain I felt, the grief and humiliation, has left me unmarked or unembittered.

None of these things can I do, because it is not within my power to change my feelings. I will tell you, though, that I *would* do these things if it *were* within my power, which means, I suppose, that I still esteem you and wish you well.

I seem to be saying that I'm prepared to be *like a friend* to you, or to try at any rate. I cannot be your friend in fact, because I am without those feelings of friendship for you that I used to have, and treasure.

I don't know if this meager portion I offer will be enough to sustain you in the midst of your great responsibilities. As a citizen, and as one who has never ceased to hold you in high regard, I wish I could offer more. You may rest assured, however, that I, as you say, want nothing from you. I shall keep both the fact and the content of our correspondence in the strictest confidence. If you wish to communicate with me further on such a basis, you may be confident of my sympathetic attention and readiness to reply.

I hail you and pray you find favor in Fortune's eyes.

And there was Marcus's hastily scrawled response:

My dear Lucio,

I feared your indifference; I welcome your anger. Only a friend could have written so honestly.

Marcus

FROM THE
JOURNAL

3

[JULY 7TH]

The terror came over me again last night, so much so that sometime during the third watch I broke into noisy sobs, awakening my Portia. She wept with me a while, and we kissed each other's tears. Then grief gave way to a sweeter passion, and I hungrily consumed her gentle offering of breasts and lips and thighs. Though sixty years of age, I am far from surfeited. That, in fact, would seem to be my problem.

Old Pius turns over and dies without a murmur, yet Marcus describes his undiminished appetite for life. *There* is a paradox to conjure with. To love life yet relinquish it without objection; how is that possible? *How?* I want to shout up at the sky. If only I could find the answer, I could break free of my fear. And, I say again, it is my fear I wish to banish, not my death.

Being unable to banish either, however, I had no wish to stay in bed and grapple with them. The sea has always exerted a calming effect upon my spirit, so, despite the hour, Portia and I harnessed a mule to the cart and set out for Fregenae, with the moon in its final quarter lighting our way. As we rode I pondered: is it not an injustice that those who are happiest with life are also easiest with death? If one's existence is rife with troubles, ought not one's passing be smooth to compensate? But logic is against the proposition, for it stands to reason that those who always want more from life than they're getting will also be the stingiest about yielding what they have.

The worst of it, of course, is that the wanting persists in the face of every gratification. Give a wanter what he wants and he will soon want something different; you can satisfy his desires but not his desiring. I speak from experience. As a boy I set very specific goals for myself, goals that seemed well-nigh impossible of realization. When, to my amazement, I achieved those goals in manhood, I found them somewhat pallid without their former luster of unattainability. If, then, death stands for something in my mind, does it stand, in fact, for my final failure to achieve the unattainable? And if it does, what then does the unattainable stand for? Have I wanted something all my life without knowing what it is? Would

I want it so much if I knew what it was? Would never attaining it—or death—be so frightening if I knew?

Unanswerable nonsensical questions, all of them. And still my fear abides.

But riding a cart of a summer's night with the moon for a lamp and your dear one beside you should satisfy a multitude of wants. And if allaying your fear is one of them, a cart ride may even do that, to an extent.

Where the track from our farm meets the river road, we turned left. The red eye of the Scorpion shone like a beacon in the sky above our destination, some three miles to the southwest. From the Aro came the rank smell of moisture and decay, the sound of crickets and frogs luxuriating in the bog of the riverbank. As we drew near the Via Aurelia we could see the lights in the Nereid Tavern and the builders' wagons outside, laden with marble and limestone. I halted the mule several hundred paces from the intersection and went to the roadside to ease my bladder. With relief attained, I resumed my seat next to Portia, but as I reached for the whip she stayed my hand and pointed across the river. In the fields off to our left, but oblivious of our presence, a slave boy, naked but for his iron collar, was chasing a naked girl whose budding breasts had barely grown large enough to define her sex. Neither he nor she could have been much older than thirteen.

Although impeded by his achingly rigid member, the boy gained on, lunged at, and brought down his prey, and they crashed to the earth together in a ferment of squeals and laughter. There was some scuffling, the sound of whispers, and then a silence as the boy stretched out on his back. Seizing his shaft with her fingers, the girl slowly took her captor into her mouth, thereby extracting a spasm of wild moans from his. After a short interval he rose violently, pushed her head away, and threw himself on top of her. She moaned as well, louder and clearer than he. In moments the flood tide of her release broke loose upon her, and she proclaimed it with a shriek that rent the moonlit air. I could see the wagon horses grazing behind the tavern raise their heads with a start, but in the fragrant darkness by the riverside all was now peaceful and still.

Portia and I watched the two children as they lay with limbs entwined amid the grass and wildflowers. We neither moved nor spoke, in part because we feared to distress them by revealing they'd been observed, and in part, I must acknowledge, because neither of us was absolutely confident that it wasn't Faunus and Egeria we had spied upon. Their coupling had seemed so feral and Dionysian there beneath the gleaming of the moon that we wouldn't have been too surprised to see the slave boy and tavern girl suddenly take wing and dart off like fireflies, turning both of us to stone as they departed, in punishment for impiety.

Fortunately, the two field sprites merely stood up after a while, and with giggles and teasings chased each other back in the direction of the tavern. Portia and I smiled at one another, perhaps envying the children for the vitality of their appetites, but in greater part savoring the sustained intensity of our own intimate communion, so recently reconsecrated in our bed.

Even with an hour or two remaining before first light, the Aurelia was thronged with heavy standard-gauge wagons heading for the City, with gravel from the pits outside Alsium, tufa from the hills above Caere, and limestone from the quarries near Centumcellae. The smell of bread baking in the Nereid's three large ovens drifted over the crossroads and mingled there with the sound of drovers shouting curses at their teams and greetings to each other.

Ever since that magical first journey with Marcus I have relished the life of the roads. And for me nothing better exemplifies that life than the nightlong hubbub around the great *mansio*-taverns on the main highways leading out of the City. It is there, and not at the City gates, that all journeys really begin; for it is there, for all practical purposes, that the City ends. Until you reach the first *mansiones*, you remain within the City's orbit: tombs block your view of the countryside every few paces, and houses or workshops rise up between the tombs. The people along the roadside all speak the City dialect and preen themselves on being "Romans," as though they dwelt on the Esquiline instead of in squalid little Seven Baths, dusty Tellenae, or sleepy Eretum. Only after the *mansiones* do the vistas widen and the genii of empty spaces emerge from hiding. I can do no more than remember them, however, because to travel beyond the *mansiones* is forbidden to men in my particular situation.

Two miles beyond the crossroads we entered the sleeping town of Fregenae. Behind us the first hints of light were fringing the slopes of the Apennines, and ahead of us, heralded by the scent of tangy dankness, lay the sea.

Another mile's travel brought us within sight of the coastline. Far to the south the beacon at Trajan's port glimmered like the morning star; far to the north the lighthouse at Alsium gave off a fading glow. Before us the dark plains of the sea stretched out in the direction of Corsica, and above the expanse of sand where our cart and mule were standing, snipes and sea doves wheeled and jinked in anticipation of their morning meal.

I took in a deep breath and held it, tasting the salt and the wetness in the air. Slowly exhaling, I cast my eyes up and down the beach, relishing the isolation and that fatuous sense of dominion that piques men's self-conceit in empty places.

But this place was not altogether empty. In the rapidly gaining light I was able to discern a strange-looking tent about a quarter mile to the north of us along the strand. It was square, with an orange top, and its sides were painted in alternating vertical stripes of faded yellow and blue.

I glanced at Portia, then flicked the whip across our old mule's haunches. When we were within twenty paces I halted the cart and jumped down. Slowly I made my way to the side of the tent facing the sea, where a flap was pulled back a short way to reveal a dark interior. The upper limb of the sun flashed over the mountain slopes at that moment, and a breeze came up as if summoned by an incantation.

I stood there for a long while, hobbled by indecision. An interrogative shrug in Portia's direction elicited only an endearing smile and another shrug in reply. We could have turned and left, of course, but curiosity was now at war with prudence and common sense. Had there been anything at all outside the tent, a team of horses, a train of baggage, I could have made inferences about what was within. But there was nothing—no people, no oxen, no horses, no baggage in any direction at any distance. All I could see around me was sand, sun, sky, sea, mountains . . . and tent. Finally, perhaps made reckless by the fate that lies just ahead, I gave in to my compulsion and summoned up the nerve to pull aside the open flap.

The floor of the tent was covered with thick carpets of intricate design, and asleep on the carpets was a very old man with long white hair and whiskers. He was dressed in heavy multicolored robes and appeared, in the meager light, to be smiling broadly.

His eyes opened wide without warning as I stood watching him, and in a perfectly casual voice he said, "Good day to you, sir."

"Good day to *you*," I managed to respond.

"If you're a robber, you can have all there is here, even my clothes. I would beseech you, however, to wait a few hours until I finish."

"I'm not a robber, old fellow, I assure you. . . . Until you finish what?"

"Dying."

"*Dying?*"

"Yes."

"Here?"

"Yes."

"Like this? All alone?"

"Is there an alternative?"

I decided to try a different tack. "May I ask your name?" I said.

He pondered for a time, looking intently at my face. "I'd rather not give my name at the moment, if you don't mind," he said.

"May I ask why you'd rather not?"

"Because I think I know you, but I can't remember if I want to."

This, as might be expected, prompted a pause in the conversation.

"You think you *may* know me . . ." I said finally, half amused and half nettled.

"Yes."

". . . but you can't remember if you *want* to know me, is that right?"

"That's substantially correct. I mean that, until I can place you exactly in my memory, I can't be at all sure that our prior association was a pleasant one and, therefore, worth renewing."

"I see," I said, nettlement giving way to amusement. "But wouldn't it be more sensible to find out if our *present* association proves a pleasant one and proceed on that basis. I might have been in a bad temper when you knew me before, after all, not quite myself."

"That's a point, I'll admit," the old man responded. "And you do seem a nice enough sort of fellow, so far. . . . Still, I'd rather not give you my name just yet anyway. There's always the possibility that *you* might not have liked *me*, you know. And when people don't like me, they don't like me a lot."

At this I had to laugh aloud. "I can't imagine anyone not liking you, even a little."

The old man nodded deferentially. "Well, it's gracious of you to say so. But, if you'll forgive my impertinence, I can't assume that a man of your age has the same likes and dislikes that he always had, now can I?"

"No," I answered, smiling, "I don't suppose you can. . . . But given that you find me a nice enough sort of fellow . . ."

"So far."

"To be sure: so far. And given that I can't imagine anyone not liking you, wouldn't it make sense for us to be friends provisionally, and then see how things develop from there?"

"Well," the old man muttered glumly, "I *was* in the process of dying, you know."

"But you look perfectly fit."

"I *am* perfectly fit," he said with a trace of pride. "I have the constitution of an ox."

"Then how could you be dying?"

"Why, voluntarily, of course."

"Voluntarily? You mean you're in the process of committing suicide?"

"Of course not," he snapped. "Suicide is for people who are unhappy."

"Or condemned," I added.

"Condemned people are a subcategory of unhappy people. I am not unhappy."

"Nor, self-evidently, are you unhealthy. Yet still you claim that you are dying."

"I'm not dying any more; you interrupted me."

"Oh. I beg your pardon."

"Well, I suppose you meant no harm."

"Exactly. It's just that I was . . ."

"Lucio!" Portia's anxious voice rang sharply from outside.

I went to the tent flap and poked my head out. "It's all right, dear," I called to her, and she waved to me with an expression of relief.

"You have a woman here?" the old man asked with marked interest.

"My wife."

"Ahh," he breathed. "Is she—forgive my asking—*old*, like you?"

"Why no," I replied, somewhat taken aback. "She's thirty-eight."

The old man smiled broadly. "Then I should very much like to meet her."

"Shall I have her come in here?"

He thought a while. "No . . . no. I'll go to her."

"Why not come as a guest to our house?" I asked impulsively. "You can die there just as easily as here, can't you?"

Again the old man thought. "Thank you," he said at last. "I would like to be your guest; your wife has a lovely voice."

I wasn't sure I fully understood the connection between my invitation and Portia's voice, but I was glad the old man had accepted. I found him a very singular fellow, all things considered. He aroused my curiosity, and my affection.

I introduced him to Portia and loaded his carpets onto our cart while she conversed with him, unaccountably, on the subject of the drying effect of sun and wind on the skin. In all my years I can't remember having ever discussed such a subject with someone I'd only just met. Portia and the old man, by contrast, seemed deeply absorbed in it, almost as if they'd known each other so long that there was no need to exchange personal information.

"What about the tent?" I asked, once the carpets were loaded.

"Leave it here," the old man replied. "Let it be my monument."

"Rather impermanent for a monument, isn't it?" I said.

"An impermanent symbol of an impermanent existence seems altogether appropriate," he responded, and resumed his discussion with Portia on the lubricant virtues of nard.

"Forgive me for interrupting . . ." I said after almost an hour.

Portia and the old man, who was lying on his carpets behind her, turned to look at me as if they were surprised to find me traveling with them. "Yes, yes," the old fellow said irritably, "you're impatient to ask about my dying. I know."

He was right, damn him.

"Dying!" Portia said in a stricken voice.

"There, there, my dear," the old man soothed. "I was giving some thought to dying when your husband discovered me, but I was clearly mistaken in my belief that the time had come, and I'm definitely not dying now."

Portia looked at him, then at me, in puzzlement.

"He said he was dying 'voluntarily,' " I attempted to explain, "which doesn't mean that he was planning suicide, he said."

"But *why?*" Portia asked, greatly chagrined, and I could have kicked myself for provoking the issue without a moment's thought for her feelings.

"Because it seemed to be time," the old man said. "My life had all been lived, or so I thought, at least."

"But you don't think so any longer, I hope."

"No, my dear lady. I don't think so any longer."

"What led you to change your mind?"

"Why, meeting you, my dear."

"As little as that?"

"Your modesty only magnifies your beauty."

I glanced over to see Portia look down at her lap and blush. "A-*hem!*" I coughed, beginning to feel like a crotchety Menelaus watching a wizened Paris seduce a matronly Helen in some gerontological version of the *Iliad.* "If I might intrude myself for a moment into this touching courtship . . ."

"Oh, *Lucio!*" Portia exclaimed impatiently.

"Don't mind him, dear lady, he's just . . ."

"Don't mind *me!*" I burst out, feeling my temper start to build. "Whose cart is this anyway?"

At this the old man began to laugh, or, more precisely, to ascend into laughter. His ascent began with what sounded like a cough, which gave way, first, to a wheezy form of chortle and then rose steadily from a phlegmy cackle, to a stertorous yawp, to a final glorious explosion of guffaws that soon had Portia and me guffawing helplessly along with him.

"Whose cart *is* this anyway?" he asked through his laughter, causing the three of us to hold our sides in merriment.

"Whose *cart* is this; that's the real question," I gasped out, and we rocked back and forth some more.

I am still at something of a loss to understand the reasons for our hilarity. I'm aware, of course, of how silly my jealousy must have seemed, and how ludicrous my sudden assertion of proprietary right. But I haven't laughed that hard and that long since I was a boy, and given my situation this hardly seems a sensible time to resume the practice.

It did give me a great deal of pleasure though; it made my heart feel lighter.

The old man had the temerity to tell us—once we stopped laughing— that lifting my spirits had been precisely his intention, and he added, before I could dispute him, that the real reason he'd decided not to die was that he knew I needed his help.

Portia and I exchanged a glance, and for a short while I brooded over the old man's latest riddle. When I turned around to ask him to explain himself, however, I found he had fallen asleep.

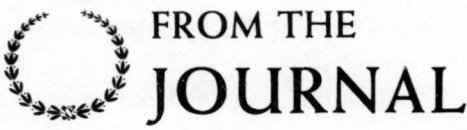# FROM THE
JOURNAL

4

[JULY 8TH]

Last night was most unusual. The old man had slept through the day; in fact, Rullo, Myron, and I had had to unload his snoring bulk from the cart as if he were a sack of turnips. We deposited him on a couch in one of the dayrooms facing the courtyard, and there he had slumbered till evening, with that vaguely insufferable smile of his on his lips.

I, too, gave in to sleep in the afternoon, but I was up after less than an hour, restless and impatient. I looked in on the old man, hoping to resume our conversation the instant he awoke; but his heavy susurrations indicated that that instant would be some time in coming. So with a bad grace I went out to my table in the garden and tried to make the time pass by writing in this journal.

It was one of those crushingly hot summer afternoons when the air clings to one's body like warm syrup, even in the shade. I wrote for a while but then sat stolidly at the table, noting the beads of sweat on my forearms and the utter stillness in the house, the stables, the pastures, and the fields beyond. The whole world, it seemed, had been bludgeoned into submission by the imperious sun; and the rasp of the cicadas had almost a plaintive tone to it, as if even the insects were feeling oppressed.

Though far from cool, my corner of the garden afforded a touch of refuge. The umbral pines behind me stood as a shield against the glare, and the scent of their dry needles filled the air with a tangy sweetness that tempered the heat. A slender column of water spurted from the small fountain in the fishpond, rising a foot or two toward the sky and then crumbling into multiple liquid pebbles of bluish gray that tumbled toward the fountain's mossy base and shattered there into spray. Just so, I thought, is the span of human life: we are shot out into the light of day and begin falling toward our dissolution even as we are still taking form. Our entire existence we are falling, and the farther we've fallen, the faster we fall, until, after a laughably few moments, we are back again in the pool of elementary substance from which we originally emerged.

One problem with having death constantly before you, I've discovered, is that you find the world teeming with bad metaphors.

Prometheus ambled into the garden from the house, paused, and sniffed

left

up at the sun, as though gauging the heat with his nostrils. It looked like Camilla had recently brushed him, for his orange coat had a creamy sheen to it, and he was carrying himself like Vanity incarnate. He surveyed the garden, noted my presence with apparent indifference, licked his chops, and started strutting casually in my direction. Halfway along he stopped to yawn, stretching out his front paws, curling his tongue, and straining the hinges of his jawbone to the very limit. It was a magnificent yawn, I had to admit, and I nodded my admiration as he continued toward me. He stopped one last time a couple of feet away and with a few emphatic strokes of his tongue smoothed a tuft of fur near his right shoulder that was not lying precisely the way he wanted it to. Then he resumed his progress, circled the chair where I was sitting, lay down on my right foot, and went to sleep.

I couldn't help reflecting on how much fuller human lives would be if people invested their more mundane errands and actions with the dramatic grandiloquence so typical of cats. Of course cats, it's said, don't know that they're going to die; they don't understand, in other words, that all they so foolishly relish is all they are going to get.

I turned again to my journal, reliving with my pen the unusual events of that morning and puzzling some more over the many conundrums the old man had disgorged. When I next looked up, I saw my daughter seated by the fountain, elbows on knees, chin in hands, eyes on me.

"Madam?" I said with mock solemnity.

She smiled.

Love, I believe, can be a truly terrible thing. Not normal love, the sort I have for my wife and son, but mad love, giddy love, obliterating love, such as Portia Camilla Aelia inspires in me. I sometimes think she's a sorceress, all nine chubby years of her. I remember the first time I held her; she was six hours old. They say that babies don't really see at first, that the external world is only a blur. But my daughter looked into my eyes when I held her, and her face said: For all these years you've belonged to yourself, but now, oh, now, you are mine.

I suppose one can read almost anything one cares to in the eyes of a newborn babe. But that expression of Camilla's, that wry, knowing, playful expression, has been visible on her face often throughout her life, was visible as she gazed at me from the fountain's base.

"Do you want to keep on writing?" she asked.

"Not if the alternative is talking to you."

Her smile broadened; she is susceptible to flattery.

"You've been writing a lot the past few days."

My breath caught in my throat. "Have I?"

"Yes. And you've been very quiet."

"How do you mean?" I asked, knowing perfectly well what she was referring to.

"I'm not certain. It's just that you don't tease me or play with me as much. Are you angry with me?"

The question landed like a sharp slap in the face, and tears sprang to my eyes. Angry with her? Oh, Jove!

"Father?"

But I couldn't speak. I looked at her: brown hair with brown bangs, brown eyes, smooth skin baked richly brown by the sun, plump cheeks, child's mouth, soldier's heart.

Was I angry with her!

Struggling to recover, I rasped out, "No, darling. No, of course not."

She looked at me quizzically, with a hint of mistrust. "Something's wrong," she said, "and you're not telling me."

Sometimes, I've heard it said, kindness can be cruelty, and other times it's vice versa. Which times are which always goes unspecified, and up to that moment I hadn't really dealt with the issue of when or how to tell my children the facts. Telling Portia had been easy, if for no other reason than that our intimacy rendered concealment impossible. But telling Decius and Camilla—that seemed harder, much harder. That seemed like dying a little while I still had time to live.

But then, so did lying outright to someone I love.

"Will you be brave?" I asked her.

It was all I needed to say. After a moment's confusion came a flash of comprehension. Then tears welled up in her eyes and she ran to me, flinging herself into my arms with such violence as to dislodge Prometheus, who stalked off in disgust.

I rocked my daughter slowly back and forth as she sobbed her anguish into my chest, and I felt vaguely peaceful, as if by telling her I had admitted something to myself.

As I held her and felt her grief, I noticed that the white glare of the afternoon light had begun to mellow toward the orange of evening, and that the sweltering stillness of siesta time was giving way to the sounds of people at work in the house and the fields.

Camilla's sobs gradually subsided, and we were content to hold each other in silence as the sun grudgingly banked its fires. Gentle portents of approaching dusk brushed against my senses: soft fragrances and delicate eddies in the air, the murmur of a breeze in the pine boughs. I felt that sense of coming into harbor, that quiet glow of rest earned after strife with which nature compensates us for her long breathless hours of incinerating heat. With my daughter in my arms my heart felt full, and with a spirit cleansed of most misgivings I gave myself up to the long sweetness of the summer evening.

We sat for an hour or more, until Venus appeared a hand's width above the horizon. So far had the old man slipped from my thoughts that I was almost startled when he strolled into the garden.

"I've been looking around your house," he said without a greeting or other preamble. "I confess that I'm favorably impressed."

"I hope you slept well," I replied, thinking to match him non sequitur for non sequitur.

"What? Slept? Oh, this afternoon, you mean. Yes, yes, I slept perfectly. I always sleep perfectly. But I've been up for hours."

He peered at me through the gloaming and seated himself on the stone rim of the fishpond. "I see you have company," he said.

"My daughter."

"I inferred as much. She appears to have been crying."

I looked at Camilla's face, and there indeed, running through the patina of dust and dried sweat, were the tracks of her tears.

"You're thinking that I have excellent eyesight for someone my age. And you're right; I have remarkably good vision. What's your name, my child?"

"Camilla. What's yours?"

"Call me Nestor for the time being, though I'm a good deal older than he was, of course. . . . Your father, I think, has just told you some news."

"How do you *know* all these things without being told them?" I cut in. "Are you some kind of magician?"

The old man laughed. "Me, a magician? Far from it. No; simple inference is the secret of my knowledge. I am a master of inference."

"Well, you're incredibly good at it, I must say."

"What's inference?" Camilla asked me.

"Inference," the old man responded, cutting my answer off, "is the power to see meanings in actions, in words, in conditions. It is the ability to relate facts to knowledge, to understand the language of the world one perceives."

"How did you become a master?" she inquired of him.

"First, by desiring to become one; second, by intense application and concentration; third, by living a long, long time without having my mind go mushy; and last, by abolishing fear."

"Why did you have to abolish fear?"

"Because fear, my dear child, is the enemy of inference. Fear clouds perception, distorts reason, and averts your eyes from truth. Fear is in league with death."

"But many men fear death," I offered, "and fearing it, shun it, as they would a noxious smell."

"Don't be thickheaded," the old man snapped. "I said fear is in league with death, but I could as easily have expressed the same thought by saying that death is what men fear. Fear and death go together. Fear *is* the act of shunning, of denying, of refusing to look at what is. The only way to shun death is to live without shunning it, or anything else, for that matter—to shun fear, in other words."

"That's easier said than done," I countered.

"It can be done easily enough," he responded, "but only if you find life more interesting."

"Than *fear?*" I asked incredulously.

"Than fear," he confirmed.

"But of course I find life more interesting."

"Oh? Then why are you living in fear?"

"What makes you think that I am?"

"Inference, my dear fellow. Inference."

"*Are* you afraid, Father?" Camilla asked me.

I hesitated a long while with my answer, noting that even old "Nestor" was silent in anticipation.

"Yes," I said finally.

Camilla reached up, kissed my cheek, and tightened her arms around my neck. "Poor Papa," she said with tears in her voice.

"So, young lady," old Nestor intruded, "what shall we do to help your father?"

Camilla looked at him blankly. "What *can* we do?"

"Why, free him of his fear."

"How?"

"Ah," the old man sighed, "now there's the crucial question."

"Yes, how?" I chimed in. "You've been awfully glib about yourself and your wonderful eyesight and perfect health and blissful sleeping habits; perhaps it's time you revealed some of the secrets of all your unparalleled . . . complacency."

Nestor shook his head sadly. "You're angry because you think I'm a mountebank, a Chaldaean. You truly believe that your death is a calamity and that nothing anyone can say will reconcile you to its coming."

"Never mind what I believe," I snarled at him. "Answer my daughter's question. *How* will you free me of my fear?"

Nestor sat in silence, with the first of the eastern stars blinking faintly in the violet sky above his shoulders. "You are afraid," he said at last, "because you do not understand the role your death plays in your existence. You do not understand how your death fits into your life. You think your death is the *end* of your life, when it is, in fact, merely a *part* of your life."

"I already know what I think," I said sullenly, and Camilla gave me a troubled look, as if to say, Perhaps you should *listen*, Father. But I went on talking. "You still haven't told us *how*, old fellow. You still haven't imparted your magic formula."

The old man grunted. "I did, in effect, tell you how."

I looked at him. "Sorry. You've lost me."

"I told you that you don't understand how your death fits into your life, and that the lack of such understanding is at the root of your fear. It follows, accordingly, that the way to free yourself of fear is to seek to understand your life and the role your death should play in it."

"Which again leaves us with the question of *how* I should go about understanding it."

The old man smiled broadly. "Ah, now, *there* is where I believe I can be of some help."

"Good. Please go ahead and try to be."

"It doesn't help matters to be surly, you know."

"I apologize. It's just that I'm impatient to have your assistance."

"You're impatient to demonstrate that my assistance is worthless. You're so awed by your death that it offends you to have anyone speak of it without due sorrowful solemnity."

He had me there, the old demon. "Look, I'm sorry," I said without much conviction.

"You're not sorry; you're merely scared," he responded in a tone of judicial severity.

And I couldn't answer him; I was afraid I would give way to tears.

There was silence, except for the swelling chorus of frogs and crickets all around us in the dark. Portia and Decius appeared bearing lamps, fruit, wine, and some bread, which they set down on the table near the kitchen door. Portia mixed wine and water in two bowls, gave one to the old man, the other to me. "Will you eat something, my husband?" she asked softly, noting the tension in the air.

I shook my head.

"Camilla, please offer our guest some meat and fruit."

My daughter dutifully climbed off my lap. "Yes, Mother," she said, and went to the table.

"Decius, fix a plate for your father, in case he changes his mind."

"Yes, Mother," Decius responded, and in his slow, lumbering, good-natured way he complied with her instructions, reminding me of nothing so much as one of those sad-eyed Ligurian retrievers at a comparable stage of adolescence, when the legs and feet seem far too large for the body. . . . There were, I noted, tear tracks on his face as well.

I sipped my wine and the old man chewed on some dates while my family watched us with uneasy eyes, as if we were two gladiators girding for a bout.

"It seems your whole family is now aware of your fate," the old man said.

I glanced at Portia, and she nodded gravely. "The boy asked where we'd gone this morning, and why. I didn't think to lie to him."

Decius, mute and miserable, stood beside her, tears brimming in his eyes. "Come stand by your father," I said to him, at the same time extending my hand to Camilla, who resumed her place in my lap. "I told our daughter this afternoon."

"I know," Portia replied. "I heard her crying."

And again, for some time, there was silence.

"Well," I said finally, "I believe we were talking about the fact that I'm scared. . . ."

The old man lifted his head, then gave a conciliatory smile. "In a sense we were, yes. But I was going to suggest an antidote for your fear."

"Yes?"

"I was going to suggest that you write your own biography."

"*What?*"

"Don't rear up like that. I'm in earnest."

"I believe you. That's what worries me."

"I don't see why it should. You're a great scribbler, after all. Perhaps a fourth of the bins in your library contain scrolls in your own hand. And, in any case, you're keeping a journal. Does changing a diary to an autobiography seem so momentous a task?"

"But what would be the purpose?"

"Why, to defeat your fear, of course. Haven't I already told you that you are afraid because you don't understand how your death bears on your life. Well, relive your life in written words. I will read what you write each day, and together we'll try to understand your past."

I said nothing for a long time, but finally murmured, "I'm sorry; I don't see how it could do any good."

The old man leaned forward and looked sternly into my eyes. "You have some time left," he said. "You can pass that time in fear, or in striving to conquer fear. You are one of the fortunate minority with the leisure, the intellect, and the means to make the last days of your life both meaningful and fine. True, you may lose in your contest with fear; the possibility of failure hovers over every effort we make in life. But no defeat, no matter how crushing, can negate the value of an honest effort. So seize this hope, man, though in your eyes it appears so forlorn. Live the end of your life as you wish you had lived all the rest of it. Let the last things you do be done well."

I looked at the old man, at my wife, at my son and my daughter, at the star-flecked sky.

Now, with the night hours past, I am back at my table in the garden with a blank scroll before me and a reed dipped in freshly mixed ink. My hand shakes a little, but apart from that I am ready to begin. And so I write:

"I was born in the Ninth District of the Sixth Ward of Rome in February, sometime around the Ides, in the year of the City eight hundred and seventy-three. . . ."

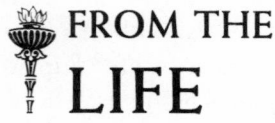 FROM THE
LIFE

5

of Lucius Aurelius Verus Celer

. . . and the most interesting question raised by that datum is: So what?

Ah, Lucio, you don't seem altogether reconciled to the concept of an autobiography.

Which in itself is rather interesting.

But also digressive.

I begin to suspect that my life is not going to allow itself to be written without a violent struggle.

Very well then: me against my life, no holds barred. With Nestor as referee.

Let's see now; I'll begin with a tactical diversion, flatter my life into dropping its guard. To wit:

The Life of the Knight Lucius Aurelius Verus Celer, Priest of the Divine Antoninus, High Priest of the Sacred Athletic Synod of Hercules, Archon of the Xystos, Overseer of the Imperial Baths; citizen of Alexandria, Athens, Elis, Pergamum, and Smyrna; Member of the Council of Antinoë, Ephesus, Hermopolis, Nicomedea, Puteoli, and Sparta; Periodonikes; twice victor in the long foot race at Olympia, thrice victor at Delphi, victor at the Isthmian Games, four times victor at Nemea, twice victor in the Actian Games, victor at Smyrna, Pergamum, Ephesus, Alexandria, Antioch, Tralles, Sardis, Laodicea, Argos, Rome, and many other places.

Well!

Achilles himself, sulking in the underworld, must envy such achievements as mine. But what I haven't mentioned—what's never mentioned in such self-congratulatory curricula vitae—is all those races in which I finished second, or third, or last, or not at all; all those occasions when I said or did something stupid, thereby causing pain to people I love; all the mistakes I made, and repeated, and repeated once more; all the short-sightedly selfish decisions I repented of a little too late . . . all my failures, in short. These you won't find mentioned among my honors or chiseled upon my tomb. These the world will readily forget, or has happily forgotten already. These I have no wish to remember. . . .

And now I know why I'm not altogether reconciled to the concept of an autobiography—I'm not altogether proud of my life.

But neither am I altogether ashamed of it.

I'm just embarrassed by much of it . . . beginning with my birth
. . . which occurred, as I said, *sometime* around the Ides of February sixty
years ago. The fact that I can't point to a specific day as the beginning
of my life constitutes the first source of my embarrassment; the fact that
I can't point to a specific man as the author of my conception constitutes
the second. The reason I lack precise information on these matters—I've
gone this far, I may as well set down the whole squalid story—is that
my mother was, in effect, a whore. She also drank heavily. She was drunk
when I was born, in fact; indeed, she had been drunk for several days
and continued to be drunk for several days more, even as she suckled
me. She had been invited—or commissioned, more accurately—to serve
as one of the amenities at, ironically enough, the coming-of-age birthday
party of one Gaius Aemilius Placidus. Gaius was the only son of Aulus
Aemilius Placidus, an immensely wealthy, inveterately jovial libertine,
who thought the best way to celebrate his son's assumption of the toga
virilis at age fourteen would be to provide him with five days of unrestricted sexual license. Because the boy's birthday fell on February fifteenth, the Lupercalia, Aulus determined to extend the festivities from
the thirteenth, Juppiter's feast, through the seventeenth, the Quirinalia.
He invited all his friends and all the sons of his friends who'd attained
to the age of manhood. The more respectable among the guests arrived
and departed in less than an hour. The more, shall I say, gregarious
among them were still there six days later.

What Aulus had done was collect every conceivable type of sexual
partner his son might enjoy, and then see to it that the boy participated
in some kind of sexual act with each one of them. The only rule he laid
down was that none of the guests could touch any of the "birthday
presents" until Gaius had tried them out himself. This naturally resulted
in Aulus's friends giving all sorts of encouragement to Gaius as he worked
his way through the throng his father had assembled for him.

And what a throng it was! You can say what you like about Aulus's
morals, but his imagination was equal to his appetites. There was a giantess
and a dwarf, a little boy and a little girl, a slender Negress from Nubia
and a dark-skinned virgin from India. There was a blonde German and
an almond-eyed Egyptian hetaera, an enormously fat Gaul and an emaciated Greek, a powdered old crone of seventy and a dewy young lad of
seventeen. There was a one-legged bawd from Sicily, a bearded slattern
from Sarmatia, and a willowy albino from Mauretania. There was a Belgic
woman with three breasts, and an apparition from Bithynia—twin sisters
joined at the hip. There was a bald woman and a deaf mute, a clubfoot

and a harelip, a hermaphrodite, a nursing mother, and a woman nine months pregnant—with me, all oblivious, inside her.

Fortunately, or unfortunately, my mother caught Gaius's eye while the revels were still in their early stages, and it was arranged that she should sit astride him while he drank from the breasts of the woman who'd recently given birth. To give my mother her licentious due, she always took a certain pride in her work. She was fond of boasting to me, in fact, that while impaled atop young Gaius she had given an exceptionally good account of herself, her gravid condition notwithstanding. Her exertions brought on her birth pangs, however, which Aulus deemed an excellent omen for her about-to-be-born baby. I have had little faith in omens ever since.

Anyway, sometime between the thirteenth and the seventeenth of February I pushed my way through the residue of Gaius's semen and spilled out into the world. Aulus was delighted by my arrival and gave my mother one gold aureus in trust for me and two to spend on herself. In other words, he gave her three hundred sesterces for entertaining just one customer, which was over fifty times what she normally charged He also offered to serve as my patron, should I ever be in need of one. But thanks to Marcus I never was.

I've always had mixed feelings about my mother. She was cheerful enough most of the time, which may have been due more to wine than to temperament. But she was never very interested in me. It wasn't that she was antagonistic, or even indifferent. It was simply that she couldn't be bothered to look after me; it diverted too much time and energy from drinking and copulation. So the task of caring for me fell, more or less by default, to my aunt Drusilla.

Drusilla, for me, will always be the ideal of female beauty. Not because she was ravishingly pretty; she wasn't. But because she combined a comely face and figure with a spirit that was fiery and indomitable. She knocked me around as roughly as anyone I've known. Even now I can recall how my ears smarted when she boxed them. But, dear gods, how I adored her. Her hair was chestnut brown and hung straight as a plumb line. Her eyes were dark, almost black, with long lashes and full parabolic brows. Her mouth was small and far too delicate in appearance to account for the rank obscenities that regularly issued from it. Her nose was straight and sharply pointed, and her body—oh, my soul!—her body was a study in contoured softness. I think I was in love with her from the time I learned how to walk, and if there was one person who for good or ill shaped me more than any other, it was unquestionably she.

Drusilla was married to Glaubus, a retired centurion, who owned and ran a cookshop-bar called the Hobnail on the ground floor of a four-story tenement situated beside the Sanqualis Gate, at the foot of the Quirinal Hill. Officially our building was part of the Ninth District of the Sixth Ward, Alta Semita, and as might be deduced from the modest number of floors, it dated back almost to the time of the deified Augustus. It was owned by a freedman, Lentulus Rutolo, who was an excellent though somewhat finicky landlord. He took loving care of his tenement, which was all he owned in the world, and the rent he charged fell slightly short of outright extortion, which by Roman standards was altruistically low. Our hallways were easily the cleanest in Latium, perhaps in all Italy, and broken shutters or loose door latches were repaired almost before you noticed they needed work. The one disadvantage of Rutolo's conscientiousness was that you could not lead a normal life in your own apartment without a constant struggle. If you closed your shutters against the sun on a hot afternoon, for example, Rutolo would soon be at your door to complain about dampness accumulating in the walls. If you kept your cooking fire going after nightfall, he would appear to make sure that you hadn't fallen asleep and left it untended. If you asked a friend to visit, you could count on him to knock on your door on some pretext or other and subject your guest to the fiercest possible scrutiny—not out of curiosity, which would have been natural enough, and tolerable, but out of an urgent need to make sure that your visitor wasn't a rowdy of some sort who might urinate in the hallway or steal the straw matting off the stairs.

Now admittedly I've never been a slave and I've never owned a building, so I'm really not qualified to pass judgment on Rutolo's behavior. But I have known many freedmen and many landlords in my lifetime—as well as several people who were both—and I never knew any of them to behave the way Rutolo did. They may have charged higher rents and they may have kept dirtier buildings, but I'd be willing to bet that they also had less exasperated tenants.

With this background in mind, the only thing one needs to know in order to understand Rutolo's dealings with my family is that Uncle Glaubus's Hobnail took up the front half of the ground floor of our building, and that Rutolo lived across the courtyard.

Rutolo regarded the Hobnail as a grave personal misfortune. No doubt when he purchased the building he had entertained hopes of evicting, or driving away, such an undesirable commercial tenant. But Glaubus was an easygoing fellow running a profitable business in an excellent location, so he paid his rent promptly at the expiration of each six-month term and laughed off Rutolo's constant threats to have him hauled up before the Praetor on some nit-picking charge or other. Thus our unhappy landlord was stuck with us, for all practical purposes—and we, by the same token, were stuck with him.

Like most bars, ours had living quarters in the rear—two small rooms facing the building's courtyard. And it was this courtyard, containing the obligatory privy for Glaubus's customers, that occasioned Rutolo's most impassioned complaints against my family. To be fair about it, he frequently had a point, for those of our patrons who had gulped down too much of our wine or sampled too much of Drusilla's cooking often sought the privacy of the courtyard and there gave up—in all the various ways conceivable—everything they had taken in. Some made it to the privy, others were overtaken by nature. In either case, there was usually a lot of unsavory noise and unwelcome aroma, both of which enraged Rutolo, whose bedroom, as luck would have it, faced the courtyard, as did ours.

Nor were eating and drinking the only bodily pleasures consummated "out back." Every so often, for example, my mother would satisfy a customer's craving for companionship, conducting the man in question to the darkest corner of the courtyard, where Glaubus had built a low platform to shelter firewood from the rain. The top of this platform was covered with canvas, and there, I imagine, the child who grew up to be me was conceived. Who the man was who participated in my conception, no one knows. Given my deep olive coloring and bristly hair, he was probably from one of the eastern or north African provinces. Given my height, he was probably short. Given my mother, he was probably drunk. At all events, he did his manly duty and paid perhaps a denarius for the privilege. Then, having initiated my life, he passed forever out of it.

My first memories are of our bar and of the people who patronized it. Glaubus had put in his twenty-five years with the legions, saved half his bonuses as the regulations require, and used that money along with his separation pay to start the Hobnail. Naturally enough, those of his customers who weren't from our neighborhood tended to be from the City's military contingents—the Urban Cohorts and the fire brigades primarily, though on occasion a Praetorian or two might condescend to grant us their custom. We attracted patrons from the other garrisons as well: Imperial police from the Caelian barracks would stop by the Hobnail after a day of drilling on the Campus Martius, and men of the Emperor's bodyguard quartered on Via Tusculana would sometimes pay us a visit after exercising their horses on the nearby Campus Agrippae.

Glaubus, being an old soldier, knew better than most people that men under arms do not go to cookshop-bars out of hunger primarily, but out of thirst. This accounts in part for the fact that we never lost even those of our patrons who made the mistake of asking Drusilla to cook them some food. Her cuisine, while not exactly lethal, packed enough of a wallop to sober all but the most liquified centurion. But many a thirsty soldier actually came to see this as an advantage; for after the requisite term out in the courtyard, he could return fully purged to our friendly precincts and begin drinking all over again. And this was no small blessing either, since what the Hobnail lacked in culinary refinement it more than made up for in the quality of its wines.

It would be no exaggeration to say that Glaubus was a connoisseur. He had grown up near Casilinum, in the heart of the *ager* Falernus, and his father, a freedman, had been overseer of one of the Septician vineyards. Glaubus's knowledge of wine, coupled with his knowledge of a soldier's taste in wine, made the Hobnail an ideal drinking place from the military man's point of view. Here were served neither the expensive and aristocratic Opimian-class vintages nor the harsh blends of Etruria and Gaul, but, rather, the solid full-bodied drinking wines of southern Latium and Campania: Falernian, of course, Caecuban, Cumaean, Surrentan—and nothing but the best of each year's growth. Every autumn, at the time of the *vindemia*, Glaubus would make a pilgrimage to the wine districts to taste and buy. The empty amphorae he took down in his cart came back full to the brim, and having eliminated all the middlemen one normally deals with in such a business, he was able to sell his high-quality wine at a price the average soldier could afford. Being an unusually massive man, moreover, he didn't have to hire somebody to keep order on those occasions when the average soldier could afford more than he could hold. In fact, he was a sufficiently intimidating figure to squelch most incipient fights with a look. Even in his fifties, he could wade into a full-fledged brawl with his truncheon and impose peace on the combatants in a matter of moments—peace in the sense of both decorum and unconsciousness.

Certain melees were too vicious to be handled even by him, however, and had to be left to run their course. These usually erupted at the conclusion of several weeks of gladiatorial games in the Amphitheater, because it was then that the marines from the Misenum Fleet barracks near the Esquiline were finally granted freedom of the City. These marines, along with a second contingent from the Ravenna Fleet, were responsible for working the canvas awning that projects from the top tier of the arena to protect the spectators from the elements. While the games were in progress, the marines naturally remained confined to the vicinity of their barracks during off-duty hours. Once the games ended, they were let loose on the City; and should some of them arrive at the Hobnail to find all stools occupied by soldiers and guardsmen, it would not be long before fists and feet started meshing with faces and foreskins.

Glaubus's strategy on such occasions was to shepherd Drusilla, my mother, and me into the back rooms and then watch contentedly from the doorway as the human tempest blew itself out. Aside from a few broken stools, the brawlers couldn't really do too much damage to the premises, at least as far as Glaubus was concerned. Rutolo, on the other hand, became virtually apoplectic at the thought of his tender stone walls being battered by hard military heads, and he once ran screaming into the midst of the fracas in an ill-advised attempt to make the brawlers see reason. To be sure, he repented of his impetuosity almost immediately and never gave in to it again as long as I knew him. He still wasn't fully ambulatory when the next free-for-all occurred, but his method of dealing with those that got going after he'd completed his convalescence was to run into the courtyard and scream at Glaubus through our back window. This was no more effective in terms of restoring order, but it was a good deal more prudent in terms of Rutolo's bodily cohesion.

But all these are fairly general recollections. When it comes to specific memories, I suppose my earliest one is about the way a stray cat lost its life. The time was spring, and I could not have been more than three years old. It was one of those muted afternoons when even the motes in a shaft of sunlight seem adrift in eternal sloth. Glaubus was unloading a small cart, and I was playing on the ground nearby. Unbeknownst to either of us, one of the neighborhood toms was crouched just in front of one of the rear cartwheels. Glaubus finished unloading, then went around to the front of the vehicle, grasped the pole, and began to pull the cart toward the storage shed. The wheel rolled over the cat's hips, crushing them like eggshells, and the animal started writhing frenziedly on the ground, spitting and snarling as though his agony were an invisible enemy straining to get at his throat. Glaubus saw what had happened and acted quickly. One heave of his shoulders set the cart moving backward, and the implacable wheel rolled over its victim's shoulders. As the poor beast's death throes ceased, its head turned, oh so slowly, in my direction. There was pain in the eyes, of course, as well as anger and incomprehension. But what really jolted me was the sorrow to be seen there, the inexpressible grief. This is unjust, the cat seemed to be saying. This can't be happening. This is *wrong*. Even as his face was proclaiming his anguished disbelief, a sense of worn-out resignation came into his eyes, and with a final sighing shudder he died.

I've heard it said that events that stay in your memory over the years must hold some special meaning for you, or else you wouldn't remember them. Perhaps the events I remember are the events that in various ways define me to myself, and perhaps my memories are merely those aspects of my experience that most vividly typify who I am. Whatever the case, I have remembered that cat and its death for nearly sixty years, all unwillingly, and I believe it was the infinite sorrow I saw in its eyes that alerted me to the specter of death. I realized then that death would always be my greatest enemy, just as I know it to be my most fearsome foe now.

I don't enjoy remembering such things. This whole project is folly. There can't be any purpose in writing more.

FROM THE
JOURNAL

6

[JULY 10TH]

We have been summoned to the Palatine, all four of us—and in a manner all too typical of the one who issued the summons. I should say of the one who caused the summons to be issued, since the document comes under the seal of Eclectus, the new Emperor's new chamberlain. Whereas Marcus would have sent a note in his own hand in care of a lone Praetorian courier, his son, Commodus, prefers to convey mandates by means of an entire troop of mounted Imperial bodyguards, sixteen bull-necked Germans, under the command of a tribune no less. The blond horde came thundering up our little roadway yesterday afternoon looking like ministers of extinction, and we all thought they had come for me. I was not going to be allowed my suicide, we thought; I was to be executed, my property confiscated, my family beggared.

I almost wish it had been something like that, instead of this tawdry little missive and its potential implications:

IMPERATOR CAESAR, *son of the deified Marcus Aurelius, grandson of the deified Antoninus, great-grandson of the deified Hadrian, great-great-grandson of the deified Trajan Parthicus, M. Aurelius Commodus Antoninus Augustus, Pontifex Maximus, of the Tribunician Power for the fourth time, Imperator for the fourth time, Consul for the third time, Father of his country, to L. Aurelius Verus Celer:*

I desire to see you, your wife, your son, and your daughter before me on the third day before the Ides of this month. You may present yourselves at the east gate of the Palatine compound at the third hour of that day. I may wish you to remain with me for a period of time, and I instruct you to make provision accordingly.

[by] Musius Eclectus, Cubicularis

My wife, my son, and my daughter!

I find it hard to bear. The idea of Portia, Decius, and Camilla within the reach of that pestilent travesty of an emperor makes my spirit wither. Of course Nestor has pointed out to me that they are effectively within the Princeps' reach anyway. But that misses the point. Because it's the

36

thought of the man actually putting his hands on them that sets my gorge to rising. Nestor claims to find it interesting that I "choose" to focus on the notion of my family being physically touched. I notice that he reads hidden significance into just about everything I say and do. I've told him that choice doesn't enter into it, that I am merely reacting as any man would to the prospect of his family coming to harm. What harm did I foresee for them, he asked me, other than the harm of being touched. I said that with such a man as Commodus anything is possible. If anything is possible, he retorted, why dwell on a single possibility. I told him to stop plaguing me; I had troubles enough already. He found this grounds for laughter. I find him decidedly irritating.

But I was curious nevertheless to know his opinion of my abortive attempt at a "Life." He started off by saying that my decision to write nothing more was perfectly understandable, and added, with not inconsiderable smugness, "You'll get over your misgivings."

I gazed at him, feeling somewhat truculent, but said nothing.

After a moment or two, with a little grimace, he declared, "I believe the time has come for me to articulate a premise."

It was such a pompous statement that I was almost angry with myself for wanting to know what the premise was.

But despite his declaration about its timeliness, Nestor seemed in no hurry to proclaim it. Instead, he launched into one of his disquisitions: "The failure to articulate premises is among the most common and pernicious of the errors people make in conducting their personal affairs. Only if you are capable, as I am, of inferring a man's basic assumptions about life from his behavior is the articulation of premises rendered unnecessary. But since few people are as gifted as I am in this respect, I always make it a point to state my basic assumptions explicitly before undertaking any attempt to enlighten the uncomprehending."

I had to give the old man credit; he had raised self-satisfaction to the level of an art form. "Those of us without comprehension salute you," I said.

"Without really understanding why," he responded, thereby winning another point.

I smoldered in silence while he favored me with a look of exquisite condescension.

"As I was saying," he resumed finally, "the first chapter of your 'Life' calls for my first premise about life in general. And my first premise is this: Every human interaction can be resolved into the basic elements of yea and nay."

I sat there blankly, having expected something a bit more monumental after the buildup. My comment was, "I believe I could do with a bit of gloss."

"Very well," Nestor responded brightly, elated, to all appearances, by the prospect of having to elaborate. "The premise describes the effects people have on one another in their personal dealings. Not the effects they intend to have, necessarily, nor the effects they profess to be seeking, but only the effects that are produced in fact. Intentions can be misconstrued, misguided, and disguised, as we all know. But effects, though often matters of feeling, are always matters of fact, and in all cases they boil down to the question: Did those involved in the interaction feel themselves to be enhanced or diminished by what occurred? This question provides the essential calculus of human relationships."

I listened and tried to puzzle out what Nestor was saying, but his arguments were too subtle—or silly—for me to grasp his entire meaning. I guess it was obvious that I was having difficulty, though for once the old man refrained from patronizing me as he doled out a further explanation.

"Let's take the initial chapter of your 'Life' by way of illustration. For most of us, it is our parents and nursemaids who interact with us first, and I take it as a given that our interactions with such people are of vital importance. Alas, as infants we have only the most primitive perceptions about those around us. But our perceptions, nevertheless, are accurate, which is to say that we interpret the actions of others as being, *in effect*, votes for or against our continued existence. I don't mean interpret in the intellectual sense; I mean it in the sense of feeling that our vitality has been enhanced or diminished. As infants, in other words, we understand instinctively the first premise I enunciated: Every human interaction can be resolved into the basic elements of yea and nay.

"Now in your particular case, lacking a father, you never experienced the yea votes many children get from the men who sire them. On top of that, your mother had little interest in you, which means the yea votes you got from her could not have been more than minimal. The only real yea votes you received, so it seems, came from a woman of volatile temper, who was probably as free with her nays as her yeas. Thus you began life experiencing less than the usual amount of succor for your natural vitality and more than the usual number of assaults against it. Like all infants, moreover, you were helpless and dependent, and this being so, it is perfectly understandable that you began to be morbidly preoccupied with your continued survival, which was but the obverse of the coin that portrayed your imminent death. Hence your first specific memory is of a creature like yourself crushed by forces beyond its control in consequence of a moment's inattention. You were right as a three year old to perceive death as your cruelest enemy; it was your misfortune to have the perception long before you were old enough to assimilate it. That is why you became, and remained, so afraid."

I looked at Nestor, who returned my gaze, and for the first time since I'd met him there was some sympathy and understanding in his eyes.

"You see, my dear Lucius," he said after a pause, "you learned to fear death before you were prepared to face it. Now you are old enough to face it, but still are blinded by your primal fear. That is why you must write out another chapter—to learn how that fear became a part of you."

I nodded that I would do as he said. And I will. Because the fear lies heavy upon me.

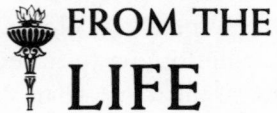 # FROM THE LIFE

7

My life before Marcus—what do I remember?

There was our street, Inter Duas Portas, the two gates in question being the Sanqualis and the Salutaris. We used to call it Twopenny Street, taking the "du" from Duas and the "po" from Portas to make "dupo," which was City slang for the two-as coin, the dupondius. Twopenny Street was an appropriate name for the main thoroughfare of our neighborhood, since our neighborhood was almost totally lacking in distinction. And to be lacking in distinction was no mean achievement, given that the neighborhood's southern boundary was Trajan's Forum and the Basilica Ulpia. Twopenny Street began, in fact, at the junction of Trajan's Forum and Trajan's Market; it ran north for about a quarter of a mile all told, skirting the western slope of the Quirinal Hill and ending at the Salutis incline just south of Campus Agrippae. As streets go it was not without its peculiarities. For one thing, it ran along at the foot of the City's tallest hill. That meant that there were buildings on one side only for half its length, because its other side consisted entirely of hillside up to the point where the Quirinal curves off to the northeast. Children like me who lived south of the curve were called "mud eaters" by the children who lived north of it, and they in their turn were labeled "brick lickers" by us.

Mud eaters was, of course, an inaccurate epithet, and I don't say that simply out of vestigial loyalty to lower Twopenny Street. It was inaccurate because the slopes of the Quirinal were never muddy (whereas the tenements of upper Twopenny Street were, decidedly, of brick). I remember how the steep hillside used to serve us as a mirror of the passing seasons. My most vivid memory is of the gradient ablaze with April poppies, thousands and thousands of them fluttering in the breeze and savoring the caresses of the pale spring grass. They were all over the hillside, from street level up to the remains of Servius's wall on the crest, and when the sun was at a certain angle the slopes took on the aspect of a two-hundred-foot-high cascade of fire, a cascade arrested in midair by some sort of magical intervention but ready to resume its plunge earthward the moment the spell was broken. As the days grew longer and hotter, the cascade modulated its color from vermilion through carmine and burnt sienna to a moribund brown, while the grass faded from lush green to bright saffron to pallid straw. Life seemed to end on the hillside in summer, and all one could see there were the skeletal remains of the living things the sun had burned away. But with the coming of autumn and its soaking rains the Quirinal revived itself, and by the Ides of January it was once more carpeted in green.

As for other features of the neighborhood, I can only repeat that there was a uniform lack of distinction. The buildings fronting Twopenny Street were for the most part tenements, older ones down at our end and progressively newer and taller ones to the north. As a rule the older tenements were better built; the newer ones, thanks to their owners' shortsighted avarice, tended to have more stories than their foundations and structural components could be expected to support. Two of them collapsed during my boyhood, and though all the people of the neighborhood rushed to rescue the survivors in the rubble, they also picked the debris clean of the survivors' personal belongings. That's the kind of neighborhood it was: larcenously altruistic.

In addition to tenements, Twopenny Street could boast several warehouses belonging to the Imperial Fiscus. Lumber and other building materials were stored there for use in government construction projects, and because this was during Hadrian's time, there was plenty of activity in their vicinity. Some of this activity could be described as pilferage—or, a more overtly larcenous form of altruism.

The crowning glory of our neighborhood was Curtio's Baths, about midway along Twopenny Street, just north of where the Quirinal curved away. It was a venerable institution, in appearance no less than longevity, and had been built during the last years of the Republic, at the time of the First Triumvirate. Pompey and Crassus were reputed to have invested money in its construction, though this may be nothing more than a neighborhood myth. Who Curtio was nobody seemed to know. Some said he was Caesar, investing under a pseudonym, but there was no real evidence for this. Others said he was a Jew and/or a eunuch, basing their assumption on the fact that "curtio" is an inflected form of "curtus," which, applied to Jews, means circumcised, and applied to horses means castrated. Whoever Curtio may have been, by my time his place had been taken by the brothers Iamblichus—Titanus and Hercules. The Iamblichus brothers were identical twin dwarfs who had come to Rome as slaves from Galatia around the time of Trajan's accession. It seemed a cruel joke on the part of their parents to have named them after giants, but when someone finally dredged up enough nerve to ask them why their mother and father had done such a thing, all the answer he got was that it was "common in our country" to name children after mythical heroes. "Yes, but why these particular mythical heroes?" the questioner persisted. And the Iamblichus brothers purportedly responded, "Because our heads looked so large when we were born that our parents thought our bodies would catch up."

One couldn't help liking the Iamblichus brothers. Certainly their former master had liked them, having granted them manumission on his deathbed and bequeathed them Curtio's Baths in his will. The brothers had prospered as a result, marrying full-size women and fathering full-size children. They ran their bathing establishment in a good-natured spirit, skimping on maintenance and cleanliness perhaps, but charging only one sestertius for a three-day ticket. And that one sestertius bought you quite a lot, all in all: in addition to the hot pool, the warm pool, and the cold pool—in all three of which, for some reason, the water tended to be tepid—you were accorded access to six pumice toilets with lemonwood armrests, tended by a solicitous slave named Rupus, who had a habit of asking you, "How are things going?" as you sat there waiting for your bowels to have mercy. You could also avail yourself of any one of the half-dozen male and female prostitutes who did business at Curtio's, and of course there was the bar, to which they were encouraged to bring you before you retired to one of the "private rooms."

Every fourth day, from the sixth hour until sunset, the baths were reserved for women, girls, and "hairless"—in the pubic sense—boys at a special family rate of two asses. Aunt Drusilla took me there regularly, hardly ever missing a quartan, and it was at Curtio's that she allowed herself to display what little affection she had for me. But I will speak of that later.

In addition to Curtio's, the warehouses, and the tenements along Twopenny Street, there were the usual number of votive shrines and altars set into the stone and brickwork. Come to think of it, there were probably more than the usual number, since the population of the neighborhood was so heterogeneous. About a quarter of the people who lived there were, like the Iamblichus brothers, from the eastern end of the Empire: Syrians, Cilicians, Galatians, and Egyptians. This group tended to favor the worship of Isis. Perhaps half the population consisted of Romans and native Italians, casual adherents of the state religion, for the most part, though some with a military background, like my uncle Glaubus, also favored Mithras. The remaining quarter of the population was a very mixed bag theologically speaking. It comprised slaves predominantly, Jews and non-Jewish Christians of various persuasions, atheists, Cynics, a Stoic or two, and worshipers of numerous esoteric dieties. Given that nearly half the free population of the neighborhood slept as lodgers in the apartments of the other half, it's remarkable that all this religious diversity didn't produce any friction, except among the sundry Judaeo-Christians. But then, no one except the sundry Judaeo-Christians took formal religious observance all that seriously.

I suppose for the sake of completeness I ought to mention the shops along Twopenny Street, though it was in these sooty emporia that the neighborhood's lack of distinction achieved its apotheosis. There was Lucus, the glazier, whose bottles and jars were of such exquisite delicacy that they could be used as lethal weapons without suffering damage of any kind. There was Pollux, the barber, a man whose skill with a razor was matched only by his aptitude for dressing the wounds he inflicted. There was Xenotes, the fuller, who considerately placed his vats of urine out on the street just to the left of his shop entrance so that no one would be troubled by the aroma of oven-fresh bread emanating from Carpio's bakery next door. There was Panterus, the coppersmith, who did rather good work actually, and on either side of him the establishments of Gabro the dyer and Postulus the carder, both of whom employed a dozen or more loudly bickering Syrian slaves, who every so often sat down and refused to do another stroke of work unless their exasperated masters granted them an increase in their peculium wage. There was Saturnius, the butcher, who boasted that he threw all unsold meat to his dogs after four days "regardless of how good it still is." And there was Males, the sandal-maker, an aged homesick Greek who kept a tattered copy of Hesiod's *Works and Days* open next to his last so that he could dream of Helicon while sewing straps onto soles. There was Petrobarbus, the cutler, like Uncle Glaubus a veteran of the legions. And there was Scarrulus, the salter, whose team of slave boys sold his delicious cooked sausages all over the neighborhood, carrying them in earthenware trays to keep them warm. Lastly there was Geminus, the reclusive perfumer, whose body was found in his shop one morning, gutted. The most remarkable thing about this was the concurrent discovery that he had been a woman. Who gutted him/her, and why, no one knows to this day.

I haven't mentioned Trypho's wineshop, Sacer's cookshop, Coriodonus's alehouse, and Eupator's tavern. They were much as you would expect them to have been—unsavory. The Hobnail was the only decent drinking place on Twopenny Street, and even the Hobnail was pretty pestiferous.

No description of the neighborhood would be complete without at least some mention of the local cats. We had several tribes of them: the hillside tribe, the warehouse tribe, and the market tribe, this last group being the northernmost branch of the large family that occupied the area around Trajan's Forum. All the cats were wild, in the specifically urban sense of that word. That is to say, they were accustomed to and tolerated the presence of humans in their vicinity and would even consent to eat the table scraps a few kindhearted old women regularly put out for them. But they would not on any account consent to be touched, or approached, by anyone, not even the kindhearted old women. They were inveterately mistrustful of people, and I don't doubt that they were right to be so. As a child, though, I found their behavior terribly frustrating—until, that is, I was befriended by one of them while it was still a kitten. This was Romulus, who became my closest boyhood companion.

I suppose it's a sad admission—that my closest companion was an animal. But I never felt deprived of human intimacy. Indeed, until I met Marcus I never even experienced it. True, most of the blame for this situation unquestionably resided with me; I wasn't much more approachable than the cats. But my faults, such as they were, were faults of omission: innate shyness, a preference for solitude, and a degree of oversensitivity. It wasn't until I was a full-grown man that I understood how provoking such seemingly innocuous traits can be to a certain kind of boy.

Such as Agricus.

Agricus was a year older than me. He had qualities that I admired before I got to know him, and that I admire now, long after our last encounter. For one thing, he was brave, insanely brave; fear only ignited his determination. For another thing, he kept faith; in spite of everything I suffered at his hands, I retained an awareness that he would never go back on his word or betray a trust. For a third thing, he was beautiful: luxuriant black hair, dark blue—almost violet—eyes, sharp clean features, a strong well-formed body. Set against all these virtues, however, was his cruelty, and his cruelty was like nothing else I have known in my lifetime. It was as if his capacity for pleasure had somehow become deformed, leaving him unable to derive enjoyment from anything except the sufferings of other creatures.

I got my first taste of his cruelty at Curtio's, when I was nine or ten years old.

The baths were always my special pleasure, mostly because they afforded me time alone with my aunt Drusilla. We would buy our tickets, go to the dressing room, disrobe, cover ourselves with the towels we'd brought, and deposit our clothes with the slave on duty in Hercules Iamblichus's office. Where we went from there depended on the season. In the hot months we went to the frigidarium, in winter to the tepidarium. This was because the warm bath in winter was about as cool as the cold

bath was in summer, thanks to Curtio's decrepit furnace. As for the cold
bath in winter, suffice it to say that it frequently featured a thin layer of
ice. I myself enjoyed the baths more in warm weather, because the
frigidarium was my favorite room. It was round and small, no more than
twenty feet in diameter. But its walls stretched upward the full height of
the building, perhaps thirty feet or more. Like most cold baths, it was
open to the sky, and since the only light in the room came from the
open ceiling, the general feeling one got was of being at the bottom of
a well. I would race to the chamber ahead of Drusilla, fold my towel,
place it on the stone bench as a cushion, and sit down. Initially, my aunt
thought my behavior was the result of childish eagerness and I had no
wish to disillusion her. But my true motive, which she divined after a
while, had nothing whatsoever to do with juvenile concerns.

I would sit there and watch the door, oblivious of the presence of
anyone else in the room. At last the door would swing open, and Drusilla
would appear, clad in a coarse gray towel. She would set down her strigil,
along with her phials of oil and soda, and, with a slightly pensive frown
and an almost virginal artlessness, unfasten the towel and let it fall away
from her body. I can remember the sudden jolt in my already bounding
pulse and the urgent ache in my member as I gripped it with my thighs
to keep my excitement concealed. And I can remember Drusilla standing
there, more bountiful than Juno, a vision of all my nameless desires.

She would walk down the steps of the shallow pool and seat herself,
the water covering her shoulders and lapping at the few loose strands of
her upgathered hair. I would half plunge, half run into the pool after her
and swim toward her eyes. She would reach out her hands for me, grip
me underneath my arms, and pull me toward her. Then, sometimes, if
she was in a good humor, she would embrace me and kiss the hollow of
my cheek. My chest would brush against her nipples, erect and hard from
the coldness of the water, and my breath would stop in my throat. I
knew great joy in those moments, and great disquiet. I would turn my
body so that my legs and hips were out to the side, and thus freed of
the danger that my secret arousal might proddingly reveal itself, I nestled
against her in a state of anxious bliss.

I have sometimes wondered why I always took such pains to hide my
excitement from her—or, rather, try to hide it, and with little success.

From the frigidarium we went to the tepidarium, where we stayed only
a few moments. In most bathhouses a spell in the warm room is a necessary
period of transition from a cold to a hot environment. At Curtio's, however, where the environmental differences were often so subtle as to escape
detection, it was only the force of custom that led us to spend any time

in the tepidarium at all. So we would quickly move on to the caldarium, which was bright with lamps and torches. As soon as we entered, I would go fetch a bucket of water from the tank and then would sit and watch as Drusilla washed her hair. When she was through with hers, she would wash mine, then rub me down with oil and briskly scrape me clean. Finally the time would come for me to spread the oil over her. She would lie on her stomach, to begin with, and as my small hands ran over her I was joyful to the point of giddiness. Then she would turn over, and once again I was convulsed by the sweetest anxiety and confusion. Sometimes she would gaze at me as I worked on her, assessing me, I felt sure, with knowing eyes. But I betrayed not the slightest embarrassment, not even as my fingers slid lovingly over her breasts.

I would finish, apply the strigil, and walk with her to the swimming pool for a final immersion. Then, all too quickly, the idyll was over.

But I was discussing Agricus's cruelty, which first touched me at Curtio's on a torrid August afternoon. By way of preface I should point out that at the time of this incident we had known each other for several years. I, as I've said, was nine or ten, he a year older. We were both mud eaters, and both of us ran with the small pack of neighborhood boys that had arrogated to itself the responsibility for maintaining the honor of lower Twopenny Street against the assaults of a comparable pack of brick lickers. Our leader was a fourteen year old named Trebbio; Agricus and I, being among the youngest in the gang, were merely low-ranking soldiers. Our relations with each other had been friendly but not especially intimate. We ran in the same pack and were therefore allied, that was all . . . or almost all. It's hard for me to remember exactly how I felt about him before my feelings were first overshadowed by hate, but I do seem to recall according him a degree of boyish admiration on account of his remarkable bravery. Once during some foray or skirmish that was otherwise unexceptional his courage landed him behind enemy lines, so to speak, and he suffered a fearful pummeling, the marks of which were visible for several months. I remember envying him his bruises, and his fortitude, and that may account for the fact that I have almost no memory of his cruelty that predates our fateful encounter at Curtio's. I do recall that he used to throw rocks at the cats in the neighborhood, and that such behavior bothered me. And I also recall an occasion when he forced a captured brick licker to swallow a handful of dirt from the Quirinal's slopes. But these incidents did not make a deep impression on me; I suppose I was too dazzled by his courage to evaluate them intelligently.

The upshot was that I was unprepared for what happened on that August afternoon. As was my custom, I had run ahead of Drusilla to the frigidarium and was sitting on my towel waiting for her when Agricus approached me. He was there with his mother, I think. He came over to me, pointed at my lap, and with a cold glint of a smile asked, "What's that?" I looked down and saw that my member was already erect in anticipation of Drusilla's appearance. "Go *away*!" I hissed. I realize in retrospect that that was probably the worst thing I could have done. He immediately caught the scent of my fear, and I will never forget the way his eyes lit up with predatory elation. "May I have some," he asked, "or are you saving it all for your lady?" I gaped at him, unable to make sense of what he was doing but beginning to discern some unspeakable horror in the empty blackness behind the violet eyes. Needless to say, my erection began rapidly to wither, and I was about to stand up and confront my tormentor when, to my utter shock and consternation, he fastened his grip on my shaft. "Don't let it disappear," he whispered. "The lady hasn't seen it yet." I couldn't speak; I felt myself sliding toward panic. I shot a wide-eyed glance toward the door, terrified that Drusilla might appear. "Don't you want her to see it?" Agricus hissed, and in an agony of humiliation I shook my head. "Then stop waving it around in front of everyone," he said fiercely, balling his free hand into a fist as he spoke and ramming it into my scrotum.

He was gone by the time Drusilla walked in. She found me writhing on the tiles next to the bench, and cared enough about me to be alarmed. I struggled to lift myself off the floor, clutching her outstretched arms for support. "Lucio, darling, what is it?" she asked me. And I answered, "My stomach, Aunt. I feel a big pain in my stomach."

To everyone's relief, except mine, the pain was gone by the time we sat down to dinner.

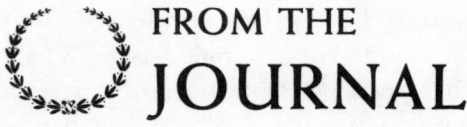# FROM THE
JOURNAL

8

[JULY 11 TH]

Early this morning, for the first time since I learned of my likely fate ten days ago, I went running. Except for the aftermath, it did me good.

I started at a slow pace down our roadway, then turned right on the river road toward Careiae and the Claudian Springs. After a mile or so the feel of sweat on my forehead and looseness in my limbs told me I was ready to pick up the pace. My breathing deepened as my stride lengthened, and I was soon in that state of vibrant equilibrium that used to carry me through the middle laps of the dolichos race—if I was running well, that is. The slap of my bare feet on the dry dirt road provided a rhythm harmonious with my heartbeat and respiration, and despite the ten days of inactivity I began to get that exhilarating sense that I could keep on running forever. The slaves working my neighbors' fields glanced up at me as I went cantering by, but quickly returned their attention to their labors. By now they are used to the crazy old man who runs when no one is chasing him. When I first came to live in the Aro Valley, they were not so indifferent. They stared then, in baffled disbelief, and turned to one another for confirmation of the evidence their eyes were reporting. One of them actually threw a rock at me—which missed—thinking that I was some sort of demon, and for a week or two the entire neighborhood was abuzz with rumors of every supernatural being from Apollo to Zephyris.

But people get used to everything, even galloping gods, and I am now regarded as a phenomenon of only marginal interest—just another loose thread in the fabric of rural life.

I galloped on until a slight stiffness just above my knees warned me that my body had softened a bit since my last run. Bowing to the constraints of old age, I slowed my pace, turning at the roadside altar to Robigus and heading back. The stiffness diminished with the slower tempo, so I loped along past our gate and made for the Nereid, thinking to have a drink there and then walk home. The sun had risen by this time and was glaring with a ferocity that foretold a day of climactic heat. I was perspiring heavily when at last I walked into the tavern courtyard.

The slaves and freedmen at the Nereid were engaged in their usual morning chores, and several wagons were being unloaded—all quite normal. But the atmosphere was not normal: there was an edginess to it, a sense of nerves exposed, submissiveness strained to the limit. At first I attributed the tension to the blistering swell of the heat, which by now had an almost malevolent quality to it, given that the day had barely begun. The people in the courtyard actually seemed to be shrinking away from the sunlight, as if it were a whip in the hand of some pitiless overseer whose brutality they could neither escape nor endure.

I walked to the shade of the porch behind the kitchen and called inside for a bowl of honey wine and cold water. A man's voice yelled back an acknowledgment and roughly issued an order. I sat down on the ground and waited, savoring the relative coolness of the shade. Within moments a twelve- or thirteen-year-old girl appeared, bearing my drink. "Superb service," I said, eagerly taking the bowl from her hands and downing a large draft. "My wife will give you a copper tomorrow morning on her way to market."

"Very good, sir," the girl replied in a numbed tone of voice as I drained the rest of the drink.

"The copper's for you," I told her, wiping my mouth with one hand and giving the bowl back to her with the other. "Tell Appius to put this on my account—Lucius Celer. All right?"

"Very good, sir," the girl said again, turning abruptly to go.

I think it was the repetition of "Very good, sir" in the same dead monotone that caused me to reach out and grip the girl's arm as she was leaving. As I turned her to face me I saw that her expression was full of fear. And now that my eyes had had a little time to adjust to the shade, I saw also that her face was marked by welts and bruises. "Are you all right, child?" I asked her, disturbed that someone her age should have been subjected to such a beating.

"I'm well enough, sir," the girl answered in agitation, yanking her arm free and disappearing hurriedly into the kitchen.

I sat there pondering what, if anything, I ought to do. Quite apart from the issue of the bruises, there was something about the girl that compelled my interest, something familiar about her face and bearing. But I realized that what went on between Appius and his dependents was really none of my affair. I wasn't any too comfortable with that conclusion, particularly when I thought of the girl's battered face. Yet for want of any plausible alternative, it was a conclusion I was stuck with.

My body felt strong as I left the Nereid, toned and cleansed by the exercise. But my spirits were low; the pain in the girl's eyes had once more put me in mind of my own troubles, which are never very far from my thoughts in any case.

I walked slowly, bowing a little beneath the violence of the sun, which was directly in front of me as I shuffled toward home. Already the heat had reached a level of bludgeoning intensity, and the dust-heavy roadside trees stood motionless in its grasp, deprived of even the hope of a breeze. This, I remember reflecting as I walked, is going to be a killing heat today. This heat is going to exact a toll.

And perhaps it was the heat that destined me to make the discovery. Perhaps the smell would not have been detectable till later in the day if the weather had been cooler.

But it was detectable, coming from the Aro, at about the midway point in my homeward walk. It was a smell I am familiar with, a smell that is unmistakable.

I stood there in the middle of the road and fought the urge to keep on walking. Having just shrunk from confronting Appius about the girl, I didn't feel I could permit myself to shirk yet another human obligation.

I followed the smell to the riverbank and needed to go only a few more paces before locating its source. I wished then, fervently, that I had not stopped walking—and I understood completely about the girl.

The slave boy was lying face up, with the back of his head in the water and his body on the upward slope of the riverbank. His eyes and his mouth were agape, his iron collar intact. His chest and abdominal cavity had been cut open; his internal organs were thick with flies. Where his penis and scrotum had been, there was a wound. The flies swarmed there, too.

I stood in the dazzling heat and gazed down at the wages of a slave boy's lust for a freeborn girl. Poor, poor innocents. They had known their appetites and their desire for one another. They just hadn't known the rules.

But they'd been taught them.

I don't know how long I stood there. I remember the weight of the sun on my forehead, the stench of carrion in my nose. I remember thinking that this couldn't have been the work of Appius; he would have made a public example of the boy if he'd decided to kill him. As master he had that right. More likely, he'd decided *not* to kill him, and the girl's family, though owing Appius allegiance as his dependents, had taken matters into their own hands and, in effect, stolen the boy from him, disposing of the "evidence" in a manner calculated to preserve a pretense of ano-nymity. Appius was not the type to practice mutilation, in any case, not even on a slave. Such savagery could have been the work only of people close to slavery themselves, so close that their freeborn status was all they could depend on to maintain the distinction between themselves and those below them. The boy had been punished for calling that distinction into question. If only he'd lived a little longer, he might have learned how much it mattered.

The summer being only a month or so along, there was still about a foot of water in the Aro. So I grabbed an arm and a leg and put the boy in the river face down, to rid his body of the flies. Then I lifted him, slung him over my shoulders, and began to walk across the fields toward home. The sun pounded at my temples as I labored on, and for some reason I began to cry. I hadn't known this boy, yet here I was struggling over the hedgerows with his body on my back. The flies found him quickly and swarmed around my head, their dronings barely audible beneath the noise of the ratcheting cicadas and the sound of my own choked sobs. I would accord him the proper rites, I told myself, as the air quivered around me and the heat haze blended sky, trees, and sun into a shimmering patchwork of yellowish blues and greens.

We should have warned them, I thought. We should have realized their danger. *We* knew the rules, after all. Why hadn't we told them to be careful about keeping their trysts a secret? We should have, we should have . . .

Fortunately, Rullo saw me staggering toward the house beneath my burden. I must have had a touch of sun by then, because my memory of my arrival home is unclear. I remember Rullo running toward me, and I remember falling down and being carried. My next recollection is of waking up in my bedroom with a wet cloth on my forehead. Portia was there, and the children, and even meddling old Nestor, who in typical fashion began talking the instant I opened my eyes.

"Behold, Atlas awakes, having borne the weight of the world on his shoulders."

"I don't feel much like Atlas," I said, sitting up and cupping my head in my hands.

"You *are* a little old for the part," Nestor bantered.

"How are you feeling, dearest?" Portia asked me, her eyes full of anxiety.

I tried to give her a grin, but it probably ended up looking more like a grimace. "I'm feeling well enough, all things considered."

"I recognized the boy," she said.

"I thought you might."

"What about the girl?" she asked.

And I told her.

There was silence for a while.

"What time is it?" I inquired, the shutters being tightly closed.

"About an hour before nightfall," Portia replied.

"I slept a long time, it seems."

"Yes."

"Let's have the shutters open," I said, and Decius did my bidding. I looked outside and saw a wooden platform in the orchard.

"I had Rullo and Myron construct a bier," Portia told me. "Is that what you wanted?"

"Yes," I answered, gingerly swinging my legs to the floor. "Here, help me up."

"Are you sure you're well enough, darling?"

"Yes, yes, yes. Let's get this over with."

"Forgive me for intruding," Nestor intruded, "but doesn't your Roman liturgy contemplate that funerals should take place after dark?"

"Our Roman liturgy contemplates that delinquent slaves should be disposed of without any funerals at all," I snapped at him. "And, in any case, I'm sure the boy won't mind if we don't adhere to prescribed ritual."

"Neither will he mind if you do, dear fellow. Which raises the question of why you are doing anything for him at all."

"No doubt you have a theory on the matter."

"Perhaps. But why don't we wait to talk of it until we've observed the proprieties and had our dinner."

"Why don't we indeed," I responded, getting shakily to my feet and, with Portia's help, going outside.

Rullo had seen to everything—sensible of the honor being accorded a fellow slave—not simply a funeral, but the fire as well.

He approached me carrying a folded piece of cloth. "This is the finger bone I've set aside for burial, Domine," he said, revealing a knowledge of the old customs that almost certainly exceeded mine. "I've put some salt on the platform," he continued, "as well as some basil and mint. Do you think that will be sufficient?"

I looked at him, a small bulky man with matted hair and perpetually worried eyes, who'd served me for most of his life. I had to confess to myself that I hardly knew him after all our years together, and as I looked on his kindly, troubled countenance I felt I had missed a great deal. "It will suffice, my friend," I answered him, and together we joined the rest of the household before the pyre.

It was up to me to speak, so I said: "We commit this boy to the fire so that his soul may be at rest. We did not know him—or, rather, we knew him only a little. We know that the fire of life burned brightly in his body, and that he died because some found the brightness excessive. We pray that his fire burned brightly enough to compensate him for the shortness of his span, and that his soul will take comfort from the fire we light for him now. We wish him peace. We salute him. We mourn him. . . . Let it be done."

Rullo handed me a torch. I walked to the pyre and inserted it into the kindling, remembering enough of the ritual to turn my face away as I did so. The wood caught quickly, and the flames went about their work. Hovering near the horizon, the sun observed our ceremony with a red unblinking eye, then slowly sank from view, leaving streaks of peach and violet as a backdrop for the sparks dancing above the boy's remains.

Rullo came up to me with a jar of water. "With your permission, Domine, the purification."

I nodded, and was splashed three times, like everyone else, with a few bootless drops. They left me feeling no whit purer, just a little bit wet.

"Isn't there supposed to be a banquet after a funeral?" Nestor asked jovially as we trooped back into the house.

"I believe I'm supposed to slaughter a pig," I responded. "But I've had enough of slaughter for a while. Perhaps some cheese and olives, and bread."

We went into the garden and sat down, while Portia, Decius, and Camilla saw to the food.

"That boy meant a lot to you," Nestor said without the usual bantering inflection.

"I never spoke to him. I don't know his name. I didn't even know he existed until four nights ago. So how could he have meant a lot to me?" I sounded angry, but both of us knew that my question was anything but argumentative.

"He represented something in your eyes, that's all. As you say, you knew nothing of the boy himself. It was only what he stood for."

"I knew something of him."

"How?"

I gave the old man a mock bow. "By inference, master. By inference."

"Ahhhh . . . Well, what did you infer?"

"I inferred that he was in the process of discovering how sweet life can be on rare occasions, that he delighted in the sweetness he was discovering, that his heart was open and his spirit free—despite his collar—that faint hints of love had touched his senses, and that he meant no harm."

"You inferred all this just by watching an act of copulation?"

"Are you saying my inferences are mistaken?"

"Well, let's consider them one at a time. First, he was in the process of discovering the occasional sweetness of life. True, but trivial. We are all in the process of discovering the occasional sweetness of life. Sweet occasions and the intervals between them are all life consists of. He was alive. Therefore, he was discovering life. We don't have inference here, merely syllogism.

"Next, he delighted in the sweetness he was discovering. All that means is that he had appetite. You watch a boy feel pleasure as he copulates and you say he enjoys copulation. There is no inference here, only tautology.

"Next, his heart was open and his spirit free—despite his collar, I think you had the mawkishness to add. Since you admittedly know nothing whatsoever about the boy, there hardly seems to be sufficient evidence for such a sentimental conclusion. I would say that inference is absent in this case, and that what we have instead is speculation.

"Next, faint hints of love had touched his senses. Now, your wife has given me a full account of what both of you saw, and there is nothing about the episode that remotely supports your assumption that he was touched by love. What is in operation here is clearly not inference, but imagination.

"Finally, he meant no harm. Again, there is no evidence for this at all. But having attributed so many becoming qualities to the boy, you were obliged to hope that he was not of a malicious temperament, if for no other reason than to keep your image of him intact. So what controlled your mind in this instance was not inference, any more than it was in the previous instances; it was merely aspiration."

He let out a breath and sat back, beaming. I could gladly have strangled him. "It seems I didn't know the boy as well as I thought I did."

"You didn't know him at all. And his importance to you doesn't depend on your having known him."

"What does it depend on?"

"It depends on how much of yourself you saw in him, and on how much of him you saw missing in yourself."

"That sounds like gibberish."

"Does it? Let's consider your 'inferences' about the boy and see how they correspond to what we know so far about you as a lad."

"Have I ever told you how tiresome I find your sarcasm?"

"Yes. Now, as to your inferences. You said, first, that he was discovering the sweetness of life."

"That has to apply to me, I suppose—according to you, anyway—for the simple reason that we know I was alive."

"True; you are an apt pupil. But what was the sweetness that you were discovering?"

"Love, I guess."

"What kind of love?"

"What do you mean, what kind?"

"Now don't go all coy on me. You're not ten years old any more. What kind of love were you describing in your account of what went on at Curtio's?"

"I don't know. You could call it erotic love, I suppose."

"I could and would and can and do. But, erotic love for whom?"

"You know damn well for whom."

"If I know damn well, then why am I asking you?"

"Because you want to put me through the discomfort of giving you the answer."

"Just so. Now please be so good as to accommodate me."

"Oh, very well . . . Drusilla."

"What about Drusilla? Give me a complete grammatical sentence, please."

"I should have left you in your tent to finish dying. How's that?"

"A complete, grammatical, and *relevant* sentence is what I'm after."

"Oh, Furies take you!" I shouted as Portia, Decius, and Camilla entered the garden.

"*Lucio!*" Portia cried. "The man is our guest!"

"Keep silent, woman!" I snapped, glaring venomously at her. Then I turned and in a low angry voice said, "I was discovering the sweetness of the erotic love I had for Drusilla."

"Excellent!" Nestor condescended. "But I see that it's now time to eat."

I sat and smoldered while the old man filled his belly. I ate only a little, conscious of the pain I had caused Portia, but unable to subdue my anger. The meal, if it could be called that, passed in bristling silence, and my family left Nestor and me to ourselves as soon as we had finished eating.

"So," Nestor said, abrasively imperturbable as always, "you were discovering the sweetness of the erotic love you felt for your aunt."

"I suppose so," I said in a sullen voice.

"Did you delight in the sweetness you were discovering?"

"No."

"Why not?"

"Because I didn't know what was going on, dammit. And because Drusilla was in many ways my mother."

"I see. So in this respect you were not at all like the slave boy of your imaginings. Now, was your heart open, your spirit free?"

"No."

"Why not?"

"I told you why not. Because I didn't understand what was happening to me. I was frightened and confused."

"Precisely. But, your senses, like those of your conjectural slave boy, had been touched by faint hints of love, hadn't they? Love for Drusilla as a woman."

I didn't answer him.

"Yet you knew there was something askew about your feelings. You were afraid to admit them. And Drusilla, though she sensed what was going on, did nothing to help you. She may, indeed, have made things worse."

I remained silent.

"You even went so far as to conceal your feelings; you hid the evidence of your emotions between your thighs. You weren't out to cause anybody trouble, after all. Like your slave boy, you meant no harm."

I felt tears begin to well up in my eyes.

"And yet you were punished for what you felt," Nestor said softly. "The one time your feelings were discovered, the consequences were almost as catastrophic as those attendant on the slave boy's lust."

I shut my eyes and held fast to my wavering self-possession.

"What all this comes down to," Nestor continued, "is a suspicion that the copulating slave boy evoked a memory of yourself at age nine or ten—an innocent, well-intentioned lad who was beginning to discover the sweetness life can offer and who was experiencing the first faint stirrings of erotic love. The slave boy was not nine or ten, however; he was old enough to understand the nature of his feelings. So as you watched him copulate and were reminded of your boyhood self, you were treated to the pleasurable fancy of having retrieved your lost opportunities with Drusilla and at last made the most of them. In watching the slave you watched the boy you once were delighting in the sweetness of your aunt's caresses, delighting because he'd been freed of the fear and confusion that arose from his immaturity. In him you saw yourself perfected, and the vision made you happy.

"But the slave's passion, like yours, was forbidden; and, alas, the boy was murdered. His secret was discovered, just as yours was, and he was punished for it, just as you were. On a sweltering summer day you found the beautiful embodiment of your redeemed boyhood lying butchered in the mud, a mound of offal, a feast for flies. Once again it was the sweltering summer day of many years ago, and the message of Agricus's fist resounded through your body: pleasure is culpable, joy is anathema. You recalled the happiness you've known in life and recoiled from the retribution looming nearer. Faced with the reeking portent of your own extinction, you did as all men do in sight of death: you honored the remains of the life that ended and mourned the illusion it wouldn't end."

I sat there with my head down and listened to him, remaining motionless and silent when he finished. What he'd said, at first blush, seemed ludicrous. But there was a flavor of plausibility to it, and it was a better explanation of my feelings than any I could have come up with. Several things he'd said had struck home, moreover, his reference to Agricus in particular.

"Why are you so silent?" he asked me.

"I'm not sure," I replied. "I think what you've said is very interesting. Much of it may even be true. But it still seems contrived somehow. I mean, doesn't it strike you as quite a coincidence that an all-but-forgotten event I just yesterday wrote about should wind up playing such a major role in my life today?"

"Not at all," said Nestor. "The sight of the slave boy and the tavern girl in each other's arms helped determine which events you would think of to write about."

"Perhaps. Yet it seems peculiar to me that I should have written yesterday about the one event in all my life that corresponds to an event that occurred today."

"Ah, but, my dear fellow, it is not the *one* event in all your life that corresponds to what happened today; it is merely the one event you've written about *so far*."

"I don't follow you."

"Well, what were you writing about, fundamentally? A loss of innocence. Such things as that occur frequently in a person's life. Indeed, losing one's innocence without also losing one's capacity for joy may be all that the process of growing up consists of. Joy comes harder as innocence fades. That is why the sight of innocence fills us with sympathy, and why the death of innocence calls forth our tears. You and the slave boy had much in common where innocence was concerned, just as did Agricus and the boy's murderers. It is always like that: those whose capacity for joy has been destroyed cannot bear the sight of it intact in others. If this were not so, the world would soon run short of cruelty."

"Fair enough," I answered him. "But even granting that there are a number of events in my life that are pertinent to what happened today, they still constitute only a minute fraction of all the events I've experienced. Isn't it odd that I should have written about one of those very few occasions?"

Nestor smiled at me. "It would have been odd if you had failed to do so."

I stared at him blankly.

"Oh, don't be so simple!" he exclaimed. "Think, man. Use your mind. As you write about your life, you will choose those from among your innumerable experiences that were most meaningful to you. *All* of those you choose to write about will be pertinent to some aspect of your experience with the slave boy. They will also be pertinent to one another in various respects. If you doubt me, think of the cat crushed by the carriage wheel. That which is meaningful to a person is that which defines him. Each event you deem important is related to every other such event through the medium of your essential self. You will encounter the dead slave boy, and his murderers, again and again as you write of your life; and other characters you haven't yet mentioned will no doubt recur as well. A man's life has many themes, and each theme reflects an aspect of the man himself."

I sat silent for a while, then lifted my eyes to confront the old man's. "You know," I said, "you're not nearly as tiresome as I was beginning to think you were."

"Praise from Caesar," he answered with a merry grin.

Portia had left a lamp burning for me in our bedroom. She was lying where she always lay, but with her face turned toward the wall. I walked over, sat down, and gently placed a hand upon her shoulder. She didn't move. With my free hand I reached over and extinguished the lamp, knowing how ugly she felt she looked when she'd been crying. "Old men are churlish, darling," I said to her. "They feel their lifeblood thinning while their bile's running thick, so they strike out like peevish geese at those around them. If they were smarter, they would cling to the people they love, instead of pushing them away. But since they're not all that bright, the best they can do, once the harm has been done, is ask forgiveness."

I find it hard to concentrate on my past when my future is bearing down on me so rapidly. I find it doubly hard when the period I'm recollecting stands out as one of the most unhappy phases of my youth. Writing about how difficult I find it to write about my past difficulties will get me nowhere, however, so I may as well get started on the difficulties themselves.

Of course, I intended to wreak vengeance on Agricus; so sharp was the sting of his offense against me, in fact, that I pledged myself to bring about his death. Unfortunately for me, he headed off my still-unformulated design for retaliation by doing me yet another injury.

It was the morning after the incident at the baths, a morning of baleful, miasmic heat. I had risen early, before first light, and made my way down the street to the tenement where Agricus lived. There was a crevice just large enough for me to curl up in between his building and the tenement adjacent to it. There I secreted myself, with a chunk of plebe bread from the Hobnail in one hand and a rock the size of a pomegranate in the other. As I crouched there, wedged in, and gnawed listlessly on my breakfast, I began to have second thoughts about the crudeness of the revenge I was contemplating. My blunt-instrument approach didn't much trouble me from the aesthetic point of view, but I could see that it left a lot to be desired on the pragmatic level. If I threw the rock and missed, I would sooner or later find myself at Agricus's mercy, which was no place for anyone to be. If I attempted to club him with the rock, I ran the risk of being discovered as I approached him, which would also involve grave consequences. It became clear to me, as I lay in wait for my enemy, that my chances of bringing off a successful act of reprisal depended on far more deliberate preparation and planning than I had bothered with up to that point. I decided, accordingly, to head back home.

I was about to dislodge myself from the crack when a small ginger cat jumped from nowhere into my lap, scaring me more severely than Agricus ever could have. The cat's attention seemed to be focused on what remained of my bread, and as his tiny needle teeth sank into it he gave out with the most violent purring noises I had ever heard. The sound he made brought to mind several dozen glass beads rolling down a cobble-stone incline, and I can't remember which astounded me more: the noise he was making or the fact that he was there at all. From the way he looked, a bit scruffy and emaciated, I took him for a stray, one of the past spring's get. But, a stray that climbed onto perfect strangers and *purred?* That made him a most unusual specimen.

He finished the bread with dispatch, settled down on his haunches, folded his front paws beneath his chest, and went to sleep on mine, all the while maintaining the most tooth-jarring racket imaginable. I stared in wonder at this unaccountable beast and tentatively ran the palm of my hand across his forehead and down his back. The purring got louder, and I hesitated before petting him again, not knowing what volume of sound he might be capable of. Another stroke did not produce any appreciable increase in noise, however, and I took this as evidence that he'd reached the top of his range. It was as I ran my hand over him the fourth or fifth time that I noticed the figure of Agricus standing six feet away from me in the street.

It was still before sunrise, and what little light there was cast a stone-gray pallor. The cat on my chest purred blissfully, his eyes tightly closed. I tried to think of some way to shut him up, but there was every chance Agricus would notice my presence if I moved so much as a finger. I could only sit motionless and pray that the noise from my orange companion didn't carry into the street.

Agricus stood with his back to me, gazing first left, then right. He didn't appear to be looking for anyone; he seemed fearful, rather, that someone might see him. Twopenny Street was deserted, however, the few hours before dawn being the only part of the day when people weren't bustling around the neighborhood.

I ran my eyes over my unsuspecting enemy and took a firmer grip on the rock I'd brought with me. I felt tempted to go ahead with my original plan, but two things stopped me: the feline sleeping on my chest and the sight of two or three streaks on the back of Agricus's thighs, streaks that looked like tracks of dark paint running down a whitewashed wall.

I had barely had time to notice these tracks when Agricus turned toward the door of the building and gave an almost imperceptible nod. For a moment or two nothing happened, but then a tall, gaunt, elderly man walked out. He was clean-shaven, distinguished-looking, and wore a woolen cloak of the most magnificent Tyrian crimson. His shoes were patrician red and bore the white crescent of a curule magistrate. I knew his face; it was a famous one, but not one I could put a name to. Whatever the name may have been, the face betrayed such utter boredom that the man almost seemed to be grieving, grieving over the unfathomable staleness he found in everything beneath his gaze.

He walked over to Agricus and placed his right hand on the boy's shoulder. Between the thumb and forefinger of his left hand he held a silver coin, which he first showed to Agricus and then let drop into the hollow of his own palm. Agricus reached up and took the coin, raising his eyes for the briefest instant to meet those of the old man. It might have been a gesture of gratitude, or it might have been simple wariness; I couldn't tell. The old man leaned over and gently placed a kiss on Agricus's head. Then he turned and walked rapidly away up the street, while Agricus stood statuelike, watching the crimson figure dissolve into the predawn gloom.

If only I had been able to understand at that moment the full significance of all I'd just seen, my vengeance would have been a very simple matter. For it is clear in retrospect that Agricus had sold himself, or been sold, on more than one occasion. Whether others besides the old patrician had pleasured themselves inside his body I cannot say. All I'm sure of is that I understood little about the scene I'd witnessed. In fact, it mystified me. The best hypothesis I could come up with was that Agricus was the old man's illegitimate son or grandson and as such was subject to his authority. I imagined that the august gentleman stole down from the Esquiline or the Aventine on specified occasions to administer discipline to his notoriously unruly descendant. In my child's mind, that was an adequate explanation for the blood streaks on Agricus's thighs, just as the coin was explicable as an indulgent patriarch's gesture of conciliation. Now that I think about it, my childish hypothesis wasn't all that wide of the mark. Its near accuracy was only metaphorical, however—and I knew as little of metaphors as I did of pederasts.

Agricus stood where the old man had left him, and he remained standing there long after his patron had disappeared from view. As I watched him from the crevice, my cat friend opened his eyes, yawned, and rose onto his front paws. He then began kneading my chest with his claws, piercing the skin beneath my tunic in a manner that generated pain with marked efficiency. Worse, he began to amplify the sound of his purring to such an extent that I gave up all hope of remaining undetected. Agricus continued oblivious of my presence, however, and as I watched him I found that, even under the circumstances, I had a tendency to get lost in admiration of his beauty. The black curls, violet eyes, delicate nose, exquisite mouth, and slender body all combined to evoke thoughts of a new Adonis. If I'd known then how great a handicap the possession of exceptional beauty can be, I might have felt a little less vindictive toward my adversary. All I knew, though, was that he had struck me and that he enjoyed a senator's favor. To me it seemed he had every advantage, while I had but few. Thus, when he finally turned and walked back into his building, it didn't strike me as all that significant that his fists were clenched and his cheeks besmeared with tears. Nor did I give much thought to the fleeting impression that for the briefest instant, as he was turning, his eyes and mine had met.

As soon as Agricus was gone, I began to wriggle out of my hiding place. Of course my cat companion remained—in at least one, and perhaps both, senses of the phrase—attached to me as I struggled free, and he maintained his position on the cloth of my tunic even after I'd gotten back on my feet. For a few moments we stared at each other, nose to nose, the cat clinging to my garment with every claw at his disposal. He'd stopped purring, and his grip on me was starting to slip, so I grasped him under his forelegs and draped him across the back of my neck like a scarf. He immediately dug his claws back into the fabric of my tunic, taking a little skin off my clavicle in the process. But he seemed to feel content in his new location, and as I set out for the Hobnail I heard again the raucous sound of his purr.

The question was where to put him. The answer, after some deliberation, was: in Glaubus's wine cellar—at least until I could sound Drusilla out on the subject of my keeping a pet. Fortunately, all was still quiet at the Hobnail when I got back there. I hurriedly dumped some crumbled-up leftover bread and some mashed-up leftover beans into a drinking bowl, threw a couple of dishrags into an old clay pot, and headed downstairs. My companion purred approvingly as we descended into the semi-darkness (or, to be strictly accurate, he purred the way he always purred, and I took that as a sign of his approval). He continued to thrum away as I set his bowl and pot down in the corner underneath the staircase, but he stopped purring, albeit briefly, when I began to detach him from the back of my neck. Once he'd settled himself on the soft rags in his pot, he resumed his cheerful buzzing, and he was soon peacefully asleep. I sat stroking him and realized, to my surprise, that my face had taken on the contours of a smile. I would call him Romulus, I decided, since we lived by the Quirinal Hill, and the god Quirinus is simply Romulus in immortal form. Romulus . . . Romulus . . . I repeated over and over again to myself, and to him, until the sound of people stirring upstairs reminded me that I had better get myself something more to eat before submitting to the long ordeal known as school.

To my great chagrin, Glaubus, along with the parents of several other children in the neighborhood, had engaged the services of one Damatrios to provide some of us mud eaters with the rudiments of an elementary education. Damatrios claimed to be an Athenian, but we, his students, always had our doubts. His accent was anything but Attic, and there were certainly enough Athenians in Rome for us to know what a real one sounded like. There was some question in our minds as to whether his accent could even be called Greek; I myself always thought it had a Macedonian twang to it. But whatever his city of origin, Damatrios had one outstanding quality as a teacher: he charged only eight sesterces a month per pupil. As to his other abilities, I can say only that we were no more ignorant after several years of his instruction than we were before our education began. And as that much could not have been said of many young aristocrats whose tutors and rhetors were among the highest paid in Italy, I guess it's fair to conclude that Damatrios gave value for money.

Our "schoolroom" was the notorious courtyard behind the Hobnail, a less than adequate site for the practice of scholarship—especially when it rained—but a quieter one than the street, which was the only alternative available. We met in the courtyard every morning from the second through the sixth hours, except on market and feast days, and Rutolo collected the exorbitant rent of two hundred and forty sesterces a year from our guardians for the use of these opulent premises.

The number of pupils under Damatrios's supervision varied from month to month, depending on the financial conditions obtaining in each boy's home. There were seldom more than ten of us and seldom fewer than six, though on particularly glorious spring and summer days the students in attendance could dwindle down to two, the two being, invariably, the shy and effeminate Tritticus, eight-year-old son of Saturnius, the butcher, and Rutolo's own son, Plettus, age eleven, who, as may be imagined, suffered more keenly from his father's passion for order than even the tenants of our building.

On this particular morning there were seven of us in attendance: the two regulars; our gang leader, Trebbio; his close friend and deputy, Donatus, also fourteen; the mud eaters' thirteen-year-old "strong man," a coarse oxlike boy named Greffo (who was so besotted with Agricus's beauty that he'd become Agricus's creature), Agricus himself, and me. The fact that Trebbio and Donatus had arrived at the Hobnail that day with Agricus and Greffo should have alerted me to the possibility of trouble. So should the fact that Agricus hadn't bothered to clean his legs or his face in the hour that had elapsed since I'd last seen him. If anything, his face looked dirtier and puffier than it had been earlier, but that didn't seem ominous to me either.

The tedious hours of recitation crawled by, passing ever more slowly as the heat gained power and weight. Damatrios harangued us, denounced us, and whacked us soundly with his staff in a losing effort to keep our attention. Finally, with the sweat pouring off him and his voice going hoarse, he surrendered to our restless apathy and set us free, with more than half of the sixth hour still to go.

To be released early from the toils of learning was just cause for jubilation. So it was in a celebratory mood that I rushed downstairs to check on Romulus. He was sleeping, but he yawned, stretched, and started to purr when I ran my hand over his body. His food had been eaten, every last bit of it, and behind his bed pot I saw four immaculate little turds. Clearly, all his needs had been satisfied, and he lay there in undiluted bliss. On impulse I bent down and kissed the top of his head. Then I ran upstairs, grabbed some bread and onions from the Hobnail's larder, and hurried over to the Quirinal for the mud eaters' regular midday gathering.

Our meetings took place on a small rocky outcropping about two-thirds of the way up the portion of the hill that was nearest the Sanqualis Gate. The outcropping could accommodate perhaps twenty of us, but that was a very tight fit. Ten or twelve was the greatest number it could hold comfortably, but that posed no difficulty, since with one thing and another it was rare that more than ten or twelve of us showed up on any given day. On this particular afternoon, however, there were between fifteen and twenty boys gathered on the ledge when I arrived, and I could tell from the cast of their eyes that I was the one they were waiting for.

I stood there facing them, a little out of breath from the climb, with sweat running in rivulets down my face and neck and chest. The sun's heat pulsed into my body in time with the labored rhythm of my heart, and fear began slithering along the coils of my intestines. I didn't need to look at Agricus to know why I was afraid; I needed only to notice the rocks held in each boy's hands.

"You're accused of betraying a brother," Trebbio said, as pig-faced Greffo, standing between him and Agricus, started pointedly massaging the large stone he had brought.

Trebbio's words stunned me.

"This morning before sunrise," Trebbio continued, affecting a magistrate's stilted tones, "you and our brother Agricus met, at your suggestion, to avenge an attack on you made by the brick licker we call Scab-nose. This Scab-nose is the son of Sacer, and he is known to rise early each day and go to the Forum Holitorium to fetch vegetables for his father's cookshop. You and Agricus planned to fall on him as he left his tenement, and fall on him Agricus did. You hung back, however, because you saw Scab-nose's brother coming down the stairs behind him. Even though you and Agricus together would have been more than a match for the two brick lickers, you were too cowardly to come to our brother's aid. You stood by while they beat him, and you watched in silence as they made a woman of him with the leg of a broken stool. Then, when you saw that they were almost finished with him, you ran away, thinking you wouldn't be punished for what you'd done."

Without fully realizing it, I had begun to shake my head in denial while Trebbio talked. I knew I couldn't exonerate myself, though. Agricus's courage was an established fact among the mud eaters, and his "wounds" from the fictitious stool leg were there for all to see. The fact that I hardly knew who Scab-nose was would not do me any good. In fact, as I realized to my horror, nothing would.

"Agricus has always been the best fighter among us—for his age," Trebbio resumed. "You, on the other hand, have never been of any particular use. The fact that you've betrayed him so foully, and the more terrible fact that you caused him to be humiliated, means that the only proper punishment for you is death. . . ."

I think Trebbio was about to say something more, but before he could continue, Greffo shouted, "Little bastard!" and sent his rock winging into my chest. I screamed and fell over backward, nearly toppling off the outcropping from the force of the stone's impact. I found I could barely move my left arm as I struggled into a kneeling position, but I was able to focus my eyes on Trebbio in time to witness the one event of that day it gives me any pleasure to remember.

Trebbio was not big for his age, nor was he unduly muscular. But there was something about the way he bore himself that made you instinctively respect him—or fear him, if that's in any way different. He was chief among us for very good reasons, in other words, and in matters that touched on his prerogatives as leader he could be brutal and fierce. When I regained my balance, I saw him standing face to face with Greffo, who was a hand's width taller and almost twice as heavy. "Did I tell you to throw a rock at anyone?" he asked in an ominously quiet voice.

Greffo seemed to shrink before him, like an inflated bladder giving up its air. "No," he answered.

"Did I give you permission to throw a rock at anyone?" Trebbio continued, and Greffo seemed to shrink some more.

"No, Trebbio, you didn't. But that little shit deserves to have his balls cut off and shoved down his throat for what he did to our darling Agricus."

Trebbio merely nodded, and Greffo thereupon began speaking in an increasingly truculent tone—the bladder reinflating. "I think it's time we stopped talking. I think it's time we turned little Lucius into a pile of chopped meat. I say let's stone him bloody, cut him open, and throw him down the hi . . ."

Trebbio, nodding agreeably all the while, had driven his knee hard into Greffo's testicles. Clutching his midsection, the pig-face sank first to one knee, then the other, while his mouth gaped open and his eyes bulged wide. Trebbio looked down at him, and brought his other knee up into his face, leaving him prostate on the ground with blood streaming from his nose and mouth. "We are a *brotherhood!*" he shouted down at Greffo's quaking body. "We are not a mob. Please remember that the next time you're tempted to overstep yourself."

Everyone stood there in silence, except Greffo, of course, who lay there and moaned.

"Now," Trebbio said, turning briskly to me, "would you care to say anything in your own behalf before the rest of us throw our rocks?"

I stared at him, then at Agricus, unable to accept the truth of what was about to happen. I was going to die because Agricus had injured me and feared I might seek vengeance. The logic of it was stunning, and I felt powerless in the face of it. I had to say something, though, if only to postpone the dreaded moment, so I said, "Everything Agricus told you is a lie."

Trebbio gave a harsh laugh. "Is that the best you can do, little coward? Turn around, Agricus, and show your comrade your wounds. . . . Now, tell me, brave Lucius, if those wounds are a lie, what in the world could be the truth?"

Agricus hastily turned to face me again when Trebbio asked this question, and only then did I realize. They made a woman of him with the leg of a broken stool . . . the old man . . . the silver coin . . . the streaks of blood . . . the equivocal instant when his eyes brushed past mine . . . *He had seen me hiding in the crevice!*

If I hadn't known before, I understood then, for good and always, the power that comes with knowledge. He wanted me dead because he thought I knew his shameful secret and would reveal it. But I hadn't known it, until then. And in my mind the most important thing in the world at that moment was to show him the power he'd given me—not use it necessarily, just show him I possessed it.

"Well," Trebbio prompted impatiently. "What is the truth of those wounds, if it's not what Agricus has told us?"

I trained my eyes on Agricus, and I can't remember having ever seen so far into another person's soul. I felt I knew him then, more intimately than anyone else I'd ever encountered. And I realized, with another strong shock of understanding, that he had no knowledge of me. Yes, it was my life that was hanging in the balance, but as between the two of us I knew that I had achieved something much better than mere revenge. A surge of fierce elation swept over me as I gloried in the thought that I held Agricus's fate in the hollow of my hand and I exulted in the knowledge that both of us saw it quivering there.

"Well," Trebbio repeated. "How did Agricus come by his wounds if not in the way he said?"

My eyes never strayed from Agricus's face. "I don't know," I said, and then braced myself to receive the first stones.

FROM THE
JOURNAL

[JULY 13TH]

I don't know whether it's a good or a bad omen, but the heat finally broke a few hours before we set off for the Palatine. I could sense a change coming during the afternoon; there was a suppressed turbulence in the air, as fugitive puffs of wind came skittering through the garden and suddenly died away, leaving trees and hedges all quivery and aflutter. There were also signs of change in the sky to the east. Instead of remaining in place, as they usually do, the clouds above the mountains started building in our direction, until by midafternoon they were arrayed in line of battle directly above our heads. Huge billowing columns of immaculate white boiled up into a sky of impenetrable blue, and the sun gave ground to the west in the face of their advance. As evening approached, the thunderheads announced their predominance with rumbles from the mountain crests, and wispy gray veils of rainfall became visible against the darkening horizon. The air grew cooler, grew denser, grew still, as a heaviness of anticipation settled over our orchard and fields. No sound came from the animals in the barnyard, and all that could be heard in the pasture was one lone calf bleating anxiously for its mother. For a long while, it seemed, all nature stood transfixed, in thrall to expectation, and the unnatural stillness deepened as the daylight paled. A gust of wind, fleeing ahead of the storm, brought with it the bracing scent of cool wet air, and once the wind had passed us we saw flickers of lightning begin to dance among the lowering clouds. Random drops of moisture fell in the lightning's wake, kicking up motes of dust as they struck the ground. And as the drops fell, the wind rose, swelling slowly and inexorably until it reached a pitch where every shrub and tree limb was bending backward in order to weather its force. There was a moment, a fleeting instant, when the tempest seemed to pause in its onslaught to gather strength. But then, with a sound like a mountain breaking open, it thundered its arrival and unloosed its full torrential power.

I was in the stable with Rullo when the storm broke, checking to see that the cart was properly loaded for the trip to Rome and reassuring myself that no necessary provisions had been forgotten. We stopped our work at the first clap of thunder and went to the stable doors to watch the rain pelt down.

"What do you think?" I asked him. "Are the gods trying to tell me something?"

Rullo furrowed his brow. "It's possible, Domine," he answered. "They say that early summer rains foretell a rich harvest. They're a good omen, in other words—at least in regard to farming." And he looked at me with a worried expression that seemed to say: I wish I could come up with something more encouraging for you.

"Well," I said, laughing, "what's good for the crops must be good for the farmer—and why would the gods bother being good to my crops if they didn't plan to keep me around long enough to enjoy the benefit?"

Rullo gave me a tentative smile. "You must be right, Domine," he said. "I don't know why I didn't think of that myself."

At that I had to laugh even louder, and I reached over and hugged his shoulders. "You're a better man than I deserve to know," I said, which clearly caused him to feel scandalized.

"Please, sir," he responded, "don't make me into something better than I am."

And I accepted his gentle rebuff; just because a man is a slave doesn't mean that he should be subjected to his master's familiarity.

I craned my neck out of the stable and looked up at the clouds, letting the rain drum heavily on my face. It felt cool and cleansing, and together with the scent of lightning in the air it made me feel calmer, more equal to the strain of confronting my fate.

Glancing over at the house, I saw Camilla and Portia in the kitchen doorway, gazing out at the rain. Camilla turned and said something, and Portia emphatically shook her head. But Camilla wouldn't take no for an answer; she began bouncing up and down on her bare feet and reaching for her mother's hands. I could see that Portia's resistance was beginning to wane a little, but she kept shaking her head and trying to affect an expression of stern disapproval. Camilla saw clearly that the balance was tipping in her favor. By now she had hold of Portia's hands, and was trying to pull her out of the doorway. I realized at last what she was up to, and tapped Rullo's shoulder so that he wouldn't miss the scene. One final all-out yank brought Portia stumbling headlong into the rain, evoking squeals of delight from Camilla, who still had hold of her hands. Portia pulled free and angrily indicated that her smock and hair were being drenched beyond redemption. I could hear the sound of her scolding voice. But Camilla ignored her mother's anger, or overrode it, rather, by dancing around her and chanting loudly,

"Father Neptune in the sea,
Send your clouds of rain to me.
When our fields are green with hay,
Send your soggy clouds away."

Portia, now soaked to the skin, watched her daughter cavorting around her for a few moments, then pounced on her, picked her up, and dropped her into the nearest large puddle. Screams and peals of laughter came from Camilla's throat, and she took off after her mother, who was beating a hasty retreat toward the house. She caught Portia a few feet from the doorway, tackling her at the knees, and the two of them fell to the ground, laughing and shrieking and splashing each other with their hands. Watching them, I felt a surge of love so powerful that it brought tears to my eyes. "I'm a lucky man, Rullo," I said. "Yes, Domine," he answered, a bit puzzled perhaps by the odd sorts of things that call forth my sense of good fortune.

It rained for an hour or more, at times with ferocious intensity, but toward sunset the cloud cover began to lift a little and the sky rapidly cleared. Soon there was nothing overhead but the deep violet dome of twilight, with Venus sparkling in the western afterglow and the giant cloud tops of the squall line marching away to the south, their summits tinted peach and persimmon by the radiant echoes of the retreating sun. The air felt clean, and fresh as spring water. It seemed we would have a good night to travel.

Perhaps it was merely that—the weather—that made all of us feel so inappropriately lighthearted in the face of so much uncertainty and danger. Or perhaps, in spite of the danger, we were simply excited by the prospect of going to Rome to see the Emperor, unsavory though he is. Even I, whose danger is greatest and whose experience of Rome and Rome's emperors is most extensive, can feel a quickening of the pulse as I contemplate returning to the City. The Urbs, as it's often said, is an addiction, an addiction it's hard to shake off. Even those who have never been to the City have heard it talked of all their lives. They are addicted too. We all are—from Britannia to Arabia, from Scythia to Mauretania, from one end of the known world to the other. Rome is the great passion, the common obsession, the goal of every townsman's journey. For good or ill it is the summit and the sum of human striving. One would have to be half-witted or insensible to disregard its fascination.

The trip to Rome would take six nighttime hours at this time of year, which meant we would have to arrive on the brow of the Janiculum no later than sunrise. Getting down the hill, across the Aemilian bridge, and over to the Palatine's east gate (the entrance reserved for petitioners, tradesmen, and others of low estate) would be a matter of no more than half an hour, which would leave us half an hour's leeway before the City's daylight ban on private wheeled vehicles went into effect. But one constantly recurring anxiety I had was that we might arrive late and be stopped on the street by some stone-headed trooper from the Urban Cohorts who would insist on detaining us at the nearest castrum while his tribune determined our fine. It wasn't the thought of the fine that troubled me; it was the idea of not getting to the Palatine at the designated hour. I could picture myself waving the Emperor's summons in the trooper's face, only to have him respond phlegmatically that every driver he'd ever caught violating the ban had always claimed some special exemption, which was really neither here nor there as far as he was concerned because it was up to the Tribune to decide on special exemptions, and even if it was up to him instead of the Tribune, he would have to take us to the Tribune anyway because our claim to exemption was not based on having the standard copper exemption disk nailed to the axle of our wagon but on an elaborate written document which he, being totally illiterate, could not even pretend to read and which in any case he was not capable of verifying without the assistance of his superiors. . . . I pictured us confined for hours inside a dusty police barracks waiting for some drunken tribune to awaken from his wine-soaked stupor. The Emperor, meanwhile, thinking me a fugitive, would be issuing orders for my arrest and sending out Treasury agents to take possession of my farm. Whatever chance I had of dying with dignity and saving my family from ruin would be forfeited irretrievably—and all because I got to the City an hour after the sun had risen.

The result of all these anxieties and imaginings was a decision to depart for Rome just after nightfall, which gave us all twelve nighttime hours to make sure of our destination. I didn't suppose we'd suffer any penalty for arriving early; the worst that could happen was that we'd end up waiting for six hours outside the Palatine walls.

Having decided on the time of our departure, I finally gave some thought to the question of Nestor. The possibility of having him come with us to the Palatine had certainly occurred to me, but after discussing the matter with Portia, I decided it wouldn't be wise for us to deviate in any particular from the instructions set out in the Emperor's summons. "I desire to see you, your wife, your son, and your daughter before me . . ." was what our First Citizen had caused to be written; so I, my wife, my son, and my daughter would be the only ones to appear. (The fact that we don't know whether we'll be provided with adequate quarters in the Palace was a second consideration; if we are to be crammed into one small room, an extra person could prove embarrassing in more ways than one.)

My decision, accordingly, was that Nestor would have to wait out our Imperial sequestration on the farm, and when I confronted him with this cruel conclusion, his response was, "I'm fond of you, friend Lucius, but I wouldn't subject myself to the pleasures of the Palatine even if every other part of the world were underwater. I didn't get to be this old by being stupid, you know."

Thus was the issue of his coming with us resolved.

Of course, with all the last-minute preparations for our departure, I hadn't had a chance to discuss with him the most recent installment of my life story. So about the beginning of the second hour of the night, when we were at last ready to leave, it was decided that he would come with us in the cart as far as the Nereid, then ride home on a spare donkey we'd bring along for his use. He had kindly offered to lend us his carpets for our journey, and I had loaded the cart in such a way that they could be laid flat over our belongings. The result was a fairly comfortable approximation of a sleeping couch, plenty large enough for Portia and the children to curl up on.

Before long everything was ready. Rullo, lamp in hand, stood with the rest of our household as the five of us took our places on the cart. Good-byes had been said already, in many cases tearfully, and there was nothing more for anyone to add. I settled myself on my seat, took the reins and whip in my hands, and turned for one last look at our house and its people. "We'll miss you all," I said. "And we'll always cherish you." Then I turned my face away and cracked the whip. It wasn't until we were past the main gate that I fully recovered control of my emotions.

The night sky helped calm me. The moon was absent, having set not far behind the sun, and as I looked up through the limpid air the firmament seemed powdered with light. Hercules, the Swan, and the Bear shone boldly to the north, while the Archer, to the south, aimed his arrow at the Scorpion's eye. Arcturus blazed in front of us, and above our heads the Milky Way spilled its luminescence from the zenith to both horizons, as if the gods had doused a star's fires and sent the smoky ashes drifting down to earth.

From the back of the cart came the sound of Portia singing softly to the children, who were cuddled up beside her. Listening to her, knowing that the three of them were there close by, took some of the sting out of my poignant self-pity, and I was able to affect a reasonably casual tone of voice when I glanced over at Nestor and asked, "What are you planning to do while we're away?"

"Read," he answered, "and smell your flowers."

"How bucolic!"

"Yes. And what, may I ask, are *you* planning to do while you're away?"

"That's pretty much up to the Emperor." I shrugged.

"But not entirely," he responded.

"No, not entirely. What do you have in mind?"

"To begin with, you should keep writing the story of your life. It's just now starting to get halfway interesting."

"Good of you to say so. But what's the point of my continuing with it if you're not going to be around to discuss it with me?"

"I'll be near to you in spirit, my friend. And, in any case, we've talked enough by now for you to keep going on your own. Slow as you are, you must by this time have some understanding of the kinds of issues that have importance. And if you still feel that you have to talk to *someone*, why, talk to your wife. Her mind can keep pace with yours, if she keeps a brake on it."

"Too true," I said. "But under the circumstances I really don't know if it makes any sense to keep on writing. I mean, what good will it do me?"

"It'll do you a lot of good. First, it will keep you occupied. Second, it will give you perspective. And third, it may save your life."

I looked at the old man. "Beg pardon?"

"You heard me," he snapped. "Can't you guess what I'm driving at?"

I scratched around in my mind for some answer to his riddle, but without success. "You've stumped me," I said.

The old man shook his head and muttered, "It's a constant wonder to me that you've managed to stay alive as long as you have."

"It'll be a constant wonder to me if I manage to stay alive much longer," I replied.

"Oh, there's no need for you to die just yet, dear boy. To stay alive, all you need to do is play a little on the Emperor's shallowness and inexperience."

"Play on them? How?"

"You were once his father's closest friend; am I correct about that?"

"Substantially correct." I nodded.

"Well, *use* that, man—use it to hold him up to his father's mark."

"I still don't follow you."

Nestor looked up at the night sky and made a gesture of supplication. "I'll spell it out for you," he said finally. "You're writing your autobiography, right?"

"Right."

"You were at one time the late Emperor's closest friend."

"Right."

"The new Emperor knows this about you."

"Yes."

"The new Emperor stands in awe of the old one."

I thought about that before responding. "Yes, he stands in awe of him. But it's awe mixed with envy mixed with . . ."

"Fear?" Nestor offered.

"Well, a kind of fear. Not a fear of being shamed or disregarded; it's subtler than that. It's more like a fear of being disapproved of . . . or maybe disliked."

"That's what I would have supposed," Nestor said.

"But how does that benefit *me?*"

"Very directly. Our Princeps is just four months into his reign; he is trying to perpetuate the form, if not the substance, of his father's magnanimous rule. Simply tell him, in front of his retinue, that you are currently in the midst of writing a personal biography of your dear departed friend Marcus. He won't dare insist on your suicide until the work is finished."

"But I'm *not* writing a biography of my dear departed friend Marcus," I objected.

"Oh, yes, you are. Everything you've written so far is merely prefatory to the history of your friendship with our late Emperor. I know you didn't realize that until this moment, but I'm sure you understand it now."

I turned the idea over in my mind. "I don't know," I said. "What if Commodus wants to see the work in progress?"

"That's easy," Nestor responded. "Simply tell him that you were planning to present him with the first few chapters next month and to ask him at that time to act as the biography's sponsor; in fact, you were in the process of organizing the material for the book when his summons arrived, but you got so busy preparing for the trip to Rome that you didn't have time to do any more work on the project."

"Isn't that going to sound a little disingenuous?" I asked. "I mean, all of us who opposed Commodus as Marcus's successor are marked for death; we know it and the Emperor knows we know it. I'm not going to sound very convincing, asking him to sponsor a book of mine about Marcus."

"That all depends on how you present the matter," Nestor replied. "If you stand before him as a man who knows he's condemned and moreover *accepts* his condemnation, I'll wager you won't find him unwilling to grant your last wish, which is to write a loving biographical tribute to his own father under his own sponsorship, a tribute that will redound to *his* greater glory, both as the son of a fallen hero and as the magnanimous ruler who has sworn himself to perpetuate the enlightened Antonine traditions. The fact that writing his father's biography could take you a couple of years won't occur to him, or if it does, the worst he'll do is give you till the end of the year to finish it. Either way, you've bought yourself a little time—as well as a good excuse for hurrying back to your farm."

There was silence for a while, as I let all he'd said sink in. Not for the first time, and far less reluctantly than before, I admitted to myself how lucky I was to have found the old man on the beach. "Perhaps Nestor isn't the right name for you," I said finally. "The more I know you, the more you put me in mind of the wily Odysseus."

The old man gave a mirthful grunt and said, "In that case you can think of yourself as a sort of Penelope, slowly weaving your shroud of words to cover the memory of a king—while death, your suitor, waits impatiently for you to be done."

"On second thought, Nestor does seems like the right name for you," I responded, and we both allowed ourselves a laugh.

We arrived outside the Nereid, and Nestor somewhat brusquely bid us good-bye, whether out of emotion or from simple rudeness I couldn't tell. Portia took his place on the driver's seat beside me, and we turned onto the polygonal stones of the Aurelia.

There wasn't much traffic at that time of night. The children at length fell asleep on the carpets, and Portia and I enjoyed a silent communion as we proceeded toward Rome. After an hour or so we passed through the sleeping village of Lorium. The road to old Pius's villa ran off into the darkness on our left, reviving memories of many long years gone by.

On we went, climbing and descending the five great hills that stand between our farm and the City. The night sky turned silently above us, while frogs and crickets sang us on our way. Soon after the start of the third watch we gained the Janiculum's summit, and while our mule slaked its thirst at the outlet of Trajan's aqueduct we looked at the vision of

Rome asleep below us. Aside from the flicker of a few scattered torches there were no lights at all to be seen, and apart from the murmurous rumbling of wagon wheels in the distant streets there were hardly any sounds to be heard either. From where we stood at that hour it hardly seemed possible that we were gazing down at the first and foremost city of the world. Even the glory of empire, it seems, must yield to the supremacy of night.

We slowly made our way down the Janiculum and across the Aemilian bridge, immersing ourselves in the hubbub of the City's nighttime traffic. Turning first south, then east, we proceeded along the southern wall of the Great Circus down to its far end, following its curve around until the east gate of the Palatine loomed up before us.

And here we wait—my family asleep, and I with my pens, ink, and scroll. Far to the southeast, where the line of the Appian Way bisects the line of the horizon, the first hints of dawn are tinting the star-pocked sky. The day will soon begin, and I am so very afraid.

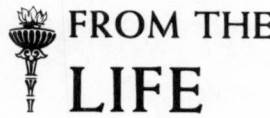
I was a good deal less afraid, thinking back on it, when I stood on the side of the Quirinal confronting the mud eaters—and I can think of at least two reasons why. First of all, I felt, however foolishly, that I was in control of the situation. Perhaps pig-faced Greffo had unwittingly done me a favor by throwing his rock before he should have, because the reality of being struck by a stone freed my mind of all the anxieties of antici-pation. Once the stone hit me, I *knew*, in almost a bodily sense, exactly what I would have to contend with—and more important, *they* knew that I was no weak sister whose spirit would break in the face of a single blow. By standing up to Greffo's stone, and to the threat of all the others, I gave the lie to the allegations of cowardice that Agricus had made against me. On some level, I think, I realized this, and the realization was a strong factor in keeping my fear within bounds.

A second factor was the sudden understanding I'd just awakened to about Agricus himself. Again it was a question of knowing something without really knowing how I knew it; but I *did* know that Agricus, having seen that I wouldn't betray his secret, would do everything he could to save my life. Of course, having started the process of persecution, he was in something of a predicament as to how he might go about stopping it; and since Trebbio might let loose the stones on me at any moment, he had to think fast and act quickly. Fortunately, he was gifted in those respects.

"Wait!" he shouted, and all the mud eaters turned to look at him. "I don't want Lucius killed just on my say-so."

Trebbio glared at him. "By Juno's crack!" he exclaimed. "It's on your say-so that we're all up here in the first place."

"I know," Agricus answered. "But maybe stoning isn't the best way to punish a coward."

Trebbio frowned. He clearly felt that his leadership was being called into question in some way, but he seemed at a loss to understand how. "I'm listening," he said in an ominous tone.

"When you kill a coward, all you end up with is one less mud eater. But if you make the coward *repay* the gang for his cowardice, then you get something of value and you don't lose a soldier the gang might need."

Trebbio narrowed his eyes at Agricus. "What's going on here, little pretty? Is this whole thing just some private quarrel between you and Lucius?"

"Oh, *no*, Trebbio!" Agricus replied, his eyes widening.

"Shall we go capture Scab-nose and his brother to see if they'll confirm your story?"

"By all means, Trebbio. Let's do that."

Our chief stared at Agricus, who bravely returned his gaze. Then he looked toward his deputy, Donatus, who gave an irritated shrug and said, "Why don't we get rid of both of them."

Trebbio barked out a laugh. "Good suggestion, my brother. Either Agricus is lying, in which case we get rid of Agricus, or Agricus is telling the truth, in which case we get rid of Lucius. But since Agricus and Lucius taken together aren't worth even half the trouble they've been causing us, I say let's stone them both and be done with them."

At this Greffo cried out, "Oh, *no*, Trebbio. *Please!*"

But our leader merely laughed at him. "Perhaps you'd like to take your darling's place, fat fellow, or maybe shield him from the stones with your excess flesh."

Greffo kept whimpering "Please, Trebbio, please," and I began to wonder whether he, too, might play a part in Agricus's secret.

"Please *what*, eunuch?" Trebbio shouted at him. "You want me to let the whole matter drop? You want me to pretend that nothing's happened?"

Greffo shook his head while tears ran down his cheeks. "No, Trebbio, no."

"Well, what *do* you want me to do then?"

"I don't know. I don't know."

"Dolt!" Trebbio spat, and it was at about this time that I began to question whether he really intended to do away with us at all.

I was no more than ten years old, but I'd been around long enough to know that older boys often get enormous pleasure out of terrorizing younger ones. I even started to wonder whether my life had really been in danger in the first place. The fact that Trebbio had torn into Greffo so ferociously for hitting me with the rock suggested that the punishment he'd had in mind for me did not involve taking my life. Looking back now, from the vantage point of old age, it seems a bit strange that my view of what went on was couched so uncritically in terms of life and death. I suppose Nestor, if he were with me, would explain that I was predisposed by my background to think in such catastrophic terms. Perhaps I was, but at least I had enough sense to feel skeptical after a while.

And that was to my credit, for even if Trebbio did not intend to punish me with death, he still had plans that posed hazards to my life.

Our leader stood silent, apparently immersed in thought, and all of us stood silent with him. I felt confident that the crisis had passed as far as my immediate survival was concerned. But as my fear of being stoned to death abated, the pain from the stone that had struck me started to throb its way though what at first had been no worse than a numbness, and ripples of achy nausea began to run up my chest and collarbone to my neck. Agricus and I exchanged uneasy glances, dismayed by the likelihood that we would soon find ourselves comrades in adversity. It was hard to believe that only the day before we had been little more than casual acquaintances.

"I have decided!" Trebbio said loudly, and all of us hung on his words. "One of these two street lice deserves to die, but neither of them matters enough for us to bother about determining which one. The point is, they've caused all of us a lot of trouble and have failed in their brotherly duty to each other. I decree that they must make good the harm they've done and heal the breach in our brotherhood. My decision, accordingly, is that they must go to the shop of Hermius the goldsmith in the Argiletum and by this time tomorrow bring back to us the golden statue of Amicitia that he displays on the pedestal by his doorway."

My mouth dropped open. The shop of Hermius was one of the most famous in the City, and the statue of Friendship that graced its entrance was the unofficial patron deity of every shop in the Argiletum. It was over two feet high, moreover, so we wouldn't even be able to lift it, let alone steal it. Trebbio couldn't be serious, and Agricus, fortunately, had the courage to confront him: "Why not just stone us now and be done with it, Trebbio," he said angrily. "Two grown men couldn't steal that statue; so how do you expect us to?"

"Maybe I don't expect you to, pretty fellow. Maybe I just expect you to die trying."

To this all the "brothers" responded with a laugh.

"I'd rather die now, thank you," Agricus announced, and the laughter immediately stopped.

Trebbio examined Agricus's face for a long moment, then turned and said to me, "Is that your wish, too, Lucius—to die now rather than try to steal the statue?"

All my fear flooded back on me; Agricus's insane bravery, or brave insanity, had landed us in a test of wills with Trebbio, a test we could win only by suffering death, and which we could lose only at the cost of our lives. I thrashed around desperately in my mind for some way to redefine the situation, but all I could come up with was, "No, Trebbio, I don't want to die today and I don't want to die tonight. Instead of having us die, I propose that you let me and Agricus steal *two* golden statues of Friendship, and then offer both of them to you and the brotherhood tomorrow."

The lame idea I had in mind was to persuade Trebbio to accept two small gold replicas of the famous statue. Such replicas could be found in goldsmith shops all over the City, and although I didn't know how Agricus and I might go about stealing two of them, I did know we'd have a much better chance of success, and survival, than if we concentrated our efforts on stealing the original.

Trebbio narrowed his eyes at me, and I felt that I could almost read his mind as he weighed the pros and cons of my suggestion. Thinking about him now, from the dispassionate perspective of many years, I can see that he had some serious deficiencies as a leader. That was more or less inevitable, I suppose, given his youth and the fact that the only qualities a gang chieftain really needed were toughness, ruthlessness, and a certain animal cunning, qualities with which he was well endowed. In the areas of foresight and human understanding, however, he fell distinctly short, and with regard to me and Agricus he had created a situation that threatened to undermine both gang solidarity and his own personal authority. Had he been a little smarter, or perhaps just a little older, he would have thought very carefully before making Agricus's charges against me a matter for the whole gang's participation. Even if Agricus had been telling him the truth, my offense remained essentially personal in nature, and in any case he should never have handed down his verdict on me before hearing my side of the story. Agricus's widely acknowledged courage and my mildly suspect reclusiveness had influenced him to take precipitate action, though, and he now found himself in a decidedly precarious position: the accuser had all but recanted his accusation, the accused was beginning to look like an injured party, the lumping of accused with accuser seemed even clumsier than it was Draconian, and just about every boy in the gang was starting to wonder whether such a frivolous pretense of justice was next going to be applied to him. If Trebbio's original object had been merely to terrorize me—and I think it might well have been— then he, Donatus, and Greffo could probably have done a better job than the gang as a whole, and without the attendant risk to his prestige. But either he hadn't been subtle enough to think of that or his malicious anticipation of my terror overcame his better judgment. In either case, he was on the verge of looking both foolish and tyrannical, so he was more receptive to my pathetic attempt at compromise than he would have been under other conditions.

"You propose to bring us *two* statues of Friendship?" he asked me.

"Yes, Trebbio. One for our altar to Quirinus and one to sell for money."

Our leader thought for a moment, then turned to his deputy for help in getting out of his predicament. "What do you think, Donatus? Two gold replicas of the statue aren't worth even a fraction of the original's value."

Ever the loyal aide, Donatus came swiftly to his chieftain's rescue. "True, brave Trebbio; but there's every chance that these two little ass wipes would bungle the job at Hermius's shop and thereby leave the brotherhood empty-handed. Perhaps it would be best for us to set them a task more suited to their limited capacities. That way we'll at least get something out of all this turmoil they've generated."

Trebbio made a show of pondering Donatus's suggestion, then announced, "Very well. We will meet here tomorrow at the same hour. Lucius and Agricus will present us with two gold statues of Friendship at that time, or suffer the consequences."

"Perhaps we should leave our stones up here, just in case," Donatus said with a malevolent grin.

"Good idea, brother!" Trebbio responded, and at his signal the stones thudded to the ground. "Until tomorrow then," he said in a tone of finality, flashing an admonitory glance in my direction before he turned and started down the hillside, with Donatus, Greffo, and all the others in his train.

Within moments Agricus and I were alone on the outcropping, the sun pounding down on us and reflecting dully off the discarded stones. My neck and left shoulder were throbbing painfully, but I found that I could still make use of my hand and arm. For some reason, I didn't feel wrathful as I looked over at Agricus; my one concern at that moment was to work out some practical plan with him for stealing the golden statues. But this concern was apparently not one he shared. For all he did was walk up to me, spit on the ground at my feet, snarl "Idiot!" and walk away.

I confess I was totally dumbfounded by his behavior. Try as I might, I couldn't think of a single reason for him to be angry at me. Only years later did it enter my mind that the cause of his anger might simply have been that he couldn't think of one either.

Dazed by the sun and sickened by pain, I slowly made my way down the hill. My only thought was to get back to the Hobnail, splash cold water on my face, and play with Romulus in the coolness of the cellar. I had barely walked inside, however, when Drusilla slapped me with such violence that I can still recall the impact of her palm against my cheek.

"Little brute!" she screamed at me. "How dare you bring a filthy street animal in here." Then she hit me again, to the amusement of all the afternoon topers in the bar.

I looked pleadingly to Glaubus for assistance, but he wasn't about to tangle with Drusilla over something as minor as a stray cat.

"Where *is* he?" I wailed, fearing the worst in the depths of my soul.

"He's back where he came from, in the street, which is where you'll be sleeping if you ever bring another animal in here."

I didn't need to listen to any more; I ran outside in panicky despair and began searching. "Romulus! *Romulus!*" I shouted, blindly pushing my way through the milling throngs of people in the street. I shouted, then sobbed, then screamed out my kitten's name, and the tears came streaming from my eyes. I hardly noticed the pain in my shoulder, and the problem of the two gold statues receded into insignificance next to my crushing sense of loss. I was ten years old and the world all at once was at my throat. It wasn't the world that tormented me, though; it was the anguish of having to fight it all alone.

 # FROM THE
JOURNAL

12

[JULY 14TH]

So far it's all been fairly humdrum.

Promptly at the beginning of the third hour I presented myself, or, rather, my summons, to the massive Praetorian on duty at the gate. He took the document in his two great paws and subjected it to such fierce scrutiny that I almost expected the ink to start running. After a long while he uttered a guttural "What is?" thereby alerting me to his Germanic origins. Pointing with my finger, I very diffidently directed his attention to the Emperor's seal and said, "Cae-sar. Cae-sar." The Praetorian glared down at the unoffending red wax, then turned to me and said, "You wait."

I watched him stride off in the direction of the gatehouse; once he'd gone inside, I looked over at my family and gave them a bemused shrug. Because of the pomp with which the summons had been delivered, I guess I'd been expecting a somewhat more grandiose reception, with a grim phalanx of guardsmen standing ready at the gate and hundreds of Imperial retainers looking down on us from the ramparts of the Augustan Palace. Thus grossly had I exaggerated the importance of my fate and the significance of my offense against the Emperor. Thus abruptly was I brought to the realization of how little I mattered in the eyes of M. Aurelius Commodus Antoninus Augustus. It seemed that I was barely worth the trouble it would take him to condemn me, and that the news of my death would occasion nothing more from him than an indifferent nod. I suppose I'd been secretly consoling myself with the notion that my passing would be tinged somehow with tragic overtones; now I see that my final hours may well partake more of the comically mundane.

After a short interval, the mountainous Praetorian returned in the company of a comparatively diminutive centurion. "Sorry about the delay, sir," the centurion said. "This fellow's new on the job. Fresh out of the Teutoburg Forest, so to speak, eh?" And he laughed boisterously, in a way that demanded—and obtained—some reciprocal sign of amusement from me. All three of us ended up laughing, in fact—the centurion because he believed he'd said something funny, I because I didn't want to be the one to tell him he hadn't, and the guardsman because he didn't want to acknowledge his ignorance of Latin.

The stench of the mundane was all-pervasive.

The centurion took charge, summoning slaves and issuing orders with all the dexterity of a practiced drillmaster. Within moments the gate was swung open and our cart brought inside. A few moments more and our belongings were unloaded. As our cart and mule were led away, a tall sallow-faced steward materialized and requested us to be so good as to come with him. We did as we were asked, and a dozen slaves carrying our belongings took station to our rear. The walls of the Augustan Palace loomed over us as we walked toward a massive portal framing a dusky torch-lit hall. The scent of cool stale air flowed into our nostrils from the semidarkness, and as we passed from the daylight there came from behind us the ponderous sound of the east gate clanging shut.

I suppose it's not excessively saccharine of me to say that our quarters could be worse. We have a window, after all, and even a view—of the slave quarters and vegetable gardens nestled against the foundation walls of the Tiberian Palace. Our window faces north, moreover, which is a blessing at this time of year. And there are no bars to keep us from climbing out of it, just a sheer forty-foot drop to a stone pavement.

Our room is about twenty feet square, the last and largest of a series of vacant cubicles fronting a single corridor, and the only one with a window. We were "advised" by the steward to remain always within its confines, though "no objection would be raised" if one of us went to fetch water occasionally from the pipe at the other end of the hall. Our room has no door on it, which may be deemed ominous or auspicious, depending on one's frame of mind. The floor is of rough brick, the walls and ceiling of whitewashed concrete, and the furniture—one chamber pot—of baked clay. For a prison cell it is not without its charms; indeed, most Romans would count themselves fortunate to occupy such commodious quarters . . . under less inauspicious circumstances.

The crucial fact, of course, is that the four of us are together, which means that our room, though harshly confining compared to our farm, is nevertheless a place to call home. We have laid down the carpets in the dark corner diagonally across from the corner where the doorway is and have dubbed that area our bedroom. Between the doorway and the window we have set up a species of table: two wooden planks from the bed of our cart supported by the two wooden chests that contain our food—salt pork and fish; onions, turnips, and beets; hard cheese, barley cakes, honey, and bread. We have removed the lids from the chests, letting the planks serve as a substitute; when it's time to eat we simply move the planks apart and reach down into the chests for our food, pushing the planks back together again to reconstitute the table and protect our remaining victuals from the flies and the light. I find it a very efficient adaptation. The four stools we brought with us provide comfortable seating around our table, and the squat congius of wine beside it should last us at least till the end of the month.

The area diagonally across from our "dining room," we have set aside for the purposes of washing and storage. As to our other needs, we decided after some deliberation to locate our complimentary chamber pot just inside the entrance to our apartment, so that it will be the first object to greet the eye of any official visitor.

Our largest crate, full of books, abaci, and writing materials, assures us of sufficient sustenance for our minds, and a leather box containing dice, counters, and knucklebones will afford us some hours of idle pleasure. Each morning, before the heat starts to build, Decius and I will exercise with each other, to keep our bodies from going stale. As on our farm, we will arise and retire with the sun; as on our farm, we will share the same food; as on our farm, we will care for and honor one another. There is no prison where love abides.

It didn't take us long to settle in, and by evening there was a definite air of domesticity smoothing down the rough walls of our cubiculum. We had eaten a pleasant dinner and were beginning to turn our thoughts toward our bed of carpets when we heard for the first time a sound I imagine we'll be listening for every moment that we're here: the sound of approaching boots.

It was a Praetorian of indeterminate geographical origin. He was above middle height, thick-necked and swarthy, with a mass of garish scars on his forearms. He didn't speak, just pointed to me, snapped his fingers, and indicated that I was to come with him. My insides turned over, but I tried not to show it. "They probably want to ask me if we're satisfied with our quarters," I said with half a smile, waving idly to my family as I stepped out of the room. It occurred to me as I followed the Praetorian's broad back down the corridor that I would dearly regret such a casual leave-taking if it turned out my time had now come.

From our cell to the place I was led was a rather substantial journey. First there were long corridors, torch-lit and smelling of pitch. Then there were stairways, steep ones, with as many as thirty steps to each. At several points we passed through arcades running high along the Palace walls. From one of these I caught a glimpse of the Great Circus yawning empty in the twilight; from another the wooden masts on the top tier of the Amphitheater became visible in silhouette against the gray blue northeast sky—like the teeth of a Titan's comb.

I paid careful attention to the route we were taking, noting small details that might help me distinguish one corridor from another if I had to find my own way. I suppose I was thinking about the vague possibility, or eventual necessity, of an escape, deluding myself that a knowledge of the Palace corridors is somehow tantamount to the attainment of freedom. Even if we escaped the Palace, we'd still be inside the compound; free of the compound, we'd still be inside the City; fleeing the City, we'd still be inside the Empire; and quit of the Empire, however would we survive? There is no escape for us, except into ever larger prisons.

But I don't suppose it can hurt for me to familiarize myself a little with this smaller one.

The Praetorian led me at last into a large well-illuminated room graced with porphyry columns and serpentine walls. At a table in the center of the room sat an exhausted-looking middle-aged man surrounded by a welter of scrolls and tablets. Several feet behind him to his right and left stood two pages in anxious attendance. The Praetorian pointed to a spot in front of the table, then placed himself a few feet behind me and stood motionless.

The man at the table was bent over some documents and seemed oblivious of my presence, but after a few moments he raised his bleary eyes to me and said, "So, Gnaeus Calpurnianus . . ."

"Excuse me?" I responded.

The man looked down at the scroll open in front of him, then back up at me. "Are you not Sextus Gnaeus Calpurnianus?"

"I'm Lucius Celer," I replied.

"Damn!" said the man. "Wrong warrant." Turning his head to his right he barked, "Lupo! Where's the information on . . . what did you say your name is?"

"Lucius Aurelius Verus Celer."

"Celer. Right. Lupo, where are you, dammit!"

In fact, the page Lupo was now down at the man's feet, frantically sifting through a pile of documents on the floor. "Here, Tribune!" he shouted in agitation, presenting a scroll, which the man at the desk immediately snatched out of his hand. "Imbeciles," he muttered to himself as the distraught page resumed his post.

The Tribune pored over the scroll for what seemed like a long time, shaking his head occasionally and delivering himself of disgusted grunts. He seemed angry and frustrated when he finished reading, and he hardly looked at me as he roughly rolled up the document and set it aside. "Look, Celer," he said at last, "your case is for the Emperor to dispose of, and the Emperor isn't here."

I gaped at him. "He isn't here?"

The Tribune gave me a cautionary look that said, Don't give me any trouble, citizen. "No. He's not here, as I just finished saying. He's at his villa in Tibur."

"Do you know . . ." I stammered, "that is, could you tell me when he's likely to be back in Rome?"

"Oh, of course I can tell you," he said with heavy sarcasm. "The Emperor always lets me know about every little move he makes. That's why I'm sweltering here in the City while he's off nice and cool among the flowers."

I decided to refrain from further questions.

He gave me a long hard look of contempt, then said, "Back to your quarters."

I started to turn away, but stopped impulsively and summoned up the courage to ask, "Do you think we might return to our farm until Caesar is again in residence here? I mean, there doesn't seem to be any point in . . ."

"When Caesar summons people," the Tribune cut in scornfully, "he likes them to stay summoned until he's through with them, if you get my meaning. I think you'd better remain right here in the Palace, so he won't get really mad at you. Don't you agree?"

I nodded, took station behind the burly Praetorian, and was led away.

Portia and the children were relieved to see me, and I made light of my interview with the Tribune: "He'll be summoning himself to the Palatine before long; that's how disorganized he is."

They laughed at my picture of a bumbling low-level functionary. And it didn't seem to faze them at all when I concluded my account by saying, "And of course he doesn't have even the remotest idea about when the Emperor will be coming back."

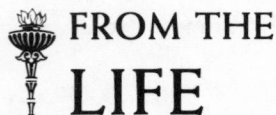 **FROM THE LIFE**

13

Despair is often a misleading emotion; it induces us to project present difficulties interminably into the future and rules out all hope of a reprieve. It is the message of a harried spirit to an anxious mind, a message that says: I cannot bear the weight of these troubles without breaking under the strain. And therein lies the confusion—for the spirit *is* bearing the weight, even as it laments that it can't. And it is up to the mind to set things straight, to instruct the spirit that it is not breaking, but merely suffering. "Nil desperandum," said old Horace, knowing that a spirit has been broken only when it is incapable of suffering any further. If you are in pain, in other words, your spirit is intact, and though the world around you may present the bleakest prospect, you remain, in essence, committed to life.

You may not realize that, however, if you are only ten years old. If you are only ten, you may succumb to your pain, and experience despair.

That, at any rate, is what I did, with Romulus lost, my shoulder a thudding agony, and the idea of obtaining a golden statue fading rapidly toward implausibility.

I trudged for hours through the neighborhood, with the heat leaching the strength from my body and the tears coursing in rivulets from my eyes. As time passed and my hopes of finding Romulus withered away, I began to sense that I was no longer engaged in a search, so much as a struggle of endurance. I had long since ceased to look for my kitten in any meaningful way; I was merely forcing myself to keep moving, oppressed by the thought that if I stopped for even an instant all my sorrow would come crashing down on me and extinguish my will to live. After a time, however, I found myself feeling too tired and bereft to care any more about my probable extinction, and so I sank down with my back against the side of some nameless building and let all the sorrow I'd been fleeing from surge through me in wave upon wave of convulsive sobs.

Left to myself, I believe I would have sat there until the mud eaters pounced on me the next day for failing to bring them their statue. I felt indifferent to my eventual fate, bludgeoned into apathy. With night coming on, my only thought was to stay where I was and wait for sleep to still my pain. And as for the morrow, well, the deliverance from pain could then be made permanent.

It turned out, of course, that I was destined to suffer, and live, a good deal longer than I was expecting to—thanks to Agricus, who located my sleeping body somehow and roughly kicked my foot by way of greeting. "Get up, you little wretch!" he said. "We've got a job to do."

Wearily I lifted my eyes to meet his. "Go away," I said.

He responded by shouting down at me, using progressively harder kicks to punctuate each word: "I told you . . . to . . . *get* . . . *UP!*"

The last kick brought me lurching to my feet with both fists flying. As I cocked my left hand for a wild punch, though, an annihilating pain swept through my arm and shoulder, causing me to scream like an animal, then double over and vomit out my insides.

"Watch where you're puking!" Agricus yelled, a wolfish smile playing over his features.

I leaned against the wall and struggled to gain control of my breathing. For some reason I found myself feeling a great deal better than I had only moments before. My head was clearer and my pain less severe. Perhaps emptying my stomach had worked a partial cure for me, or perhaps the only therapy I'd ever really needed was to take a few swings at Agricus. One way or another, I was back in the world, and concerned to make sure I would stay there.

"Are you finished?" Agricus asked impatiently, and I nodded that I was. "Then let's get going," he said, heading off at a fast pace down the street.

He led me across the Via Flaminia in the direction of Campus Martius. We passed the Saepta Julia, skirted the slave barracks of the Neronian Baths, then turned into an empty-looking district of dilapidated tenements and cavernous warehouses. Several blocks along we entered the courtyard of one of those huge tenement complexes constructed by the lawyer Regulus some fifty years before. This particular one was a full seven stories high and consisted of five identical apartment buildings squeezed in around the pentagonal courtyard where we were standing. The smell of urine and stale wine lay heavy on the stagnant air, and from somewhere high up came the sound of a woman's screams. "Either her quim's too small or his poker's too big," Agricus said, with a carnal laugh. I focused my attention on the screaming, which sounded hysterical, and more fraught with horror every moment. It did not call to mind any visions of quims and pokers; it suggested, rather, that some mother's child had just been found dead.

"Come on," Agricus said, and led me to a stairway. We made our way up the first two flights surrounded by total darkness, but the third-floor landing turned out to be a porchlike affair, open on one side from waist height to the ceiling and overlooking what appeared to be a well-tended kitchen garden. The garden was enclosed on three sides by a stone wall, one section of which abutted the building some five or six feet below the landing. Agricus climbed up on the waist-high sill, got a grip on it with both hands, and gradually lowered himself until his feet made contact with the wall. As soon as he had a firm footing, he worked the fingers of his right hand into a crack in the tenement's brickwork to secure a hold. Then he motioned to me with his left hand and whispered, "Climb down. I'll keep you from falling."

I had a moment's misgiving as I clambered onto the sill; Agricus was not the ideal choice to serve as guarantor of my safety. But then I thought of the strange new bond between us, and lowered myself toward him without any further qualms.

Once on top of the wall it was a relatively simple matter to continue our descent to the ground. The gibbous moon was now fully risen, moreover, so there was plenty of light for us to see by. Agricus led me to the open side of the garden, open, that is, except for a six-foot-high fence of wooden slats. Using his flexed knee and bent shoulder as steps, I had little trouble scrambling over; he followed so close behind me that he came down almost on my back.

We were in a small yard at the rear of what looked to be a shop of some kind. Directly in front of us a heavy bolted wooden door hung slightly askew from its upper hinges. Agricus went to the door and started tugging violently on its hinged side. "*Help* me, dammit!" he said in a hoarse whisper, and I hurried to add my efforts to his. After a short interval the lower hinges came loose, and the door's bottom corner swung open about a foot. Using all our strength, we were able to widen the opening enough to make it possible for us to squeeze inside. This accomplished, we paused for a moment or two to catch our breath, and Agricus, the sweat running off him, made a comment that did nothing to diminish my ever-mounting sense of anxiety: "When it's this easy to break into a shop," he said, "the chances are good that there's some kind of animal on guard inside."

I was about to ask him what he meant exactly by "some kind of animal," but before I could get a word out he was wriggling his way into the interior of the shop. As I watched his feet disappear into the blackness beyond the doorjamb, I had a strong urge to flee in the opposite direction. Just as the urge was being converted into an intention, however, the sound of Agricus angrily whispering "Come *on*, can't you!" brought me back from the dream of escape to the nightmare of squeamish complicity.

Being smaller than Agricus, I was able to squeeze inside with little difficulty, and my first glimpse of the shop's innocuous-looking interior served to ease somewhat my near-panicky apprehensions. Before me stood rows of wooden chests, a single row against each side wall and a double row back to back in the middle of the shop. Agricus handed me an iron rod and pointed to the aisle on the right; he then set to work prying open the first chest on the left. I stared stupidly at him until it dawned on me what I was supposed to do; then I went rapidly to work.

Opening the chests was a relatively simple matter; the only problem was that there were a lot of them. The first few I looked into contained candlesticks; next came lamps, then unguent boxes, bracelets, tripods, scales and weights, dishes, cups, platters, salvers, and finally phalluses. As I ran my eyes over chest after chest of crafted metal I had little sense that I was sifting through untold treasure; I was too intent on finding our statues for one thing, and, for another, the pale moonlight coming through the slats of the shutters caused the mounds of gold and silver before me to appear no more lustrous than tarnished steel.

I finished with the side row of chests and started work on those in the middle, many of which had leather shipping tags indicating they'd come from places like Parthia and India, outside the Empire's boundaries. The third or fourth chest I opened was empty, or so I assumed. There may have been a flicker of movement down in the darkness of its interior, but I took that as a trick of the uncertain light and hurried on to the next chest down the line. I was within two or three chests of the end of the aisle when I came at last upon one that was full of statues. "Agricus!" I called in a loud whisper, and he was instantly at my side.

There were all kinds of statues in the chest, deities and genii of every conceivable description. We found one Friendship right on top, but as we worked our way downward it began to seem likely that we wouldn't find another. The floor around us was littered with statues and statuettes: Minerva next to Fortune, Mars on top of Aesculapius, Isis beneath Cybele. Only when we had reached the bottom of the chest did a second Amicitia appear, and even Agricus allowed himself a loud sigh of relief. "Let's get out of here," he said, and I was only too ready to accommodate him. Gripping my statue tightly in my right hand, I was about to follow him out the gap by the door when my eyes fell on a statue of Eurydice as Maenad that Agricus must have thown on the floor. In spite of what happened because of that statue, I remember it with excitement to this day. It was erotic, unquestionably, but crafted with such masterful subtlety that its sexual fascination appealed as much to the mind as to the loins. Its face was what transfixed me, however, for its face, alive with a kind of lubricious indolence, was the face, made golden, of my much loved and hated aunt Drusilla.

Hypnotized, I set down the statue of Friendship and tenderly lifted the image of Drusilla from the floor. My member ached with a shameless urgency, and I could feel raw passion rising in my blood. The likeness was not exact, I noticed; the statue's features were more classic and conventional than my aunt's. But the body was hers in every detail, from the curve of the thighs to the pucker of the nipples. And I possessed her. I could do with her as I willed.

Lost in wonder and arousal, I contemplated the image of Eurydice/Drusilla for an interval outside of time, and it was only the swaying of a shadow that brought me back to reality. It was a ropelike shadow, bulging slightly at the top, and it swayed slowly back and forth against the background slits of moonlight on the floor in front of me. I could feel the hairs bristling on my neck as the shadow kept on swaying, and I thought of the flicker of movement I'd noticed at the bottom of that empty chest. Almost against my will my head turned, slowly, slowly, slowly, until a ladder of horizontal scales came into view. Slowly, slowly I climbed the ladder with my eyes, until at last there were other eyes to look at—maddened eyes, demented eyes—the eyes of a hamadryad cobra.

Again there was an interval outside of time. The instant our eyes met, the snake reared back and gave off a sound like waves breaking on an ocean shore. We stared at each other, I in horror, he in rage, while I struggled to remember the exact location of the door. I dared not take my eyes from his, but I knew he wasn't directly athwart my line of escape. My line of escape would be inside the range of his strike, though, so I would have to move very, very fast, if I could summon the will to move at all.

I don't know how much time passed with the snake and me mutually entranced. But all at once Agricus stuck his head through the door opening. "What the deuce is . . ." he began, finishing the sentence with "Juppiter and Zeus!"

With a loud hiss the snake turned toward the sound of his voice, and I leaped away to the side. Instantly the flared head came lunging in my direction. I felt a current of air as the gaping mouth blew past my cheek. Then I moved, while the snake raised his head to strike again.

The door opening loomed in front of me, an infinitely distant few feet away. Down came the lethal head as I flung the top half of my body outside, my legs thrashing frantically behind me. With a gasp of horror I felt something catch and take hold of the bottom of my tunic, the part of it that was still inside the shop. Sobbing, I yanked it free, and all at once found myself on the ground outside, intact and unscathed.

Agricus stared at me, wide-eyed, unbelieving, then stared at the hole from which I'd just come. Without a word we both sprang for the fence, and we didn't stop for breath until we were back on the stairway.

For a long time we sat on the landing, panting and sweating. I was still so scared that I almost expected the snake to come vaulting over the garden wall into my lap, and I was anxious to put a lot more distance between him and me as quickly as I could. It seemed miraculous that I was still alive—and still whole, moreover, apart from what felt like a minor scratch on the back of my left calf. Leaning over to inspect that part of the leg, I pulled my tunic up to get an unobstructed look. As I pulled, the scratchy feeling proceeded up my calf to the well between the sinews of my knees.

"Don't move another inch!" Agricus said in an urgent tone, bending over and plucking a curved white sliver from the hem of my garment. "You untoothed him!" he said exultantly, holding the broken fang up to the moonlight. I stared at it in appalled fascination, then anxiously ran my hand along the back of my calf. The skin had been broken in a few places, but not deeply enough to draw blood. No venom, it seemed, had made its way into my body.

"Damn, but you're lucky," Agricus said, having examined my leg for himself.

"I know," I responded, noticing for the first time that I had such a death grip on my statue that the fingers of my right hand were starting to cramp.

Then I realized.

"What's the matter with you?" Agricus asked, as I held the statue out in front of me and stared at it with unmixed horror.

He followed the direction of my eyes until he, too, was gazing at the statue. "What have you done?" he exclaimed angrily. "How could . . ."

But then he looked more closely—at the statue, at me, at the statue again, and again at me. He began to laugh.

This time my spirit did break.

I knew that nothing, not even another snake, could ever compel me to go back into that shop.

I was destroyed, I was undone—a fool who had run out of luck. With numbness seeping through my mind, I turned and headed down the stairs, leaving Agricus to bay his amusement at the moon.

I wandered in the general direction of home, indifference washing over me as it had that afternoon. At length I was standing in Twopenny Street, opposite the crevice where I'd hidden at the beginning of the day. It occurred to me, through a haze, that this was the first place I should have looked for Romulus. And indeed, when I stuck my head in the opening, he greeted me with a loud meow.

I dropped down into a sitting position and lifted him onto my chest, savoring the percussive rattle of his purr. I felt strangely content having found him, and sensed I could now face the wrath of the mud eaters with equanimity. The game was over, and I'd lost. But at least I'd have a friend with me at the end. That was sufficient consolation.

I must have slept for a while, because when I next opened my eyes a pale dawn was drifting down on the dusty tenements along the street. As in a dream I saw Agricus approaching me. He looked tired and drawn. Before long he was standing over me, his face a mask without expression. From his left hand he let fall two objects: a statue of Friendship and the head of a one-fanged snake. In his right hand another statue of Friendship gave off a leaden gleam.

Looking down, his face still blank, he pointed to the statue I'd come to think of as mine, the statue of Eurydice resting next to Romulus in my lap. He looked at me, I looked at him. Then I picked up my statue and placed it in his hand.

Next to Friendship in the dust, the snake's dead eyes stared up at me, while Romulus purred blissfully on. I felt the loss of my statue, felt it with a gnawing ache that defied common sense. But despite the ache, I was not inclined to begrudge Agricus his trophy as he turned and strode wearily into his building. We'd just been through a lifetime, he and I, and been linked together in ways that I but dimly understood. Another full lifetime has passed since he exacted his tariff from me, but I've never once doubted he charged a fair price.

 **FROM THE JOURNAL** **14**

The hours of a summer's day pass slowly, like the puffs of cloud I can see from our window, slipping eastward by imperceptible degrees across the shimmering dome of heat that lies on the City. Here in our quarters we surrender ourselves to lassitude, all effort being too arduous and all repose too alluring while the sun holds sway. Retreating from the light, we have gradually taken on the habits of nocturnal creatures and have found, to our gratification, that our eyes can see almost as well by the glimmer of a lamp as by the glare of the empyrean. We rise at dusk and retire at dawn, to doze and dream and drift our way across the molten day, "pendent twixt sleeping and waking," as the poet puts it. From outside in the compound come the sounds of life in its normal courses: the thump and scrape of a mattock cleaving the soil in a nearby garden, the splash and splatter of water being spilled onto a brick pavement, then, a moment later, the scratchy rasping of broom bristles sweeping it clear. Next, the low murmur of intimate conversation can be heard, as two old women pass on their way beneath our window; only the loud crunch of the gravel beneath their sandals preserves their exchange of confidences from profanation by my prying ears.

As the sun moves beyond the meridian, new sounds float up through the viscid air. Squealing shutters slap closed and the latches securing them fall shut with a *clack!* Blinds clatter down, doors swing to, keys turn in locks, and clanging gates are bolted to their posts. Little by little the sounds of human activity diminish, until there is not much more to listen to than the ratcheting of the cicadas and the sigh of a fleeting breeze. At last a semblance of stillness descends on the Palatine, as even the summit of Empire accedes to the summer heat. Then there are no sounds at all to be heard as one swelters, save for the anxious beating of one's own heart.

Yes, the heart goes on beating: thud-thud-thud with mindless persistency. And sometimes while it's beating, if the children are asleep and the heat hasn't leached us of desire, Portia and I will join together in a silence heavy with breathing and perspiration. In her, and her body, I find some consolation for our demeaned condition.

I've written little more of my—or Marcus's—biography, and nothing more of this journal, since the day we arrived here. In fact, I've been flagrantly indolent in just about all respects, having yielded, for the time being, to a sense of futility and self-pity. I try to conceal my feelings from my family, with what success I can't be certain. They, too, must contend with apathy and tedium; I will not sap their resolution by flaunting my petty despair.

Ye gods, I feel such contempt for myself. Indeed, the most grievous consequence of our confinement, so far, seems to be the loss of any tolerance I ever had for my own moral infirmities. After sixty years of desiring and obtaining and squandering and salvaging, I am farther from peace of spirit than I've ever been. After six decades of searching I've found nothing of either Marcus's selflessness or Agricus's courage in the murky quagmire of my soul. I still yearn for some chimerical form of "fulfillment," even, more ardently, it seems, than when I was a boy. And when I think on my life and the sum of my accomplishments, I want to weep for shame. How meager, how paltry, are the relics of my existence, especially when I consider the plenitude of my opportunities. Like some retrograde travesty of the Divine Augustus, I found marble palaces to build on and have left only hovels of brick. Were I not still so greedy for life's pleasures, I would acknowledge my imminent death as nothing more than a long overdue comeuppance.

Where lies the defect in my nature? Perhaps I've expected too much of life. Perhaps the morass of banality that is the setting for most men's existence is all someone with my deficiencies can demand as an arena for his own. For some reason, I've always resisted the notion that I am cut from the same coarse cloth as the common run of humanity. And perhaps the real penalty for such arrant snobbism is to be confronted constantly by its speciousness.

So be it: I am no one special. The divine fire burns no brighter in me than in the meanest goatherd.

Ah, ah, how that rankles! How that has always rankled! And I would dearly love to know why I recoil so violently from such an admission. All my life, all around me, I've known people who pass their years in a state of tolerable contentment even though they are without, to all appearances, any claims or pretensions to distinction. Are these people merely poseurs, who harbor in secret the most grandiose notions of self-importance? Or are they truly what they seem: creatures who feel no need to justify their existence with pleas of exceptionality?

Alas, I have long since realized that the first hypothesis holds true in only a small percentage of cases. Clearly, and unaccountably, most people in this world don't question the propriety of their presence here, though they may have doubts with respect to others. I, by contrast, see others as aspects of the natural order, and reserve all my doubts for myself.

Perhaps I'm just tired, unto death, as it were. I seem to have spent my whole life in a vain effort to break loose from the fetters of service and obligation. I have wanted only to be left alone, in good health, with plenty of money, and love, so that I may do precisely what I wish to whenever I choose.

Small wonder I'm tired.

Fool! Ass! Dolt! Oaf! At sixty years of age you are less enlightened than a child of six, and your aspirations are even more puerile.

Look, *look* at your family if you doubt the truth. It is *you* who has brought them here, *you* who has failed them, *you* who has so arranged matters that their lives are in danger and their bodies confined. Yes, behold them, treading out the airless days in this vile injurious place, and ask yourself why you ever got yourself entangled in the matter of Marcus's heir. Was it perhaps because you foresaw some hint of advantage, not to mention some prospect of advancement? Befriend the next Emperor and who knew what might happen. Debts might be lifted from your shoulders, cares might be banished from your mind. Who could say? Even a senator's stripe might have been in the offing. And you could then have lived as you wished—free of care, free of doubt, free of death.

Ah, simpleton.

I know now why I haven't written in this journal for so long: it opens my eyes to myself. Henceforth, I think I'll keep my eyes on the past when I'm writing, if indeed I can bestir myself to write at all.

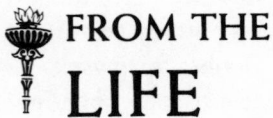
Trebbio and the rest of the mud eaters were at first incredulous when Agricus and I presented them with our golden trophies. There was much narrowing of eyes and wrinkling of noses as the statuettes were passed from hand to hand, and we could hear words like "brass" and "painted" being freely bruited about. Gradually, however, the suspicious mutters and skeptical frowns gave way to a marveling silence, as if the genius of Friendship herself had descended incarnate onto the hillside.

It is no exaggeration to say that my fortune was made—with the mud eaters at any rate. In one brief instant I was transformed from a mildly suspect nonentity into a fully established personage. And as for Agricus, well, if there'd ever been any doubt that he was destined one day to assume Trebbio's mantle of leadership, it was forever dispelled at that moment.

With regard to Agricus and myself, the next year or two saw a strengthening of that peculiar bond that passed for friendship between us. He continued, as before, to treat me with a volatile blend of disdain and condescension, but sought out my company as if I were his closest confidant, which I guess I may have been. I for my part continued to regard him with a mixture of deference and loathing, but welcomed his companionship as a source of endlessly diverting stimulation. I remained, moreover, both intrigued and repelled by his cruelty, which partook at times of pure malevolence, but often stemmed from simple callousness as well. I think what intrigued—and repelled—me most about it was its apparent randomness: the lash seemed to fall on whichever back was nearest. Only after many months of close association with him did I begin to discern some pattern in the randomness, and this pattern proved even more intriguing than his unpredictability. It was a subtle thing to start with, just a fleeting hint, the shadow of some leaning. So I watched him more closely until one salient fact became apparent: boys he'd attack if they came within his orbit, but girls and young women he'd go hunting for. Using his beauty as a lure and a beguiling pose of boyish innocence as a snare, he was able to arouse both passion and adoration in the haughtiest female breast. Indeed, it was the most uppish females he favored as his prey, and because I by contrast was profoundly unnerved by such creatures, his power over them became a source of constant wonder.

There was the slave girl Fabia, for example, who was fifteen, perhaps, when I was thirteen or twelve. She was from somewhere in the eastern provinces and worked as a prostitute at Curtio's, taking a peculium of one sestertius out of the four denarii Hercules Iamblichus charged each of her clients. Now four denarii was a lot of money to be charging in a neighborhood like ours, and in an establishment like Curtio's, but Fabia was never short of customers. I myself thought her exquisite, and admired her ardently, though from an impecunious distance. She was tiny, not even five feet tall, with honey-brown curls and the face of a wood nymph. Her skin had the glow of a succulent olive, and her plump figure would have met Plato's standards for the ideal form of Carnality. She was proud, of course, and vain of her standing at Curtio's. Both Iamblichus brothers regarded her as being almost more royal than servile, as the size of her peculium amply demonstrated, and if a slave in her profession can be said to reign over anything, Fabia reigned at our neighborhood baths.

To Agricus, inevitably, her high estate came to represent both a challenge and an affront, and he told me one day that he was going to "cut her down to size"—which was a somewhat maladroit choice of phrase given that Fabia was diminutive to begin with.

Even though I witnessed the implementation of most phases of Agricus's plan—if indeed it was a plan at all, and not just a spate of brilliant improvisation—I still don't really understand how he managed to subdue Fabia's pride. His first tactic was to present her with a gift—a perfume bottle—elaborately wrapped in a crimson cloth. I watched him offer her the package in the bar at Curtio's, and flinched involuntarily when she laughed in his face. If it had been me she had laughed at in that way, I would have shriveled up and sunk into the ground. But Agricus was not so fainthearted. He flashed that brilliant grin of his and said, "I brought you only a small token of my devotion, oh, Fabia, but with your smile and lilting laughter you give me back riches beyond compare."

Poor Fabia. Quite aside from the fact that her laughter, so far from being "lilting," was hardly more than a shrieky bray, she had been endowed with only marginal intelligence. Then too, she was very young—older than Agricus, to be sure, but in malice ten years his junior. She laughed more softly when he'd finished his little tribute, but brayed again when Titanus Iamblichus shooed him and me out of the bar.

"The hook's in," Agricus said to me as we walked out to the street.

His next ploy, a day or two later, was to hide his gift to Fabia in the bin where she kept her clothes. This done, he proceeded the following night to hide in the bin himself. Several more days passed, and when I finally saw him again on the street his face was alive with lupine satisfaction. "Meet me on the hillside at dawn tomorrow," he said. "I've got a little treat for you."

I knew Agricus well enough by then to refrain from asking questions, but, sure enough, he and Fabia were already on the rocky outcropping when I arrived there the next morning. Fabia was naked, moreover, reclining on a blanket.

"Look, dear," he said to her, "here's my good friend Lucius, the fellow I've been telling you about."

I received from her a nod of condescension, which I barely noticed, given the profusion of other things to look at.

"I've been talking to Fabia about how inexperienced you are with women," Agricus continued, "and she's agreed to let you watch us, if you don't make too much noise."

At this Fabia giggled, then bestowed upon Agricus a gaze of besotted infatuation.

My first and, given Agricus, customary reaction was to suspect that I was about to be humiliated. Staring at Fabia's body, though, I decided to endure whatever the Fates had in store.

Agricus still had his tunic on, but he lay down beside Fabia and began rubbing her crotch and kissing her breasts. I watched with the most concentrated attention, and thought my skull might burst when the girl began to give off little moans. Gradually her moans got louder, her breathing heavier and rough. Agricus, by contrast, seemed calm and self-contained, working on her as though he were the courtesan and she the paying customer. All at once he stopped what he was doing and sat up, to Fabia's visible dismay. "Look here," he said to me, "you're not going to learn anything standing over there. You'd better come closer."

I did as I was instructed.

"This is what a woman smells like," he said, proffering the fingers of his right hand.

I took a few diffident sniffs at them and picked up a hint of mustiness on their tips.

"No, no, no!" Agricus exclaimed, dropping his hand onto mine and gripping it. "You can't really smell the aroma unless you dig it out yourself."

With that he thrust my fingers into Fabia's cleft, and held them there so forcefully that I couldn't even with effort pull them free. The girl's already shaken poise seemed to slip away utterly in response to this uncouth intrusion. "Move your fingers around," Agricus whispered salaciously. "Work them into her as far as they can go."

"Agricus . . ." Fabia began in an uncertain voice.

"Be still a moment, dear," he responded, and forcibly pushed my hand inward.

"Agricus, please . . ." she whimpered, causing him to lift his eyes and fix her with a glare.

"I asked you to be still a moment," he said in an ominously quiet voice. "Now will you do as I ask you or not?"

"But it hurts, Agricus," she replied, tears beginning to well in her eyes.

"Oh, it hurts! I'm so sorry," he said in a tone of exaggerated solicitude, and without letting go of my wrist he bent over and kissed her on the cheek. "Don't be so rough, Lucio!" he barked out reprovingly, letting me withdraw my fingers a little from the warm moistness where they were lodged.

I was over my shock by then, but still somewhat at a loss as to the proper course of action to follow under the circumstances. On the one hand, I didn't much like the idea of being used as an instrument of my compeer's malice. But on the other hand, quite literally, there was the silken grip of Fabia's genitals. In the event, it was the other hand that prevailed, because it began, almost of its own volition, to explore that deliciously spongy inner flesh that, but for Agricus, I could never have even hoped to touch. My heart raced as my fingers moved, and as my fingers moved my shaft strained blindly toward the steamy warmth enfolding them.

Now, like the effusion of a swamp, Fabia's scent began flowing into my nostrils, with an effect on my body that was well-nigh incendiary. So great was my arousal, in fact, that several moments passed before I realized that Agricus had released my wrist. The instant the realization hit me, though, I jerked my hand out of her, as if in fear that she might lop it off.

Agricus, meanwhile, had removed his tunic and crawled past me, naked, in the direction of his victim's shoulders. Stopping just beyond them, he ranged his body above her face so that all I could see of him was his legs and buttocks. "I've gone all limp, dear Fabia," I heard him say. "Won't you please kiss me till I'm hard again?"

There was silence for a moment, then a sound like someone wading through a pool of mud. Agricus's buttocks began to rise and fall with a languorous rhythm, and I leaned back and craned my neck around in order to observe the act that till then I'd been able only to imagine. It was not quite as erotic as I'd expected it to be—it rarely is for an observer. Fabia's mouth looked grotesquely distended, and the back of her head seemed pinned to the ground by the force of Agricus's increasingly vehement thrusts. She didn't seem to be enjoying herself very much, and her meager pleasure was soon diminished further when a ripple of spasms ran across her lover's body and he let out a long guttural sigh. Immediately she started coughing and choking, but Agricus grabbed hold of her head to prevent her from dislodging him from her mouth. Then, all at once, he screamed and lurched backward, ending up in a sitting position with his wilting member cushioned between his palms. "You *bit* me!" he said unbelievingly to the still-choking Fabia.

"I couldn't brea . . ." she started to wail between coughs and throat clearings, but Agricus's fist slamming into her cheek put an end to the attempted explanation.

"You should never have bitten me," he said to her as she cradled her cheek and began to whimper.

I thought for a moment he was going to kill her, and I was about to try to restrain him when he turned without warning and gave me a demoniacal wink.

"Oh, please, *please* forgive me, Agri darling," sobbed Fabia. "I'm so terribly sorry if I hurt you; it was just that I couldn't breathe."

"Well, why didn't you say something?" Agricus shouted angrily, and poor Fabia could only gape at him.

"I couldn't," she blubbered out finally. "You were way too deep in my mouth."

Agricus made a show of considering the validity of such an excuse, then said, "Do you really want me to forgive you, Fabia?"

She looked up at him, her eyes liquid with hope. "Oh, please, dearest sweetheart. I can't bear to have you angry at me."

"Very well," he said with judicial deliberation. "But I want you to do me a favor in return."

"Anything, my sweetest. Anything."

Agricus slowly turned his head in my direction. "Make a man of my friend here."

Both Fabia's mouth and mine fell open.

"But Agri-poo, darling . . ." Fabia started to object.

"What's the matter?" he snapped at her. "One more poker in your coin box won't make that much difference."

Fabia stared at him reproachfully, then cast a glance at me and curled up her nostrils. "But he's so ugly . . . and scruffy looking," she complained.

"Under his tunic he's as beautiful as me though," Agricus replied reassuringly. (And, of course, he had reason to know.)

I watched the two of them debate about me, torn between the throbbing in my member and my reluctance to collaborate in the slave girl's further degradation. To be sure, her comments about my appearance offered me a convenient excuse for the depredations my body was contemplating, but my brain kept reminding me that the girl was being systematically victimized, and for no other reason than that Agricus disliked her.

Victimized or not, though, Fabia did not seem unduly troubled by the prospect of inducting me into the ranks of the intromitted, and after heaving a sigh of resignation she summoned me over to her with a wave of her hand. Trancelike, I answered the summons, and stood trembling with anticipation as she displayed herself on the blanket. Quite casually, she reached up under my tunic and took hold of my little peg.

"He's not even hard," she reported to Agricus in a tone of irritation.

"You'll remedy that, no doubt," he responded cheerily.

"Come closer to me," she said in a curt tone of voice, giving my peg a little tug. "And take off your tunic."

I glanced uncomfortably at Agricus, who gave me a gleeful nod of encouragement.

"Come on!" Fabia prodded, and in moments my tunic was off.

"Now don't be frightened, little fellow," she said in the rote-sounding tones of a bored professional. "I'm just going to spread some mouth-honey on your little puppy here, make it sit up and do lovely tricks."

And without further preamble she went to work on me, producing sensations that were almost too intense to be pleasurable. After a brief interval, though, she drew away and said wearily to Agricus, "He's not going to get hard; he's too excited."

"Work on him," Agricus responded. "Use your professional expertise."

Fabia glared at him, and I heard her mutter "Ye gods" as she returned her attention to my problem.

"You lie down on your back, little fellow," she said, "and see if your puppy likes sniffing around my cave."

She arrayed herself over me and placed the tip of my poker in a place that felt enticingly warm and wet. "Sniff up and down little puppy," she said, having just failed to stifle a yawn, and then moved my peg around so that it got wet too. "Stick your nose way inside, little puppy," she went on, as with a quick thrust of her wrist she embedded perhaps half an inch of me in the slippery folds of her quim. "Ah, that's so nice," she said in a transport of boredom. "Now look around little puppy," she continued, moving her pelvis a little way back and forth. The puppy did as she instructed and was greatly inspired by what it saw. "Umm, that's a good little fellow," Fabia droned on, lowering herself a bit, so that fully half my peg was engulfed by her inner flesh.

From that point on events unfolded far too quickly. I could feel my shaft going rigid while the crown of my member began to swell. Seasoned practitioner that she was, Fabia knew exactly what was happening and saw to it that it happened fast. Raising her body an inch or two off me, she flexed her muscles and stretched my rope taut. I gave a whimper of ecstasy as her wetness pulled me upward, then erupted in spasms as she sank down the length of my shaft.

She started to disengage herself from me before my spasms had abated, but even so I felt she'd vouchsafed me some inkling of grace.

"Well," said Agricus as I lay there gasping. "How does it feel to be a man?"

"Confusing," I answered him.

He laughed at that, handed me my tunic, and said, "Let's go get some breakfast."

I looked at him, then at Fabia, and in a hesitant voice replied, "All right, I guess, if you're hungry."

And to my astonishment he started down the hill.

"*Agricus!*" Fabia shrieked, and he turned nonchalantly in her direction. "Why are you leaving me like this? You said you'd forgive me if I did what you asked."

"And I do forgive you, oh, Fabia," he responded in an equable tone. "It's just that your body smells of compost and I'd rather not get close to you again."

Even in the early-morning light I could see the color drain from Fabia's face.

"I never liked you, you know," he continued calmly. "For four denarii I'd rather poke a goat."

Fabia stared at him in mute horror, and I thought at first it was only the anguish of rejection that I was seeing on her face. It turned out, though, that something more serious than rejection was contributing to her loss of equanimity. "*AGRICUS!*" she screamed at him. "I can't get back up to that second-floor window by myself."

"I know," he replied with a sunny smile. "I hope they don't beat you too badly when they catch you outside."

This callous response left Fabia speechless, and Agricus turned to me, his eyes triumphantly agleam. "Shall we go, my brother?" he asked in a carefree tone.

And I didn't know how to answer him.

There I was, still quivering from the caresses of Fabia's flesh; and there was Fabia, to all appearances just as capable of giving pleasure as she'd ever been. Now the way Agricus had arranged things, my chances of ever again being treated to Fabia's ministrations were going to be nil, even if she survived her punishment and resumed her calling. Four denarii was a formidable sum of money for a boy like me, and as a boy I was in any case debarred from buying her. If I stayed with her now, though, and offered to help her sneak back to her quarters, I could possibly trade her service for service. It was ignoble of me, I know, to be thinking in such terms at such a juncture. But I was possessed by Priapus, and my desire was overwhelming.

"Uh, I think I'll stay up here a while longer," I stammered, causing Agricus to narrow his eyes at me. But then, in an instant, he realized the trend of my thinking, and a wolfish smile spread over his face. "Take good care of yourself," he said with a cursory wave, and turned and strode off down the hill.

Slowly, abashedly, I brought my gaze around to Fabia, who sat there looking lacerated and old. She contemplated me with wretched eyes, searching perhaps for a hint of reprieve in my expression. She didn't find one though and, bowing to the inevitable, let out a long tired sigh of submission. Her voice was bitter as she leaned back to show me her body. "I suppose your puppy's hungry again," she said.

And we proceeded from there to do business.

 # FROM THE
JOURNAL

[AUGUST 11TH]

The Emperor has returned.

That, at any rate, is how I interpret all the tumult and fanfare that erupted in the Palace compound during the third watch of the night. We, of course, were not awakened by it, having just finished our "midday" meal. It startled us a bit, though, since we've become accustomed to a Palatine whose voices are soft and bucolic, unlike those that come from trumpets in full paean, horses in full gallop, and centurions in full spleen.

The worst of the hubbub lasted the better part of an hour, and its slowly diminishing reverberations continue audible even now, with the sun nearly halfway across the sky.

It's either the Emperor, therefore, or Jove himself who's graced this ancient hilltop with his presence. I could hope that it's Jove, but after sixty years one begins to run short of comforting illusions.

Needless to say, I can't sleep. But it's more excitement than anxiety that keeps me from my rest. Not that my fear has abated one whit; if anything, it's grown more keen. But the shackles of anticipation at last are loosening, and they have weighed on me more heavily than any fetters wrought by fear.

See! Even my pen feels lighter: it floats across the scroll dispensing metaphors.

And that's not the only reed of mine that's afloat on a tide of animation. Look there: my wife sleeps lying on her back, her legs carelessly flexed, one breast billowing free. The children, too, are deep in slumber. This is no time for writing in journals. . . .

I hadn't realized, I guess, just how oppressed my spirit was by the condition of our lives this past month. But that, I suppose, is the way that one bears the unbearable: by tamping down one's self-awareness. At all events, I feel rejuvenated, if not reborn, and all my sensations, fear not excepted, have the tangy vividness of life made new.

What more shall I do with all this resurgent vitality? I must do something; if I simply sit here like a slug and await the sound of approaching boots, I shall go mad. But what are my alternatives? I feel far too agitated to write much more, and my family is buried in sleep. If there were only something useful . . . ah, *ha*!

I have read it all now, every word that I've penned on my life—or Marcus's life, as old Nestor would have it. And I find the tale a trifle baffling. Set down as it is, it has a strangely alien quality, as if the subject were someone other than myself. Yes, the boy is father to the man, but this boy, this Lucius fellow, I hardly know him. It almost seems like I've been invested by some magic with his memories, but not with any of the feelings such memories should evoke.

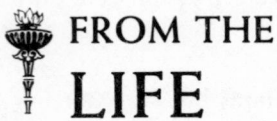
I first met Marcus—if "met" is the appropriate word—a year or two after
Fabia had made a man of me . . . or ended my boyhood, at any rate.
Agricus, by that time, had succeeded to the leadership of the mud eaters,
and it was thanks largely to the bold and imaginative way he exercised
his office that he, Marcus, and I came to know one another.

It was Agricus's conviction that a gang such as ours had commercial as
well as social functions to perform, and while he had no objection to the
practice of pummeling brick lickers, he felt there was a higher calling to
which we should all aspire, i.e., larceny. Perhaps he owed this particular
orientation to Trebbio, who'd been the first to send him out to steal. My
feeling, however, is that his eyes had focused on money a long time
before our theft of the golden statues—and for perfectly obvious reasons.
Money had been potent enough to purchase *him*, after all; and if it was
sufficiently powerful to transform his mother into his procurer, why then,
few were the wonders beyond its ken. Certainly Agricus, during the time
that I observed him, gave clear signs of having an almost mystical fascination with a coin's capacity to determine conduct. It was mysterious
enough in his eyes that small round pieces of metal stamped with portraits
and mottoes could be converted at the whim of their possessor into food
or drink or the pleasures of a comely body. But there was an even greater
mystery within the objects, because if you possessed enough of them the
whims you might chance to indulge in became a matter of widespread
interest, and people started cajoling you to bend such whims in their
direction. Thus the coins' power could be tapped not merely by spending
them, *but simply by having them to spend!* Witness the Equestrians, for example—free birth and 400,000 sesterces were just about all you needed
to join their illustrious ranks. And witness the highest—and therefore
most bribeworthy—Imperial officials, denominated by nothing other than
their salaries: sexagenarii, centenarii, ducenarii, as if their stipends
were . . . no, *because* their stipends *are* far more indicative of their standing
in the hierarchy than any titles descriptive of their official functions.

Thus the iron link between money and power gleamed golden in Agricus's eyes, and we mud eaters, in consequence, found our attention shift-

ing—or being shifted—from the delights of mere hooliganism to the subtleties of generalized theft.

It was in the course of an act of thievery, in fact, that Agricus, Marcus, and I became acquainted.

One of Agricus's sharper perceptions was that a theft, to be successful, must result eventually in the acquisition of those small round pieces of metal. In other words, it was no good stealing things if no one would give you coins in exchange for them. Trebbio had discovered this when he tried to sell one of our stolen statues of Friendship. The first goldsmith he approached had tried to rob him of the trophy then and there, at dagger point, and Trebbio had barely escaped from the shop with his life. The second, third, and fourth prospects had refused to have anything to do with him, and the fifth turned out to be a cousin of the merchant we had burglarized, who started screaming for the Urban Cohorts the moment he saw the statue. Discouraged and disgruntled by these developments, Trebbio, with about ten of us to back him up, had next quick-marched down to the Porta Capena in order to haggle with the Jews. They explained to him, as nicely as possible, that the statue was nearly valueless anywhere within ten miles of the City, but they offered to take it off his hands for six denarii. Trebbio demanded ten at a minimum, and settled tamely for seven. Thus Agricus and I—and Trebbio too—had nearly gotten ourselves killed for the grand total of twenty-eight sesterces. And once all our time and aggravation were factored into the equation, the reward seemed more meager still.

It was clear, therefore, that if one was going to steal, one had to steal either coins or objects that could be readily exchanged for coins . . . objects, ironically enough, such as bricks.

Agricus became our leader during the seventeenth year of Hadrian's reign, when the program of wide-ranging public works initiated by that Emperor was approaching its climax. One consequence of all the construction work then in progress was a sharp increase in the price of building materials, and though my memory is uncertain as to specific numbers, I do believe that most builders were paying as much as ten sesterces per hundredweight of bricks. One builder was paying only six, however, and the person he paid it to was our new leader.

Looking back on our operation, I can see that Agricus's decision to traffic in bricks was uncommonly shrewd. For one thing, it ran counter to form, which is to say, bricks, although valuable, are not generally considered objects of value, and are therefore not guarded and protected the way such objects usually are. Stealing them was a simple matter of scaling a wall and lobbing them over it, then collecting them in wicker baskets and taking them to our thrift-conscious builder.

Fifteen of us mud eaters could transport perhaps three hundred pounds of bricks at a time, but we could fling perhaps a thousand pounds over a wall before we got tired. Thus, if we were feeling energetic enough to make five trips, we could clear as much as eighteen denarii in a single afternoon. A few simple calculations will reveal that after only four days of such diligent thievery, each of us could find himself with more than sufficient means to purchase even such undreamed-of luxuries as Fabia!

The work, in short, was lucrative—by our standards, at any rate—and the pickings easy. Agricus nevertheless saw to it that we ran no unnecessary risks, which was simply good business practice from his point of view. Minimizing risks meant, first, moving our operations in random patterns from one brickworks to another, and, second, concealing the fact of our thefts as much as possible. We always stole from the largest stacks, for example, and stripped away only the outermost bricks on their sides. Thus a stack eighty bricks long, sixty wide, and thirty high, would measure seventy-nine by fifty-nine by thirty when we got through with it, and though some of us felt that seventy-six by fifty-six by thirty would look equally unsuspicious, Agricus, brave as he was, remained adamant for caution. He was right, of course. Crime, like any other enterprise, requires care and concentration if it is to succeed, whereas we, being boys, kept persistently drifting toward sloppiness. Thus, even if Agricus's meticulous approach verged now and then on the finicky, it still, using Cicero's phrase, served as a "salutary corrective." So salutary was it, in fact, that the major risk was borne not by us but by our penny-wise builder, who stood to lose a few foolish pounds above the neck if anyone noticed that the bricks he was using bore the works marks of every single brickyard in Rome.

As a rule, we stole when it suited us, taking into account such factors as the weather, our gang wars, and the condition of our finances. It was Agricus's habit to turn each of our forays into a sort of outing, having us bring along food—and even a girl or two from Curtio's sometimes—to lend a sense of enjoyment to the expedition. By doing this, he raised a banner of fun over the toil and potential danger of our endeavors, which not only gave us more pleasure in our thievery but also made us better thieves. Indeed, thanks to our leader's foresight and intelligence, we had all the advantages of criminals with but few of the anxieties, and it seemed to us impossible that anything other than an unlucky coincidence could subject us to retribution for our crimes.

Of course it was precisely such a coincidence that occurred.

At that time, perhaps the largest brickworks in the region around Rome was owned by Marcus's mother, Domitia Lucilla. It was located just to the west of the Via Salaria's fifth milestone, and covered a vast area between the Posternian Cemetery and the river Anio. Unaware of, and indeed indifferent to, the identity of its owner, Agricus and I and about a dozen of our brothers set out for this works one brilliant December afternoon, with the air smelling tangy from wood smoke and the light from the sky tinted gold. By the time we arrived at our objective, the sun was within a hand's width of the horizon, and the chill of approaching darkness flowed up from the ground beneath us like vapors from a marsh.

The wall around the works was of brick, appropriately enough, and fully eight feet high, but it posed no obstacle to us. Greffo's back and shoulders served as our stepladder, and it was his job to stay outside the wall and gather up the bricks we flung over it (being careful to use one of the wicker baskets as a helmet while he did so).

We dropped down inside the compound and set silently to work, having plundered so many brickyards by then that all talk was unnecessary. The eight or nine of us who were fastest on our feet ran to the stacks and brought armloads of bricks back to the wall, where the three or four of us who were slowest stood ready to toss them over to Greffo. After ten or twelve round trips, the "runners" began to tire, and one by one went back over the wall, with the help of a boost from the "tossers."

I, unsurprisingly, was the fastest of the runners, and the one least prone to fatigue. Agricus, by contrast, was slow of foot, so he usually worked with the tossers. It was a point of honor with him, however, to be always the last one to flee.

On this evening, I, with lungs straining and body pouring sweat, was in the middle of my twelfth, and last, sprint to the brick stacks. As I ran I took note of the crescent moon in the bloodred sky near the western horizon and listened to the pounding rhythm of my bare feet. Set against this rhythm were the muted thuds of tossed bricks landing outside the wall, and it was only as I drew near the stack I'd been stealing from that I realized those thuds were getting louder. Instinctively I stopped and listened. Turning, I saw to my horror that the tossers had stopped to listen too. How, in that case, could I still be hearing bricks strike the ground, more rapidly, rhythmically, and resoundingly every moment?

Clearly it wasn't brick falls I was hearing, and a sickening tremor of terror washed over me as I grasped all at once what it was.

"Lucio! Get back here!" Agricus shouted, and I turned and ran harder than I was ever to run again, with one major exception. Glancing over my shoulder, I could see only stacks of bricks in the rapidly dwindling light. But then, just above the tops of the stacks, I caught sight of three disembodied heads bearing down on me, three frightening specters on invisible horses, moving at a steady gallop down the long corridors of brick. I saw that two of the heads were sheathed by helmets, and that was all I cared to see. Turning my eyes away, I focused all my concentration on the movement of my legs.

"Come *on*, ox brain!" Agricus shouted to me, while clasping his hands to make a step for Rutolo's son, Plettus, who was the last boy still inside the compound apart from Agricus and myself. Lying flat on top of the wall was Greffo, his arm reaching downward to help Plettus up. Just as the first helmeted horseman broke into the clear, their two hands met. I saw Agricus strain to boost Plettus upward and Greffo stretch to establish a grip. Then there was the brief soft *whoosh* of a *pylon* cleaving the air.

The spear entered Plettus's back between the shoulder blades and passed easily through his body to the wall, where its point embedded itself with such force that the shaft was left quivering all up and down its length. Plettus threw his head back in a silent roar of agony, then went limp, and Greffo, struggling to lift his now dead bulk, finally sobbed and let him go. For a moment the boy hung there, impaled like a chop on a skewer, but then the weight of his body pulled the spear point out of the wall, and he fell.

By now I had reached Agricus's side, and the other two horsemen had come into view. *"Throw the bricks!"* Agricus shouted, while rushing over to Plettus's body. For an instant I didn't comprehend his meaning. Then I saw him yank the *pylon* out of our dead friend's back and turn to face our assailants. Reaching down, I took a brick in each hand, reflecting imbecilically on how lucky it was that our comrades had left some behind. The two helmeted horsemen were now within fifty feet of us, and roughly brought their mounts to a halt. In one smooth motion, they climbed down and drew their short swords. With a shock I realized that they were *singulares*, men of the Emperor's personal guard, and had I known how to, I would at that moment have prepared myself to die.

The two soldiers exchanged a brief word while I gaped in disbelief at their massive arms and thighs. The taller of the two began walking slowly toward us, the moon's light flashing from the steel of his sword. "Wait till he gets close," Agricus hissed at me, and I waited as long as I could.

He was no more than ten feet away when I threw the first brick, which struck him flush on the chest but didn't even cause him to alter his pace. Agricus and I shot each other a desperate glance, and I saw his fingers opening and closing around the bloody shaft of the *pylon*. "Good-bye, Lucio," he said to me, and charged toward the soldier with a high-pitched scream.

Fortune favors the bold, it's said, and in this case our adversary was so surprised by Agricus's attack that he could do no more initially than side-step and trip him. The next instant, though, his sword arm was rising to the sky, and only when it reached the top of its arc did I hear a mild voice call out, "Dracena! Stop!"

It was the third horseman, a boy no older than me.

It was Marcus.

If it were possible to travel through time, I believe I'd make my first journey back to that moment, almost as much for reasons of curiosity as for those of sentiment. I say this because my recollection of that first encounter has remained so vivid in my mind that I would like to compare it with the original experience and see how well it corresponds.

I was cold, or chilled, more precisely, standing there in the December twilight with sweat lying like soft sleet on my body. The moon's crescent shone wildly in the flawless indigo of the sky, and a faint sigh of wind from the riverbank brought with it the scent of pork on an olivewood fire.

The four of us—Agricus, the *singulares*, and I—stared at the slender form astride the horse, and the guardsman who'd been about to strike reluctantly lowered his sword.

The horse came to a halt in front of us, and the boy we were watching dismounted. He was a little taller than I was and his hair was an unruly mop of curls.

He approached me, and I took in a breath, not out of fear so much as anticipation.

"Whose bricks are these?" he asked me in a placid voice, indicating the dozen or so on the ground near my feet.

Though the light was meager, I could sense that he was studying me, with a calm fascination I couldn't begin to make sense of. His eyes sparkled in the near darkness, and I could see that his lips were curved into a gently pensive smile, a smile that suggested he was more concerned with how I would sound than with what I would say.

I struggled to come up with something clever, but in the end could offer nothing more than the simpleminded reply, "They're mine."

"In that case, perhaps you'd be willing to sell them to me," the boy responded without missing a beat.

I narrowed my eyes and peered at him, convinced he was playing a joke on me.

"Will one denarius be sufficient?" he asked, reaching for the pouch at his belt.

I stared blankly as he fished a coin out and extended his hand.

"All right?" he prompted in an amiable tone, and I looked down at the coin that was resting in his palm.

"Who *are* you?" I asked unthinkingly, raising my eyes from his hand.

"I am Marcus, of the Annii Veri. And you?"

"*The Annii Veri!*" Agricus erupted, scrambling quickly to his feet.

Marcus turned to him. "Yes, brave fellow. The Annii Veri."

At that point Agricus's face underwent a strange transformation, as, first, amazement, then elation, then calculation fleeted over his features, and were replaced at last by a mask of impassivity that I had never before seen. "Then you are the son of Annius Verus," he said.

"I have that honor," Marcus answered with a nod.

"And you are named for your grandfather."

Marcus nodded again.

And so the pieces all fell into place. This boy was not just anyone. He wasn't even just any patrician. His grandfather had been three times Consul, the last time when I was five years old. His father had been Praetor when I was three. And he himself, well, everyone knew that he was Hadrian's chosen one—the successor to the dead Antinoüs, some said, taking "chosen" in its most licentious sense, but a likely successor to the Princeps' seat as well, whether catamite or not.

Agricus strode over to Marcus and lifted the silver denarius from the young nobleman's palm. "I thank you, Marcus Annius Verus," he said. "I am Agricus, a freeborn son of Rome, and this is my friend Lucius, freeborn as well. We are deeply grateful to you and humbly accept your patronage."

I turned and gaped at Agricus; the boy had said nothing at all about taking us on as his clients.

"It is I who should be grateful to you," Marcus said with a knowing smile. "After all, who else would sell me such high-quality bricks at such a reasonable price?"

"It is our privilege, Marcus Annius Verus," Agricus responded, returning Marcus's smile in a way that engendered in me the first of what were to be myriad pangs of jealousy over the years.

"Call me Marcus," the young patrician said, reaching out and calmly taking from me the one brick I still held. "I already know who my ancestors are."

"Marcus it is," Agricus replied promptly, as the boy scrutinized the brick in the last dying quiver of the western afterglow.

"I see that you've already been good enough to stamp these bricks with the mark of this particular works," Marcus said, an arch expression playing over his features. "My mother will be grateful to you for adding to her supply."

So *that* was how he happened to be there.

"It's a service we're always happy to provide to members of your family, Marcus," Agricus responded baldly.

At this Marcus broke into laughter, and even the two *singulares* gave in to a smile.

I don't know why, really, but anger suddenly overcame fear at that moment, and pointing to Plettus I burst out, "Too bad he can't be laughing with us."

In an instant the laughter and smiles were gone; there was only Agricus's angry glare.

Again Marcus looked at me, with that same quiet fascination I had seen in his face before. "It *is* too bad," he said. "And that is one reason why I laugh."

Nobody had ever talked to me in paradoxes before, and I have to confess that I didn't think he made much sense. But in response to my puzzled frown he merely patted me on the shoulder. "Your rebuke is well taken," he said gently.

For a long moment he contemplated my face; then he turned to the two *singulares* and said, "Take the dead boy and this excellent fellow Agricus back with you to the City." Returning his eyes to mine he continued, "I hope to convince young Lucius here to ride back on my horse with me."

Of course I went with him; I was already under his spell. And of course Agricus was filled with wrath.

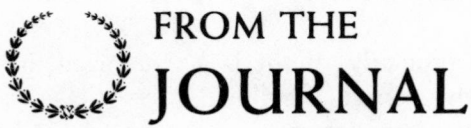

FROM THE
JOURNAL

[AUGUST 12TH]

The Emperor's summons came sooner than I expected, and was delivered in a manner I hadn't anticipated. I am still not fully recovered from the experience. Nor is my family.

It was toward the end of the night's second watch; we were preparing to eat. All afternoon and all evening the sultry air had been filled with unfamiliar and discomforting sounds, as if the hitherto pastoral world outside our window had been diabolically transformed into the most profane of Roman back streets. The sounds were made up of laughter and screams primarily, in all conceivable combinations. A child's scream of anguish, for instance, would be followed by an old crone's taunting laughter, and a man's bellowing guffaw would call forth a woman's irate screech. Men and women would shriek curses into the darkness, then cackle as others cursed back. After some hours of this the screams and laughter began to sound indistinguishable, as if joy and horror had become compounded in the roisterers' minds.

It was thus with no great appetite that my family and I contemplated our simple meal. That didn't matter, though, since we were not destined to eat it.

Screams and laughter had not been among the sounds I'd been listening for since the Emperor's return to the Palatine. My ears had been alert, rather, for the creak of a door swinging open at the far end of the corridor and the brisk rap-tap of a Praetorian's boots as they approached our room.

Perhaps the door down the hall was open to begin with; at all events, I never heard it creak. What I did hear, instead of two boots approaching at prefect's cadence, was several pairs of sandals coming toward us at a disorderly trot. Next I detected the clink of cloak rings against the rough casing of breastplates, and the flap of leather waist strips against hard-pumping thighs.

I guessed who they were before the first of them exploded into our room, and one glimpse at their blank, cold-eyed faces confirmed my grim conjecture. They were *frumentarii*, soldiers of the secret police, dressed in their customary manner—full armor and bare heads. (It is said that they never wear helmets because they never work in daylight, but those who say it are careful not to do so within their hearing.)

Without a word they grabbed us and shoved us out into the hall, their large calloused hands like clamps on the back of our necks. Either by chance or by cruel calculation, they seized Portia and the children first, so that I was forced to witness them being propelled down the hall in front of me. Thus I hardly felt the policeman's heavy fingers on my own neck as he pushed me along, so lacerating was the vision of pointless cruelty that assailed my streaming eyes.

I hated no one at that moment so fiercely as myself, and took a perverse pleasure in the extent of my own impotence and humiliation. But I took no pleasure of any sort in the sight of my wife and children being brutalized; all I could feel about that was a fiery and all-engulfing shame.

We passed for what seemed like hours through the murky corridors of the Palace, a ragged single file, a caravan of pain. As I stumbled along I thrashed around in my mind for some word of encouragement I might shout to my family. But I could think of nothing . . . nothing except "Be brave!" which, called out to them by me, would have been both superfluous and hypocritical.

At last we entered a brightly illuminated audience chamber, which was crowded with the well-coiffed, well-dressed, well-oiled, well-powdered, and heavily scented courtiers of the Emperor's entourage. Some laughed as we were brought in, but one woman, clearly maddened by drink, began for no apparent reason to scream. She was Portia's age, or a few years younger, and was dressed in what looked to be sheaths of multicolored silk. As her screaming continued, the people nearby drew away from her, but casually continued their conversations as they moved.

Bit by bit the woman's screams gave way to sobs, and she sank to her knees with her body trembling. Then, with such violence that I gave a start, she leaped to her feet again and shrieked out, "I've been poisoned!" At this all the courtiers laughed, and a bilious-looking senator came over to her and slapped her hard across the face. "Shut up or I'll send you home!" he shouted, then turned and walked away. A trickle of blood ran out of the woman's mouth as she glared at his retreating figure, and with a tentative motion she brought her fingers up to her chin. When she drew them away there was blood on their tips, and as she gazed at it her features curved into a lascivious smile. For some moments she stood there leering at her fingers, but at last she turned and walked idly past me out of the room. It was only as she went by that I realized with a shock that this demented creature was Marcus's second daughter, Lucilla.

How cruel the gods can be to the children of the great!

And how cruel the children of the great can be to those of us more lowly born!

Scant moments after Lucilla's exit there was a trumpet fanfare from the far end of the room. Our four *frumentarii* instantly forced us to our knees, and the one who was guarding me tightened his grip on the back of my neck to such a point that I let out an involuntary moan. An aisle opened in the middle of the hall, as senators and courtiers craned their necks to see their Emperor make his entrance.

And make his entrance he did, preceded by six *cornicines* with cheeks bloated and trumpets blaring, by no fewer than twenty-four lictors bearing their fasces, by several dozen of his "friends," and by a veritable walking menagerie, including mastiffs, hounds, leopards (on leashes), bears (in chains), and apes, appropriately enough, running loose.

At the rear of this garish procession was Commodus himself, in many ways the most impressive part of the spectacle. Unlike Marcus, he was tall and of robust build, with powerful shoulders and sinewy arms. He was naked to the waist, moreover, and glistening with oil, his curly black hair and beard circling his features with a leonine grace. Over his shoulders was draped the pelt of a leopard, and cinched around his waist was the skin of a wolf. On his feet he wore sandals of beaten gold.

He made straight for the spot where the four of us were kneeling, and as he got nearer the *frumentarii* applied forward pressure on our necks, so that our heads appeared to bow.

The trumpeters, lictors, *amici*, and other creatures in front of him broke ranks and stepped aside to afford him free passage to where we knelt, and he strode bombastically to within a few feet of us before coming to a grandiose halt. For some moments he just stood there, with legs spaced wide and thumbs hooked into the pelt around his waist. Then, abruptly, he barked out *"HA!"*

There was total silence in the hall.

"HA!" he barked again, with all the contempt and malice that can be borne by a single syllable.

"HA! HA! HA!" he repeated, and gave a signal that caused the *frumentarii* to release their holds on our necks.

"So," he said, giving voice to his first perceptibly human utterance, "how do you feel now about betraying me?"

I raised my eyes to look at his, and saw in them something of that same anxious truculence that had characterized Agricus's expression on the Quirinal as the mud eaters cradled their stones.

"I am not aware of having betrayed you, Caesar," I replied, being careful not to contradict him.

"You're not *aware* . . ." he shouted, then turned his head and played to his audience. "Behold, my friends: a man who betrays all unknowingly—in his sleep, perhaps, amid his snores."

This sally was greeted with rapturous laughter, and even some scattered applause.

"So," he said, returning his gaze to me, "you're not *aware* of having betrayed me."

"No, Caesar."

"Do you deny, then, having counseled my father to deny me?"

This modest rhetorical conceit brought forth a chorus of admiring gasps, intensified perhaps by the idea of my infinite perfidy.

"I have never counseled any father to deny his son, Caesar."

"Meaning, I suppose, that I am not the son of our late beloved Aurelius Antoninus."

"You are unquestionably his son, Caesar."

"Then why did you counsel him to deny me?"

Now, as never before, I had to be nimble in thought and word. "Caesar, I never, to my knowledge, spoke ill of you to anyone."

"You *lie!*" he bellowed. "You haven't had a good word for me since the day I was born."

"If Caesar will permit me to . . ."

"Right from the start I saw it," he continued, "when you used to tutor me in athletics—even then you disapproved of me."

"It has never been my place to approve or disapprove of someone of your rank, Caesar."

"Be *silent!*" he shouted, then took up his theme once more. "Right from the very start . . . And don't tell me you really liked me, either."

I looked at the man and realized, a bit belatedly, how unequal he felt to the task of being emperor. The question was how to exploit that realization.

"Look at me," he continued, turning around to face his court. "Am I such a bad First Citizen?"

"No!" they all bawled in rough unison.

"Am I so much worse than my father?"

"Better!" they cried out.

"You see," he said, turning back to me. "You see how unfair you've been. . . . But don't take their word for it. Don't even take mine. Consult, instead, the evidence of your senses."

I looked at him uncomprehendingly.

"I'm *here!*" he said finally, in exasperation. "I came in from the country." But still his meaning eluded me.

"That is to say," he continued through clenched teeth, "I'm here in Rome . . . in the middle of August . . . attending to affairs of state."

I struggled with all my power to understand precisely what he was saying, then ventured timidly, "Surely, Caesar, the whole world will marvel at your sense of duty."

"You admit that I'm no less conscientious than my father," he declared triumphantly.

"It is not for me to make comparisons, Caesar," I responded, letting out a small sigh of relief, "but clearly no one could be more conscientious than you."

"You admit that you were wrong about me."

"I never doubted your devotion to Rome, Caesar," I said, and, deciding to take a modest gamble, added, "I just never thought that you'd make a great runner."

There was a breath of quickly suppressed mirth in the chamber, as all present waited to see what the outcome of my impertinence would be.

For a long time there was deathly silence, as the Emperor considered my jest. But at last he threw back his head and roared out sweet laughter, and everyone else made haste to join in.

Still laughing, he turned and walked away from us, as the *frumentarii* again forced our heads to bow. Then, having hustled us back to our quarters, they went their way.

That was in the middle of the night.

But now it is the middle of the day, and though the summer heat feels like sulfur in our lungs, my Camilla is shivering still.

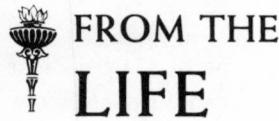
I don't think I had ever before engaged in a conversation like the one I engaged in with Marcus as I rode along on the rump of his mare. For one thing, I had never before been astride a horse, as Marcus inferred, no doubt, from the grim tenacity with which my arms were clasped around his waist. For another thing, no one had ever before taken such an interest in the details of my life. Had I known more about Marcus, or been less anxious about our means of locomotion, I might have noticed the deftness with which he drew me out: the tact with which he framed some questions and refrained from asking others. Never once, for example, did he ask me about my background or my past; his questions pertained exclusively to my present: where did I live, whom did I live with, what was my family like, what was my building like, what was Twopenny Street like as a neighborhood, how had I come to be "in the brick business" (as he put it), who were the brick lickers and the mud eaters, who was the dead boy Plettus, on and on and on. It was only after he had dropped me off at the Sanqualis Gate that I realized he'd asked me nothing about Agricus. Callow as I was, it never occurred to me that he'd already gleaned what he wanted to know from the facts of their first enounter.

The *singulares* deposited Agricus and Plettus's body at the gate scant moments after Marcus arrived there with me. "Perhaps I'll come visit you two sometime," he said to us as his mare shied away from the corpse at our feet.

"We'll look forward to that," Agricus replied exuberantly, and the three horsemen turned and rode off.

There was nothing exuberant in Agricus's expression when he turned to face me, though. Instead, there was such loathing that I reflexively drew away from him. "I hope you don't think you're too good now to help me carry Plettus back to his father," he said.

It still amazes me that I was too dense to fathom the reasons for his anger.

I have said that Agricus preferred to prey on women who were proud, and I've confessed I was aware of his predilection. Thus I might have suspected the shape his revived hostility to me would take. But, as always with Agricus, I was prepared for neither the form nor the magnitude of his malice.

He must have started devising his scheme at the time of Marcus's first visit to Twopenny Street, which occurred some two months after our initial meeting. I remember the day exactly; it was the Lupercalia, a bright and bitter February morning, unclouded, thanks to the holiday, by soul-numbing thoughts of school. I walked out of the Hobnail in high good humor, with frost on my breath and a cup of cold cooked beans for Romulus in my hand. Popping a bean or two into my mouth as I walked along, I savored the catastrophic pungency of Drusilla's cuisine. And when a scruffy-looking curly-headed boy approached me with his hand out, I moved instinctively to protect my food.

"Oh, come now," the boy said, smiling, "can't you spare even one little bean for a hungry friend?"

Then I realized who it was.

He was barefoot and dressed in a threadbare tunic, but he seemed to be utterly indifferent to the cold.

"What are you doing here?" I asked in astonishment, forgetting my place for a moment, and its subservience to his.

"I said I might come visit you," he responded. "Now how about that bean?"

I hesitated an instant, but decided to let events run their course. "Here," I said, extending the cup toward him, "take all you want."

Luckily for him, he wanted only a few, but even they were sufficient to start tears streaming from his eyes. "Immortal gods!" he exclaimed in a choked whisper.

"My aunt Drusilla's famous around here for her cooking," I told him.

"I don't doubt it," he replied with a stricken nod.

"Do you like the taste?" I inquired.

"It's very . . . distinctive," he answered me. "Do you know where I might get a drink of water?"

I showed him to the nearest City spigot and tried to keep from laughing while he gulped down the better part of two sextarii.

"Thirsty weather," I said when he'd finished drinking, and we both broke into laughter.

"Where are you headed?" he asked me.

"To feed my cat, Romulus."

"You're going to feed him *those*?" he gasped, pointing in horror at the cup.

"They're his favorite food," I told him.

"He must be a remarkable animal."

"He is indeed. Perhaps you'd like to meet him."

"What I'd like to do is watch him eat, if you don't mind."

"By all means," I said.

"Thank you," he replied easily. "As long as it's understood that I won't be invited to eat myself."

And at that we laughed again.

Romulus liked Marcus; but then, Romulus liked everybody, even Agricus.

"He purrs very forcefully," Marcus said, watching him wolf down Drusilla's beans.

"I told you; that's his favorite dish."

"You mean he's not going to fall over dead?"

"He doesn't usually," I responded, and our laughter erupted yet again.

"What's so damn funny?" a harsh voice sounded behind us. And of course it was Agricus, who'd apparently just come downstairs.

"We were talking about how much Romulus likes Aunt Drusilla's cooking," I said, turning toward him.

"And who's this little mouse turd with you?"

"That's a fine way to talk about one of your best customers," Marcus interjected.

Agricus narrowed his eyes at him. "Marcus?" he said incredulously.

"The very same."

Agricus darted his glance back and forth from Marcus's face to mine. "How long have you been in the neighborhood?" he asked in a suspicious tone.

"Why, I've only just arrived."

"And you went to *his* house first?"

"Who, Lucio's? No. I met him by chance on the street."

At this Agricus seemed to relax a little. "So," he said, "you've come to mingle for a morning with the lower orders?"

"Not to 'mingle,' and not just for a morning," Marcus responded.

"To do what then, and for how long?"

"Why, to visit friends, for as long as they will have me."

For several moments Agricus subjected Marcus to a skeptical scrutiny, but at last, with a tight-jawed grin, he said, "Are you still in the market for some low-cost bricks?"

With one gust of laughter all the tension was dispelled, and at Agricus's suggestion the three of us headed off to give Marcus a tour of our Twopenny Street domain.

We took him everywhere—first to the mud eaters' meeting place high up on the side of the Quirinal, then to the secret shrine where the gang maintained its tutelary deities, the golden statue of Amicitia foremost among them. Next we showed him around lower Twopenny Street and took him inside Curtio's Baths, where he met Fabia, who was doing business at her same old stand, but looking a good deal the worse for wear, in my opinion.

"Who's this you've got with you?" she asked me, treating Agricus as if he weren't there.

"Fabia, *darling!*" he broke in. "Can you have forgotten me *already?*"

"Who is *this?*" Fabia repeated, ignoring him and pointing at Marcus.

"This is our friend, uh, Dionysus, from Sicily," I replied, realizing that Marcus might want to remain incognito.

"He's cute," Fabia said. "Is he old enough?"

I looked blankly at Marcus, who looked blankly back at me. "Well," I said finally, "*are* you old enough?"

"I cost only three denarii if you are," Fabia volunteered. (Apparently all the wear and tear had diminished the poor girl's value—or else she really did find Marcus "cute.")

"Uh, how old do I have to be?" Marcus inquired.

"Old enough for the toga virilis," I informed him.

"Ah, well, then I don't qualify, I'm afraid," he said with an evident sense of relief. "And, in any case, I don't have three denarii."

"Then get your pukey face out of here and stop bothering me," Fabia snarled sweetly. "And take your scummy-looking boyfriends with you."

Marcus's eyebrows shot up at this, but he seemed more intrigued than offended. Whatever his inward reaction, Agricus came promptly to his aid. "Don't worry," he said. "I know a goat down the street who'll give you a lot more value for your money."

This jibe was more than Fabia could tolerate, apparently, for all at once she was rushing toward Agricus with a dagger in her hand. "Beast!" she screamed. "Pestilent dung fly!"

Agricus wisely took to his heels as she bore down on him, but as he ran from the bar he shouted laughingly over his shoulder, "You see! I *knew* she hadn't forgotten me."

As soon as Marcus and I rejoined him on the street, the three of us consulted as to what Marcus should see next. In the end, Agricus and I decided to take him on a quick tour of brick-licker territory, a choice that involved some risk, to be sure, but not overmuch, given the teeming bustle of midday traffic.

The excursion proved uneventful, but it took a little longer than we'd expected, and since it was well into the seventh hour by the time we got back to Agricus's building, we were all fairly hungry. The next logical place to go was therefore the Hobnail.

"I thought we'd agreed that I wouldn't be compelled to eat with you," Marcus said with a grin as we walked along.

"What?" said Agricus sharply. "Have you two been trading invitations?"

"On the contrary," Marcus replied in a playful voice—thereby forestalling an angry retort from me. "Young Lucio was kind enough to let me sample the food he was taking to Romulus. When I tasted it, and learned that his aunt had cooked it, I immediately begged him never to ask me to his home for a meal."

Agricus gave an unpleasant laugh, but he seemed more than halfway mollified. "That was a mistake on your part, Marcus," he said. "His aunt may not cook too well, but she sure as Juppiter can satisfy your other appetites."

I stopped in my tracks and glared at him. "What's that supposed to mean?"

He stopped and glared back. "Are you too stupid to guess?"

"Are you too spineless to say?"

The next word out of either of our mouths was going to start us trading blows, and Marcus acted quickly to prevent a scrap. "The lady in question seems to inspire strong passions in both of you," he said placidly. "Do you think you could put off battering each other bloody until I've had a chance to meet her?"

Agricus and I continued to glare at each other, but some of the fire had gone out of our confrontation.

"I *am* your guest, after all," Marcus continued. "Who's going to look after me if you two start brawling in the street? I might get kidnapped by brick lickers, or seduced by Fabia or even force-fed Drusilla's beans."

Still we continued to glare, but at last Agricus gave a wave of disgust and spat out, "Oh, drop it."

So we continued on to the Hobnail.

"Who's this?" Drusilla asked in a less than friendly voice when we arrived.

"A new boy in the neighborhood," I told her. "His name's Dionysus, from Sicily."

"And what's he doing here?"

"I thought I might share my supper with him."

"You did, eh?"

"He thought he might share his supper with me, too," Agricus interjected, his most endearingly boyish smile in place on his finely wrought features.

Drusilla regarded him coolly, but with a degree of interest that made me queasy with foreboding.

"I have a few asses, matron," Marcus ventured. "Perhaps you might let me purchase a little food for my friends and myself."

Drusilla turned and gave him a closer inspection. "You speak very well for a boy from the provinces," she said. "And I notice you have the fingernails of a patrician."

This was the only time I can ever remember seeing Marcus blush. He was even so abashed as to lower his eyes.

"Never mind," Drusilla said with a laugh. "Dionysus of Sicily or aristocrat of Rome, I don't suppose you can eat enough to beggar us." And with that she went off into the scullery to conjure up our food.

"She's magnificent!" Marcus said breathlessly as soon as she'd left the room.

And Agricus confided with a leer, "I couldn't agree with you more."

Sitting there beside them, I suddenly felt chilled and alone. They were my friends, I knew, and there was nothing in what they'd said to take exception to. But that didn't seem to matter somehow, because at that moment—and indeed for all that remained of that day—I didn't feel very friendly toward either one of them.

[AUGUST 13TH]

We are going home.

I look at those words on the scroll before me and tears well up in my eyes.

We are going home.

It is the last watch of the night and all is stillness on the Palatine. And in less than two hours . . . we are going home.

For almost the last time, I look out our window at the northwestern sky, at the stars and the boughs of the pine trees. That window, that hard concrete square, has been the frame for my picture of the world for over thirty days. To think that I will soon be able to run my eyes around the full circle of the horizon again, to watch the sun come up as well as set, to feel the wind blow and the rain fall . . . Two hours is too long to wait.

But I will master my impatience, or, rather, my circumstances will master it for me. And I will bend my thoughts to this journal, so that the hours may fade away.

I could not have foreseen—or at all events I did not foresee—the strange form our deliverance would take, if it is permissible to describe as "strange" the person of the present Emperor.

He came to our room at nightfall, unarmed, to all appearances, and attended by only a single Praetorian. My poor Camilla, on seeing him walk through the doorway, gave a whimpering cry and shrank back into our "bedroom" corner.

"What horrible tales have you been telling that child about me?" the Emperor shouted in my face, causing Camilla to curl herself into a ball and start sobbing.

"I have not spoken of you to her, Caesar," I replied, my voice quivering with anger.

"Then why . . ." he roared, before catching himself and resuming in a lower voice, "why does she draw away from me so fearfully?"

"Perhaps the magnificence of your presence overawes her," I responded. "You are, after all, descended from many gods."

Commodus considered this reply mistrustfully, then looked at Portia and said, "Can you not comfort her, woman?"

"I can try, Caesar," she answered in a firm voice, and hastened to Camilla's side.

"And this would be your son," the Emperor said, striding bombastically over to Decius.

"Yes, Caesar," I responded. "That is my son, Decius."

"Decius, eh," the Emperor said with forced heartiness, clapping the boy on the back. "I'll wager your father's bequeathed you his speed of foot, judging by the looks of you. Do you hope to wear the olive crown at Olympia one day and stand alone with Zeus in the temple, like he did?"

"No, Caesar," Decius answered bravely. "I am clumsy and slow, and my only ambition is to live my life as a farmer."

Commodus seemed a bit deflated by this response, while I for my part reacted with a pang of remorse. With that one simple question the Emperor had shown more interest in my boy's future plans than I've bothered to exhibit for quite some time; having obtained the answer he did, moreover, he now knows just as much as I do about the matter of my son's aspirations. Thus do those we hate sometimes remind us of how hateful we can be to those we love.

"Well," said the Emperor, somewhat flustered, "it's a noble calling: working the land. I, uh, congratulate you on your choice of vocation."

"Thank you, Caesar," Decius solemnly replied.

"Now then," said Commodus in a magisterial tone, "to the business at hand."

We all looked at him in anxious expectation.

"It has come to our attention," he resumed portentously, "that you, Lucius Celer, are writing a 'Life' of the late Emperor, my father."

Had I not remembered where I was and who was addressing me, I believe I would have gawked.

"Is this correct?" he concluded in an ominous voice.

Once again I called on my mind to think quickly. "Well, Caesar," I said, "I believe it would be more accurate to say that I've been setting down some of my personal recollections of him, before old age clouds my thinking. My direct association with him was only of some few years' duration, as you no doubt know, but despite my relative insignificance in his life, I've ventured to hope that my reminiscences might be written under your aegis, so to speak, as a tribute to your father's sacred memory."

I was out of breath when I finished speaking, and prayerful that I hadn't left anything out. Judging from the Emperor's demeanor, it didn't appear that I'd done too badly, for his mood seemed a good deal lighter.

"In other words," he said, "your reminiscences, as you call them, pertain only to the years before my father became Quaestor at age seventeen."

"Yes, Caesar," I responded, since I certainly wasn't about to say no.

The Emperor pondered for some moments. "How far along are you?" he asked me.

"I've gotten as far as the second year of our friendship," I lied, not wanting him to think that my labors could still be nipped in the bud. "The first several scrolls are at my farm, if you'd like to see them," I added, continuing the bluff.

Again the Emperor lost himself in thought. "You have our permission," he said finally, "to complete the work you've begun, and we direct you to present us with the fruits of your efforts not later than the last day of next month. Until that time we reserve judgment on your other crimes. You may leave the Palatine at sunrise."

And with that he turned and walked out.

The four of us gaped at one another for several moments after he'd left, then rushed together and embraced with laughter and tears. A month-and-a-half reprieve has been granted us, when death seemed sure and near. And the reprieve isn't all we've been granted, for with it has come an almost equal boon. Yes, life is precious, and yes, one lives as one can. But life is sweetest by the hearth. And so I say again with my pen the words I am singing in my soul: We are going home.

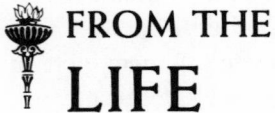
The statue of Eurydice.

I hadn't thought about it much since the morning I exchanged it for a statue of Friendship. I didn't really miss it either, not having possessed it long enough to feel its absence. And besides, I had the genuine article to admire in its place, the real flesh-and-blood Drusilla: a bit thicker in the waist, perhaps, a bit longer in the tooth—but every inch the woman she'd always been, and maybe more.

I remember once, when I was very little, I was playing in the Hobnail's courtyard on a summer evening. Drusilla appeared, to fetch some firewood probably, but when she saw me she came over and gave me a kiss. She had just returned from the Baths, I remember, because she smelled of fresh oil and attar of roses. For a moment she cupped my cheek in the palm of her hand and looked down at me with love. I remember gazing up at her and drinking in the shimmer of her beauty. "Your eyes are sad, little fellow," she said, and I smiled at her to show her she made me happy. When she smiled back, though, her eyes were suddenly sadder than mine. "I am barren," she said, which meant nothing to me, and then, "You are all I will ever have," which meant a great deal.

"You are all I will ever have." Her voice was both grateful and wistful, as if having me, though desirable, was far less than all she desired.

And why do I write "as if"?

She kissed me once more and went inside, leaving me to my solitude beneath the fading light of the summer sky. Never again was she to reveal to me such secret feelings. Never again, perhaps, was she to acknowledge them to herself. Had it been otherwise, we might have enriched each other's lives as have many another woman and child. But it was only the way it was, and we were destined to waste the fate that had brought us together.

It was nothing momentous, really—that statue of Eurydice. I came into the Hobnail one sleepy afternoon to find it standing untended on the top of the bar. The place was empty, and very quiet, and it may have been that Glaubus was away on one of his wine-buying trips to the south. Yes, of course he was; I remember the October light, the tepid caress of the languid air. He was down in Cumae or Surrentum or someplace, watching the grapes get picked, and the time was some eight months after Marcus's first visit to Twopenny Street.

Dear noble Marcus—swept away now like Drusilla, like Agricus, like Glaubus and Rutolo and Hercules Iamblichus . . . like that slave boy I saw, once, consumed by desire in a field by a river beneath the moon.

I think Marcus loved her most, or maybe best. He wanted nothing from her, was fulfilled by what she was. His visits to the neighborhood became after a while merely visits to the Hobnail, and he would sit there for hours at a time . . . and watch. Not stare, but watch—and not merely watch, but talk and joke and laugh and listen, and sometimes even try the food. But always he was aware of her; as she in her impudent way was always alive to his awareness. She would muss his hair and pinch his cheeks and lean way over to let him see. But he would merely continue to smile at her, or beam at her, more precisely, like a supplicant whose prayers she answered even before he gave them voice.

And sometimes Agricus would appear, to glower at all the conviviality. He would stand just inside the entrance and cast a withering eye on the bar's patrons. If his mood was filthy enough, he would unsheathe his cruelty and brandish it about, turning at last on some unlucky soul and carving him up like a well-roasted joint. His wit more than compensated for his malice on such occasions, and his victim had no recourse but to bleed in silence and try to smile while the others laughed. I say "try" because often it wasn't possible to smile; and even if you got your lips to curve a bit, you felt your facial bones would splinter from the strain.

I know all about that.

I stared at the statue of Eurydice for a long while. I think perhaps I was in a state of mild shock. It had no business being there; I knew that much in the depths of my soul. Not only did it not belong where it was, but also it was in the worst place it could be.

And yet I could not have said why.

The statue belonged to Agricus; that was one thing that was wrong with it. And it resembled Drusilla; that was another. I had traded it for a statue of Friendship, regarding the trade as a fair one because of the service Agricus had rendered me. If it was back within my keeping—as it was, effectively, at that moment—it could mean only one thing: my bargain with Agricus was being squared by some other means, by some other person, without my consent.

All this I felt without being able to articulate. My knowledge was limited to two facts: the statue on the bar and the malice of Agricus. Something had been building between us ever since Marcus's first appearance in our lives, something gangrenous and swollen with poison. Agricus seemed to have come to hate me all over again, but for no reason I could think of. And though I'd borne patiently with his taunting and ridicule, thinking perhaps that I'd done him some unwitting wrong, his animosity toward me had only intensified. Nothing I said or did had been sufficient to placate him, so I'd come to believe that he was bent on doing me harm. And there was something about the sight of Drusilla's graven image on the bar that told me the harm was in the process of being done.

I remember most clearly the silence, the sensation that all time and motion had ceased around me and that I alone existed in the world. I mean, of course, in the visible world, for the air was heavy with creatures unseen. I walked softly into the back rooms, which were as empty as the bar; then I stood for a long time and stared at the door to the cellar.

I knew as I stood there that I had come to a pivotal point in my life—not because of what I was about to discover, but because I had resolved to discover it. I could have walked out of the bar and let the dark truth lie. But it was as if I was being told something by the silence surrounding me, something about myself and my place in the world. I could have ignored what the silence was telling me, could have turned my back and walked away. Curiosity played no part in the matter; I already knew what my eyes would show me. But if I didn't see it for myself I would never be sure it was so, and if I never was sure it was so, I would never act on it, and my life from that point on would in most ways be counterfeit.

It was thus with a sense of the inevitable that I made my way down the cellar stairs. And once I'd seen what I had to see, I made my way up again and walked out the door of the Hobnail as if it had long since ceased to be my home.

 FROM THE
JOURNAL

22

It seems impossible, but here I am, back in my garden, with Prometheus purring at my feet. Everything is as I left it: the fountain is still playing out its uninspired metaphor, the scent of the pines is still pungently sweet, and the sky . . . ah, the sky . . . the sky is still cause for jubilation—so much so that I can barely set down two words in succession without stopping to look up at it.

Of course it is not precisely the same sky I looked up at when we left here, for, though nothing could alter its majesty, there have been subtle changes in its tone. The sun no longer rides so high on the meridian, for example, and its estival glare has given way somewhat to a preautumnal glow. Then, too, the clouds are pushing ever more boldly west from the mountains, and in a matter of two or three days we will start to get those brief but violent evening downpours that signal the equinox is near.

What a joy it is to be back in the middle of it all, to be in the world and not merely on it! I could barely contain myself as sunrise approached this morning; indeed, the steward who came to lead us to our wagon found us standing fully laden in the middle of our cubiculum, ready to follow him the instant he recovered from his surprise.

We walked out of the Palace to find a daytime-exemption disk already nailed to the axle of our wagon and our mule already in harness. In less time than it took the Praetorian on duty to see to the opening of the gate, both we and our belongings were in place on our cart. I cracked the whip the moment the gate started to swing, and if that mule of mine had balked for even an instant I believe I might have jumped down and pulled the wagon myself. Happily, though, the beast was in a tractable mood, and he ambled forward with Portia, Decius, Camilla, and me, all silently imploring him to pick up his somnolent pace.

The sun overtook us as we labored up the Janiculum, and we paused at the middle fountains of Trajan's aqueduct to let the mule ease his thirst. Below us the City glowed white and ocher amid the long morning shadows, with the Temple of Jove on the Capitoline sparkling in the pristine light. I let my eyes traverse the scene before me and tried to envision the cluster of rude huts so fiercely coveted by the old Etruscan kings. For nine hundred years, oh, Rome, you have stood at this ford of the Tiber, and for two hundred years you have stood at the summit of the world. That you are great I must acknowledge; that you are good I must deny. But then, where would I find someplace better? Not in this world, nor in this life. You are the proudest of mankind's creations, oh, mighty Urbs, and as such you should cringe in shame.

But the sun and the earth are divine creations, and to be bathed in splendor by the one while heading homeward across the other was, for me, like sailing in glory over waves of gold. We climbed the parched brown hills of August and watched our shrinking shadows lead us westward over the Aurelia's stones. Our bodies soaked up the heat from the sky as if it were a healing unguent on the sores of our confinement; and when we topped the hill above the Aro Valley and caught our first glimpse of the Nereid Tavern and our farm, our joy was almost painful in its intensity. I pulled to the roadside, reined in the mule, and sat in the sun with the tears streaming down and savored the vision before me. Now, I thought, we have all it is possible to have.

There were more tears when we drove through the gate of our farm, and there was more joy as well. But there was also a baffling puzzle. Rullo informed me that old Nestor left here on foot six days ago, ostensibly to visit the Nereid. He hasn't been seen or heard of since.

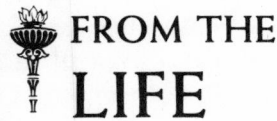

FROM THE LIFE

23

I had no particular plan in mind when I left the Hobnail, just a determination never to return there. And it wasn't only the sense of having been betrayed—or, rather, doubly betrayed—that hardened my resolve; it was a feeling that I no longer belonged in the place I'd called home, and perhaps had never belonged there to begin with.

But if I didn't belong at the Hobnail with Drusilla and Glaubus, then it followed logically that I didn't belong anywhere or with anyone; and it may have been this perception, more than anything I'd seen that day, that accounted for the heaviness I felt in my chest and the sense of constriction that afflicted my throat with each breath.

I had seen the truth at the foot of the cellar stairs, and the truth was that I was alone. I couldn't have said what that meant to me at the time, but I was all too aware of how it felt. And knowing how it felt, I entered upon the one phase of my life when death held no terror for me at all.

The one friend I could think of to turn to was Romulus, but he was out on the prowl when I got to the crevice beside Agricus's door. Lacking the will to take further action, I squeezed into the crack and waited for him to return.

It came to me as I sat there that a part of my life was ending—the part that had begun the first time I entered that crevice to lie in wait. Then, my sole purpose had been to avenge myself for a humiliation; now my humiliation was complete. Agricus the Invincible had triumphed over me again, and he hadn't needed his invincibility to do it. He had simply bettered me, or bested me, more precisely; and there was every sign that he could go on besting me whenever he felt so inclined. But not even Agricus could defeat a foe who fled before the next battle. So I would flee, and deny him further triumphs. It was bad enough being where I didn't belong, without having my teeth kicked in for good measure. Far better to flee with my incisors intact, even if I had to leave my pride in the mud behind me.

And what was I giving up, really? Not all that much: a fragile illusion that Glaubus and Drusilla were my family, and infrequent glimpses of my mother in her cups. That was about the sum of it. As for the mud eaters,

I was already outgrowing them. And as for the neighborhood, it wasn't worth the two pennies of its name. What else was I leaving then, aside from Romulus? Why, nothing whatever—nothing, that is, except all I'd ever known or cared for.

Well, not quite everything, I realized with a surge of hope. There still was Marcus.

Yes, of course!

Dear Marcus: who liked me, was gentle to me, was my friend—who loved Drusilla much as I had loved her, who had smiled and accepted my rebuke about Plettus, who'd even chosen me over Agricus for the honor of riding on his horse.

Marcus Marcus Marcus: his image flooded through my mind. I would go to him, bow to him, entreat him to be my protector. And he would respond with kindness, find a place for me, bring an end to my travail. Sweet and noble Marcus—how I yearned for the shelter of his magnanimous spirit.

And how I dreaded the possibility that he might not care a damn about me either.

For a while I was lost in anxious speculation about the way he would receive me, if he consented to receive me at all. Then it occurred to me that I would have to locate him in order to find out. The last time I'd seen him he'd told me that he would be spending the harvest time at his uncle's estate, a place called Lorium, off the Via Aurelia. But he hadn't told me how far away Lorium was from Rome. No matter; I would travel the distance required. Reaching under the neck of my tunic, I grasped the leather thong from which my bulla hung and pulled the little locket out. It, too, was made of leather, unlike Marcus's, which was made of gold. But gold or leather, a bulla's meaning is always the same: the boy who wears one is freeborn.

I undid the clasp on mine and let it fall open in my palm. Inside its hinged hemispheres was the capital available for my journey: two denarii, a sestertius, and six asses. I didn't know how far that would take me, and I could only hope I reached Lorium before I found out.

Romulus appeared toward evening, looking prosperous and self-satisfied, but with breath that reeked of fish sauce. "Who've you been stealing from today, old fellow?" I asked him as he climbed up and settled himself on my chest. By way of reply to my question, he yawned, licked his chops, closed his eyes, and started up that racket of his that passed for a purr. I ran my palm over his head as he lay there, savoring the texture of his fur. Then in a low low voice I confided, "I have to leave you soon, my

one faithful, because I love you too well to take you with me. This street
is no longer my home, you see, even though it is still yours. True, with
me gone, there'll be no more of those beans you love so much, but
everything else you like to eat will continue to be yours for the stealing.
And your friends the lady cats will still be here, though you must never
trust them for even an instant, because females are the slaves of desire
and they'll betray you whenever the fever rises in their loins. And you
mustn't trust Agricus either, because he's more than half female himself,
though no one knows that except for you and me and a swarm of lecherous
patricians. What it comes down to, dear Romulus, is that you mustn't
trust anyone ever again, because there's absolutely nothing to be gained
by it. You've got your home here in this crevice, you've got girl cats to
poke by the dozen, and you've got food wherever you care to look for
it. You've got everything you want or need, in other words. So let those
who aren't as fortunate trust *you* if they've a mind to, but don't you ever
trust them. Life is better by far on your own, little fellow. But of course
you've known that now for years. . . . I only wish you'd been capable of
telling me."

Outside our crevice, night was falling, and with it a misty whispering
of rain. Inside, where Romulus and I were huddled, all was dry except
for my eyes. Circling my arms around his burly haunches, I settled myself
to get some sleep. And thus the two of us passed my last night in the
squalid little district that no longer passed for my home.

Had anyone bothered to take them the next morning, the auspices for
my journey in search of Marcus would not have been favorable, not if
steadily heavier rain and rapidly rising wind counted for anything. I woke
up cold and hungry, and alone, to boot, Romulus having apparently gone
off on the prowl while I'd slept. Ah, well, I sighed, less than half in jest,
his defection makes it unanimous.

But the problem of my hunger was quickly solved, as things turned
out, because one of Scarrulus's slave boys happened to be going by my
crevice at just about the time I awoke; the odor of hot sausages in his
earthenware tray may even have helped awaken me.

"You! Boy!" I called out, and he turned toward my voice with a startled
expression. "One with bread," I told him, holding out two asses in my
palm.

Standing there soaking wet, he narrowed his eyes and peered at me.
"What are you doing in there?" he asked.

"Keeping dry," I answered him, "which is more than I can say for you."

The boy looked up at the sky, as if my reference to the rain was the first news he'd had of it. He peered at me a second time before handing me the food I sought.

"Thank you," I said, taking a healthy bite while he continued to stand and gape.

"You're welcome," he replied uncertainly, before at last setting off again down the street.

I couldn't have explained it to anyone at the time—nor can I fully explain it to myself even now—but I found that I was feeling almost cheerful as I sat there and chewed on my breakfast. I guess boys in their teens are pretty resilient creatures, as indeed they'd better be. And I guess, also, that on the other side of the tarnished coin that depicted the loss of my home and family there was a shinier, more hopeful scene: one stamped with the challenge of starting anew, gilded with the promise of adventure, and agleam with a newfound sense that I was emerging from boyhood into the likeness of a man—an unformed man, to be sure, an untested and untempered one; but in purpose, in enterprise, and in some-times reckless action, a passable replica of what I aspired to be. I think I felt a bit like the young Theseus on the day of his departure from Troezen: yes, the road to Athens is fraught with danger, and yes, he must travel it alone. But set against his peril is his eagerness to discover the world and at last define himself—no longer in terms of daydreams, but of deeds. Does he feel some fear as he leaves his birthplace? He'd be foolish indeed if he didn't. But the fear is only a tax imposed by nature on those who take risks, and given the glory of risking, the boy knows it's not much to pay.

With the rain pelting down, I made my way south across the City to the Aemilian bridge. Once on the far side of the Tiber, I began walking along the Via Aurelia and soliciting rides from farmers who were heading home in empty carts from the vegetable market in the Campus Martius. Before long a kindly old fellow with the foulest breath imaginable took pity on me, and with him I traveled about six miles out of Rome, as far as the ancient bridge over the Galleran stream. There the old man had to turn off toward his farm. But when I stepped down from beneath his wagon's awning and submitted myself once more to the storm, I had a piece of information in my possession that more than compensated for the harshness of the weather: Lorium was only five miles farther on.

By then it was midmorning, a slack time for traffic outbound from Rome, so after almost an hour of futile waiting I decided to continue on by foot. About a mile farther along I stopped at a roadside tavern and spent two asses for a bowl of hot honey wine and some bread. This nourishment fortified me for the miles I still had to travel and, incidentally, put an end to an acute case of the shivers.

Seeing that I was soaking wet, the tavern keeper kindly let me sit by his fire. "Going far?" he asked me with an amiable smile.

But I, with my city dweller's ingrained wariness, merely smiled back and answered, "As far as I can."

I couldn't have known it then, but before the day was out that statement was to prove truer than I'd thought.

The problem I encountered beyond the tavern was simple but not easily soluble: how to find Marcus on an estate as vast as his uncle's. And Lorium *was* vast: it flanked three miles of the Aurelia to an average breadth of some six miles on either side. That made it a domain of nearly 100,000 jugera, and though there were dozens of roads and tracks across it, there was only one true area of habitation apart from the tiny village where the main farm road intersected the Aurelia. Alas, this village was deserted when I got there, presumably because the rain had stopped and everyone had rushed off to help with the harvest before it started again. The wise choice at that point would have been to wait where I was till the villagers returned. But by that time both my wisdom and my patience were in equally short supply. So I tossed a sestertius into the air and then set off up the right-hand road when it came down showing heads.

I walked for the better part of an hour, with the wind whipping down from the north to further chill my sodden tunic. The fields on either side of the road had been harvested already, so there was nothing to protect me from Boreas's wrath. My teeth chattered and my shivering resumed, while the fierceness of the cold gave an added edge to my fear that I might be walking in the wrong direction. That fear was soon displaced by an even sharper one, however, when I looked down the road and saw two horsemen charging toward me. Who were they? Robbers? Soldiers? I had no idea. In rapidly mounting panic, I scanned the surrounding fields. There was no cover anywhere, except far away to my left, where a line of trees at the base of some hillocks suggested the presence of a stream. I gauged the distance to the tree line to be not quite half a mile, which wasn't much farther than the horsemen were from me. I remembered enough of trigonometry to know that I was closer to the tree line than they were, but I also knew enough of horses to realize that I had no real chance of escape. For want of better alternatives, though, I took to my heels, looking one last time over my shoulder to confirm what I knew I would see: the two horsemen veering off the road to pursue me.

The fields were muddy, but the footing was good, and I wondered prayerfully as I ran full tilt whether the horses were having more trouble with the furrows than I was. The answer was, they weren't, because now, for the first time over the noise of the wind, I could pick up the sound of their hoofs. They were close and gaining, and the tree line was still far away.

I bent all my will on my running, while invoking the aid of the gods. But the hoofbeats only got louder.

At last, with about three hundred feet still to cover, I felt a horse's hot breath on my neck, and with a sudden stunning impact I was sent sprawling to the ground. My own breath flew out of me when I fell, and my skull took such a heavy jolt that when I set about trying to rise I couldn't sort out up from down. Shaking my head to regain my bearings I struggled to my knees, but no sooner had I reached a half-upright position than a massive forearm came clubbing into my mouth.

"We don't stand for crop thieves on this farm," a voice said, and the next sound I heard was a sword being pulled from its sheath. A rough hand grabbed my hair and yanked me upright. "We'll see how much you'll steal with both your hands cut off," the voice said.

I was too bludgeoned and too dazed to be terribly afraid, but I knew when a hand gripped my forearm that I was about to experience murderous pain.

"Hold him steady," came a second voice.

But then the first said, "Whoa!"

A man's face, large and coarse and ruddy, came swooping close to mine. "Don't I know you?" the mouth said.

I blinked and blinked and fought to clear my senses, till at last I could see who it was.

"Dracena?" I choked out.

"The very same," the *singularis* replied.

And it was indeed the very same soldier who had come within a flicker of killing Agricus at the brickworks.

"Perhaps you'll forewarn us the next time you pay us a visit," he said with a fearsome smile. And without another word passing between us, he picked me up and gently placed me behind him on his horse.

Less than a quarter of an hour later we reached the top of an easy rise. "Was it worth the journey?" Dracena asked. For there, no more than a quarter mile away across the pastures, were the gardens and porticoes of the stately villa where my friendship with Marcus would shortly be put to the test.

FROM THE
JOURNAL

24

[AUGUST 17TH]

A horseman in military uniform came galloping through our gate this morning, and my first reaction was, of course, one of dread. But when the horseman dismounted and approached the house, I noted with relief that he was far too young to be running errands for the Emperor. And in fact he was merely a dispatch rider with the Imperial Post, a courier on his way to Rome from Massilia bearing letters and administrative dispatches. One of those letters, it seemed, was for me, although offhand I could think of no personal friend or acquaintance who was licensed to use the *cursus publicus*.

And yet I might have guessed from whom the letter came.

Massilia, the day before the Ides of August
My dear and most excellent Lucius,

I pray these presents find all of you safely back home, and I am confident my prayer will be answered. If it has been answered by the time you read this, then you must acknowledge my talents as a rumormonger. Or did you guess how word of your biographical exploits happened to reach the ears of the mighty?

Fear not, Lucio; you have friends you do not know of, myself not least among them. And you shall see me again ere long. But meanwhile take no thought of flight, I adjure you. For flight from a danger must needs entail flight toward a place of safety, and you as yet have nowhere to flee to. It is in order to supply this lack that I am now embarked, however. So stay put where you are until you have my summons.

And keep writing that "biography," just in case.

Yours in the Eyes of the Mind Eternal,
"Nestor"

I read the letter several times, then put it down, picked it up again, and read it over twice more. Was Nestor senile? Was he mad? How could anyone in the possession of his senses announce in writing his intention to mediate my escape from the Emperor and then commit what he'd written to the care of the Imperial Post?! It was insupportable, the work of a deranged mind and an irresponsible spirit.

Or was it?

I picked up the letter and read it over once again, and yes, on the premise that Nestor is nothing more than an aged eccentric, it was inexcusably reckless of him to write and send it. But what if he's something more than that? His access to the *cursus publicus* suggests that he might be. And so does his insinuation that it was through his good offices that Commodus came to believe I was writing a biography of Marcus. Then, too, there is his cryptic comment to the effect that I have friends I'm not aware of, himself "not least among them." But how can it be said that I am unaware of *him*? Unless by "myself" he has reference to his still undisclosed real identity. What was it he said at the time I first met him— "I'd rather not give you my name, *because I think I know you. . . .*"

Well, then, who could this "Nestor" be? I haven't had so many friends in my life that I should forget one who was close enough once to risk his life for me now. But I can think of no one, no matter how I rack my brains—no one, that is, who still has a life left to risk.

And what did the old fellow mean by "Keep writing that 'biography,' just in case"?

Did he mean in case I need a pretext to prolong my life? Or in case I need the wisdom to accept my death?

Perhaps he had both contingencies in mind.

In any case, on I write.

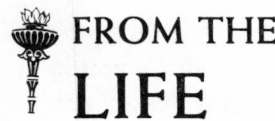
I can think of few moments in this "Life" of mine when I felt as wretched as I did while Dracena's horse descended the small hill overlooking the villa at Lorium. I was cold, I was soaked, I was mud caked, I was drained; my head throbbed, my body ached, my knees trembled, and my mouth was bruised and swollen. Other than that, as the old joke goes, I felt perfectly fine, and I was able to derive some small satisfaction from the knowledge that Agricus was missing out on all my misery.

As with the crossroads village, the villa appeared deserted as we approached it, but so imposing was the picture it presented that the absence of mere human beings seemed somehow apropos. Set amid cypress, oak, and fig trees, and ringed by neat hedges of boxwood and rosemary, the principal edifice in the cluster had for its façade a colonnade not less than a hundred feet long. And when a shaft of sunlight pierced the cloud rack and fell on this line of columns, I realized with a shock that each and every one of them had been fashioned from Pentelic marble. What am I doing in a place like this, I wondered uneasily; such magnificence seemed clearly reserved for those who dwelt on Olympus, or in Elysium.

We rode along the length of the colonnade and turned at its far end onto a mall flanked by a long stretch of boxwood hedges on one side and a shorter line of columns on the other. This second colonnade was about half the length of the main one, and together the two formed a huge marble L—which I prayed might be more omen than coincidence. As we passed the tip of this L a large formal garden was revealed, with fountains and flowers and ornamental shrubbery in well-tended profusion. Far away on the other side I picked out what I assumed to be the slave quarters and stables, but I got only a brief glimpse of these structures before my view was blocked by the massive walls of the villa's main residence.

"Here we are," Dracena said, dismounting and lifting me down after him. "I suppose the boy's out helping in the fields," he continued. "I'll show you to the hot baths so you can clean up before he comes back."

He led me through the gleaming Pentelic portico into a large vestibule, from which we passed through a flowered courtyard ringed by small bedrooms. At the top of a flight of several steps, we proceeded down a long corridor to a breathtaking chamber decorated from floor to ceiling with intricate mosaic designs.

"The dressing room's through that door," Dracena said, pointing diagonally across the hall, "and the hot baths adjoin it on the right."

I nodded that I understood.

"You should find everything you need in there," he added, "except a willing woman." And with that he turned and strode off.

I stood motionless after he left, drinking in the artistry displayed on the floor and walls. It dumbfounded me to think that Lorium and all its wonders actually belonged to a man who was an uncle by marriage of a boy who was my friend. And yet I didn't feel entirely out of place. I felt, rather, as I had a year or two earlier, when Glaubus treated me, and himself, to an afternoon at Trajan's Baths. I'd been awed by that establishment, just as I was awed by Lorium. But I'd also had a sense of being welcome there, like a pilgrim at some distant shrine. And I had that same sense again as I stood cold and wet in the precincts of my friend's uncle's household: the sense that I was accepted—even though I could never belong.

I crossed the chamber and went though the door Dracena had indicated. The room in which I found myself, though tiny compared to the hall of mosaics, was in many ways far more impressive. Not only were each of its walls painted with pastoral scenes of startling verisimilitude, but its floor, which was of otherwise unexceptional clay tile, felt warmer to my feet than the stones of Twopenny Street on a summer afternoon. Of course I'd heard of hypocausts, but hearing of them and having one all to myself were quite different matters; and I couldn't shake off the eerie feeling that the little room was about to be thronged with portly half-naked plebeians, all of them perspiring freely, conversing loudly, and belching explosively, while the air turned rank with the effusions of their flesh.

The silence and my solitude continued undisturbed, however, and after some moments I turned my attention to the features of the room. The pastoral wall paintings, on closer inspection, proved to be depictions of the seasons of the year, and in the background of each there was a portrayal of Juppiter carousing in one of his copulatory disguises: a satyr in Spring mounting Antiope from the rear, a swan in Summer gliding between Leda's thighs as she reclined in a shallow pond, a bull in Autumn with Europa impaled beneath him on the slopes of Mount Ida, and a column of fire in Winter consuming a buxom Semele, whose face suggested the last extremities of sexual release.

I'd seen erotic paintings before, but few of such artistic mastery and none with the erotic focus confined to the background. That placement seemed perverse to me somehow, as if the artist and his patron were the kind of people who would roast an entire bullock and then eat only its brains.

Of course it was the painting of Leda and the swan in the midst of their aquatic ecstasies that framed the doorway to the baths, and on either side of this portal there was a gleaming lemonwood table. The one on the left offered towels of immaculate Egyptian linen arranged in three neat piles according to size. The one opposite presented an array of small silver cups and delicate colored-glass bottles. A closer examination revealed that the cups contained soda ash, while the bottles gave off the muted scent of perfumed oil.

I stood for a long time contemplating all these munificent bath provisions and struggling with the question of whether they were intended for the use of such as me. In the end, fixing on a course of the boldest timidity, I took one small towel with me through the door beneath Leda's bliss.

I now found myself inside a torch-lit room that was warmer, and darker, by several magnitudes than the dressing area I'd just left—with my clothes still on my body, as I noticed belatedly at that moment. Wincing in embarrassment, I yanked off my tunic, hung it on a peg by the door, and wrapped my one meager towel around my waist. Once all this was accomplished, my embarrassment quickly yielded to the soothing sensation of heat on my aching sinews, and as the heat seemed to be flowing from somewhere in front of me I advanced a few tentative paces into the chamber before halting to take note of my surroundings. The walls of the room were of soot-darkened brick that all but negated the already feeble light of the torches, but my eyes adjusted rapidly to the dimness and I saw I was in a kind of foyer. Several feet ahead of me was an ancient-looking arched portal built of large undressed stones. Through this portal streamed the warmth, and beyond it, to the best of my ability to make out, was a much larger room, with whitewashed walls and a floor of polished marble. Looking toward that room, I all at once felt apprehensive, and a spate of nameless anxieties went skittering through my mind as the massive stones of the portal beckoned me to draw near. Having no real cause to be anxious, I felt doubly ashamed of my jittery nerves. But, ashamed or not, I stayed rooted where I stood, straining to pick up some sound or movement that might define my sense of danger. There was nothing to be seen or heard, however, so I crossed at last to the portal and leaned my head forward in order to peek beyond.

I don't know if the two gray-bearded men on my left saw me before I saw them or vice versa, but in either case I became aware of their presence some fifteen feet away from me far too late to escape their gaze.

"Good day to you, my fine fellow," said the younger-looking of the two. "Come forward and make yourself known."

I squelched an urge to turn and run, and forced myself to respond to his soft-spoken words of command.

"I am Lucius, from the Alta Semita," I breathed meekly as I approached the two of them.

"And I am Titus, from Lanuvium," my interlocutor replied, the kindness in his eyes offsetting somewhat the formality of his tone.

I came to a halt a few paces in front of him and shot a furtive glance at his companion, who was regarding me with the cool impassivity of a surgeon assessing a wart. Wrapped in towels, and with one foot resting on a stool, this silent figure compelled me to hold his gaze, though his visage was so intimidating that I wanted only to hide from it. He was sixty or even older, big boned, pale skinned, and fleshy, just shy of being fat. But his eyes so far overshadowed his body as to render it almost invisible. I had never seen eyes like those—dark and pitiless, yet sparkling with Promethean intelligence. Such eyes had clearly glimpsed far too much of the world to be blinded by illusions; they didn't *see* so much as *know*, and in their knowing there was an implacable sense of reality that filled me with disquiet. It seemed plain to me that they had long since come to view man's domain from some vastly larger perspective, one that enabled them to range at will over a multitude of more ennobling scenes. Now, accordingly, whenever duty or expedience required them to turn their contemplation back to the inanities of the mortal world, the shift was accomplished with great reluctance, and the mortal world held sternly to account for it.

"I am Publius, from Hispania," the mouth below the eyes announced. "Do you fancy a sip of wine?"

And without waiting for my answer, the speaker lifted a glass decanter from a large bowl of ice beside him and poured some crimson liquid into a gold cup held out by his companion.

"Come," said this somewhat less intimidating gentleman, as he proffered the cup.

"I wouldn't taste it just yet if I were you," said the man with the terrible eyes. "Fresh from the ice, it will be a trifle too cold." (It struck me, then, that the ice he'd so casually alluded to must have come all the way from the Apennines—at least a full day's journey from where he sat.)

"You needn't postpone your pleasure long, though," said the man named Titus, "the heat in here being what it is."

I nodded acknowledgment and waited, gazing blankly at the contents of my cup to avoid those cauterizing eyes in front of me. Moment succeeded moment in the torrid silence, and streams of sweat began coursing down my body, mixing as they descended with the dry mud adorning me to produce little rivulets of dark brown silt.

"I would think that it's ready for tasting now," the spectral gentleman declared from the recesses of his towels; and in a trance of cowed obedience I brought the cup up to my lips.

"Cumaean!" I exclaimed after taking a sip, surprised out of my reticence by the unexpectedness of so familiar a taste in so unfamiliar a setting.

Instantly both pairs of eyes homed in on me, and I cringed to my marrow beneath the weight of their redoubled attention.

"Would you care to guess its age?" said the less fearsome of the two elders after a glance at his compeer.

"I'll try," I answered nervously. Recalling the tutelage of my uncle Glaubus, I lifted the cup to my nose, inhaled the bouquet, and once more took a dram or two of the liquid into my mouth. It was smooth, as only the very best vintages could be, and as ripe for drinking as it was ever likely to get. Putting its maturity together with its quality, I reviewed in my mind the vindemiae from the time I was six to the time I was nine. Only when I was eight had the Cumaean vintage been truly exceptional. And so in a tentative voice I responded, "I believe that it's now six years old." (It still perplexes me that out of such accidents of cognizance men fashion their opinions of their fellows.)

"You have an acute palate for someone so young," said the icy-eyed Publius. "May I ask you how it was that you came by it?"

It took me several moments to untangle his locution sufficiently to understand what he was asking, but once I understood, I made haste to reply. "My uncle taught me about wine, sir. My uncle Glaubus."

"Ah," said Publius. "He is a cognoscente?"

"No, sir," I responded confidently, not knowing what the word meant but feeling certain that I'd never heard it applied to Glaubus.

"He is *not* a cognoscente, you say?" Publius asked with a frightening increase in the intensity of his concentration.

"No, sir," I stammered. "He's the proprietor of a bar."

There was a brief instant of silence; then both men erupted in guffaws.

"That clarifies the matter very succinctly," said the one named Titus, laughter still agitating his body, and I risked a glimmer of a smile, praying as I did so that all the merriment boded well.

"But wait!" said Publius abruptly, and the resultant silence fell like a boulder. "You then must be that Lucius of whom Marcus has spoken."

I stared at him, my jaw hanging slack. "By your leave, sir," I quavered, "do you mean Marcus Annius Verus?"

"I call him 'Verissimus,' " he responded, "because he is perversely devoted to the notion of truth. He has spoken of you often."

Spoken well or ill? I longed to ask. With affection or indifference? But I stayed silent—afraid to question, afraid to know.

"You are welcome here," said Titus. "I am Marcus's uncle, Antoninus."

I took his cordiality as an encouraging sign, though my confusion over his suddenly altered appellation must have been apparent.

"Were he not so self-effacing," Publius explained, "my friend here would have described himself as Titus Aurelius Fulvus Boionius Arrius Antoninus, sometime Consul Ordinarius and Consular Magistrate for Etruria and Umbria, newly designated Proconsul of Asia, *and* uncle of Marcus Annius Verus . . . by marriage."

At this the two men exchanged grave signs of mirth.

"I, on the other hand," Publius continued, "am simply a guest here, like yourself—though regrettably somewhat longer in the tooth."

I was unfamiliar with such metaphors, so the humor went over my head; had it not been for the two men's rueful smiles, in fact, I doubt that I would have realized that some jest had eluded me.

After the inevitable awkward pause, Titus Antoninus inquired blandly, "Did you have any difficulty getting here?"

Given my mud-caked condition, even I could appreciate how tactfully the question had been phrased.

"I had a little trouble finding the place," I replied, seeing nothing to be gained by going into greater detail. "The worst problem was that I couldn't find anybody to ask for directions."

"Everyone's out helping with the harvest," said Titus Antoninus. "We've had a demon of a time getting the crops in and the grapes picked, what with all the rain. Every able-bodied creature on the estate has been lending a hand."

"Except you," Publius amended, "out of kindness to an enfeebled friend."

"Out of respect and affection, if I may presume to correct you."

Publius gave a grateful nod, then turned to me and asked, "So how did you manage to find 'the place,' despite your 'problem'?"

"I, uh, met Dracena on one of the roads."

"Good thing he didn't take you for a crop thief," Titus Antoninus said without the least trace of irony. Then, after a quick glance at Publius, he continued, "But I suspect you're eager now to wash the dust of travel from your body. Shall I point you in the direction of the caldarium and the swimming bath?"

"Yes, sir, thank you," I responded, appreciating his graciousness almost as much as the opportunity he'd given me to escape his friend's gaze.

"They're through this door on my right," he said, indicating, "the caldarium first and the swimming bath adjacent. You'll find strigils and anything else you might need on the shelf beside the tub."

"Thank you," I said again, starting to edge toward the door. "By your leave, I'll go now and wash."

"Bene lava," said Publius, with a smile like that of a skull.

"Thank you," I stammered yet another time, adding a quick, "Good afternoon to you both," before fleeing from his death's-head grimace.

The caldarium was a spacious chamber paved with mosaics no less dazzling than the ones I'd seen before, and the so-called tub, steaming in an alcove at the back, was a marble cistern large enough to accommodate a skiff. Using one of the half-dozen silver ewers arrayed around the base of this vat, I doused myself repeatedly with hot water, delighting in each cascade of warmth as it washed away a bit more of the soil and grit of my bold little six-hour odyssey. I next dissolved some soda ash in a water bowl and thoroughly cleaned my hair, immersing myself in the steaming marble cauldron once I'd finished. I luxuriated a while, and then, without too much diffidence, availed myself of several towels, which were even more plentiful in the caldarium than they'd been in the dressing room. Once dry, I oiled and strigiled myself and went though the door to the swimming bath.

This was the loveliest room I'd yet seen. The walls depicted scenes from the *Aeneid*, and in the little alcoves that punctuated the paintings there were Greek statues of such delicacy and grace that only by touching them could I confirm that they were made of stone. The most exquisite aspect of this exquisite sanctum was the pearllike glass in the panels just beneath the beam-and-coffer ceiling. This glass alternated with short pillars that bore the ceiling's weight, and through its translucent screen came the wanng light of the autumn afternoon. I think a cloud must have fled from before the sun just after I entered the chamber, because even as I was in the act of taking in all its wonders it filled up like a tide pool with the orange radiance of Helios's day-end fires. Dumbstruck, I sat down on a bench and gaped like a bumpkin at the glory ablaze around me. I felt ravished by the transcendent scene, and stricken by its cruel impermanence. Try as I might, I could not grasp the reality of my presence in the midst of so much beauty, and the thought that Twopenny Street and Drusilla were barely half a day behind me transformed my confusion very quickly into tears. Sitting there, I felt like some ragtag Icarus—too close to the sun for my wings to sustain me, too far from home to descend back to earth; and as I looked through my tears at the fantastical chamber before my eyes, I was gripped by a sense of irreparable loss. Never before had the idea of belonging somewhere meant so much to me; never before had I felt so out of place. It's said that the truth of our aloneness is the most painful lesson we can ever learn; but I wouldn't go quite that far. In my case, at all events, the pain was merely all I could bear.

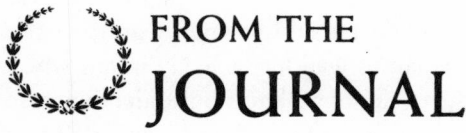
[AUGUST 18TH]

I had a strange and unnerving dream last night. I dreamed I was running, naked, as at Olympia, along an empty road beside the sea. The road was of soft-packed dirt, firm enough to cushion each footfall yet so resilient as to transform my normal stride into a series of effortless bounds. The sun shone down from the zenith as I ran, and the sky was immaculate blue. I dreamed that I'd been running for miles without the least fatigue or stress, and I felt I could gallop along forever down this road by the shining sea. But then there was a columbarium by the road, and I stopped to see whose ashes had been walled up there. There were no ashes, though; in place of cinerary urns there were people in the niches, living people laid out on marble slabs. All at once it was evening, and the sky was heavy with clouds. The people in the niches looked up at me with sympathetic smiles; they seemed to be gentle and kindly. Then the moon appeared, full and brilliant above the cloud tops, and from its reflections glistening on the nearby water emerged the figure of a woman. She was majestically statuesque, with large marmoreal breasts that leaked milk from their distended nipples. I sensed that I knew who this woman was, but I couldn't be sure because her face was obscured by shadows. She walked out of the sea in my direction, and my member went stiff as she approached. There was a scent of wildness in the night air around me, and when I glanced at the columbarium I saw that all the niches were empty. The woman strode up to me, so tall and regal that my eyes were gazing directly into the silken curls above her cleft. Placing her massive hands on my shoulders, she drew me toward her body. I buried my face in the fleece of her venereal mound and realized with a shock that the scent of wildness I'd been smelling was in fact the scent of the sea. The very next instant I found myself tumbling through an ocean of stars, like a plume of milkweed riding on the wind. I wasn't afraid, though, because the woman still enveloped me; indeed, my staff was now buried deep inside her while my lips sucked fiercely at her breasts. On and on we tumbled through the star sea. But all at once I found myself completely alone. Stark terror welled up in my body, and I struggled like a drowning man to come awake. Alas, I could do no more than dream that I'd awakened, and in that nightmare of waking I found myself still hurtling down the corridors of night. My soul shriveled up when I grasped the reality of my abandonment, and I began to wail like a sickly infant who's been left on some hillside to die. The ocean of darkness bore silent witness as I spiraled screaming toward its depths, and had my own plaintive whimpers not at last truly roused me from my slumbers, I believe I'd have fallen forever—an agonized pinpoint of sentience crying out for compassion to the concourse of uncaring stars.

What am I to make of a dream such as this? What do such awesome visions portend? If old Nestor were here, he'd probably tell me to go back over my "Life" in search of answers. And I, in turn, would probably tell him that all my "Life" seems to do is raise new questions.

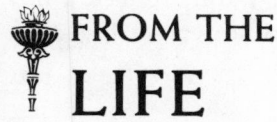

It turned out, perhaps unsurprisingly, that I needn't have worried about either the extent of Marcus's friendship or the enthusiasm of his welcome. The warmth of his greeting was so unrestrained, in fact, that I was tempted to view him as somewhat profligate with his affections. (And when I confessed that unworthy suspicion to him some months later, he laughed so hard I feared he might do damage to his rib cage.)

I was sitting disconsolate by the swimming bath when he burst in— even wetter and more dirt encrusted than I had been on my arrival.

"*Lucio!*" he shouted, running headlong toward me and grappling me into his arms.

"You're glad to see me?" I said in wonderment as he planted kisses on both my cheeks.

"Glad?" he responded. "I'm absolutely brimming with joy."

"Then I haven't presumed too much in coming here?"

"*Presumed!*" he said in an affronted tone, taking hold of my shoulders, "Did *I* presume too much all those times I came to you?"

I shook my head, too choked with feelings to remind him that his impromptu visits to the Hobnail were hardly comparable to my intrusion onto his uncle's estate. "I just . . . didn't . . . know . . ." I said, struggling to lift my voice above the clamor of my emotions.

"Didn't know what, dear fellow?"

". . . didn't know . . . how you felt."

"About you, you mean?"

And I could barely manage a nod in reply.

"Gods of the sea and air!" he exclaimed. "What did you think I felt?"

I shrugged miserably, not knowing what to say.

"Do you seriously mean to tell me that there's still some question in your mind about my love for you."

I raised my eyes to his, and the props of my self-control began to give way. "You *love* me?" I asked, as my eyes started streaming.

"Well of course I do, you spittlewit. What ever on earth made you doubt it?"

"I didn't doubt it," I murmured, returning my gaze to the floor. "I just never imagined it."

Marcus put his arm around my shoulders, as my tears formed a tiny puddle on the tiles. "Lucio," he said softly, "I treasure you as I would a brother."

"I don't understand," was my muted response.

"What don't you understand?"

"I don't understand the reasons for your affection. I can't think what I've done to make you love me."

"But you haven't *done* anything at all," he answered with a trace of impatience. "You've simply *been* what you are."

I turned and looked at him. "What I am," I said, "is a fatherless plebeian, a mongrel of the lower orders."

"Only the unborn are fatherless, Lucio—and all of us are mongrels in one way or another."

"But by no means all of us are *humiliores*," I retorted, "especially in this house."

Marcus raised his eyebrows and gave me a rueful smile. "I ask your pardon," he said. "If you are, perhaps, too conscious of your place in life, I am, perhaps, too careless about my own. But even if it's true that a great gulf divides us in the eyes of the world, it's also true that the love between us can bridge it. So I tell you, Lucio, once and for always, that my affections aren't subject to my rank, and that the way the world perceives us must never determine the way that we regard each other."

I have to confess that I received these eloquent protestations with a somewhat skeptical ear, and perhaps for no other reason than that I wanted so badly to believe them. My skepticism wasn't directed toward Marcus's sincerity, of course—that was never less than absolute; it was directed, rather, toward the basis of his affections. I suspected, in other words, that he had resolved to feel love for me instead of letting a feeling of love evolve, and whether my suspicions on this count stemmed more from a sense of my own unworthiness than from a clear perception of Marcus's eccentricities is a question that has spanned almost fifty years without yielding a conclusive answer.

Not that I was ungrateful or at all unwilling to accept the friendship he offered. I simply had a sense that I'd come by his love much too easily, and that he, with his immoderate passion for virtue, had simply seized on the first presentable plebeian who crossed his path in order to assure himself that the stain of aristocracy hadn't seeped too deeply into his soul.

And so I said to him, "What is it about the way I 'am' that you should have come to love me?"

"Ah, now, that's easy," he replied with a smile. "For one thing, you are without pretense. . . ."

"That's more a function of circumstance than of character."

"Untrue," he declared with an emphatic shake of his head. "I've seen beggars ask for pennies with all the condescension of the Babylonian kings. Pretense resides in the soul, not the purse. . . . Now may I continue?"

I gave him a grudging nod.

"So, as I said, you are without pretense. And in a similar vein, you are without malice."

"Now there I flat *know* you're wrong."

"Tut-tut," he said, shaking his head again and raising a remonstrative finger. "Malice resides in actions, not just feelings, so you can spare me a recital of all your petty resentments and secret hates."

I looked at his complacent grin a moment, then gave in with an irritated shrug.

"Now then, you are also without deceit. . . ."

I shrugged again. "My good qualities, it seems, are nothing more than the absence of certain bad ones."

"I haven't gotten to your good qualities yet, and I may never get to them if you keep interrupting me."

"I'm sorry," I said in a sulky tone.

"And besides," he continued with a tiny flicker of irritation, "you are by no means without your blemishes, mistrustfulness being foremost among them."

"I have reason to be mistrustful," I cried out in abject self-pity.

"So do we all, Lucio," was Marcus's earnest response. "But sooner or later we must decide if the betrayals we guard against are really so anguishing as to warrant the terrible antidote of perpetual suspicion."

I looked at him, at the dark hollows where his eyes lay hidden by the gathering dusk. "Some of them are," I said dully.

"Or is it that some of them *were*?"

I looked more closely into his shadowed orbits, and my tears resumed their flow. "What do you mean?" I asked, though I could have guessed if I'd cared to.

"I mean, I suppose, that the worst part of any betrayal is the sense that one was foolish in reposing trust; for it is that sense, magnified by the sting of perfidy, that leads one to question all love."

"True enough," I said in a broken whisper.

"Well, consider then," he continued, "that your error may not have resided so much in trusting per se as in trusting wrongly. And if that was the case, then the only betrayal you suffered was a betrayal of yourself."

"Do you offer that as a source of consolation?" I asked with imperfectly muted sarcasm. And in the near darkness I saw Marcus's lips again take on a smile.

"I offer it as a spur to cogitation, my friend; because I think I can guess the nature of the 'betrayal' you think you've suffered, and if I'm right in my conjecture, then you haven't been betrayed at all."

"You side with Agricus then!" I flared up at him.

"With him no less than with you, dear Lucio. Now tell me, am I right in thinking that Drusilla's taken him to her bed?"

I was silent a long moment, then spat out an angry "Yes!"

"Aha! There, I *knew* it."

"Congratulations."

"Oh, Lucio, don't wallow so much in your desolation. If you feel betrayed, it's only because you 'trusted' your aunt and Agricus to resist the power of their obvious mutual attraction. But neither one of them ever took any vows of abstinence from each other, nor, in all probability, did either of them give too much thought to what you might make of their copulation. Their 'betrayal,' if any, was of Glaubus, not you, though I doubt that your uncle would be so misguided as to view their conduct in such a light."

If I had had anyone else to turn to at that moment of my life, I believe I would have said good-bye to Marcus and headed off. My anger with him was as venomous as it was unreasoning, and the fact that he was my only refuge in the world did little but add to my fury. How dare he exonerate those goatish traitors; how dare he speak them fair and censure me! If he was in sympathy with their iniquities, he might at least have had the breeding not to admit it; and if he differed with me about their moral culpability, he might at least have had the good grace not to be right.

"Have I spoken too much truth to you, Lucio?" he asked.

"Yes!" I blurted abruptly.

"Well then, it probably won't hurt if I confide a bit more."

"I'm not sure that I want to hear it."

"In that case you'd better cover your ears and start whistling."

I sat immobile as the darkness took hold all around us.

"If you *ever* trusted Agricus," he said quietly, "and I mean trusted him as a friend, then you're a fool and well punished for your folly. If you ever trusted Drusilla, on the other hand, then you're simply a susceptible little boy. In either case, you could not have trusted either of them for long without willfully ignoring the promptings of your reason. You're too smart, in other words, to persist in trusting such people—too smart, that is, unless your *desire* to trust them was so overwhelming as to lead your mind astray."

I sat silent, unable to refute him, unwilling to agree.

"Is it so hard a lesson to learn," he went on, "that you cannot impose moral obligations unilaterally, any more than you can coerce love? Our hearts just do not respond to such unnatural pressures. And so, however fervently you may have wanted your aunt and your compeer to show their love for you in certain specified ways, the only ways they were actually able to show it were their own. You do not accept their ways of showing it, though, and insist, instead, that you've been betrayed. But who of the three of you has turned his back on the other two, and who of the three of you sets conditions as the price of his love? If it is hard for you to accept the truth that Drusilla and Agricus desire each other, that is no moral failing of theirs. And if it is impossible for you to acknowledge the fact that they can satisfy their desire without negating their feelings for you, then you are demanding more of them than you have any right to expect."

The weight of emotional logic in Marcus's words bore down on my spirit like lead, and it was the resultant pain and exasperation that led me to lash out at him as viciously as I did. "You're awfully knowledgeable about the subject of desiring Drusilla," I said.

My heart froze the instant the words were out of my mouth, and I still shudder to think what might have become of me had I been dealing with a soul less generous than my friend's. I stared at his motionless silhouette, while the innuendo I'd just uttered reverberated through the suddenly inimical silence. Moments passed as we faced each other, two shapes slightly darker than the darkness all around. At last, with a heavy sigh, Marcus shouldered the weight of my reckless insinuation and absolved me of the thwarted love we shared, saying in a muted tone, "Aren't we all, dear Lucio. Aren't we all."

Then he held me as I sobbed out my brokenhearted pain.

 FROM THE
JOURNAL

[AUGUST 19TH]

Is it possible, I wonder, that the dreams I've been having lately bear some relation to what I've been writing about my life? The question occurs to me because the dreams have been unusually vivid and disturbing. The one I had last night, for instance, seemed to echo in some obscure manner the words I'd written earlier in the day. In this dream I was fleeing from some unknown danger, running across the dusty caldera of an immense extinct volcano. All at once I saw Marcus running beside me, not the fourteen-year-old Marcus I've been writing of in my "Life," but the dour and weary sixty-year-old Emperor I encountered on the Danube last fall. This aged Marcus seemed to be racing with me for some reason, or perhaps "keeping pace with me" would be more precise. When I slowed down, he slowed down; when I speeded up, so did he. Always he stayed abreast of me, and some ten or twelve feet to my left. His face was stern, though free of anger, and the message I read in his eyes was: I am running this race for you. He seemed to be asking me to trust him, in other words, but though I wanted to I didn't feel I could; and when he realized this, he fell dead on his back in front of me, letting blood from his mouth spurt skyward in a gusher. This angered me, and I shouted at him to get up and finish our race; but his only response was to spew out more of his vital fluid. My anger at that point became ungovernable, and I began to shriek curses at him, whereupon he began very slowly to come back to life. And that so terrified me that I gave out with a cry of fright and woke myself up.

I've consulted my copy of Aristotle's *On Divination by Dreams*, as well as an abstract of the new treatise on the subject by Artemidorus of Lydia. Neither work provides much enlightenment, I'm sorry to say. So I suppose my only recourse is to go on writing and dreaming until the connection between the two functions becomes apparent. Or until Nestor informs me that I'm simply too dense to comprehend it.

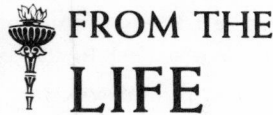

FROM THE LIFE

I feel a touch of shame whenever I think back on that conversation by the swimming bath at Lorium. There I was, throwing myself on Marcus's mercy, imposing on his good nature, yet still having the effrontery to demand that he attest to the sincerity of his love. This done, I proceeded to attack him, or, rather, to further test his love for me by subjecting it to additional strain. I suppose, looking back on it, that my behavior was all very natural and understandable; it is when we feel least sure of ourselves that we are most suspicious of others' affections. But however natural my actions were, they could hardly be thought of as laudable—especially when contrasted with those of my friend.

It is a measure of the person Marcus was that he responded to my insolent assault on him with a simple invocation of the longings we had in common. You see, ran his underlying message, not only is our friendship real enough for you to be cruel to me without regard to our social standing, it is even so real that such anger as might come between us is instantly transformed into a shared sorrow that draws us closer together.

Of course my present understanding of what passed between us then is for the most part a product of hindsight; my perceptions *in medias res* were considerably more confused. About the only thing I was sure of, in fact, was my inability to view the coupling of Agricus and Drusilla from Marcus's philosophical perspective. It was enough, however, for me to know that such a perspective existed, and that it shaped the judgments of the one who now meant more to me—or so I'd convinced myself—than either of the couplers ever had or ever would.

I sobbed for some time there in the darkness by the pool, until Marcus gently reminded me that the dinner hour was approaching and he had yet to bathe. So with some effort I composed myself, and together we made our way back to the caldarium, which was bright with lamplight by then and fairly teeming with slaves. None of these serviles seemed disposed to offer Marcus any attendance, and it took me a moment or two to realize that their strange behavior was most probably the result of his own instructions. He raised no objection to my assisting him with his bath, though, and once he was oiled and strigiled we both donned clean tunics and headed out a side door in the direction of his quarters.

Though he'd seemed cheerful enough since we'd left the swimming bath, he'd also become very quiet, and I began to worry that he was already tiring of my presence. I thus felt compelled to ask him whether anything was wrong as we made our way down the torch-lit corridors.

"Oh, no, certainly not," he answered with a sunburst of a smile. "I've just been ruminating about all the fun we're going to have now that you're here."

This declaration served to diminish my anxieties to some extent—at least for the remainder of the evening.

We came at length to the flowered courtyard I'd passed through with Dracena. I might have guessed that Marcus's chosen "quarters" would consist of one of the tiny cubicles that ringed this enclosure. Nor were the room's furnishings in any way inconsistent with its dimensions: the floor was packed dirt, the walls rough brick, the seating one stool, the amenities one earthenware bowl and ewer, and the illumination one lamp. The only aspect of the room's appointments that couldn't be ranked as a bare necessity was a rickety old table littered with scrolls, tablets, styli, reeds, and inkpots—and I could imagine the moral convolutions Marcus must have gone through before permitting himself such a flagrant luxury.

The sleeping accommodations were of a piece with the rest of the room's decor: they consisted of two plank-and-skin pallets, one sitting by the far wall with Marcus's rumpled cloak spread across it, and the other, which had just been provided, apparently, leaning upright beside the doorway.

"Well," said Marcus, beaming with pride, "what do you think?"

Scrupling to tell him the truth and hurt his feelings, but scrupling also to tell him lies while concealing my own, I chose a third course and replied simply, "You patricians really know how to live."

He stared at me an instant, then burst into delighted laughter. "I'd forgotten, Lucio, that you are an ironist."

"Yes, but I'm told it's curable."

"The gods forbid, dear comrade. May you die an old man, with your irony intact."

"That sounds more like a curse than a benediction."

"Only because you're foolish enough to despise your own gifts."

I was about to point out to him that others had been known to despise them as well, but I decided on reflection that even my lust for self-pity was in danger of suffering satiation.

From Marcus's quarters we made our way through several rooms I hadn't seen before and down a long corridor, from the far end of which issued the noise of conviviality and the aroma of roasting meat. Light from a legion of torches danced toward us along the naked walls, growing ever brighter and more lurid as we approached our destination. A glance at Marcus told me that he understood my sense of rising excitement, and when we passed at last through the portal at the corridor's end, I found myself engulfed by a scene so remarkable that I can still conjure it in my memory down to the most minute detail.

We had entered a large and densely crowded chamber whose white marbled walls were tinted russet by the smoky light of the torches. Though the far end of the room consisted of a colonnade open to the nighttime chill, its interior was awash with warmth, the sources of heat being the eight-foot-square cooking pit in the center of the scene and the three or four hundred cheerful revelers who were gathered around it. Rising from the pit tenuous columns of smoke coiled their way through the scarlet haze, diffusing at last into the general clamor that beat against the walls. And it was this din, I believe, more than the heat or light or sheer magnitude of the spectacle, that most affected me as I took the whole scene in. The pure volume of sound was enough to make a profound impression, but what struck me even more was its tenor—for it was downright, nakedly happy: full of exuberant laughter and untrammeled fellow-feeling. I had never heard such a chorus of vitality before, and as I stood and stared and let the sounds wash over me I came to the joyful realization that there were more kinds of families for me to choose from in the world than those defined by the oppressive bonds of blood.

And so a glow of quiet gladness streamed through my body as I contemplated the vision before me, and it was indeed a vision that rewarded contemplation. Above the coals of the cooking pit, for example, the roasting carcasses of a bull, a boar, and a ram turned slowly on heavy iron spits. Sweating slaves with massive shoulders manned the cranks that kept them turning, while a dozen less muscular retainers tended smaller skewers around the pit's perimeter. Basted and sizzling on these were suckling pigs, flatfish, plump pullets, and kid. Behind the cooks some twenty or thirty servers crouched by their stacks of wooden platters, and interspersed among them the carvers stood ready at their boards.

While the meat and poultry roasted, dozens of servants circulated among the couches with trays of boiled eggs, onions, apples, chestnuts, and figs; a dozen or two more darted here and there bearing flagons of wine and water.

Those who feasted were several times more numerous than those who served, and scores of tables, stools, and dining couches had been provided to accommodate them. So densely was everyone packed in that I couldn't at first detect any semblance of order in the arrangements. After several moments of observation, however, I saw that the couches, at least, had been laid out in roughly defined concentric circles, with the cherry red embers of the cooking pit pulsing restlessly at their common focus. The innermost of these circles was peopled with men exclusively, and rather large men at that. From their size, from the prevalence of leather corselets among them, and above all from their close proximity to the roasting meat, I deduced that they had to be soldiers, though why they were present in such numbers on an occasion such as a harvest feast amounted to something of a mystery.

Surrounding these burly figures was a far more populous circle made up of ruddy-faced men, women, and children clustered together in family-size groups. Almost all of these people were dressed in homespun, and perhaps two-thirds of the men displayed the close-cropped hair of former slaves. They, it seemed likely, were all one-time chattels of Marcus's uncle who'd been raised to the rank of tenants on manumission and been given small plots of land to farm in return for a share of their crops. Of course their former master, by transforming them from his slaves into his dependents, had at the same time transformed himself from their owner into their patron, and as such he had the right to claim their services at various times such as the harvest. Judging by the looks of good cheer on their faces, they had rendered those services right willingly—as well they might have, given the advantages they enjoyed as clients of so eminent and properous a protector.

No less cheerful, to all appearances, were the rest of the men in this middle circle. They, I assumed, were neighboring smallholders, who, though they owed Titus Antoninus no service, had nevertheless supplied him with their own and their families' temporary labor. In return, I imagined, they stood to get cash or a cartful of produce—not to mention all they could eat at this lavish banquet.

The outermost circle was rather less densely populated than the inner two, but the people in it made a greater collective impression on the eye. This may have been due in part to their proximity to the torches on the walls, but I think it was more directly attributable to the richness of their jewelry and attire. The men's tunics were not dull brown or gray like those on the backs of the rustics, but white, with the brilliance of fuller's chalk, and emblazoned with crimson borders. The golden rings of the Equestrian order glowed warmly on a score of fingers, and the broad stripe of the senatorial class ran boldly down ten or twelve sleeves. Among the women, jeweled brooches flashed from the shoulders of several dozen

ankle-length stolae, and the garments themselves, though of unadorned
wool in isolated cases, were for the most part cut from dazzlingly colored
silks and linens; crimson, saffron, and violet being the dominant hues.

On the right-hand side of this outer circle a cluster of some fifteen or
twenty people dominated the entire scene. Nine or ten of these—Dracena
prominent among them—were fully armed *singulares*, arrayed unobtru-
sively but unmistakably in a protective crescent around the others, who,
with one notable exception, were all reclining on oversized couches. The
exception was the fearsome Publius, who was seated or, given his demeanor, enthroned on a high-backed chair, with his right foot resting
on a stool just as it had been in the baths. Marcus's uncle was immediately
to his left, with a stern-looking, plainly dressed woman and a somewhat
corpulent young man on the couch beside him. Three elderly men with
long beards reclined on the couch to Publius's right, and on the couch
to the right of them was a boy about my age, a sickly looking girl some
three or four years older, and a thirteen- or fourteen-year-old imp of a
female, who was staring quite openly in my direction.

"You've met my uncle already, I believe," Marcus said, and I nodded
that I had.

"And the Emperor as well, so they tell me."

"What Emperor?" I asked, as my heart started pounding.

"The Roman Emperor, you dimwit."

"The *Roman* Emperor?"

"Yes. Our First Citizen . . . You've heard of him?"

"Heard of him, yes; met him, no."

"You mean to tell me that you don't recognize that gentleman seated
in the chair?"

"I recognize him all too well; his name is Publius."

Marcus smiled broadly. "Is that what he told you?"

"You mean his name isn't Publius?"

"Oh, it's Publius all right; in fact, it's Publius Aelius Hadrianus."

"Hadrianus?" I asked, my voice fading to a squeak.

"Rings a bell, does it?"

I nodded numbly, sensing a sudden shakiness in my knees.

Marcus gazed at me, his eyes full of merriment. "What's the matter,
Lucio? Haven't you ever seen an emperor before?"

I gaped at him, then at Publius, then at each of them in rapid succession.
"You mean . . ." I began.

"You guessed it," Marcus responded. "Your bathmate Publius is none
other than Imperator Caesar Traianus Hadrianus Augustus—Emperor,
Princeps, and master of the Roman world, poor fellow."

I was so stunned I could think of nothing more magniloquent to say than, "What's wrong with his foot?"

"He has gout."

"Oh," I commented, staring awestruck at the afflicted extremity.

"Well," said Marcus after a decent interval, "now that we've exhausted your curiosity about the most powerful man in the world, shall we take our places and have a bite to eat?"

"Our places?" I asked blankly.

"On the end of that left-hand couch, next to that little brat who's been staring at us."

We made our way across the room, saluted Emperor and host (both of whom actually graced us—or Marcus, at any rate—with indulgent smiles), and sat down next to the little brat who immediately started in with Marcus by saying, "It's nice that you finally condescended to join us."

"Lucio," Marcus addressed me, ignoring her completely, "may I present my cousin Marcus Galerius, at the far end of the couch, and his sister Aurelia, beside him. . . . Marcus and Aurelia, my dear friend, Lucius."

The two accorded me friendly nods, which I returned, I hope, without too much hesitation.

"You know perfectly well, Marcus," the imp interjected, "that he's really much more interested in meeting me." And I blushed to realize she was right.

"Oh, Annia, you're here," Marcus said in mock surprise. "Please forgive me, but it's so easy to overlook someone of your dwarfish dimensions. You should really be more forthright about making your presence known."

"You've heard what they say about the wit of Stoics, cousin," she retorted; "it's close akin to the wisdom of sheep."

"Such wisdom may yet be within your ken, little dewdrop, given sufficient diligence and study."

"Too bad the same thing can't be said of you," she shot back at him. Then, turning to me, she said, "I am Annia Galeria Faustina, daughter of Titus Aurelius Fulvus Boionius Arrius Antoninus and Annia Galeria Faustina, his wife."

"*Youngest* daughter," Marcus corrected.

"Ignore him," Annia said.

"But he's my friend," I objected.

"For that I pardon you."

"And my host as well."

"He can't be your host, you pea brain; he's a guest here himself."

"Pea brain!"

"This is my father's house," she continued, oblivious of my indignation, "and I, therefore, am much better qualified to be your host than he is."

"Hostess, you mean," I suggested truculently.

"Ah, you've noticed," she replied, flashing me a smile that was all the more dazzling for having been so unexpected.

"You think I'm pretty, don't you?" she asked me, and I could only drop my eyes and blush.

"I like your friend, oh, beardless sage," she announced to Marcus, eliciting laughter as a response. "And your friend likes *me* even more."

"It was inevitable, Annia, that someone would like you eventually," Marcus rebutted—and my blushes deepened and spread.

To tell the truth, Annia Galeria's dark hair, slender figure, and deep-set obsidian eyes had made more than a trifling impression on me. Indeed, I was well on my way to being captivated by her—and far too young, alas, to realize that part of what was captivating me was her haunting resemblance to my aunt Drusilla.

[AUGUST 20TH]

How mysterious the tides of memory! They sweep even the grandest passions from the surface of the mind and leave them to lie undiscernible beneath the ceaseless eddies of recent recollection. But then a chance wind arises to fret the currents of the past, and all the intervening decades recede in a rush from your thoughts; the dark waves of bygone years roll swiftly away toward the skyline, and there on the shore, shimmering in the radiance of remembrance made new, stands the lost love you'd almost forgotten, and the pain you must once more endure.

How long has it been since I last thought of Annia? How long has it been since she died? Three years? Five?

Dear gods, there are some wounds that never heal, and some sorrows that never diminish.

Annia Annia Annia—I mourn for us yet, as I would for a stillborn child.

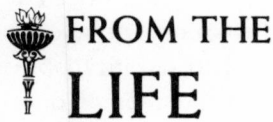# FROM THE
LIFE

And so I began a new life at Lorium, one filled with the joys of discovery and the pangs of adolescent love. The keystone of this life was learning, for Marcus immediately co-opted me into the classes given by his tutors, classes for which I'd been singularly ill-prepared by the dronings of Damatrios in the Hobnail's courtyard. With respect to Greek studies, I was absolutely hopeless; and because the tutor in that subject was no less a personage than Alexander "the Grammarian," it was quickly agreed between Marcus and me that at those times when he and his cousins were struggling with Xenophon beneath the great scholar's exacting eye, I would be off by myself somewhere working on my egregiously awkward Latin composition. I wasn't much more competent in the area of law, unhappily, but the tutor, Quintus Junius Rusticus, being a Stoic as well as a jurist, had no objection to my listening to his lectures and gleaning what I could from them. In two disciplines only did my level of learning approach that of the young patricians, yet even in these I would have found it almost impossible to attain any semblance of intellectual equality without the patient indulgence of our teacher. This was Sextus, a wise and gentle nephew of the famous Plutarch. He hailed from Chaeronea, where Philip of Macedon and Sulla of ill fame won their greatest victories, and he'd been educated in Athens. Though Greek by birth and Greek by learning, he spoke and wrote the most exquisitely lucid Latin I've ever heard or read—and I've heard Fronto and read Virgil in my time. Ah, how I wish my beloved Sextus were alive today, to teach rhetoric and philosophy to my children in the way he taught them to me! Alas, he died in the plague thirteen years ago; but statues in his honor still stand on the Arx and in the Palatine Library, just as shrines to his memory still stand in the hearts of his former pupils, whose minds he so unassumingly enriched.

At Lorium, as on Twopenny Street, the pursuits of scholarship consumed the entire morning, though at Lorium we were allowed a short respite at the fifth hour, when a modest *prandium* was laid out for us in the dining hall's colonnade. There Annia and Aurelia would join us for a few quick nibbles before returning to their Latin syntax. I was in no fit state to resume my own studies after they left, however. Had I been at all familiar with Ovid, I would have realized that the emotional turbulence that always overcame me was a perfectly normal, not to say inevitable, consequence of such tantalizing encounters; fleeting glimpses of one's beloved are among the most sharply barbed of Cupid's arrows, after all. But I was only fifteen when the little god's volleys first struck me; I knew no more than that they lodged deep, and stung.

There were two more hours of academic endeavor after our *prandium*, but then we boys were free, within certain limits, to do exactly as we pleased. Before we could take full advantage of our freedom, though, one of us had to be taught by the other three to ride a horse. I say *a* horse with the intention of being literal, since there was only one animal on the entire estate who was sufficiently docile not to intimidate me. This phlegmatic beast, inaptly named Incitatus after the famous equine Gaius Caligula once adlected into the Senate, had a profound aversion to any gait more strenuous than a trot. That was fine with me, though it often caused Marcus and his cousins to seethe with exasperation, especially when we devoted our afternoons to excursions away from Lorium. I suppose their feelings of impatience were entirely natural under the circumstances, but if the pace of our excursions was sometimes maddeningly slow, the abundance of readily accessible destinations somewhat made up for it, particularly since the only restraint on us was the requirement that we make our way homeward by nightfall. Annia, by contrast, led a far more cloistered existence, and I guess it was fortunate that she wasn't at liberty to share our adventures. The flames of my youthful passion might have flared too brightly, if I'd been continuously exposed to the creature who'd kindled them. Or perhaps I should say, they might have flared too brightly much sooner.

Not that she was ever very distant from my thoughts as things actually stood. Indeed, no matter how interesting the sights we saw or the people we encountered, the moments when I wasn't musing about her were pathetically few. Only one sight impressed me sufficiently, in fact, to banish her image from my mind for any appreciable length of time; and what I learned from the experience was that even love must give way on occasion to a vision of the infinite.

It was one of those dazzlingly crystalline autumn afternoons when the colors of nature seem to blare out at you like trumpets. The Apennines to the east looked almost close enough to touch, and the sun to the southwest flashed white and gemlike in a sky of fathomless blue. The air savored of mountain meadows, and though it was cool enough to nip at your skin now and then, you could feel the sunshine dancing on every breeze.

We had set off westward from the villa, crossing the Aurelia at the Marcian stream and entering the outskirts of Fregenae after little more than an hour's ride. This village was our ultimate destination as far as I knew, for Marcus had said as much, adding only that when we got there I would be vouchsafed "a modest surprise." Of course I knew right away from the smiles he exchanged with his cousins that the surprise in question was likely to be anything but modest; but I still wasn't prepared for the magnitude of what lay in store.

I guess one reason I loved Marcus so dearly was that he loved me so well. Most boys would simply have shown me whatever there was to see that day without taking the trouble to prime me first. Marcus, however, knew exactly what the moment of revelation would mean to me, and so with typical loving forethought he took care that my spirit was properly prepared.

We rode through Fregenae at an easy trot, attracting a few curious glances here and there, but nothing in the way of concerted interest. At the end of the short main street we came to a grove of umbral pines that stretched away far into the distance on either side. "Your surprise is just beyond these trees," Marcus told me, with his eyes agleam, and the four of us proceeded into the grove.

Every one of my senses was keenly alert as Incitatus trudged forward through the thin shafts of sunlight that dappled the ground. High above us the pine boughs swayed in the quickening breeze, and on each whispering zephyr rode the faintest suggestion of salinity. This trace of saltiness in the air, coupled with the ever-increasing sandiness of the soil, should have alerted me to the nature of Marcus's surprise. I was girding myself for some pitfall, however, some hidden obstruction or practical joke; so the moment of discovery, when at last it came, had precisely the impact intended.

I dropped the reins as Incitatus stepped out onto the beach, hardly noticing as he drowsily slowed to a halt. My eyes scanned the vast sweep of the horizon, and my mouth fell open in wonder. Directly in front of me was the sun sparkling off the water, and beside me was Marcus, savoring my entrancement.

"You're going to attract flies, you know," he said to me, and in the midst of my rapture I caused my mouth to close.

But then I caused it to open again, announcing simplemindedly, "This is the *sea!*"

"An inspired guess," Marcus commented.

I got down off Incitatus and walked in a daze toward the water, while Marcus continued along beside me on his horse. "That's Corsica over the horizon," he said, pointing, "and Hispania six days' sail farther on."

"Whatever you say," I responded, too entranced to give much thought to the import of his words.

Thinking back on it now, I feel a little foolish about reacting so convulsively to my first encounter with Mare Nostrum. And yet I can still to this day experience the thrill of that pristine moment—and not merely in the context of recollection. The feeling runs over my body every time I walk along the seashore and survey the endless reaches of water stretching away from me to the sky. No matter that I long ago learned the sad truth that beyond those awesome horizons there are only other poor wretches like me. For it is the horizons themselves that enchant my spirit; whatever lies beyond them I leave to the makers of maps.

Grateful as I was to Marcus for revealing such a wonder to me, my first, and then obsessive, desire was to share my excitement with my love. (I sometimes blush for myself when I think back on the boorish self-absorption with which I all too frequently repaid his kindnesses.) So rabid was I to get back to Annia's side, in fact, that even Incitatus got a taste of my impatience. Again and again, and in mounting frustration, I hammered my heels into his ribs. If I made any impression on him, though, it certainly wasn't of the variety to produce an increase in his speed.

But despite his impenetrable lassitude, we reached the villa well before dusk, and after ridding myself of him at the stables, I ran like Hermes to the northern end of the main colonnade, where Annia sometimes read before dinner.

She was there.

"Hello, friend Lucio," she called to me with a twinkling smile, while I made a belated effort to disguise my haste to be near her.

"Hello," I answered in an unconvincingly casual tone, slowing down to an easy lope and then leaning against the nearest pillar in a pose of idle indifference.

"I've been thinking about you," she said, letting her eyes drop down for an instant, "wondering what you've been up to all afternoon."

If there was a reproach implicit in this statement, it was drowned out by the thudding in my chest. "We went to the sea," I said proudly. "Have you ever seen it?"

She raised her eyes to mine and gave me a slow vulpine smile. "I've traveled on it," she said.

My sense of deflation was impossible to conceal. "When?" I asked.

"Two years ago," she replied, still smiling. "We went to Greece."

"Oh," I said, momentarily at a loss.

"We sailed from Brundisium to Apollonia, across the Adriatic."

"That must have been exciting."

She lifted her eyebrows and gave me an emphatic shake of the head. "I spent the entire journey retching. Does that count as excitement?"

"Is being seasick really that awful?"

"I would have been only too glad to die."

"I'm glad you didn't," I declared unthinkingly, then blushed scarlet.

Annia dropped her gaze again as her lips curved into a bitten-in smile. "I'm glad I didn't, too," she answered me, and then further demolished my composure by bringing her eyes back to mine.

For a long while we just gazed at each other, fledgling spirits all atremble to try their wings.

"I've never seen anything like it," I said finally, yielding to the tension. "The sea, I mean."

"You'd never seen it before?" she replied with a trace of coolness, sounding somewhat miffed or disappointed.

"No. And I never imagined it was so . . ."

"So . . .?"

"I don't know; so awesome, I suppose. So overpowering."

"How funny you are," she said, her spirits quickly reviving.

"Funny?"

"Making such a fuss about something as boring as the sea."

"It's just that it was so new to me," I pleaded in extenuation, despising myself for a hopeless bumpkin.

"Oh, I didn't mean there was anything wrong with the way you felt about it," she explained in a solicitous tone. "In fact, I think I rather envy you."

"Envy me?"

"Your sense of wonder, Lucio . . . and your innocence."

Had her voice slowed for a moment to caress the sound of my name? My impression was that it had, and the thought made me downright giddy.

"What are you thinking about, Lucio?" she asked in a winsome tone.

"About you," I answered helplessly.

"What about me?" she inquired, her eyes hypnotic.

"I don't know, really."

"That you're dying to kiss me, perhaps?"

So now one fledgling at least was beginning to beat its wings.

"Yes, perhaps," breathed the other.

"Well, I won't stop you, you know. . . . I won't even mind."

And in the space of an instant our lips were together.

"Ah, Lucio," she sighed as they parted, "I feel the goddess rise in me sometimes when I'm near you."

There was no need to ask her which goddess she had in mind, nor, indeed, was there time—given the haste with which she disclosed the fact that she wouldn't mind if I kissed her again.

Our idyll could not be prolonged, alas, because the time for dinner was fast approaching. So less than a quarter hour after our first kiss I floated blissfully back to the cubicle I shared with Marcus. He was bent over his studies, as usual, scribbling away in the rapidly fading light. But he looked up as I sauntered in, and in a casual voice remarked, "You're looking very pleased with yourself."

"I've had a wonderful day," I responded, "thanks in no small part to you."

He acknowledged my tribute with a gracious nod, but then gazed down at his pile of scrolls with a deeply troubled air. "You're letting yourselves in for a lot of anguish," he said finally, "—both of you."

If there'd been anything scolding or censorious in his tone, I might have refused to listen to him. But there wasn't a trace of judgment or disapproval in it, merely sincere affection and profound concern.

"If the genders were reversed," he continued, still staring at his desk top, "there might be a glimmer of hope for the two of you. But the way things are . . . I just don't see what can be done."

"I'm not sure I know what you mean," I said, as fear started crawling over my body.

"*Annia* would know," he snapped with asperity, turning abruptly to face me as he spoke. "She's a damnable willful fool!"

"Speak plainly to me, Marco," I pleaded, feeling panic burgeoning inside me.

"She's patrician, Lucio; you're plebeian."

"Well, I haven't thought of marrying her, you know."

"*Marrying* her!" he erupted. "Lucio, you risk your life by merely touching her."

"By *touching* her? You can't be serious."

He raised his eyes and looked plaintively at the ceiling, then turned back to me and intoned in a mournful voice, "The rules are stricter among *honestiores* than they are on Twopenny Street."

"What rules?"

"The same rules that forbid your aunt to couple with a slave, Lucio. . . . Please forgive my bluntness, but you ask and I must answer."

I stared at him in shocked disbelief. "But freeborn women sleep with slaves all the time in our neighborhood," I expostulated. "Nobody gives it a thought."

"That's in your neighborhood, Lucio. People here would give it quite a lot of thought. And even on Twopenny Street they'd think a bit if a freeborn woman took some slave to be her husband."

"You mean my rank's no higher with respect to Annia than a slave's would be with respect to my aunt?"

Marcus averted his eyes from me. "I've told you," he said, "the rules are stricter here."

I sank stunned onto my pallet and stared for a long time at the wall. "What do I do?" I asked finally.

"What do you feel?" Marcus rejoined.

I turned and showed him the misery in my eyes.

"Ye gods!" he sighed despairingly. "We'd best pray she's less smitten with you."

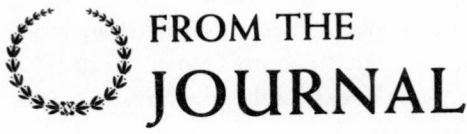 # FROM THE JOURNAL

[AUGUST 21ST]

At last it has dawned on me—*the slave boy!*

Finally, and belatedly, I believe I understand what compelled me to act as I did when I came upon his body on the riverbank. And the best part of my sudden enlightenment is the corollary realization that old Nestor was *wrong*. It wasn't the incident with Agricus at Curtio's that caused me to invest that poor butchered boy with so many aspects of myself; it was the doleful consequences of my social inferiority to Annia.

How wondrously strange are the mind's evolutions. To think that an all-but-forgotten passion should have echoed mutely inside me for all these years and still have possessed sufficient resonance to launch me into unwonted spasms of grief—all without my having any awareness of its influence.

Perhaps old Nestor wasn't so wrong after all; perhaps the incident with Agricus played a role of its own.

Not that I really think it did, of course. But if something so shrouded in time as my love for Annia could govern my actions for a day just last month—and without my even realizing it—then almost anything is possible in the realm of what shapes and inspires me.

And so perhaps old Nestor was correct about something else as well— the notion that by writing of my life I might begin to know myself.

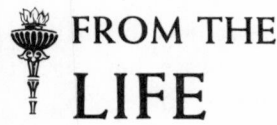
There was only one sensible way to resolve the problem of Annia and me, and that was to put distance between the two of us. With my heartsick acquiescence, accordingly, Marcus, petitioned his uncle for permission to return to Rome ten days earlier than planned, alleging as his excuse a desire to consult the works of two obscure Greek rhetors, Pargas and Dynalectios, whose writings were available only in the Ulpian Library. Given his standing as "Verissimus," he was instantly taken at his word and granted leave to depart; and indeed there'd been nothing even remotely short of the truth in his representations. He *was*, for some unfathomable reason, genuinely interested in that particular pair of Attic worthies, and the Ulpian Library in Trajan's Forum *was* the only place outside of Greece and Alexandria where their writings could be found. Marcus was no fraud when it came to truth-telling; he was just extremely canny about which truths he told. (I'd have been very interested to know what he'd have answered, though, if Titus Antoninus had thought to ask him why he was in such an all-fired hurry to consult the works of two such undistinguished droners.)

I, alas, lacked Marcus's gift for selecting the best truths to tell; but even he, I think, would have found it hard to break the news of our departure to Annia.

I myself found it much, much worse than hard.

I went to the trysting place well in advance of our normal meeting time and there made an effort to collect my wits. I felt like a thirsty traveler who'd arrived on the banks of a clear cool stream only to discover that the water in it wasn't fit to drink. Oh, the temptation to gulp some down anyway! How could anything so seemingly pure and unsullied be in any way inimical to one's well-being? It wasn't possible; it wasn't fair.

Yet there it was all the same. So as the golden autumn evening waned around me, I resolved that, thirsty as I was, the tainted liquid would never more pass my lips.

And in that one regard, at least, my hour of trial proved an intensely self-revelatory experience. For even though I was very much in love with Annia, there was still no question in my mind as to whether or not I would forsake her. Of course, one might say, that was simply a matter of survival—and so it was. But matters of the heart have often been known to prevail in such cases, and the fact that in my case they weren't going to taught me something about the kind of person I'd become.

Alas, I reckoned without the kind of person Annia had always been.

She appeared at the appointed hour, her dark eyes shining and her black hair glistening with oil. I was about to speak to her, but she forestalled me, raising a finger to her lips and guiding it slowly over to mine. I could not keep myself from kissing that finger, nor the hand and wrist and arm from which it projected. As my mouth moved, my resolution crumbled, and by the time my lips reached her shoulder no power on earth could have kept them from hers. Moist and yielding, they parted to receive me, and in reckless defiance of its toxins I drank long and deep from the forbidden spring. Ye gods but those poisons were sweet to the taste—as sweet, very nearly, as they were bitter to forswear.

"I have to return to Rome tomorrow," I gasped when our lips finally parted, fearing that I might never again have will enough to blurt it out.

She looked into my face for a moment, then drew her head back and regarded me with an expression of wary skepticism. "What do you mean?" she asked coldly.

"Please don't be angry with me," I pleaded. "You must know that I don't want to go."

"Then you must tell me why you have to," she responded, her eyes flashing with indignation.

"Because Marcus is going."

"So?"

"So! He's my patron, Annia; where he goes I have to follow."

Her lips curled into a sneer. "Like a dog, you mean."

I stared at her, too shocked and wounded to reply; while she stared back at me, a little astonished, I think, by the venomousness of her words.

Yet it didn't occur to me to take umbrage at what she'd said. Indeed, shocked as I was, I was also so ashamed of myself for having skirted the truth and placed all the blame on Marcus that the sting of Annia's scorn felt almost soothing.

As if that weren't enough, Annia herself was immediately convulsed with contrition. "Oh, Lucio, please forgive me," she said in a tearful voice, thrusting herself against me and tightening her arms around my waist.

"It's all right," I answered dully. "You've every right to feel contempt for me."

"Oh, no no *no*," she protested, raining kisses on my face and neck and shoulders. "I don't feel contempt for you, Lucio; truly I don't. I couldn't, ever."

Her solicitude was an even more poignant torture than her disdain had been, while her kisses were inducing such a fever of passion in me that I felt like I was about to split in half.

"Annia, stop," I moaned without conviction. Summoning the strength from somewhere, I added, "There are more reasons than one why I'm leaving tomorrow."

"Tell me," she said, pulling back a little way in order to look me in the face.

"You're a patrician," I said bluntly. "I'm not."

Her eyes widened in response to this statement, and lines of acute irritation appeared on her brow. "And why should that matter so very much?" she asked in a truculent voice.

"You know why, Annia," I answered her.

She glared at me in mounting exasperation, clearly dumbfounded by the notion that something as arbitrary as a social convention could keep her from having what she wanted. "I don't care," she said finally. "I love you and I'm not afraid to admit it."

"But I am, Annia. *I am!*"

She took a step backward and fixed me with a stare full of loathing. "No, you're *not!*" she shouted. "You just don't love me enough to face the risks."

Now there, I confess, she'd presented me with quite a conundrum. Because it dawned on me, once she'd spoken the words, that the fact she'd just alluded to lay at the very base of all that was transpiring between us.

And it was a fact. She, unlike me, was ready to plunge herself into our passion for each other with no thought for consequences or constraints. True, she had less to lose than I did, but that was probably beside the point. What was to the point was the absolute nature of her emotional involvement, and the unaccountably equivocal nature of my own.

We stood staring at each other for several moments, until a fierce transformation came over Annia's face. "It's *Marcus!*" she hissed ferociously. "Isn't it?"

"Marcus?" I responded in a muddled tone.

"Of course it is," she resumed, all but ignoring me. "He terrified you with all this patrician-plebeian nonsense and then cooked up some pious-sounding excuse to get the two of you back to Rome."

I looked at her, at a loss.

"I'm right, aren't I?" she said, her eyes narrowing.

"It's not his fault," I countered lamely. "He was concerned for our welfare."

"You *imbecile!*" Annia shrieked, and with such unexpected violence that I actually flinched away from her. "Don't you see that he's jealous!"

"Jealous? Jealous of whom?"

She looked up at the sky and raised her clenched fists to her temples. "Of *me*, you hopeless innocent. Of *ME!*"

I could only gape at her in astonishment. Up to that point, it had never once occurred to me to question Marcus's *bona fides*. And despite Annia's accusation, I still wasn't inclined to view it with doubt, even though I sensed that there might be a grain of plausibility in what she'd said. I trusted Marcus; that was all there was to it. And by the same token, I didn't trust Annia as much.

On such uncharted rocks has many an ardent love been known to founder.

"Oh, I hate you," Annia wailed, the tears finally starting to fall. "I hate you both."

And with that she slapped me as hard as she could, one hand after the other, and then ran away, sobbing, in the direction of the stately residence where we'd so recently been unlucky enough to meet.

[AUGUST 22D]

The heat lay especially heavy last night, and after I'd sweltered for a couple of hours it occurred to me that we might all find some relief in the garden. Portia applauded the idea of our moving outdoors, and when we looked in on the children to find that the sultry air was depriving them of sleep as well, the decision to flee the house was made. In keeping with this decision, Decius and I went rummaging around the storeroom in an effort to locate some spare plank-and-skin pallets beneath all the cobwebs. We succeeded finally, but nearly got pitchforks in our throats when Rullo and his son mistook us for thieves. I thanked the two of them for their vigilance, explained our presence in the storeroom, and sent them back to their beds, all the while feeling acutely foolish for having roused them. It was only my status as their master that stopped me from giving voice to a full-fledged apology.

We set up the pallets near the fountain and spread thin blankets over them, all of us longing to get some rest. But the air in the garden proved almost as stifling as the air in the house, and sleep seemed as far away as ever.

With relief from the heat denied us, there was nothing for us to do but labor for breath and gaze up at the sky; the fact that the sky was unusually beautiful afforded us but little consolation. After a time, though, I noticed two shooting stars streaking across the Milky Way near the Swan, and our attention quickly shifted from the oppression of the swelter to the detection of other such wisps of incandescence.

"What are they, Father?" Camilla asked me as all our eyes scanned the firmament.

"Sparks from the wheels of Phaëthon's chariot, so I'm told."

"But you don't believe that, do you?"

"No," I answered after deliberating a moment. "But it's as good an explanation as any other I've heard."

"There's one!" Portia cried out, pointing just east of the zenith. And there one was indeed: a long-lingering filament of light that stretched all the way from the Dragon's snout to the Eagle's eye.

"How beautiful!" Camilla sighed.

"Could they be the departing souls of the dead, Father?" Decius asked in his usual diffident manner.

"The departing souls of the dead? Where did you get that idea, son?"

"I don't know, Father; it just came to me now as that shooting star went by."

I sat up and looked over at him, thinking, for some reason, that he was just about as old as Annia and I had been when we first failed at love.

Annia and Marcus . . . Drusilla and Agricus . . . four streaks of brightness in transit across the sky, four radiant spirits departing into the night . . .

"That's a nice conception, Decius," I said finally.

"Thank you, Father," he murmured in response.

And yet again I feel ashamed when I think how little I know him.

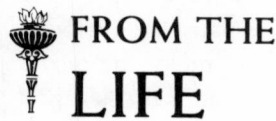# FROM THE
LIFE

And so I returned to Rome less than twenty days after I departed, although to say that I "returned" is in some respects less than accurate. Because the Rome to which Marcus now introduced me was as different from the Rome I'd grown up in as horses are different from goats. This new Rome, centered on the Palatine and the Caelian, was wondrously free of the noise and squalor that characterized the central wards. No stench of chamber pots corrupted its air, no blocks of tenements obstructed its light. The masses of sweating humanity that shoved and swore their way through the defiles of the City's core might just as well have been in Persepolis for all one knew of them on these fragrant hilltops. Here amid groves of pine and cypress, amid showers of cyclamen and amaryllis, the mansions of Rome's noblest families stood like temples to the sylvan gods. And though Diana and Faunus were nowhere present in these dwellings, the families' renown could be worshiped instead.

Of course the people who comprised these families bore but little resemblance to the rough and rowdy street folk from whom I had sprung. In fact, about the only thing that "they" had in common with "us" was the citizenship of Rome. And if I'd felt out of place at Lorium, where the atmosphere of rural simplicity had muted somewhat the social distinctions between me and my hosts, I saw myself as an outright intruder on the Caelian, where the mood of sober urbanity greatly accentuated them. So keen was my sense of inferiority to begin with that there were stretches of time when I couldn't be prevailed upon to utter a single word. Even direct questions sometimes failed to wring a response from me; instead of answering them, I would turn to Marcus with an expression of helpless discomposure on my face, and leave it to him to furnish the replies. Sensitive as always to my feelings, he forbore to chide me about such overweening diffidence, but he did sometimes plead with me to risk a phrase or two now and then. "After all, Lucio," ran his reassuring theme, "the worst that can happen if you garble your words is that you'll be horsewhipped and flung off the roof."

The chance that I might garble my words was not what lay at the root of my anxiety. What unnerved me was the prospect that in speaking I would reveal what I truly was—a low-born, coarse-tongued impostor.

And therein lay the cruelest irony. For it became clear as the years went by that a flair for Latin rhetoric was about the only patrician attribute I was ever going to possess. Compounding the irony's cruelty, moreover, was the fact that most patricians of Marcus's stamp had a marked preference for speaking Greek!

Luckily for me, though, Marcus's mother, Domitia Lucilla, did not number herself among them. She spoke the same sort of homespun Latin that I did, and regarded Graecophonic Romans as insufferably affected. The fact that the Emperor Hadrian was foremost among such *Graeculi*, as she referred to them, in no way diminished the force of her disdain, and so great was the Princeps' regard for her that he never used the offending tongue when in her presence.

That she was held in such high esteem by so exalted a figure was not in any way surprising, since, in addition to being highly intelligent, regally good-looking, and unimaginably wealthy (some thievery in her brickyards notwithstanding), she was also a quite genuine exemplar of all the old Republican virtues. Because she'd loved her husband during his lifetime, for instance, she'd chosen to observe the equally quaint custom of remaining faithful after his death; and though her fidelity was buttressed to some extent by a certain skepticism as to the motives of her suitors, it was nevertheless a faith well kept. Not that a rich widow's ingrained wariness of the fortune hunter was the only consideration that kept her set against remarriage; there was also her conviction that no man could ever compare with Annius Verus as a husband, and that his sacred memory would, therefore, prove a better conjugal companion than any creature of flesh and blood.

Then, too, she was single-mindedly devoted to Marcus, so much so that the thought of putting someone in his father's place distressed her more on his account than her own. Whether Marcus shared this aversion to the idea of a successor is hard to say. He certainly gave no hint of it if he did, but then again, he had no reason to, given the stalwart rigor of her virtue.

He was singularly blessed, in my opinion, to have had a mother as adoring as Domitia Lucilla, especially since her adoration was never expressed in any terms but those of profound respect. She may even have been a bit in awe of Marcus, secretly surmising that she and Annius Verus could never have brought forth a son of such peerless perfection without the active intervention of some god.

The high regard in which she held her firstborn child proved to be of considerable benefit to me, for as his vouched-for friend I was immediately accorded the status of *persona grata*. The fact that I was plebeian seemed, and indeed was, immaterial to this august lady, she being far too much of an aristocrat to ever look down on someone who wasn't.

Her daughter Cornificia—Marcus's younger sister—was equally free of snobbish airs; she was also the most artlessly good-hearted creature I'd ever met. With her buckteeth and bulging eyes, her flat chest and scraggly hair, she was a thirteen-year-old vision of all the tortures that puberty can devise. Miraculously enough, she was able to joke about her adolescent afflictions, perhaps because she felt secure enough in the love of her family to keep them in some kind of perspective. Marcus she revered as one would the most indulgent of fathers, while Domitia Lucilla stood as her closest friend and confidante. Blessed with the keen intelligence of both the Annii Veri and her mother's line as well, she was neither a figure of fun nor an object of pity. She stood, rather, as living proof of the fact that no stain of homeliness can withstand the gentle solvent of human affection.

Given three such loving people, it wasn't long before even my monumental diffidence started to give way, and as autumn yielded to winter, the idea that I might presume to regard myself as a member of the family— in certain limited respects at least—began to seem less and less outlandish.

Of course I remained terribly lovesick, and many were the nights when I woke from dreams of Annia with the residue of my passion cold and sticky on my thighs. On other nights I'd lie wakeful for hours, the talons of desire tearing at my innards while her siren image beleaguered my thoughts. Sooner or later I would bend to the will of Eros and let my hand stray downward to the region of my loins. There, at the vortex of all my longing, I would stroke the swollen canker of my lust—stroke and stroke, until spasms of poignant pleasure washed over me and let me descend at last into the merciful inanition of sleep.

The worst of it was that, within ten days of my return to Rome, Annia returned there too, and to an estate less than half a mile's walk from Domitia Lucilla's. Adding torment to injury, moreover, was the fact that her brothers returned home with her, and promptly resumed their studies with Marcus's tutors. Not that there was anything in any way objectionable about the two of them; they were as bland and affable as could be. But their arrival each morning at "my" place of residence was a constant reminder of the lacerating fact that Annia, though still beyond my grasp, was once more within my reach.

Titus Antoninus, it seemed, had gone off to assume his proconsulship of Asia without taking his wife and children with him—not from any want of familial feeling, to be sure, but out of concern for his elder daughter, Aurelia Fadilla, whose indifferent health rendered her unfit to face the rigors of a month-long journey, especially with winter coming on. Taking her best interests and other pertinent factors into account, Titus had decided that her mother and siblings should remain with her in Rome until the spring. At that time, if she was stronger and the weather set fair, the entire family could join him at his post in Ephesus.

The Proconsul was wise to err on the side of paternal caution, for with the sailing season officially over and northeasterly gales on the rise, even men such as he felt a qualm or two about embarking on the November seas. The reward for his prudence was forthcoming six months after his departure, when he and his family were reunited; the penalty for it was paid a good deal sooner, when Annia and I gave up trying to stay apart.

And in all fairness to the two of us, we did most diligently try. That we failed was a simple consequence of the fact that we lived in an aristocratic milieu that was too small by several magnitudes to keep our paths from crossing—and crossing repeatedly at that.

Am I making excuses for us? Yes, I am. But I do so because we *did* make determined efforts to avoid each other, and we *did* stay at arm's length when our efforts first came to naught. Had we been older or wiser or a little bit less infatuated, we might have realized what we were up against. Had we been bolder or cooler or a little bit more sophisticated, we might have dared to face down all the risks. With a pinch of dissemblance and a scruple of deceit, after all, we might have contrived to fulfill our desires in secret; we might have gorged ourselves on each other to our hearts' content and then discovered, once our passion was spent, that there had never been much between us but swollen appetite.

Many are the things that might have been, but the things that were remain; and the way things were in Rome that winter, both Annia and I were trapped. The fact that our love was forbidden merely stoked the lust it fed on; the fact that our ardor was untamable merely stressed the need to hold it back. Madness forbidden, wildness restrained—the paradoxes were too much for us. Am I making excuses then? No, I'm not. There is no excuse for lovers who can't moderate their passion; there is no excuse for eagles who take wing and claim the sky.

Marcus, of course, was wise enough to have foreseen our predicament and sensible enough to refrain from giving advice. He knew, perhaps better than I did, that the game had to be played by its players to its conclusion, and having acquainted me with its rules and assured me of his love, he gracefully withdrew from the arena. In behaving thus he provided me with more support and comfort than could ever have flowed from his active intervention. He also demonstrated once again the depth of his genius for friendship.

To be sure, even if he'd been inclined to involve himself in the turmoil of my ill-starred affair, he'd have had precious little time to indulge the inclination. For in addition to his studies and family responsibilities, he had a host of official and sacramental duties to attend to. He'd been a knight since the age of six and a priest of the Salii since the age of eight; and since the Emperor had never made any secret of his intention to place him in the direct line of succession to the Principate, he'd had dozens of other titles and offices conferred on him over the course of each consular year. Natually, innumerable public officials, Imperial bureaucrats, fellow patricians, senior Praetorians, hand-picked *singulares*, and high-ranking slaves had been detailed to assist him in the discharge of his responsibilities. But he claimed he needed at least one close personal friend to attend him as well—in order to "keep my spirit from bloating and my irony in check." So I took on the role of his trusted equerry.

Of course I was delighted to be of some assistance to him, even if I couldn't quite rid my mind of the suspicion that the fact that I'd be delighted had loomed larger in his calculations than any sense that he required my services. Whether he required them or not, though, he quickly made use of them, and to such an extent that I could barely catch my breath. Only a few days after Annia's return from Lorium, the Plebeian Games were upon us, and the next fortnight proved so hectic that the glimpses I frequently caught of her sometimes failed to wrench my soul.

Sometimes—but by no means the first time.

I remember the incident clearly. It occurred on the day before the Nones in the Theater of Marcellus, just before the first performance of the games. The November morning was resplendent, the travertine galleries were packed, and the largely plebeian audience was merry to the point of unruliness. Less merry were the ushers, who spent much of their time chasing impudent slaves out of the upper tiers to the standees' precincts on the roof, and much of their energy breaking up the fistfights that erupted between rival claimants to the vacated seats. Adding to the ushers' difficulties was the presence, so typical in a plebeian crowd, of large numbers of small screeching children, all of whom seemed to regard urinating on the steps of the aisles as a point of infantile honor. Maneuvering adroitly to avoid the resultant puddles and the more violent altercations, chestnut and sausage vendors rushed about hawking their wares at the top of their voices. Soldiers of the Urban Cohorts, meanwhile, alternately glowered dire menace at the rowdiest brawlers and struck martial poses for the comeliest women, striving in the process to maintain that air of military impassivity best suited to their fully armed presence in force around the perimeter of every tier.

I remember that the play to be performed was Afranius's comedy in Roman costume *The Stepson*, any Greek work being out of the question at the commencement of a plebeian festival. I remember, also, sitting just behind Marcus, whose place was in the last of the fourteen front rows reserved for the knights. I was leaning forward, as I recollect it, chatting with my patron about something or other that had to be seen to after the performance; and though the matter we were discussing could not have been inconsequential, both Marcus and I found it hard to focus on it in the face of the constantly rising clamor of expectancy that pervaded the theater. Down in the orchestra the Praetor and the vestal virgins were making their way to their seats, prompting senators and magistrates to rise from their own with due signs of respect. The plebeian aediles, meanwhile, were already in place at the ends of the parodoi leading to the stage, which meant that their announcement of the play would be forthcoming in a matter of moments.

Everyone in the audience now craned his neck to see the presiding and suffect consuls make their entrance into the theater—everyone including myself. It was while I was peering down at the aisle between proscenium and orchestra that my unsuspecting eyes were transfixed by hers.

She was in the far left-hand corner of the orchestra's semicircular arc, no more than eighty or ninety feet from where I sat. It seemed to me that she was the only person in the entire theater whose gaze was directed away from the stage, but then, my senses were so muddled by the shock of seeing her that nothing was very clear except her eyes. Had those eyes been glittering with anger, the force of the shock might not have been as great; had they glimpsed me and gone blank with indifference, I might not have become so unstrung. I'd sworn to myself over the course of many a restless night that if ever again those orbits fixed on me, I'd let nothing in their obsidian depths make inroads upon my composure— not spite, not resentment, not even hate. What I'd failed to reckon with was the chance that they might fix on me when I wasn't on guard and prepared for them—when, in other words, I had no mask of equanimity clamped tight upon my face.

It was over in a fraction of an instant—first my blink of recognition, than her lightning flash of triumph. I hastened to put my naked countenance in order, but the exultant gleam in her smile made nonsense of the effort. "Your wide eyes have betrayed you," said her dark eyes; "in the act of seeing, you have been *seen!*"

Thus in one brief moment were all the fruits of my flight from Lorium rendered forfeit.

And what, in all my boyish transparency, had I so irrevocably revealed? Not merely that I loved her; we'd both known that all along. But that I loved her a good deal more than I'd been willing to admit—to myself, much less anyone else. Not half an instant after her message reached me, I realized what had just transpired, and with a rueful smile I acknowledged my defeat. This sign from me immediately brought a mist of solicitude to her eyes, and that, more than any flash of triumph, made my downfall absolute. She loved me dearly too, it seemed, enough to be touched by my gesture of submission. And it was the fact that she loved me dearly that spelled disaster for us both. One can withstand the heat of passion, after all; there are many ways to cool the blood. But passion admixed with tenderness sheds that warmth which inspirits life. To turn one's back on it is to turn one's face toward the wall.

I was to see Annia twice more during the games: once from a distance as I watched the knights' parade, and once from within twenty feet as I escorted Marcus to the Feast of Jove. The ludi finally ended, however, and I was granted some semblance of reprieve.

But the respite proved brief. On the Nones of December Domitia Lucilla gave a dinner for her late husband's sister, the purpose being to celebrate receipt of the welcome news that Titus Antoninus had at last arrived safely at his Ephesian post.

Of course I was fully prepared to encounter Annia on this occasion, and of course my preparedness did neither of us the slightest good. Indeed, I personally might have been better off if her presence in the triclinium had come as a complete surprise: then, at least, I'd have been spared all the anxieties of anticipation.

Those anxieties were by no means inconsiderable; in fact, they became so acute as the appointed hour drew near that I gave serious thought to feigning illness and slinking away to my bed. Both Marcus and Annia would have seen right through such a craven ploy, however, and Domitia Lucilla would have been left with an unlucky eight around her table. My sense of shame, therefore, combined with my sense of obligation to brace me for the sight of my beloved. And as Marcus and his mother stood arm in arm at the mansion's threshold, ready and eager to welcome their guests, I crouched alone in the door porter's gate shack, a dazzling new tunic adorning my dread.

One mark of adolescent infatuation, I've noticed, is that every look ignites a spark; but when Annia stepped down from her litter that evening, her glance met mine like a blade striking a grindstone. Almost two months had passed since we'd been face to face with one another, and the period of separation had served only to put a jagged edge on our passion. To make matters worse, the canons of etiquette conspired to place us side by side on the left-hand dining couch, since Marcus, his mother, and sister, as hosts, reclined on the right, while his aunt and two eldest cousins, as ranking guests, took the couch of honor in between. My place was, of course, at our couch's lower end, with Annia on my right, next to her youngest brother and Cornificia opposite. Marcus, beside her, glanced over at me as the slaves went around with the wine and water: his smile commiserated, but his eyes were resigned.

"You're looking decidedly . . . aristrocratic," Annia said softly, her own eyes intent on a fig she was eviscerating.

"I feel more plebeian than ever, though."

"Was that said to discourage me?" she probed after a pause.

"I feel more in love than ever, too."

We reclined in silence for several moments, my confession echoing in both our minds.

"Have you talked to Marcus about that?" Annia asked eventually.

"Yes."

"And . . .?"

"He wishes us well, but fears for our welfare."

"How very benevolent of him!"

I turned to her, making no effort to conceal my fretful anger. "What in Jove's name would you like him to do for us, Annia? If it would help us at all, I know he'd gladly do it."

She regarded me appraisingly as I upbraided her. When I'd finished, she asked, "Do you get as angry at him, Lucio, when he speaks ill of me?"

"He never does," I retorted, then remembered with a pang his bitter outburst at Lorium: "She's a damnable willful fool!"

A film of wetness blurred the brightness in Annia's eyes, even as my own must have softened with the realization of my unwitting lie. "Don't mind me," she said finally, with a hint of a sigh. "I simply envy him your adoration."

Immediately I felt myself blush and was utterly at a loss for some adequate response. "Annia . . ." I began.

"Please be still for a moment," she said in a muted voice, struggling as she spoke to blink back her tears. "I just never imagined that the first thing we'd do would be to quarrel."

Her shaken composure left me feeling abashed. It hadn't occurred to me that we'd quarrel either, but now that we had I was not in the least surprised. And it was always going to be that way with Annia and me: always at the core of my feelings for her would be the sense that despite— or, perhaps, because of—our lust for one another, we were doomed to transact our love as antagonists. It seemed that we lacked somehow any root compatibility of interests, as if our contrasting ranks had so cut across our passion as to sever such cords of affinity as might have bound us together. Nor, now I think about it, is that just some idle metaphor: for the diffference in our social standing set us hopelessly—though not quite rationally—at odds. Annia felt aggrieved because my love for her was not so unqualified as to transport me beyond all mundane concerns for my personal welfare; I felt aggrieved because her love for me was not so selfless as to purge her breast of all yearnings that might aggravate my plight. If anyone had told us that we were demanding the impossible of one another, we might conceivably have agreed. But such was the pitch of our adolescent ardor that we each saw the other as wreathed in light; and from those radiant creatures who shone so in our eyes, the impossible was not much more than the least we'd come to expect.

The dinner proceeded at a leaden pace, on our side of the table at any rate. Annia was slow to recover her customary vivacity, and when she did at last, it seemed a trifle forced. We exchanged inanities as our food was served us, and they stung more cruelly than any gibe because they defined the extent of our estrangement. As the evening wore on I descended from pique to remorse to indifference to despair, and Annia, to all appearances, descended with me. What distance had failed to accomplish in the space of months, proximity had achieved in a matter of hours—or so I thought. I mistook deflation for disintoxication, and didn't realize the true immensity of my error until Annia, while submitting to my formal good-night kiss, whispered tersely, "Tomorrow—the eighth hour—at the bend of the Claudian Aqueduct."

FROM THE
JOURNAL

36

[AUGUST 23D]

I am restless and short-tempered today. Perhaps it's because of the heat.

Or perhaps—with a bow to Nestor—it has something to do with all the memories of Annia I've been dredging up.

Whatever it is, it's taking its toll. I feel as surly and loutish as an old boar in heat, and I find myself lecherously preoccupied with the plump slave girl, Gaia, who is weeding the beets and parsnips not ten feet from where I sit.

Granted I might be forgiven my preoccupation, for sweat has long since soaked through the fabric of her smock and is now coursing in limpid rivulets down the chasm between her breasts. Her downy skin glistens like polished walnut, sleek and lubricious with all the unguents of youth. I can imagine her thighs and the bliss between them; I yearn to be enveloped by the softness of her flesh.

How old can the siren be? Fifteen? Sixteen? And how often have I known her to smile at me with more warmth than befits her estate. Is she ambitious? In the master's bed she would have the master's ear. Is she complaisant? That smile proclaims she is.

She is mine if I want her . . . she is willing . . . she's a slave . . . I could reward her handsomely . . . she would be grateful . . . she would be pleased . . .

Oh, ye gods, I was within a heartbeat of summoning her to my side. Oh, foul, corrupt old hypocrite that I am. For fifty years I've watched those with power abuse those without, and flatter themselves all the while that they were doling out largesse. For fifty years I've sworn to both the gods and myself that I would never, *never*, use my freeborn status to exploit those below me. I, who have sipped the bitter potion of subservience and borne the callous scourgings of disdain, I of all people should be the last to assert my dominion over others.

Oh, Juppiter, Mithras, Isis, and Jehovah, oh, all ye gods that may yet be or ever were—in all my life I've never burned so with self-loathing . . .

. . . and all in response to a *thought*?

I do not understand myself. Why should the stirrings of nature in my viscid old blood arouse such furious remorse? Look there—the buxom child is still placidly weeding the garden; my carnal thoughts have left her undefiled. What crime have I committed, then, that I should be so liberal with the lash?

I think again of the slaughtered slave boy—and of Nestor, the magician of the mind. Is this another instance of my past emerging in my present? Do my memories of Annia converge in some way with my craving for this sprite? Here is the second slave child in as many months to fill my heart with anguish—and without my having done the slightest wrong. Is she the true object of my pity? Am I the true subject of my contempt? Or are my memories the real protagonists in this bucolic summer scene, and Gaia's charms old sorrows now made flesh?

Nestor, Nestor, where are you? I am beset by questions, and only you can raise the siege.

FROM THE
LIFE

37

The question, of course, was: Should I tell Marcus that Annia had proposed an assignation? The answer, of course, was: Yes, I should. And that answer, of course, was wrong. It has long since become clear to me, looking back on the episode, that my sole purpose in telling him was to secure his permission for—or at least his acquiescence in—a resumption of my affair. Naturally enough, I took pains to convince myself that I "owed" it to him to be open and honest, and after forty-five years I still wince at the memory of my cowardice masquerading as a sense of duty—especially because the masquerade was such an ignominious failure.

Marcus was far too wise, it turned out, to assume any responsibility for the continuation—or termination—of our romance. He refused to play Atlas to my Hercules, in other words, and put the burden of decision right back where it belonged. "If you don't show up this afternoon," he confined himself to saying, "she will never speak to you again."

"Then I must go see her, mustn't I?

"Only if you want her to keep on speaking to you."

Though somewhat deflated by this reply, I was still unwilling to abandon my quest for abdication, and so responded, "What I want isn't important, Marco; it's what I ought to do that matters."

This eruption of disingenuousness provoked even him to raise his eyebrows, but he was quick to lower them again and say, with a smile, "Only Socrates is wise."

"What?"

"Because only Socrates understands how little any of us knows about the 'oughts' of others."

"But surely, Marco," I expostulated, "you must have an opinion."

Still smiling, he replied, "My opinion, Lucio, is that you desperately want to see her."

"But should I, Marco, dammit all—should I?"

His eyes were sympathetic, but his answer was only, "Ask Socrates."

Ludicrously enough, I felt somehow betrayed by him, and I sulked off to my rendezvous (for there was never really any question about which choice I would make) in low but smoldering dudgeon. The weather fit in nicely with my foul humor: low scudding clouds, chill northeast winds, and rain now and then in angry spasms. One such spasm was in progress when I arrived at the appointed spot, and, wrapping my cloak tight around me, I took shelter within a clump of pines.

Though it was called "the bend," the part of the Claudian Aqueduct that Annia had chosen for our tryst was in fact a massive right angle some sixty feet high that framed the southwestern corner of the Claudian Temple's precinct walls. Since these walls were themselves a good twenty feet in height, and since the distance between them and the aqueduct's arches was barely seven paces, the umbral pines and boxwood that grew at their base provided an ideal setting for youthful assignations—assuming that the weather was halfway decent. Alas, the fact that the bend was the scene of many amorous encounters was hardly a well-kept secret; among children of the rich, its convenient location on the Caelian's eastern slope had made it downright notorious. Had the weather been just a trifle less dreary, accordingly, there was every possibility that Annia and I would have encountered some other couple on that December afternoon. And it was precisely the risk that we'd be seen by someone that I was brooding over as I crouched, all ashiver, at the base of the temple walls.

Thus, even before Annia's arrival, I had a grievance all ready to dispute with her.

She appeared soon enough, skipping gracefully down the hillside in a brilliant yellow cloak of Spanish wool—a garment so distinctive, I noted fretfully, as to announce her presence with more fanfare than a cohort of trumpeters. I stood up as she drew nearer and noticed that she'd put enough powder and rouge on her face to make her look like something out of the back alleys of the Subura. That she'd been equally lavish with her perfumes and oils was evident a few moments later when, spying me amid the pine trees, she threw herself into my arms with a high-pitched cry of "Lucio! Oh, my darling!"

"Not so loud!" was my passionate response; but if it put her off at all, there was no way to tell from the ardor of her kisses.

"Lucio, Lucio," she murmured breathlesssly, grabbing my right hand and guiding it to her cleft. "Now, at last, we can fulfill our love."

Gingerly I moved my fingers over the sparse growth of hairs that fringed her venereal gates. "Did anyone see you come here?" I asked.

"No, of course not, darling Lucio," she answered me, reaching under my tunic and coiling her icy fingers around as much of my member as the wintry air had left unshrunk. "By Minerva's sword!" she gasped, intending, I'm sure, no irony. "I'd no idea they were so *tiny!*"

"It's the cold, Annia," I said in a tone of strained indulgence. "They tend to shrink up in the cold."

"Oh . . . well"—she beamed salaciously—"I know a place where it's nice and warm."

"How far is it?" I asked from the depths of my obtuseness. And she laughed, with good reason, but too loud.

"No farther than your fingers," she whispered, arching her hips so there'd be no mistake about which hand.

"How did you manage to get away from your house?" I asked, persisting with my romantic interrogatories as my fingers started to probe.

"I told everyone I was going to spend the afternoon with Cornificia," she said as her breathing became shallower.

Instantly my fingers stopped moving, and the rest of my body—with one shrunken exception—went rigid. "But what if someone asks Cornificia how the two of you passed the time?"

"Oh, we agreed that she's to say that we went to make an offering at the Temple of Venus. . . . Isn't that clever?"

"What do you mean, 'you agreed'?" I asked, my voice constricted.

"I mean we *agreed*, silly—we made up."

"You mean," I managed to say, "that Cornificia knows about our meeting?"

"Well, I had to tell someone, Lucio darling. How else could I free myself to come here?"

Convulsed by a sense of anxious fury, I yanked my hand from her crotch and turned away from her.

"Lucio! In Jove's name, what's the matter?"

I was almost too enraged to answer her—almost but not quite. "How *could* you have told Cornificia?" I snarled with my back to her.

I could hear the hurt and anger building up in her voice as she responded shrilly, "Well of course I swore her to secrecy, Lucio. What do you take me for?"

I didn't trust myself to reply.

"Why are you behaving like this?" she wailed at me. "You can't pretend that you didn't tell Marcus."

"That was different," I snapped.

"*Why?*" she cried, the sound of choked sobs parenthesizing the fateful word.

"Because I trust him," I responded.

"And I trust Cornificia. . . . So there!"

I whipped around and glared venomously at her. "*Damn* you, Annia. When it's my life that's at stake, it's only who *I* trust that matters."

"How dare you speak to me like that," she gasped, her eyes widening in horror. "How *dare* you!"

"Oh, I beg your pardon," I retorted with heavy sarcasm. "I forgot for an instant that I was speaking to my social superior."

At this her eyes widened ever farther, her nostrils flared, and her lips curled into a sneer. For a long moment we just glared at each other, but then she turned her back on me and angrily strode away.

There have been few occasions in my life when I've been as dispirited as I was when I returned a half hour later to Domitia Lucilla's mansion. As bad as I felt when I got there, though, it was nothing compared to the misery I experienced when I found out that Agricus was there as well.

FROM THE
JOURNAL

38

[AUGUST 24TH]

Once again an Imperial courier has come galloping up our road, and once again I have before me a cryptic letter from our erstwhile houseguest.

Augustonemetum, in Aquitania,
the fourteenth before the Kalends of September

My dear and most estimable Lucius,

You must begin, now, to make provision for the dissolution of your estate and the welfare of your dependents, particularly the serviles. I instruct you in this wise because I know how scrupulously you attend to the needs of your familia and how reluctant you would be to abandon them to the mercies of the Imperial Fisc. You cannot, alas, manumit them, because your flight from the Emperor's writ would render their manumission void. You must, accordingly, sell them to someone who treats his slaves with a degree of humanity. If you know of no such person, you must find one. Do not, however, sell to anyone who knows you personally or is aware of your precarious circumstances; to do so would fatally compromise any plan for your escape. If you can do no better, go to the slave emporium at Ostia and engage an agent. Your familia is not so numerous as to occasion significant comment there. You will want to stipulate that the familia be sold as a block, and you will, furthermore, want to satisfy yourself as to the fitness of any would-be purchaser. Be sure to inform the agent that you *are going to strike the bargain, not he; and if he responds by insisting on a fixed fee instead of a commission, so be it. Only by dealing directly with the buyer will you be able to assess his suitability; and since the common practice when an agent strikes the bargain is for the buyer to bribe him into accepting a lower price, you will probably end up with a greater net profit.*

Now, as to the details of the sale: bargain vigorously but let the buyer wear you down; demand concessions on the matters of timing and terms of payment as you give ground on the matter of price; insist specifically that the buyer come to your farm to inspect the chattels in question; tell him you must get as much work out of them as possible before giving them up, that you can't waste a full day of their labor by bringing them to market; instruct him to bring gold sufficient to cover half the eventual purchase price when he comes to make his inspection, and demand payment thereof on execution of the contract of sale. (He will probably bring only a third or less, but that's standard practice, so don't make an issue of it.) The contractual provisions should themselves be fairly standard, but the contract itself should be postdated no earlier than the Kalends of October, it being agreed between you and the buyer that the date on the contract is the date he may take possession. Tell the fellow that you're willing to harvest early and take a loss, but that you're not willing to harvest before the end of September and end up ruined. Your attitude throughout the negotiations should be that of a man sorely distressed for money, and you should stipulate in the contract that the buyer must pay your agent the remainder of the purchase price on the very same day he takes possession. (Be sure, by the way, to provide the agent with written authorization to deduct all registration fees, excises, and title charges from the total sum he receives; otherwise the sale will be void. He will deduct his own exorbitant fee as a matter of course, never fear; but since you're not destined to receive any part of the final payment, it hardly matters.)

One final point: you must devise a stratagem to keep your buyer from boasting to everyone about his brilliant bargaining triumph, at least until you, your wife, and your children are safely on your way. (The agent will chatter, inevitably, but whatever he says will most likely be lost in the flood of business gossip that daily overruns the port.) It is vitally important to keep word of your transactions from the ears of the many functionaries who might speculate as to their underlying significance. So think deeply and devise well. If my tired old brain comes up with anything, I will advise you in my next letter.

Until then I remain,

Yours in the Eyes of the Mind Eternal,
"Nestor"

Oh, yes: how goes your study of your past?

Now this, to my noneternal mind, is a truly astonishing document. I am to undertake to sell all my slaves, but I must keep my actions secret in the process. Not only that, but I must "devise a stratagem" to keep a person I don't know from discussing his private business arrangements with people he does—until such time, moreover, as I and my loved ones are "safely" on our way.

On our way *where*, I'd like to be told, and to what conceivable end.

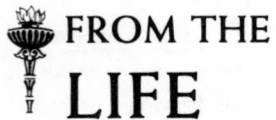
It was altogether typical of Agricus that he should have thrust himself back into my life at that worst of all possible moments; no less in keeping with his nature was the fact that he derived such obvious relish from my resultant discomposure. As much as the sight of him unsettled me, however, the effect of his presence on Cornificia had been a good deal more pronounced. Chances were he'd reduced her to helpless twitters the instant they met.

At all events, she was so utterly distracted by the time I made my appearance that she filled the main reception room with a cry of "Ah, dear Lucio, did all go well with you and . . ." She caught herself at the last moment, fumbled around for some unincriminating end to her sentence, and finally came up with, ". . . your horse?"

This starkly inapposite greeting aroused Domitia Lucilla's curiosity, and turning in her chair to look at me, she asked, "Why on earth would you choose to go riding on a day like this, Lucio? You who are reluctant to mount a horse even when the weather's fine."

Stunned by the specter of Agricus and shaken by Cornificia's near betrayal, I was in no condition to devise an apt response. But Marcus, as always, came to my rescue.

"I made a bet with him," he said. "I wagered my bearskin cloak that he couldn't get Incitatus to carry him to the brow of the Janiculum and back in the space of an hour."

"You must have been very confident of the outcome, dearest, to risk the loss of your favorite capote."

"Oh, I was, Mother—extremely confident. Given Lucio's horsemanship and Incitatus's vigor, I didn't expect to see either one of them back here till after dark."

"Yet here they are now—or here Lucio is, at any rate—and the ninth hour's barely begun."

"Yes, I see, Mother. It seems I made an improvident bet."

"Only if he and the horse have actually been to the Janiculum and back," Agricus offered with a nasty smirk.

"Oh, I forgot; you two know each other," Domitia Lucilla said. "You come from the same *vicus* of the Alta Semita."

"Very true, revered lady," Agricus was quick to respond. "We have been close friends for many years."

I gave him a blank stare, then turned to Domitia Lucilla and said, "We grew up together, madam, but we were seldom if ever close."

A shocked silence greeted my words, almost as if I'd spit full in Agricus's face—which in fact I almost had. His lupine cunning was more than equal to the occasion, however. After blinking away my rebuff, he declared, "Alas, most noble lady, it is true that the love between me and my friend here is no longer what it was. I did him a wrong once, you see, a wrong I've long wanted to set right. Of course I don't expect him to believe that I desire sincerely to make amends; if I were in his place I'd have doubts of my own. But I swear to you, Lucio—and your aunt will bear me out—I went to the Hobnail to return the statue I took from you on the very same day that you ran away from Rome."

I gaped at him, totally at a loss. Yet even in the midst of my anger and confusion I had to admire his genius for feigning virtue. It was clear, without question, that his touching little recitation had won him the sympathy of both Domitia Lucilla and Cornificia; I would now, in their eyes, look churlish if I spurned his attempt at conciliation. I'd probably look churlish in Marcus's eyes as well, because, though he had a far better understanding of the situation, and few if any illusions about Agricus's morals, he'd long since made it clear to me that he didn't regard his affair with Drusilla as being in any way abhorrent.

Thus, denied all succor for my righteous indignation, I was forced to sort out my muddled feelings for myself—a task that would have taxed my capacities to the limit even if I'd had time to think about it. I didn't, of course, thanks to Agricus, who'd so arranged things that all eyes were upon me and all ears awaited my response. If I didn't say something soon, accordingly, I risked giving the impression that I was simply too peevish to speak.

But what was I to say? Here I had just returned from a lacerating, and to all appearances terminal, quarrel with the girl I loved, only to find myself confronted by my lifelong nemesis dispensing protestations of benignity like a priestess of Pax. Could he really be operating on the assumption that my animosity toward him stemmed from an almost forgotten exchange of statuettes? No, he could not. He knew exactly what had prompted my enmity, just as he knew precisely what had driven me from Rome. It was he, without a doubt, who'd left the statue of Eurydice on the Hobnail's bar, where I would be sure to see it. He'd certainly known, moreover, the conclusions I would come to once I'd pondered the meaning of its presence. True, he could not have known what, beyond tormented, my reaction would be, and he might not have planned on my seeing him and Drusilla prod-in-quim. But he'd known what he was doing, and had certainly understood that my departure from the neighborhood occurred in consequence. The only thing that wasn't altogether certain was his motive, although to my mind it was certain enough, my patron's perceptions notwithstanding.

To me, Marcus's contention that Agricus's and Drusilla's coital revels had been motivated by carnality alone had never been all that convincing. Still, I couldn't summarily dismiss the idea. I had to admit that from Agricus's twisted perspective the golden Eurydice might have stood as a quid pro quo: gleaming image for steaming flesh. I had to acknowledge, furthermore, that my flight into exile was probably not a reaction he'd premeditated. But even assuming he'd intended a trade-off, and even admitting he hadn't meant to drive me away, I knew without question that malice had figured prominently in his actions.

Now here he stood: professing his love, proclaiming his friendship, parading his charm. I still didn't trust him a dupo's worth, but this wasn't the moment to publicize that fact. I still didn't like him or his methods, but I itched for some inkling as to why he'd appeared. I decided, accordingly, that I would have to play his game. So with my face deformed by a bogus smile I turned to him and declared, "I believe what you've told me, friend Agricus."

Of course he didn't for a moment believe what I was telling him, but he had no choice but to grant me my little deceits. If he had the nerve to feign virtue, after all, he could damn well feign belief as well.

There was a sigh of satisfaction from the two women as Agricus and I clasped arms; Marcus, however, had to struggle to keep from laughing. "This joyful moment calls for wine and feasting," he said at last, and Cornificia squealed, "Oh, yes!"

Standing there, looking into Agricus's eyes, I could see the old hostility glittering deep within. But there was something new in his gaze as well, and when he muttered through his teeth, "You've done quite well for yourself," I knew in a flash what it was—grudging, but unfeigned, admiration.

At Marcus's suggestion, the five of us adjourned to Domitia Lucilla's sitting room, where food and drink were speedily provided. As the wine flowed, the mood became more festive, and the voice most alive with elation was that of my newly reacquired "friend," three-fourths of whose listeners sat enraptured as he regaled them with tales of plebeian life. With night coming on, the lamps were brought in, and a glow of good feeling began to pervade the room. Cornificia gazed gooey-eyed at her new-found vision of love, while Domitia Lucilla trained on him her warmest matriarchal smile. Agricus, without too much feigning, basked in the heat of the women's adoration. Marcus, meanwhile, observed the entire scene from a perspective of philosophic amusement.

As for myself, I stayed wary. Knowing Agricus as I did, I felt certain he had one or two more surprises in store for me, and the cocksure glances he now and then cast in my direction confirmed the logic of my forebodings. What was he doing here? That was the crucial question. Had he come looking for me, or for Marcus, or for us both? What was the pretext for his visit? What did he hope to achieve?

I watched him: he was master of the situation. He'd conquered Cornificia with his beauty, Domitia Lucilla with his poise, Marcus with his bravura, and me with his guile. He held the reins, he held the stage, he held the initiative; while I sat paralyzed in front of him like a mouse transfixed by a snake.

As the evening wore on I grew more and more uneasy; it seemed somehow that my world was coming apart. Annia was lost to me. Agricus was at my throat. And Marcus, my dear Marcus . . . couldn't he tell that I needed his help?

Etiquette be damned, I thought; he should ask my enemy to declare himself. He should force him to state his real purpose. Surely the forms of hospitality had by now been sufficiently observed. I beg you, beloved patron, command this miscreant to confess what he is about!

But no, alas: Marcus didn't comprehend my sense of peril—although for that I could hardly reproach him. I would have been hard put to explain it myself, and it's only in retrospect that I begin to discern some basis for my belief that havoc impended.

It seems quite simple, really. Agricus, with his seductive wiles, had driven me from the only family I'd ever known. And now that I'd found a new one, there he was again. Of course the question occurs to me: Why should his good standing in the eyes of those I loved have caused me to tremble so for my own? Did I regard myself as worth so much less than him that I would suffer irreparably by comparison? Who was comparing us anyway? And who had decreed that those I loved were obliged to choose between us?

Who indeed?

Was I the true villian, then, not he? Had there always been so little love in my life that I couldn't bear having to share it? Or was it, rather, that I'd imputed to Agricus my own emotional gluttony, and now feared that he'd devour all the morsels of affection I coveted for myself?

Neither hypothesis makes much sense, I confess, as I think back on all that transpired. But good sense was no more my strong point then than good courage is right now. So the fantastical possibility persists: that Agricus was to blame for nothing, and that the wrongs done were not his but mine.

It's more likely, of course, that the wrongs done were ours, and reciprocal, though, damnably adept as he was at looking out for himself, it's hard to believe I ever did him much harm. As damnably inept as I was at machination, moreover, I probably did the most harm to myself— which would have been very much in keeping with my established pattern.

Certainly I didn't do myself much good that evening; because as Agricus's display of narrative wit approached its climax, so did my own anxiety and exasperation. For several hours I'd been watching him ingratiate himself with the people whose love was my only refuge, and as much as he'd ascended in their estimation it seemed to me that I'd declined. If I didn't speak soon, I felt with a chill, I'd be supplanted entirely in their affections. So, apropos of nothing, and in a strident, grating voice, I cut into Agricus's recitation with, "What was it exactly that prompted you to make your way up here on such a wet and wintry day?"

Ah, woe unto the rabbit who trifles with the snare. I knew the instant I spoke that Agricus had me in his grasp. His eyes proclaimed as much, just as the eyes of the women proclaimed their perplexity and dismay. Marcus wore a frown of deep chagrin; and my own face, I imagine, looked like that of a just-speared fish.

Who was I, in the house of another, to ask a guest to explain his presence? An ill-mannered upstart and dolt at the very least—and one who wished with every atom of his being that he could uspeak the words he'd just spoken.

But wish as I might, I could not. And my enemy, pausing for several moments to let the echoes of my blunder fill the room, brandished the well-honed weapon of his advantage.

"What prompted me," Agricus began, savoring every syllable, "was a sense of obligation to you."

Unmerciful gods! I thought, he's going to milk this till the udders bleed. And having thought that, I confined my response to a simple "Oh?"

"Yes," he resumed, donning all the trappings of comradely solicitude. "Something's happened that you should know about, so I came up here in the hope that I might find you."

"How fortunate for me that this region of the City isn't entirely unfamiliar to you," I said with all the reckless malice of the despairing; and the effect on Agricus was immediate and pronounced. Never before had I thought to use the weapon of his secret shame against him. I was surprised, in fact, to discover it so ready to hand. But I'd been humiliated enough for one evening, and I wanted to warn him not to push me past endurance.

"It's about your mother," he said, hurriedly shifting the focus of our exchange away from him and back to me. "I've been waiting till we could speak in private to tell you the sad news."

"Tell me now," I answered him. "There is nothing concerning me that I wouldn't have these people know."

Just a hint, old nemesis, just the lightest touch of the blade on your throat.

"Very well, as you wish," Agricus responded, still struggling to recover his self-possession. "But then, you must have guessed the truth already."

"She is dead?"

"She died two days ago."

"Ah, I see."

What was I supposed to do now? Feign grief? No, impossible. Much better to feign stupefaction. That was closer to the indifference I felt.

Everything now occurred in its predictable sequence. Domitia Lucilla and Cornificia rushed forward to condole with me, Marcus expressed his stoical sympathy, I declared that I would go back to Twopenny Street to see to my mother's rites, and Agricus was rewarded for bearing ill tidings with an invitation to spend the night. Given my afternoon's debacle with Annia and my evening's collision with him, I hardly cared if he stayed or went. It's true I didn't much relish the idea of sharing a bedroom with him, but being dispirited to the point of apathy, I consoled myself with the thought that the worst he could do while I slept was take my life.

# FROM THE
JOURNAL

[AUGUST 25TH]

Here I sit, fool that I am, in what must be—or Jove help the other lodgers—the dingiest room in the most unsavory inn on either side of the Decumanus Maximus in Ostia. Dingy though it is, this airless cubicle rents for the remarkable sum of six silver denarii a night, vermin included, and according to the innkeeper it is thanks only to the most freakish quirk of fortune that a room at this price—or indeed at any price—was available for our use. The previous occupant succumbed to a stroke, it seems, not half an hour before Decius and I walked in, in search of lodgings. "The gentlemen passed on very quietly," the innkeeper assured me, "so you needn't even bother to turn the blankets."

I daresay I needn't; it was probably the smell of the blankets that brought on the poor man's stroke in the first place. But I'm in no position to quibble about a bit of filth. We're in Ostia, after all, at the height of the sailing season, and this piquant little hostelry was no less than the sixth or seventh at which we inquired. Of course two or three of the other inns had had some sleeping space available in their stables, and at a nightly rate of only one denarius per person. Apart from horses and their droppings, however, such stables tend to be the exclusive domain of felons and their victims—and since I had no wish to enlist myself in either of those two categories, I judged it prudent to keep on looking.

Here we are then, sweltering but secure in this louse-infested closet, a refuge that should prove just barely tolerable for the space of a single night. Tomorrow morning, the gods being merciful, old Syrus should have a prospective buyer or two lined up for me, and after an hour or so of haggling over preliminary terms and conditions, Decius and I should be free to quit these precincts and set our sights for home.

I still have grave doubts about the wisdom of this venture we're embarked on. It seems lunatic to me that I should be undertaking to dispose of my entire familia on the strength of a bizarre letter from some eccentric octogenarian whose identity I can't even guess at. In fact, as Decius and I were riding down our road toward the Nereid this morning, I came very close on more than one occasion to halting and turning back.

What kept me going forward? I don't really know. Perhaps it was my sense that I ought to make at least some provisional arrangements for Rullo and all the others. Or perhaps it was my lingering hope that, regardless of how far negotiations proceed between me and any would-be buyer, I will never really be obliged to put my hand to a contract of sale.

Ah, well, there's no need to grapple with such issues just now; I'd be better off directing my attention to the host of hungry insects who seem convinced that I'm their bedtime snack. Decius, alas, has already served as their supper; the poor boy hasn't had a peaceful moment since he lay down on his cot. I think I'll profit from his example and take my night's rest in this chair. True, I won't be able to sleep very well in a sitting position, but at least I'll force a few ticks and bedbugs to exert themselves a little if they want to get at my flesh.

There's another reason that second cot isn't beckoning me, and that is, quite simply, I'm not all that tired . . . although by all rights I ought to be. Any sixty-year-old equephobe who sets out at dawn on horseback, makes a twenty-mile journey, transacts important business, finds suitable lodgings, and then wolfs down an indigestible dinner should by nightfall be either out on his feet or dead. I, on the other hand—though I can't pretend to be brimming over with energy—feel reasonably robust and alert. Perhaps my unwonted animation is merely a reflection of the difference between the bustling vitality of Ostia and the sleepy tranquillity of our farm. A more likely explanation is that I feel revived by my sense that at last I'm actually *doing* something to help shape my eventual fate. Then, too, there is the relief I feel at having found someone as trustworthy as old Syrus to act as my agent. On top of that, there is the sense of satisfaction I've been deriving from my belated efforts to get to know my son.

I must admit I had some misgivings about asking him to accompany me on this trip. What would we have to talk about? Would he wind up being in the way? I certainly didn't want to be saddled with looking after him, but was there any reason to suppose that he required looking after?

In the end I based my decision on the perception that a journey to Ostia and back was so trifling in terms of time and distance that I ought in all fairness to grant Decius the benefit of the doubt. He seemed so elated by the prospect of going with me, though, that I immediately began to repent of having invited him. I even gave some thought to withdrawing the invitation, but on reflection I had to acknowledge that the mere fact that he was keen to take a trip with me did not necessarily cast doubt on his fitness or his mentality.

And in truth I needn't have worried; he has proved to be a thoroughly agreeable traveling companion: good-natured, self-sufficient, and always anxious to be of assistance. I would even go so far as to say that this journey has gone much more smoothly with him along than it ever would have if I'd been on my own. He is good with the horses, for one thing, which compensates somewhat for my fretfulness; and whereas I tend to be a bit standoffish with the people we encounter, he seems to have a gift for disarming them. On the ferry across the Tiber, for example, he got to chatting with the boatman about all kinds of things: river navigation, boat construction, port operations, and the like. By the time we reached the Old Harbor landing he'd garnered quite a few bits of information about life on the lower Tiber. One of those bits—elicited perhaps intentionally?—was the name of "the only honest slave trader in the entire Ostia emporium."

Now under normal circumstances I wouldn't have attached much importance to a stray fragment of ferryman's gossip, but in this case the datum in question was of such great potential significance that I'd have been foolish to disregard it. True, if the boatman had had the least inkling that we were going to Ostia for the express purpose of selling slaves, I would have immediately suspected some collusive arrangement between him and old Syrus. But Decius had been entirely discreet about the reason for our journey, and the old man's name was merely one of several the boatman had mentioned in order to illustrate his assertion that "there aren't more than half a dozen trustworthy merchants between the Pons Sublicius and the sea!"

Of course there was still a fair possibility that the boatman's information might prove inaccurate, but a rumor of honesty was at least something to go on—something more, at any rate, than my blind conjectures about the best way to proceed.

As things turned out, just about the whole of Ostia was acquainted with Syrus Siculus, although some referred to him as Syrus the Sicilian and others as Siculus the Syrian. There was no disagreement as to how he could be found, however; everyone we asked for directions told us that on reaching the slave market we should look for the big wooden sign that showed the Tigris and the Euphrates flowing past Mount Etna. Beneath it, they assured us, was the stall of the man we were seeking.

Finding the sign posed no difficulties whatever, since it was not merely "big" but enormous—perhaps eight feet by four. Finding the man whose origins it depicted was not quite as easy, though, since he was asleep in the stall's dark interior and proved to be every bit as small as his sign was large. It wasn't until our eyes adjusted to the dusky light that we were able to discern his outline among the shadows, and it wasn't until we'd cleared our throats several times that we were able to rouse him from his midday nap.

He was fully alert once awakened, however, and after rising to greet us got directly down to business. No more than a quarter of an hour later our business was concluded, so rapidly had he educed and extrapolated all the relevant information. Honest or dishonest, he clearly knew all there was to be known about the buying and selling of slaves. He was so knowledgeable, in fact, that he aroused my interest in the subject, an interest I would never have suspected I possessed. And it wasn't just the breadth of his knowledge that intrigued me; it was the man himself. Wizened and squinty, he was an utterly bald little fellow of decidedly monkeyish mien whose copper-colored skin looked far too smooth and supple for someone of his years. Coupled with his singular appearance was a quick mind and an ebullient disposition, and when he asked us if we'd like to share some wine with him, I was quick to respond that we would. "Splendid," he exclaimed, and in moments there were three bowls, a pitcher of water, and a flagon of Falernian on the counter in front of us. "Have a stool," he said, handing us each a bowl, and as we seated ourselves in the shady coolness of the stall's interior, he embarked on the story of how he had become a dealer in slaves.

He'd been born servile himself, it seemed, the son of house slaves in Antioch; and he'd been educated by his father, who kept the master's accounts. But the master had a penchant for speculating in the corn trade, alas, and when two of his ships went down in a freak summer storm off Cyrenaica, he was obliged to sell off almost every slave in his household, including Syrus and his parents. Their new master was a Sicilian from Panormus, a Roman senator, and the holder of vast estates. He made the mistake of opposing P. Aelius Hadrianus's accession to the Principate, however, and his vast estates were summarily confiscated when he went into exile, as were some thousands of his slaves. Many of these, Syrus among them, were sold in a block to an Ostian wholesaler, the only ones remaining in Sicily being those, like Syrus's father, who did specialized, highly trained work, and those, like Syrus's mother, who weren't fit for the galleys or the mines.

Thus, at the age of ten or so, he was separated from his parents and sent to a slave pen in Ostia, to languish there until such time as he was sold. No one was interested in buying him, though, because he was so stunted and scrawny, and at last the wholesaler had to accept the fact that he had an unsalable commodity on his hands. He put Syrus to work performing menial chores around the stall where he ran his business and soon discovered to his considerable delight that the boy had some background in the keeping of accounts. In an instant Syrus went from being worthless to being valuable, becoming invaluable with the passage of the years. He so endeared himself to the wholesaler that he received, not merely his freedom, but also a share of the business.

Here he was, then: a former slave who'd made good, and listening to his exuberantly related life story I couldn't help but be glad for him. I'm confident now that his reputation for honesty is well deserved. He's a man who feels favored by Fortune, after all; he has no need to lie and cheat.

And I guess I feel rather fortunate myself that his name became known to me when it did. I'm more than a little gratified, moreover, to know that I have Decius to thank.

Accompanied, or, rather, harried, by Agricus, I left Domitia Lucilla's house at dawn and began my melancholy pilgrimage back to the Hobnail. It felt strange to be returning from the home I'd chosen to the home I'd fled, and I wondered as we walked toward the Forum whether the passage of a mere two months had left me as much a stranger in my old world as I was an anomaly in my new one.

But with Agricus beside me I didn't have much time for such reflections. He was at me in his customary manner the moment we passed through the mansion's front gates. "Why aren't you wearing your new bearskin cloak?" he asked with a smirk.

"What bearskin cloak?" I snapped back at him though I would have been better advised to stop and think.

"Why, the bearskin cloak you won from Marcus yesterday by dint of your remarkable feat of horsemanship."

"Oh, that," I said dismissively, trying to sustain the charade. "He'll probably give it to me when I get back tomorrow."

"*Tomorrow!*" Agricus responded, setting the subject of the cloak aside in order to pursue a more promising line of attack. "You're not planning to linger among us plebeians any longer that you have to, I see."

I turned and glared at him. "Why should I linger among those who have no love for me?"

"Oh, it's love you're after, is it?"

"Among other things."

"Such as?"

"Such as friendship, and kindness, and some semblance, at least, of loyalty."

"My, my, but you sound aggrieved."

I glared at him again. "Not without reason."

He gave a soundless laugh. "Why do I get the impression that I'm the one you feel wronged by?"

"I can't imagine, Agricus; unless by some quirk you've developed a conscience."

This time he laughed out loud. "It seems to me that I did you a favor, Lucio."

"Not intentionally, you didn't."

"Intentionally or not, it worked out for the best."

"Then let's just leave it that I'm guilty of ingratitude."

"And what else, if you'll pardon my asking?"

"What do you mean, what else?"

"I mean, what else are you guilty of that Marcus and Cornificia know about but the Lady Domitia doesn't?"

I had an impulse to start throwing punches at him, but quite apart from the likelihood that he'd block them and retaliate, there was the certainty that such a reaction would betray the fact that he'd struck a nerve. A small chill went through me as I contemplated the prospect of his learning about my involvement with Annia. Then *he'd* have a secret to use against *me*, and I'd have no way of restraining his malevolence.

"Your interest in me is touching," I replied.

"Well, you know, Lucio, I've always been concerned for your welfare."

"Concerned against it, you mean."

"No, not a bit. You take this matter we're discussing now, for example— pure altruism on my part. Just consider: I make the long trip from the Hobnail to the Caelian in order to tell you about your mother. You're not there when I arrive, though, and no one mentions where you've gone. When you do finally show up, looking like the contents of a jackal's entrails, three very interesting things happen. First, Cornificia starts to ask you a question, but then stops; second, the Lady Domitia asks you a question you clearly don't want to answer; and, third, Marcus supplies an answer that is clearly of his own devising. What am I to make of all this, concerned as I am for your well-being? Obviously you're engaged in a forbidden activity of some sort, but whatever it is, it's not so forbidden that Marcus and Cornificia can't condone it and act as your abettors. Now I ask myself, What sort of activity would be anathema in the eyes of someone like the Lady Domitia yet relatively innocuous in the eyes of her children? Immediately the image of Priapus flashes into my mind. But wait—the Lady Domitia is no thistle-faced prude; she wouldn't object if her plebeian house guest engaged in a little venereal sport. Not at all. Let him plunge his poker into every quim on the Caelian—provided, of course, that he doesn't profane the sacred fissure of a patrician. Aha! I say to myself, could that be the sort of activity that my foolish friend Lucio has been engaged in? But no; what highborn maiden with a grain of pride would submit herself to his scruffy caresses? Not a one. A high-born maiden *without* a grain of pride, however? Well, such a creature would be capable of almost anything. . . ."

I just kept walking as he yammered on, silently cursing the fate that had allotted me so clever an antagonist. His deductions were uncannily accurate; I had to admit that. But even though they'd shaken me, I was careful to let no sign of discomposure appear on my face. They were merely guesses, after all, and without the name of my loved one to tie them together they posed no significant threat. Let him speculate all he wanted to, I concluded, striving frantically to reassure myself. But then I remembered the way Cornificia had gazed at him—and I cursed my darling Annia more fiercely than even my fate.

"I've given this whole matter a good deal of thought, Lucio," Agricus resumed at last, "and I believe that you *are* poking some patrician wench."

"You're free to believe whatever you want to, pretty face."

"Don't trifle with your betters, little fellow," he shot back at me, his voice taking on an angry edge. "We both know that I could confirm my hypothesis without all that much trouble."

"You could confirm it only if it were true. And besides, we both know things about you that don't even require confirmation."

He frowned a little at this, but gave a shrug and said, "Look, I'll make a bargain with you."

"That would require a belief on my part that you could be trusted to keep your word."

"Such a belief would be justified."

I didn't reply to this.

"Do you doubt me?"

"Let's just say I'm unconvinced."

"Well, let's just say, also, that you'd better strike a bargain with me anyway."

"I'd better, eh?"

"Yes, Lucio—you damn well know you'd better."

"No, I damn well don't!"

"In that case I'll make it simple for you: if there's to be war between us, the winner will be him with the least to lose."

The bastard! I thought. The cunning, conniving *bastard!*

"There doesn't have to be war between us, though," he continued, moderating somewhat the tone of menace in his voice. "We can cooperate with each other whether you trust me or not."

"Can we now?"

"Yes, easily. You've got a weapon to use against me if I betray you, after all; just as I, given provocation, could inflict a few wounds on you. The way things stand between us will serve as an ironclad guarantee of our good faith. And if that isn't good enough for you, bear in mind that you really don't have any choice."

I turned to look at him and saw a cold glint in his eyes that warned me not to furnish the provocation he'd alluded to . "What sort of bargain did you have in mind?" I asked resignedly, hoping that the question wouldn't be taken as a sign of outright capitulation.

"I want to go back to the Caelian with you," he replied in a matter-of-fact manner.

"You *what?*"

"I want to go back to the Caelian with you. Is that so incomprehensible?"

"The fact that you want to isn't."

"What is, then? The idea that I'd actually go?"

"No. The idea that I'd let you go with me."

"You left with me. Why not return with me?"

"Because, among other things, it's not a guest's place to have guests of his own."

"But it's not *your* guest I aspire to be."

I turned to look at him and was greeted by a smile that made me shiver.

"Have I alarmed you terribly, little Lucio?"

"Suppose you tell me what you're up to," I responded, trying not to sound as alarmed as I felt.

"The beguiling Marcus has his pet plebeian. Why shouldn't the ravishing Cornificia have hers?"

I whirled without thinking and sent my fist into his cheek. "Don't judge everyone by yourself!" I shouted as he went sprawling. Then, with a surge of apprehension, I braced myself for his retaliatory assault.

It never came, though. He simply rolled into a sitting position and started to laugh. "Ah, just think, Lucio," he sighed, ruefully shaking his head, "if you'd done that two months ago instead of running away to Marcus, our prospects today would not be anything like as rosy."

"There's no such thing as 'our' prospects," I objected.

"Oh, yes there is, little comrade. You and I are going to rise or fall together. You'd better get accustomed to that idea."

"You're contemptible!" I spat out ineffectually.

"Not so contemptible, I hope, as to rule out our rising conjointly to the heights."

"Wouldn't you find the depths more congenial?"

"Devastating, Lucio," was Agricus's derisive rejoinder. And as he got up and brushed himself off he added, "You have a genius for vituperation."

"Better that than a genius for malice."

He turned and frowned at me. "Malice?" he said.

"You mean there's some other explanation for the fact that you've been tormenting me all these years?"

His face took on an expression of mixed amusement and incredulity. "Is that really what you think?" he asked.

"Don't tell me that I've misjudged you," I replied with heavy sarcasm.

For a long while he stared at me. "Not as much as I've misjudged you," he said at last.

"Meaning what, precisely?"

"Meaning that for someone of your intelligence you are really remarkably stupid."

"Enlighten me then."

He paused and slowly shook his head. "I don't believe I can."

"Then at least stop tormenting me."

"I would, but you give me no choice."

"That's ridiculous!" I retorted.

"You see! You're incapable of enlightenment."

"No! *You're* incapable of talking sense."

He gazed at me appraisingly for a moment or two, then responded, "I'll talk sense to you, Lucio—the kind of sense that even you will understand."

"I appreciate your condescension."

"Well then, try to appreciate a few other things as well. Try to appreciate the fact that my mother and I have no Hobnail to support us, and that we've always had to earn our rent money in whatever ways we could. Try to appreciate the fact that Marcus is as important to my future as he is to yours, if not more so, and that I played as great a part in securing his friendship as you did. Can you understand, Lucio, why I would want to share in the fruits of that friendship? Does it make sense to you that I would resent your eagerness to exclude me?"

It hardly seemed possible, but for an instant I thought that I'd detected a trace of wetness in the corners of Agricus's eyes. Tears from him would not have come as much more of a surprise than the words he'd actually uttered, though; and more surprising even than the way he'd expressed himself was the fact that his statements, at first blush, seemed valid.

Valid or not, however, they didn't much diminish my feelings of antagonism toward him, and when he read that in my expression, his own features instantly hardened. "I tried," he said. And I was foolish enough to retort, "You failed."

We stood there for several moments, the confession of enmity between us as fateful as a confession of love. Agricus *had* tried; I understood that even then. He'd reached out as far as he was able and revealed as much of himself as he dared. No doubt the effort had cost him something; no doubt my rebuff had cost him more. But even now I can't reproach myself for refusing to be conciliated. He'd said nothing to indicate that he regretted any of the countless acts of cruelty he'd been guilty of in the past, and his plea of destitution sounded suspiciously like an excuse to go on committing such acts in the future. On top of that there was his crassly opportunistic attitude toward Marcus, and his offensive assumption that it corresponded to mine. It didn't, of course—of that much I was certain. Such advantages as I enjoyed by virtue of my relationship with Marcus had always in my mind been entirely incidental to the love I bore him. Agricus, by contrast, had no interest whatever in Marcus the individual; it was Marcus the future Princeps whose friendship he coveted.

And it was this perception more than any other, I think, that confirmed me in my mistrust of him. Yes, he'd reached out to me, but with no more true affection than if he'd reached for a rung on a ladder. In his eyes I was merely an instrumentality, a means to which Marcus was the end. That he should have imputed his own squalid motives to me was ironical in the extreme, but by the same token more or less inevitable. For his obsession with self-advancement was so all-consuming as to blind him to the fact that greed for love is just as commonplace a vice as greed for gain. He was far too rapacious, in other words, to realize that I might have squalid motives of my own.

"It seems we weren't destined to be friends," he said finally.

"I don't think destiny's to blame."

"Perhaps not. But wherever the fault lies, we've both got to get along as best we can, even if that means getting along with each other."

"Fortunately, it doesn't."

"That remains to be seen, Lucio. Neither one of us can decide the issue on his own."

"You may be right about that, but *my* decision has already been made."

This pathetic attempt at a bluff on my part made no more of an impression on Agricus than the punch I'd landed. He looked me calmly in the eye and responded, "So has mine."

At that point there was nothing more to be said, and for the remainder of our walk back to the Hobnail we stayed silent. Just outside the shop, Agricus stopped, and again fixed his eyes on mine. "Until tomorrow," he said, and then walked off down the street.

I watched him stride away from me, knowing for a certainty that the threat implicit in his last two words was by no means an idle one. Did I have nerve enough to defy him? Would I dare return to the Caelian that very evening and let him do his worst when he learned I'd gone? No, I confessed with a pang of self-contempt. I knew him too well and feared him too much to arouse his vindictive passions. He would return with me to the place to which I'd fled to escape him, and I would cope with his presence as best I could.

It's a wise coward, after all, who knows when the time has come to grovel.

[AUGUST 26TH]

Old Syrus didn't have a potential buyer waiting for us this morning. But he did come provided with the *name* of a potential buyer—and what a name it is!

It seems that no less a personage than Gaius Aemilius Placidus is in the market for some fifteen or twenty home-born slaves, in family units preferably, to work a run-down farm near Tuder, in Umbria. This farm, some 1,500 jugera in size, came into Gaius's hands by virtue of the death of his wife's second cousin, a spendthrift drunkard who was not merely penniless when he died, but in debt to Gaius to the tune of over 277,000 sesterces. The Tuder estate was all that was left of this profligate fellow's once considerable holdings; it was there that he'd tippled away the last few years of his existence, selling off his slaves one by one in order to keep himself supplied with cash for all his extravagances. Needless to say, as the number of slaves available to work the land dwindled, the land began to yield to nature's encroachments, and for the last nine months or so it had suffered the calamities of utter neglect. Gaius, accordingly, was in need of experienced farm workers who could reclaim the property and make it pay a profit. Not that its profitability mattered a great deal to a man of his abundant wealth. But since it was all he had to show for his outlay of over 277,000 sesterces, no one could blame him for wanting to make the most of it.

I had to admit to Syrus that the situation as outlined seemed well suited to the needs of my familia, and he in turn was quick to assure me that Gaius's overseers had a reputation for humanity. Of course, he added, Gaius was far too important a man to involve himself personally in the details of such a comparatively minor transaction. Even his estate manager couldn't be bothered with them, and had simply commissioned one of Syrus's fellow slave traders to handle the entire matter from start to finish. This meant, he said, that the reputation of Gaius's overseers would in all probability be the only security I'd have for the well-being of my familia—admittedly a negative consideration. But the fact that the transaction was being handled on both sides by traders rather than principals had a positive consequence, and that was that certain fees and excises could be "dissembled," as Syrus put it, leaving a larger portion of the gross purchase price available for traders' commissions, and for me.

The prospect of added gain did nothing to allay my misgivings about subjecting those who've served me so well to the authority of a total stranger. "Mightn't it be possible to find out which overseer Gaius has in mind for the Tuder estate?" I asked, my concern manifest in my voice. "I realize that I'm making complications, but couldn't we say that I insist on having my slaves inspected prior to sale by the man who's going to be working them—simply in order to insure myself against any subsequent claims that I misrepresented their quality?"

Syrus frowned a little, "Your concern for your people does you credit," he said. "But for the buyer instead of the trader to inspect in a case like this is distinctly out of the ordinary."

"Is it so much out of the ordinary that it can't be considered?"

Syrus brooded, then appeared to come to a decision. "In a world full of wonders," he said, "who am I to refuse to consider something just because it's out of the ordinary? I'll do better than consider it, my commendably solicitous friend; I'll pledge my word to arrange it. Now what do you say to that?"

"I say that you are one of the wonders you just alluded to."

"So are we all, my dear fellow, did we but know it."

So are we all indeed—and more so in this particular instance than even old Syrus might imagine. My affection for him is such that I almost let my astonishment show when he first mentioned Gaius's name. In the end, I decided that the details of my association with that fine old patrician patriarch were too private, and too unseemly, to be shared with anyone outside my family.

Not that anyone inside my family was at all familiar with them at that particular point. It wasn't until Decius and I were across the Tiber and more than halfway home that I overcame my embarrassment and acquainted him with the squalid facts.

There is a fine inscrutable irony in the thought that the boy whose semen flushed me from my mother's womb should have grown into the man whose gold may shortly purge me of my slaves. Would it matter to him, I wonder, if he knew that we were linked by fornication? Would he perceive the irony of our situation, and ponder its antic meanings?

Probably not.

Decius was thoroughly fascinated by the story, and overcame his usual diffidence sufficiently to solicit additional details. I must say I found his intense interest a little disconcerting. It was almost as if he felt starved for knowledge of me.

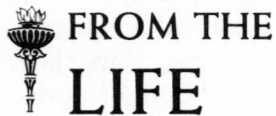 **FROM THE**
LIFE

I suppose it shouldn't have come as all that much of a surprise, but I was taken aback anyway when Glaubus informed me that he'd seen to my mother's rites on the day after her death. That, of course, was the day before Agricus slithered up to the Caelian on the pretext that her rites were impending. He'd duped me again, in other words, and so dramatically improved his own position in the process that I almost had to admire his duplicity.

"Agricus fetch you here?" my uncle asked me in an amused tone of voice, and with a sullen nod I acknowledged he had.

"Where'd he find you?"

"At Marcus's house," I confessed.

"Is that where you've been all this time?"

"Pretty much—there and at his uncle's farm."

"What'd you run off for?"

The question was not unexpected, but the angry answer I had ready was for Drusilla's ears, not his. So I confined myself to replying, "Agricus."

Glaubus was silent, his massive chest and shoulders looming like a boulder above the counter where he stood. There wasn't much light in the Hobnail so early on a winter's morning, and what little there was clung like sooty gauze to the corners of the ceiling. A few pallid, reflections played over the smooth skin of my uncle's skull, but beneath the heavy shadow of his brow his face was in darkness. "Your aunt's pretty peeved at you," he said at last. "I hope for your sake you give her a better explanation than you just gave me."

Better, but no different, I almost retorted.

"She's still asleep," he continued, "but you may as well go wake her up and get the bloodshed over with."

"All right, Uncle, I will," I said, forbearing to add that if any blood was about to be shed, I didn't intend it to be mine.

I entered the smaller of the two rear rooms and paused to let my eyes adjust to the gloom. The shutters were closed, the air heavy with the odors of sleep. I let the sound of my aunt's breathing guide me to her couch, then stood looking down at her for a long, long while. She was buried deep in slumber, her mouth hanging open and her knees beneath the blankets drawn up toward her chest. No, I thought, it's not my blood that's going to be shed this morning, and as if in confirmation a strange wildness started flooding through my veins. She lay there before me, defenseless, disarmed—and as the wildness built up inside me I struggled to give it a name. Anger, of course, but also heartbroken love; vindictiveness, most certainly, but also the tenderest solicitude; a desire to kill . . . ? Yes. But a darker desire as well, so dark as to go undefined.

The wildness constricted my chest, clutched at my throat, thundered in my ears; and I watched in horrified fascination as the hand on the end of my arm reached out and slowly pulled the blankets back to reveal my aunt's naked form. The smell of her rose to my nostrils as I gazed at the nipples from which no milk had ever flowed. From her breasts I ran my eyes downward, past the flaccid thickness of her waist to the dark thatch of hair between her drawn-up thighs. Time went by as I probed every crease and studied every contour of her nakedness. Fragmented memories spilled through my mind: the cold bath at Curtio's, the hot bath later, the hot oil, my small hands on her breasts, the statue of Eurydice, the dead snake's staring eyes, and yes, the sight of Agricus's buttocks rising and falling, rising and falling, in the dark dankness of the Hobnail's cellar, in the dark dankness of this woman's flesh.

Feeling the chill of the morning air on her now uncovered skin, Drusilla started groping for the blankets I'd stripped away. Her hand slid down her hip to her knee, then felt around behind her thigh and up to the small of her back. A frown of irritation came over her face as her fingers continued their futile search, and at last, with a little moan of exasperation, she opened her eyes, and saw me.

There was an instant of concussive shock as the enormity of what I'd done came through to both of us. There she lay, exposed to the indignity of my gaze; and there I stood, incriminated beyond all hope of absolution by the irrefutable evidence of the blankets clutched in my hand. We stared at each other through a haze of blighted affection that stung our eyes almost to tears. Almost, but not quite. For one must not weep in the presence of an enemy, especially an enemy one has loved.

I was in an indefensible postion; I had no recourse, therefore, but to attack. "Is *this* what Agricus got so hard about?" I said, sneering at her body.

She retaliated instantaneously, shooting her hand up under my tunic and taking a cruel grip on my prod. "You're pretty hard yourself, you little sneak," she hissed, sinking her nails into my tumescence, "but you won't be hard again soon."

She squeezed and gouged with what felt like all her strength, while her right hand went for my scrotum. This is Agricus at Curtio's all over again, I thought in rising panic, and then my wildness overwhelmed me.

I have never hit anyone as hard: my fist smashed into her mouth with such force that I still bear two tooth marks on my knuckles. The blow stunned her, just long enough for me to land another one on the side of her jaw. I felt her grip on me loosen, then tighten, then loosen again as her eyes started to roll. Blood spurted from her mouth and her right hand came clawing up toward my face. I grabbed it with my left and sent one last blow crashing into her temple. That finished her. Her hands went limp, and with an anguished whimper I fell backward, released.

My wildness had saved me, but now I began to shiver uncontrollably. For several moments I sat there and stared at the damage I'd done to Drusilla's face, but then the thought of Glaubus assailed me, and my breath stopped in my throat.

Now panic reigned. I leaped for the shutters, jerked them open, and flung myself into the courtyard. Regaining my feet, I crouched low and listened for Glaubus's footfall, but there was no sound at all to be heard—none, that is, until through the open shutters there came a strangled animallike howl.

The courtyard was a cul-de-sac, so I had but one chance of escape. Scrambling over to the gateway leading to the bar, I risked a peek down the darkened hall. There came Glaubus, lumbering toward the courtyard, but then swerving left into Drusilla's cubiculum. I began running the instant he disappeared inside, and if I'd delayed so much as a heartbeat, I don't think I would have survived. For Glaubus, shocked by the sight of Drusilla battered and bloody, came staggering backward a step or two into the hall, and I just did get past him before his bulk blocked the way. He lunged for me as I darted by, but like the snake in the goldsmith's shop, he got hold of nothing more than the hem of my tunic, which mercifully ripped away and let me consummate my escape.

I shot out of the Hobnail and took off down Twopenny Street with all the speed I could muster. My fear spurred me on, of course, to run as hard as I was able, but what really made me fly was a sense of anni-hilating horror.

 FROM THE
JOURNAL

44

[AUGUST 27TH]

Although I've tried my best to come to terms with the fact that time passes more quickly as one grows older, I still can't help but feel daunted by the way the seasons have been wheeling by of late. Their progression seems so headlong to me that I often feel like a leaf being blown by some mighty wind down a long darkening tunnel toward my extinction. This, admittedly, is not the most lighthearted approach one could take to the subject of one's mortality; but the subject itself is hardly conducive to exultation.

What is the cause, I wonder, of all these morbid musings? Could it be the stiff breeze that has come sweeping down from the northwest today, bearing upon it the first faint hints of autumn? Yes, it could, absurdly enough. For I don't feel ready, somehow, for the onset of colder weather; the prospect of winter frightens me. Perhaps that's because by November or December my world will have irrevocably changed. Even if I'm still alive, this farm and all its people will be lost to me. I'll be a fugitive in some alien land, cut off forever from the sky, the earth, and the consolation of my home.

Ah, how sorry I feel for myself, how filled with tears and rheum! Yet I cannot entirely despise my acquaintance with despair. To lose what one loves is painful, even to the most stoical of souls. Why add self-contempt to one's burden of sorrow. The fleeting seasons are insult enough.

There's a saying among runners who compete in the Greek games that "every great foot racer is really a fugitive at heart." This, like most Greek sayings, never made much sense to me. So one summer, at Elis, I summoned up sufficient nerve to ask old Kallistos of Sidon, who'd won the stade race at the 222d Olympiad, to explain exactly what it meant.

"What it means," he responded from the lofty reaches reserved for those who've worn the olive crown, "is that the mark of every great runner is a love of running, and that the source of this love is the runner's sense that he is making an escape."

"An escape from what?" I asked, blunt minded.

And in a tone of pointed condescension he replied, "From everything that will ever slow him down."

This explantion, alas, left me feeling only marginally enlightened, but I didn't dare ask him to elaborate further. I see now that one reason I was so slow to comprehend the saying's metaphorical significance was that the need to flee had arisen so often in my actual experience. How could the threat of being slowed down metaphorically make a meaningful impression on someone who'd repeatedly faced the real prospect of being brought to a terminal halt? It couldn't, obviously, or at least it didn't; but as I think back now on the way I felt while fleeing from Glaubus and the Hobnail, I realize that I experienced the metaphor long before I ever heard it expressed.

I knew the moment I reached the street that nothing and no one could catch me. I was aware, in other words, that I was safe. But the horror I'd just been part of was still in hot metaphorical pursuit, and so, donning Mercury's winged sandals, I galloped on.

Oh, how I ran that morning, or rather, how I flew! Down Twopenny Street, past the Ulpian Basilica, through the crowds in Trajan's Forum and the Forum Julium, along the north colonnade of the Basilica Aemilia, past the filigreed drum of the Temple of Vesta, and the massive podium of the Temple of Venus and Rome. I sobbed as I ran, sobbed for what I'd done to Drusilla, sobbed for what she'd done to me. I sobbed for my uncle Glaubus, whom I felt I had somehow betrayed, and for the Hobnail, which he'd let me call my home. I sobbed for Rutolo's precious walls and

Curtio's tepid baths, for the grimy shops along Twopenny Street and the sun on the Quirinal's slopes; I sobbed for the mud eaters and the brick lickers, for the purring of Romulus and the warm cave of Fabia's flesh. I sobbed for my foolish mother, who had died without troubling to live, and for my unknown father, whose only bequest was my seed. I sobbed above all for myself and all my longings, for the hopes I now knew were forlorn. My dreams of redemption had been proved cruel illusions, my birthright of love stood revealed as a sham.

I ran as I sobbed; as I sobbed I ran—blindly, obliviously, past the Colossus of the Sun, the Amphitheater of the Flavians, and the precincts of the Deified Claudius. At last a wave of exhaustion assailed me, and I staggered and fell to the ground. My sobbing continued unabated as I lay with my face in the dust, and perhaps a quarter of an hour passed before I gave any thought to where I was. The instant I raised my eyes, my sobbing abruptly ceased. For I discovered, to my utter astonishment, that I had come to rest at the precise spot where Annia and I had quarreled the day before. I gaped up incredulously at the graceful arches of the Claudian Aqueduct, then turned my head to confirm the presence of the Claudian Temple's walls. I had indeed returned to the Bend, and the mystery of my presence there seemed so awesome to me that all the sorrow and horror I'd experienced receded entirely from my thoughts. Some wheel had come full circle, it seemed, in the space of a single day, and though it began and ended with Annia, she was no more than its outer rim. In its interior, arranged like wooden spokes, were the people who had determined the shape of my life: Drusilla, Glaubus, Agricus, Marcus, and even my shadow of a mother. I lay at the hub, connected to Annia yet kept rigidly at a distance from her by all those radiant souls.

What a strange and magical metaphor I'd created in making my metaphorical escape. Or perhaps it was some god's creation, some god who had guided my feet. Whoever its author, there it was: the circle described by my life. And though it didn't fully compensate for my lost birthright and my shattered dreams, it did instill in me a firm sense that I'd be wise to go on living.

[AUGUST 28TH]

I ran this morning—if such comical exertions can be described as running—for the first time since early July, and it is clear to me that after
fifty days of comparative inactivity my muscles have lost most of their
tone. I suppose such physical deterioration is inevitable in a man of my
years, but the degree to which I've degenerated still comes as something
of a shock. Sound mind–sound body remains an attainable ideal, after
all, even for dotards like me; and if I'm to deal effectively with the
challenges of the months to come, I had better take steps to repair the
ravages of the months just past.

Many steps, in fact, or, rather, paces, or strides—but not too many
or too soon. The northwesterly stream of coolness that washed over us
yesterday made this morning's air so invigorating that only my professional
experience kept me from overextending myself (though I suspect my body
will lodge a protest in any case when I lift myself out of bed tomorrow).
I was wise enough to start off at an easy walk; nor did I break into a trot
until I reached the altar to Robigus two miles up the road. I loped along
toward Careiae, relishing the hush of nature that anticipates the sun and
breathing deep those same hints of autumn freshness that I'd bemoaned
so piteously only twelve hours before.

The moment was utterly idyllic but decidedly short-lived, for no sooner
did I start to ascend the gentle incline leading to the Via Cornelia than
my wind ignominiously gave out. I labored on for a few hundred paces
as my legs turned to granite and my knees rusted stiff, but at last I had
to bow to the overwhelming evidence of my decrepitude. Slowing to a
feeble trudge, I turned and headed for home, acknowledging as I did so
the sad truth that old runners who aspire to be fugitives at heart had first
better tend to their lungs and legs.

My life, if not my emotions, became a good deal less turbulent in the months following my visit to the Hobnail. Marcus readily forgave me for what had happend there, or, rather, he declined to blame me; and I seized on that as forgiveness in order to mitigate my own sense of culpability.

"You burst a blister," was the way he put it. "Now, at least, it won't leave a callous on your soul."

"But I hit her, Marco," I whined remorsefully, seeking to extract from him every last ounce of exculpation he could provide. "I hit her *hard*."

"I daresay you did," he answered me, "and it speaks well for your sense of priorities."

Though this response left me feeling less than totally absolved, I judged it advisable at that point to let the matter rest. Marcus couldn't undo what I'd done, after all, and had already given me every benefit of the doubt. What it came down to, alas, was that no matter how charitably my actions might be interpreted, I would be left with an irreducible residue of guilt. This, it seemed, I would have to live with; and if the burden ever became too heavy I could always turn to Agricus's favorite maxim for consolation: "Better to live with remorse than to die without transgressing."

Perhaps it was that maxim or something like it that accounted for Agricus's readiness to forgive my transgressions against him. I might almost say, his eagerness; for he not only overlooked the fact that I'd returned to the Caelian without him, but even evinced a degree of respect for me because of the injuries I'd inflicted on Drusilla. "You should see her *face!*" he confided in an admiring whisper several days after the event (having himself just brazened his way into Domitia Lucilla's presence and been reproved for his impudence with an invitation to stay for dinner). "She looks even worse than *Cornificia!*"

I responded to this cruel comparison with a look of revulsion, even as the unsuspecting object of Agricus's ridicule gazed at him in cow-eyed adoration from across the table. What an upside-down world this compeer of mine inhabited: I'd battered his mistress, so he admired me; a sweet young girl felt love for him, so he derided her. Perhaps such inverted reactions are common to all those who profess the misogynist's creed, or perhaps they're common to every man living, but only misogynists confess them. Thinking back on the force of the blows I'd dealt Drusilla, I had to wonder whether it was Agricus's emotional deformities that repelled me so inordinately or the horrible prospect that I might have a few of my own. With respect to Drusilla, certainly, my record was a good deal worse than his, and with respect to Fabia it wasn't a great deal better. That left my liaison with Annia as the only grounds for distinguishing between us with respect to women in general; and my liaison with Annia was of course a thing of the past.

The conclusion seemed inescapable: though I'd always been pleased to define myself as my aunt's adoring nephew and my sweetheart's devoted swain, there was little evidence of devotion or adoration in my treatment of either one of them. That both had loved me was in no way open to question; that their love had been properly returned was very much open to doubt. It's said that the difference between being loved and feeling loved accounts for half the misery in the world; but might not the real culprit be the difference between feeling love and loving? "By your deeds shall ye be known," as the Jews are fond of saying; and by my deeds I now knew myself to be much less the antithesis of Agricus than I was his virtual twin. The only difference between us, indeed, was that he seemed to glory in his misogyny whereas I found mine a source of grief.

I told no one my terrible secret, not even Marcus, but carried it hidden inside me like a tumor. The weight of it was an unremitting burden on my spirit, a burden that came close to crushing me evey time Annia chanced to cross my path. She was blossoming into womanhood with a speed that would have disconcerted me even if we'd been lovers; the fact that we were hopelessly estranged turned my dismay into torment. The swell of her breasts beneath her clothes invariably produced a corresponding distension beneath my own, while the details of her countenance took on proportions of such exquisite harmony that what had once been mere prettiness was raised to almost intimidating heights of beauty. It seemed that for every adolescent affliction poor Cornificia had suffered, my Annia had been vouchsafed a blessing; and my only consolation for this cruel twist of fate came when Agricus finally met her and failed to make any discernible impression. He, to be sure, displayed a roughly comparable indifference to her, and I was forced to the conclusion that they were both so vain of their beauty as to render the company of any peer uncongenial.

It was Marcus who was now at the center of my world, so the events of greatest moment in his life perforce became the focus of my own. The first, and officially most significant, of these was his assumption of the toga virilis, which in accordance with tradition took place two days after the Ides of March, during the Liberalia festivities. In anticipation of this, his formal entrance into a man's estate, he served as honorary prefect of the City from the beginning of the Latin Festival on the Kalends of February until its end on the day before the Nones. On the Nones itself came the momentous announcement of both his and Cornificia's betrothals, she to C. Ummidius Quadratus, of the distinguished consular family, and he to Ceionia, daughter of the brilliant voluptuary who, with the new title of "L. Aelius Caesar," was about to become the adopted son and designated successor of the fierce-eyed Emperor himself. The choice of Ceionia had been dictated by Hadrian, and it had the effect of confirming Marcus's place in the direct line of succession to the Principate. Naturally the identity of my dear friend's wife-to-be did not come as any great surprise to him, nor did it inspire in him any great amount of joy. "She's as virtuous as her father is decadent," he told me. "We're going to bore each other senseless."

Ten days or so after the betrothal announcements, Domitia Lucilla—at her son's instance, no doubt—was kind enough to give a dinner in honor of my lamentably approximate day of birth. Annia was not present on this occasion, mercifully enough, but Agricus, unmercifully, was, along with Cornificia and several of Marcus's cousins. Since this was the first time in sixteen years that anyone had bothered to observe the anniversary of my parturition, it was for me a uniquely memorable event—and not least because it marked the first time I ever saw my beloved friend get drunk.

Now there were few things less compatible with what I knew of Marcus's nature than outright inebriety, so when the first signs of his intoxication became discernible, I was loathe to give credence to my senses. Only on longer acquaintance did I learn that he was capable on isolated occasions of sitting down in a given spot and very deliberately drinking himself blind—and that was precisely what he did that night.

He waited until after dinner, of course, but as soon as Domitia Lucilla retired to bed he and I and Agricus retired to the library and went speedily to work on a large flagon of Falernian. There we sat: Marcus increasingly tipsy, I increasingly bemused, and Agricus in a virtual trance of calculation. As the hours passed, our conversation turned, predictably enough, to the subject of Marcus's engagement. "It's a matter of duty, or, rather, she is," he said, badly slurring his words; "and duty as we all know, is . . . *duty!*" Having said this, he gave us a smile that was probably intended to appear wily but which showed on his face as something between a yawn and a wink. "I get a quid pro quo for doing my duty, though," he continued. "The Emperor's agreed to let me go to *Greece!*"

There was a long pause while we all reflected on this portentous news. "Right after my birthday," he resumed at last, adding almost offhandedly, "You fellas wanna go with me?"

Agricus and I gaped at him in astonishment, while he gazed woozily back at us. "Tell you what," he said as his head started lolling, "you can gimme your answer in the morning." And with that he toppled over in a heap.

After staring at his crumpled form for several moments, Agricus and I glanced warily at each other.

"When's his birthday?" my nemesis inquired.

"The sixth before the Kalends of May," I responded, appalled at the thought of all the advantages he stood to derive from Marcus's inebriation (my self-serving assumption being that he would never have been invited to accompany us had it not been for the influence of drink).

"Well, what do you think, dear comrade?" Agricus said after a pregnant interval, his lips curving into an altogether insufferable smile. "Shall we take our friend up on his generous offer, or shall we stay here in Rome and steal bricks?"

 # FROM THE
JOURNAL

[AUGUST 29TH]

Oh, how I ached when I arose this morning—or, rather, when I attempted to rise. Anyone observing my efforts to attain an upright position would have counted the spectacle most amusing. It seems that at sixty years of age one must pay a heavy penalty for one's lapses into sloth, that penalty being to feel at least twenty years older. I knew from experience, however, that the worst would be over once I'd gotten to my feet; and as I hobbled out of the house and down the road I was happy just to be ambulatory.

Luckily for my knotted muscles, yesterday's autumnal briskness was absent from this morning's air, and with each step I took, the humid warmth of summer worked its way a little deeper into my flesh. By the time I reached the river road I had raised a bit of a sweat, and by the time I passed old Robigus's altar I was ready to lengthen my stride. For some reason, though, I happened to notice the date of the Robigalia, which is inscribed on the altar's base: A.D. VII Kal. Mai.; and having noticed it, I slowed down, then came to a stop.

It's merely a coincidence, I suppose, that the local numen of wheat blight should have his festival on the eve of Marcus's birthday. And I suppose it's merely coincidence that of the sixteen priestly colleges in the *pontificium* it is the Quirinales who are charged with the duty of propitiating him. I suppose, also, that since I wrote about Marcus's birthday just last night, it was only to be expected that I would notice the date on the altar's base today. And I suppose that, having noticed that date, it was only natural of me to wonder whether something more than mere co-incidence accounts for its connections with Marcus and me.

Was it coincidence, one might ask, that I ran straight from the Hobnail to the bend of the Claudian Aqueduct? (And is it coincidence, come to think of it, that when the Quirinales make their sacrifice to Robigus on the eve of Marcus's birthday they do so beside the Via Claudia?)

Aristotle said that a coincidence is a connection made in the mind of an observer between events that are unconnected in the external world.

Marcus, however, said that a coincidence is a perception made by the mind of an observer of a connection that can't be explained by reference to the external world.

I'm no philosopher and I don't pretend to be qualified to choose between these conflicting views. All I know is that, having experienced my coincidence this morning, I ran up the hill to the Via Cornelia and didn't once run out of breath.

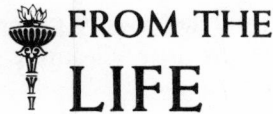
The period between my sixteenth birthday in mid-February and Marcus's fifteenth in late April passed, it seemed to me, with agonizing slowness. This, I suppose, was as much a consequence of my impatience to set off for Greece as it was of my eagerness to be gone from Rome. True, the specter of Agricus cast something of a shadow over the impending journey, but not even he could dim the shining prospect of Hellas that lay at journey's end.

Then as now the allure of Greece was like that of no other place in the world. I'd heard the Hellenic provinces spoken of every day of my life, or so it seemed, and in the realm of thought and beauty they had provided most of my standards of comparison. If, like most Romans, I considered it regrettable that a land as glorious as Greece should be inhabited by a people as inglorious as the Greeks, that was largely because, like most Romans, I secretly envied them their heritage. What nation on earth has ever been worthy of such a legacy? None, if Plato is to be believed; not even the nation that bequeathed it.

I dread to think how much more slowly the hours would have passed that late winter and early spring had Marcus and I not been so frantically busy. We barely had time for our studies in the month that preceded the Liberalia and were often obliged to neglect them in the month that followed. No matter how hectic our lives became, however, we never failed to devote half an hour or so before bedtime to the pleasures of planning our trip. Huddled together in the lamplight, we would study maps and itineraries, read aloud from the geographies of Strabo and Pliny, and pore over Polemon's guidebooks until fatigue at last overcame us. Our researches extended not just to Greece, but to all the regions of Italy we'd be passing through en route to our point of embarcation at Brundusium: Latium, naturally, Samnium, Campania, Lucania, Apulia, and Calabria.

The Via Appia would serve as our basic route of march, at least as far as Beneventum. There we would have to choose between the old road and the newly completed Via Traiana. Thanks to Marcus's quid-pro-quo discussions with the Emperor, our choice would be unrestricted; we were under no compulsion to adhere to any particular schedule and could take any main road, side road, or sea lane that struck our fancy, the only Imperial proviso being that Marcus had to be back across the Hydruntine Straits by the end of the sailing season in October.

What lay before us, in other words, was almost six months of utterly unencumbered freedom, the kind of freedom few people are vouchsafed for even six days; and given the magnitude of the opportunity afforded us, Marcus insisted early in the course of our discussions that our journey must have a theme. I straightaway suggested "Exploration!" which wasn't precisely apt but which Marcus provisionally accepted pending consultations with Agricus. He, to my considerable exasperation, immediately came up with the far more felicitous concept "Discovery!"

Of course I was sorely tempted, and on more than one occasion actually opened my mouth, to ask Marcus what on earth his reasons were for inviting that twisted miscreant to travel with us. My unaccustomed good sense in refraining, ultimately, from such an impertinence was attributable in good part to the painful memory of the blunder I'd made by asking Agricus to explain his presence in Domitia Lucilla's house; but in even greater part it was a function of my steadily growing awareness that Marcus's actions, though often incomprehensible, were seldom if ever devoid of purpose.

Winter yielded to spring, oh, so grudgingly that year, with the first part of April not just wetter than March but distinctly colder as well. As the Ides approached, the rain abated, but rare was the day when enough sunlight pierced the cloud rack to offset the chill winds swirling down from the north and northeast.

My ever-mounting fever of impatience did not offset them either, but like an ague merely caused me to shiver the more. Day after day I scanned the skies, searching for some sign that more temperate weather was near at hand; then night after night I cursed the little clouds of frost that continued to form as I breathed out my fretful sighs.

My impatience was irrational, for the date of our departure was in no way contingent upon the docility of the elements. Apart from unforeseen problems, in fact, that date was more or less predetermined. We couldn't leave Rome until after Marcus's birthday on the sixth before the Kalends of May, and it would have been unlucky to leave during the Ludi Florales, the festival that began two days later. Thus, unless we were willing to delay our departure until the six-day games ended, the fifth before the Kalends was the only date open to us. Since we were not at all willing to accept such a delay, Marcus took the wise precaution of acquainting the household auspex and haruspex with the details of our plans. They thereupon consulted their respective bird calls and sheep entrails and very obligingly reported to Domitia Lucilla that the date we'd chosen for the commencement of our journey was "incomparably auspicious." That clinched the matter.

Thus the fifth before the Kalends it was going to be, whether the sun shone or the wind blew or the rain fell; so my impatience to feel spring's warmth in the air must have been a function of all the blunders I'd made while fending off winter's cold. Nonsensical though it seems, I'm driven to the conclusion that I'd come to associate my estrangement from Drusilla and Annia with the time of year during which the ruptures occurred. It was not enough, accordingly, for me to be quit of the scene of those calamities; I ached to be free of their air and sky as well.

Eagerly though I'd anticipated it, the eve of our departure proved to be a day of decidedly mixed feelings for me. I was happy, on the one hand, that our preparations were completed and our journey was about to begin; but I was also very apprehensive about the dinner in honor of Marcus's birthday that was to take place in the evening. The cause of my apprehension was Annia, of course, for she could no sooner absent herself from the festivities than could I. It was not merely her cousin's birthday, but his leave-taking as well; and as Annia was herself about to set off with her mother and siblings to join her father, the Proconsul, in Ephesus, the party for Marcus represented the last opportunity that she and her Roman relatives would have to congregate together for at least a space of years. This circumstance served to diminish somewhat the magnitude of her impact on me, for so many relatives were present that it was tolerably easy for me to avoid her (impossible though I found it to keep my eyes on anyone else).

Ye gods but she looked stunning that night—virginal yet lubricious, demure yet carnally inclined. Every so often some admiring fellow would undertake to flatter her, and as a blush came shimmering to her cheeks, a rill of delighted laughter would spill from between her lips. Such enchanting intimations of approval invariably produced a stream of additional compliments, and as Annia acknowledged them one by one, an almost feverish glow of excitement began to suffuse her features. With her eyebrows arched and her breathing shallow, she would drink down her devotee's praises; and her eyes, which had been sparkling, took on a glaze that was very like wonder. She plainly wasn't accustomed to being barraged by adulation, and it's possible, I suppose, that she had just that evening become aware of the power her beauty conferred. Regardless of when she became conscious of it, the process of exercising it was clearly one that afforded her exquisite pleasure.

Oh, how I yearned to submit to that power!

I wanted her—unreasonably, immoderately, ineffectually, and too late. The boundlessness of my desire for her was matched only by the point-edness of her indifference to me. I felt at last that she was well worth risking death for, and if anyone had been percipient enough to tell me that by giving rein to such feelings I was merely seeking to deprive myself of the joys implicit in my forthcoming journey, I would have laughed—or wept—in his face.

Suitably miserable, I mounted Incitatus the next morning and rode for what proved to be the last time through Domitia Lucilla's front gates. On my left was Agricus, looking insufferably smug atop a chestnut stallion, and behind the two of us rode Marcus and Dracena, the latter's presence being attributable to both the Emperor's dictates and our own common sense. The open road was no place for boys accoutered as we were—with horses and satchels and not a few coins—to be traveling unescorted, especially if one such boy was in line to succeed to the Principate. None of us objected to Dracena's presence, certainly, and one of us at least was more than glad of it.

We made our way down the southern flank of the Caelian and turned east, passing beneath the Marcian Aqueduct and through the Capenine Gate. We were now on the Via Appia; our journey had officially begun.

And begun slowly, I might add, because the Queen of the Roads was, as usual, thronged. Ahead of us in the outbound lane empty farmers' wagons in endless procession rolled toward the new-risen sun, their pre-dawn cargoes of food and flowers already on display in market stalls throughout the City. Inbound came a no less imposing cavalcade of builders' *plaustra*, their axles groaning beneath the dead weight of gravel and stone. Pitted against these two lumbering columns, travelers on horse-back, like those in litters and carts, had little choice but to plod along at the wagons' torpid pace. By the Appia's third milestone, however, the Latin, Tusculine, and Ardeatine forks had siphoned off some of the traffic, and we began to make slightly better time.

Not that we were in any great hurry, of course; our first day's destination was barely six hours' ride from the Caelian. Still, it was a relief to be able to ease up a bit on the reins, and our horses, who'd understandably been rather skittish while hemmed in by rickety carts and lurching *plaustra*, calmed down appreciably as the volume of traffic continued to abate.

At the third milestone the massively ostentatious tomb of Crassus's daughter-in-law Caecilia Metella loomed up like a citadel on our left. This mausoleum, Marcus informed us in mordant tones, had been conceived not so much as a tribute to the decedent's memory as a monument to her survivors' grief, the sincerity of which was reaffirmed every time one of them reflected on the monstrosity's cost.

And with that as his point of departure, Marcus proceeded for the next few miles to maintain a running commentary on almost every tomb we passed, a commentary that was not merely witty and informative but, to my mind at least, quite remarkable. It turned out that his family had been connected in one way or another with just about every person or group whose monument stood beside the road, and in a few cases he himself had been personally acquainted with the deceased. In most cases the connection was far more remote, but whether the ashes belonged to the freedmen of some senator who'd been a political ally of Marcus's grandfather or to the wife of some knight who owed his rank to Marcus's uncle, there was always some link, however tenuous, between those who'd passed on and the youthful patrician who would one day have charge of their posterity. It crossed my mind then that since I, too, had ties to Marcus, each such link now extended to me; and a strange feeling of fulfillment welled up inside me, as if I'd been initiated into some mystery, or accorded some special grace.

Needless to say, such a feeling somewhat undermined my efforts to be gloomy; and the elements conspired against me too, because a morning mist had by now transformed the April sunlight into a gently pervasive radiance that wreathed every tomb, every tree, and every traveler with a mantle of chastened gold. Assailed by such insidious splendor, I started feeling happy in spite of myself, and it's a tribute to the fundamental mopishness of my temperament that I didn't come right out and smile.

[AUGUST 30TH]

I ran again this morning, without intolerable discomfort, then sponged myself off, and had my usual barley-cake-and-sausage repast. I'd just about finished eating when Decius and Rullo came into the house with the disturbing news that there were signs of rust in the wheat growing on the far side of the river. Immediately I thought of Robigus and the mysterious workings of coincidence; but when rust appears in your fields, there's not much time for rumination. I was out the door in an instant, my mind intent on gauging the direction of the wind. Rullo and Decius agreed with me that it was blowing from the southeast, so we hurriedly collected some pitch and torchwood and set off at a fast clip toward the Aro. We'd gone no more than a hundred paces, however, when we noticed a horseman coming down the river road from the direction of the Aurelia. He was a tall fellow, imposingly erect, whose hair and beard were so dark that they almost glistened. He was clearly too old to be a *tabellarius* of the Imperial Post, and the fact that he wore no uniform or insignia all but eliminated the possibility that he'd been dispatched by the Emperor. Still, I felt certain that he was on his way to see me, and, sure enough, he turned left at the fork and came cantering up the road we were descending.

"I'm looking for the knight Lucius Celer," he said as he drew near us, smoothly bringing his stallion to a halt.

Hard and rough as his voice was, it seemed almost meek and gentle in comparison with his face, which reminded me immediately of Dracena's. The fellow might well have passed as Dracena's double, in fact: his eyes were just as cold, his lips as thin, his nose as flattened, and his scowl as fierce. Of course, my friend the *singularis* had, pursuant to regulations, kept himself clean-shaven; and against this horseman's luxuriant mat of curls he could have opposed only a meager crop of slicked-down strands. In all other respects, though, the resemblance was well-nigh uncanny, and I think it was the great affection I'd long ago felt for Dracena that today led me to speak to this redoubtable stranger with less than my usual reserve.

"I am Lucius Celer, sir, and I welcome you to my farm. Alas, I have a rather pressing matter to attend to at the moment, so if you'll be good enough to continue on to my house and have one of the women there provide you with some refreshment, I'll join you at my very first opportunity."

The horseman glanced at the torchwood and jugs of pitch we were carrying and said, "Found a trace of rust, have you?"

"We think we may have, yes. Are you familiar with the problem?"

"I should say so, and vice versa," he replied with a bleak smile. "Maybe you'd like me to have a look."

"Why, thank you, that's very kind," I responded, and almost before I'd finished speaking he had in one smooth motion dismounted.

"Would you mind if the horse waited at your house?" he asked me.

"No, of course not," I answered him, whereupon he gave the animal a casual slap on the rump, which sent it galloping off up the hill.

"Hadn't we better get going?" he said as the three of us stood there staring at the stallion's retreating form.

"We had better indeed," I replied, and we resumed our march.

"My name's Junius Aemilius Spaeto," the fellow said as we stepped briskly along a few feet ahead of Decius and Rullo. "I'm one of Gaius Aemilius Placidus's overseers."

I almost stopped dead in my tracks, but wisely kept walking and started thinking instead.

"Something the matter?" Spaeto inquired.

"No no, nothing at all. It's just that, well, I'm embarrassed to confess it, but I wasn't expecting Gaius Placidus to send someone so soon."

"Oh, he's a great believer in expedition," Spaeto said without the least trace of admiration.

I glanced over my shoulder at Rullo, who, the gods be thanked, was intently discussing the rust problem with Decius. Turning back to Spaeto, I said, "To be quite honest with you, I haven't yet told my familia of my plans to sell them. . . ."

"That present something of a problem, does it?"

"Well, yes and no. That is, it occurs to me that if you would consider remaining here as my guest for a day or two, you could actually watch my people as they go about their work. . . ."

"I was instructed to do that anyway," Spaeto announced, oblivious, or indifferent, to the presumption implicit in such a statement.

"Ah, splendid," I said. "Might I impose on you, in that case, to keep the purpose of your visit here, uh, unspoken?"

He looked down at me with that fierce mien of his, but then in a perfectly accommodating voice replied, "It's your farm."

I took that as an affirmative response.

I was so shaken by the overseer's unexpected arrival that when the preliminary diagnosis of rust was confirmed, I almost overlooked the need to appear more distressed than I felt. I remembered in time, however, and though I didn't manage to shed any counterfeit tears while watching the infested wheat burn, I did succeed in looking desperately concerned while we inspected the remainder of the crop. I guess, though, that I've become a farmer at heart over the course of the years, because when Rullo confirmed my impression that there was no sign of blight on this side of the river, my sigh of relief was as genuine as it was deep.

With my anxieties about rust allayed for the moment, I can once more concentrate on worrying about my slaves. The time is fast approaching when I'll have to tell them they're to be sold, and I heartily dread the prospect. Meanwhile, I have this formidable fellow Spaeto here taking their measure with his gimlet eyes. Do they suspect, I wonder, that he's observing them.

Does he suspect that I'm observing him?

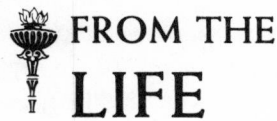# FROM THE
LIFE

51

As the sun climbed higher, the morning mists began to burn away, and by the time we reached the eighth milestone all that was left of them was a milky softness in the unblemished blue of the sky. Now the whole verdant amphitheater of the Alban Hills stood revealed to us, its slopes dotted with stately villas whose marble colonnades and russet tile roofs gleamed like opals amid dark green spires of cypress and pale ocher swaths of plowed soil. From out of the west a quickening breeze came riffling through the poppy-strewn meadows that flanked the road, carrying with it a scent of pear blossoms that blended deliciously with the vernal bouquet of spear grass and the fragrance of new-mown hay. Indifferent to these dulcet aromas, Incitatus trudged listlessly along toward the Mons Albanus, a trail of malodorous droppings his only response to the gentle splendor of the morning.

At the twelfth milestone we entered Bovillae, the Appia's first post station, and paused at the old limestone *mansio* there to let our horses drink. Just beyond the town came the first of the highway's major intersections, with the route to Castrimoenium curving off on our left toward the hills and the road to Antium branching off on our right toward the sea. After this crossroads the Appia began its long, gradual ascent toward the upper reaches of the Alban Mount, the massive walls of Domitian's country estate dominating its eastern embankment from the sixteenth milestone on. Sybaritic in conception, Neronian in conceit, this monument to that mistrustful Emperor's profligacy overawed the landscape it surveyed; and when, after half an hour's steady ride, we emerged from the villa's shadow into the dazzling sunlight of the Alban heights, the sensation we experienced was one of disproportionate relief.

Looking behind us, it was now possible to discern the marble-crowned hills of the City almost twenty miles to the north, while ahead of us stretched the long, unswerving viaduct that would bring us within an hour to the ancient Latin *municipium* of Aricia. It was as we neared the far end of this viaduct that we began our encounter with that infamous legion of the lame, the halt, the shiftless, and the indolent known euphemistically as "the beggars of the Arician vale." Taking advantage of the narrowness of the roadstead and the steepness of its final grade, these noisome mendicants pressed in on both our flanks and exhorted us in a most peremptory manner to honor the gods through the medium of our *liberalitas*. To say that they were importunate would be like describing a wounded boar as miffed, and it came as no surprise to me when Marcus said that the local aediles were often obliged to drive the whole lot of them off the roadway by force of arms. Shielded by Dracena's menacing presence, however, we ran their gauntlet without any serious incident; although Dracena discovered later in the day that someone at some point had relieved him of his short-sword's silver pommel.

Once in Aricia we purchased some dates, some cheese, two loaves of bread, and a sextarius of Alban wine at the market adjacent to the Appia's second post station; and thus provisioned we pushed on the last few miles to our first day's stopping place—the estate just outside Lanuvium where Titus Antoninus, Proconsul of Asia, had been born half a century before. This estate was modest compared to Lorium: no more than a thousand jugera, and had belonged at the time of Titus's birth to his maternal grandfather, the consul Arrius Antoninus. Since then it had passed through Titus's mother to Titus himself; and who knew but one day it might pass to his daughter Annia, or even to his distinguished nephew by marriage. At the time, though, Marcus was merely a wayfarer there, as were we who rode with him, and as Annia would be, too, in a few days time.

Did that qualify as another coincidence? Not quite. But it was connection enough to occasion a twinge of despair.

A reception committee of sorts was on hand to welcome us to the estate, thanks, no doubt, to Annia's mother, who'd sent word of our impending visit to her caretaker. We found that ancient specimen waiting for us at the villa's gate along with a wide-eyed, thumb-sucking boy no older than five and a mongrel so far advanced in pregnancy that she could barely sit up. This motley triad had obviously been keeping vigil by the gateway for quite some while, but apart from the dog—whose tail started wagging—they reacted to our arrival in a manner so matter-of-fact as to verge on utter apathy.

Hand in hand with the child, the old man led us to the villa's main residence, which had apparently been boarded up for the winter. Aside from the kitchen, only one section of the house was ready for habitation, and since that section consisted of public rooms exclusively, a degree of improvisation had been called for in the arrangement of our accommodations. Thus we found four oxhide pallets set out for us in the main dining hall, along with a generous supply of bedclothes and towels. The informality of the barrackslike setup was much to Marcus's liking, and for Agricus, Dracena, and me such quarters afforded a near-patrician standard of comfort. The hall was large, light, and airy, for one thing, in marked contrast to the cramped dinginess of the cubicula we were accustomed to; and it overlooked the Roman campagna, for another, providing a view from its south-facing colonnade that literally stopped my breath for a moment the first time I took it all in.

Before me in the near-to-middle distance a patchwork of vineyards, woodlands, and fields sloped gently away toward the sea, its several components forming a harmonious mosaic of subtle greens and browns. Beyond this bucolic prospect a broader vista unfolded, with purple mountain ramparts to the east, slate-blue ocean to the west, and the vast emerald plane of the Pomptine Marshes in between. Rising from the marshes' southwestern extremity, a massive promontory stood astride the far horizon, its contours barely discernible through the shimmering midday haze. This shadowy eminence, Marcus informed us, was renowned as the island of Aeaea, the fabled realm of the goddess Circe, who'd transformed Odysseus' shipmates into swine before succumbing herself to the wily hero's charms. In actual fact, my friend continued, it was not an island at all, but a peninsula; and its name was not Aeaea but Circeii.

Of course I wasn't about to question the accuracy of Marcus's statements, but I knew in my heart that they somehow fell short of the truth. For island or not, the distant colossus had effectively cast a spell on me, a spell so potent that, gazing out at its looming presence, I all at once felt the spirit of Eurydice take wing from its crest and come flying toward us on the southwest breeze. In my spellbound condition, I must have breathed out some sort of prayer, because the wind, which since our arrival had been flowing in a fairly steady stream, suddenly rose to gale force and went howling down the length of the colonnade. "An airy demon," Dracena muttered apprehensively as the squall abruptly subsided, and I could readily sympathize with his unease. We stood silent a while in the wake of Eurydice's passage, then gazed once again at the witch's domain. Out there on the horizon, it held both the sea and the land in thrall, with only the sky undaunted. High above its massive shoulders the sun danced defiance on the meridian; and it took a soul as impious as Agricus to sully the sacral moment with a curt declaration of "Lunch!"

Ignoring my angry glare, he shouted down to the slaves in the kitchen courtyard for some drinking bowls and water, which were duly brought up to us. Seating ourselves on the ledge of the colonnade, we mixed our wine and consumed our provisions while our legs dangled blithely in the air. Then, with the sun and the breeze washing over us, we considered how we might best pass the afternoon.

"Why don't we go look at the ships," Marcus suggested.

"The *ships?*" Agricus responded irritably. "Why, the sea's at least four hours' ride."

Marcus smiled at him. "I mean the ships anchored in Diana's lake, old gruff-and-grum, which is barely half an hour from where we sit."

"Would it surprise you to learn that I don't know what you're talking about?" Agricus inquired in a testy voice.

"The surprise would be hearing you admit it," Marcus retorted.

Even Agricus had to laugh. "Well, I *do* admit it!" he said. "Now please be so good as to enlighten me."

"I'll do better than that, dear fellow," Marcus answered him. And after ascertaining with a glance that Dracena and I sought enlightenment too, he got to his feet and led us all out to the stables.

We made our way back to the Appia, rode a mile or so toward Rome, then turned onto a steep and narrow woodland track. This brought us, after a quarter of an hour's climb, to a ridge crest that proved to be the rim of a long-extinct volcano. Far below us in what once must have been the fiery depths of the caldera, Diana's mirror, Lake Nemorensis, glittered turquoise in the afternoon sun.

"I don't see any ships," Agricus announced indignantly.

"I don't either," Marcus replied, a secretive smile playing over his features. "But you must admit it's a lovely sight."

"I didn't ride all this way just to look at scenery."

"No, of course you didn't; feel free to avert your gaze."

And with that Marcus guided his horse onto a muddy trail that zig-zagged its way down the crater's precipitous slopes. Dracena and I immediately set out after him, and Agricus, after the obligatory display of recalcitrance, came cursing along behind us.

The western quadrant of the crater's basin was already in shadow by the time we reached the lakeside, but Marcus led us northward along the shore and we soon regained the sun. There was still no trace of a boat anywhere on the water's surface; indeed, it wasn't until we were within hailing distance of Diana's sanctuary that we saw any signs that boats might once have been present. Flanked by two lines of ornate bronze mooring posts, a crumbling concrete mole extended out perhaps a hundred paces from the shore. Nothing man-made floated beside it, however, just a dead mouse and some rotting fragments of wood.

"It looks like your ships have sailed off to Taprobana, Marco," Agricus jeered.

"That would be a most remarkable feat on their part," Marcus replied, dismounting smoothly and striding off up the ramp of the dilapidated dock.

Dismounting, the three of us followed him, picking our way gingerly among the cracks and creases in the concrete. We were about halfway along when he reached the far end and turned to face us. A smile of undisguised amusement spread over his features as he stood there observing our laborious progress. As we drew nearer he called out, "Prepare to be purged of unseemly doubts, ye apostles of incredulity."

"Oh, get on with it!" Agricus snarled.

Marcus, his amused smile yielding to one of outright merriment, extended his arms at a slight angle from his body and pointed to the surface of the lake. "Behold!" he intoned portentously.

We just stared at him and shot each other glances of unease.

"Be-*hold!*" he repeated with even more emphasis, thrusting his hands down toward the water on either side of him as if he were a sorcerer invoking some wraith.

So we stared at him again, until curiosity overcame bewilderment sufficiently to start us moving toward the side.

Always beaming, he watched us edge our way over and peer down into the depths.

"By the gods!" Dracena exclaimed in a whisper, as the hairs on the back of my neck stood up.

Even Agricus succumbed to amazement, fairly shouting out the question all three of us had in mind: "What in the name of Neptune is *that?*"

"Why, a ship, dear fellow. Whatever else?"

"Furies take you, Marco! Stop playing coy, and tell us what we're looking at."

"You mean I've finally managed to arouse your curiosity?"

"It's my animosity you're arousing, damn you. Now tell us . . . what . . . that . . . *is!*"

"That, my beloved Agricus, is nothing more or less than one of Gaius Caligula's Imperial barges."

"*One* of his barges? You mean there are others like this?"

"There is one other like this," Marcus replied, his eyes atwinkle, "and it's over here on my left."

If the exaggerated caution with which we'd negotiated the length of the crumbling mole had been comical to behold, the headlong recklessness with which we now traversed its width must have seemed downright hilarious—especially since one of us charged across the pier in such feverish haste that he very nearly propelled both himself and his boyhood companion into the water. Only Dracena, with his quick reflexes and powerful arms, preserved us from that chilly denouement; while Marcus, to his eternal discredit, sank to his knees in the grip of indecorous laughter.

"Oh, shut up, Marco!" Agricus shouted, after cursing me roundly for my clumsiness. Marcus just kept on laughing, though, and Agricus, rather than rail at him, turned his attention back to the colossus whose superstructure loomed like a leviathan some ten feet below the surface of the lake. "What are they *doing* here?" he asked when Marcus's hilarity finally subsided.

"Preparing to sail for Taprobana, I should imagine," Marcus replied, wiping the tears from his cheeks.

Agricus gave him a look of disgust. "When you're through being precious," he said, "may we impose on you for the answers to one or two questions?"

"By all means. What is it you don't understand?"

For the first time in my life I saw Agricus's jaw muscles working in response to mere verbal provocation. But he soon unclenched his teeth sufficiently to ask, "Why are there two Imperial barges sitting on the bottom of this lake?"

"Well, that's rather a long story, my friend. Are you sure you've got the patience to listen to it?"

"If I get bored, I'll masturbate," Agricus sneered.

With a playful grimace, Marcus responded, "In that case I'll be brief."

He rose from his knees and began walking at a leisurely pace back toward the landward end of the mole. "As you'll notice," he said, signaling with a wave of his arm that we should accompany him, "the barges extend the full length of this dock—nearly a hundred paces. And although it isn't possible to confirm the fact visually from here, I hope you'll take my word for it that, given the width of their decks, you once could have walked from that line of mooring posts over there on the right to this line over here on the left—a distance of almost two hundred feet—without even getting your toes wet! Now what do you think of that?"

"*I* think that I'm beginning to feel an urge to play with myself," Agricus answered. "Do *you* think that you could dispense with the statistics long enough to give us the historical facts?"

"I'm interested in the statistics, Agricus," I objected; only to be squelched by a cruel, "Of course you are, Lucio; they spring from your master's lips."

With my ears burning, I shrank into humiliated silence, and the sympathy in Marcus's eyes only added to my sense of shame.

"You're in an uncommonly truculent mood this afternoon, my friend," he said to Agricus. "Does being away from Rome disagree with you?"

For a long moment the two of them stood motionless, assessing each other from the citadels of their respective wills. I'd never before heard Marcus threaten anyone, even obliquely, and I felt a warm rush of love for him for coming to my defense (although by doing so he'd unwittingly confirmed the validity of Agricus's gibe).

"Am I being truculent?" my adversary asked disingenuously. "I can't imagine how I could have conveyed such an unfortunate impression."

"Very forcefully is how," Marcus answered him in clipped tones. "But I'm pleased to hear that it's merely an impression."

"And I'm pleased that you're pleased, dear comrade, since your pleasure is always uppermost in my thoughts."

Again there was a moment of cool mutual appraisal. "Try considering the pleasure of others as well, then, if pleasing me is truly your foremost desire."

"Oh, it is, Marcus . . . and I do on occasion consider the pleasure of others—more scrupulously than you might imagine."

Marcus gazed at him with an unmollified expression, but relented finally and resumed his old self-effacing grin. "I believe I was relating the history of these barges," he said.

"No," Agricus interjected, eager to demonstrate that he'd yielded no ground. "You were merely expatiating on their dimensions."

"Ah, so I hadn't yet got to the best parts of the story."

"Nor even to the good parts, if you'll forgive my candor."

Marcus bowed deeply. "I'll pardon you your candor most readily, but can you ever find it in your heart to forgive me my prolixity?"

"Done!" Agricus responded, returning Marcus's bow and adding, "Feel free to go on at the greatest possible length; I promise to keep my hands well clear of my genitals."

This remark seemed to bring their confrontation full circle somehow, and as the tension dissipated in smiles, Marcus took up the thread of his narration, with all his customary rhetorical finesse.

"The Emperor Gaius, ever jealous of his preeminence, became extremely upset one day when somebody happened to mention the so-called King of Diana's grove. Gaius was aware, of course, that a sanctuary consecrated to the virgin huntress existed here, but the details of her ancient cult worship were as unfamiliar to him as they probably are to the three of you. He learned from his courtiers that Diana's high priest was called Rex Nemorensis, a title that struck the demented Emperor as decidedly subversive, particularly when he considered the proximity of the rival monarch's dominions to his own inviolable sanctuary on the Palatine. By what right did some obscure lakeside priest presume to style himself a king, Caligula demanded to know. And he was duly informed that because the high priesthood of the sacred grove had since time immemorial been the prize of individual combat, it had also immemorially carried with it the honorific title Rex.

"As you might expect, this information served merely to aggravate Gaius's anxieties; but his courtiers hastened to reassure him by pointing out that Diana's high priesthood was a prize of such little account that only runaway slaves could vie for it. In fact, the only real benefit the so-called kingship of the grove conferred on whoever 'reigned' there was immunity from recapture and punishment. That was why, in ancient times at least, all fugitive slaves who fancied themselves proficient with the sword used to converge on the sanctuary as Diana's feast day drew near. There, starting on the night of the last full moon before the Ides of August, lots would be drawn; and he whose lot was chosen would be permitted to enter the grove and do battle with the incumbent high priest. If the reigning Rex killed him, another contender for the office would take up the challenge the following night—and so on, if necessary, until the eve of Diana's feast. If the Rex was still alive by then, he would be accorded another year of rule; but almost invariably the wounds inflicted by the succession of unsuccessful candidates would take their toll, and on the Ides of August a proud new King would be crowned.

"Hearing this account of the primitive ritual, the Emperor Gaius felt greatly relieved, since even he could suffer the existence of a rival sovereign whose reign was destined to last no more than a year. Imagine his dismay, then, when he was told that the incumbent King had been reigning since the time of Augustus. 'Augustus has been dead these twenty-five years!' he shrieked, terrified by the prospect that some invincible demigod had taken possession of the sacred grove and stood ready now to challenge him. But his fears, as usual, proved groundless, just as the reasons for the reigning King's longevity proved mundane.

"What had happened was that the bond between master and slave had undergone tremendous change in the centuries since the cult first flourished, and most particularly in the hundred or so years just preceding Caligula's Principate. Much of this change had been codified, moreover, for example in the lex Aelia Sentia of Augustus. And even as the master's absolute power over his familia was being subjected to successive legal restraints, so, too, the practice of manumission was being accorded ever greater legal respect. The ultimate consequence of all these changes was that fewer and fewer slaves felt the need to run away, and those few who did flee were rarely desperate enough to trade their fugitive status for a fighting chance at one scant year of grace.

"None of this was of interest to Gaius, however; all he knew was that there was a king of sorts within three hours' ride of the City, and that this king was senior to him by at least a quarter century. The situation was manifestly intolerable, and Gaius gave orders that it should be rectified forthwith. The man to whom he gave these orders was none other than his wily old uncle Claudius, who played the fool well enough in his time to survive his nephew and actually become one.

"Caligula's plan was megalomaniacally simple: on Diana's feast day, the King of the grove was to be 'deposed' and his place taken by the Divine Gaius's personal champion, a gladiator by the name of Pertinax, who would reign as the Emperor's surrogate. In conjunction with this sacrilegious act of usurpation, the goddess Diana, in the person of her cult image, was to make a formal renunciation of her virginity and apply for the honor of becoming one of Gaius's immortal consorts, pledging as her dowry dominion over the sacred grove.

"Poor Uncle Claudius: it was his job to organize a triumphal celebration of these blasphemous activities, and even though it was July already, woe betide him if all the necessary preparations were not completed by the Ides of August. The logistical difficulties were formidable enough, but Caligula in his madness soon added to his uncle's list of labors a task that verged on the impossible.

"It seemed only right to the Emperor that the goddess Diana should receive him and make the requisite gestures of submission well before he arrived outside her sanctuary. And what better or more public spot could there be for such an act of obeisance than the unsullied middle of the lake? There could be none, of course, and Caligula promptly presented his uncle with a demand for two luxuriously appointed barges of predictably grandiose dimensions—one for the goddess and the other, slightly larger and more sumptuous, for himself.

"At first Uncle Claudius despaired; he even went so far as to plead with Caligula to kill him then and there. But the Emperor threatened him with far, far worse than death if he failed in his sacred duty. So Claudius scurried off in panic and began his forlorn struggle to accomplish the near impossible.

"Improbably enough, he succeeded, although the seaworthiness of the vessels he managed to provide was in no way comparable to their magnificence. They survived a single transit of the lake, however, and having served their intended purpose in Caligula's odious spectacle of profanation, they were made fast to this very mole, which, like the vessels themselves, had been constructed especially for the occasion.

"Less than six months after this disgraceful exhibition of impiety, Ca-

ligula was assassinated and the title of Princeps was thrust upon his astonished uncle. A more or less inevitable period of uncertainty and ferment
ensued, but when it was over old Claudius's position was secure; and one
of his first official acts after consolidating his power was to restore Diana's
grove to its ancient sanctity.

"Claudius saw no reason to wait till the next Ides of August, for in his
opinion the gladiator Pertinax, having totally ignored prescribed ritual
when he cut down the incumbent rex, was nothing but a false pretender
to the high priesthood and an arrant intruder in the grove. In early March,
accordingly, less than two months after Gaius's murder, he gave orders
that a centurion in his personal guard, a mountainous German—and
former slave—by the name of Arminius, should be schooled in the rites
of the Nemorensian cult and sent to do battle in the sanctuary. Whether
Arminius actually observed the ritual when the time came is open to
question, but he did most definitely separate Pertinax's body from his
head. This was a source of great satisfaction to Claudius, who undertook
to expunge all trace of Caligula's obscene pretensions by personally heaving a thirty-pound stone through the flimsy bottom of each of those
stupendous barges he'd striven so frenziedly to build. Once this purgative
deed was done, he left the grove to Arminius, who settled down to a
long and peaceful retirement in a woodland setting pleasantly reminiscent
of his native Germania. Gaius's barges, meanwhile, settled down to a
long and peaceful process of disintegration, a process that continues to
this very day."

We stood silent for some moments after Marcus finished his narration,
pondering the strange interplay of sanctity and insanity that had marked
the history of this ancient domain. In my own case, fascination with the
Imperial barges had been entirely supplanted by curiosity about the sanctuary and its servile High Priest, and I made no effort to disguise my
eagerness to explore the interior of the grove.

"Is there still some sort of king reigning in there?" Agricus asked, as
we turned to look at the line of gnarled oak trees on the hillside above.

Behind that leafy barricade, the sanctuary lay secluded in silence.

"I can't really say," Marcus replied.

"Let's scare up one of the resident priests and find out."

"I don't think there are any resident priests nowadays, Agricus. Such
priests as there are probably live in the village, if this shrine's like most
of the other old ones in Latium."

"Well then, let's just go on up and see for ourselves."

Marcus frowned and shook his head. "We'd better not trespass without
knowing what's what," he said. "Why don't we go back to Aricia, have

a bite to eat, and inquire about visiting the grove. The moon's almost full tonight, so if no problems arise, we can come back here at nightfall and see Diana's sanctuary in just the way a candidate for the high priesthood would have seen it."

This proposal met with our unanimous approval, approval that—in Agricus's case at least—was expressed with an altogether abnormal degree of enthusiasm.

 # FROM THE
JOURNAL

52

[AUGUST 31ST]

After passing a fitful night, I rose at the first hint of daybreak and set off at an easy pace down our road. At the river fork I turned left for a change, instead of toward the altar to Robigus—not because I'd recently had more than my fill of that vexatious little numen, but because a left turn would take me toward the sea; and the sea, I felt, might supply a remedy for the vague sense of disquietude that had denied me the benefit of a good night's rest.

Once across the Aurelia I gradually lenthened my stride, and by the time I reached Fregenae I was moving along at a clip that could only be deemed immoderate for a man of my accumulated years. Down the Decumanus I galloped, with padlocked shops and shuttered windows the only witnesses to my passage; and I was fairly flying when I plunged into the pine grove that skirted the far end of the street.

Though sunrise was barely half an hour off by then, an umbral gloom still prevailed amid the trees; but I had no need to slacken my pace, because just enough daylight filtered down through the pine boughs for me to see where I was going. After fewer than fifty paces I broke clear of the grove and went bounding over the soft sandy beach toward the water's edge. There firmer footing awaited me, and in the grip of a kind of madness I launched myself northward along the shoreline, running as I'd run once at Delphi, in the first giddy fullness of my youth.

But to have persisted long in such violent exertions would have proved the last reckless folly of my old age, and so even though I felt strong enough to keep on going for a good long while, I forced myself to slow down to a walk.

What had come over me, I wondered, as I strode along the beach, noting with no small degree of pride that I wasn't too badly winded. What inner demon had caused me to take wing like that? Was it the fugitive in my runner's heart? And if so, from what did I believe I was escaping?

Or, rather, from whom?

From all those who might tend to slow me down?

From all those who might encumber me when the time comes to flee?

From all those I will soon be delivering into the charge of a hard-eyed stranger?

From all those I am abandoning?

Behold! Father Nestor, wherever you are—I have just solved the riddle of my nocturnal malaise.

It was shame that kept me from my rest—abject and well-deserved self-reproach, unleavened by even a granule of prospective repentance. And it was shame, most probably, that sent me charging through village and pine grove like a satyr intent on a nymph. It was shame, I daresay, that led me to act the part of Mercury and go skittering along the shore at full extension—an arguably suicidal and indisputably asinine piece of behavior. And it is shame that I am feeling right now, as I contemplate the uncertain fate of those who have served me so well and so long, the fate to which I, their protector, am subjecting them, and of which the dark-visaged Junius Spaeto will be the minister.

That formidable gentleman was awaiting me when, shortly after sunrise, I trudged back into the barnyard, my overtaxed legs growing stiffer by the moment. Had I come all the way home on foot, I believe I'd have been suffering considerable discomfort by that time; but having been foolish enough to ignore my body's limitations in the first place, I'd then been wise enough not to compound my foolishness, and on reentering Fregenae had procured a ride on a farmer's cart as far as the Via Aurelia.

"I saw you set off this morning," Spaeto said, somewhat to my surprise. "And then it came to me that you must be *the* Lucius Celer."

I gazed at him, more than a little bit mystified. "*The* Lucius Celer?"

"The runner, I mean—the *periodonikes*."

Flattered through I was by this unwonted nod of recognition, it served only to increase my sense of mystification, because not one Roman in a hundred cares a fig for Greek athletics, and not one in a thousand knows the Greek word for an athlete who can boast of victories at the four great Panhellenic festivals. "You must have a good memory for athletic minutiae," I said, "because whatever semblance of renown Lucius Celer the runner might once have enjoyed, he's been rusticating in well-deserved obscurity for more years now than a dog has fleas."

Spaeto frowned at this, as if such protestations on my part amounted to little more than an indulgence in false modesty. "I saw you win the boys' dolichos at the fourteenth Capitoline Games," he announced in a tone of almost sacerdotal solemnity. "I was only seven years old at the time, but I've never forgotten that race or the glory of your victory."

"Neither have I," I confessed as I struggled to maintain my composure.

Spaeto could not have known it, of course, but that glorious victory I won at age sixteen had been but a prelude to the most agonizing defeat of my entire life.

For some strange reason I felt an impulse to tell him that, to take him into my confidence. Naturally I refrained from doing so; I'd only just met the man, after all. As the day wore on, though, and the two of us toured the farm together to watch my slaves at work, it became clear to me that our relationship had shifted somehow to a slightly different footing. I don't know why, really—apart from his one short burst of loquacity in regard to the race I'd run, Junius Spaeto has remained an impenetrably taciturn stranger. But there's a solidity about the fellow, an absence of cant, that makes me want to confide in him, ridiculous as that may seem.

Perhaps it's just wishful thinking on my part. Perhaps I *need* to like him in order to assuage the guilt I feel about betraying my familia's trust in me. Low as is my opinion of myself, I refuse to believe that I'm drawn to him simply because he voiced some admiration for my bygone prowess as a runner. No, there must be something else about him, some compelling inner quality that I'm responding to.

I have to remain wary, though; it may well be that all I see in him is the strength of character in which I myself am so deficient. It's a common failing of human nature—to stand in awe of someone merely because he happens to display the one particular virtue one finds most lacking in oneself.

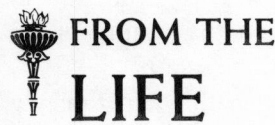
The Golden Boar Tavern stood hard by the Appia's second post station in Aricia and did a thriving business, thanks largely to the ceaseless procession of wayfarers who travel the Queen of the Roads. We arrived shortly after sunset, and after feasting ourselves on cooked beans and onions asked the prosperous-looking *caupo* where we could find a votary of Diana's shrine.

"At the far end of the table you just rose from," he informed us, pointing out a disheveled, emaciated, sallow-faced individual who was either well advanced in years or in extremely poor health. His name was Ascanius, the *caupo* told us. He was a dull-witted freedman who made a meager living as a tanner (which explained his sickly appearance) and who earned a few extra sesterces from time to time by snaring the wild dogs and rabbits to be sacrificed to Diana each month on the rising of the full moon. "When I was a boy they offered her deer and boar, like they're supposed to," the *caupo* went on in a mournful voice. "She was worshiped properly in those days. . . . But now all these eastern cults are in fashion, and the old gods are being scanted." He paused to ruminate on this sad state of affairs, then resumed in a tone of mounting indignation that led me to suspect that the ever greater vogue many oriental creeds were enjoying had more than once roused him to obloquy in the past. "It's what comes of allowing the Palatine to be overrun by a passel of eunuch Greeklings," he declared, teetering incautiously on the brink of sedition. "And I'll wager it won't be long now before the goddess finds nothing but frogs and field mice on her altar."

The enormity of this prospective sacrilege so infuriated the *caupo* that he succumbed to a series of aguelike nods and eye blinks such as usually foretoken the onset of a seizure; and perhaps it was his state of advanced agitation that led him to conclude his philippic by exclaiming, "I only pray to Jove that I'll be a heap of ashes long before that black day comes!"—which was a somewhat reckless declaration given his faith in the ancient gods.

Barring divine intervention, though, it seemed altogether likely that the *caupo* would enlarge ad nauseam on his pietistical theme; so we took advantage of the awed silence that followed his plea for extinction to thank him for his hospitality, congratulate him on the quality of his cuisine, and extricate ourselves from his conversational grasp.

Down at the far end of the table we found Ascanius the tanner deeply engrossed in the consumption of a bowl of soup, and the blankness of the stare with which he greeted the first of our questions regarding the sacred grove was almost enough to make us wistful for the *caupo*'s fulminations. With the aid of persistent interrogation, however, we managed to extract from him the guarded opinion that there could be no objection to our visiting Diana's shrine, provided only that we stayed well clear of "the oak."

"What oak?" Agricus asked tersely, hoping, no doubt, that bluntness might mitigate the effects of Ascanius's limited comprehension. But his strategy, alas, proved ineffective. Despite the peremptory locution he'd used, our slow-witted tanner still had considerable difficulty relating the question asked to the conversation in progress.

"Eh?" he said.

"*What* oak must we stay well clear of?" Agricus elucidated slowly.

"Why, the oak with the mistletoe growing on it, of course," Ascanius replied in a testy voice, being obviously afflicted by that provincial narrowness of mind that attributes the currency of common knowledge to even the most obscure details of local lore.

"And why must we stay well clear of it?" Marcus inquired—a reasonable enough question in my opinion, but one that clearly strained the limits of Ascanius's patience.

"Because that's where old Quintus stands guard," he responded, making no effort to conceal his contempt for our ignorance.

It was my turn, so I plunged right in and asked, "Who's old Quintus?"

He stared at me in disbelief and appeared to conclude that the four of us and our feebleminded questions represented a potentially dangerous phenomenon well outside the normal range of human experience. "He's the Rex," he said in a somewhat constricted voice, shooting wary glances at each of us as he rose from his seat and started edging toward the doorway.

"And why does he stand guard by the oak?" Agricus inquired. But at that Ascanius simply turned and bolted from the tavern, leaving the four of us to contend as best we could with a distinct sense of mortified bemusement.

"Oh, never mind him," Marcus said finally. "I'm pretty sure I know why the Rex stands guard there." And with that he led us out of the Golden Boar into the vernally cool and moonlit night.

"Are you planning to share your precious knowledge with us?" Agricus asked as we made our way to the hostelry's stables.

"Well, unless I miss my guess," Marcus replied, ignoring the snideness with which the question had been phrased, "the mistletoe oak the tanner referred to is the source of the so-called golden boughs that serve as the high priest's symbol of office."

"You mean the tree's branches are like the fasces of the magistrates?" I asked.

"They're somewhat like the fasces, Lucio, but far more significant. Unless a candidate for the high priesthood manages to obtain possession of one of them, he cannot legitimately challenge the incumbent to do battle."

"But in order to get close to the tree," Agricus interjected, "he must first get the better of the incumbent, who stands guard right next to it. Are you seriously suggesting that before he can fight the incumbent for the high priesthood he has to fight him for the right to challenge him to a fight?"

"I believe, my dear Agricus," Marcus responded patiently, "that most candidates attempt to secure their golden boughs by means of stealth and calculation."

"Why don't they just go after the high priest first, and cut a branch off the oak tree afterward?"

"Perhaps because some of the subordinate priests are keeping watch on them, Agricus. I don't really know."

"Well, I certainly wouldn't bother with any tree limbs if I wanted to be the rex. I'd just barge right in and kill the old king."

"No doubt," Marcus commented.

"I believe I *do* want to be the Rex, come to think of it. . . . Perhaps I'll make a bid for the high priesthood this very night."

We were about to mount our horses when Marcus made the uncharacteristic mistake of rising to Agricus's bait. "Alas, you're not a runaway slave," he said.

"I left Rome this morning, Marco, and it wouldn't be hard to find a brick licker or two who would testify that I'd run away."

"But it would be altogether impossible to find one who could testify that you are a slave," Marcus retorted, thereby compounding his original error.

It must by then have been clear to Agricus that he had his prey on the hook. At all events, there was a hint of dark elation in his voice when he responded, "True enough, Marco. But, for my servile status, I would rely on the testimony of a few well-chosen *honestiores*."

"I'm afraid I don't follow you."

"Just take my word for it, dear fellow. If a gladiator and a Praetorian could pass muster as runaway slaves, then so, most assuredly, can I."

At this point Marcus wisely decided not to pursue the matter further, but as we rode out of Aricia toward the track that would take us to Diana's grove, I could tell from his obvious discomposure that he'd chosen the wise course far too late.

Sure enough, we had no sooner turned onto the narrow upward-winding trail than Agricus in a taunting voice renewed his attack: "You won't mind, I hope, if I usurp the throne of the reigning Rex this evening."

"Oh, not at all," Marcus responded, attempting to sound unconcerned. "But I will miss having the pleasure of your company on the remainder of our trip."

"But you'll *have* the pleasure of my company, Marco; you won't have any occasion to miss it."

"You can't seriously expect to travel on with us tomorrow, dear comrade, if you're intent on becoming the monarch of Diana's grove tonight."

"Oh, yes I can, Marco, my boy. Because a monarch, you see, goes wherever he likes whenever he wishes, leaving his underlings to manage his dominions."

Again Marcus took refuge in silence, and again a palpable tension pervaded the still night air.

The moon was well risen by the time we reached the crater's rim, and it shone down resplendently on a world leached of color by its frosty brightness. Awash in this lunar radiance, the western half of the lake gave off sparkles of shimmering quicksilver; the eastern half, by contrast, lay in thrall to the crater's shadow. On the far nothern shore, just inside the shadow's borders, the faint flicker of a cooking fire marked the site of the goddess's shrine.

"Behold!" said Agricus. "A beacon to guide me to my kingdom."

But this time Marcus did not respond to the provocation.

The trail wound downward through the trees, and shafts of moonlight penetrated the leafy branches to make a silver gray patchwork of the forest floor. As we descended, the brooding silence surrounding us became steadily more pronounced, so much so that I, for one, began to feel thoroughly oppressed by it well before the descent was complete. We finally gained the lakeside and rode north along the shoreline as we'd done a few hours before. As before, we dismounted on reaching the ruined mole and tethered our horses to a poplar growing by the water's edge. Marcus then led us up the gentle incline toward the phalanx of oaks that defined the eastern boundary of Diana's sanctuary. It was merely a matter of coincidence, I suppose, that at the very moment we entered the sacred grove the alignment of earth and sky was such that we also passed from moonlight into the shadow of the volcano's rim.

Apart from night sounds, it was very quiet in the darkness amid the trees, and I shivered a little at the thought of the legions of desperate ruffians who'd prowled these woods over the centuries. This is no holy place, my senses warned me; this is a place where life is sacrificed to fear and where death, declaring himself propitiated, rejoices most in his unappeasable fury.

With Marcus still in the lead, we threaded our way through the oak grove single file and soon reached a small grassy clearing. There, between us and the steeply wooded slopes of the volcano's crater, stood half a dozen crude stone chapels as well as several clusters of statues. This was the sanctuary proper, but even in limpid starlight it failed to inspire much veneration. It was clear, somehow, from the seemingly haphazard placement of the sacred images and from their utter lack of affinity with the natural surroundings, that deep religious feeling had played a less than prominent role in the shrine's foundation. Gazing at the sinister banality of that forest clearing, I had a strong suspicion that Diana's cult was merely an adjunct of its high priesthood's murderous rites, not vice versa, as was generally supposed; and any modicum of sympathy I might have had with the *caupo*'s outraged piety vanished abruptly, along with my anticipatory sense of awe.

But I hadn't much time to savor my disillusion. For my companions, after pausing to survey the sterile array of icons, hastened off toward the southern end of the grove, where the fitful light of a hearth fire sent sickly shadows skittering upward through the trees.

We kept to the edge of the clearing, moving rapidly but making no noise; and before long there was nothing between us and the firelight but a cluster of aged oaks. Taking Marcus's lead, we bent down and made our way back into the grove, crouching lower and lower the nearer we got to the flames. By the time we reached our objective, we were virtually on our hands and knees. And that was just as well, because not twenty feet away from us, in the middle of a clearing that was smaller and even less numinous than the one where his cult had its being, sat Rex Nemorensis himself.

He did not make a regal impression; on the contrary, he seemed to be an extravagant caricature of a king. Dressed in tattered furs and deer-skins, he sat half-slumped by his hearth fire—a brutish apparition whose scraggly hair was flecked with dead insects and bits of vegetation, whose rheumy eyes were red-rimmed and vacant, and whose matted beard fell in a greasy cascade to his paunch, just below which a filthy hand slid idly up and down the swollen shaft of his penis.

"You see," Marcus whispered to Agricus, "the service of a virgin goddess is not without its drawbacks." Whereupon all four of us had to struggle to stifle our sniggers.

"It seems I'll have to institute a few reforms in the liturgy," Agricus responded. "And one of the first things I'll do is cut down that eyesore of a sacred oak."

Following the direction of his gaze, our eyes came to rest on the tree he was referring to—and though they didn't become sore exactly, neither were they soothed by the sight of that celebrated spire.

It was an extremely old tree; that much was obvious—but surely not as old as it looked. A victim of its own sanctity, it had, with two massive exceptions, been utterly denuded of branches to a height of some twenty feet. The surviving lower boughs had themselves been picked clean of smaller offshoots—none too ceremoniously, from the look of things—and displayed only a few paltry leaves and some clusters of mistletoe at their extremities. The entire tree trunk, indeed, from the roots up to the lowest branchings, bore the marks of repeated mutilations. And the distance of the uppermost wounds from ground level aroused in me not only great admiration for the mettle of those who'd inflicted them but also great doubt as to the wisdom of provoking the grotesque biped who presumably was responsible for the one nearest the top.

For several moments we observed the unkempt figure in silence. Then Marcus, a bit offhandedly, whispered, "Well, I don't know that this sight is worth all the trouble we've taken to see it, but at least we can travel on now without feeling we passed up an opportunity."

"Not quite yet," Agricus responded. "There's still the matter of my accession to be attended to."

"You can't seriously be interested in usurping *that* throne."

"A domain's a domain, Marco. You'll be given yours one day; I'm usurping mine tonight."

"But this is no domain, Agricus. This is an empty travesty, a pathetic antique."

"It'll have to suffice, dear boy. It's the only domain that's ever likely to come my way."

Marcus glared at him through the shadows, his face a study in anger and frustration. "It's out of the question," he said finally.

Agricus's eyebrows rose. "You wouldn't by any chance be asserting your rank here . . . or would you?"

"I have too much respect for myself to do that."

"Well then, you'll just have to forgive me if I indulge myself in a modest display of overweening ambition. . . . Won't you?"

"On no account and under no circumstances."

"You won't forgive me? What a terrible pity."

"It won't be necessary for me to forgive you. I intend to stop you."

Agricus's features now curved into a cold and predatory smile. "Oh, really? . . . How?"

"Personally."

"And by what means?"

"By whatever means necessary."

"You speak boldly, with Dracena here to back you up."

"Dracena won't interfere."

"He will when I'm about to kill you."

"Well, perhaps. At all events, it will do you no harm to weigh his possible intervention in your calculations."

Composed and expressionless, Dracena neither moved nor spoke.

"You respect yourself too much to assert your rank, yet not enough to fight your own battles?"

Marcus now said something that shocked me: "I always fight my own battles, Agricus; I just sometimes need help to win."

Agricus was clearly impressed by this echo of his own ruthlessness, but he drew his dagger anyway and said, "Well, this will certainly be one of those times, little fellow, so why don't the three of us get started."

So quickly that I hardly saw it move, Dracena's hand came chopping down on Agricus's wrist, causing the dagger he'd just drawn to drop into the bushes. But startled as I was by Dracena's quickness, my surprise was as nothing compared to the shock I felt when a spear came from nowhere and lodged below his right shoulder.

"Damnation!" he hissed, instantly yanking the *pylon* free. No sooner had he spoken than the coarse voice of Ascanius the tanner rang out from the trees: "Alarm, Quintus! Alarm! In the woods in front of you. They mean to take your life!"

Hearing this cry, the unkempt creature near the fire sprang to his feet, revealing himself to be rather larger and more muscular than he had seemed in a seated position. Staring wildly around him, he ran behind the sacred oak and reappeared a moment later with a sword of truly prodigious dimensions grasped in the same filthy right hand that had just been at work on his member. His staring eyes now scanned the boundaries of the clearing, and all too quickly fixed on us. In the next instant his eyes widened even farther, his nostrils flared, his sword rose high, and a roar of rage issued from his throat.

Then he charged.

"I can't move my arm!" Dracena snarled, as a second *pylon* went whizzing by my ear.

Though I didn't fully understand how it had happened, it was painfully clear to me that we were in serious trouble. Agricus was disarmed, Dracena was disabled, Ascanius was invisible, and a large maddened recluse was bearing down on us with a sword that could cut through an ox. "I think I'll forgo my new kingdom," Agricus announced to us as we all four took to our heels.

I was scared silly, I don't mind confessing; so much so that I sprinted off without so much as a thought for my companions. Only once did I look back, and what I saw was the Rex pausing long enough in his pursuit of us to embrace his friend Ascanius in a manner that can most decorously be described as intimate. This tender scene lent a new dimension to my anxieties about getting caught, and from that point on I gave all my attention to fleeing.

I was a little surprised and more than a little abashed when I discovered on reaching the mole that I'd left my three comrades far behind me. I was much relieved, however, to see that Ascanius had lacked the wit to steal our horses before initiating his ambush. (Only later did I realize that what had probably prompted him to attack us had been the sight of Agricus drawing a knife.)

But the question of Ascanius's motives was still far from academic at that point, so I hurriedly untied the horses and went rushing back to assist my friends.

They appeared almost instantly, wide-eyed and out of breath. "Ye *gods*, you can fly!" Marcus gasped as I ran up to them. But there was no time for extended conversation. Within moments all three of them had mounted their horses and galloped away, leaving me, in my turn, to trail behind as I struggled frantically to impress upon Incitatus the importance of a burst of speed.

The moon was approaching its zenith when at last we reached the crater's rim, which was far enough from the sacred grove so that we all felt reasonably safe.

"Did you really intend to use that knife on me?" Marcus inquired of Agricus as the four of us gazed down at Diana's archaic domain.

There was a long silence before my nemesis finally responded.

"I'm not a fool, Marco," he replied with a heavy sigh. "All I wanted was to be a king."

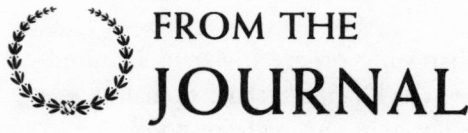

FROM THE
JOURNAL

[SEPTEMBER 1ST]

This has been a horrendous day, and yet I feel somehow enhanced by it.

It began prosaically enough. I rose, with some effort, for breakfast, my every joint and sinew protesting vigorously. Henceforth, I resolved, I shall refrain from impersonations of swift-footed Mercury and adopt lame Hephaestus as my exemplar (in spirit at least, since my body may yet recover).

After breakfast I went with Decius to set some rabbit snares in the lettuce—a task I do not relish but which I perform myself so as to minimize the poor creatures' suffering. My snares are more elaborate than most and much more difficult to set. But they kill instantaneously almost every time they're tripped; and having seen what horrors of pain and panic trapped animals must endure, I can't begrudge our errant herbivores a few extra hours of added toil.

We'd almost finished our work when Decius suddenly stood bolt upright and stared off in the direction of the house.

"Something?" I asked after a few moments' silence.

"Listen," he said in an urgent whisper. "Do you hear a sound?"

I stood up myself and cocked an ear—but heard nothing, at least at first.

"*There!*" Decius half shouted. And I listened again.

"You mean that chirping noise?" I asked finally, referring to what sounded like the distant peeping of several new-hatched chicks.

"Yes, Father," he replied in an uneasy voice. "But I don't think those are the cries of birds."

Now both of us listened with all our concentration; but for the moment, it seemed, the sounds had utterly ceased.

Then all at once we heard them again, slightly louder and more distinct. "You're right," I said, a sense of dread beginning to rise in my belly. "Those aren't bird sounds."

We shot each other an anxious glance, and squinted once more into the distance.

"Do you see the dust cloud, Father?" Decius asked, his voice stricken.

And as he spoke, I saw it—a pale brown billow rising high into the air above the road between our farm and the river. The next instant I was running—as hard as I could in spite of my prebreakfast resolution. The nearer I got to the house, the clearer it became that the sounds I was hearing were women's screams; and thus the spur of fear propelling me was cruelly reinforced by the lash of desperation.

I was gasping for air by the time I reached the roadway, but I paused only long enough to deduce from the scores of fresh hoofprints that the dust cloud we'd seen was the work of at least three-dozen horsemen.

Up the hillside I struggled, sobbing for breath as the sun drummed down on my brow, and by the time I staggered into our barnyard I was almost insensible with exhaustion.

"Halt!" came a Teutonic-sounding voice, and in my near prostration I not only halted but also collapsed to my knees. "You are Celer?" the voice demanded.

Hardly able to breathe, I could do no more than nod by way of reply.

"Tell the Emperor we've captured his man," the voice commanded with a hint of pride, and with that my worst apprehensions were confirmed.

I knelt there, trying not to succumb to the impulse to weep, and before long there was another, more familiar, voice, bellowing down at me from on high. "It seems from the look of you that you're not quite the runner you used to be, Lucius Celer . . . but still, the sight of you on your knees does not displease me."

Struggling to speak—and to avoid even a trace of irony once the words came—I managed eventually to gasp out, "I bid you welcome, Caesar, to my humble farm."

"Ha!" he barked contemptuously. "How dare you presume to welcome us. You, a dead man in all but fact."

With my breathing now somewhat less labored, I was able at last to look up toward the Emperor's face. It was impossible to make out his expression, though, for his head was haloed by the sun and his features were in shadow. "Yet while I live, Caesar," I ventured, "the fact remains that you are welcome."

"How very hospitable of you," he retorted. "But does this welcome of yours entail anything other than words? A bowl of wine perhaps? Some cordial conversation in the shade of your garden?"

"By all means, Caesar. Anything here that can afford you pleasure is yours, without question, to command."

"And so is everything else here, it so happens."

At this I lowered my eyes again. "I am aware, Caesar, that whatever I possess in life I possess by your grace and sufferance."

"Does that include your low opinion of me, by any chance? Did you come by that by my grace and sufferance?"

"It grieves me, Caesar, to think that you doubt my reverence for you."

"I daresay it grieves you, my slick-tongued friend; it would grieve just about anyone who dwells within reach of my authority. But it wouldn't grieve you too much to think badly of me in secret, now would it?"

"As your deified father often said, Caesar: 'He who looks down on another must first be blind to himself.' "

The Emperor's response to this was swift and angry. "I know exactly what your game is, Lucius Celer," he shouted. "I see how cleverly your answers evade my questions, and how you mock me with my father's words. I'm not a fool, you know, nor a mere posturer, as you may think. *I am my father's son!* Yet still you deny me the respect that is my due."

"I live in constant fear of you, Caesar," I shot back in exasperation. "Is that not respect enough?"

It was insane of me to have said such a thing; in fact, it was downright suicidal. In the dead silence that followed my outburst I remembered with a stab of anguish that such rash words could recoil on my wife and children.

But the very next moment there was a hand on my shoulder, and Decius gently asking me, "Shall I kneel beside you, Father, or help you to your feet?"

I almost wept in gratitude on hearing his voice, and promptly felt my courage start to revive. "Help me," I managed to say, and sooner than I would have thought possible, I was standing, unsteady but erect.

"What a touching display of fealty," the Emperor sneered. "You could benefit, Celer, from your offspring's example."

"I readily acknowledge that, Caesar," I responded, looking around me for the first time at the distressing scene in the barnyard. Over by the stables my slaves stood encircled by Praetorians, the women clinging, terrified, to their children and each other as the men, desolate, listened to their whimpers and stifled sobs. Portia and Camilla, meanwhile, stood ashen-faced near the house, with a soldier on either side of them and Spaeto glowering just behind.

"And your wife could benefit as well, by the look of things," Commodus continued, tossing his head in Portia's direction. "We found her alone in the garden with that tall fellow on our arrival—while you, it seems, were hard at work out in the fields."

For the briefest instant I felt a pang of jealousy, but it was speedily negated by the thought of all that Portia and I have found in one another.

"I am as much my wife's inferior in fealty, Caesar," I tacitly rebuked him, "as I am my son's and my daughter's."

"Then who is this dark-maned fellow, pray, who enjoys such free and easy access to your lady?"

It dawned on me then, at long last, that even though my dear wife's virtue had in no way been compromised by Spaeto's presence, my own chances of survival almost certainly had, and I found myself utterly at a loss as to how I should reply to the Emperor.

"By your leave, Caesar," Spaeto himself interceded, "I own the land across the river, and I'm here today because I've discovered signs of rust."

"Ah, so you're just a good neighbor," Commodus scoffed. "But I'll wager the rust you're discovered flows monthly down the lady's legs."

At this all the Praetorians broke into raucous laughter, while Portia cringed and our slaves looked on aghast.

"I wouldn't know, Caesar," Spaeto riposted coolly, "for it is wheat rust that occasions my visit. Indeed, if you'll look out there beyond the river, you'll see that I've already burned off one of my fields."

Commodus squinted off in the direction of the Aro, as Decius and I held our breath. "You mean to tell me that our friend Celer here would not have noticed that entire wheat field on fire when it's just across from one of his own?"

"There are any number of reasons for putting wheat to the torch, Caesar," Spaeto responded. "And in the absence of a specific warning, Celer would have had no reason to suppose that his crop was in any danger. . . . He and I have had our differences over the years," he continued, improvising masterfully as he went along, "but we are neighbors nevertheless. That is why, when my overseer informed me on my return from the City last night that blight had been discovered and a field set ablaze, I felt it incumbent upon me to come right over here this morning."

The Emperor regarded him skeptically for some moments, and he gazed impassively back. "Enough of this!" Commodus barked at last, turning his attention once again to me. "The purpose of my visit here is to inspect my father's biography. . . . Have you completed it?"

"No, Caesar," I replied, flinching inwardly. "I regret to inform you that I have not."

"I assumed as much. But you *will* complete it, though, and deliver it to me personally by the Nones."

"But that's only four days from now, Caesar," I had the temerity to object.

"I'm fully conversant with the intricacies of the calendar, thank you.

Just consider yourself fortunate that I'm in residence at Lorium for the time being, so you won't be obliged to ride all the way in to Rome."

With that, he signaled summarily for his stallion, and his guardsmen rushed to mount their own. "Until the Nones then," he said once he'd mounted, glaring down at me with eyes full of wrath. Then he galloped off with his massive Germans in column behind him, a pall of dust and some piles of fresh manure the sole remaining evidence of his unexpected incursion.

I rushed to Portia the moment he was gone, embraced her and Camilla, and reached out for Spaeto's hand. "You risked your life for us just now," I said to him. "I can't begin to thank you sufficiently."

"Well, the way I look at it," he replied with a thin-lipped smile, "if *that* fellow dislikes you so much, you must be an exceptionally worthwhile person."

"Oh, he dislikes me, all right. He's disliked me with a vengeance for many years."

"I more or less inferred that from his behavior," Spaeto responded, locking his eyes onto mine. "But as much as he dislikes you now, just imagine how he'll feel when he finds out you've up and fled."

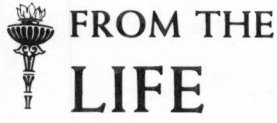
(The Emperor be damned!

I can't possibly finish Marcus's "biography" by the Nones, and even if I were capable of such a feat, there still wouldn't be much point in my attempting it. The manuscript's degree of completeness has as little bearing on my ultimate fate as its style or content, after all. So I may as well just keep on scribbling away in my customary manner and pray as I scribble that my fate may prove less dismal than I am anticipating.)

A lamp had been left burning for us beside our pallets in the villa's dining hall, and by its faint fluttering light Marcus attended to Dracena's wound. Observing the solicitude with which he cleaned and dressed the ugly puncture, I was assailed by an altogether unworthy suspicion that he and the *singularis* might be lovers. The source of this perverse notion is still a mystery to me, and I'm ashamed to have entertained it. Perhaps it was the spurious rumor about Marcus being the Emperor's catamite that gave rise to the idea. Or perhaps it was Annia's assertion that he was jealous of her hold on me. In retrospect, though, it seems fairly clear that *I* was the one who was feeling jealous, and that the cause of my jealousy was all the earnest attention being lavished by him on someone else.

There was, it now appears, a darker side to the love I bore him—a fierce possessiveness and rabid greed for affection that led me, all unthinkingly, to tar him with the same brush of sodomy I'd been holding in reserve to ward off Agricus.

Thus do the contrivances of fear work to undermine the foundations of affection.

We all slept well that night, to no one's great surprise, and when, on our awakening, Dracena reported some return of motivity in his upper arm, we decided that we should continue our journey.

Our next destination, Forum Appii, was the Appia's fourth post station and the northern terminus of the Pomptine ship canal. Our intention was to arrive there in time to take passage on the night boat, which would carry us through the marshes to Tarracina while we slept. Since the town was only half a day's ride from Lanuvium, however, we had five or six hours of free time to dispose of, and Marcus had a plan to insure the best use of them. "Why don't we go to Ardea and see the elephants," he chirruped.

"What elephants?" Agricus inquired in a wary tone.

"Why, the Emperor's elephants, naturally. There's a whole herd of them in the Imperial Game Preserve, just outside the town."

"They're not underwater or anything, are they?"

"No." Marcus laughed. "They're all walking about on dry land. I promise you."

And so it was decided.

From Lanuvium to Ardea the road descended steadily, and we trotted along at a comfortable pace with the warm sun on our backs and a sea breeze caressing our cheeks. We arrived in Ardea well before midday, bought some honey cakes for our lunch, and rode west out of town until we reached the main entrance to the Imperial Game Preserve. Marcus identified himself to the gate guards and asked them to direct us to the Procurator's office. They readily obliged, and after proceeding a mile or so into the park grounds we came to the cluster of modest buildings that made up the administrative headquarters of the southern district of the preserve. The largest of these, the guards had told us, housed the office of the Deputy Procurator, and in case we had any trouble determining which the largest was, we had only to look for the building with the bas-relief elephants above its doors.

Thanks to these explicit directions, we quickly located our objective. While Marcus was inside introducing himself, Agricus, Dracena, and I craned our necks and scanned the fields in the hopes of espying some elephants in the flesh. Our efforts proved unavailing, however. Indeed, the closest thing we saw to an elephant was a pair of cows in a pasture behind the headquarters building grazing tranquilly among the poppies.

It wasn't long before Marcus rejoined us, accompanied by the Deputy Procurator himself. This boulder-shaped gentleman looked very much the part of an elephant warden. He was broad-shouldered, barrel-chested, big-bellied, and short-legged. He was also almost totally bald, with a ruddy bulbous nose and a beetling sunburned brow. His name was Scaurus Diodorus, and he proved to be as gruffly good-natured a guide as we could have wished for.

"Excuse me, sir," I asked once his horse had been fetched and the five of us were under way, "are all the elephants in hiding?"

He shot me a glance to see if I was serious, then burst into stertorous laughter. "Not so they can't be found, my boy; of that much I can assure you. What prompts the question?"

"Well, we haven't seen any so far."

He laughed again. "You'll see some soon enough," he said, "enough to last you a lifetime."

We cantered along for several miles, then at Scaurus's command slowed our horses to a walk. "One thing you don't ever want to do," he confided, "is come upon a herd of elephants so fast that you scare them."

"Why?" Agricus inquired. "Would they charge at us?"

"No," Scaurus replied, grinning broadly. "But they might start fleeing in our direction."

We soon came to a halt several hundred paces from a line of trees that seemed to serve as a natural boundary between scrub growth and forest.

"There they are," Scaurus said softly, pointing toward the base of the trees. The four of us began straining our eyes to make them out. "They eat leaves and bushes mostly," he continued, oblivious of the fact that none of us had yet caught sight of them. "Quite a lot of leaves and bushes, when you come right down to it."

"There's one!" Dracena roared all of a sudden, and at the sound of his voice several dozen massive gray heads rose from the distant underbrush and gazed bemusedly around.

"We'd better not make too much noise," Scaurus tactfully cautioned us. "None of those animals is domesticated, you see. They're all destined for the Amphitheater sooner or later."

"Then where are all the ceremonial elephants?" I asked. "The ones I've seen in triumphs and in parades."

"They're kept near Rome, in a compound by the Tiber, all the way at the other end of the preserve. The only time any of them come down here is when animal combats or hunting spectacles are scheduled in connection with the games. We use the best-trained ones to cull the largest specimens from this herd and help keep them calm on the way to the City."

"Can we get any closer?" Agricus inquired eagerly.

"Yes. But let's take it very slow and quiet."

"You wouldn't think such enormous creatures would be so skittish," Marcus observed.

"They're not all that skittish, really," Scaurus responded. "It's just that they're so damnably large that even a little skittishness can cause a lot of problems."

Moving at the slowest possible gait, we continued to approach the herd, but now it was our horses who began to show signs of skittishness.

"They're not used to the smell," said Scaurus, whose own horse seemed perfectly calm. "If you want to get any closer, we'd better proceed on foot."

The four of us exchanged glances of mild to acute apprehension, but dismounted nevertheless and headed off through the underbrush with Scaurus in the lead.

We closed to within fifty paces of the elephants—who appeared unaware of, or indifferent to, our presence—and kept inching ever nearer, until the true scale of the massive creatures became intimidating in the extreme. At a distance of twenty paces or so Scaurus at long last whispered that we were close enough, and to the extent that I could breathe at all, I breathed a sigh of relief.

For a while we crouched there, gaping in awed fascination at the browsing behemoths. I found it almost impossible to assimilate the fact of their size, and despite their lumbering gentleness and obvious amiability, I felt nearly faint with fear.

Before I actually passed out, however, Scaurus determined that we'd tempted fate long enough, and with a wave of his arm he signaled that we should withdraw. I lost no time complying with his instructions, and set off at such a rapid pace in the direction we'd come from that I soon left my four companions far behind me. So headlong was my progress through the underbrush that I paid hardly any heed to the putrescent stench that was floating on the air, and no heed at all to the fact that it was getting stronger with every step I took.

If I'd been going any faster I'd have crashed right into the unsuspecting beast. In actual fact, though, when it reared up in front of me and trumpeted its dismay I was able to come to a skidding halt.

It was a small elephant, and for that I thanked the gods. Several moments passed before I noticed the much larger one on the ground beside it and came to the realization that I'd located the source of the stench.

Unlike me, the small elephant quickly got over the shock of our encounter, and walked slowly around the body of the big one, pausing every so often to prod the noisome carcass with its trunk. When this prodding produced no response, the animal walked around the body again and tried nudging it with his foot. It occurred to me that this was by no means the first time the poor creature had attempted thus to elicit some sign of life from its mother, and when the nudging, too, ended in failure, the downcast animal began to shake its head and rock from side to side in a heartrending pantomime of grief.

I felt pierced through with sympathy for the disconsolate creature and almost forgot how frightened I was—despite the fact that the beast was at least as tall as me at the shoulder. Watching it shift its weight from side to side and mournfully wag its great head, I felt an agonizing need to provide it with some comfort or consolation. All I had to offer, though, was the honey cake I'd purchased for my lunch.

Moving my hand very slowly, I reached inside my tunic for my purse, opened it, and probed for the sticky square. Once my fingers located the cake, I, again very slowly, lifted it from under my garment and held it out so the elephant could see what it was.

But he (for I'd come by then to assume he was a male) displayed not the slightest interest in my offering. The two of us simply stared at one another—I too shaken to flee, and he too despondent to eat.

"You'll have to put it in his mouth if you really want him to eat it," came Scaurus's voice softly from behind me. "But judging from the smell of his mother, he's not going to live long enough to digest it."

I turned my head slightly and saw that Marcus, Agricus, and Dracena were there as well. "Can't we save him?" I asked plaintively.

Scaurus shook his head. "Elephants nurse for five years, my boy; and this one's no older than two. But even if he was three or four, I can tell by the look of him that he's already been far too long without food."

I turned back to look at the grieving animal, and tears welled up in my eyes. "What happened to his mother?" I asked in a whisper.

"It's hard to say. Old age maybe, worms, lung lesions—or it could be her heart just gave out. She's been dead at least four days, though," he added, sniffing the fetid air. "Of that much I'm certain."

I stood there gazing at the elephant as he rocked from side to side. "Did you say I could put the honey cake in his mouth?" I asked Scaurus finally.

"It won't make bit of difference to him, son, but you go right ahead if it'll make you feel any better."

"What do I do?"

"He's too far gone by now to really notice what's going on, so I'd walk right up to him and plant it on his tongue."

Although my fear hadn't left me, a stronger emotion kept it well within bounds. I therefore did as Scaurus suggested and approached the suffering calf.

He kept rocking and shaking his head, unaware, to all appearances, that I was standing at his side. As close as I was now, I could see the skin hanging from his ribs and smell the odor of death each time he exhaled.

I reached up with my right hand and put my arm across his neck. Half-dead though he was, the force of his constantly shifting bulk almost knocked me to the ground. I was able to regain my balance after a moment, however, and with my left hand I placed the honeyed wheat cake in his mouth.

He swallowed it instantaneously, but gave no sign it had afforded him any solace.

"We've got to get going, Lucio," Marcus said in a gentle voice. So I took my arm off the animal's neck and began to walk away. Before I'd gone three paces, though, I heard a sighing sound behind me, and I turned to see the elephant with its head on the ground, kneeling on his two front legs.

"That's the end of him," said Scaurus. "He'll be dead inside an hour."

I was still in tears when the boat left Forum Appii.

[SEPTEMBER 2D]

A dreadful realization jerked me awake before dawn this morning and sent me lurching out of the house and across the fields. With my body sorely depleted by yesterday's overexertions, I couldn't sustain too rapid a pace. That turned out not to matter very much, though, since if I'd reached the lettuce fields any sooner than I did, there wouldn't have been sufficient light for me to see by. Even as it was, the sky in the east had brightened just barely enough to permit me to distinguish rocks from bushes. Just barely enough was more than sufficient, however, given the urgency of my errand. So after arming myself with a good-size stick, I hastened off to start tripping my snares.

My haste served no real purpose, of course, at least in terms of the welfare of any rabbits. For I was panting and cursing and stomping around so noisily that even the fiercest of boars would have long since fled the vicinity. In addition to all the other noises I was making, little whimpers of relief kept escaping from me as one snare after another proved to be still intact. But it was precisely because the next one might not be that I kept hurrying along in a fever of anticipatory remorse.

The next to the last one was not intact, alas, and after staring for a moment at the havoc it had wrought, I stumbled off to disarm the one remaining.

That accomplished, I returned to attend to my victim, what pieces of him I could find. I had mad thoughts of constructing a miniature pyre for him and of committing his butchered body to the flames. But since I wasn't quite far gone enough to indulge in such excesses, I simply sat down on the ground in the end and leavened my guilt with my tears.

An infant elephant, a slave boy, and now a poaching rabbit: three deaths I failed to avert—the first because of my impotence, the second because of my negligence, and this last because of my folly.

To think: all my crops and livestock will belong to the Emperor in a few days' time. If only I'd known that yesterday, that poor rabbit would be thriving still.

And the true horror, of course, is that I *did* know that yesterday—all yesterday afternoon. But I neglected to consider the full implications until this morning. Not content with acting the fool, I proceeded to compound my folly—defending a lettuce crop and then realizing too late that I and my prey are allies.

I suppose I shouldn't berate myself too harshly; the Emperor's visit left us all in a state of shock.

Except for Spaeto, that is. He was the soul of equanimity.

"How did you know that we intended to flee?" I asked him once my people and I had recovered our wits a little, and once he and I were alone.

"I didn't know—at least not till the Emperor came barging in."

"You mean that the Emperor knows, too?" I asked in frozen horror.

"No, no, no," he responded, with a squinty smile. "It's just that as soon as it became clear to me that you were in his bad graces, everything else made sense."

"Everything else?"

"Forgive me, friend, but you are not terribly adept at dissembling your intentions. To begin with, you insist that my patron, Placidus, inspect your slaves before buying them, even though for purposes of farm work he'd be perfectly content to take them on an agent's warranty. Pursuant to your insistence, however, he dispatches me here, and no sooner do I arrive than you entreat me to conceal the purpose of my visit from your familia. Now all this strikes me as rather eccentric, but I pay no particular mind. Who am I to judge my betters, after all? After a day or two, though, several things become clear to me: first, your farm is prosperous and you yourself are in no discernible financial distress; second, everyone here is suffering acutely from nerves; third, you are as attached to your dependents as they are devoted to you; and fourth, it is I who am being inspected, not they. In light of all these perceptions, the question immediately occurs to me: Why is he divesting himself of his familia? And the only answer I can come up with is: I don't know. But then your friend Marcus Commodus comes rampaging into your barnyard, and part of the riddle is speedily solved. You have incurred the displeasure of our First Citizen, it seems, and face the prospect of suicide, or worse. But wait— this can hardly be news to your dependents. And in fact, distressed though they are by the Emperor's invasion, they do not appear to regard it with surprise. But then, why should they? You'd have had no earthly reason to conceal your plight from them, nor could you have concealed it for very long if you'd bothered to try. But why, in that case, won't you tell them that they're going to be sold? You're selling them for their own good, after all, and to a buyer whom they will assume you're prepared to vouch for. Being consigned to a new master is vastly preferable from

their point of view to being confiscated by the Imperial Treasury. So why
do you persist in concealing your intentions?"

I gaped at him in dumb admiration for a moment, then said, with
conviction, "Please go on."

"Of course you wouldn't want the Emperor to learn of what you're
doing," Spaeto continued. "He might think you were denuding your
estate. But since you're acting in your slaves' own best interests, one would
think that you would trust them not to speak. And yet you do *not* trust
them. And that, in my mind, immediately raises the prospect that your
own best interests are at stake as well—that your intention, in other
words, is to escape."

As I listened, awestruck, to Spaeto's impeccable logic, I struggled in
my own mind to calculate the extent to which I could take him into my
confidence. I suppose the fact that he'd risked his life for me should have
already resolved the question to my satisfaction. It hadn't though, at least
not entirely. So I asked him, "What led you to lie to the Emperor on our
behalf?"

He frowned at this, his expression evincing both melancholy and anger.
"My father was a slave for most of his life," he said, "but he refrained
from marriage until he was manumitted, because he didn't want to have
any children unless they could all be born free. . . ."

He was silent a moment, and the muscles along his jawline rippled
fiercely.

"I've seen slaves treated badly," he resumed at last, "and I've seen them
treated well. Only rarely, though, have I seen them treated with
love. . . . And in each such case I hold the master in high regard."

Hearing this testimonial, I was convinced finally that I could confide
in him, and I spent most of yesterday afternoon and evening telling him
about Nestor.

"He'd better get back here before the Nones," Spaeto observed, "because you're going to have to start running by then whether he shows
up or not."

"You're right," I acknowledged. "But where do we run to without him?"

"The nearest boat, I should imagine. Boats don't leave any tracks."

"And then what?"

He pondered. "I'd make for Corsica, to begin with. It's large, it's not
very populated, and there are mountains to hide in from one end to the
other."

"Corsica," I reflected. "It sounds like as good a place as any."

"Or as bad, since it's very much part of the Empire. Still, if you can
get that far, you might get farther."

"How do I obtain a boat though, without 'leaving tracks'?"

"I'll see to that for you," Spaeto said simply. "I'll take a couple of your slaves with me to Fregenae, and say we want to go fishing."

"Are you sure you ought to take that risk?" I asked him.

He gave me a stern look and answered, "What has 'ought' got to do with it, my friend?"

I could make no fitting response to that, other than "I wish that I could thank you somehow."

"You can: make good your escape."

But all at once I thought of a serious objection to his scheme. "I haven't told any of my slaves that we're going to be forced to flee. If you take two of them with you to Fregenae, they'll suspect and tell the others."

To this Spaeto responded with a smile that betrayed just the least trace of condescension. "There'll be no need for them to tell anybody anything," he said. "Your slaves have known of your intentions for quite some time."

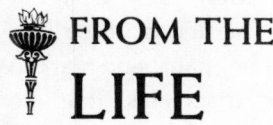
If the blessings of youth consist of anything more than supple limbs and
the illusion that death is remote, then a sense that the world is yet to be
discovered must surely be numbered among them. It is novelty more than
variety, after all, that lends life its savor; and when every single thing is
new, as on a boy's first outbound journey, tears and heartaches become
mere incidents of the odyssey, and the sorrows of one day are relentlessly
trodden under by the excitements of the next—and by the vexations of
the intervening night hours, too, on some occasions.

In our case, the nocturnal boat trip down the Pomptine canal proved
to be something of an ordeal—for those of us, at least, who'd been
hoping to get some sleep. Mosquitoes were the first problem we had to
contend with, untold swarms of them, bold and voracious enough to
stick their needles right through the fabric of our clothing. At the boatman's suggestion, we wrapped ourselves in our cloaks after smearing our
hands, feet, and faces with river mud. This preserved us from further
mosquito attacks, but left us beset by the boatmen themselves, who
seemed intent on making as much noise as possible to no discernible
purpose or effect. When we reached the midcanal post station at Ad
Medias, our crewmen changed places with the crew of the northbound
boat, so that both companies might arrive back at their home ports in
the morning. Our progress was quieter from that point on, but no more
restful, since it turned out that one of the reasons the crewmen from
Forum Appii had made so much noise was to keep the teams of mules
on either side of the canal roughly abreast of each other as they towed
the boat along. The crewmen from Tarracina showed considerably less
interest in coordinating the efforts of the mule drivers, however, and did
not shout at them at all, except on those by no means rare occasions
when the boat plowed into one bank or another of the canal. When this
happened, the Tarracina boatmen more than made up for their previous
reticence, spewing great gobbets of colorful language out into the darkness, while the deck passengers, who'd been flung together into a writhing, snarling heap by the force of the impact, struggled to disentangle
themselves from one another and resume their fruitless efforts to get some

rest. One corpulent female passenger, snoring blithely away near the bow, was actually sent rolling right overboard by the first of these collisions, and she might possibly have drowned, given her panic and marked obesity, had she not discovered, after a plenitude of screams, that she was standing in water that reached no higher than her chest.

Smarting from the discomforts of the journey, we arrived outside Tarracina feeling grimy, itchy, surly, and fatigued. Worse still, the flesh surrounding Dracena's wound was becoming tender and showing signs of inflammation. He, of course, denied feeling any pain and protested, on the contrary, that his arm was almost fully back to normal. Marcus wisely did not make an issue of his condition, but I think it was with Dracena's health in mind that he proposed the villa of his cousin Libo, near Formiae, as our destination for the day. He hadn't seen Libo for several years, he said, but he'd heard some interesting stories about him, almost all of which contained references to the beauty and opulence of his seaside estate. Formiae, moreover, was an attraction in itself, boasting a splendid theater, sumptuous public baths, and one of the most celebrated brothels on the Italian peninsula. It had the further advantage of being just five hours' ride from Tarracina, and that was an important consideration in terms of Dracena's health.

Before recommencing our travels, we sought out Tarracina's public baths, and in the warmth of the caldarium washed away two days' worth of dried sweat, horse smells, and dust. After bathing we wrapped ourselves in towels and took breakfast in the solarium, wolfing down fresh-baked bread with honey, dates, and cheese. We then retired to what Marcus referred to as the "throne room" and there passed a merry quarter hour telling each other the most vulgar stories we could think of while the sluice water flowing beneath us carried away the detritus of our bowels.

Cleansed, nourished, unburdened, and refreshed, we embarked on a cursory tour of Tarracina's sights, foremost among which was the Temple of Jove on the citadel. From the temple's steps we could see the coastline stretching away southeastward toward the Caietan peninsula, just south of our destination, while northeastward the Via Appia snaked its way past the saline waters of Lake Amyclanus and the vineyards of the ager Caecubus toward the ancient town of Fundi at the foot of the Auruncian Mountains. It was a glorious day—immaculate sky, crystalline air, and enough of a zephyr to temper the sun's vernal warmth.

"I suggest we take the Via Flacca," Marcus said, pointing to the road along the coast. "It's a slightly more direct route, and I seem to recall that it goes right by my cousin's estate, just before rejoining the Appia at Formiae."

There were no dissenting voices, so after savoring the view a while longer we made our way down from the citadel and started off.

Despite being the more direct route from Tarracina to Formiae, the Via Flacca was little traveled, and that was a simple consequence of the fact that there were no towns along the road, merely some scattered seaside villas. Being little traveled, it was also unpaved and lacking in such main-road amenities as taverns, water pumps, post stations, and drainage. It did have clearly marked milestones, though, and it wasn't long before we began running races between them.

Agricus started it by challenging Marcus, and at my signal the two of them went charging off. I was not about to exhort Incitatus to bestir himself for such a frivolous purpose; I meant to save whatever scant reserves of speed he had for use in dire emergencies. (The fact that even at my boldest I remained the most tentative of horsemen might also have played a part in my decision not to participate.)

It was clear as soon as Dracena and I again got within earshot of our two companions that the victory had gone to Marcus, for Agricus was angrily insisting that the outcome of their wager could only be decided on the basis of best two out of three.

"I don't seem to recall any mention of a second or third heat," Marcus responded equably.

"That's because it goes without saying, Marco. It's *always* best two out of three."

"Oh? In which jurisdiction?"

"Why, Rome, naturally."

"I've spent most of my life in Rome. Why is it that I never heard about this ordinance of yours until now?"

"Because you've been entirely out of touch, Marco—living up there on the Caelian."

"Lucio hasn't been entirely out of touch, though," Marcus riposted with a sly smile. "Let's ask him if its 'always' best two out of three."

"Oh, fine. And when was the last time Lucio ever sided with me?"

"Are you seriously suggesting that one of us might be capable of subordinating the truth to his personal feelings?" Marcus asked with heavy irony.

"It's possible," Agricus replied baldly.

"Well, let me offer a sort of compromise," Marcus said after giving the matter some thought. "Instead of asking Lucio to decide the issue for us, I propose that you race him yourself."

"Oh, no," I interjected. "I'm infantry material; no cavalry charges for me."

"Infantry's precisely what I had in mind," Marcus answered me. "Agricus will ride; you will race on foot."

"You must be mad," I protested.

"No, not at all," Marcus replied. "Given a fair and reasonable head start, I've no doubt you'll win my wager for me. . . . Are you agreeable, Agricus?"

My nemesis flashed me a nasty look and responded warily, "How much of a head start did you have in mind?"

"Oh, I don't know. I think it's fair to say that a horse can cover a mile more than twice as fast as a man. So if we were to give Lucio only a half-mile lead, your prospects should be nothing less than rosy."

After favoring me with another unfriendly glance, Agricus inquired, "Do I win the bet if I beat him?"

"You win the bet," Marcus affirmed. "Just as I do if he beats you."

Agricus calculated for several moments and then said, "Done!" which prompted me to ask, "What precisely is at stake here, and what do I stand to win or lose?"

Marcus and Agricus exchanged quick secretive smiles, and Marcus responded, "What's at stake here, dear Lucio, is nothing more nor less than my virginity."

"How's that again?"

Marcus's smile broadened. "It's very simple, really. If Agricus wins, we both go to the brothel in Formiae, and I pay; if I win, neither of us goes to the brothel in Formiae, and Agricus owes me six denarii."

"And what do I win if you win?" I asked.

"I'll split my booty with you," Marcus answered simply. "Three denarii apiece."

"Fair enough," I said.

"There is the distinct possibility that you might lose, however," Agricus made haste to remind me. "In which case, Marcus and I will go to the brothel without you."

"What does that mean, exactly?" I asked, glaring at him.

"It means, little whippet, that while Marcus and I are slipping our staves into the warmest, wettest quims in all Italy, you'll be back at Libo's villa with your poker in your fist."

"Easy there, dear fellow," Marcus said with a laugh. "You'll hurt your own chances if you give him too much of an incentive."

"Oh, I don't know," Agricus sneered. "He's a lot more proficient with his fist than he'll ever be with a woman."

And on that cordial note, we turned our attention to the details of the race.

The stretch of road we were on was ideally suited to our purpose. It ran straight and level toward the sun, a light brown strip between the blue Tyrrhenian deep and the green Fundian plain. From the fifth milestone, where we were, it was possible to see some two or three miles down the Via Flacca; and that was just as well, given the mistrustful glances that Agricus and I kept casting at one another. So deep-seated were our mutual suspicions that it took almost half an hour of collective debate to work out ground rules for the race that could accommodate them. The end product of our deliberations was an intricate series of interconnected movements such as the high priest at the most elaborate of sacrificial rituals might have gazed upon with wonder and envy. The honor of initiating these newly devised solemnities fell to Dracena, who rode his horse out to the quarter-mile marker and kept an eye on Agricus while Marcus and I cantered out to join him. On our arrival, Marcus became responsible for keeping an eye on my adversary, and Dracena accompanied me in turn to my own starting point a quarter of a mile farther on. There I dismounted and removed my belt and sandals, while Dracena waved back to Marcus that we had arrived and were making ready.

"This race is yours, boy," he said to me as Marcus acknowledged his signal.

"What do you mean?" I asked, running in place for a moment and then shaking out my legs.

"Remember the day you came to Lorium, and my comrade and I chased you down?"

"I remember all right—all too clearly."

"You were no more than half a mile away when we first caught sight of you, and I'll swear it took us at least a mile of riding to catch you."

"Really?"

"Yes, really. And I'll tell you another thing . . . uh, oh . . . get to the mark; the boy's just raised his arm."

"I'm ready," I said, crouching down slightly and leaning forward. "What else were you going to tell me?"

"Just this," Dracena replied, his eyes fixed intently on Marcus. "That horse Agricus has underneath him . . . ."

"Yes?"

"You outraced him once already."

"What do you mean?"

"That's the same horse my comrade was riding that day. . . . Now GO!"

My old trainer Polyaenus always insisted that a distance runner had to know three things in order to win the dolichos: who he was running against, how he should run to defeat them, and what he was running for. This last prerequisite always struck me as somewhat superfluous, and so I asked him one day what anyone would ever run for except to win. "One runs to win, unquestionably," he answered me, "but what separates the greatest runners from the mere professionals is a sense that one's victories have meaning."

Alas, I'd not yet encountered Polyaenus when Dracena shouted "GO!" and of the three things I needed to know in order to run well, I knew only the first and least important. I was completely unaware, moreover, that races are won as much by the mind as by the lungs and legs. Thus, when I dashed off down the Via Flacca that forenoon, I was encumbered by a grievous weight of ignorance. My lungs and legs strove courageously to serve me, but my mind and my purpose were grievously obscured.

Though I set off at a fast clip, I'd gone barely fifty paces before Dracena went galloping by on his way to the finish-line milestone. I was a little unnerved by how quickly he'd overtaken me, and began half unconsciously to speed up the tempo of my stride. I settled before long into what felt like a comfortable rhythm and went bounding along beside the sea (as in my dream of a fortnight past!) confident that I could sustain such exertion indefinitely.

The hoofbeats of Marcus's horse became audible as I bore down on the three-quarter marker, and rapidly grew louder once I passed it. The fact that I'd reached the marker well ahead of him might have warned me that I was forcing the pace, and so might the fact that I was starting to feel a trifle winded with almost half the race still to run.

"Victory is in sight!" Marcus shouted to me as he went charging by, and I responded with a jaunty wave—a foolish piece of bravado that caused me to break stride.

Victory *was* most assuredly in sight, however: no more than two hundred paces dead ahead of me. I had only to maintain a steady cadence in order to seize it.

But my lungs and legs, having been neglected so long by my mind, were now, alas, beginning to labor, and with roughly a hundred paces still remaining I heard the sound of hoofbeats once again.

They were gaining on me at what seemed an alarming rate, but when I sought to lengthen my stride I found that I could not do so and also maintain my rhythm.

At fifty paces I began to panic, and at twenty-five I was hopelessly out of control. Legs leaden, arms flailing, chest heaving, I ran the last few steps like a man in the midst of a seizure; and when at last I staggered past the milestone it was with the dust raised by Agricus's stallion filling my mouth and stinging my eyes to tears.

"Victory! *VICTORY!*" Agricus exulted, while Marcus smiled a smile of resignation.

As for myself, I gave serious thought to flinging my feckless body into the sea. The only thing that deterred me was the thought that Agricus might be the one to effect my rescue.

[SEPTEMBER 3D]

No wonder I felt such compassion for a mob of lowly rabbits: my soul is every bit as timorous as theirs.

I was sitting in the garden yesterday morning, writing in my journal, when all at once it occurred to me that my scribblings constituted a peculiarly damning sort of evidence, not simply against Spaeto, my new-found benefactor, but against my slaves and my loved ones as well. They are all of them now coconspirators, engaged in a plot to thwart the Emperor's will. Yet there I was, busily documenting their treasonable activities, and for no good reason I could think of.

The awful realization surged over me just as I set down Spaeto's statement that my slaves had long been aware that I was contemplating an escape. I sat there horrified, staring at the scroll in front of me as if it were a dagger flecked with gore. My next thought was to commit all my most recent journals to the fire without delay, and in order to give effect to that intention I hurriedly gathered up the scroll and started walking toward the house.

So oppressed was I by a sense of the urgency of my errand that I went striding from the sunlit brilliance of the garden directly into the shaded twilight of the kitchen without pausing for even a moment to let my eyes begin to adjust. As a consequence, I also went striding right into Spaeto, who noticed me bearing down on him at the last instant and was able to cushion the force of our collision by grabbing hold of my shoulders. I thank the gods for his strength and quick reflexes, for even as it was, I felt like I'd crashed into one of those massive oxhide shields that the legionaries used to tote around with them.

"You're looking decidedly resolute, this morning, Lucius Celer," he said with gruff good humor, and I hastened to explain to him both my grim demeanor and my new resolve.

"I think you may be overindulging a little in your anxiety," he said once I'd finished. "But even if your fears are well founded, I don't see any need for such drastic action."

"You don't?" I responded blankly.

"No, I don't."

"But surely some sort of action is called for."

"Yes—the action you've already taken."

"What action is that?"

"The action of recognizing the potential danger."

I considered this a moment, then asked, "You really think that's suf-ficient?"

"More than sufficient, given the circumstances," he replied with an emphatic nod.

"The circumstances?"

"Yes. There's little likelihood that Commodus and his Teutons are going to favor you with another visit before you and your family set off for Corsica. And even if they were to come galloping up your road again, you'd still have plenty of time to consign that journal of yours to the hearth fire before the first towhead burst into the house."

"I'd have plenty of time," I amended, "only if I heard them coming."

This attempt to split hairs elicited a sardonic smile. "They're not exactly stealthy in their movements," Spaeto said.

"No," I acknowledged with a rueful laugh, "they're not."

But my laughter ceased abruptly when another consideration impinged on my thoughts. "What if I should be captured during the course of our escape, though?"

" 'What if' is a game for philosophers, my friend; you can't insist on guarantees. All you can do is assess the risks confronting you and deal with such contingencies as arise. In this case the risks seem small to me; and since I am one of those who might be incriminated by your writings, my opinion should carry some weight."

"But why take any risks at all," I asked, "when the flames could reduce my words to harmless cinders?"

Spaeto frowned at me. "If I had children, as you do, Lucius Celer, and the wit to commit my thoughts to writing, I would no sooner burn what I'd written than I would fling my life's savings into the sea."

Although this emphatic declaration did not allay my fears entirely, it did raise some doubts in my mind as to the wisdom of acting on them. The degree of conviction in Spaeto's voice, moreover, suggested to me a corollary of the thought (confided not so long ago to this very almost-burned scroll) that we value most in others the qualities we find most lacking in ourselves; we also discount most in ourselves the qualities that others most admire.

With the question of incinerating my journal set aside for later decision, Decius and I, with Spaeto and Rullo, spent most of yesterday afternoon and evening assessing the problems involved in our projected escape. The more we considered the matter, the more desperate the enterprise seemed, but given the constraints of time and distance it appears we have no feasible alternative. The prospect confronting us is in no way palatable, however: four people woefully ignorant of the sea attempting to cross a hundred and fifty miles of open water in a small sprit-sailed boat. The very thought of such a journey sends shivers over me. Even assuming we arrive in one piece on Corsica, how are we going to manage once we get there? Autumn is coming on. Where will we find shelter? Who will take us in? We can't remain long in the populated regions along the eastern coast, but once we flee to the interior we'll be at the mercy of brigands and brutish shepherds. How will we survive all the dangers awaiting us? How will we subsist without help? My mind recoils at the thought of what fate may hold in store.

Nestor, Nestor, where *are* you?

But it makes no sense, or so I'm told, to dwell for any great length of time on purely conjectural calamities—no matter how likely they are to occur. As Spaeto observed, one can only assess the risks and deal with the contingencies.

One can also feel frightened, however.

But frightened or not, I may as well resume yesterday's journal entry at the point where that rabbity fit of timorousness interrupted me. There's enough on this scroll already, after all, to incriminate each of my faithful abettors several times over. I doubt I can further imperil them by appending a few expository details.

I was astonished, of course, when Spaeto told me that my slaves had long been aware of my intention to attempt an escape. I was more than a little anxious, moreover, to know how they had come by that awareness, and how Spaeto had learned that they'd come by it.

"Slaves know everything," he said in answer to my first question, and when I pressed him to elaborate, he responded, "Can you guess what slaves talk and think about most?"

I shook my head.

"Why, their master, of course."

"Their master?"

"Yes, their master."

"It makes sense, I suppose," I said after thinking it over.

"It makes more than mere sense, my friend. Consider: if somebody owned *you* outright and had absolute power to dictate everything from the details of your day-to-day existence to the shape of your ultimate fate, wouldn't you make that person the subject of the most exhaustive and meticulous study?"

"Yes, I believe I would," I answered him, smiling.

"Well then, you begin to understand how a slave thinks; and that understanding, however rudimentary, sets you apart from the vast majority of slaveowners. Few of them realize how naked they are to their serviles' gaze, or how clearly and in what minute detail they are perceived. A slave *knows* his master, far better and with far more precision than his master will ever know him. Indeed, he must know him better, no matter how benevolent the dominus may be. On the diligence of his observations, his welfare and even survival may depend; and for every detail of temperament he overlooks, he yields to hazard a precious fraction of his already minimal autonomy. That's why those who serve us scrutinize us so closely, and why they often know more about us than we know about each other or ourselves."

I stood silent, reflecting on all he'd said and wondering how truths that seemed so obvious now he'd uttered them could have eluded my perception for so long. I knew, of course, that I was by no means unique in my obtuseness, but typical, rather, of slaveholders as a class. Yet it bothered me more than a little to think that I'd been so egregiously myopic. (Only later did it occur to me that my failure to perceive my slaves' scrutiny might have been due more to careful dissimulation on their part than to culpable blindness on my own.)

And I still wasn't sure how, by scrutinizing me, they had learned that I was plotting an escape.

"Child's play," Spaeto snorted when I asked him. "First and foremost, there was your secretiveness. A man who's preparing for death doesn't start keeping things from his slaves. He doesn't take unexplained trips to Ostia or give shelter to unexplained guests. A man awaiting death opens himself up to those who serve him; he doesn't shut them out. He announces what provision he's made for their future welfare and tells them how they're to dispose of his remains. Unlike you, he devotes most of his time to the final ordering of his affairs. Unlike you, he has his wife and children constantly at his side.

"And just consider your wife and children from your serviles' point of view. Are they grieving over your imminent death? They are not. On the contrary, they seem to be in an advanced state of nervous apprehension, as if anticipating some adventure fraught with danger. How can one explain such odd behavior in the family of a man who's about to die? One can't easily. Unless, of course, the man has plans to stay alive."

"It all sounds very convincing," I acknowledged when he finished.

"The most convincing part is yet to come," he replied. "It must have been Nestor's letters that confirmed your slave's suspicions."

I narrowed my eyes at him. "But I never showed them Nestor's letters, and on top of that, only three of them can read."

At this Spaeto merely smiled at me, which caused me to narrow my eyes even further.

"You can't seriously be suggesting . . ." I started to object, beginning to feel more than a little bit scandalized.

"I can't? Why not?"

"Because I locked up those letters in the library."

"Oh? And where did you lock up the key?"

"I didn't need to lock it up; I always carry it with me."

"Always?"

"Well, not when I go running."

"And not when you go to bed, either."

I paused a moment, frowning in thought. "How can you be so sure they read those letters?"

Again Spaeto smiled. "How many times have Imperial couriers come galloping up to your house in recent years?"

"I don't see the connection," I responded, after puzzling briefly over his question.

"Just give it some thought. Literate or not, every one of your slaves knew pretty much what the Emperor had in mind for you, and they also could guess pretty accurately what you had in mind for yourself. What they couldn't guess, however—and didn't know, because you weren't telling—was what you had in mind for *them*. And because it was a matter of no small importance from their point of view, I'm sure they made it their business to find out. Slaves being slaves, they probably would have read Nestor's letters out of simple curiosity in any case."

I stared at Spaeto, flabbergasted. "You mean they've known all along?"

"I don't know about all along, but they've certainly known for some time."

"And how did you know they knew?"

Spaeto gave me another smile: somber, yet gentle and paternal. "Because the alternative to flight in your case is death, my friend. And given your serviles' regard for you, if they hadn't known you were planning an escape, they'd all have been downcast and grieving."

"You're *right!*" I gasped in wonderment as the full import of what he'd said hit home. "I never really thought about their feelings for me before."

Spaeto nodded almost mournfully. "I know, Lucius Celer. If you had, you might have shown them some trust."

And it came to me, when he said that, what a cruel and pointless travesty of wariness I'd been engaged in all this time. "I don't deserve their love," I said aloud to myself as a shroud of remorse settled over my spirit.

"Love is a gift, my friend," Spaeto corrected me. "It's meant to be accepted, not deserved."

"I know," I said as my eyes brimmed over. "But I'd like to deserve it just once, all the same."

⚜ FROM THE
⚱ LIFE

59

By defeating me and thereby winning his bet with Marcus, Agricus had, among other things, somewhat complicated our day's itinerary. He and Marcus clearly could not show up at Libo's front door and then excuse themselves an hour or two later in order to attend to some unspecified business in Formiae. That would be both embarrassing and rude. But delaying Marcus's defloration until the morning was equally out of the question: first, because the brothel probably wouldn't be open till after noon and, second, because our next destination, Capua, was a full day's ride and then some from Formiae's fleshly delights. The obvious solution, given the close proximity of Libo's villa to the town, was for us to proceed to Formiae directly. And this we did, Agricus making it clear on our arrival that my exclusion from the venereal revels remained a foregone conclusion.

His intransigence on this issue came as no great surprise, of course, but he seemed also almost obsessively intent on establishing himself as the sole mediator of Marcus's sexual initiation. That wasn't surprising either; officiating at such rites of passage had become rather a specialty of his. He'd presided at my own first intromission and had probably served as the scabbard for several others. His expertise in these matters was as undeniable as it was degraded, just as his behavior toward me was as unastonishing as it was antagonistic.

In truth I wasn't all that distressed by my exclusion. I didn't even feel much rancor. A bet had been made, and I had come out the loser; that was all there was to it. Had our positions been reversed, I felt sure, I'd have shown him no more consideration than he was showing me.

No, my quarrel was not with Agricus, for once. It was with Marcus. But what the quarrel was and how it had arisen were questions I found hard to answer. To be sure, I hadn't thought about them much while we were on our way to Formiae, since I was still smarting from the sting of my defeat. Once Marcus went off with Agricus to essay his inaugural prod, however, I felt a need to grapple with them. And it was while perched on the sea wall of Formiae's harbor that I finally puzzled out some answers.

290

Dracena was with me, stretched out in the sun by my side. Unlike me, he'd forgone the pleasures of the brothel voluntarily, claiming that he wasn't "in the mood." I could well believe he wasn't. He looked terrible, his face haggard and chalky white. It was clear that he'd begun to run a fever, and his overall condition had deteriorated so markedly since Tarracina that I would have been gravely concerned about him had I not been so preoccupied with myself.

And in the fullness of my petulance, I felt ill used by *him* as well. He'd assured me of victory, after all, encumbered me with excess confidence and pride. Yes, he and Agricus and Marcus had each done me some signal disservice that day, or so I chose to believe. And my choice, though perverse, was understandable, since the alternative to feeling anger was feeling shame.

But was it really within my power to opt for one and disclaim the other? Or were my anger and shame so hopelessly commingled as to render the choice mere illusion? Like many youths short on experience, I had sought to impose some order on reality by viewing it not as a flux but as a complex of separable components, each of which could be analyzed and understood in isolation. Sitting on Formiae's sea wall, with the sun trending westward and the smell of the sea in the air, it dawned on me that emotions, at least, were not compatible with this conception. They didn't come singly, or so I now perceived, or even in twos and threes. They came in masses, like shiny filaments all coiling and intertwined. My shame and anger, for example, were bound up inextricably with feelings of love and betrayal and grief. I was ashamed I'd lost the race to Agricus because I loved Marcus and had failed him by failing to win. (True, I'd never before run so great a distance without the impetus of fear to sustain my speed; but it was clear to me that if I'd given the least thought to the question of pace, I could have won the race, and the bet, rather easily.) I was ashamed, moreover, because in failing myself and Marcus I'd given yet another victory to the enemy who'd betrayed me with my aunt; and the grief that betrayal had caused me was thus rekindled.

At the core of my discomfort, though, lay a betrayal of a different kind, one far subtler but no less cruel. Indeed it may well have been crueler. For no matter how painful the scars left by an enemy, they are as nothing compared to the wounds inflicted by a friend, even if they've been inflicted unthinkingly.

In what way had Marcus wronged me? That was the riddle I found so baffling. He'd seen me run from the King of the grove and been impressed by my speed of foot. He'd chosen me as his ally in a contest against my foe. He'd made me his share-alike partner in the division of any spoils. And he'd forgone all signs of reproach when I stupidly lost the race.

How then had he transgressed against me?

Ah, yes; how painfully simple.

By regarding me as his equal.

It was an old, old sin of his, and one he had never repented. He'd confessed it by the swimming bath at Lorium in words I remembered well: "I tell you, Lucio, once and for always, that my affections aren't subject to my rank, and that the way the world perceives us must never determine the way that we regard each other."

"Once and for always," he had said to me, and once and for always it had remained.

In his eyes at any rate.

But the world's perceptions could not be summarily invalidated by means of his personal fiat. Such fictions as we chose to maintain with each other could in no way offset clear-cut facts.

We *weren't* equals, no matter how stridently we protested that we were. In reality, I was totally dependent on him, for love and family no less than shelter, food, and clothes. He might choose to ignore that reality; and yes, like a fool, so might I. But it would inevitably intrude itself upon our friendship, and each time it did so I'd be betrayed.

The nature of the betrayal now stood revealed to me: Marcus had given me too much credit. He'd seen me as an equal participant in the wager, when in fact I'd been no better than a pawn. Unlike him and Agricus, I'd had nothing substantial at stake. If I'd won, I'd have received three denarii from him, a meaningless sum in the context of his overall largesse. And having lost, what had I forfeited? The doubtful pleasure of watching his fall from grace. Agricus, by contrast, had stood to lose six denarii, which for him was a tidy amount. And Marcus, whom I'd failed, now passed from innocence 'twixt the thighs of some Formiaen whore.

It came to me at long last that underlying the wager my two companions had made was a far more significant contest, one involving their values and outlooks and more. Beneath their constant badinage, I now perceived, raged a battle of wills between finely matched equals. For Agricus, unlike me, was dependent on no one at all. With his beauty and courage and utter lack of scruples, he was as self-sufficient as anyone could be—an opponent worthy of Marcus's virtuous mettle. I, on the other hand, was a juvenile parasite, gorging on my patron's indulgence. And this, perhaps, was the point Agricus had meant to drive home by keeping me out of the brothel: quim is for men who are manly, was his message; whereas you, it is clear, are a boy.

Marcus's transgression, then, was a simple one. He had judged quite correctly that I was capable of outrunning Agricus's horse and he'd procured me an opportunity to profit by doing so (not incidentally, at Agricus's expense). Believing me his equal, he didn't see how, by running, I might demean myself. Believing me his equal, he'd accorded me freedom to choose. But he'd been badly mistaken about me, and that was the crux of his crime. I could not compete on his and Agricus's level; with them I was out of my depth. Though the time might come when I would shed my dependence, that time had not yet come. And until such time as it did, I'd do well to remember my place.

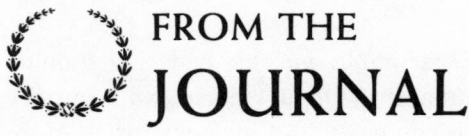
[SEPTEMBER 4TH]

Nestor has returned; the gods be thanked.

He reappeared yesterday evening, his corpulence astride some poor mule and his smugness more in evidence than ever. I was so glad to see him, though, that I went so far as to embrace him when he dismounted.

"Have we been introduced?" he asked as I clasped him to me.

"No," I replied; "but given the problems confronting us here, we've more or less dispensed with such formalities."

"A wise expedient. I take it that matters have reached a pitch of some slight urgency."

"They have indeed. I'm supposed to deliver what there is of Marcus's 'biography' to the Emperor at Lorium on the Nones."

"The Nones, you say. Well then, I'm glad I didn't dally on my way here."

"So am I, let me assure you."

He smiled at this and took hold of both my shoulders. "Be of good heart, Lucius Celer. Those friends unknown I referred to in my letters have been busily at work on your behalf, and your biographical pretenses have provided them with time sufficient to bring their labors to fruition."

"They've cut things rather close though, those unknown friends," I said with a trace of a shudder.

"Knowing providence would prove a staunch ally," he responded, his smile broadening as his hands gave my shoulders a playful shake.

I escorted him inside to the kitchen, where he was greeted with elation by both my family and my slaves. "It seems that my absence from this household has greatly enhanced my standing within it," he said after submitting happily to Camilla's kisses and my wife's embrace. "I'm led to wonder, therefore, whether this warm reception is meant to welcome me back or applaud me for having gone away."

"A bit of both," I answered him, "given the nature of the business that took you from us."

"Fair enough," he affirmed. "And now, may a weary traveler prevail upon the master of the house for a bit of sustenance?"

"He may indeed. In fact, I was expecting him to. Only . . ."

"Only?"

"Only I hope the weary traveler won't wait until after he's eaten to acquaint us with his plans for our escape."

"Oh, I wouldn't use words like 'escape,' my dear fellow," he said, his eyes focused over my shoulder, "especially with such a formidable-looking stranger standing just outside the door."

I whirled around in momentary fright; but the stranger in question was merely Spaeto, newly returned from Fregenae, where he'd been making arrangements to hire a boat. "I'll hazard the guess that you're the old man they call Nestor," he said, taking a few steps into the kitchen.

To this Nestor replied with a prolonged inquisitorial squint, which finally terminated with the statement, "And I will hazard the guess that you are my host's newest friend."

They both took such pleasure in displaying their powers of deduction that I couldn't refrain from teasing Nestor a little by asking him, "Would you care to hazard a guess as to my newest friend's name?"

To this he responded with an elaborate pantomime of concentration— furrowing his brow, scratching his head, and pulling abstractedly on his beard. At last he emerged from his portentous deliberations and, looking me straight in the eye, declared, "Judging by the look of him, I would say that his name must be . . . Spaeto!"

A *whoosh* of intaken breath soughed through the kitchen, as nearly everyone present gave vent to a gasp of amazement.

"How did you *do* that?" I practically shouted at Nestor.

"Very simple," he responded, bestowing upon me one of his most extravagantly insufferable smiles. "By chatting with two of your field slaves as they helped me coax my mule up to the house."

There was a gust of laughter then, as Nestor and Spaeto clasped hands. "I am in your debt, Junius Spaeto," the old man said, "no less than our well-beloved Lucius. But for you, it seems, all of my efforts on his behalf would have gone for naught."

"Yet but for you, venerable sage, I would not have had the good fortune to have met him."

This reply set Nestor to beaming. "Venerable sage," he repeated to himself, "that has a nice ring to it." And with that he reverted once more to the subject of food.

There would be no putting him off; I knew that from experience. So I resigned myself to the fact that I would have to fill his belly before learning what was in his mind.

It turned out, of course, that discretion was as much a factor as gluttony in his reluctance to discuss our escape. Even after he'd sated himself and drained his wine bowl, he refrained from all talk of his plans. "I could do with a breath of air," he said finally, indicating subtly that only Spaeto and I were to accompany him.

The three of us made our way out of the house into the twilight and set off down the road toward the Aro as the last tinges of afterglow gave way to stars in the western sky. For a while we walked along in silence, with Nestor seeming preoccupied and grave. He found his voice as we neared the river road, though, and turning to me said, "For by no means frivolous reasons, dear Lucius, I can tell you very little about the arrangements I've made. You in turn may confide very little of what I tell you to your family, and to your slaves you may say absolutely nothing."

Unreasonably enough, I bridled at this, prompted, no doubt, by my recent feelings of guilt. "But surely I ought to tell them something," I protested. "They've known for ages that I've been thinking of escape, and they've proven their loyalty a hundred times over."

Nestor frowned at me. "Of course they've known for ages," he snapped. "Slaves know everything. And of course they are loyal to you, no less than you are to them. I say again, however, that as to the details of this escape you've been pondering they must know *nothing*, not even which way you'll turn at the river road."

"Why such inviolable secrecy?" I asked sullenly.

"Because, my dear fellow, there is so much more at stake in this enterprise than you can possibly imagine."

I stared at him. "Is that the full extent of your explanation?"

"There is one thing more I will say," he replied after a moment spent coolly assessing me, "and that is that you yourself will shudder at the risks we've taken once you know all the facts of the case."

This response did little to mollify me, and I was about to press my point further when Spaeto forcefully intervened. "Speaking for myself, friend Lucius, I want to be told as little as possible about your plans, and I daresay your slaves will share my feelings. The less they know, the safer they'll be once you've departed, after all. The *frumentarii* will have little trouble tracing them, and some of them, surely, will be interrogated under torture. Whatever they know will be wrung from them, and if they know too much they'll all be implicated as your accessories and butchered. Much as they love you and pray for your deliverance, your fate once you leave here can have no further bearing on their lives. You've provided for them splendidly, and they revere you for it. Don't try to atone for not trusting them in the past by denying them their rightful future, and incidentally jeopardizing your own."

Spaeto was right of course, and had argued with unanswerable logic. I accordingly turned to Nestor when he'd done speaking and in a chastened voice said, "Please forgive me for being so contrary. I seem to be having some difficulty keeping my wits about me."

"Understandable," Nestor replied with a smile, "and forgivable, especially since it's not for your wits that we esteem you."

"You must tell me one day what it *is* for."

"No, my dear man. The truth is, one day you must *learn*."

Leaving that cryptic thought to bemuse me, Nestor turned his attention to those few meager details of our escape he deemed it meet I should know. "There's a merchant ship awaiting us at Alsium," he said, "which, unless I'm mistaken, is no more than three hours from here by cart. Given that you've been summoned to attend the Emperor on the Nones, we must leave here tomorrow night, and not later than the end of the second watch. You may take as much with you when we leave as will fit inside your wagon, but be sure to include among your belongings all your writings, all your correspondence, and all your winter clothes."

And that was all I was going to be told, apparently, for Nestor's next words were addressed to Spaeto. "You've contracted for a boat, I understand."

"That's correct," Spaeto replied.

"I have in mind a use that boat might be put to, a use that entails a degree of risk."

"Go on," Spaeto said.

"Your plan, as I understand it, was for Lucius and his family to flee to Corsica. That's a good plan, apart from one flaw."

"And that flaw is . . . ?"

"And that flaw is, it's too obvious. The *frumentarii* know as well as you do that Lucius has little chance of escaping except by sea; and Corsica is the nearest safe landfall off this part of the coast. It's a large island, mountainous, and for the most part sparsely populated. It's therefore one of the first places the *frumentarii* would look."

Spaeto gave a slightly embarrassed shrug. "You're right, of course. But Corsica was the best idea I could come up with."

"I am not reproaching you, man," Nestor protested, "far from it. Indeed, I believe we can turn your flawed idea to our advantage—if, that is, you feel you're in a position to assist us."

"So far I feel I am," Spaeto responded, "but I can't promise that you aren't going to scare me off."

"Well, let's find out," Nestor said, grinning. "My idea, very simply, is this: all but four of Lucius's slaves should set off northward at nightfall tomorrow. The four who remain should correspond roughly in age and sex to Lucius and the members of his family. At dawn on the Nones, some six hours after we depart for Alsium, you and the four of them should arrive in Fregenae with your baggage, board the boat you've contracted for, and sail straight off toward Corsica, preferably while there are several villagers around to watch you go. Once you get three or four miles out to sea, turn northeast and make for some empty stretch of beach. Then scuttle your boat near the shoreline and proceed to the prearranged place where the rest of your party will be awaiting you. The result, with any luck, will be that once all of *you* are inconspicuously on your way to Placidus's farm in Umbria, the *frumentarii* will come sniffing around Fregenae and conclude that all of *us* are conspicuously on our way to Corsica."

"It sounds like a good plan," Spaeto observed after considering it. "And you haven't managed to scare me off."

With our strategies determined, the three of us returned to the house and there confronted several dozen eager and anxious faces. I found it painfully difficult to withhold all information from them, but I confined myself to saying, "My beloved friends: In the morning we shall prepare for the future. While this night lasts, though, let us cherish one another and savor in memory all we've shared. Take your rest, have no fear, and be sure of my unreserved love. I in turn will never forget the love that you have shown me.

"Accept my blessing, and my all-too-inadequate thanks," I concluded hurriedly.

For the affection in my serviles' eyes was more than I could endure.

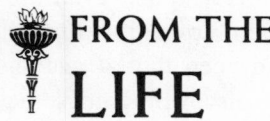
It was late in the afternoon before Marcus and Agricus rejoined us. Judging by the former's expression of bedazzlement, Formiae's courtesans had more than lived up to their reputation. Judging by the latter's expression of smugness, they'd had the benefit of some detailed advice. By combining Agricus's knowledge of Marcus with their own widely celebrated expertise, the brothel operatives had no doubt contrived to work some insidious variations on the immemorial themes. Whatever form those variations may have taken, my friend had clearly been unsettled by them. It was a tribute, I suppose, to the powers at Venus's command that the Marcus I now saw before me was not quite the Marcus I had known. Gone was the neophyte Stoic, beguiled by the romance of the mind; in his place stood a candidate for wantonness, enraptured by the logic of the flesh.

"How was it?" I asked him, although given his wide-eyed vacancy the question was wildly superfluous.

"Quite remarkable," he answered me, adding, after further deliberation, "Quite . . . *remarkable.*"

"He took to it like a fish to water," Agricus interjected, "and displayed considerable natural aptitude."

"You must feel very gratified," I remarked without overmuch affection.

" 'Vindicated' would be closer to the mark," he replied, fixing me with one of those looks of his that evoked every indignity I'd ever suffered at his hands.

"We'd better get going," Marcus decreed all at once, either thoroughly out of patience with our interminable bickering or utterly oblivious of the fact that we'd been talking to each other. "We don't want to descend on Cousin Libo just as he's about to have his supper."

We rode westward out of Formiae, retracing the route we'd taken in, and about a mile outside the town an imposing vine-covered archway rose up on our left, flanked by topiary hedges that suggested some sort of fish. "Here it is," Marcus said, having somewhat recovered from his daze. "The Villa of Dancing Dolphins."

"Those hedges are supposed to be *dolphins?*" Agricus asked incredulously; and I echoed him, "Those dolphins are supposed to be *dancing?*"

"You see, my friends," Marcus said to us with a rueful smile, "even the wealthy have their sorrows. I'll wager my cousin spent upward of 20,000 sesterces for some slack-jawed Greek servile who'd been touted to him as a horticultural genius. Imagine his anguish on discovering that the fellow was capable of no better work than this."

"I cringe to think of it," I said; and Agricus added, "The pathos tears at my heart."

"Ah, what hard, uncompassionate souls you are," Marcus responded with a bogus sigh, leading us through the archway and down a long cypress-lined path that led to his cousin's mansion.

"Who are you and what do you want?" asked the elegantly clothed young slave who was lounging beside the front portal when we rode up.

Marcus gave the arrant fellow one of those half-quizzical expressions of his that served as his standard response to asininity, but his tone was graciously forbearing as he replied, "Would you be so kind as to inform your master that his cousin Marcus Annius Verus has come to call on him?"

"Is he expecting you?" the slave demanded to know.

Though Marcus's nostrils flared a little, he responded in a voice that continued equable. "Alas, I'm not familiar with the contents of his mind. Perhaps I ought to investigate the matter and report back to you."

This touch of irony was well outside the slave's range of wit, and he retorted curtly, "Never mind; I'll go and ask him myself."

With that he stood up, carefully smoothed his saffron tunic, and went into the house, leaving the four of us to gape at one another in dumbfounded disbelief.

"Do you think it's safe to dismount?" Agricus asked, not entirely in jest.

"Oh, it's safe enough," Marcus responded with an impish grin, "but some might not think it polite."

"In *that* case . . ." Agricus began, and instantly he, Marcus, and I scrambled off our horses' backs.

We hit the ground laughing, and even Dracena was moved to smile. But our hilarity was quickly cut short by the sudden emergence of Libo from the house.

Marcus had told us that his cousin was "pushing fifty," but the tall, well-built, fair-haired figure who now rushed forward to greet him could easily have passed for forty in broad daylight and for thirty by the light of the moon. Whatever his age, his appearance was singularly impressive—not a line on his tan patrician face or an ounce of fat on his lean athletic frame.

"Beloved Cousin!" he exclaimed, enfolding Marcus in his sinewy arms. "What a joy it is to see you!"

Although slightly taken aback by Libo's effusiveness, Marcus managed to give some convincing signs of reciprocal enthusiasm. He lost no time, however, in turning his cousin's attention to us. "May I present my good friends Lucius and Agricus, of the Alta Semita," he said, "and my trusted companion and comrade Spurius Dracena."

He'd barely finished speaking before Libo came bounding over to me. "Beloved brother!" he said, his eyes wide with unaccountable affection.

"You do me great hon . . ." I started to respond, but my obeisances were cut short by a bone-crushing embrace and concussive kisses on both my cheeks. I could see Agricus smirking as my ribs nearly succumbed to the force of Libo's welcome; but then he realized all at once that his ribs were next, and his eyes started darting every whichway in a vain search for some avenue of escape. He had no choice but to submit in his turn, however, while I rejoiced in the fact that the last smirk, for once, was on him.

Only Dracena, who had wisely remained in place upon his horse, escaped the full fury of Libo's salutations, though even he was almost yanked from his sanctuary when our host seized hold of his proffered hand.

Greetings having been accomplished without disabling injury, Libo conducted us into his house, pausing at the threshold to say to the slave who'd accosted us, "Pallas, dear brother, please see to the horses and baggage."

To this request the insolent fellow responded by raising his eyebrows and rolling his eyes, as if Libo were making insupportable demands on him. But his master disregarded this silent protest.

The villa, though considerably smaller than Lorium, was in many ways just as impressive, for the maximum architectural effect had been derived from its close proximity to the sea. The entrance hall, the dining room, the swimming bath, and most of the bedrooms looked directly out on the Caietan Gulf and on the ranges of sun-tinted mountains that receded from its eastern shore. In the bedrooms and dining room, moreover, the view had been consummated by delicate hemispherical colonnades, which, by extending the chambers outward, served to foster an illusion of motion over the waves. On entering one of these rooms, accordingly, you could sit or recline with your eyes fixed on the water and imagine yourself at the bow of some fantastical seagoing palace, some fabulous floating pavilion bound for regions beyond the sky.

Since the villa was so impressive, I would not have been surprised to find its inhabitants somewhat humdrum by comparison. They were anything but—Libo's wife, Vibia, in particular.

To say that she was plump would be euphemistic; she was opulently, unabashedly fat. But her fleshiness, far from detracting from her allure, greatly added to it, though she was in no sense short of it to begin with, despite being well over forty. Like Annia, she had sparkling dark eyes and lustrous black hair. Unlike Annia, she used a great deal of powder and rouge. Her lips were stained blood red and called up ravishing images of corruption. Her clothes were a gauzy virginal white and left little to the imagination. Allied with all these charms was a sharp tongue and a patently lascivious disposition. Indeed, Marcus likened her personality to that of a "concupiscent shrew."

I found her positively delectable.

Libo appeared to regard her as a scourge.

Together they had produced twin daughters, Livia and Arria by name, who at that time had just turned nineteen. It was clear that they viewed Libo as something like a god and their mother as something of an embarrassment, though they were far too well-bred to let their aversion degenerate into open disrespect. In terms of physique and coloring they were very much her antithesis and very much the image of their father. In terms of physiognomy, on the other hand, the resemblances were reversed. Combining as they did the best aspects of Vibia's features and Libo's build, they'd grown into strikingly handsome women. And when we all convened for dinner that evening they looked like a brace of young she-lions as they arrayed their lissome bodies on either side of their father's couch.

Agricus gazed carnivorously at them from our couch across the table, while I gazed surreptitiously at Vibia as she reclined on the couch in between. Despite the intense carnality of my feelings for her, I didn't conceive of the possibility of a tryst. She was a patrician matron, after all, and I a low-born guest in her husband's house. (Naive as I was, it didn't occur to me that coupling with a wife-and-mother might be far more acceptable in aristocratic society than dallying with a daughter, or son.)

Naive or not, I dearly envied Marcus his place beside Vibia on the middle couch, especially since, given his recent defloration, he seemed barely less besotted with her than I. Dracena I envied less because he looked so worn out and ill, but even so, if he'd offered me his place on her couch in exchange for my vigorous health, I would have seriously considered the proposal.

Not that the third place on my couch was occupied by anyone disagreeable. On the contrary, the ninth person at the dinner table was a
gentle old Theban named Thiasos, who served as Arria's and Livia's tutor.
I rather liked him, especially since he was kind enough not to converse
in Greek.

After what seemed like quite a lengthy delay, a first course of seafare
appeared. It was carried in by three sullen-faced slaves who unceremo-
niously deposited their trays on the central table and left.

"Perhaps it would be more expedient if we were to help ourselves,"
Libo said in an apologetic tone. So we all leaned over and filled our
plates, having already accustomed ourselves to mixing our own wine and
water.

"How polite and long-suffering our poor guests are," Vibia gibed at
her husband. "Don't you think that they're entitled to some sort of explanation?"

"I'm sure we don't want to bore them with the details of our domestic
arrangements, dearest," he replied in obvious embarrassment.

"Better to bore them than to subject them to the unexplained rudeness
of our so-called slaves."

To this Libo responded with a feeble laugh, while Livia and Arria
sought to comfort him with soulful commiserative smiles. "Speaking of
rudeness," he said somewhat lamely, "I was reading from Cicero the other
day, and he made a number of very telling comments about good manners
in one of his letters to Atticus."

"How unutterably enthralling," Vibia remarked, turning her eyes away
from Libo just quickly enough to catch me ogling her.

"Yes, isn't it," Libo continued, turning to Marcus as though seeking
his assistance. "Did you know, dear Cousin, that the villa next to ours
used to belong to that illustrious republican?"

"You don't say so!" Marcus marveled obligingly.

"Oh, yes indeed. In fact, it's been pretty well established that Mark
Antony's henchmen murdered him in that very house."

"At least he died quickly," Vibia interjected, "whereas all of us here are
condemned to die a slow death from lack of proper attendance."

"Ah, dearest Vibia," Libo sighed, an edge of irritation becoming audible
in his voice. "I sometimes think that *you* will be the death of *me*."

To this statement Livia and Arria responded with evident distress,
reaching out almost in unison to give their father's hands a solicitous
squeeze.

"These sea acorns are remarkably delicious," Marcus said in an effort
to steer the conversation into more innocuous channels.

"They certainly are," I seconded him; and even Agricus chimed in with "Yes indeed."

"It's providential they're to your liking," Vibia said, suggestively licking fish sauce off her fingers, "since it will probably be quite some while before our servile 'brothers' will trouble themselves to bring in the second course."

"That's *enough!*" Libo erupted with sudden vehemence, as Arria and Livia glowered censoriously in their mother's direction.

"One course is most certainly not enough," Vibia retorted.

"You know perfectly well what I'm talking about, Wife."

"That's quite true, Husband; and I think it's high time our guests knew, too."

For several moments Libo glared at her, his jaw muscles working. Then he appeared to come to a decision, and turning to Marcus he said, "Dearest Cousin, I must confess to you that this house is an *ekklesia.*"

"An *ekklesia?*" Marcus repeated, clearly as much at a loss as I was as to Libo's reasons for using the Greek for "public assembly" to describe his own private domain.

"It's not a political matter, I assure you," Libo hastened to add. "It's purely a question of religious observance. Believe me, we all acknowledge Caesar's authority here and pray for his continued good health. Our Redeemer repeatedly enjoined us to render all due obedience to him, in fact."

"I'm sure that was very public-spirited of him," Marcus responded. "However, I think it only fair to inform you that the Emperor's health has been considerably less than good of late."

Libo looked devastated by this information, and in a quavery voice declared, "Well then, we shall all pray most strenuously for his complete and speedy recovery."

To this Livia and Arria reacted with emphatic corroborative nods, while Vibia, with remarkable delicacy, broke wind.

There ensued an awkward silence, during which we all tried to avoid the appearance of sniffing the air. I myself risked a fleeting glance in Vibia's direction, and went hot around the ears when I saw that she in turn was gazing at me.

"Excuse my ignorance, Cousin," Marcus said finally, "but why do you call your house an *ekklesia,* and who exactly is your 'redeemer'?"

"Please forgive me for not elaborating to begin with," Libo said in a painfully apologetic, almost obsequious, tone. "I call this household an *ekklesia* because we are a community of souls, and our Redeemer is the son of the one God."

"Oh, you're *Christians!*" Marcus exclaimed delightedly. "How very intriguing. I can't think why I didn't figure that out for myself."

"We're not *all* Christians," Vibia interjected, wiping her wet fingers on the diaphanous white muslin that imperfectly concealed her breasts. "And not all of us who are are truly devout."

"To which category would you assign yourself, gracious lady?" Marcus asked her.

"I, sweet Cousin, am the most devout of non-Christians, largely because Christianity has wreaked such havoc among my slaves. . . . I take it you've noticed their peculiarly unservile behavior by now."

Not wishing to take sides in a long-standing marital dispute, Marcus gracefully sidestepped by saying, "I seldom pay much attention to the way slaves behave."

"You would if they stopped attending you," Vibia responded. "Especially if their master encouraged them in their derelictions."

"I do *not* encourage them," Libo protested.

"You certainly don't *discourage* them," Vibia answered back.

"They are children of God, just as I am. It is not for me to treat them like brute beasts."

"And what about how you treat *me?*" Vibia spat out, her voice rising markedly in both volume and pitch.

"You have chosen to exclude yourself from our community of souls, my dearest. There is nothing whatsoever I can do about that."

"*Exclude* myself!" Vibia shrieked, rising, with no small expenditure of effort, to her feet. " 'Exclude' myself you dare to say. How in the world can I have 'excluded' myself when I'm exactly the same woman I've always been?"

"Except that there's a good deal more of you," Libo commented under his breath.

"I heard that," Vibia said, striking a fairly believable pose of injured pride. "And I suppose that you would say I'd just 'insulted myself' by hearing it. But the fact is, oh, my ageless and beautiful husband, that I didn't start putting on weight until six years ago, when you began to turn away from me and this whole Christian farce of yours began."

"I didn't turn away from you," Libo shot back at her. "I simply received the holy spirit when it descended upon me."

"Holy spirit!" Vibia sneered. "I'd call it the fear of growing old."

"Rubbish, woman."

"You were forty-two and flabby, Husband, and your daughters, whom you'd never had much time for up to then, had just recently started to bleed. Doesn't it strike you as odd that ever since the 'holy spirit' made its celebrated descent upon you you've been exercising like an athlete, shamelessly pampering your daughters, and studiously ignoring me."

"You're imagining things, dearest. And besides, we've been through all this before. Out of consideration for our guests I think we should . . ."

"Out of consideration for our guests we should provide them with some semblance of hospitality. But we can't, because no sooner had you been 'redeemed' than you set about establishing this *ekklesia* of yours, this empty façade you call a Christian community. And when the slaves showed no interest at first, you lured them in with promises of Christian 'brother-hood,' which to them meant no more than less work."

"That's ridiculous," Libo objected, though he clearly knew that there was more than a grain of truth in what she said.

"No more ridiculous than this Christian love you keep prating about, this love which seems to prevail everywhere but in our bed."

"Really, Vibia, you're going too far," said Libo, as all the rest of us looked on in various stages of indignation, embarrassment, or lust.

"You're always maundering on about how this Christ of yours has assured us of forgiveness for our sins," Vibia continued, totally ignoring Libo's protest. "Well I for one am not aware of having committed any sins I need forgiveness for. . . ."

She paused and glared wrathfully at her husband and daughters, who sat frozen before her on their couch. "What are your sins, Libo?" she said finally. "For what crimes are you in such desperate need of forgiveness?"

And with that she stalked out of the room, leaving her guests, her family, and her daughters' Greek tutor in a state not too dissimilar to shock.

"Perhaps we should have the rest of our dinner served to us in the library," Libo said finally in a numbed tone of voice. "It's unlucky to have eight around the table."

Unsurprisingly, our conversation once we'd retired to the library was marked by little in the way of animation, and it wasn't long before a consensus emerged that it was time we went to bed.

Libo had placed four separate bedrooms at our disposal, but Marcus, out of concern for Dracena's condition, chose to pass the night in company with the *singularis*. I myself was by then more or less accustomed to Agricus's constant presence, so I wouldn't have minded much if we'd ended up sharing a room. He claimed to be looking forward to a little privacy, however, though I suspected he was secretly hoping to lure Livia or Arria, if not both, to his bed.

That such hopes would most probably prove vain I was about to discover in a most exotic fashion.

It had been a long day on top of a nearly sleepless night, and it didn't seem possible somehow that Tarracina and the Pomptine ship canal were barely twelve hours in the past. Much had happened in those twelve hours; I had lost a race, Dracena had lost his health, Marcus had lost his virginity, and Agricus had emerged victorious once again. Some things never changed.

Though I was tired, I didn't feel ready for sleep, so for a long while I stood by my bedroom's colonnade and looked out at the moonlight on the mountains and the moonbeams on the sea. I felt lonely and ruttish, in need of a woman's warmth. But there were no women accessible apart from those that I could conjure in my mind. With fatigue overtaking me, I finally lay down on my pallet and gave some halfhearted consideration to placating my desires with my "fist," to use Agricus's endearing locution. But in the end I thought better of it, an instance of self-restraint for which I was shortly to thank the gods.

Before long I dozed off, with thoughts of Annia's slender body conveying me toward my dreams. I awoke some time later with one of Vibia's nipples lodged firmly between my lips.

"I saw you eying me at dinner, you little mongrel," she whispered as her body sank down atop mine.

I knew right away that I'd stopped dreaming; the weight of her billowy flesh and the smell of her powdered skin were far too real for any nighttide fancy. And their reality was unquestionably to my liking, apart from the nagging scruples I had with regard to my role as a guest.

"Excuse me, gracious lady," I said, having managed by dint of supreme exertion to roll her onto her side, "but great as is my desire for you, I'm obliged to remember that your husband is my host."

Her response to this was to press her wet mouth against my ear and hiss, "What if I told you that he is being unfaithful to me at this very moment?"

I gave some thought to that contingency while she nibbled and sucked on my lobe. Then, with the greatest reluctance, I replied, "That would not make him any less my host."

Undiscouraged, Vibia sent her tongue slithering deep into the recesses of my ear, and on withdrawing it breathed, "What if I told you that he has not one mistress but two, and that both of them sprang from my loins?"

"You can't be serious!" I responded in a shocked whisper, as her mouth found its way to my neck.

"Oh, can't I?" she retorted, and began licking my chest.

"You *can* be serious?" I asked in mounting arousal, as she ran her tongue across my stomach.

"I'll give you a choice," she said breathily, as her head moved lower and lower. "I can lead you to his bedroom and let you see for yourself. "Or . . ."

"Or?" I repeated, no longer caring much whether incest was afoot or not.

"Or you can take my word for it," she whispered, taking all of me into her mouth.

I decided at that point to give her the benefit of the doubt.

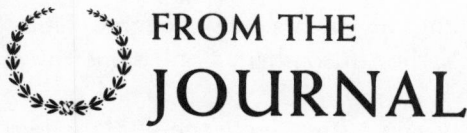

FROM THE
JOURNAL

62

[SEPTEMBER 5TH]

We are away.

We left for Alsium at midnight, arrived there at the beginning of the fourth watch, and sailed from the harbor at first light. Our ship is called the *Liberta*, aptly enough, the wife of its original owner having been a freedwoman. It is at present owned by its captain and several of his relatives, one of whom—a brother-in-law, I believe—fancies himself enough of an artist to devise color schemes for the family's vessels. In my opinion the fellow is laboring under a serious misapprehension, for the alternating green and red bands that ring the *Liberta*'s hull are not only unsightly in themselves but look positively garish in conjunction with the golden yellow of the stern gallery and the vivid purple of the steering oars and trim. Our captain seems perfectly content with the ship's out-landish appearance, however, most probably because the way she looks has no bearing on her seaworthiness or speed, both of which are pur-portedly first rate.

She is a good-size ship, perhaps two hundred fifty tons burden, with a standard square-rig mainsail, a spritsail, and a mizzen. She carries a cargo of oil and a crew of thirteen. Her captain, who bears the illustrious name of Aeneas, is a bellowing red-haired Tarentine whose moods seem to alternate between jolly exuberance and apoplectic rage. And though the crew doesn't appear to take these volcanic humors of his too seriously for the most part, they waste no time in complying with his commands.

As far as I can tell, they all regard Nestor, my family, and me as ordinary travelers, not as fugitives from the Emperor's writ. Even the captain appears to view us as unexceptional. I had assumed for some reason that Nestor had privately chartered the vessel he said was awaiting us at Alsium. I realize now that he did no such thing, and that it would have been very imprudent of him if he had. What he did instead, ap-parently, was seek out a reputable-looking merchant ship bound for some suitable destination and then negotiate, in the usual manner, terms of passage for himself and for us. Given that the *Liberta* was fully laden when we boarded her, he must have had to pay some sort of premium for the time she spent waiting for us in port, but needless to say he has confided none of the details of his arrangements to me. To be sure, once we were safely clear of the harbor this morning, he was gracious enough to let us know that we are on our way to Narbo, in southern Gaul, some three or four days' sail west by north.

I suppose I shouldn't be so huffy about his secretiveness. He is our rescuer, after all, and has thus far managed our escape with the utmost efficiency. Everything is going perfectly, as a matter of fact. We are on a fast, well-run ship impelled by soft southerly breezes across a tranquil summer sea. Our quarters on the afterdeck are comfortable and clean, and we even have a collapsible awning at our disposal to ward off excessive glare or eventual rain. A few miles away to starboard lies the coastline from which we have fled, and above it the sun is just now breaching the crest of the Apennines.

Yes, everything is unquestionably going well; but this is the last time I will ever see the sun rise over my homeland.

It is well risen now, and perhaps an hour has passed since I put down my pen and succumbed to tears. Oh, ye cruel and unfeeling gods, why must we always leave so much behind us in order to carry on with our lives? It is unjust. It is unfair. I feel I've lost almost everything dear to me in the space of the last twelve hours. As the sun set yesterday I had a house, a farm, and a familia of trusted slaves. Now I have a collapsible awning, a few square feet of deck space, and a conscience heavy with remorse. Somewhere, many miles beyond our wake, a small boat is heading westward out of Fregenae. Aboard is my friend Junius Spaeto, once more risking his life to save mine, and four of those trusted, and trusting, serviles, serving as doubles for my family and me.

All the rest of my slaves set off for Umbria yesterday evening, taking leave of us in a ferment of kisses and sobs. The girls who have been Camilla's playmates all her life wept inconsolably when it came time to say good-bye to her, and as for Camilla herself, I have never before seen her so distraught. The women slaves in their turn clasped her fiercely to their bosoms, then clung to Portia as though to life itself. Tears streamed down Decius's cheeks throughout the whole sad succession of farewells. I was often unable to speak as the people of my familia filed by me one by one for a last embrace. Along with my blessing, I gave them each a coin: a sestertius for each child, a denarius for each woman, and an aureus for each man—poor compensation for all the service they've rendered me, and all they may yet suffer on my account. To each and to all I sought to convey some measure of the love they must now know I feel;

and when Gaia, the buxom young creature I once coveted to my shame, responded to my valediction by sinking to her knees and raining tearful kisses on my hands, I felt such anguish and contrition that I came near to breaking down.

Very quickly, the time for their departure was upon us, and I watched my people march dolefully through the gateway. For a long while the sound of their lamentations lingered behind them, until it faded little by little into the star-flecked stillness of the night.

For the next few hours I threw myself into the details of packing our belongings and loading them onto the cart. I didn't want to think about the good-byes that were still to be said.

At midnight all was in readiness, and the good-byes could no longer be postponed.

There is a certain rightness, I suppose, in the fact that it was Rullo and his family who appointed themselves to stand as surrogates for me and mine. His older son is Decius's age almost exactly, and his younger one is precisely Camilla's height, despite being a year or so her senior. (For a nine year old, the boy was most understanding about the need to attire himself in girl's clothes come the morning, although I doubt he would have been so amenable if his playmates hadn't already left the farm.) Rullo's wife, Lollia, is a good deal older than Portia, and has dark hair rather than fair. But a hooded cloak will more than compensate for any want of a close resemblance, especially since in most other respects, such as closeness and loving devotion, the family as a whole is very much the image of my own.

What could I say to the four of them when the time came? How could I convey some small fraction of the love and the sorrow I felt? In the end, I could think of nothing to say or do. I just stood there, struck mute, searching their faces in the lamplight for some sign that I was managing somehow to communicate the flood of feelings that my body could barely contain. I embraced the sons decorously enough, then embraced the wife as well, but when it came time to put my arms around Rullo, my feelings all at once overflowed.

For a long time we held fast to one another as I wept on his shoulder like a child. Then finally, with an effort, I staunched the flow of tears and, pulling my head back a little, saw that Rullo's eyes, too, were brimming over. We gazed at each other for several long moments and exchanged the saddest of smiles. "Be well," I said to him, and he answered me, "Be well."

Then one final embrace, and I let him go.

It only remained now for me to say good-bye to Spaeto.

"I fear for you, my friend," I said. "Perhaps you had better come away with us."

"Then who would care for your familia?" he replied with a smile.

"Who will care for them if the Emperor tracks you down? He'll trace my slaves easily enough, and when he finds them, there you'll be."

At this Spaeto laughed. "You forget, friend Lucius, that we're dealing here with the Imperial bureaucracy." And seeing my puzzled expression, he continued, "The Emperor in all his grandeur won't go searching for your slaves himself, you know, and he certainly won't send his Teutonic bodyguards to do his searching for him."

"I still don't follow you," I said.

"It's very simple," he replied. "The people who are going to trace your slaves are not the same people who've seen my face. If anyone 'tracks me down,' as you put it, it will be the *frumentarii;* and the *frumentarii* don't know me from Julius Caesar."

"That's true, I suppose."

"Of course it is. Now go, Lucius Celer, before your anxieties do you in."

With that, he turned to my family and gave Portia, Decius, and Camilla each a kiss. "Lead them away to their refuge, oh, venerable sage," he said to Nestor, who clearly still relished the appellation.

To me his parting words were, "Know, Lucius, that I am ever your ally and friend."

There was a crack in the plaster of our bedroom ceiling, a jagged line that ran nearly to the window from the corner above our bed. Sometimes after Portia and I had made love, or when sleep was eluding me, I would stare up at that fissure in the lamplight and imagine it a river or a road. I would embark then on imaginary journeys, or else start retracing some journey from my past. Invariably sleep would overwhelm me before I journeyed very far, and I'd find when I woke in the morning that the route of my travels was once more merely a fault in the plaster.

What route shall I travel now, oh, ye gods?

And where, oh, where shall I find rest?

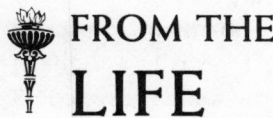 **FROM THE LIFE**

63

Since it was still quite early in the morning when we were ready to depart from Libo's villa, a nice question of etiquette arose as to whether Marcus should cause our host to be awakened so that we might formally take our leave and personally thank him for his hospitality. I had had to resolve a somewhat similar problem just before dawn, when I awoke to find myself pinned to my pallet by the bountiful weight of our hostess's body. My problem was compounded by the fact that I badly needed to ease my bladder, and complicated by the recumbent lady's odor, which was a peculiarly arousing blend of perfume, oil, and venereal effusions. I knew that my friends and I had to get an early start that day if we were to reach Capua at anything like a reasonable hour; so, clearly, I couldn't lie there and luxuriate beneath the fragrant folds of Vibia's flesh. Of course, with regard to her—as opposed to Libo—the question was not so much *should* she be awakened as *how*, though I really didn't have that many options. With my arms and legs effectively immobilized, the only maneuverable parts available to me were my member and my tongue. Fortunately, Vibia's ear was well within range of the latter, which served very efficiently to rouse her from her slumbers. Once she was roused, however, she hastened to avail herself of the former, with the result that I experienced considerable distress when I finally paid heed to my bladder's demands.

But such torment as I suffered was hardly significant in light of all the pleasures I'd enjoyed, and it was with decided reluctance that I withdrew for the last time from the clinging warmth between Vibia's thighs.

Marcus, of course, was already up and doing by the time I emerged from my room, while Agricus and Dracena were getting dressed. Though dawn had long since broken, we were, to all appearances, the only people awake in the entire villa; and the question of waking Libo arose as we sat in the pantry breakfasting on honey and bread. "I can't go barging into his bedroom," Marcus expostulated; and remembering what Vibia had said about who might be in his bedroom with him, I was not at all disposed to disagree.

"Leave him a note," Agricus suggested.

"Fair enough," said Marcus, "but with whom?"

I nearly restrained myself, but in the end the urge to advertise my sexual conquest overcame my better instincts. To maintain a discreet silence about Vibia seemed inadmissible somehow, especially in light of the humiliations I'd suffered the previous day. "I know someone we could give the note to," I said.

The three of them turned to look at me, and Marcus responded, "Really? Who?"

"Oh, just someone who can be relied on to make sure Libo receives it," I replied, feeling a little coy but also—all at once—a little anxious. Marcus might not approve of my sleeping with his cousin's wife, I belatedly realized; perhaps my conquest was not something to be bragged about, but concealed.

I'd gone too far by then to reconsider my original decision, though, a fact that Agricus, ever alert to any chinks in my self-possession, was quick to exploit. "Where are you keeping this anonymous someone?" he asked pointedly.

I couldn't come up with an evasive answer quickly enough to head him off.

"She's in your room, isn't she, you little turd?" he said with a trace of envy in his voice. "You got your prod into one of those twins."

"Such unseasoned pullets are not to my taste," I responded loftily.

That was all Marcus and Agricus needed to hear. "Vibia!" they exclaimed simultaneously, both delighted, apparently, to have solved my trifling riddle. And Marcus added, "I saw you making cow eyes at her, you satyr; though I have to admit I found her pretty enticing myself."

"Sow eyes would have been more appropriate," Agricus commented gallantly. "But then, a person of Lucio's minimal charm can't afford to be too selective."

"Feel free to assume the grapes were sour," I shot back at him, "since you plainly weren't charming enough to find out for yourself how they taste."

"I plainly wasn't desperate enough, you mean."

"Comrades, comrades," Marcus intervened, imperfectly suppressing a smile, "let us not indulge in impropriety. We must remember that the husband of the lady in question is not only our host but also the cousin of no less eminent a personage than myself. I suggest, therefore, that we refrain from all further reference to her until we're well on our way to Capua. In the meantime, though, I can see no harm in taking advantage of Lucio's, uh, connection with the lady to transmit to Libo our sincere thanks for his—and of course his wife's—hospitality."

Thus it was that I returned one last time to the room where I'd spent the night. But Vibia was no longer there, alas. I suppose simple prudence had impelled her to return to her private quarters, since worse than embarrassment might have resulted if she'd been discovered asleep in my bed. Her prudence had landed me with a problem, though, for what was I now to do with Marcus's note? Reporting the problem back to Marcus seemed out of the question, because that would raise doubts in his mind— or so I thought—about my claims of coitus, and expose me at the same time to the full force of Agricus's ridicule. I see now, though I didn't realize it then, that by imputing to Marcus a readiness to doubt my veracity I had begun already to alter my view of him. In one or two subtle respects he had become less a friend to be trusted that a patron to be cultivated; and there is no question but that this portentous change in my perception of him had taken place in less than a day and a night.

But what in fact had caused it?

I'm still not sure I know.

Certainly the realization that I was so dependent on him played a part. But my dependence, on the other hand, was nothing new. The change in our relationship, however subtle, was far too insidious to be explained solely in terms of an increase in my awareness. Something more concrete had occurred, something terrible and dark, to tarnish the chastened steel of our mutual trust. And though my mind recoils from the idea, the fact is that only one significant event took place during the day and night hours immediately succeeding our departure from Tarracina: Marcus had stuck his pristine prod inside a woman.

But to return to the problem of his note—it seemed to me that I had two choices: I could leave it anywhere and report that I'd delivered it direct to Vibia, or I could slip it under some likely-looking bedroom door and report the same thing.

Emboldened by the belief that Marcus would probably never be the wiser, yet still possessed of some scruples about getting the note to its intended recipient, I opted in the end for the under-the-door approach. I don't know to this day if the door I chose was the right one, or if Libo ever received Marcus's words of thanks. I do know what I told my companions when I rejoined them, however—that it had taken every last ounce of my self-discipline to resist Vibia's efforts to lure me back into bed.

We'd fixed on Capua as our day's destination for the simple reason that Marcus had no friends or relatives to receive us in the next three towns along our route, whereas he did have contacts among Capua's leading citizens.

In the event, we covered barely forty of the less than fifty miles between Formiae and our goal before Dracena toppled from his horse.

It seems clear in retrospect that Marcus, Agricus, and I had been somewhat negligent with regard to his deteriorating condition. But a good part of our negligence was directly attributable to him. He not only refused to talk to us about his wound, but became positively bearish if we presumed to express our concern. The result was that we more or less kept our distance from him, although Marcus had made it his business to maintain an unobtrusive watch.

As we rode toward Capua that day we saw signs that he was getting worse. Sweat poured off him though the weather was cool and cloudy, and I noticed at one point that his body was wracked by shivers.

Naturally, I felt worried about him, but I was afraid to speak or act. He was a soldier, after all—a *singularis*, the elite. Who was I to tell him how to deal with a commonplace battlefield wound?

The question became moot when he collapsed, of course. And in a way it was fortunate he did. For he fell from his horse within sight of the Auriga Tavern, a decidedly unprepossessing establishment that we might otherwise have simply passed by. And had we done so, we would never have come to know Hieronymous.

 **FROM THE JOURNAL** **64**

[SEPTEMBER 6TH]

We are adrift in featureless silence, the dull gray plane of the sea blending by subtle degrees into a phlegm-colored overcast that seems to encroach on us constantly without ever drawing near. The sails hang limp from the yardarms and the steersman lies snoring by his oars. Perhaps half a dozen of his fellow mariners are similarly fast asleep, sprawled out like casualties of battle on the deck planks and hatches. Of the crewmen who are awake, a few have cast fishing lines over the gunwales and sit cleaning and gutting their catch between bites. The rest are engaged in a quiet but intense game of knucklebones, the stakes being rather higher, I imagine, than comports with good comradeship or good sense.

According to Captain Aeneas this unnerving combination of flat calm and hovering mist is called a "day glaze" and is not at all uncommon in these waters at this time of year. Such conditions pose no threat to the safety of the ship, he assures me, and rarely persist much longer than three or four hours.

"Where are we, do you suppose?" I asked him this morning, trying not to sound excessively concerned.

"Oh, probably halfway 'round Corsica, and drifting west by south."

"When do you think we'll get some wind?"

This elicited a hearty laugh. "Not too soon, I hope."

I tried to make some sense of this paradoxical reply, but had to confess, "I don't understand."

"Just look around you," said the Captain, indicating with a sweep of his arm the off-white blankness that enveloped us. "If we catch a breeze before we can get a bearing on the sun, we won't know which way to point the prow. We might even have to reef sail and drop anchor."

"Those sound like fairly drastic measures."

This craven display of landlubber's ignorance provoked a roar of merriment. "Not *so* drastic, Poseidon save you. If it's a soft breeze, we won't lose much by spurning it, and if it's a full-fledged gale, I may be able to smell which way it's blowing."

"You can *smell* the direction of the wind?"

"I'd be a poor ship's captain if I couldn't, my friend, since it's no more

difficult than solving a simple riddle. You see, given the time of year and
our approximate location, I pretty much know what sort of winds we're
likely to encounter. Northwesterlies are the most common in these waters,
and on their currents you can catch the fertile scent of Gaul. Southeast-
erlies are fairly common also and savor of Africa's sand and heat. The
northeasterly flows are often gusty and bear the cool wet imprint of the
Alps, while on winds from the Hesperides there floats the dry tangy
fragrance of Hispanic flax."

"Remarkable," I commented.

"And, regrettably, quite imprecise," Captain Aeneas responded with a
smile. "But you know how it is with us seamen: the uncertainties of our
profession are such that we all like to imagine we know a great deal more
about nature's caprices than the gods have thus far seen fit to reveal.
Without such pretenses we'd find ourselves either living in constant fear
or else refusing to venture out of port. Good fortune, good seamanship,
and many long years of experience aren't always enough to sustain us
throughout a voyage. We need a little arrogance as well, a degree of out-
and-out conceit. Because there are times—and they're by no means infrequent—when the elements get the upper hand of us and tempt us to
surrender to despair. At such times it isn't enough simply to throw up
our hands and appeal to the mercy of the gods. We must continue to
act as if we are masters of the situation and refuse to believe that we're
helpless to shape our fate. We *are* helpless, of course, in every ultimate
sense; but if the gods haven't forsaken us entirely, we can still prevail by
insisting that we are not."

"Are you trying to tell me that there's some dangerous weather in the
offing?" I asked with a ludicrously disproportionate degree of concern.
And Captain Aeneas guffawed so loudly by way of response that several
snoring crewmen were startled out of their sleep.

"I wouldn't much mind if there were some foul weather impending,
you fretful fellow. I'd almost prefer a raging storm to this damnable day-
glaze calm."

And so the reality of our situation is that we are in no particular danger
and that these conditions of limited visibility won't persist too much
longer.

My fantasy is, however, that they will persist for the rest of our lives.

I remember, not so long ago, gazing at the fountain in our garden and
musing about the way a condemned man all at once finds the world to
be teeming with bad metaphors. I sit now, gazing at the rheumy vapors
that envelop us, and observe that a reprieved man inhabits a world where
the metaphors are far more brutal and to the point.

Where are we? We are nowhere. Where do we journey? From void to void.

Yes, in actual fact we are at sea on the good ship *Liberta*, and we are en route from Italy to southern Gaul.

But our ultimate destination remains unknown to us, and our ultimate fate is no longer in our own hands. We have become blindly subservient creatures, shepherded along by a muzzy-minded old man.

Is this, then, the degraded form of existence to which we must henceforth resign ourselves? Have we fled from death only to embrace in turn the most sordid and abject dependence?

And why do I say "we"?

It is my spirit, not anyone else's, that is oppressed by all this nothingness.

It is I, and not my loved ones, who feels unanchored and unmanned.

Could it be that my ever tenuous sense of myself was so bound up with the status accruing to me by virtue of my land, my slaves, and my rank in the social order that, once stripped of those trappings of autonomy, I find myself merely a husk?

It may well be the case, for I search in vain within myself for some store of fortitude to sustain me in my hour of trial. I can see no future dignity beyond this opaque gray metaphor that encircles us.

I feel myself beginning slowly to yield to despair; and over the bitterness of my incipient despondency there hovers the unmistakable staleness of failing nerve.

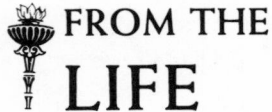
Unhealthily situated near the Volturnus River bridge, where the Via Latina joins the Via Appia, the Auriga Tavern was an offense to the eye and the nostrils that aspired, as Marcus put it, to the highest standards of squalor. It was a monument to the keen business instincts of a certain M. Lucilius Bassus, a Capuan of Vespasian's time, who perceived that a tavern located at the junction of the two major roads leading southward from Rome would greatly enhance the wealth of any man astute enough to build it, and who, accordingly—to quote in part from the lengthy *pro-memoria* chiseled above the Auriga's front portal—"caused this *mansio* to be constructed with his own money in the year of the four Emperors and lived here."

"Whatever in the world possessed him?" Agricus wondered aloud as we eased Dracena down from Marcus's horse.

"You mean, to build this place?" I asked, grasping the half-conscious *singularis* under his armpits.

"No. To live here once he built it," Agricus replied, getting a grip on Dracena's legs.

"Well, it's a good thing he did build it," Marcus avowed, doing his best to hold up his bodyguard's midsection, "since it's at least two more miles to Casilinum."

"I have a feeling we're going to wish we'd traveled the extra distance," Agricus said as the three of us heaved and hauled our burden into the tavern.

And in the event he was very nearly right, for our first impulse once we stumbled inside was to wheel right around and stagger out. Even Marcus found the ambience repellent, and went so far as to inquire of the grotesque-looking *caupo* if he could recommend any reasonably priced inns in Casilinum.

"There are no inns in Casilinum," the *caupo* announced with a prevaricatory smile that afforded us an unobstructed view of his decomposing teeth. "But by the grace of Mercury we happen to have a room available here, and I'm sure you'll find our prices exceedingly moderate."

Marcus, Agricus, and I exchanged uneasy glances, as if we were contemplating a plunge into some pit. Then Marcus said, "Perhaps you'd show us the accommodations you have in mind."

"By all means," the *caupo* replied, grinning at us like a wolf flaunting a bad case of gum disease, "but since the room is upstairs and in the rear, your companion there might prefer to wait here in the bar while you're conducting your inspection."

So eminently sensible a suggestion, phrased with such commendable tact, of course met with our unqualified approval, so we stretched Dracena out on a bench the *caupo* provided for us and followed our would-be host into the murky interior of the inn.

The room he had in mind was in happy, and unexpected, contrast to the rest of the establishment. It was located above the stables, for one thing, and therefore smelled considerably more salubrious; although admittedly this was the first time I'd ever found the blended odors of horse manure, horse sweat, and urine-soaked straw to be comparatively aromatic. The room enjoyed the additional advantage of overlooking the tavern courtyard, which meant that it was a good deal brighter and better ventilated than both the tavern itself and all the dingy little cubicles that lined the corridors through which we'd passed. Indeed, our proposed accommodations fell not far short of being downright airy and spacious, remarkably so in light of the modest tariff of only six sesterces per night, which was probably a reflection of the fact that the room had until quite recently formed a part of the stables' hayloft.

Agricus was quick to seize on this as a bargaining point in our discussions with the *caupo*. "You mean you intend to charge us one and a half denarii to sleep with our horses," he exclaimed indignantly, "when you know perfectly well that stable accommodations should never be more than half-price."

"These *aren't* stable accommodations," the *caupo* protested. "Look— there are six separate beds in here, each one covered with fresh straw. You don't find amenities like that in any stable."

"Nor do you find horse turds under your floorboards in any cubiculum," was Agricus's retort. "And besides, there are only four of us here; why should we have to pay what you charge for six?"

"You don't have to," the *caupo* responded smoothly. "You're completely at liberty to go find yourselves lodgings somewhere else."

To me, at least, this seemed a persuasive point, especially with Dracena lying prostrate on a bench in the bar and with the room under discussion being so comfortable and modestly priced. But I knew better than to interfere with Agricus's machinations; that was Marcus's prerogative, if he chose to exercise it.

But he didn't choose to, and Agricus persevered with his haggling. "Of course we could go elsewhere," he said in a conciliatory tone of voice, "but that would be neither convenient for us nor profitable for you. Bear in mind, sir, that evening is already nigh and that this room will probably stay empty if we don't take it."

"The room costs six sesterces, and you can take it or leave it as you see fit," the *caupo* replied.

"Yes, but it only costs one sestertius *per bed*, and what I'm trying to say to you is that you can *guarantee* yourself revenue from at least four of those beds by coming to an agreement with us now. And just think: if two more travelers show up later on, you can charge them a sestertius apiece and rake in the full six you were aiming for originally."

"Are you some kind of lawyer's apprentice?" the *caupo* asked him warily.

"You flatter me, sir," Agricus answered with a show of affability. "But I'm just a weary traveler with a shrunken purse and an ailing companion."

"Now there you are!" the *caupo* flared up. "What other 'weary traveler' is going to be willing to spend the night in the same room with someone who's diseased?"

"Believe me, sir, he's not diseased, merely disabled—a wound he sustained while hunting is taking a long time to heal."

"That's what *you* say. But he looks pretty diseased to me."

"Well, he doesn't look healthy; that much I have to acknowledge. And so in all fairness to you, perhaps we should offer you five sesterces for the night."

"All right, *all right!*" the *caupo* shouted, throwing up his hands. "In all fairness to me, you can stay here for five sesterces. But I'll have the money in advance. Right now?"

"Of course," Agricus responded with courtly poise, whereupon Marcus stepped forward and counted out five brass coins.

"That was a truly brilliant display of perversity on your part, Agricus," he said once the *caupo* had gone storming out of the room (though a smile belied his condemnatory tone). "In order to effect a savings of one paltry sestertius, you came dangerously close to depriving us of these accommodations, which we badly need and which would have been cheap enough at twice the price."

"Well, you know, a sestertius here, a sestertius there; it mounts up," Agricus responded airily.

"You're right about that," Marcus agreed, whereupon the three of us headed downstairs to the bar, where perhaps a dozen other travelers were already seated at the main table. Despite the unappetizing aspect of the victuals set before them, they seemed to be suffused with good cheer, and the focus of their joviality was a robust-looking, dark-bearded man of Jewish appearance who was holding forth on the subject of women's favors and provoking in the process repeated bursts of laughter from his auditors.

"I tell you, my friends," he was saying, "there's not a man among us who can't be reduced to infantile jelly by the sight of a billowy breast and a pouting nipple, provided, of course, that they aren't dependent from the body of his wife. Now why should this spousal exception be the rule, you ask me. Why should your wife's breasts of all the breasts in the world fail to excite the sharpest quiver in your member? Are they not sweet and succulent as pomegranates? Do you not delight in their curving softness and their impertinent upward tilt? What is the reason underlying this terrible irony of our natures? Stated succinctly, it is this: the breast a man possesses is never the breast he seeks. But what breast does he seek, you ask me; and I answer you, the breast that gave him nurture."

This outlandish observation elicited several gasps, a few sighs, and two or three muted grunts from the people seated at the table; and the fellow who'd made it leaned back and roared with laughter.

"Ah, you weren't serious," one of his listeners said with a hint of relief in his voice.

"I am always serious," the dark-bearded man replied, "deadly serious, in fact."

"And yet you are always laughing," someone else remarked.

"I laugh out of a sense of piety, my friend."

"A sense of piety?"

"Yes. I am a Jew only by birth, you see. My true religion is laughter."

This was all Marcus needed to hear, and with great enthusiasm he plunged into a dialogue with the self-styled apostle of mirth, a dialogue about life and death, good and evil, significance and insignificance, appearance and reality, action and contemplation—the full complement of philosophy's weightiest concerns. The bearded man, whose name turned out to be Hieronymous, seemed to understand instinctively the sort of person Marcus was; and I sensed a strong attraction between them, a mutual fascination even, that took on a quality of vibrant radiance as they explored, thought by thought, the terrain of each other's minds. Agricus and I and the rest of the people in the tavern listened in dumb amazement as the colloquy proceeded, and when Hieronymous told the story of the crazed old Jew who in fact was none other than his father, I think even Dracena listened to him entranced.

No one spoke when the story was over; indeed, no one uttered a sound. It came as something of a shock, therefore, when Hieronymous started to bellow with laughter. We, his audience, were a little taken aback by this; in fact, his hilarity seemed to us to border on sacrilege. But then, almost as one, we remembered that the subject of the parable he'd just related had been precisely his conversion to the worship of Risus, and all of us, Dracena not excepted, began to roar with merriment at the thought of our own solemnity. "The god is here! The god is here!" Hieronymous shouted with tears streaming down his cheeks. "Let us praise him with our guffaws." And with such a funny-sounding invocation to inspire us, we did just that.

I don't know how long we spent laughing in that squalid bar that night, but I do know that when we finally got Dracena settled in our room we found that his fever had broken. Hieronymous, who'd helped us carry him up the stairs, took a look at his wound and pronounced him out of danger. "It will run with pus for a day or two," he said "but he should be strong enough to continue on with you by the Nones."

"The god of laughter interceded to restore his health," said Marcus, not entirely in jest. "Perhaps we ought to offer Risus a sacrifice."

Hieronymous found this idea as amusing as he found most everything else. "Risus accepts no sacrifices," he declared. "Indeed, he laughs at them. All he demands of us is that we cultivate our sense of humor."

He then turned without warning to me and added, "And you, my young friend, would be well advised to stop neglecting yours."

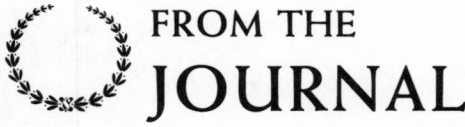
[SEPTEMBER 7TH]

True to Captain Aeneas's prediction, yesterday's oppressive glaze conditions have dissipated, and we are beating our way westward through
choppy seas in the face of a stiff north-by-northwest breeze. The water
beneath our keel is a dark and angry blue, a reflection of the fathomless
azurite of the empyrean, and on each fresh gust of wind rides an astringent
portent of the autumn and winter that are to come.

By all rights I shouldn't be attempting to write under these conditions;
the pitch and roll of the ship makes it virtually impossible to keep my
pen in smooth motion across the scroll. I realize I'm courting seasickness,
but even the risk of nausea does not deter me. I feel compelled to continue
writing, or, rather, I feel compelled not to stop. Why? Because this journal
and my so-called biography constitute my sole refuge from the painful
tedium of my inadequacy. Here in the privacy of this scroll I can at last
allow my self-pity free rein. Here I can bewail my fate and lament my
lot with infantile abandon, gnash my teeth and tear my hair without
arousing any but my own superfluous scorn. Here, best of all, I can revile
myself without threat of contradiction and revel incontinently in the
contempt I feel for the spineless, feckless creature I have become. When
I grow weary of laying the lash across my back, I can turn to the story
of my early life for further amusement and titillation. In writing my "Life"
I can not only escape from the present into the past but also observe the
curious process by which a child failed to develop into a man.

Oh, if only my wife and children loved me less, I could slip in silence
over the side. But their misguided affections restrain me, alas. And so I
go on living, which as a punishment is altogether fitting, but as a torture
is unconscionably cruel.

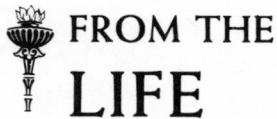 **FROM THE LIFE**

We remained three days at the Auriga Tavern while Dracena convalesced, and despite his protestations that he was well enough to be left unattended, we ventured no farther than Casilinum, across the river, on the first of the intervening days. We wouldn't have gone even that short a distance away except that Hieronymous offered to sit with the *singularis* in our absence. When we returned from our brief tour of the not particularly edifying Oscan town—which, despite its lack of distinction and our *caupo*'s lying assertions, was favored with no fewer than *four* inns and taverns—we found that our wounded companion had recovered his strength sufficiently to sit on the edge of his bunk and lose a few asses at dice to our ever jovial Judean surrogate. His convalescence was proceeding so rapidly, in fact, that by the next morning he was declaring himself fully fit to resume the journey, and it was only with the greatest difficulty that Marcus persuaded him (if a direct order qualifies as a form of persuasion) to remain in bed. In exchange for his grudging acquiescence and his solemn pledge not to exert himself unnecessarily, Marcus granted his request that he be left to himself and not "hovered over" by any of us or by Hieronymous. "If it's my fate to lie here for hours on end and play the slacker," he said, "then I'd just as soon no one was present to witness my disgrace."

Marcus, Agricus, and I thus found ourselves with an entire springtime day to dispose of, and it didn't take us long to fix on Capua, barely half an hour's ride away, as the place where we could most profitably, and profligately, spend the time.

We'd intended to visit Capua anyway and indeed had been on our way there when Dracena toppled from his horse. The town's reputation for license and excess stretched as far back as the Punic Wars, after all, when Hannibal's victorious army marched in to spend the winter there and emerged some four months later a debauched and drunken mob. Nearly three hundred and fifty years had passed since the disorderly departure of Hannibal's troops, but Capua, from all we'd heard, had retained its pristine decadence intact.

Our original plan had been to ride into the town and find our way to the house of a certain Sextus Severianus, who was one of the local magistrates and also a former political protégé of Marcus's paternal grand-father. We had little doubt that Sextus would accord us the warmest of welcomes, but given Capua's enticing reputation for depravity and the fact that we wanted to get back to Dracena's bedside by nightfall, we decided to forgo his hospitality and sample the municipality's pleasures on our own, in anonymity.

We invited our new friend Hieronymous to come along with us, and he with great alacrity accepted. I for one would have felt a bit forlorn if he'd declined, and so would Marcus and Agricus unless I'm much mistaken. Since our first encounter with him, we'd spent almost all our waking hours in his company. Indeed, apart from the time consumed by our trip to Casilinum, he'd hardly been out of our sight. Whether it was downstairs at meals or upstairs in our room above the stables, the four of us kept up a lively and sometimes heated colloquy, the subject of which, broadly speaking, was the meaning and purpose of life. As in most such discus-sions, the heat generated greatly exceeded the light shed, but thanks to Hieronymous's unfailing exuberance and wit our exchanges seldom flared into open animosity, even when Agricus's position on a given question was sharply at variance with my own.

It seems hard to believe, looking back on it, that on the morning we set off for Capua with him we'd known Hieronymous for not much more than a day. Come to think of it, it didn't seem all that believable at the time either. For not only had the three of us come to regard him as a friend on such short acquaintance, but we'd each done so for entirely different reasons. Marcus responded most readily to his intellect. He was enchanted to find a mind, no less keen than his own, that was so dissimilar in its orientation yet so accessible to reason and so fluent in the language of ideas. I, by contrast, was drawn to his genial warmth and paternal self-assurance, though I was also a little in awe of his perspicacity. How he had contrived, barely an hour after our first meeting, to discern that my sense of humor was in danger of languishing from lack of use was still an utter mystery to me—unless, of course, I'd been moping around most unconscionably at the time, which to the best of my knowledge I had not.

As for Agricus . . . well, who ever knew with any certainty what his real feelings were? There isn't much doubt in my mind that he liked and respected Hieronymous, but as to his reasons for doing so I can only speculate. Our new friend had a faintly roguish quality that would have appealed to Agricus's amoral nature, and he seemed to be substantially unencumbered with illusions, which was a quality that Agricus admired. Other than that, it seems safe to assume that my nemesis wasn't altogether immune to Hieronymous's affability, but such affection as he felt for him was always muted, if not concealed. Hieronymous, for his part, was well aware of the distance Agricus maintained between them, and he scrupulously respected it, never once, to my knowledge, indulging in the easy familiarity and playful banter that characterized his interactions with me and Marcus. Perceptive as he was, our exponent of sacred laughter must have seen right away—as Marcus and Annia had when they first met him—that Agricus was not remotely interested in giving of himself or receiving emotionally from others. (I, on the other hand, who arguably knew him better than any of my three friends, never quite managed to assimilate that essential fact of his personality. Perhaps I was clinging to a belief that he would somehow see the light one day. Or perhaps I just couldn't accept the fact that such light as he shed was never going to shine on me.)

Understanding as I, to some extent, did why we three boys were attracted to Hieronymous, it occurred to me then, as it does again now, to wonder what it was that attracted him to us. Marcus was an attraction all by himself, of course, by virtue of lineage no less than intellect; and it's possible, I suppose, that Hieronymous's primary interest was in cultivating him as a patron. Such a crassly cynical hypothesis does both him and Marcus a disservice, however, and is probably a more accurate reflection of my own mean-spirited nature than it is of his actual motivations. Then, too, there is a far more plausible explanation for his interest in the three of us: the fact that we, as a threesome, were in some ways rather interesting.

I sensed as much even back then—that there was something slightly out of the ordinary about the interplay of our personalities, something that someone like Hieronymous could not help but recognize and enjoy. It wasn't just that we combined plebeian and patrician elements in our adolescent triumvirate—although in that respect we were unquestionably unique—but we were well matched as individuals, too. There was Agricus, the beautiful predator, Marcus, the Stoic prince, and I, the . . . what? Odd, but I can't seem to think of an accurate way of characterizing the person I used to be. The baffled innocent, perhaps. Or perhaps the suffering fool.

But whatever I was, and whatever we three may have been, the fact remains that we were drawn to Hieronymous no less than he was drawn to us, and the logical outcome of our mutual attraction was that he should join us on our excursion to Capua. It was fortunate in this connection that he, like us, was wedded to no particular schedule or itinerary. Indeed, as he informed us on more than a few occasions, he regarded all schedules and itineraries as anathema. He was, he said, a highly professional amateur traveler, by which he meant that he traveled for the love of traveling but also made his living at it. How he managed to make his living at it I never completely understood, even though his guiding principle was nothing if not intelligible. This principle, baldly stated, was: Buy cheap and sell dear. And that is precisely what Hieronymous did. He went from town to town and from market to market on the back of his long-suffering mule, and at each locality along his route he would engage in activities that bore an uncanny resemblance to bartering and haggling. His stock in trade, so to speak, consisted of rugs, lamps, pots, figurines, and several kinds of semiprecious stones, all of which—apart from the stones—he carried around in a large cloth sack that sometimes doubled as his blanket at night. What he did with these items was sell them for more than he'd paid or exchange them for items of greater value—tasks much easier to elaborate than to accomplish. He accomplished them though, with unfailing regularity, and solely by virtue of his skill as a bargainer. To me it seemed that he was making a living out of thin air, but he assured me that there was no wizardry involved. Perhaps there wasn't. But if it wasn't wizardry, it was artistry, and of a very high order indeed. And one consequence of his having such a remarkable gift was that he was completely at liberty to spend as much time with us as he liked.

And so off we went, on a brilliantly sunny morning, down the Via Appia toward the most brazen of Italy's cities—a place where, we felt confident, we would satisfy every one of our carnal lusts.

The first of these to be satisfied, as it turned out, was our appetite for alluring aromas and vibrant colors, since the Appia, as it traversed Capua's outskirts, was flanked as far as the eye could see by fields of roses, violets, and lilies. These myriad flowers were the raw material of Capua's famous perfumes and salves, and as we rode along with the sunlight enhancing every blossom and the warm air suffused with honeyed smells, I found myself wondering if Elysium itself could be any lovelier.

Marcus, to all appearances, was no less dazzled by the riot of color and fragrance than I, but visions of paradise were the farthest thing from his mind. "It's hard to believe," he said, "that this road was once lined with crucified slaves."

"I hope for their sake that they didn't suffer from hay fever," Agricus commented after a pause, and Hieronymous, at least, found the remark amusing.

Marcus blushed a little. "Sallust doesn't mention hay fever," he said with a sheepish smile, "but then, he was never the most thorough of historians."

"In what connection does he not mention it?" Hieronymous asked.

"In connection with the slave uprising led by Spartacus, which began in Capua two centuries ago and was finally crushed by Pompey and Crassus. . . ."

"Who crucified all the rebel slaves they'd captured during the fighting," I offered, having read Sallust's chronicles myself.

"Correct," said Marcus. "And who lined the Via Appia with them all the way from Capua to Rome."

"So," said Hieronymous, "you find yourself surrounded by sweet-scented beauty on a glorious spring day, and it puts you in mind of dreadful suffering and death."

"Precisely," Marcus responded with enthusiasm, sensing an imminent resumption of our ongoing metaphysical debate. "To the contemplative mind the essence of beauty is its impermanence, its mortality, so to speak. And so from beauty a philosophic observer may proceed in easy stages, first to impermanence, then to mortality, onward through suffering to the road's end at death."

"Is that where we're headed this morning?" Hieronymous quipped. "I could have sworn we were on our way to Capua."

"So we are," Agricus interjected. "And when we arrive there we're all going to die little deaths at the hands of the beast with two backs . . . or was that not on today's agenda, Marco?"

"I do believe it crossed my mind," Marcus replied, blushing again, much more deeply.

"Ah, now I see the connection," Hieronymous said. "You wish to confirm all the discoveries you made at the brothel in Formiae."

"Of course he does," Agricus declared. "In fact, 'Discovery' is the theme of this entire journey."

"Yet you seem to be of two minds about what you are discovering," Hieronymous continued. "For how else are we to explain all this talk of mortality and crucifixion?"

"He used to believe that his actions were governed purely by Reason," Agricus asserted with a nasty smirk. "But in Formiae he discovered Passion, and so now he isn't so sure."

"What do you have against Passion, my young friend?" Hieronymous asked.

"Passion is Reason deformed," Marcus replied, his expression deadly serious. "Until Formiae I was ignorant of its power."

"Ah," sighed Hieronymous. "You've begun the work of coming to terms with the importunate demands of the flesh."

"So it would seem," Marcus responded rather ruefully. "And judging by the fever that's been raging in my blood these last few days, that work is going to prove arduous in the extreme."

We rode on past the fields of flowers and soon caught sight of Capua's huge old amphitheater, which our ailing Emperor had recently restored. Close by stood the city's monumental western gate, which by no great coincidence had recently been renamed in our ailing Emperor's honor.

Once through the gate we made our way to the municipal stables, where we deposited our three horses and one mule (Hieronymous having wisely left his sack of merchandise back at the Auriga in Dracena's care). We then proceeded on foot to the town's forum, which we found to be overflowing with people. It turned out that we'd arrived in Capua on a market day, and the result was that we spent the best part of our first few hours there shopping our way from stall to stall.

Now shopping, as a general rule, is not an activity in which I take compulsive interest, but in an emporium as rich as Capua's and with a shopper as shrewd as Hieronymous to do my haggling for me, I soon found it to be a surprisingly congenial pursuit. What made it even more congenial was the fact that what most of the vendors were selling was food; and so our progress through the market became a sort of protracted—and highly palatable—midday meal, during the course of which we sampled at least a dozen different kinds of comestibles. And it may well have been closer to *several* dozen, given the remarkable variety of foodstuffs on display. There were cheeses and nuts of every sort, fruits and vegetables of every description, bread and cakes of all shapes and sizes, spices, herbs, and other condiments without end. There were fish fresh from the river and fish culled from the sea. There were octupi, eels, and squid as well as shellfish, snails, and frogs. There were olives of many varieties, soaked in vinegar, wine, or brine. There was beef and pork (salted, slaughtered, or on the hoof), game and poultry (alive or freshly killed), doves and pigeons (in little wooden cages), and suckling pigs (ready for the fire). There was *mulsum* by the jug, oil by the amphora, honey by the comb or the pot, and wine by the congius or the cup. There were calves' brains and slabs of tripe, mushrooms and baskets of truffles, sausages still sizzling from the fire, meat pies still hot from the oven, and milk still warm from a she-goat's teat.

Needless to say, our appetite for food and drink had been satisfied most abundantly by the time we finished sampling and shopping our way across the forum. And there wasn't much doubt in my mind as to which appetite we would endeavor to satisfy next.

Capua's famous Seplasia was a narrow street that ran due south from the forum's southwestern corner. The first few hundred feet of its length were lined with shops offering carpets and tapestries, and Hieronymous, who traded in that sort of merchandise, declared the Capuans' craftsmanship to be of a very high order. Farther down the street were the shops of rope makers and metal workers, the din emanating from the latter making it almost impossible to concentrate one's attention on the finely wrought bronzes their proprietors had on display. Beyond all the banging and clanging the Seplasia became even narrower, and exotic odors began to permeate the stagnant air, blending with and overlying one another in heady combinations. Here were clustered the sellers of perfumes, cosmetics, and salves, their dingy little shops all conveniently close to the three run-down buildings that transformed the Seplasia's southern end into a dark and grimy cul-de-sac. These, at last, were Capua's celebrated brothels.

Justly celebrated, I should say, because, unlike most such establishments, they offered sexual services that were not entirely devoid of erotic feeling. I don't mean by this that those who provided the services lusted more for a customer's flesh than for his money. They did not. But they did supply sexual gratification with a fair degree of professional skill, and with relatively few displays of aggravated boredom or disgust.

Before any of us could be properly gratified, though, we had to decide which of the three brothels we would patronize and which of that chosen brothel's strumpets appealed most to our individual tastes. Marcus was so taken with one of the strumpets lounging in front of the brothel on our right that the first question was effectively rendered moot. And as things turned out, we hadn't really needed to bother ourselves about it to begin with. No sooner had we followed Marcus into the right-hand building than his chosen strumpet led us straight through a narrow passageway to a large reception room in the building next door. Here, in what we'd thought of as the middle brothel, a dozen or so of her colleagues were arrayed in various states of languorous repose. When several more of them ambled in through a passageway on the other side of the room, it at last became clear to us that Capua's celebrated brothels had all been consolidated into one. That one more than lived up to the city's scabrous reputation, though, most particularly from the viewpoint of my poor besotted friend Marcus.

The strumpet he fancied was called Phoebe, and Phoebe, as the saying goes, was quite a handful. It wasn't just that she was tall—less than a palm's width shy of Dracena's stature at the least—she was also muscular, and by no means unpleasant to look at. The most distinctive thing about her, apart from her height and physique, was the fact that she was dressed almost entirely in the skins of wild animals—*small* wild animals, I should say, given the extent to which her own pelt remained accessible to public view. All in all I could well understand the reasons for Marcus's abject infatuation with her. And so, to all appearances, could she, as she stared at him carnivorously through eyes that had been boldly accentuated with mascara. I must say that I didn't much envy him her concentrated attention, for to my mind she was more than a little intimidating. With her lips stained the color of blood, her face stark white with paint and powder, and her curly black hair glistening with oil as it cascaded down past her shoulders to her breasts, she resembled nothing so much as a frenzied maenad; and I was secretly glad that it was Marcus, not I, who'd been cast in the role of her Orphic suitor.

For myself I chose a waiflike creature named Niobe, whose doleful brown eyes were so large as to constitute a virtual deformity. She, like several of her sister prostitutes, was dressed in a lewd travesty of the toga, one that was draped in front so as to leave her right breast and pubic thatch exposed, and cut short in back as to reveal her narrow buttocks. It should have been obvious to me right away why I'd been drawn to her, but it wasn't until I was lodged deep inside her that her resemblance to Annia registered in my mind.

Agricus's choice of partner somewhat surprised me, for instead of selecting one of the haughtier—or at least more arrogant-looking—harlots on display, he fixed on a rather mousy little creature by the name of Ariadne, who could easily have passed for a boy of ten or eleven had she not been wearing the same revealing sort of "toga" as my own slender ox-eyed Niobe.

Hieronymous's choice was more in keeping with my expectations—a beefy pale-skinned German girl who for some unfathomable reason had been given the name Thetis by the brothel's proprietors, though she no more resembled a sea nymph than did Hieronymous himself.

With the selection process completed, we requested and—for a small additional consideration—were given a room with four couches. At Hieronymous's suggestion, moreover, we provisioned the room with four sextarii of wine from the brothel's bar and two bowls of assorted fruit from its pantry. We then, most wholeheartedly, addressed ourselves to the matter of our pleasure.

Within half an hour, half the wine had been consumed, and our four concubines were feeling its effects no less than we. Marcus's Phoebe had divested herself of her animal skins, and my Niobe's amethyst toga had been transformed into a small puddle of color on the white tile floor beneath our couch. Agricus had lifted Ariadne's togalike garment so high above her waist that it hung like a saffron garland from her neck, and Thetis, at Hieronymous's playful urging, had shed every last stitch of her clothing as well, revealing slablike breasts and a superabundance of reddish freckles.

More wine flowed, and on one couch after another the coital festivities commenced. At some point in the midst of my own exertions I happened to glance for a moment in Marcus's direction. He was lying on his back, his hips straddled by Phoebe's thighs, and she was riding him, with her head thrown back, her body shining with perspiration, and her breath hissing out at an ever more rapid tempo through the spaces between her tightly clenched teeth. She was a magnificent vision of orgiastic abandon, and Marcus, beneath her, writhed and grimaced as if he were impaled on the point of a spear. The sight of them toiling so ardently in the grip of their passion inspired me to bring my own labors more speedily to fruition, and before long all eight of us in that squalid little room lay breathless, sweating, and spent. It was then that Agricus demonstrated once again that he was master of every situation.

"I propose a change of partners," he said with a rakish smile.

"And *I* propose that I be given a little time to catch my breath," Hieronymous replied in a tone of near exhaustion that was very much in keeping with his words.

"It gives me great pleasure to inform you that your proposal is entirely compatible with my own," Agricus said in his most suave and ingratiating manner. "For the change of partners I have in mind pertains only to your Thetis and Marco's Phoebe."

He paused, obviously pleased with himself, while the rest of us tried to figure out what he was driving at.

"In other words," he resumed finally, "I propose that your Thetis lie with Marco's partner and that Marcus's Phoebe lie with yours."

There was a brief silence as the gist of what he was saying sank in.

"That will cost you four denarii extra," Phoebe announced in a rather adamant tone of voice, while Thetis, blushing becomingly, gave vent to some girlish titters.

"Done!" said Marcus, who, but for the effects of all the wine we'd been drinking, might have first given Hieronymous an opportunity to bargain her down.

"What about Ariadne and me?" my Niobe protested plaintively, and in a manner suggesting that her interest in Agricus's couchmate was based, to some extent at least, on a passion for more than mere money.

"Done!" Marcus repeated somewhat tipsily, having just drunk down yet another bowl of wine.

And thus it was that he, Hieronymous, and I were transformed temporarily from participants into spectators. Reclining comfortably on our couches, we watched in fascination as Agricus put our four prostitutes through their paces, generating in the process several exotic conjunctions of upper and lower orifices that I'd have assumed offhand to be anatomically inadmissible. Eventually, though, he exhausted his inventory of lesbian caresses and we all resumed our heterosexual revels.

Marcus was too drunk by this time to achieve any meaningful semblance of tumescence, but his devoted Phoebe ministered so tenderly to his wilted little prod that I could hear him whimpering with delight all the way across the room. He was almost too drunk to walk when the time came for him to bid his devoted Phoebe a fond farewell, but with some assistance from me and Hieronymous he managed to negotiate the distance between her parting endearments and the welcoming whinnies of his equally devoted horse without falling down, passing out, or throwing up.

The sun was hovering close to the western horizon as we made our way from the municipal stables to Hadrian's Gate and the Via Appia, and all but its upper limb had disappeared by the time we reached the fields of flowers that had dazzled us so in the morning light. Marcus, who'd been jabbering on quite cheerfully about his "beloved" Phoebe during our walk from the brothel to the stables, had become very quiet once we set off on our return journey to the Auriga Tavern. Although he teetered slightly in his saddle, he appeared to be having little difficulty staying mounted, and the animal was so docile and responsive to his will that the four of us were able to move along at a fairly respectable trot. All at once, however, he reined the stallion in with a violent jerk and half jumped, half tumbled to the ground. Then he began to run: blindly, wildly, through the field of lilies and violets that bordered the side of the road.

"Go after him, you dimwit!" Agricus shouted at me as I sat stunned on Incitatus's back and watched Marcus go sprinting away. "I said go after him, dammit! What's the matter with you?"

"I heard what you said," I responded, bringing Incitatus to a halt. "But I don't like the sound of you giving me orders."

And having made that point, I dismounted and headed off in pursuit of Marcus.

He had a considerable head start on me, perhaps a hundred paces or more; and even if I wasn't quite as drunk as he was, I was still a long, long way from being sober. I gained on him, though, at a modest but respectable rate, and after half a mile or so the gap between us had narrowed to not much more than fifty feet. "Marco!" I called to him as he lurched onward through the field of fragrant blossoms. "*Marco!*" I called a second time when he gave no sign of having heard my initial shout. I was about to yell his name yet a third time when he suddenly turned his head and looked back at me. Alas, given his advanced state of inebriation, he was in no fit condition to be running in one direction while looking in another, and therefore stumbled, staggered, then fell sprawling to the ground.

I ran up, knelt beside him, and turned him over so I could see his face. He was badly winded, and his chest heaved with every sobbing breath he took. "Are you all right, Marco?" I asked him. "Why did you go running off like that?"

He said nothing at first, just looked at me as if I were a stranger. Then all at once a terrible anguish came into his eyes, and with a roar that must have cruelly strained his vocal cords he bellowed out a long, de-spairing "N–O–O–O–O–O–O!"

"What is it, Marco?" I asked, fearful that he'd injured himself in some way, or taken leave of his senses. "Please tell me. Are you in pain?"

He looked at me, wild-eyed, staring, and grabbed my shoulders with both hands. "I don't want to be virtuous any more," he said in a frantic whisper. "I don't want to go on being good. . . . In the name of the gods, please, *please*, help me."

"Of course, Marco," I responded, feeling utterly at a loss as to how to deal with him. "Just tell me what you want me to do."

"*Please!*" was all the answer I got from him, and then "Please . . . please . . . please . . . please . . ." until the words gave way to violent sobs.

Without thinking, I put my arms around him and held his quaking body close. "It's all right, Marco," I murmured ineffectually. "Everything's going to be all right."

But he kept on sobbing, knowing much better than I did how little chance there was of a reprieve.

[SEPTEMBER 8TH]

We are back on dry land at last. *Wet* dry land, I should say, given the cloudburst that greeted us as the *Liberta* made her way through the gathering darkness to her berth in Narbo's harbor. That was more than two hours ago, and the rain is still beating down on the cobblestones outside our inn. Such a downpour seems benign enough now that we've arrived safe and sound at our destination. But earlier today, while we were still out of sight of land, a comparable deluge put us all in great fear for our lives. Even I, who just yesterday would have been only too happy to sink forever beneath the waves, was badly frightened when the weather turned suddenly violent. It's one thing to contemplate death while the seas are relatively calm, I've discovered, and quite another thing to look it in the face when the wind and waves are threatening to tear your ship apart.

The experience was not without its compensations, however. It not only disabused me of the notion that I sincerely wanted to die, but also opened my eyes to the fact that I'd been disgracefully neglectful of my family.

I was crouched down against the gunwale near the prow, clinging for dear life to one of the capstans as the storm built toward its frenzied climax. Portia, Decius, and Camilla were huddled together opposite me, all three of them looking every bit as terrified and wretched as I was myself. It wasn't their expressions that awakened me to my neglect of them, though; it was the fact that both Portia and Camilla were clinging to Decius, while he in turn fought with what looked like all his strength to keep hold of one of the cleats nailed to the deck. The scene struck me so forcefully that my abject fear was displaced almost entirely by a sense of unutterable shame. How could I have permitted myself to abdicate my role as paterfamilias so ignominiously? *I* was the one my wife and children ought to be clinging to. And if I lacked the strength—of character, no less than sinew—to keep them from being washed overboard by the storm, then *they* were the ones who ought to have a sturdy capstan to hold on to, instead of one meager iron cleat.

It came to me as I looked over at them that they no less than I had been uprooted, that they no less than I had suffered a loss. I'd been so engrossed in my own despairing anguish that I'd neglected to give any meaningful thought to theirs. And the result, I felt certain, was that I'd added immeasurably to their burden of woe.

Ah, well, we are all out of danger now; Captain Aeneas has brought us safely into port and through the storm. And if my family can somehow find it in their hearts to forgive me for my unconscionable self-absorption—assuming, of course, that they're aware of it (which for some inexplicable reason they don't appear to be)—I'll bend every effort to make up for the way I've behaved.

Ye gods, they must be mad to keep on loving me. Please let me, henceforth, prove more deserving of their affection.

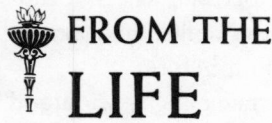
It didn't take Marcus long to recover his composure. In fact, the sound of Agricus calling out his name nearby was all the incentive he needed to staunch his tears and assume his familiar mask of equanimity. "Quite a spectacle I've been making of myself," he remarked as we both got to our feet. "If anyone but you had seen me carrying on that way, I'd have felt thoroughly mortified."

He made this statement in such a matter-of-fact manner that its underlying significance at first was lost on me. It was only later, after we'd responded to Agricus's cries and rejoined Hieronymous and our horses on the roadside, that I realized he'd paid me a quite considerable compliment (assuming, of course, that his statement had been inspired by our mutual affection and not by my social insignificance).

"I heard you shout 'No!' out there a little while ago," Hieronymous said to him as the three of us mounted up again. "Was that an answer to a question or a statement of principle?"

"It was a cry for mercy," Marcus responded with an embarrassed smile, "but I couldn't shout quite loud enough."

On our return to the Auriga we found Dracena sitting silently in the bar, looking rested if not quite robust. Upon seeing us, he immediately began to expatiate on the theme that his health would suffer far more from continued enforced inactivity than it would from a day on his horse's back. Marcus, who by then was beginning to feel considerably more hung over than drunk, was not disposed to argue with him, and so the decision was made to set off come morning for Beneventum.

"I hope you'll ride on with us," Marcus said to Hieronymous as we were about to head upstairs.

"It will be my very great pleasure," Hieronymous replied.

And with that we all retired, to try to sleep off the effects of having sated too many carnal appetites.

From Casilinum to Beneventum, the Appia trends steadily upward, and at about the midpoint of our journey we came to the famous Caudine Forks. The road here was squeezed in at the foot of two fairly respectable mountains, and seeing the terrain at first hand it became easier to understand why an entire Roman army, trapped in the defile, had tamely surrendered to the Samnites almost half a millennium before.

Beyond the Forks the road continued to rise, traversing a wide and fertile plain until it reached the Appia's twentieth post station, at Caudium. There, after watering our horses and sharing a loaf of bread, we basked for an hour or so in the bright spring sunshine, having still not recuperated fully from our exertions of the previous day. We were about to bestir ourselves and resume the march when three hulking Praetorians galloped up to Caudium's one lone tavern and gruffly ordered the *caupo* to prepare food and drink for a party of forty. Recognizing one of the three as an old friend from his garrison days on the Palatine, Dracena struck up a conversation with them and reported back to us that the party referred to was traveling to Ephesus by way of Brundisium and consisted of the wife and children of Titus Aurelius Antoninus, Proconsul of Asia. Marcus immediately shot me a look, which Hieronymous did not fail to notice. As for me, my mouth went dry and my heart picked up its tempo. The prospect of seeing Annia again filled me with the most lacerating kind of joy, the kind that only one's first love can engender. I knew it would be unspeakably painful to see her again, but I also knew it would be worth whatever agony it cost.

I had to be careful, though, to keep my surging emotions concealed from the watchful eyes of my old enemy. If he ever discovered the identity of my patrician *inamorata*—whose existence he'd already deduced—I felt sure that he would use the knowledge to torment and eventually humiliate me. Perhaps I did Agricus an injustice by imputing so much malice to him, but the picture of him and Drusilla panting and grunting in coital rapture was still painfully fresh in my memory, so I was not disposed to give him the benefit of any doubts.

An all but interminable hour passed before the three Praetorians reappeared at the head of a column of wagons, litters, and horsemen; and during the course of that long hour the *caupo* of the tavern along with his wife, his children, and his slaves rushed frantically about from house to house in an effort to round up enough bread, wine, olives, and cheese to feed their fast-approaching visitors. The entire village of Caudium was not significantly more populous than the procession headed its way, so the *caupo*'s task was not an easy one to accomplish. Since the Proconsul's family and dependents were traveling on official Imperial business, moreover, and under a warrant of the *cursus publicus*, neither the *caupo* nor the townspeople had any guarantee that they would be compensated for the food and wine they were contributing. They could only pray that the

Proconsul's wife would be aware of their situation and take pity on them; but how much pity she took, if she took any at all, was entirely a matter of her discretion. (Marcus, who observed the villagers' feverish preparations and anxious faces, was to institute changes in the *cursus publicus* that alleviated somewhat the burdens placed on small communities like theirs; and it gives me a modicum of pleasure to know that a mundane experience I once shared with him led eventually to the implementation of a benign new policy throughout the Empire.)

Annia's two brothers, who were riding just behind the Praetorians, were the first familiar faces to appear, and as Marcus rushed forward to greet them I nervously scanned the wagons and litters to their rear for some sign of Annia's presence. Of course the curtains of the litters were drawn, but given the likely order of march and the fact that there were only two litters in the column, I concluded that her mother was traveling in the second one and she and her sister were ensconced inside the first.

My conclusion proved correct. Annia's brothers, having greeted Marcus with boisterous whoops and hearty embraces, next led him to the first of the approaching litters and drew the curtains aside. Immediately the air was rent by the delighted squeals of two young women, and I caught sight of Annia's laughing countenance as she leaned forward to give Marcus a sisterly kiss. The moment I saw her my heart soared and my spirits sank. No woman anywhere could hold a candle to her. She was perfect—in terms of wit, of vivacity, of willowy physique, and of unsurpassed beauty. I might just as well aspire to the affections of Juno or Minerva as delude myself that I stood any chance of rekindling the love I'd been too cowardly to consummate. She was irretrievably lost to me, and I would have to content myself henceforth with pale imitations of the passion, the exhilaration, and the ecstasy that she alone could inspire.

Under the Praetorians' supervision, the lady Faustina's slaves placed her litter at right angles to that of her daughters and from the baggage wagons produced three folding tables—two fairly small ones that they put within easy reach of the litters' occupants and one a good deal larger that they set up a few feet away. To this large table the *caupo* and his dependents brought all the food and wine they had managed to scrape together and provided a dozen or so stools as well, stools that were intended for the three Praetorians, Annia's two brothers, the lady Faustina's secretary, auspex, physician, and hairdresser . . . and, regrettably enough, the five of us.

As slaves set about mixing the wine and preparing plates of food for the three women, Marcus presented Hieronymous to them. Our new friend made an immediate favorable impression, delivering himself of several gallant and witty remarks which caused the lady Faustina to blush deeply even as she gave vent to delighted laughter. To Annia and her sister he addressed somewhat more circumspect comments, being well aware that the amount of flattery one lavishes on a woman should in most cases be directly proportional to her age.

Now it was time for Agricus, Dracena, and me to present ourselves— an ordeal I'd been dreading. The lady Faustina was, of course, gracious and friendly, and displayed that rare ability, peculiar to the wives of important men, to summon pertinent information from her memory about people she'd met only in passing and talked to hardly at all. She remembered, for example, that Dracena had at one time served in the Praetorian Guard, that Agricus was a favorite of Domitia Lucilla and Cornificia, and that I was "appealingly shy." Having said that much about me and favored me with one of her warmest smiles, she proceeded to add—in all innocence, I feel sure—"Aren't you the young man who got on so well with my daughter, Annia?"

There was a brief silence. Had the lady Faustina and I been characters in one of those Atellan farces that are so popular with the Roman mob, her question would have been my cue to hasten downstage and say in an aside to the audience, "When she asked me that I very nearly fainted." And even though the two of us were involved in a farce of an entirely different kind, I very nearly fainted nevertheless.

With that one question, I felt all too certain, she had delivered me into the hands of my enemy. And had there been any doubt in my mind, I needed only to cast a glance at Agricus, whose smile was at its most lupine pitch of intensity.

"Yes, Lady Faustina," I finally managed to reply, "I derived great pleasure and edification from your daughter's company. I've even presumed so far as to think of her as my friend."

"Nicely put," Marcus said, flashing me a supportive, and sympathetic, smile.

"Yes!" the lady Faustina agreed. "That was very nicely put indeed. I can readily understand why Annia feels such fondness for you."

"Thank you, Lady Faustina," I responded, wishing fervently that the earth would open at my feet and swallow me up for good and all.

All etiquette required of me at that point was to acknowledge Annia and her sister with a respectful nod and withdraw. Once my eyes came to rest on Annia's face, though, I felt extremely reluctant to shift them away. For one thing, she was blushing most becomingly, and for another, she kept her own eyes cast down in a manner I found infinitely vulnerable and sweet. "I'm awfully glad to see you again," I said with perfect sincerity. And Annia, by way of response, raised her eyes to mine and favored me with one of her gentlest smiles.

Throughout the meal that followed my mind was constantly spinning. On the one hand, there was the lady Faustina's catastrophic disclosure, which placed me more or less at Agricus's mercy. But, on the other hand, there was Annia's forgiving smile, which meant that all might not be lost as far as she and I were concerned.

I had no further opportunities to speak with her that afternoon, but the lady Faustina invited Marcus and the rest of us to travel along with her party to Beneventum and spend the night there with her and her children as guests in one of the Imperial villas that Publius Aelius Hadrianus had placed at her disposal. I felt almost giddy with anticipation as we rode toward our destination, and almost faint with anxiety as I contemplated the innumerable atrocities that Agricus was now in a position to perpetrate. No doubt to aggravate my apprehensions, he rode along with a smile of supreme contentment disfiguring his features and said nary a word the entire afternoon. Marcus, however, expressed a tactful degree of solicitude, not so much because of all that had happened so far but because of everything that now seemed all too likely to occur. I myself declined to dwell for long on the many embarrassing complications that might arise. The paramount fact from my perspective was that Annia still felt some measure of affection for me. That was worth all the complications and humiliations that the next several hours might have in store.

The Emperor's villa at Beneventum sat on a high bluff overlooking the river Calor and was Imperially furnished and staffed. It afforded not just the standard amenities but a number of luxurious refinements as well. All five of us, for example, were provided with fresh new tunics to wear at dinner that evening and then add to our traveling wardrobes. These tunics were sewn and embroidered with gold-colored thread, which went nicely with the olive crowns of beaten gold that we were given to wear on our heads (but not to keep for ourselves, alas). Annia, her mother, and her sister, having several dozen chests of clothes to choose from, did not require Imperially provided finery to maintain Imperial standards of dress, and when they took their places in the open-air colonnade that served as that evening's dining chamber, even an Empress might have envied them their attire. Annia was arrayed in a stola of pure white silk that clung to her body like wet gauze. My little prod went rigid as I stood there looking at her, causing a slight bulge to appear in my gold-threaded tunic.

"Better control yourself," Agricus murmured to me as she took her place on the left-hand couch. "You know how violent I tend to get when you start showing off your erections."

I turned to glare at him as my member rapidly reverted to detumescence. His face was a study in malicious glee. "Someday," I said through clenched teeth, "you are going to provoke me beyond endurance."

"A frightening prospect," he responded in a tone of indifference. Then, addressing himself to Annia, he immediately launched his first attack: "I understand from my good friend Lucius here that you have an all-consuming passion for things plebeian."

To her very great credit, Annia perceived instantaneously that Agricus was not merely lying, but lying with malicious intent. "That depends," she answered him coolly, "on the particular plebeian and the particular *thing* you have in mind."

"Ah," Agricus responded, "I see that your beauty is matched by your intelligence."

"Whereas yours is matched by your impudence," she retorted, to my immense satisfaction.

"Am I really that good-looking?" Agricus asked in a labored attempt to seem charming.

"Obviously you think you are," Annia shot back.

"Oh, I apologize, dear lady, if I've in any way offended you," Agricus protested, punctuating his words with a bow of exaggerated contrition.

"Why?" she snapped. "When offending me was clearly your intention."

"Never!" Agricus exclaimed with a gasp of bogus incredulity. "Please believe me."

"I'll believe you, but only if Lucius will corroborate what you say."

"Which I won't!" I announced emphatically.

Whereupon Agricus, his first assault having been decisively repulsed, withdrew temporarily from the field, his malice having served no other purpose than to bring Annia and me closer together. Indeed, with my love for her now buttressed by both gratitude and admiration, I ceased to concern myself about Agricus altogether and instead focused all my attention on the prospect of arranging an assignation. At that point, I confess, I no longer cared much about the risks involved; my desire to possess Annia was so clamant that I felt ready to outface even death in order to satisfy it. The question had ceased to be: Can I get away with it? and had become simply: How can it be managed?

But to this question there weren't any readily apparent answers. The Emperor's villa was large, and the quarters occupied by the lady Faustina and her children were in an entirely different wing from those allotted to Marcus and the four of us. Of course Annia and I couldn't possibly concert plans for a tryst over the dining table, if for no other reason than that Agricus would overhear them. No; I had to come up with some workable stratagem on my own, one that would take Agricus and all other impediments into account.

After a good deal of careful thought, I opted for a course of action that, while not particularly imaginative, at least possessed the virtue of simplicity: I would wait until the moon rose at the beginning of the night's third watch, and then undertake a systematic search. As fate would have it, though, the need to search was substantially obviated even before I went to bed, thanks in good part to Hieronymous, who, for reasons of his own, had plied the lady Faustina with compliments throughout the course of the dinner. By the time we finished eating, our hostess was fairly glowing with good humor, and she invited all of us to retire to her sitting room and partake of some elderberry wine. I thus had a fairly accurate conception of Annia's whereabouts when I rose from my bed soon after midnight and silently went in search of her. "I will come to you," I'd managed to whisper in her ear as we chastely exchanged a kiss good night; and the answering spark of excitement in her eyes was all the light I needed to guide me to her.

She was waiting for me—perfumed, powdered, and naked beneath the bedclothes. I said nothing as I lay down beside her, just ran the tips of my fingers over her body, savoring the smooth coolness of her skin and the scent of musk and roses that enveloped the two of us like a cocoon. My lips sought hers, then strayed to her throat, her shoulders, and her breasts. A long hiss of intaken breath escaped her as my tongue ran over her nipples, and a stifled cry of ecstasy as it probed her most secret part. "Now, Lucio, now," she whispered fiercely, her fingers coiling through my hair. "I want you inside me *now!*"

I required no additional urging, and in moments my body was ranged above hers, my hips between her wide-spread thighs. With a quivering hand she reached for my swollen member and placed its crown inside her. I was grateful then for my exertions of the previous day. Had my passion not been satisfied so recently, I would have spilled my seed inside her then and there.

But alas, I wasn't destined to spill my seed at all that night, for as I strove to enter her more deeply, she winced, went stiff, and tried to pull away.

"What is it, darling?" I asked her, feeling almost too aroused to breathe.

"Nothing," she answered, placing my peg inside her once more.

Her body remained stiff, however, and got stiffer with each slow thrust of my hips.

"I'm hurting you," I whispered anxiously.

"It doesn't matter," she whispered back, and with her fingernails digging into my buttocks, she pulled me forward once again.

Now for a man to deflower a virgin he must either know what he is doing or else be driven by such insensate lust that the pain he's inflicting doesn't deter him. I, very plainly, did not really know what I was doing, and aroused though I was, I wasn't aroused enough to keep on doing it. Annia's body was now so taut with distress that I began to have serious misgivings and nagging second thoughts. As my ardor waned, my member wilted, moreover, so the question of defloration was rapidly becoming moot.

"Don't stop!" Annia pleaded as my poor little prod slipped out of her.

"I'm sorry," I answered, and then let my tongue and lips give her some of the pleasure, at least, that my fragile manhood had denied her.

Afterward we held each other, and she wept in my arms. "This was our last chance," she whispered despondently as the first streaks of dawn began to tint the eastern sky.

And I prayed to the gods that the future might prove her wrong.

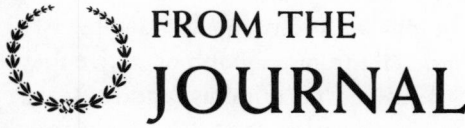
[SEPTEMBER 9TH]

The rain ended during the night and the day dawned cloudless and cool, with blustery winds whipping down from the northwest. Our first order of business upon rising was the purchase of a wagon and a pair of horses, a task I was only too glad to leave in Nestor's capable hands, and which he accomplished with considerable dispatch. Fortunately for us, the teamster from whom we purchased our horses happened to have a *carruca* for sale as well, one that precisely suited our purposes. It is large enough to accommodate the five of us and all our belongings, and it comes equipped with a leather canopy, the sides of which can be raised or lowered depending upon the weather. Of course the teamster's original asking price was little short of exorbitant, and it remained unreasonably high, in my opinion, even after Nestor had expertly bargained him down. But having now traveled some thirty miles in our new conveyance, I can see that our money was well spent. For one thing, we are no longer dependent for shelter at night on a succession of verminous inns; and that means, among other things, that we can cover as much distance as we wish each day without concerning ourselves about the availability, or indeed the existence, of suitable accommodations at the places where we choose to call a halt. In a sense, we have a home again, and that, perhaps, is one of the reasons why I'm feeling much less doleful than I was. Another reason is that I'm heartily sick of all the moping I've been doing lately and have resolved to cultivate a more cheerful disposition from this day on.

With our means of transport secured, we proceeded to the harbor and, with the help of Captain Aeneas and his crew, transferred our baggage from the *Liberta* to our wagon. We then bid our sailor friends farewell and headed west out of the city.

I've never been in Gaul before. Come to think of it, I've never been anywhere at all in the western Empire. On the basis of one day's travel, however, I find little in the appearance of this province to distinguish it from Latium and Campania. The Latin spoken here, apart from a few regionalisms and inflections, is virtually identical to the Latin one hears in Rome; and the local coinage, though minted for the most part in

Lugdunum and Mediolanum, doesn't differ significantly from the coins struck on the Capitoline. Public buildings are pretty much indistinguishable from those that dominate the Imperial forums, though of course they are not quite as old on average or conceived on quite as grand a scale. And the countryside, too, is reminiscent of west-central Italy, apart from a slightly greater preponderance of pine growth and a somewhat inferior soil.

It is getting dark now, and we are camped on a spit of land in a gently flowing river. The wind, which blew gustily in our faces all day long, has died down with the setting of the sun. Portia and Camilla are tending the cooking fire while Decius tends to the horses; and Nestor, still somewhat depleted by our four days at sea, is already fast asleep beneath the canopy of our *carruca*. No doubt he'll bestir himself the moment that dinner is ready, but while he sleeps all is serene.

I'm not sure why exactly, but I'm feeling much more reconciled to our exile now than I've been at any time since we left our farm. Perhaps the comforting similarities between home and Narbonensis have softened the shock of our dislocation, even though the blunt truth of the matter is that the more familiar our surroundings, the greater the distance we are from safety.

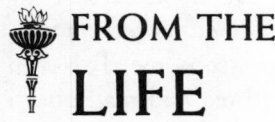
It was ironic in a way that Titus Antoninus's family caught up with us on the very day we were to arrive in Beneventum; for it is at Beneventum that travelers headed for Brundisium must choose between the newer, easier, and faster Via Traiana and the older, somewhat neglected, and decidedly slower Via Appia. All other things being equal, the first route gets you to Brundisium a full day and a half ahead of the second, and that is why almost every traveler prefers it. The five of us were in no particular hurry, though, and the Via Appia—we'd been reliably informed—was far more scenic, and hazardous, than its more recently constructed rival. Of course it was precisely the Via Traiana's popularity that made that stretch of the Appia a more dangerous route to travel. For you could frequently find yourself the sole wayfarer on the road as you proceeded from one post station to another, and as such you were easy prey for bands of robbers, not to mention the more predatory elements among the local population. For adventurous young fellows like Marcus, Agricus, and me, however, such hazards served only to make the Appia more attractive. We had Dracena with us, after all, and vainly regarded ourselves as more than a match for any gang of miscreants we might be fortunate enough to encounter. In fact, the only real drawback associated with taking the Via Appia was that the lady Faustina and her party were going to take the alternate route. And even that drawback, as Marcus gently reminded me, could in some ways be viewed as a blessing.

In the end, as was his custom in matters relating to Annia and me, he left the final decision in my hands—an act of courtesy on his part that I could have willingly done without. Still, I can't honestly pretend that choosing between the Appia and the Traiana was all that difficult on the merits. Indeed, as I've already suggested, the sole argument in the Traiana's favor was that Annia would be traveling on it. The only real issue in the final analysis was whether Marcus would take the blame in Annia's eyes for a decision that had really been made by me; and he, being the good friend he was, readily agreed to endure her displeasure on my behalf, yet again. I was aware, even at the time, that my behavior was both craven and dishonest, the more so since Annia to all appearances had assumed from the very outset that she and I would be taking different roads out of Beneventum. Hadn't she said, "This was our last chance," as I lay dejectedly beside her in her bed? Obviously she understood our circumstances a good deal better than I did. Or she understood me. For even if the decision to depart Beneventum on the Via Appia had really been Marcus's rather than mine, there would still have been nothing to prevent me from choosing the Via Traiana on my own—nothing except my servile attachment to Marcus and my cowardly refusal to cast my lot with Annia instead.

We took leave of the lady Faustina and her children shortly after sunrise, and I had an impulse to whisper "I'm sorry" in Annia's ear as I leaned forward to kiss her good-bye. I quashed it, though, on the theory that I had no right to solicit yet another sop for my conscience from the very person I had sinned against the most. Her eyes were red as she bid me farewell, and her expression was free of all reproach. Was it possible, I wondered, that she had matured so much since our rendezvous at the Claudian Aqueduct that she'd come to understand the essential hopelessness of our situation and no longer felt the need to attribute blame. Had she, like Marcus, become an early convert to magnanimity?

I didn't know.

All I was sure of as I reluctantly took my leave of her was that I was unworthy of her affection—not because of my status as a plebeian but because of my shortcomings as a man.

Perversely enough, the sun was shining and the sky was clear as we made our way down the Appia toward Aeclanum. But I should say "up the Appia," for with Beneventum behind us we were embarked upon our transit of the Apennines.

We arrived at the Appia's twenty-fourth post station in Aeclanum around noon, but remained only long enough to water our horses and purchase some food. We couldn't afford to tarry there, because the twenty-fifth post station was a good thirty-five miles farther on, at Aquilonia, and the alternative to getting there before nightfall was riding through the mountains with nothing but starlight to illuminate any lurking dangers. Adventurous though we were, we weren't fools enough to go looking for trouble; and so we ate as we rode, and maintained a steady pace.

Having had no sleep to speak of during the night just past, I had trouble remaining awake after we'd eaten. The warm sun, the crisp air, and the leisurely rhythm of Incitatus's hoofbeats on the road combined with a full belly to lull me into somnolence. I repeatedly slumped forward as we rode along, only to be jarred awake each time my head came in contact with Incitatus's neck. Of course Agricus did not fail to make my rude

awakenings the occasion for some predictably scabrous comments on the
subject of Annia and me. "He still reeks of quim," was one of his gentler
sallies; "that's why he keeps leaning over to smell his horse." Much to
Agricus's disgust, I responded to his gibes with little more than a weary
nod. I was dispirited to the point of apathy, and his taunts barely penetrated my shell of despairing indifference.

The Appia kept taking us higher, and by midafternoon we found ourselves riding along a ridge line above a narrow river valley, with mountain
peaks on the horizon all around us and sunlight glinting off the water far
below. Just beyond the road's one hundred seventy-fifth milestone we
passed over a small stream that served as one of the valley river's tribu-
taries. Part of the stream's flow had been diverted by means of lead pipes
into a concrete basin, and we halted beside it in order to stretch our legs
and let our horses drink. We'd made excellent time up to that point, and
with a good four hours of daylight still left to us we had less than fifteen
miles still to go. The carpet of spear grass and wildflowers along the
roadside looked wonderfully inviting in the warm spring sunshine, moreover, and since there was no longer any doubt that we could get to
Aquilonia by nightfall, we decided to permit ourselves the luxury of a
rest.

Tired as I was, I rejoiced at the opportunity for a respite, and within
moments I was lying on my back amid the cyclamen and poppies and
gazing up at the pale blue sky. From far away came the faint whisper of
countless leaves rustling in the wind, while closer by a vagrant breeze
gently buffeted the grass and wildflowers. High above us, a bird of prey
floated, almost motionless, on a current of air, its wings outstretched and
its gaze fixed firmly on the ground. No doubt its presence overhead was
pregnant with all sorts of meanings; but as the lady Faustina's auspex had,
like Annia, taken the Via Traiana out of Beneventum, he was not available
to interpret those meanings for us.

Annia, Annia, Annia—cowardice, futility, and despair.

My eyelids felt heavy, and I allowed myself to doze. I couldn't have
slept for more than a quarter of an hour, though, because when I opened
my eyes I saw that neither the sun nor the bird had significantly altered
their positions in the sky. Despite the short duration of my nap, I found
myself feeling somewhat rested; and for some strange reason I felt a bit
less despondent as well. Perhaps the moment was just too idyllic for
concentrated melancholy; perhaps nature on that vernal afternoon was
simply too fragrant and benign.

I don't really know.

But I was not about to question the improvement in my spirits, especially when Hieronymous, lying on his back beside me, broached the subject that usually caused me the most lacerating pain.

"So you've conceived a raging passion for a patrician girl," he said. "That must be what's been eating away at your sense of humor."

"That among other things," I replied.

"Why does it sadden you so?" he asked. "Are you so far gone that you want to marry her?"

"I haven't thought about marriage."

"I should hope you haven't. That young woman would make your life miserable if ever you took her to wife."

"Why do you say that?"

"Because she's rich, beautiful, patrician, and the youngest of four surviving children—which, phrased less euphemistically, means that she's spoiled rotten."

"That's true, I suppose. But it doesn't lead me to love her any the less."

"As well it shouldn't. If I were in your place, I'd love her, and make love to her, at every opportunity."

"That might be dangerous, or so I've been told."

"The antidote to danger in this instance is discretion, not abstinence. Why deprive yourself of a pleasure you hunger for so ravenously just because it involves an element of risk?"

"That's more or less the same conclusion I came to myself."

"But . . . ?"

I paused, considering the extent to which I could take Hieronymous into my confidence, and then responded, "But . . . I reckoned without her maidenhead."

This elicited a silent laugh. "You thought, no doubt, that someone might have been there before you, to clear the way."

"No. I didn't really think at all. I was surprised, in fact, when I saw that I was hurting her."

"And so you stopped?"

"I had no choice," I replied, feeling a blush start to spread from my ears.

"Why? Because she pushed you away?"

"No," I said, cringing inwardly with acute embarrassment. "Because my prod went limp."

"Ahhh," Hieronymous sighed. "It had never encountered such an obstacle before?"

"No," I admitted.

"What a pity," he declared. "You were no more than a hair's breadth away from paradise, had you but known it. One determined thrust and you'd have been home."

"I'd never been with a virgin before."

"So you've already confessed. But next time, at least, you'll know what to do."

"Assuming there is a next time."

He turned his head toward me and with an incredulous frown on his face said, "Don't tell me you're considering celibacy."

That made me smile, albeit ruefully, "I don't know if I'll ever see her again; that's all."

"Well, I hope for your sake that you're not going to abstain until you do."

"I hadn't planned on it," I said with a touch of bravado.

"I'm happy to hear that," he responded. "Even if she's as adept at loving as her mother, there's no reason for you to play the eunuch while the two of you are apart."

I almost mistrusted the evidence of my ears. "As adept at loving *as her mother?*" I squeaked. "You mean to tell me that . . . "

"Yes, I mean to tell you that . . . " he replied with just a trace of self-satisfaction.

"Ye gods!" was all I could manage by way of response.

"You appear to be somewhat nonplussed."

"I *am* somewhat nonplussed."

"And what, may I ask, is nonplussing you?"

"The notion that you and the lady Faustina actually slept together last night."

"Oh, you needn't be nonplussed about that, my young friend; we hardly slept at all."

"But she must be nearly *fifty!*" I exclaimed, causing Hieronymous to erupt with mirth.

"Maturity in a woman is not without its advantages," he said once he finished laughing. "Last night with the lady Faustina, for example, the problem of a maidenhead never arose."

I couldn't keep from laughing myself when he said that, but I quickly reverted to more serious concerns. "All right, let's leave her age out of it. There's still the matter of her being a proconsul's wife."

"And what of that?"

"What do you mean, 'And what of that'? What do you think would have happened to you if you and the lady Faustina had been discovered in the act?"

Hieronymous pretended to ponder that possibility, and then, in a tone of extreme gravity replied, "If the lady Faustina and I had been discovered in the act, I believe I would have been in very serious danger of losing my erection."

I responded to this jest with a grimace of impatience. "You would have been in even *more* serious danger of having your erection lopped off."

"Don't even think such a thing," Hieronymous winced. "One circumcision in a lifetime is enough."

Although this elicited a laugh from me, I was quick to protest. "You're not taking this matter seriously."

"I wish I could say the same for you," he retorted. "For it's my impression that you are entirely too concerned about who puts what inside whom."

I considered this a moment, then said, "That's possible, I suppose."

"I'm glad to hear you acknowledge it. And bear in mind, if you will, that the beast with two backs leaves no scars on its victims' bodies."

"Unless, of course, one counts a swollen belly as a scar."

"Ah, *ha!*" he barked, "you've hit on yet another advantage enjoyed by those of us who frequent older women."

"I take your point. But the woman I want to frequent is decidedly far from mature."

"There are ways around that sort of difficulty," Hieronymous said with a knowing smile.

"I'd appreciate it if you'd tell me what they are," I responded.

"Another time," he announced while gracefully rising to his feet. "For I see our friend Marcus is preparing to remount his horse."

[SEPTEMBER 10TH]

This was a pleasantly uneventful day, replete with warm sunshine, good roads, and bucolic scenery. Indeed, there was only one occurrence that could conceivably be regarded as noteworthy: one of our horses showed signs of going lame. But Decius quickly remedied that condition by first finding and then removing a small shard of pottery that had somehow become lodged below the animal's left rear fetlock.

I shudder to think how much more difficult this journey would be for the rest of us if Decius were for some reason absent from our ranks. He has a wonderful way with animals and is much more knowledgeable about managing and caring for them than I had ever realized. Neither Nestor nor I is of much use at all, and Portia and Camilla are of course of less use still. Decius, on the other hand, is not merely competent in this regard, but possessed of a remarkably even disposition as well. His presence exercises a calming effect on all of us, the value of which, given the way I've been behaving of late, cannot be overstated. It troubles me somewhat that, much as I've come to appreciate and even admire him over the course of the last few months, I still don't feel that I really know him. There is a vague, barely perceptible strain between us that renders most of our interactions unduly formal if not downright stiff; and I'm at as much of a loss as to how it originated as I am for a way of rooting it out. Perhaps it would help matters if I discussed the subject with Portia; at all events, it certainly couldn't hurt.

In the meantime, our odyssey continues. We passed through Carcaso this morning, and by midday tomorrow we'll be in Tolosa, on the banks of the Garumna. Nestor continues to treat our ultimate destination—and indeed all our intermediate ones as well—as a secret far too dark and deep to be shared. He can't keep me from making educated guesses, though. If we follow the river to its mouth we shall arrive at Burdigala. And once in Burdigala our next logical step would be to take ship again and sail northward into the Atlantic Ocean. I pray, therefore, that we will *not* follow the Garumna to its mouth. I've had quite enough of the sea on this journey to last me the rest of my life.

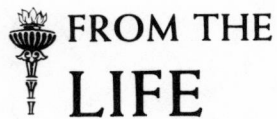
I found myself in a strangely turbulent frame of mind as we resumed our progress toward Aquilonia. On the one hand, I burned with curiosity to know what Hieronymous had meant when he said that there were "ways around" the risk of my impregnating Annia (in the unlikely event I ever got near her again). But, on the other hand, the possibility that I could indulge my passion for her to the fullest without suffering dire consequences filled me with a kind of giddy apprehension. What he was saying, if I understood him correctly, was that with the exercise of a little discretion I could safely copulate with any woman who would have me, even if she were the Emperor's wife! And if he was right about that, what was I to make of all the solicitous warnings Marcus had voiced to me from the moment Annia and I had met? Did they contradict what Hieronymous was saying, or did they mean simply that Marcus doubted my ability to "frequent" Annia on an ongoing basis and also remain discreet? The clear implication underlying Hieronymous's words—and actions!—was that patrician women were no different from all other women; they simply had to be enjoyed more cautiously. But this was directly at variance with my somewhat callow perception that patrician women, indeed all patricians as a class, were somehow a race apart—aristocrats in the literal Platonic sense, not just normal human beings who happened to have been blessed with wealth and social standing by an accident of birth. I must confess that I found Hieronymous's position on the subject to be little less than revolutionary, and as usual I turned to Marcus for a definitive opinion and a clue as to how I should behave.

I had plenty of time to mull the issue over before I raised it with him, though, because for the first few miles the five of us, as was our custom, remained in a fairly tight cluster as we rode along. After an hour or so it became clear to me that if I wanted to converse with him privately I'd have to either wait until we arrived in Aquilonia or split the two of us off from our three companions while we were still en route. Fortunately, a meaningful glance in Marcus's direction coupled with one or two discreet nods toward our rear was all it took to alert him to my desire for a confidential talk. Incitatus, as always, was only too glad to slow his gait, and Marcus tightened the reins on his stallion just enough so that he, too, fell a few paces behind our three fellows. He then listened intently as I conveyed to him, in suitably muted tones, the substance of my most recent conversation with Hieronymous.

"What do you think?" I said upon concluding my recitation.

"What do *you* think?" he came back at me. "That would appear to be the more significant question."

"I don't *know* what to think," I answered him truthfully, "but if Hieronymous really did sleep with the lady Faustina last night, that indicates to me that there must be something in what he says."

"Well," Marcus said after pondering my words for a moment or two, "I certainly can't pretend to be an expert when it comes to the subject of women; so if I were in your place I'd be disposed to give substantial credence to the statements Hieronymous has made."

I did not regard this as a satisfactory response, not just because it was uncharacteristically equivocal and diffuse, but also because Marcus was plainly uncomfortable with the subject under discussion. Belatedly it occurred to me that I'd just informed him bluntly that his aunt was an adulteress and his new traveling companion a rake. Why shouldn't he feel uncomfortable? And yet his discomfort seemed to partake more of embarrassment than of rage or disapproval. For a moment I entertained the bizarre notion that Hieronymous had been so bold as to ask his permission before undertaking the lady Faustina's seduction. But this idea seemed so outlandish that I summarily dismissed it and contented myself with asking simply, "Would you rather we didn't talk about this?"

"Oh, no, no," he was quick to reply. "It's just that I don't feel adequate to advise you. I agree with Hieronymous that your view of my fellow patricians is somewhat . . . idolatrous. And I agree also that patrician women are just as, if not more, susceptible to seduction as their plebeian sisters, regardless of the social standing of the would-be seducer. What I'm not at all sure about, however, is how all this relates to you and Annia. Yes, it's true, or so I believe, that the risk of a 'swollen belly' can be minimized or even eliminated by means of various amatory techniques; but it's also my understanding that such techniques require considerable experience and self-control on the part of those who practice them, the kind of self-control that is not particularly compatible with feelings as intense as yours with regard to Annia. Now Hieronymous must be at least forty years old, and he's plainly very experienced in the ways of love. For him, therefore, it makes perfect sense to run the risks attendant on possessing any woman he desires. The same thing can't as readily be said of you, however; and you differ from him in yet another respect. Hieronymous does not fit anywhere near as neatly into the Empire's social hierarchy as do you and I. As a freeborn Judean of Jewish blood he most nearly resembles a defeated enemy of Rome who's been granted all the privileges of Roman citizenship upon yielding to the Emperor's authority. He is not a plebeian, because he enjoys the legal rights that pertain to *honestiores*. But he is not a patrician either, because he doesn't practice the State religion and is therefore ineligible for political office. His status, in other words, differs dramatically from yours in at least three respects: his feelings are less intense, his experience of women is more extensive, and his social standing is higher. It seems to me, therefore, that the risks he ran in connection with the lady Faustina are not precisely comparable to the risks you run in connection with Annia."

Intelligent and lucid as Marcus's disquisition had been, it was not at all what I'd been hoping to hear. But then, with Annia on her way to Ephesus and me on my way to Greece the practical consequences of the words he'd spoken seemed minimal at most. "I don't imagine you find my analysis of your situation all that encouraging," he said after we'd ridden along in silence for a while.

"It's not your analysis I find discouraging," I responded. "It's the fact that I think you're right."

As the afternoon waned, clouds started building to the north and east, and once the sun had set the air turned decidedly chilly. May in the mountains, I began to suspect, would prove to have much in common with March by the sea; and sure enough, it wasn't long before all five of us bowed to the elements and broke out our woolen cloaks.

Far more worrisome than the cold was the fact that, with dusk fast approaching, Aquilonia was nowhere in sight. Given the clouds that were rapidly overspreading the sky and the fact that the moon wasn't due to rise until the night's third watch, a well-nigh Stygian darkness was about to overtake us. Had we miscalculated the distance to Aquilonia? Had we by some mischance strayed from the Via Appia onto some desolate stretch of secondary road? Under normal circumstances we could have assured ourselves that we hadn't lost our way simply by referring to the milestones. But though the stones themselves had survived intact through several centuries of rain, wind, and snow, the information that had once been chiseled on them had long since been worn away. As a matter of law, the milestones' upkeep was the responsibility of the nearest municipality— in this instance, Aquilonia. But as a matter of fact, the law was rarely observed and even more rarely enforced, especially when a municipality was small, poor, and far from any important city.

In the absence of any sensible alternative, the five of us rode on through the rapidly gathering darkness, with one of us at least feeling more and more uneasy. Shortly before dusk gave way to darkness, however, we rounded a bend and saw Aquilonia clinging to a mountainside no more than a mile or so ahead. Instantly our anxious frowns gave way to smiles of relief, and we covered the distance remaining, not at a gallop exactly, but at a highly spirited trot.

Aquilonia, we discovered on our arrival, was nothing more than a quarter-mile string of tumbledown stone houses on a steep incline, with the Via Appia its one and only street. Where the houses ended, the mountainside on which they were perched continued its ascent toward the lowering clouds, which concealed its upper reaches from view. The Appia, meanwhile, curved sharply away to the right, descending the mountain's east-facing slope until it, too, disappeared in the gathering gloom.

The sense of excitement and anticipation engendered when we first caught sight of the town began to ebb rapidly as we rode through it. All the houses appeared to be deserted; there were no lights to be seen or any sounds to be heard. There was only the chill darkness and the mournful moaning of the wind.

"Country people tend to rise and retire with the sun," Hieronymous said in an unavailing effort to reassure us.

"Either that or they've all fled," Agricus responded, his voice sounding strained and hollow in the face of the pervasive silence.

We rode on, repeatedly casting wary glances to our sides and rear, as if we were expecting some savage apparition to come leaping out at us from the dark interior of every house we passed.

It wasn't until we reached the far end of town that we saw any sign of life. The building looked much like every other building we'd seen, but it had one distinguishing characteristic: slivers of light showed through the slats of its shutters.

"I'd better go in and have a look," said Dracena, sliding smoothly off his horse's back. The rest of us, without hesitation, stayed put.

A swath of lamplight spilled onto the Appia's polygonal stones as Dracena opened the building's door. Then the door swung shut behind him, leaving us once again in the dark.

For some time we waited in silence, the only sounds being those made by our horses as they nervously shifted their weight from hoof to hoof.

"We should either go in after him or get ourselves out of here," Agricus said as the suspense became steadily more wearing.

But before we could make any response to this suggestion, the door opened and Dracena reappeared. "Welcome to the Via Appia's twenty-fifth post station," he said in a hearty voice; and I slumped a little as the tension drained from my body.

The interior of the post station was warmed by a robust hearth fire and illuminated by some fifteen or twenty lamps. It was also somewhat crowded, given the presence of perhaps a dozen adults and at least half that many children. These people, it turned out, were the entire population of Aquilonia, which once must have been at least fifty times larger. They did not appear at all forlorn, however; on the contrary, they seemed full of rude good cheer. Their ruddy faces testified to lives lived out of doors, lives devoted for the most part to the growing, hunting, and gathering of food. Judging from the peasant stockiness of their bodies, they grew, hunted, and gathered with considerable skill. And it came as no surprise to us to learn that they were all related to each other, either by blood or by marriage.

"You are welcome here," said one of the older men. "And there's room for your horses in the stable across the road."

"I'll go see to the horses," Dracena said to Marcus with a grin. "You stay here and get acquainted with our hosts."

There was a moment of awkward silence after Dracena walked out the door, but the uneasiness was quickly dispelled when one of the women asked, "Would you like some lamb stew?"

"You are most hospitable," Marcus responded. "We've come a long way, as it happens, and we're very hungry indeed."

At this several of the women began bustling about, clearing spaces for us at the long table in the back of the room and setting out bowls, cups, and large wooden spoons.

"You say you've come a long way," the older man said in a deferential tone. "Where did you begin your journey?"

"Well," Marcus replied, "we set off this morning from Beneventum, but we began our journey some eight or nine days ago in Rome."

This reference to the City caused something of a stir among the villagers, and one or two of the women whispered, "You see; I told you so" to other members of the group.

"And where are you going?" the man asked.

"We are bound for Brundisium," Marcus answered him, "and from Brundisium we sail for Greece."

This response seemed to confound the Aquilonians' expectations somewhat, and after several moments of murmuring among them the same man said, "Pardon me, but if you are bound from Rome to Brundisium, what are you doing here?"

Marcus looked slightly taken aback by this question, but then he

realized what had prompted it and proceeded to explain the reasons for
our choice of the Appia over the Traiana.

"You chose the Appia because it's the longer and more hazardous route?"
the man asked with a touch of incredulity in his voice.

"The more interesting route," Marcus amended.

At this there was much frowning and shaking of heads among the
villagers. Obviously the notion that travel might in some way be compatible with pleasure or edification was new to them.

"No more questions for now," one of the bustling women told our
interlocutor. And then, turning to us, she said, "Come, strangers, sit
down and have some food."

We did as we were bidden, and before long Dracena rejoined us. The
villagers remained clustered together on the other side of the room and
stared at us with expressions of mute fascination as we wolfed down our
stew.

"This lamb is delicious," Marcus said to them when he'd finished eating,
and immediately his bowl was refilled.

The significance of this transaction was not lost on Hieronymous, who
drank down the contents of his cup and declared, "This wine is delicious,
too."

Within moments his cup was full again.

And the fact of the matter was that neither he nor Marcus was merely
being polite. The food and wine *were* delicious—not overly subtle, perhaps, but delicious nevertheless. The stew contained onions, white beans,
peppercorns, and garlic cloves in addition to the meat, and the gravy in
which all these ingredients swam was thick, dark and teeming with basil,
bay leaves, and fragrant herbs. The wine was new, raw, redolent of fertile
soil, and very potent. My uncle's customers would have heartily approved.

After we'd eaten, though not quite drunk, our fill, Marcus began asking
some questions of his own. Our hosts, it turned out, were all that was
left of a community that had until some twenty-five years before numbered
well in excess of a thousand souls, not counting slaves. And the cause of
this drastic depopulation was nothing other than the newly completed
Via Traiana. Aquilonia, it seemed, had been almost entirely dependent
for its economic existence on the steady stream of travelers making for
Rome from Brundisium and vice versa. In addition to the post station,
the town had been able to boast of no fewer than eight inns and taverns,
all of which had been regularly filled to capacity during the months
between March and November. Our hosts had been one of a dozen or
so farm families who provided food for the hostelries' innumerable patrons.
There'd also been a market, where less affluent wayfarers and the Aqui-

lonians themselves could purchase all the surplus food that hadn't been sold to the *caupos*. In addition to food and lodging, moreover, Aquilonia had been able to offer its transient visitors the services of three blacksmiths, two wheelwrights, six stables, three scribes, three barbers, one physician, and a fluctuating number of prostitutes. With the completion of the Via Traiana, however, the town's lifeblood dried up. Virtually overnight the Via Appia was transformed from the main thoroughfare between Rome and the east into a rustic back road linking Beneventum and Tarentum; and traffic between these two provincial cities was but a tiny fraction of what it had been when the Appia was the only route connecting Latium and Campania with Apulia and the Hydruntine straits.

With calamity staring them in the face, the Aquilonians had appealed to Trajan and then Hadrian for assistance. But the town was not well represented on the Palatine or in the antechambers of the Senate, and it received only marginal relief. Their appeals having accomplished so little, the inhabitants of Aquilonia gradually bowed to the inevitable and began to disperse. Most of them migrated to Beneventum or Tarentum, though a few of the wealthier ones set their sights on Rome. All that was left now was an old post station and a street lined with empty houses. By providing the Empire's citizens with a faster and safer route between Rome and its eastern provinces the Emperor Trajan had all unknowingly wiped out a thriving community. And I suspected that there were few otherwise farsighted decisions made on the Palatine that did not produce some such lamentable result.

Listening to our hosts relate the story of their town's demise, we were struck by the absence of sorrow and rancor from their voices. Marcus raised this matter with them at his first opportunity. The somewhat surprising response he got was that they and the other farm families who'd grown the food for Aquilonia were, if anything, better off now than they'd ever been while the town was thriving; and this proved to be not quite the paradox it seemed. The farm families, always more or less self-sufficient, had never had much use for the metal coins that both townspeople and travelers somewhat disdainfully presented to them in exchange for food. True, it was sometimes possible to trade crops or livestock for some of the services the town's artisans provided, but such services were seldom essential to the farmers' welfare, and, in any case, the artisans more frequently payed them in cash. Thus the farm families had to work long and hard for what often amounted to a negligible reward, even if one or two of them adopted the townspeople's values and foolishly prided themselves on being "rich." But of course there wasn't much else for them to take pride in, because Aquilonia, like many provincial towns, had

always tended to look on those who tilled the soil of its hinterland as
bumpkins; and though the farmers secretly returned the scorn the townspeople heaped on them, the fact remained that they and their forefathers
had slaved their lives away for centuries on end in the service of those
who showed them little respect. That had simply been the way things
were.

But then came the Via Traiana, and the flow of travelers through
Aquilonia was reduced all at once to a trickle. Many fields, accordingly,
lay fallow the following spring, and many farmers unthinkingly joined
with the townspeople in bewailing the "terrible misfortune" that had been
visited upon their community. When the next spring came, there were
fewer Aquilonians to buy the food the farmers grew, and the number of
jugera under cultivation was therefore reduced again. By the third spring
the town was almost deserted, and the farmers—many of them still
laboring under the delusion that something catastrophic had occurred—
confined themselves to raising only as much as they and their families
required in order to subsist. It wasn't until a few more years went by that
they began to realize they were living as well as they'd ever lived while
expending only a fraction of the effort. And there was another unexpected
bonus as well—there were no longer any townspeople around to look
down on them.

Now, some twenty-five years after the Traiana's completion, the dozen
or so farm families had only to feed themselves and maintain the Aquilonia
post station pursuant to the very occasional directives issued by the Imperial Curator of Roads. Since our host family's lands were adjacent to
the town, they had taken on the responsibility for the station, and, indeed,
had made it their home. Judging by their burly figures and round smiling
faces, life for them had never been so good.

Marcus, while listening to this odd story, became progressively more
pensive. Later that evening, just as I was dozing off on the bed of clean
dry straw our hosts had laid down for us on the post station's floor, he
looked over at me and in a low voice said, "You know, Lucio, the more
I think about it, the less the prospect of wielding power appeals to me."

FROM THE
JOURNAL

[SEPTEMBER 11TH]

We are camped just outside the walls of Virodunum, on the west bank of the Garumna, after a day's journey that was blessedly uneventful in almost all respects. In fact, if we hadn't been directed to detour around Tolosa when we arrived at the city's south gate just before noon, our day's progress would have been entirely without incident. Tolosa, it seems, takes its daylight ban against wheeled vehicles within the city walls very seriously; and since we had no particular need or desire to explore the place on foot, we simply crossed the Garumna and proceeded on our way.

The weather continues fine and I continue to be struck by how little difference there is between this part of Gaul and the countryside around Rome. The scenery is a bit less dramatic and the people a bit less cosmopolitan. But in most other respects we could just as easily be traveling from Nomentum to Ardea as from Narbo to Aginnum.

I know we are going to pass through Aginnum, because Nestor, in response to my more or less daily inquiry about where the deuce we're headed, let slip the suggestion that I would be able to formulate a more accurate hypothesis as to our ultimate destination "once Aginnum is behind us." Thanks to this indiscretion I now feel it's reasonable to conclude that our final goal lies somewhere in Lugdunensian Gaul or Brittania. But having reached that conclusion, I still only want to know more.

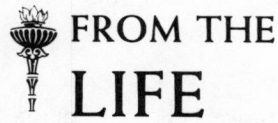
I awoke at first light the next morning, wrapped my cloak tightly around me, and tiptoed outside to ease my bladder. Fog had descended on Aquilonia during the night, fog so thick that after walking just a few paces up the road I could no longer see any sign of the post station or the town. Frost formed on my every breath and steam rose where my urine struck the ground. But though the air was decidedly cold, it was also delightfully fresh, and after relieving myself I stood for a little while savoring the muted dawn and the perfect silence. It scarcely seemed credible that only a day and a night had passed since Annia and I had said our good-byes. It felt more like a month since I'd last seen her, and I concluded from that that I was still very much in love—which was not a very startling conclusion.

I found on my return to the post station that it had come to vigorous life. My four companions were up and about, the straw we'd slept on had been taken away, and a fire had been kindled in the hearth. Before long we were feasting on honey cakes, bread, and goat cheese, and warming our insides with hot spiced wine.

When it was time to leave, Marcus offered to pay our hosts for the food and lodging they'd provided. But the older man who'd regaled us the previous evening with the story of the town's recent history merely shook his head and said, with a deferential smile, "As I indicated last night, we have little use for money here nowadays."

Marcus acknowledged the truth of that observation, and in a characteristic gesture of generosity presented the man and his family with his gold-hilted dagger as a gift. Judging by their expressions, it was worth more to them than several dozen talents of silver.

The fog was beginning to lift a little when we finally rode out of Aquilonia, and by the time we reached the river Aufidus some six or seven miles on, it had burned off almost completely. By midday the sun's heat had intensified dramatically, and all five of us felt a bit parched by the time the Appia crested the southern slope of Mons Vulturis. Happily for us and our horses there was a spring just beyond the crest, and, having slaked our thirst, we sat down and rested beside it. Before us, stretching away to the eastern horizon, lay the pale green reaches of the Apulian plain. The Apennines were now behind us; the lands that had once been Magna Graecia lay ahead.

In deference to Marcus's deferentially expressed wishes, we'd chosen Venusia as our day's destination. There, some two hundred years before our arrival, the poet Horace had been born, the son of a freedman; and no poet, not even Virgil, ever gave Marcus greater pleasure. We had it on good authority, moreover, that the house where the poet first drew breath was still standing. There was also the tomb of the great soldier Claudius Marcellus to add further to the town's appeal.

The date, as it happened, was the seventh before the Ides of May— the first day of the Lemuria—though none of us was aware of that fact when the day began. Since our departure from Rome we'd given little if any thought to the particularities of the religious calendar, or the secular calendar, either, for that matter. It wasn't until our arrival in Venusia that we realized the day was ill-omened—the feast in propitiation of all the ghosts who've been otherwise forgotten or ignored. In Rome, people no longer paid much attention to such antiquated observances, but the Venusians made quite a fuss about this particular one, and for reasons that could later be regarded as a portent of the troubles we were to experience there.

We rode into Venusia toward the latter part of the afternoon, inspected Claudius Marcellus's tomb (which stood on the north side of the Appia, just inside the western gate), and then proceeded on through town in search of Horace's birthplace, asking directions of the few people who were in evidence on the streets. The last person we asked was an old woman, bent and toothless, who pointed to a crumbling hemispherical edifice no more than fifty paces ahead. After thanking her for her assistance, Marcus asked her one additional question: "Why does this town seem so deserted?"

The old woman looked at him in a manner suggestive of either impatience or contempt, but then responded, "This is the first day of the Lemurian Games, so most everyone's out at the amphitheater."

"The Lemurian *Games?*" Marcus repeated, his incredulous tone reflecting the difficulties all five of us were having with the bizarre notion of athletic contests in honor of anonymous spirits of the dead. That made about as much sense as celebrating the birthdays of people one had never heard of; it was an altogether eccentric sort of activity.

The old woman had no interest in dispelling the fog of confusion in which she'd enveloped us, however. She simply waved a hand at us in disgust and scuttled off.

"Well," said Marcus as we all sat dumbfounded on our horses' backs and watched the irascible crone's retreating form, "we know where Horace was born, at least."

But did we?

True, the building the crone had pointed to bore the following inscription on one of its dilapidated walls: HERE ON THE SIXTH DAY BEFORE THE IDES OF DECEMBER IN THE YEAR OF THE CENSORSHIP OF M. LICINIUS CRASSUS THE DIVINELY INSPIRED POET QUINTUS HORATIUS FLACCUS FIRST DREW BREATH. But the crumbling hemispherical structure the inscription presumably referred to was clearly the inside back wall of some bathhouse's frigidarium, and we all regarded such a setting as a thoroughly improbable birthplace for a divinely inspired poet, especially since the poet in question had been a man of great candor and humor who had repeatedly—and, some said, defiantly—acknowledged his father's servile birth in his writings. Was it likely that such a man, if he'd truly been born in a frigidarium, would never once have made mention of that fact in the satires and epistles that flowed from his pen? The answer was no; it was not at all likely. What seemed far more probable in our collective opinion was that the house in which Horace had been born either no longer existed or could not be identified with any certainty; and it struck us as being no less probable that the proprietors of the bathhouse had simply proclaimed their frigidarium his birthplace one fine day on the assumption—probably correct—that by doing so they would attract as customers more of the Appia's quota of weary and dusty travelers than competing Venusian establishments with fewer historical pretensions.

Of course Venusia, like Aquilonia, must have suffered severe economic dislocation when the Via Traiana was completed, and quite apart from the absence of people in the streets, the town's buildings and public places had a run-down neglected quality to them which strongly suggested that its days of glory were a thing of the past. Venusia still existed, though, and given the games in progress, it had also retained at least some of its former vitality. How its citizens had managed to keep their native city alive struck us as something of a mystery. It was a mystery that was shortly to be solved.

We continued on eastward through the town on the assumption that the amphitheater the old woman had mentioned would be clearly visible from the Appia, and, sure enough, there it stood: on the left side of the road just beyond Venusia's eastern gate. The only signs of activity, though, were on the right side of the Appia, where several hundred people were scattered about on the grassy inclines that flanked a sandy field some two hundred paces long by thirty or forty paces wide. At the near end of this field stood a row of three-foot-high wooden posts that bordered the base of an isoceles triangle laid out in concrete on the ground. At the apex of this triangle, the point nearest us, was a small circular pit about three feet deep, and perhaps two-thirds of the way down the right-hand side of the field stood a shaded enclosure containing ten or so concrete seats. The only other distinguishing features of the flat stretch of sand were two six-foot-high iron posts set midway between the grassy inclines, one of them down toward the far end of the field and the other some ten paces beyond the base of the concrete triangle.

Perhaps a hundred paces to the right of this area was another, much larger, sandy field, also flanked by grassy slopes, which featured a low concrete partition running lengthwise down its middle for roughly two-thirds of its course. In between these two long stretches of sand stood a rather large templelike structure built in the old-fashioned Ionic style and several smaller buildings of similar design.

"If I had to make a guess," Hieronymous said as the five of us took in the scene, "I'd say we were looking at a stadium, a gymnasium, and a hippodrome."

Of course there was very little guesswork involved in his observation. The more interesting question, now that we'd located the site of the games, was: Why were they being held? And to get this question answered we made our way over to the stadium, which to all appearances was the only one of the three facilities where anything was going on.

We dismounted near the grassy incline on our right and surveyed the people closest to us in search of someone who looked not only knowledgeable but approachable as well. One of the two or three people nearest us was a tall, bearded, and decidedly muscular man, who was lying face up on the grass of the embankment luxuriating in the mellow warmth of the afternoon sun. He was Hieronymous's age or a little older, with light brown hair and a wealth of scars on his sinewy arms and legs. His nose was nearly flat, having obviously been broken many times, and a good part of his left ear was missing. As for his face, well, it looked even more scarred and battered than his arms and legs, and at least half his right eyebrow had been effaced by the remnants of a gash that only a skilled surgeon could have managed to stitch closed. Remarkably enough, this living record of innumerable lacerations and abrasions looked blissfully comfortable and serene as he lay there on the grass, and if he hadn't sensed our proximity and opened one eye to see who we were, I don't think we'd have had the temerity to bother him with our questions. The way events unfolded, though, it was he who asked us a question first.

"What's the matter?" he said. "Haven't you ever seen a pankratiast before?"

With that inquiry he'd answered at least some of the questions we would have liked to ask him; and I'm a little surprised in retrospect that none of us managed to deduce his profession from his appearance the moment we first saw him. Greek games, or some facsimile thereof, were in progress, after all, and the man addressing us was clearly an athlete of some kind. He was also, clearly, a specialist in the sporting arts of personal combat and, more specifically, in the *pankration*. A wrestler would not have amassed so many scars, and a boxer's wounds would have been confined to the head and upper body. Only a practitioner of what some people called "competitive brawling," the combat sport in which all imaginable holds, kicks, and blows are permitted (except the bite and the gouge), could have accumulated so large and so varied a collection of wounds. Over and above his wounds, however, there was something in the eyes of the man reclining in front of us that forcefully suggested he'd been a fierce competitor in his time. For in his sport, victories are won only by inducing one's opponent, by means of a choke hold or the threat of a broken limb, to raise his hand high and surrender, and there was nothing in this fellow's face to suggest, even remotely, that there was any conceivable set of circumstances in which he could be driven to admit defeat.

"Well?" he said with just a trace of impatience as he rose to a sitting position.

"Excuse us," Marcus responded, "but we're somewhat confused about the games in progress here, and we were hoping you might be willing to enlighten us."

This statement elicited a mordant smile and the following reply: "You're from the Urbs, I take it."

Marcus acknowledged that we were.

"May I know your names?" the man asked, whereupon Marcus introduced each of us in turn.

"I am M. Ulpius Domesticus," the man said once Marcus had finished, "and my native city is Colophon. . . . Now then, what precisely is it about these games that confuses you?"

"Just about everything, to be perfectly honest."

At this M. Ulpius Domesticus gave a silent laugh. "No doubt you find the idea of an athletic festival in honor of the lemures somewhat nonsensical."

"I'd say, rather, that we find it somewhat puzzling."

M. Ulpius Domesticus laughed silently again, and then said, "Believe me, the games make perfect sense once you know the story behind them. Do you have the time to hear it?"

"Most assuredly—if you feel disposed to tell it."

"Very well," said M. Ulpius Domesticus. "Make yourselves comfortable, in that case, because the tale is by no means a short one."

Leaving our horses to nibble on the lush green grass underfoot, we seated ourselves on the ground in front of our new acquaintance.

"You're aware, no doubt," he began, "that all the towns on the Via Appia between Beneventum and Tarentum have suffered severe declines since the new route to Brundisium was completed some twenty-five years ago."

We nodded that we were well acquainted with that aspect of recent history.

"You may also be aware that the triumvirs Antony, Octavius, and Lepidus settled some thousands of their legionary veterans here in Venusia after they triumphed over Caesar's assassins almost two centuries ago. Ever since then the Venusians have deemed themselves to have an exceptionally intimate connection with the Urbs. Many Venusians, in fact, regard themselves as being more truly 'Roman' than even Capitoline Jove. And so, when the number of travelers passing through their territory diminished to almost nothing, they lost no time in sending a deputation of their most distinguished citizens directly to my namesake, M. Ulpius Traianus. Given the illustrious role their ancestors had played in bringing about the Republic's demise, the Emperor gave them a sympathetic hearing. Given the fact that the new road bore his own illustrious name, however, he did not respond with enthusiasm to the Venusians' artless suggestion that parts of it be rendered permanently impassable. Having foreseen the possibility that the Princeps might prove refractory in this regard, the Venusians advanced what to their blunt minds seemed a far more moderate proposal: that all travelers using the new road be required to pay a toll for the benefit of towns along the old one. This suggestion, too, failed to win the Emperor's favor. Finally, as a last resort, the Venusians pleaded with Trajan to grant them a large sum of money by way of compensation. But he, whose patience by then was beginning to show distinct signs of wearing thin, announced—conceivably with vindictive intent—that he would come to their assistance by building them a new amphitheater. Dazzled by this pledge of Imperial munificence, the Venusians sang the praises of their august benefactor and set off on their homeward journey, totally disregarding the fact that their beloved municipality had about as much use for an amphitheater as it had for a Trojan horse.

"M. Ulpius Traianus had spoken, however, so the Venusians' amphitheater was duly built, none of the town's leading citizens having had the nerve to approach the First Citizen a second time with a request for some other form of largesse. They did summon up the courage to present their case in writing to the Emperor's Principal Private Secretary for Petitions, though, and this eminent functionary wrote back to them that his master was graciously disposed to award them three days of gladiatorial and wild animal combats to commemorate the construction of their new arena. The reply concluded by saying that Trajan would be much obliged to the Venusians if they would demonstrate their gratitude for his liberality by undertaking not to renew their entreaties for assistance during the remainder of his mortal lifetime.

"Not even the Venusians were obtuse enough to disregard such an admonition, and after inaugurating their new amphitheater with the only event that has ever taken place here, they settled down and waited for the Emperor's mortal lifetime to end, which, inevitably, it did. And no sooner had Hadrian acceded to the Principate than a delegation of Venusians was on its way to Rome. The new Emperor, being a somewhat more cunning man than his predecessor, and being enamored of all things Greek as well, responded to their supplications by bestowing upon them all the facilities required to stage a full-fledged Panhellenic festival. He also initiated biennial games in his own name and under his own patronage, and let it be known that he would underwrite any additional athletic festivals the Venusians chose to initiate themselves. Grateful though they were, the Venusians, for reasons that remain shrouded in mystery, interpreted the Emperor's words to mean that any games they organized had to be in honor of deities, genii, or incorporeal spirits who might otherwise be denied their full quota of observances. So they searched the pontifical calendar for feasts and holidays that were sufficiently obscure or outdated to warrant widespread neglect. They found three: the Fordicidia in April, the Lemuria in May, and the Furrinalia in July; and the Emperor, true to his word, straightaway provided them with all the funds they needed to establish three annual athletic festivals.

"They responded to his generosity with great enthusiasm, of course, but were now confronted with the task of seeking out athletes who'd be willing to compete in their newly founded games. Now normally all one needs to do in order to lure athletes to an athletic meeting is offer prizes of money to the eventual victors. When the Venusians approached the most prominent competitors in the Greek festivals, however, they found to their dismay that none of them would participate in their new contests without receiving an exorbitant sum of money in advance. The games calendar was already filled to overflowing with athletic festivals of long standing, moreover, throughout the Empire and in Greece. The Venusians soon realized that their festival was doomed to form part of the so-called Novice Circuit—that loose collection of obscure competitions in out-of-the-way provincial towns that attract old athletes past their prime and young ones still rounding into form. I, as you will have deduced already, fall into the first of these categories. But happily for me, I am here as a judge, not a competitor. If you tarry a while longer, you will be able to observe me in the exercise of my office."

"You mean an event is about to take place here?" I asked simple-mindedly.

"The *games* are about to take place, my young friend, though not, as yet, in earnest."

"I don't follow you," Marcus said.

"What I am telling you," M. Ulpius Domesticus responded patiently, "is that even though the men's competition doesn't start until tomorrow, the games begin officially with the boys' events this afternoon."

"But hardly any spectators are here yet," Marcus observed, prompting M. Ulpius Domesticus to smile forbearingly and say, "Games on the Novice Circuit are famous for their small crowds, and smaller prizes."

"But if the crowds are so small, what purpose do all these newly founded festivals serve?"

"Well, they attract a fair number of athletes, for one thing, who must eat and drink and find someplace to sleep; and they also attract an occasional trainer or two in search of nascent talent. It's by no means unheard of, moreover, for spectators from nearby towns to show up, most particularly when one of their fellow citizens is competing. But far and away the most important purpose the games serve—amply funded as they are by an Imperial endowment—is providing the Venusians with an inexhaustible source of honoraria in return for the efforts they expend in staging and presiding over the competitions. I, for example, am one of only a few *xenoi* who perform official duties at these games; almost every other judge and functionary here—and they are countless as grains of sand—is a citizen of Venusia. And, depend on it, if any one of them had been sufficiently conversant with the brutal subtleties of the *pankration*, I myself would not be here in an official capacity."

"Is there going to be a *pankration* competition for boys this afternoon?" Agricus asked, with a hint of blood lust in his voice.

"There is indeed, right after the boys' foot races are run."

"The boys' foot races," Marcus repeated reflectively, and then inquired of M. Ulpius Domesticus, "How young must a young man be in order to qualify as a boy?"

M. Ulpius Domesticus assessed him a moment before replying. "You're not by any chance contemplating a competitive role for yourself in these games, are you?"

"I'm not, as it happens. But what objection would there be if I were?"

"Oh, there'd be no 'objection' of any kind. It's just that many of the competitors on the Novice Circuit tend to be a little bit . . . unmannerly."

"How unmannerly can anyone be while running a foot race?" Marcus asked.

M. Ulpius Domesticus, after favoring him with a cryptic smile, responded simply, "You'd be surprised."

That ominous-sounding response was more than enough to dissuade me, at least, from contemplating active participation in the games.

Marcus persisted, however, in wanting to know how "boy" was defined in an athletic context, and M. Ulpius Domesticus was pleased to accommodate him. "For all practical purposes," he said, "No one under sixteen is qualified to compete as a boy on a professional level; and no one over nineteen is supposed to. In actuality, a fair number of 'boys' ward off the stiffer competition that comes with athletic manhood until they are well into their twenties."

"But a boy of sixteen or seventeen might conceivably have some success against them?"

"If he was fast enough, yes; and if he could cope with their unmannerly tactics."

That, apparently, was all Marcus needed to hear. To my chagrin but not my surprise, he turned to me and said, "Well, Lucio, what do you think?"

"I'm willing," I replied immediately, trying to conceal the acute sense of reluctance I was attempting at the same time to ignore.

"Brave fellow!" Agricus remarked in a sarcastic tone.

"That he is!" Marcus retorted, enfolding my shoulders in an exuberant bear hug. Then, turning back to M. Ulpius Domesticus, he asked, "Where do we apply for permission to participate?"

From that point on, things happened fast. M. Ulpius Domesticus escorted us to the shaded enclosure and there introduced us to the Venusian aedile who was in overall charge of the games. He in turn referred us to the prefect in charge of the stadium, who directed us to the tribune charged with supervising the foot races. This functionary summoned his deputy for boys' foot racing, who, after consulting several of the wax tablets an elderly slave carried around for him announced that "so far" only seven competitors had been entered officially in the three races. That meant, he went on to say, that there were still two starting positions available; so if I qualified in all other respects I could compete. He asked me my name, my native city, if I was freeborn, if I enjoyed the rights of Roman citizenship, and if I was a member of one of the athletic synods, while his slave dutifully noted my responses on one of the wax tablets in his custody. Since I was not a member of an athletic fraternity, I had to have a sponsor and pay a fee. Marcus, of course, was quick to assume that role and bear that expense.

No sooner had the formalities of my registration been completed than a herald blew a blast on his trumpet and called on all competitors entered in the stade race to congregate at the starting posts. Once all eight of us were gathered there, the tribune in charge had us pick one white stone each from a golden cup. On each stone a number had been drawn in black ink; mine bore the number 2, which corresponded to the 2 that had been painted on the second starting post from the right.

It was at this point that the first in a succession of events I was unprepared for took place.

All seven of my opponents stripped naked.

[SEPTEMBER 12TH]

Today we passed from Narbonensian Gaul into Aquitania, and the look of the land has subtly but unmistakably changed. This region resembles Latium far less than the countryside around Tolosa and Carcaso. It is greener, looks much more fertile, and is partitioned by a series of low wooded ridges that run eastward for miles from the banks of the Garumna. Between these ridges lie fields and orchards awaiting the harvest. And what a harvest it promises to be! The peaches and plums we've seen hanging from the trees today look absolutely magnificent and taste even better than they look. So, too, do the apples, pears, and cherries, even though they are not yet fully ripe. In the fields we've seen peas, asparagus, artichokes, lettuce, cabbage, haricots, barley, and wheat luxuriating in the warmth of the sun and the richness of the alluvial soil. This area is nothing less than a garden, and its people in consequence look prosperous and fat.

We covered about thirty-five miles today and are camped once again beside the Garumna. Aginnum is some ten miles ahead, and Nestor was gracious enough to inform us at dinner this evening that we would be turning north when we get there tomorrow. Burdigala and the great ocean, accordingly, can be excluded from our conjectural route of march. I begin to suspect that our ultimate destination lies someplace in the province of Britannia, but I still haven't the faintest notion where precisely, or *why*.

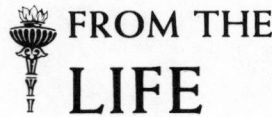

Having devoted over twenty years of my life to the Greek games, I find it hard to credit the idea that there was once a time when I didn't know that all professional athletes are bound by prescript and tradition to compete in a state of nature. Indeed, it's no exaggeration to say that, old and crotchety as I now am, I'd be righteously indignant if I were ever to see a participant in an officially sanctioned competition sporting so much as a loincloth, even if the athlete in question were the lowliest neophyte taking part in one of the most obscure festivals on the Novice Circuit.

My recollection of how shocked I was as I stood by the starting posts at Venusia that afternoon is quite distinct, however. Like most Romans, I regarded the idea of appearing naked in public with profound embarrassment and repugnance. I was as yet unacquainted with the aesthetic pleasures the Greeks derive from the sight of finely tuned athletes contending with one another to the utmost of their abilities while attired in nothing more than a film of oil.

And oil, or, rather, the lack of it, was the next urgent problem I had to contend with. My seven opponents, having already stripped to the skin, were now emptying small phials of clear viscous liquid into their hands and smoothing it over their own and each other's bodies. This custom, too, was altogether new to me, though it came, in time, to be the one aspect of athletic ritual I cherished most. That young men who are about to compete with each other at an often savage pitch of intensity should prepare for this violent strife by gently, and sometimes lovingly, applying a layer of oil to the backs and shoulders of their rivals seems to me the very essence of the sporting ethic. It serves as a tangible, and often needful, reminder that athletes are meant to excel their adversaries, not destroy them.

Alas, having come without any oil of my own, and being still very much of two minds about whether to divest myself of my clothes, it seemed likely that I'd be excluded from the prerace rituals as well as the race itself. As fate would have it, though, the young, sandy-haired, pimply-faced whippet of a boy who'd drawn starting post 3 took note of my woebegone expression and said to me, "I've got a little extra oil here, if you could use some."

To say that I felt grateful toward him hardly conveys the depth of my sense of indebtedness, most especially because the business of oiling myself and being oiled by him served to distract me somewhat from the excruciating embarrassment attendant on taking off my tunic. "Thank you," I said with heartfelt sincerity once my body was fully coated, hoping that my tone of voice would compensate to some extent for the painful inadequacy of my words.

"It's only a little oil," he replied dismissively, being almost as uncomfortable with my abject gratitude, to all appearances, as I was with my utter nakedness.

"Take your places," came a voice from behind me, and I turned to see an austere-looking middle-aged man standing in the three-foot-deep pit at the apex of the concrete starter's triangle. In his right hand he gripped the ends of eight taut lengths of twine, which ran from his fist through shallow grooves in the concrete to starting gates. Brass staples at half-foot intervals kept the twine confined within the grooves and served to guide it up the sides and over the tops of the gates. These "gates" consisted of two simple wooden slats, one vertical, about four feet high, and the other horizontal, about two feet long. Each gate resembled the right half of a slightly elongated letter H, except that the twine running from the top of each standing piece to the tip of each crosspiece made the starting line as a whole look like a row of transparent pennants. The bases of the crosspieces sat in tiny beveled niches on the sides of the uprights, but were not attached to them in any other way. Thus—as I finally managed to figure out—when the starter gave a yank on his eight taut lengths of twine, the tips of all eight crosspieces would be pulled simultaneously upward, causing the bases to fall from their niches in the uprights and causing the crosspieces as a whole to drop into a perpendicular position so that they no longer barred each runner's path. The moment that happened, the race was on.

"Runners . . . prepare!" said the starter portentously, and I noticed my fellow competitors planting their toes in the two closely spaced channels that ran the length of the concrete triangle's base. As far as I could tell, all eight of them lodged the toes of their left foot in the front channel and the toes of their right foot in the rear one. I copied their actions and then, taking yet another cue from their behavior, bent slightly forward at the waist and halfway extended my arms.

All, I assumed, was now in readiness, and no sooner had I made that assumption than the starter yelled, "Go!" and the crosspieces dropped.

Had I not felt quite so befuddled by all that was going on, I might have been disheartened by the fact that by the time I hit full stride, all seven of my opponents were a pace or two ahead of me. Thus—and for by no means the last time that afternoon—it was brought home to me that there was a lot more to running a foot race than merely running. To begin with, one obviously had to master the techniques involved in breaking out of the gates and accelerating to maximum speed. Failing this, one would inevitably have to address oneself to the techniques of catching up. But mastery of these requires, for the most part, far less in the way of training and experience than do other aspects of foot racing. All that's really needed to master them, in fact, is a strong competitive drive and a considerable capacity for speed—assuming that one is running only a sprint, which, happily enough, was precisely what I and my opponents were doing.

Oddly enough, I never much doubted my ability to overtake my seven adversaries; the only question in my mind was how quickly did I have to do it. If, as seemed likely, the starting and finishing lines had been laid out on the stadium floor in conformance with the canons of symmetry, I could reasonably expect to find the latter some ten paces beyond the twin of the six-foot-high iron post I'd just then passed. That, at all events, was the only plausible working hypothesis I could come up with.

It was always my preference during my athletic career to run the stade race "from behind." In theory this is not a wise tactic, since at the top professional levels any sprinter who breaks into the lead may well prove impossible to catch. My experience, however, was that the sight of a runner ahead of me more often than not called forth my fiercest competitive instincts. And it gave me another advantage as well. For it is virtually impossible, in a sprint, to lose a lead and then regain it to win the race; and that, to my mind, means that he who leads from the start must almost always be running scared, which is not the best way to compete. True, if one can focus one's mind and spirit so intensely on victory that one loses all awareness of the competition, one can lead from start to finish and run brilliantly. But it is not at all easy to achieve that intensity of focus race after race. The mind is easily distracted, the spirit easily unsettled. Far more reliable as an incentive to victory, from my point of view at any rate, is an opponent who shows you his buttocks and makes you eat his dust. Such an opponent soon ceases to be a fellow athlete contending with you for a prize and becomes instead a sworn enemy, boastful and cocksure, who is clearly intent on showing you up.

At the time in question, I was a long way from articulating these tenets of competitive strategy, but the emotions underlying them don't really require articulation in order to produce the observed effects. Without thinking much about my feelings, or even being fully aware of their

existence, I set off in hot pursuit of my opponents, suffused with resentment and seething with vindictive wrath. Small wonder that I overtook
all seven of them some twenty paces before the iron post and then went
on to win by some three or four strides.

I think everyone in the stadium—most assuredly not excluding me—was
more than a little bit stunned by what I'd just done. Those present, at
all events, greeted my victory with a salvo of stony-faced silence that
substantially diminished the pleasure I took in it. Marcus's enthusiasm
almost made up for the other spectators' ungenerous reaction, however.
He came running down the field to where I stood catching my breath
(pointedly ignored by my seven defeated opponents), and seizing me in
a violent embrace shouted jubilantly, "You were magnificent, Lucio, absolutely magnificent!"

Basking in the warmth of his congratulations, I walked with him back
to the shaded enclosure on the southern side of the field, where the
stadium prefect brusquely presented me with a gold aureus and a nicely
wrought tripod of bronze.

"What does one do with a tripod?" I asked as my traveling companions
examined the fruits of my first victory.

"One squats on it," Agricus offered with all his customary civility.
Whereupon Marcus, affecting to ignore him, said, "I think it's meant to
serve more of a traditional than a practical purpose. Achilles awarded
tripods at Patroclus's funeral games, if I remember correctly."

"He also awarded horses and slave girls and prize bulls," Hieronymous
remarked, his voice playful.

"Yes," said M. Ulpius Domesticus, "but he was not so thoroughly
schooled in parsimony as our friends the Venusians."

"Perhaps they'll reward you with a slave girl after the next race," Hieronymous suggested.

"Only if he wins it," Agricus was quick to stipulate.

"Can there be any doubt but that he will!" Marcus exclaimed, and no
sooner had he spoken than the herald summoned all competitors in the
diaulos race to the starting line.

"Be careful rounding the turning post," M. Ulpius Domesticus cautioned
me as I took leave of my companions, and had I been wise enough to
take the time, I could have profited enormously by persuading him to
explain what he meant.

But it turned out I was in need of guidance of an even more elementary
sort. For after walking several paces toward the starting gates my opponents and I had just used, I realized that none of the other runners was

moving in the same direction. The explanation was that the diaulos—
and the dolichos as well—always starts from the end of the arena where
the stade race ends, since it is toward that end that the judges' enclosure
is situated. What had confused me more than anything else, I suppose,
was the absence of a concrete starter's triangle and a row of wooden gates
at the stade finish line. But it came to me, after I'd turned in great
embarrassment and gone scurrying off on the track of my fellow competitors, that such an elaborate starting installation was not really necessary for the longer races, and that the two lines of concrete toe channels
that had served as the stade finish line were all that was required to insure
a fair and uniform start. And thus it was—almost before I'd had a chance
to catch my breath, it seemed—that the second race began with the
utterance of a simple verbal command by the starter.

The diaulos is a bit too long to be sprinted. A race of just over two
stades, it will sap the strength of any runner who attempts to go all out
from start to finish. The trick is to run fast enough to stay within striking
distance of the lead while conserving sufficient strength to sprint the final
three or four hundred feet. When the race began, I was feeling so breezily
certain of my ability to make up lost ground (and so grimly determined
to eschew the tactical blunders I'd made in my race against Agricus and
his horse) that I resolved to stay back on the outbound leg and then trust
to a burst of speed to propel me into the lead once I'd rounded the turning
post.

The strategy was a sensible one, but it reckoned without the unmannerly designs of my opponents.

I should have guessed that something was amiss right from the start,
when all seven of my adversaries lagged along with me at my deliberately
lethargic pace. For reasons I doubt I could have articulated, I did not feel
comfortable having them bunched so tightly around me. But with my
mind focused primarily on the business of winning the race, I subdued
my uneasiness with the thought that if they didn't soon open up a lead
on me, they'd be doomed to ignominious defeat.

I know now, of course, that the turning post is often the turning point
of a race. Back then, however, I wasn't even aware that all turns in the
stadium events must be to the left. Had I not drawn starting position
number 2, in fact (which was well toward the right side of the field), I
might quite conceivably have tried to go around the turning post in the
wrong direction.

I don't to this day have the slightest idea which of my seven opponents
it was who actually committed the act, but all at once, as I was about to
come out of the turn, I felt a sharp push against my right shoulder and

then heard the loud bonging sound of my forehead hitting the hollow iron post. I must have lost consciousness at that point, because the next thing I remember was Marcus's face hovering over me as the spectators down at the other end of the stadium lustily cheered whoever it was who'd won the race.

"Why didn't they cheer me like that?" I asked half in jest as I rose to a sitting position and cupped my battered brow in my hands.

"I think it has something to do with you being a stranger in these parts," Marcus responded, and then asked, "Are you all right?"

"I think so," I answered him, and too quickly rose to my feet.

"Whoa there, easy, dear friend," he said, grabbing hold of my arm as I staggered and almost fell down. "Perhaps you'd better confine yourself to the role of spectator for the remainder of the afternoon."

I did not feel at all reluctant to take this prudent advice, but the instant we rejoined our companions at the other end of the field Agricus set about goading me as only he in his bottomless malice could.

"How gracefully you run," was his opening gambit. And when Marcus sprang to my defense, saying, "He was flagrantly and brutally fouled," Agricus merely smiled that peculiarly grating smile of his and sneered, "Poor lamb."

At that moment the herald sounded the call for the dolichos race, and I was just angry enough to flash my nemesis a look of defiance and stride off toward my starting position.

"Lucio . . ." Marcus started to object, but then merely shrugged his shoulders and lapsed into silence.

Agricus displayed no such restraint. "Stay well back of the pack," he called to me after I'd gone a few paces.

"*What?*" I snapped, swinging around to look him in the face.

"You heard me," he responded blandly. "Stay well back of the pack."

"Why should I?"

"Just take my advice, Lucio. Trust me."

I could hardly believe my ears. "*Trust* you!"

"You won't regret it, I promise."

"Because I won't do it," I retorted, and turned away.

I was fuming when I took up my position on the starting line, not simply because Agricus had had the effrontery to favor me with his unsolicited advice, but even more because the advise he'd offered was manifestly correct. I *had* to lag behind my seven opponents; I had no other choice. If I ran alongside them, they would clobber me again, and I clearly couldn't hope to run ahead of them for the full twenty lengths of the field that comprised the race. No, the only course open to me was to stay well back until past the last turn and then sprint for all I was worth. It galled me to my marrow, though, that in opting for that strategy I was condemning myself to appear my enemy's tool.

The race developed unremarkably enough, my seven opponents seeming quite content to leave me unmolested as long as I stayed submissively in the rear. To be honest, the painful tedium inherent in running so long a race soon diminished my competitive ardor almost to the vanishing point, and by the seventh or eighth lap, I must confess, I wanted the race to be over a good deal more than I wanted to win it.

It was about then that I began to notice droplets of blood scattered about in the footprints we'd been making in the sand. Immediately I looked down at my own legs and feet to see if I was the one who was bleeding. But I wasn't. And at the start of the ninth lap one of my competitors went limping off the field. That explained the blood, or so I thought. On the second leg of the lap I noticed that two other runners had developed pronounced limps. And the red splotches on the sand were beginning to proliferate at such an appalling rate that at several points I very nearly slipped. Surely all this blood wasn't a normal concomitant of the dolichos race; no athlete would repeatedly subject himself to an event that entailed mutilation.

What the deuce was going on?

The tenth lap was upon us, and speculation rapidly gave way to a conviction that, quite apart from anyone's bloody feet, no prize was worth the extreme discomfort attendant on continuing to run. This was my first encounter with the "death pain" that all professional runners come to know and abhor. I never got used to it and I never understood how I managed to overcome it repeatedly and finish each race. The fear of humiliation probably played a large part in inducing me to sustain my efforts, but when the pain was upon me, humiliation seldom seemed too terrible a fate.

On this occasion, as on most others throughout the course of my career, I just gritted my teeth and doggedly kept on putting one foot in front of the other, the finish line rather than victory having become my primary goal. But my six remaining opponents, though still some fifteen paces ahead of me, were all repeatedly breaking stride, so it was clear that the race could be mine. Coming out of the last turn I swung wide to the right, to give my struggling adversaries as wide a berth as possible while overtaking them. They were all in such great distress, it turned out, that I was able to coast the last hundred feet or so and still win going away.

The spectators responded to my second victory of the day with a silence considerably more ominous than that with which they'd greeted my first; and their muteness grew more menacing still as each of my six opponents came staggering across the finish line and collapsed onto the sand.

"I wouldn't stay around here to collect your prize if I were you," M. Ulpius Domesticus said to Marcus and me as I gratefully pulled my tunic on over my head.

Why not? I was about to ask, but before I could get the question out, I felt Marcus grip my elbow and start guiding me toward our horses.

"Hurry *up*, in the name of the gods!" Dracena snarled from behind us after we'd walked a dozen or so paces. And if I hadn't been frightened up till then, the sound of fear in *that* imperturbable voice struck terror deep in my soul.

I turned my head to look back only once, and saw a large crowd of people clustered around the starting line. I didn't turn my eyes again in that direction until I was mounted on Incitatus. Then I saw to my horror that the crowd was now very purposefully headed toward us. The next moment I heard the sound of Dracena's palm landing hard on Incitatus's rump, and my slothful steed bolted forward with such vigor that I nearly fell off his back.

We rode hard out of Venusia, and kept riding until it was nearly dark.

"Would someone please tell me what's going on," I pleaded when we finally slowed down a little to let our horses breathe.

"Agricus put oil in the toe channels," Marcus said in a tone of irritation.

"On the starting line?"

"On the starting line."

"But why?"

"In order to avenge your humiliation in the diaulos, little fellow," Agricus explained in a voice that fairly oozed self-satisfaction.

"What does putting oil in the toe channels have to do with avenging anything?" I asked angrily. "And who in Hades designated *you* to be my avenger?"

"No one designated me, dear boy. I simply volunteered my services. I can't stand to see you being humiliated by strangers."

"I'm convulsed with gratitude," I said.

"It was nothing more than a labor of love, really."

"Since it involved inflicting pain on others, I don't doubt it. . . . Now would you be gracious enough to explain how you achieved your results."

"It was simple. I asked Ulpius Domesticus if there was any way you could get even with your opponents. He told me that in the old days, when he was just beginning his career, he'd heard that a dolichos race had been fixed on Delos once so that a runner from the island could be assured of winning the prize. He said that the islanders put a little oil in the toe channels where the foreign competitors were to stand. This oil caused small pebbles and larger-sized granules of sand to adhere to the foreigners' feet, where they gradually opened up small cuts and nicks. He said that, the way he heard it, the local boy was the only runner to finish the race."

"And so you took it upon yourself to revive this venerable practice on my behalf."

"Exactly. While everyone else was busy celebrating your defeat in the diaulos, I provided myself with a stray cruet of oil and sowed the seeds of your glorious victory."

"Did it never occur to you that I could win just as easily without your help?"

"That possibility may have crossed my mind, precious. But, alas, having now indulged our penchant for righteous retribution, we'll never really know for certain if you could have won on your own."

At this point Marcus reentered the conversation, saying angrily, "Have I ever mentioned to you, Agricus, that you have a positive genius for malice?"

In response, my inveterate enemy merely smiled his nastiest smile and said, "Flattery, my dear Marco, will get your fleet-footed little vassal precisely nowhere."

If we hadn't been riding at the time, I would have made that statement the occasion for a few well-aimed blows to Agricus's venomous mouth. The way things were, though, I had to content myself with spitting full in his beautiful face.

[SEPTEMBER 13TH]

Things have been going so smoothly for the most part that a day of vexations was probably long overdue. I only hope, now that the sun has set on it, that we are not due for another for a long time to come.

I should have known we were in for a difficult time of it right from the outset, when Portia, Camilla, and I awoke with severe symptoms of diarrhea. Perhaps those peaches and plums we gorged ourselves on yesterday were a bit too rich for our blood, or perhaps the river water we've been drinking is slightly impure. Whatever the cause of the disorder, the effect on our bowels has been well-nigh catastrophic, and my poor little overworked bunghole feels like it's been voiding thistles for a not so solid month.

Complementing our intestinal malfunctions is a newly discovered defect in the brake-release mechanism of our wagon, a defect we became aware of when we attempted to start on our way this morning and found that the vehicle's front wheels would not turn. Decius was able to effect a makeshift repair of sorts, but every time we hit a bump the brake would lock again, and he'd have to jump down, crawl underneath the wagon, and pry it into an open position.

To cap this endlessly frustrating day, one of our horses went lame on us some five miles beyond Aginnum. And since the other horse couldn't possibly pull our heavily loaded wagon by himself, Decius had to unhitch both him and his limping companion, ride him back to Aginnum, and then return with a newly purchased gelding who could join him in the traces.

While Decius was seeing to all these matters, I attempted to sell our lame animal to the farmer whose house stood about a half mile down the road from where we'd been forced to stop. He wasn't interested in buying a lame horse, he said, but intimated that he'd be willing to "take him off [my] hands." I insisted on some sort of payment, though, and after considerable haggling settled for a dozen artichokes and a half-dozen cabbages. (It's fortunate, in light of all the expenses we've recently incurred, that Spaeto was able to pay me half the purchase price for my slaves before we left Italy. Our own resources are just about exhausted, and were it not for the gold pieces I obtained from him we'd be virtually penniless in a matter of days.)

Decius returned in midafternoon and we once again got under way. Now, as night is falling, we are camped by the river Oltis, with the city of Vesunna some two days' journey away. After Vesunna comes Iculisma, I assume, then Segora or Limonum, and the Liger valley. I feel certain—for the moment, at least—that we are headed for the Channel.

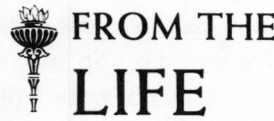
I did not derive much satisfaction from spitting in Agricus's face, largely because in doing so I failed to cause him much distress. In fact, he always seemed pleased when he succeeded in provoking me to aggression against him.

On this occasion he went so far as to laugh a little while wiping my spittle off with his sleeve. "Victory has made you a bit pugnacious, it would appear," he said. "Take care lest you succumb to fatal hubris."

I had no response to this insincere admonition, and that may have been because it wasn't altogether wide of the mark. I had to admit to feeling a certain pride in my newly confirmed athletic prowess; for the first time in my life I saw myself as having some claim to distinction, and I'd be lying if I claimed further that the idea had in no way turned my head. That much I had to grant my perennial adversary—he was always able to see into the darker places of my soul. Like the traditional slave in a triumphal procession who repeatedly whispers in the victorious general's ear that all glory is fleeting, Agricus stood as a constant reminder to me of the base and selfish instincts that only my sense of inadequacy kept safely within bounds. I don't for a moment suppose that he intended to serve such a beneficent function, but neither can I deny him the credit for having served it.

We arrived at the Appia's twenty-eighth post station in Bantia not long after nightfall, but at Dracena's insistence remained only long enough to feed our horses and ourselves. Dracena reasoned that since the Venusians could not have failed to notice the direction in which we'd fled, there was a good likelihood that they were still in hot pursuit. That being the case, we had little choice but to keep on riding, until dawn at least, and possibly all the way to the Tarentine Gulf.

We had no apparent need to proceed at a gallop, however, since the horses of our hypothetical pursuers would be no more capable of maintaining their headlong pace than were our own animals, at least three of which had been bred specifically for speed and endurance. It was while discussing this particular subject that Marcus, Agricus, Dracena, and I finally gave some thought to the question of how in the world Hieronymous, on his aged and apathetic mule, had managed to keep up with us over such an extended distance. The answer, of course, was that his aged and apathetic mule was still placidly grazing outside the stadium at Venusia and that he himself had appropriated some unsuspecting spectator's stallion for his personal use. "I overheard Agricus's conversation with Ulpius Domesticus," he explained, "so when I saw him putting oil in the toe channels I knew right away that I'd be needing a more spirited mount."

"Wonderful!" Marcus responded in a tone of exasperation. "With you and Agricus along on this journey, we may as well all take up highway robbery and be done with it."

"That's fine with me," Hieronymous retorted, "but let's not take it up on *this* highway, please, or we shall all most assuredly starve."

This provoked a few smiles but little more, and we rode along in silence for several miles before Marcus recovered his good humor. I wasn't sure why he'd reacted so irritably to Hieronymous's capricious act of theft. To me, our jovial companion's actions made perfect sense. Indeed, what else could he have done under the circumstances? Being clearly associated with the four of us in the eyes of the local populace, it would not have been at all prudent of him to wait around in Venusia after we'd fled in the hopes that he wouldn't be recognized. Since his mule couldn't possibly have kept up with our horses, moreover, or maintained a lead over theirs, he had no choice once he decided to flee with us but to provide himself with a horse of his own. Perhaps Marcus was miffed because Hieronymous hadn't consulted him before taking the action he did, or perhaps, sensing—after Capua—that his own "virtue" was not as impregnable as he'd thought, he was more than usually concerned about others observing the forms of both custom and law. His uncharacteristic rigidity on this issue called to mind the way he'd reacted to Agricus's fanciful plan to depose the king of the grove. At that time, too, he'd displayed a certain stiff-necked devotion to the established order and an equally pronounced aversion to acts of anarchic self-assertion. It caused me no little uneasiness to entertain the possibility, but I had to wonder as I considered his behavior whether he might have been more decisively shaped by his aristocratic breeding than he liked to imagine or admit.

He didn't continue out of temper, though, and soon was once more observing the rites of badinage with Agricus, Hieronymous, and me.

"Lucio tells me that you're conversant with the mysteries of impregnation," he said to our disciple-of-laughter-turned-horse-thief as soon as our conversation took its inevitable turn toward the topic of sex.

"Ah, yes," Hieronymous replied in mock despair, "but what good does it do me?"

"It must have kept you out of trouble on a number of occasions."

"Perhaps, perhaps," he responded in a tone of exaggerated melancholy. "But as the apostate Jew Saul once wrote to the gentile Christians at Corinth, 'Yea, though I understand all mysteries, and all knowledge, and though I have all faith, so that I could move mountains, but have not love, I am nothing.' "

"This Saul fellow didn't mention laughter?" Agricus asked in an arch tone of voice.

"This Saul fellow was something of a fanatic and therefore had little or no sense of humor," Hieronymous replied.

"Why cite him then?" asked Marcus.

"Because even those without laughter may not be entirely lacking in wisdom."

"What does all this have to do with impregnating a woman?" I asked impatiently.

"It has this to do with it: one should never impregnate a woman one does not love."

"That sounds like a moral proposition," Marcus objected.

"I think the practical ramifications greatly outweigh the ethical ones, my young friend."

"Speaking of practical matters," I persisted, "how does one go about observing this prohibition you've just enunciated, without abstaining entirely from venery, that is?"

"My but you're inquisitive on this subject," Agricus commented. "One might almost imagine that you knew some female who'd be willing to endure your goatish caress."

"Oh, *do* give it a rest, Agricus," Marcus snapped. "Can't we have just one discussion on this journey that doesn't degenerate into personalities."

"My profuse apologies," Agricus responded, his expression blank but somehow ominous.

Marcus, after exchanging icy stares with him for a moment or two, turned back to Hieronymous and said, "Please proceed with your answer to Lucio's question."

"With the utmost pleasure," said our merry companion. "Now then, the object of the exercise being to avoid impregnation, we must first consider the agents that cause impregnation to occur. These are: a woman who is fertile and a man who can fill her with his seed. But since no woman is fertile during the period of her monthly bleed, one good way of avoiding impregnation is to refrain from copulation at all other times. Of course this approach calls for a degree of self-restraint far greater than most men are wont to display; for who in his right mind would forgo the pleasures of a woman's body simply because she wasn't letting blood? Only a foolish few. But the rest of us need not despair, because even if a woman is fertile at the time of coition, she cannot conceive unless a man fills her with his seed, and he cannot fill her with his seed if his prod is impermeably sheathed."

"Impermeably sheathed with what?" I hastened to inquire.

"With the lining of a sheep's intestine, believe it or not."

"With *what?*"

"With the lining of a sheep's intestine, I say. The Persians have been sheathing their prods with sheep gut ever since the time of Alexander. It was Alexander's great general Antigonus, in fact, who introduced the practice into Greece, where it still enjoys considerable popularity."

"But what with all the, uh, undulations attendant on the sex act," the ever-pragmatic Marcus broke in, "how does one keep the sheath from coming off?"

"A very penetrating question," Hieronymous punned unconscionably. "But the answer is ready to hand. One simply stretches the open end of the sheath as wide as possible and makes a hem in it. Through this hem one then threads a length of string. One then applies the sheath to one's person (taking care to enclose the testicles), pulls the ends of the string taut, and ties, out of deference to Alexander, a not-quite-Gordian knot. With one's scrotum serving as an anchor of sorts, one is then prepared to 'undulate' to one's heart's content without the slightest fear of insemination."

"Remarkable!" I sighed, wishing that such information, and some such device, had been available to me when I could have made some use of it. But then another thought occurred to me, and I said to Hieronymous, "Doesn't the sheath interfere somewhat with one's pleasure?"

"In answer to that I can only reply 'Compared to what?' Does it interfere more with one's pleasure, for example, than the fear of impregnating a woman one doesn't care for (and probably has no business sleeping with)? Does it interfere more with one's pleasure than fathering a child one doesn't want but may have to acknowledge? On the assumption, however, that your question pertains to pleasure in its narrowest physical sense alone, then the answer is 'Yes,' the sheath does interfere with it somewhat, but not nearly so much as abstinence or fear."

"Where can one obtain these sheaths?" Marcus inquired. "I myself seldom carry sheep entrails around with me as I go about my daily business. In fact, I didn't until this moment imagine that they could be used for any other purpose than divination."

Hieronymous laughed. "You will find, my fine young nobleman, that we of the eastern provinces, though far inferior to you Romans in the arts of war and statecraft, are far ahead of you in the domain of sensuality and pleasure. As with all conquering races, your attention is focused on the blunt realities of sword and statute, while we, who can only envy you your power (having long since relinquished our own), must content ourselves with the subtle abstractions called passion, beauty, and art."

"Aside from the matter of passion," Marcus commented, "I'd say you got the better of the bargain."

"Oh?" said Hieronymous. "And what is it about passion that you object to?"

"The fact that it is Reason deformed."

"That sounds more like an article of Stoic faith to me than it does a reasoned argument; and if any human trait qualifies as Reason deformed, I would say it is faith most decidedly, and passion most certainly not."

"How do *you* conceive of passion then?"

Hieronymous pondered a moment. "Well, my young friend, I conceive of Passion *and* Reason as the two defining aspects of Mankind's consciousness; and I believe that as this consciousness develops over the centuries men will find that the distinction between its two components becomes steadily narrower. I believe further that when our consciousness has developed to the point where Reason becomes perfect understanding and Passion becomes pure sensation, the distinction will entirely disappear. Passion and Reason will become as one, in other words, and we men shall become as gods."

"Excuse me," said Marcus, "but are you seriously suggesting that mankind as a whole is capable of achieving *divinity?*"

"Not mankind as we know it today, most certainly, but mankind as it may eventually become."

"Well, I can't really dispute the point with you, but it all sounds pretty fantastical to me."

"Fantastical? Not at all. And if you'll be good enough to direct your gaze to the heavens, I will demonstrate its impeccable plausibility."

"The heavens?" Marcus said. "You mean the sky?"

"I mean the sky," Hieronymous responded. "Just look at it for a moment—there, on the northern horizon, where Cassiopeia and Cepheus are pleading with Perseus to defend their daughter, Andromeda, from Poseidon's sea monster. Do you see the constellations I'm referring to?"

"Yes," said Marcus, "I see them."

"Good!" said Hieronymous. "So you can also see the Milky Way, in which they are located."

"Yes, I can."

"Excellent. Now Democritus tells us that the Milky Way consists of stars very much like our own sun, and thanks to Eratosthenes and Aristarchus we know that our sun is at least three million miles away from us. Aristarchus tells us, furthermore, that the sun's diameter is roughly 60,000 miles, and we know from observation that it subtends an arc of roughly one degree in the sky. If a body 60,000 miles in diameter and 3 million miles away subtends one full degree of arc, how far away must a body of the same size be in order to be indistinguishable from similar bodies all around it? I'll save you the trouble of working through the logic and mathematics of the problem and confine myself to saying that if we arbitrarily assign to the indistinguishable body a wildly inflated angular width of one one-thousandth of a degree, we will discover after performing the necessary calculations that said indistinguishable body is some 3,000 *million miles* distant from the earth.

"This inconceivable figure is based not on fancy but on Reason and empirical observation, and even though our estimates of relative size and distance are a long way from being precise, the magnitude of the universe as we perceive it still baffles the mind."

"That's all very interesting," said Marcus, "but what does it have to do with mankind achieving divinity?"

"That's a fair question," Hieronymous replied, "and if you'll bear with me a little longer I'll endeavor to answer it."

"I'll bear with you," Marcus responded.

"According to my people," said Hieronymous, "the world began about 4,000 years ago, and well over 3,500 of those years passed before the Greeks made their discoveries about the scale of the universe we inhabit. I expect it will take mankind at least that many years again to discover what the stars are made of and why they shine with such radiance. Perhaps another 3,000 years will suffice to solve the mystery of how the universe began, and 10,000 years after that we may be able to make some educated guesses about the purpose for which it was created. . . ."

"You believe, then, that there was a creator?" Marcus asked.

"I believe that the universe is a mystery, and that mankind must progress in the direction of divinity for countless millennia before the human mind becomes capable of comprehending it. Let me refer you to the work of Democritus again in order to illustrate my point. Democritus tells us that all matter is composed of individual indivisible 'atoms,' inconceivably minute particles of fundamental substance that combine in arcane ways to form everything that exists. Everything! From the adamantine steel of a soldier's sword to the soft skin of a woman's breast. How is that possible? And what are these indivisible bits of matter composed of themselves? I put it to you that not even Aristotle could make sense of such questions. And I put it to you further that whenever we look around us and try to divine the fundamental structure of the world or cast our eyes skyward for the purpose of defining it, we encounter realities that are so radically at variance with our commonsensical preconceptions that we must either throw up our hands and ascribe the whole of existence to some deified image of ourselves or else bow our heads and acknowledge that we are as children in our understanding and that eons must pass before our minds are mature enough to grasp the truth."

"All of this sounds perfectly compatible with the tenets of Stoicism," said Marcus. "What you're saying, if I understand you correctly, is that mankind's progress toward divinity will proceed hand in hand with the development of our ability to reason. So I still don't see how passion can possibly play a constructive role in the process."

"Ah, but you forget," said Hieronymous, "that man's desire to understand is the greatest passion of all. Unique among all living creatures, he contemplates the world around him and the inevitable end of his sojourn in it and asks himself: *Why?* All his religions and superstitions are simply more or less misguided attempts to answer this one burning question. We know we must die and so we lust to understand. And it is this unique quality that leads me to believe that our ultimate destiny may be godhead. For if it is true that we have some spark of the divine inside us, that spark resides, I believe, in our passion to comprehend our place in the universe. Indeed, my reason goes so far as to suggest to me that this singular passion may well be the seed implanted in us by the mystery we call 'God' so that we will strive unceasingly in the direction of his divinity."

"What a shame that none of us will be around to experience it when our descendants finally arrive," Agricus remarked in a voice full of scorn.

"That *is* a pity, I agree. But there are consolations available. For the mystery we call 'God,' having condemned us, in his wisdom, to live out our lives in a ceaseless struggle to reconcile the conflicts between Passion and Reason, provided us, also, with a divine means of reconciling them when all mortal means prove unavailing."

"I think I can guess what that means is," said Marcus.

"I'd be very surprised if you couldn't," Hieronymous replied.

"Well, *I* haven't the slightest idea," said Agricus testily.

Whereupon Marcus and Hieronymous enlightened him with a hearty gust of laughter.

[SEPTEMBER 14TH]

I am beginning to feel extremely anxious about Camilla. Her diarrhea continues severe and she appears to be running a fever. Portia and I, fortunately, seem to be over the worst of our indisposition, and Nestor and Decius have been spared its discomforts entirely. Camilla, however, is still unable to digest any food. Whatever she eats, she voids within half an hour, and that together with her unremitting cramps has had the effect of draining all the color from her face. Poor little mite; she says she feels chilled, and despite the fact that Portia has wrapped her in a blanket and is holding her close against her body, she shivers almost incessantly. It hasn't helped matters that the weather's turned cold and wet, but Nestor assures me that if we just keep feeding her a little lightly salted bread every couple of hours she'll have her health back by tomorrow or the day after. I don't know why he's so confident of her recovery, but I'm only too glad to take his word for it. I think I might go mad if anything were to happen to her.

And I dread to think what dire straits we'd all be in if Decius weren't hale and hearty. He spent half the night under the wagon repairing the brake release, and today we had no problems with it at all. It's a good thing, too, because the terrain in this particular region of Gaul is rather hilly, and I had to make use of the brake on at least three separate occasions, when we might otherwise have come down a steep grade much too fast.

As for our new gelding, I am for the most part quite satisfied. He's strong and gets on well with the gray. His only shortcoming is a certain tendency toward skittishness when we encounter wagons coming fast in the opposite direction. Perhaps he'll calm down, though, as he grows more accustomed to his new circumstances.

Here we are then, camped by the river Duranius, with the city of Vesunna some thirty miles down the road. We've covered almost two hundred miles since we left Narbo six days ago, and if we continue on at this rate we should reach Coriallum, on the Channel, well before the end of this month. Perhaps Nestor will enlighten us as to our ultimate destination when we get there. For the moment, though, I'm far more interested in what he has to say about the state of my little girl's health.

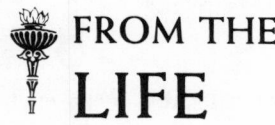
It felt strange to be traveling at night, with Hieronymous expanding jauntily on his philosophy of life and Agricus writhing angrily beneath the weight of his every pronouncement. Neither Marcus nor I could understand why our companion was taking such violent exception to what Hieronymous had to say. The discussion was little more than an exercise in teleology, after all, and though Hieronymous's premises struck me as rather intriguing in some respects, they were still nothing more than ideas, which—from Agricus's point of view, at any rate—were seldom of such practical significance as to warrant an emotional response. I suppose, looking back, that one thing Agricus objected to was Hieronymous's implicit assumption that life was something more than the interval between birth and death. For though he'd never bothered to articulate his own opinions on the subject, I always took it for granted that he saw life as an exercise in futility and conducted himself accordingly. Thus the notion that there might be some purpose to it (a purpose that could be realized through laughter, of all things) must have seemed to him unendurably offensive. He certainly acted as though it did at any rate, just as Hieronymous seemed to delight in playing on his prickly indignation.

I myself was much less interested in the metaphysical implications of Hieronymous's outlook than I was in the moral ones, and so I asked him if morality had a place in his overall scheme.

"Since God is a mystery," he replied, "God's morals are a mystery as well."

"You don't believe in morality then?"

"How could I not believe in it? It's a fact of life, like piles."

"I'm afraid I don't follow you."

"My dear boy, the world is positively awash in morals, just as it's awash in laws and religions and all the rest of our social artifacts. And it's a good thing that's so, given that most people are neither equipped nor inclined to think for themselves."

"And what do you have to offer to those of us who are so equipped and inclined?" Marcus interjected.

"What do I have to offer?" Hieronymous responded. "Why, nothing.

Nothing at all. You're on your own, just as I am. You have to grope and agonize and feel your way along."

"Employing what criteria of judgment?"

"Why, your knowledge, your wisdom, and your desires. Whatever else?"

"You take a ruthlessly pragmatic approach then?"

"As opposed to a patently mindless one, yes. Since I must live with the consequences of my decisions, and live with myself as well, I am not about to abdicate the responsibility for making those decisions or delegate it to social artifacts that were not formulated with my particular purposes in mind. I accept nothing on faith and I acknowledge no higher authorities. My passion and reason in tandem are the sole arbiters of my behavior. And any man who claims otherwise is either a fool, a hypocrite, or a slave."

Marcus and I exchanged bemused glances, having never before heard Hieronymous express himself with such fervor. His outburst seemed out of character somehow, just as Marcus's sudden and heated objection to his theft of a stallion had seemed out of character for him, and just as Agricus's more recent display of volatility had been a marked departure from his standard demeanor of disparaging indifference. I must admit that I found these anomalous eruptions somewhat unsettling. Quite apart from the fact that they clashed with all the comfortable conclusions I'd come to about who, and what, my three companions essentially were, they suggested also that a colloquy of sorts was in progress among them that I was not merely excluded from but incapable of apprehending. Of course I wasn't totally oblivious to the interplay of their contending credos; it was obvious that each in his own way was promoting his personal view of life. But my perception of the competing dogmas was clouded at best, and if I'd been called upon to characterize each one of them, I doubt I could have come up with anything more definitive than Duty, Autonomy, and Revenge.

We arrived in Silvium toward the fourth watch of the night and found, predictably enough, that the entire town was dark and shuttered. Since we had now put a good many miles between ourselves and the irate citizens of Venusia, Dracena allowed that prudence had been adequately served. Thus the only question confronting us was whether we stop where we were or continue on toward Tarentum. I was all for stopping; since our departure from Aquilonia I'd run three miles, ridden what seemed like a hundred, and sustained a mild concussion into the bargain. Enough was enough. Marcus pointed out, however, that if we did stop we'd either have to roust everyone in the Appia's twenty-ninth post station from their sleep—with who knew what adverse effects on their aptitude for hospitality—or sit around for a couple of hours until they awoke as a matter of course. None of us found the second alternative at all attractive, and given the fact that we'd already antagonized one municipality in the region, the first didn't much commend itself either. We opted for a course of action proposed by Hieronymous: that we ride on till daybreak, find a comfortable place to rest near the roadside, and resume our progress toward Tarentum come afternoon. For sustenance we still had most of the loaf of bread we'd purchased in Bantia, and for drink there were always the water pumps along the road. So we set off from Silvium tired but tolerably content, and for the next dozen or so miles watched the sky in the east before us evolve from the star-flecked blackness of night through the muted gray violet of dawn and the pale persimmon that heralds sunrise to the delicate lambent blue that mantles old Sol in his ascendance. The warmth spilling down from the firmament made me even sleepier, and when we finally came to a halt by a grove of cedar and cypress, I fairly dove off Incitatus's back onto the fragrant fir carpet in their shade.

The next thing I knew, old Sol was trending westward from the zenith.

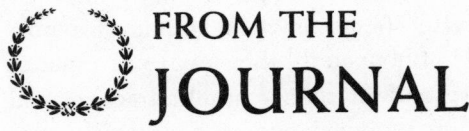 FROM THE
JOURNAL

82

[SEPTEMBER 15TH]

I had the most horrible dream last night. I dreamed that Marcus and I were strolling on the Caelian and by chance ended up at the Bend of the Claudian Aqueduct. No sooner had we arrived there than he turned to me and said, rather abruptly, that he had a great deal of work to do. Without another word, he strode away. As I, by contrast, had absolutely nothing to occupy me, I started to feel time weighing heavy on my hands. My first thought was to go back to Marcus's house and pass the hours until he was through working in pleasant conversation with Domitia Lucilla and Cornificia. But then, with a shock, I remembered that both women had been dead for well over twenty years. I tried to think of someone else in the world who meant something to me, but there was no one else besides Marcus. Portia, Decius, and Camilla didn't exist, for some reason. It wasn't that they were dead; they just didn't exist, and I felt utterly alone. There was no one in the world I cared about or who cared about me. There was no point in my continuing to live. The pain of my loneliness was so terrible, in fact, that I very much wanted to die. And it was as I began to consider how I might kill myself that I awoke.

For several moments I lay motionless, listening to the rain beat down on our wagon's canopy. Gradually I became aware of Nestor's snoring—a mundane sound I found immensely reassuring. With his every stertorous exhalation the dream's grip on me loosened. I turned slowly onto my side and breathed in the fresh and familiar smell of Portia's hair. Her back was toward me and in her arms, mending nicely, as Nestor had promised us she would, was our darling Camilla.

It had been no more than a dream.

I slept very little the rest of the night and for some reason have been feeling vaguely oppressed all day long. Perhaps it's the endlessly gray and wet weather that's nagging at me, or perhaps it's the phase of the moon. Who knows? There is nothing in the waking world to account for my sour disposition. The wagon is serving us well, the new horse is quite satisfactory, and we are making good progress toward our unknown destination. We passed through Vesunna today and should get as far as Iculisma tomorrow. In the context of our generally equivocal circumstances, all is well.

It's common knowledge, though, that dreams sometimes turn out to be foretastes of things to come.

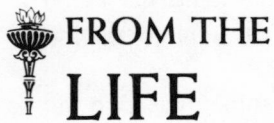 FROM THE
LIFE

83

Although the sun was well west of the meridian by the time we awoke from our nap, we covered the thirty miles remaining between us and Tarentum at pretty much our customary pace. The town was an important seaport and would not be closing down at sunset like some isolated village. That was how we reasoned, at any rate, little realizing that, so far from closing down, the place would in many respects—most of them unsavory—be coming to life.

In the event, dusk was fast approaching when we gained the west bank of the river Galaesus and got our first view of the city, a mile or so to the east. And with that one glimpse it became clear to me why Tarentum had stood with Athens and Syracuse at the summit of the pre-Roman world. The city occupied the entire tip of a westward-pointing promontory, with an immense natural anchorage on one side, sheltered from the sea by a string of islands and breakwaters, and an equally large deepwater lagoon on the other, where three or four good-size ships and some dozen smaller ones were berthed. Several hundred feet of water separated the tip of the promontory from the mainland opposite, and above this channel a bridge of high arches carried the Appia across.

Tarentum thus combined all the best features of a fortress and a harbor, and even though she had long since yielded her standing as chief port of southern Italy to Brundisium, she had nevertheless retained at least the semblance of her former glory.

Darkness had fallen by the time we reached the bridge, and once across it we proceeded with all deliberate speed to seek out the nearest tavern. We hadn't had a proper meal since our departure from Aquilonia, after all, and even Marcus confessed to an acute sense of hunger. The first establishment we came upon was called the Smiling Satyr, a name that proved peculiarly apropos. The five of us were so ravenous that it wasn't until we were seated and had placed our order that we began to take note of the tavern's other patrons, almost all of whom were already taking note of us. What struck me first was the presence of a dozen or more boys my age or younger who were dressed in loose-fitting chitons of saffron, crimson, or puce. It took me a little longer to notice that just

about everyone else in the place looked like either a pederast or a gladiator. Only those who looked like pederasts were in fact what they
appeared, though, those who looked like gladiators were really pederasts
in disguise.

Of course Agricus in such a setting quickly attracted more than his
aliquot share of attention, and Marcus, too, was subjected to no mere
modicum of scrutiny. Even I came in for a number of salivary leers, and
a question arose in my mind, at least, as to the wisdom of dining in the
company of people who seemed hungry for our very own flesh. It didn't
much help matters that, prompted by the widely reputed excellence of
Tarentine shellfish, we'd elected to begin our meal with oysters. For these
bivalves enjoy wide though, in my experience, unsubstantiated acclaim
as aphrodisiacs, and when a large bowl of them was placed in the center
of our table, the assembled pedophiles took that as a sign of our complaisant availability. Having hit on such a gratifying interpretation, they
proceeded in quick order to cast Hieronymous as our pander and Dracena
as our keeper. And in a matter of moments, the most repugnant of the
gladiatorial apparitions was discussing with our jolly Judean his ithyphallic
interest in *me*.

Never one to neglect the comedic potential of a given situation, Hieronymous responded to the hulking brute's expressions of interest in a
most accommodating manner. "I can tell," he said, pointing across the
table to where I sat, "from your choice of young Adonis over there that
you are a man of the most discriminating taste. I must in all honesty
inform you, however, that the boy has been having some trouble with
his bowels the last few days, so your enjoyment of him may entail a
certain element of risk."

"If he voids while I'm with him," the behemoth growled, "I'll wring his
pretty little neck."

"Just so, just so," replied Hieronymous. "It was with precisely that
possibility in mind that I took care to acquaint you with his condition.
He is rather a valuable commodity, after all."

"How valuable?" the ruffian inquired.

"Well, he's available by the night or by the hour. What would be your
preference?"

"My preference would be to purchase him outright. And I'll pay you
6,000 sesterces to seal the bargain."

This pronouncement brought all conversation in the tavern to a halt.
Hieronymous, the brute, and I were now the center of attention, and
one of us at least was beginning to feel more than a little anxious. That
same one was also at something of a loss as to why, with Marcus and

Agricus present in the room, the brawny sodomite had conceived such an obsessive passion for *him*. There's no accounting for tastes and all that, but this fellow's cravings seemed positively perverse. And a real question had arisen with respect to Hieronymous's ability to counteract or redirect them.

"Six thousand!" he said in a tone of rueful amusement. "He cost me twenty, and he wasn't even broken in."

This figure of 20,000 sesterces strained the credulity of everyone present, not least of all the brawny sodomite. But however implausible the figure was, the fact that Hieronymous had quoted it effectively communicated an unwillingness to sell.

Realizing there was nothing he could about it, the fellow heaved a sigh and said, "Oh, very well then. What will he cost me for the night?"

"Please excuse me," Hieronymous replied, "but he does have this intestinal condition, and since you said you'd wring his neck if it got the better of him while in your company, I risk losing all I've invested in him if I deliver him into your hands."

An insidious gap-toothed smile spread over my would-be ravisher's face. " 'Wring his neck' was only a figure of speech," he said. "Now be a good fellow and tell me his going rate for the evening. I promise to restore him to you none the worse for wear. . . . A little stretched in places, perhaps, but nonetheless none the worse."

This crude jest brought forth a roar of boisterous laughter from all those gathered around our table, and to me it began to look like Hieronymous was running out of room for maneuver. Well after the fact, he freely admitted that that indeed had been the case, and that he'd actually begun to feel for his dagger beneath his robes. But both he and I were spared the consequences attendant on spurning the brawny sodomite's patronage by the sudden and inexplicable intervention of my lifelong foe.

"*You!* Lout!" he shouted at my admirer, having risen from his seat. "How dare you insult me in this fashion."

This outburst took the lout he was addressing—and indeed all the rest of us—completely by surprise, and for several moments the fellow just stood there stupefied and stared at him. "How have I insulted *you?*" he inquired finally in a tone at once truculent and defensive.

"By lavishing so much attention on my rival here, who is my inferior in all respects, especially those pertaining to love. Purchase *me* for the evening and I will punish you for your cloddishness with caresses that will leave you whimpering with delight."

The target of this seductive diatribe listened carefully to what Agricus had to say, and then, in an almost comically brisk and businesslike manner, turned to Hieronymous and asked, "What's the going rate for *him?*"

"For *him?*" Hieronymous responded, momentarily somewhat rattled. "Why, for him I always charge one hundred."

"One hundred sesterces?"

"Uh, no. One hundred denarii."

The mention of such a sum in such a connection immediately elicited a chorus of gasps and murmurs from the onlookers, but because Agricus's prospective customer had professed himself ready to lay out 6,000 sesterces to purchase me, there couldn't be much question about his readiness to lay out four hundred to sleep with him. It became fairly clear that what we were probably dealing with was not a gladiator—who would rarely have six hundred sesterces to dispose of, let alone 6,000—but a rich voluptuary who engaged in occasional slumming. All the gladiatorial posturing and regalia most likely concealed a timid, henpecked paterfamilias with large estates outside Tarentum and a penchant for pretty boys. Agricus, with all his experience, had almost certainly seen through the masquerade before the rest of us, and his forceful intervention began to make perfect sense. This fearsome rowdy was probably no more than an easy mark, an identity he speedily confirmed by agreeing without discussion to pay one hundred denarii for one night in Agricus's arms.

The bargain having been struck, Hieronymous seized the opportunity to get us all out of that tavern by saying to our gladiator, "I maintain a little love nest here in town where for only ten denarii extra you may enjoy your sweet-faced darling in perfect comfort and seclusion."

I had to give both him and Agricus credit for their genius at improvisation; but what I wondered about most as the six of us trooped out of the Smiling Satyr and down the street was whether the prospect of one hundred denarii would tempt Agricus to consummate the tryst he'd helped arrange.

No more than fifty paces away was another and, as it turned out, no less appropriately named tavern, the Sea Nymph. Hieronymous, who was still craftily improvising, stopped us a short distance from the entrance and said to Agricus's customer, "Please wait here a moment while I go make sure that all is in readiness." He walked into the Sea Nymph, leaving Dracena, Marcus, and me to stand around in acute embarrassment while Agricus's mark caressed him and cooed endearments. Every so often I would sneak a look at them, curious as to my enemy's reaction to being petted like a girl in front of Marcus. But so far as I could tell he was indifferent. His face was utterly impassive, his demeanor one of unalloyed repose. He was even holding his admirer's hand, and would actually nod from time to time to show that he was attending to the burly fellow's burblings.

Hieronymous at long last reappeared, and from his expression it was clear that he had matters well in hand. Thus, while Dracena went off to the Smiling Satyr's stables to retrieve our horses, the rest of us marched into the Sea Nymph and breathed in the smell of roasting lamb. The succulent aroma brought home to me that, aside from two or three oysters, we still hadn't attended to our hunger. As it happened, Agricus's masquerade gladiator was feeling a little peckish himself. And the result, unaccountably enough, was that he stood all five of us to dinner. As the meal wore on and the wine flowed, moreover, a succession of cracks began to appear in his gladiatorial façade. By the time a bowl of fruit was placed on our table, his head had come to rest on Agricus's shoulder, and on his face was fastened a blissful smile. If the idea had been a little less implausible, I would have sworn that he was in love. His air of swaggering bombast had given way almost entirely to a mood of ursine benevolence that could almost be counted as sweet. I tried to imagine what would prompt a man of his obvious means to tart himself up like a gladiator and throw his money around like it was sand. The disguise suggested that he was ashamed of his pedophilia, and the militaristic bluster indicated a certain lack of self-confidence. By the time the meal was over, I was beginning to feel distinctly solicitous toward the fellow, and even went so far as to hope that, come the morrow, the four hundred sesterces he was laying out for Agricus would seem to him money well spent—assuming, of course, that Agricus was actually going to go to bed with him, right under Marcus's nose, so to speak.

To all appearances, he actually was. For with dinner eaten he leaned over and whispered in his besotted client's ear some formula of words that made the fellow's eyes bulge, and shortly after that the two of them were on their way upstairs.

Marcus, Dracena, Hieronymous, and I watched them go, then sat for several moments in silence. Finally Marcus turned to Hieronymous and, in a voice that wasn't exactly brimming over with warmth, inquired, "What sort of percentage are you entitled to in this line of work?"

To this implicit rebuke Hieronymous, to his credit, did not respond with a laugh. On the contrary, he was profusely apologetic. "I behaved like a proper fool," he said. "I let the whole business get out of hand."

"What on earth did you have in mind?" Marcus asked.

"Not nearly enough, as you have no doubt already discerned. My general idea was to jolly everyone along for a while and eventually extricate us from the situation by demanding exorbitant fees. I thought it would be a fairly simple matter to overtax the resources of the lowlifes we were dealing with, but I failed to reckon with the possibility that I might run into an utter spendthrift."

"It wasn't the sort of possibility that one could readily foresee," I said, all the food and wine—not to mention what I thought of as Agricus's disgrace—having put me in a magnanimous frame of mind.

"That's very forbearant of you," Hieronymous responded. "I really didn't mean to put you in such an equivocal position, and I most earnestly beg your forgiveness."

"Let's consider the matter closed," I declared, and then, glorying in my supreme fatuity, added, "All's well that ends well, after all"—the assumption being that all had already ended.

It hadn't, of course, though it wasn't altogether imbecilic of me to assume otherwise. For even though there were several demonstrably "approachable" women hovering around our table, the four of us by that time were game for nothing more exotic than a good night's sleep. Declining, therefore, to avail ourselves of the Sea Nymph's nymphs, we made our way up to the lodgings Hieronymous had arranged.

And from somewhere down the corridor came the sound of a grown man whimpering with delight.

I don't know how long I slept before Agricus woke me, but I do know I was sleeping like the dead. When I first awoke, in fact, I didn't know where I was, nor could I imagine who was tugging on my arm and whispering urgently that I should "Come! Come and see!"

Semistuporous, I rose and followed him down the corridor through the inky dark. Just ahead of me, a door was pushed open, and the light of an oil lamp reached my eyes.

"Shhhh," Agricus cautioned me, his finger to his lips, as he pulled me inside the room and closed the door. His gladiator was sitting naked on the floor, his back against the bed, his chin resting on his chest, and his legs straight out and slightly spread. Agricus, I now noted, was naked, too, and the expression on his face was one of trancelike excitation.

"Go closer," he whispered, once more pulling on my arm. "Go closer so you can see."

There was an odor in the room I didn't like, and Agricus's strange excitement was beginning to make me feel uneasy. I took two cautious steps toward the figure on the floor.

"How come he's so sweaty?" I asked, noticing the sheen of a liquid on his belly.

By way of answering my question Agricus climbed onto the bed, gripped the tops of his gladiator's ears with thumb and forefinger, and slowly pulled his head back to reveal the hilt of the dagger that was lodged in his throat.

I sucked in a breath as a few more trickles of "sweat" ran down from the wound to the dead man's chest and belly. Agricus had driven the blade in just below the underside of the jaw; the point of the dagger now protruded an inch or two from the back of his victim's neck.

"What have you *done?*" I whispered in horror.

Still gripping the dead man's ears, Agricus smiled vacantly and replied, "I've avenged myself, Lucio; I've repaid my degradation with blood."

"But *why?*" I asked him. "He wasn't the one who degraded you."

"No, Lucio," Agricus responded, his smile becoming terrible to behold. "He was the one who set me free."

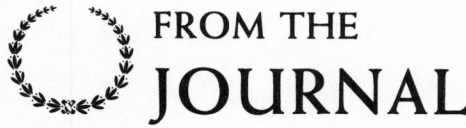
[SEPTEMBER 16TH]

I must try to remain calm.

I must keep reminding myself that the situation is not by any means irretrievable.

But how could I have allowed such a thing to happen?

In retrospect it all seems so . . . *foreseeable.*

But perhaps that's the way it is with most accidents: once they've occurred, the events leading up to them seem to have so clearly foreshadowed the calamitous results that one feels remiss for having failed to take effectual precautions.

And yet the precautions we did take seemed eminently prudent at the time. We were on a slight downgrade when the brake again locked, and before Decius went underneath the wagon to work it loose we carefully placed large stones in front of all four wheels. How could we have foreseen that the wagon would move backward up the hill? We couldn't really; it was just so improbable.

I knew, though, that the gelding acted skittish in the face of oncoming traffic. And it didn't require much prescience on my part to anticipate the possibility that a local farmer would drive a team of horses past us while Decius was under the wagon. It's common knowledge that skittish horses often rear up when frightened, and it's altogether obvious that if they're hitched to a wagon when they rear, the wagon will inevitably move backward. That Decius would work the brake loose just as the farmer and his horses went by us up the hill was unlucky but not unforeseeable. So why didn't I foresee it?

The wheel passed over his right leg just above the ankle. Nestor says the bones are shattered. The way he says it makes my stomach turn.

I examined Decius's leg myself. There's some discoloration, to be sure, but no bleeding. The wheel rim didn't even break the skin. I feel certain that any broken bones can be set. Decius says the pain is nothing terrible. If the fracture were really serious, he'd be in agony.

So calm down, Lucius Aurelius Verus Celer. Just calm down. Take a few deep breaths. We'll have an informed opinion before too much longer.

The surgeon we've been directed to here in Iculisma is away somewhere attending to a distempered bull, but his slave says he'll be back within the hour. . . .

Then we will know the worst.

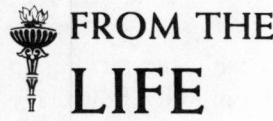
The first thought that occurred to me after I got over the shock of discovering that Agricus had committed murder was that I had to acquaint Marcus with what had happened and at the same time make sure that no one else found out. That thought in turn raised the question of whether Agricus could be relied on to stay silent and stay put if I left him unattended. He had just committed a wildly irrational crime, after all. Did I dare let him out of my sight?

I looked at him: he still had his victim by the ears and was still smiling his terrible smile. Perhaps a direct question would elicit a response that reflected his state of mind. So I asked him straightforwardly, "What do you intend to do now?"

"You know," he replied in a carefree voice, "I haven't given it too much thought."

"Well, what do you think you might like to do?"

He pondered, then answered, "I don't know, really. I feel so cheery, I'd almost like to sing and dance."

"Aren't you the least bit tired?" I asked, hoping I didn't sound like I was trying to prompt him.

"I am a bit tired, now you mention it," he responded. "Not as tired as old Dionysus here, but tired enough to make the idea of a little nap attractive."

"His name was Dionysus?"

"Dionysus was just a pet name I gave him. I never quite got around to finding out his real one."

That response seemed marginally rational, at least, so I decided that I could risk leaving him alone.

"Well, if you're going to take a nap," I said, "I guess I'll go back to bed myself."

"You do that," was Agricus's rejoinder, his facial expression and tone of voice reverting all at once to their usual pitch of scornful condescension. "But if you should happen to run into Marcus on your way, be sure to tell him for me that I'm not anywhere near as crazy as you would have him believe."

Though I was stung to discover that he'd been feigning distraction and playing me along the whole time, I was relieved to see that he was once again his old cold and calculating self.

"With your permission," I said, going over to the table and picking up the flickering lamp, "I'll go get Marcus now and let him judge how crazy you are at first hand."

"Splendid!" said Agricus. "Dionysus and I will await your reappearance with bated breath. Won't we, old fellow?"

And as he caused his victim's head to move up and down in a travesty of an affirmative nod, I turned my back on him and walked out of the room.

When I returned with Marcus a few moments later the scene was essentially unchanged. Agricus was still on the bed and still had hold of the dead man's ears. "You should have let me dispose of the King of the Grove, Marco," he said, smiling exultantly. "I would have gotten this sort of thing out of my system."

Marcus took in the scene and disgustedly shook his head. "Did you really have to take some poor fool's life to make your point?" he asked.

Still smiling, Agricus responded, "You must admit I've made it well."

"And what do you suppose you've proved?"

"I've proved that I'm prepared to go to any lengths to accomplish a given objective, the objective in this case being to establish what might be called my usefulness beyond the peradventure of a doubt."

"I don't much like your methods," Marcus said.

"Of course you don't. But can you deny that I get results?"

To this Marcus made no reply; he simply shook his head again and then asked me to go fetch Hieronymous and Dracena. Of course I complied with his request, but I was even more loathe to leave him alone with Agricus than I'd been to leave Agricus by himself. The words they'd just exchanged had clearly had reference to prior conversations between them that I had not been privy to. I could guess pretty readily, however, the ultimate purpose that Agricus's demonstration of "usefulness" had been intended to serve. But was it really possible that Marcus contemplated some sort of long-term relationship with him? Did he really see a place for him and for his ruthless proficiency in obtaining "results" in the life of duty and selflessness he was preparing for? Obviously he did. And that raised the far more problematical question of what possible role he could envision for me.

By the time I returned with Hieronymous and Dracena, Agricus had relinquished his hold on the dead man's ears, but he remained, to all appearances, intensely elated. On seeing what he had done, both men reacted with pronounced consternation and annoyance, but also with a degree of resignation, as if they'd been half expecting him to do something of the sort sooner or later.

"I know this is beginning to sound a little monotonous," Hieronymous said to Marcus, "but I think we ought to be leaving town as soon as possible."

Marcus frowned deeply. It was clear that, quite apart from his vexation with regard to the fact of murder, his sense of propriety was grievously offended by the prospect of having to resort once again to the ignominious expedient of flight. This was the third time that Agricus's actions had landed us in a dangerously awkward situation, and if the observation had been at all relevant to the question of how we were going to extricate ourselves, I would have pointed out that the results he was so expert at obtaining were oftentimes results we deplored.

But the immediate question was how we could best accomplish our escape from Tarentum. Heading off down the Appia toward Brundisium was the most obvious possibility, but not necessarily the most attractive one. To start with, we'd made no secret of the fact that Brundisium was our destination, and that meant that anyone of a mind to pursue us could readily guess the direction in which we'd fled. Compounding this problem was the additional fact that Brundisium was only forty-five miles distant; and since there were no guarantees that we'd find a ship ready to sail for Greece the moment we got there, our putative pursuers might very well arrive at dockside before we were safely at sea. Set against those difficulties, though, was the possibility that we might not have any other alternative. Unless we were prepared to pass up our golden opportunity to visit Greece, we pretty much *had* to go to Brundisium soon or later, and the longer we waited the more widely disseminated would be both the news of Agricus's crime and the presumption that we were its perpetrators. Agricus hadn't killed just anyone, after all; he'd killed a man who was rich. And as Tarentum's ranking magistrates would inevitably be men of means themselves, they were more than likely to regard his action as something of a personal affront.

Thus, going in *any* direction by land afforded us but little hope of making good our escape. There was a small chance, however, that we might be able to flee from Tarentum by sea. And with that possibility in mind we stole out of the Sea Nymph, collected our horses, and made our way down to the port.

There on the waterfront Fortune smiled on us, although it looked at first like she had turned her back. The small boats in the inner harbor were clearly too small to accommodate all of us, and all but two of the larger ones—we discovered on making inquiry—were bound westward for Africa, Mauretania, or southern Hispania. Of the two that were heading in an easterly direction, one had Alexandria as its destination and the other Hieronymous's native city of Caesarea, in Palaestinae. Either would have suited our purposes very nicely, but neither was due to sail that morning. In fact, the only large ship that was preparing to weigh anchor at sunrise was bound for Mauretania, and it began to look like we would soon have to make the hard choice between pressing on toward Greece in the face of great danger on the one hand and taking ship for the opposite end of the Empire on the other.

But thanks to the watchman on the ship set to sail for Mauretania, we were spared the necessity of making such a choice. Seeing us returning glumly from our canvass of the other vessels there, he advised us of the presence of an Imperial grain ship in the outer harbor. She had called at Tarentum to repair some storm damage she'd sustained while passing through the Straits of Messina, and was bound in ballast for Alexandria to take on a cargo of wheat. To the best of the watchman's knowledge, her repairs were substantially complete. Indeed, she had been rowed to the outer harbor a few hours before sunset, and from the way her sails were rigged he'd concluded that she'd be weighing anchor at dawn. All we had to do, he continued somewhat ruefully, was "persuade" her captain to break the rule forbidding anyone other than Imperial officials and their families to travel as passengers on grain ships. If we had enough money to do that, he said, the captain could easily put us ashore at some agreed-upon point as the ship made its way down the coast of western Greece.

Marcus thanked the fellow for his assistance, and the five of us then proceeded with all speed to the outer harbor. There we had no trouble locating the grain ship he'd referred to, since it was festooned with blazing torches and swarming with activity. It was also enormous—so huge that the dozens of crewmen scurrying over its decks and rigging looked much like dwarfs. I would have said, at a guess, that the ship was every bit as large as the barges we'd seen resting on the bottom of Diana's lake. But even more impressive than its size was its solidity. This was no mere ceremonial vessel designed to float empty across the placid surface of a glorified fish pond; this was a working freighter intended to transport perhaps a thousand tons of Egyptian grain across 1,500 miles of open sea to the mouth of the Tiber and the mouths of the Roman populace. Probably every crumb of bread I'd ever eaten at the Hobnail had been made from grain brought to Italy in a vessel like this. And there was a distinct possibility that at least some of the bread I'd gobbled down had started its journey to my belly in the bowels of this very ship!

She was called the *Isis* and carried brightly colored carvings of the goddess on her bows. At her stern a massive gilded goose head and neck curved upward from the waterline to a height of some fifteen feet above the poop deck, in the middle of which—unoccupied for the moment— was the helmsman's station, with its twin tillers joined at right angles to the thirty-foot-long steering oars. Forward of the poop was the gray stucco ship's cabin, with its red tile roof, brick chimney, and hemispherical blue-shuttered windows. Forward of that was the yawning cavity that constituted the hold, empty except for a pile of extra spars, several stacks of firewood, fifty or sixty sealed amphorae, two water tanks, a chicken coop, three canvas lean-tos, and half a dozen goats.

Locating the captain in the midst of all the frenetic activity was a labor that occupied Agricus, Marcus, and me for the best part of a quarter hour, but we finally tracked him down in the pungently malodorous bilge, where he was inspecting a newly retimbered section of the hull. His name was Archimedes, a small, wizened, sharp-eyed man who obviously had a lot on his mind.

"We're almost a month behind schedule," he explained as the three of us tried as best we could not to breathe through our noses, "so say what you have to say in as few words as possible."

"I and my four companions would like to take passage on your ship," Marcus responded tersely, taking the captain at his word; "and we're prepared to pay."

"That's very liberal of you," said the captain, tapping the freshly caulked planking with a mallet, "but there's an Imperial rescript that forbids me to carry passengers."

"I thought in this case that we might persuade you to make an exception."

The captain stopped his tapping and gave an order in rapid-fire Greek to the bosun, who'd been holding a lamp for him to see by. Then to Marcus he said, "You thought you might persuade me . . . how? With an offer of money perhaps?"

"Only if my eloquence failed to convince you," Marcus replied with a straight face.

The captain looked at him, then smiled dryly. "Do you happen to know why that Imperial rescript was issued?" he asked.

Marcus confessed that he did not.

"Well, I'll tell you," the captain said. "It was issued because so many would-be passengers like you gave bribes to so many *magistri navium* that a significant percentage of the grain ships like this one were built to carry got dumped into Alexandria's harbor to make room for passengers and their effects."

"Ah, I see," said Marcus.

"I'm glad to hear it," said the captain. "Now do you have any idea what would happen to me if the Prefect of Corn Supply learned that I'd disobeyed the commandment of the rescript?"

"Something bad, I imagine."

"Something very bad. Something so unspeakably bad that I'd have to be an even greater fool than I am to take the risk."

"But," countered Marcus, "since you're on your way to Alexandria half-empty, the terms of the rescript can't possibly apply."

"Correction, my brainy young friend—the terms of the rescript can't *logically* apply. But, alas for you and me, it makes no distinction whatever between voyages to and voyages from the province of Egypt."

"That makes no sense," Marcus objected.

"In that respect," said the captain, "the rescript bears a strong resemblance to a number of other Imperial decrees. . . . I'm sorry, but there's nothing to be done."

Marcus pondered a moment. "What if I were to tell you that I was traveling under a license of the *cursus publicus*?" he said finally.

"Then I'd wonder why you didn't say so in the first place."

"That's understandable. But if I were to show you the diploma granting me the privileges of the *cursus*, what then?"

The captain scrutinized him. "If you have such a diploma, you'd be welcome aboard the *Isis*."

"I do have one," said Marcus. "Do you want to see it right now to confirm the fact?"

"That won't be necessary," the captain replied with a sly smile. "Because if it turns out you're lying to me, you and your friends will all be leaving the ship as quick as a wink, even if we happen to be well out to sea."

"Fair enough," said Marcus. "May I take it, then, that we have your permission to stay aboard?"

"You may," said the captain, "until such time as you fail to produce that diploma."

"I'll produce it immediately upon demand," Marcus responded. "I don't much fancy the prospect of swimming all the way to Greece."

"Well you'd better resign yourself to swimming at least part of the way, young fellow. Because this ship is bound for Alexandria, and we'll be proceeding there as fast as we can without calling at any ports along the way."

"I'm sure we'll be able to work out the details of our passage to our mutual satisfaction," Marcus said diplomatically. "But for now, I imagine, I had better attend to the details of getting the rest of my party aboard."

"You never told us you were licensed to use the *cursus publicus*," Agricus said in an angry tone as he, Marcus, and I made our way up into the blessed night air from the bilge.

"Perhaps I'm not," replied Marcus smiling smugly.

"You'd better be," said Agricus. "That fellow will throw us overboard if you've been bluffing."

"You're not afraid, are you?" Marcus inquired with a malicious grin.

And Agricus merely glared at him by way of reply.

[SEPTEMBER 17TH]

We are in the midst of a waking nightmare.

I know now why Nestor had that look on his face when he told me that the bones in Decius's leg were shattered.

But when I first heard the physician's diagnosis I refused to accept it.

I still don't have full confidence in the man, even though he claims that he served his apprenticeship under the renowned surgeon Aretaeus.

We're told that he's the only truly qualified physician in a thirty-mile radius. Perhaps that's why he looks so haggard and so much older than his thirty-seven years.

I have yet to see him smile.

Not that there's anything for him to smile about.

His face remained blank while he examined Decius's leg, even though the examination was in some ways as harrowing as anything that followed. Every time he touched Decius's shin or manipulated his foot the boy cried out in agony, and by the time the examination was concluded the poor lad was thoroughly soaked in perspiration, while his mother, who'd been cradling his head and murmuring words of encouragement throughout the entire ordeal, was so white that I feared she might faint—as I myself was on the verge of doing. Nestor, fortunately, was knowledgeable enough about these matters to have removed Camilla from the scene before the examination began. He took her with him to a local wainwright's shop to have our wagon's defective brake replaced. Too late, of course. Had we not been in such a hurry to get wherever it is we're going, we would have stopped and had the work done as soon as the brake proved faulty. It would have cost us at least half a day's delay, to be sure; but the calamity that has now overtaken us will cost us a great deal more.

I still can't quite grasp the reality of everything that happened once the surgeon completed his examination. He motioned me aside and said, "I want you to get the boy into a standing position and then help him hobble over there, to the stable."

I looked across the courtyard in the direction he'd indicated and nodded agreement.

"As soon as we get him inside, I want you to keep him standing and as steady as possible."

Uncomprehendingly I nodded again.

"I'm going to knock him out with a sharp blow to the jaw," he continued, and all at once the horror of what was about to happen hit home.

"You're going to knock him out?" I repeated stupidly, not wanting to acknowledge what I already knew to be true.

"I'm going to try," the surgeon answered me. "Now I've got to go wash down the table in there and have my slave lay out my tools and rig up some torches for me to see by. I should be ready for your son by the time you get him across the yard."

I stood there staring at him and ever so slightly shaking my head, trying somehow to negate the meaning of the words he'd just spoken. *"Why?"* I asked finally. "Why must such a thing be done?"

The surgeon looked at me and, in a deadened voice, replied, "Bone splinters have severed at least one artery, probably two. If we don't act now, and quickly, your son will surely die of blood poisoning, if the hemorrhaging doesn't kill him first."

I nodded vacantly, and the surgeon gripped my shoulder for a moment to give me courage. He then walked off through the twilight to the stable.

I watched him go before walking back to the bench where Decius sat with his mother, his injured leg stretched out from his body. "He wants to try to set the bones," I lied, "but it's getting too dark out here, so he says we should come inside."

Decius nodded submissively, and with Portia's and my help stood up. I tried to think of another lie, a lie that would shield her from the shock of what was about to happen by inducing her to go somewhere else. But my invention failed me, and of course there was no way I could warn her without also alerting Decius. Thus, I did not prepare my wife for the terror of the truth.

The surgeon wasted no time; the instant we were inside the stable door his fist connected with Decius's jaw, and the boy crumpled. As Portia looked on stunned, I helped the surgeon lift him onto the still-wet table. The brands in the wall sconces flared garishly, and on a bench beside the table the surgeon's slave was setting out his tools.

"What are you going to do?" Portia asked in a horrified whisper as the slave tied Decius down with thick rope and the surgeon lifted a hacksaw off the bench.

"Nothing that either of you needs to witness," he replied, and gave me a look indicating that I should take her outside.

"What is he going to do?" she asked me as I put my arm around her shoulders and rapidly led her away.

"He is going to take off Decius's leg," I answered, with what I hoped was merciful bluntness.

She sagged against me and let out a convulsive sob. "In the name of the gods, *why?*" she asked, though I could tell she knew already that it was pointless to argue or object.

"To save Decius's life," I answered her simply.

And then both of us cringed as the courtyard resounded with his screams.

How fitfully my son sleeps! How far from sleep am I! We two, Decius and Lucius, stand the watch while Camilla slumbers in the old man's arms, oblivious of his snores. And Portia, my gentle Portia, has yielded at last to exhaustion. Her head rests on the pallet where Decius lies. She's kept vigil beside him all night, kneeling like a penitent so as to catch any word he might utter, attending to him with all the inexhaustible solicitude that a loving mother can lavish on a stricken son. If she were to open her eyes at this moment her gaze would fall on the pitch-and-blood-stained dressing that conceals his terrible wound.

I am unable to sleep. So I sit here beside my mutilated boy, blaming myself for the fate that has befallen him, but every so often taking refuge from self-reproach in the chronicle of my adolescent misadventures, among them the first of the many races I ran on my two strong youthful legs.

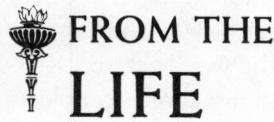
Given Captain Archimedes' expressed intention to sail from Tarentum to Alexandria with all speed and without calling at any ports along the way, it was a good thing for us that the most direct course from Italy to Egypt lies through the Ionian islands and right along the western coast of the Peloponnesus. This was to our advantage, the captain informed us, because small boats from almost every port regularly came out to greet passing freighters like the *Isis*. They would tie up to the ship's hull and ride along for as long as it took their pilots to sell all the local olives, wine, cheese, honey, fruit, and vegetables they'd carried out from their towns. For a consideration, the captain said, these boatmen would be only too happy to take us back to shore with them; and for a somewhat larger consideration they would even undertake to transport our horses.

This was good news from our point of view, since the question of how we were going to get from the *Isis* to Greek soil had been more or less ignored in our haste to escape Tarentum. The question of why Captain Archimedes was in such a rush to get to Alexandria had gone unanswered as well, but he enlightened us once the ship cleared the outer harbor.

The sun had not yet risen, since the *Isis* had cast off her mooring lines at the merest suggestion of first light. The crew had rowed her out into the harbor and hoisted her topsail and her sprit. When we were abeam of the main barrier island, the captain had ordered the mainsail up, and the rowers had shipped their oars. There was a slight but steady quartering breeze off the land, just enough to keep us going, and the sea for the moment was blessedly calm. Thus, with the heel of the Italian "boot" emerging from the morning mists to port and the city of Tarentum receding into those same mists astern, the captain could at last breathe a little easier and engage in conversation.

"There was a big fire in the shipyard at Syracuse," he explained. "That's why we ended up at Tarentum. Tarentum's the only port between Sicily and Brundisium where ships this large can be repaired. If I could have trusted the old girl's ribs to open water, I might have tried to make the crossing south to Cyrenaica and gotten the work done in the yard at Ptolemaïs. But since she'd had part of her hull stove in, in the storm we ran into off Rhegium, I didn't dare sail out of sight of land. I had to hug the coastline in case the temporary bulkheads we'd slapped together didn't hold. Now I'm way behind schedule. I've got to get to Alexandria, take on a load, get clearance to sail, fight the wind all the way back to Ostia, have my manifest audited once I get there, off-load my cargo, get clearance to sail, and then repeat the whole process again and get another full load of grain back to Ostia before the sailing season ends. . . . I estimate I have about one chance in ten of making it."

"What will happen if you don't?" Marcus asked.

"The Prefect of Corn Supply will be gravely displeased with me."

"And what then?"

"His displeasure could cost me every penny I possess."

"Do you possess many?" Agricus impudently inquired.

"Barely enough to make all the difficulties of the grain trade endurable."

Before long the sun rose, the wind picked up, and the *Isis* showed her speed, which, with an almost empty hold, was considerable. After chatting some more with the captain, Marcus and I made our way up to the bow and together leaned over the gunwale to watch the prow cleave its way through the waters of the Tarentine Gulf.

"How do you like sea travel so far?" Marcus asked me as the spritsail strained at its trim lines and salt spray glanced off the bows.

"I like it fine," I answered him, "but I don't know how I'd feel if we were out of sight of land."

"You'll know before long," Marcus responded with a laugh. And with no great zest I laughed along with him.

But it wasn't until late afternoon that the peninsula began to recede astern; and I must admit that, excited though I was by the thought of Greece just beyond the southeastern horizon, I cast many a forlorn glance back at Italy as it faded from view.

Soon the stars came out and the wind died down. After a savory dinner of pulse and roast kid, Captain Archimedes conducted us on a mariner's tour of the springtime sky.

"Now see there, just above the horizon and fine off the bow, that's the red-eyed Scorpion that was sent by Artemis to punish Orion for his presumption in lying with Eos, goddess of dawn; and off the starboard bow you can see Asclepius the healer holding his sacred silver snake; and then there's Herakles, kneeling before the crown of Ariadne. See how he has the red-eyed Dragon's head pinned under his right foot; and there, on either side of the Dragon's tail, are the greater and lesser Cretan Bears, who fed and sheltered Zeus when he was hiding from his father Kronos. . . ."

"Do you see the figures he's referring to?" Agricus asked me in an irritated whisper.

"You have to use your imagination," I told him.

"Ah . . . you don't see them either."

"Well, I sort of see them, in rough outline."

"I don't."

"You're both looking too hard," Marcus interjected.

"Or not pretending hard enough," was Agricus's retort, as the voluble Greek captain rambled on.

I didn't realize how tired I was, but I suppose my fatigue worked to my advantage, for no sooner had the ship's purser shown us to our sleeping quarters than I lay down and was dead to the world. I slept straight through till morning, moreover, thanks in good part to the captain's kindness in allotting us berths amidships, where the *Isis*'s pitching motion was least pronounced.

The sun had already risen by the time I awoke, and so had my four companions, whom I found eating bread and honey on the poop deck with the captain. Naturally I had to endure a fair amount of chaff about my slugabed behavior, but the day was too bright, the air too bracing, and my breakfast too tasty for me to mind.

As the sun climbed toward the meridian the wind at our backs blew with ever greater force, and the *Isis* fairly galloped over the waves, her prow rising and falling with a slow yet exuberant rhythm. Around midday we were joined in our headlong progress by a school of dolphins, who bounded and frolicked through the water alongside our bows, as if the *Isis* were some long-lost cousin who'd returned at last from the antipodes. Dozens of crewmen gathered at the gunwales to throw chunks of bread and small fish to the gamboling creatures and cheer them on as one after another leaped halfway out of the water to snare a morsel in midair.

"What do you suppose they're all acting so cheerful about?" Agricus asked me grumpily, casting a look of sour disapproval at the sleek gray acrobats of the deep.

And though I didn't share his feelings of reprehension, I could well understand his sense of rankling envy.

My second night aboard the *Isis* passed much like my first, but the manner of my waking differed greatly. For Marcus shook me from my slumbers in the first gray light of dawn and with his finger to his lips indicated that I should follow him up on deck. We emerged into an eerie silence compounded of still air and virtually flat-calm sea. Marcus beckoned me over to the gunwale, put one arm around my shoulders, and pointed with the other to the craggy silhouette of an island some five miles off the starboard bow. I looked at the island and tried to discern some distinguishing feature. But I couldn't, and so after a few moments I turned back to Marcus and gave a helpless shrug. His eyes wide with excitement, he pointed more forcefully at the island looming up ahead and then explained his intense animation with one single whispered word: *"Ithaca!"*

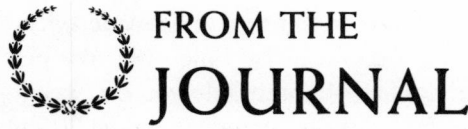
[SEPTEMBER 18TH]

When the physician examined Decius's wound this morning I couldn't tell if the frown on his face was one of concentration or concern. He said "the leg" was beginning to heal, but advised us very forcefully to remain here in Iculisma for at least one more day. When I asked him why, he gave me a look compounded of weariness and irritation and answered, "To make sure that the leg is healing cleanly." That response immediately raised a host of other questions in my mind, but given the expression of sorely tried patience the first one had elicited, I thought better of asking them at that time.

Nestor betrayed no surprise when I told him what the physician had said, but he pondered the information for quite a while before making any comment. When he did speak at last it was in a voice uncharacteristically weighted with uncertainty and misgiving. "I'm sorry to have to raise this subject at such a trying time," he said, "but I feel that I must now reveal to you our general destination."

I looked at him expectantly, and waited.

"It is Britannia," he said finally, "and I feel obliged to tell you this only because it lies across the Channel."

"I thought it might be Brittania," I said. "But why does the fact that it lies across the Channel compel you to confirm that?"

Nestor dropped his eyes and then, with obvious reluctance, lifted them again to meet mine. "For reasons you may be able to surmise, but which I cannot yet divulge, we must sail to Britannia from Coriallum."

"Yes?" I prompted him.

"It is a difficult crossing at the best of times, and a long one—over seventy-five miles."

"And . . . ?" I said, my voice beginning to harden a little with impatience.

"And . . . the later the date we arrive in Coriallum the more difficult it will be to find a boatman who'll be willing to attempt the voyage."

All at once, and with a sickening shock, I realized what had led Nestor to disclose our destination. "You're telling me that I may have to choose between Decius's welfare and my family's survival."

"Now there's no reason to suppose that the problem will develop into as Draconian a dilemma as that. I just felt that you should be made aware of the constraints that have been imposed on us by time. We *must* get across the Channel before the weather closes in, and only you can weigh the risks inherent in delaying here against those attendant on departing prematurely."

"But the physician seemed to indicate that we can leave tomorrow, if all goes well," I said in an almost supplicatory tone.

And though Nestor was compassionate enough to accord me a corroborative nod, the heaviness in his expression left me filled with disconsolate forebodings.

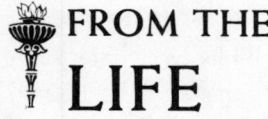 FROM THE
LIFE

89

Still with his arm around my shoulders, Marcus in a low voice began singing the Homeric dactyls:

> "The Phaiakians' ship rode the waves
> Straight and true, carrying a man
> Of god-like mind and wise counsel,
> Who in his time had much endured
> And many sorrows suffered. . . ."

"He sounds a lot like me," I interjected.
"Don't be irreverent," Marcus responded, and then resumed:

> "His is a rugged country,
> Too steep for horses, narrow
> But not unpleasing withall,
> For grain grows here, and the vine,
> And rain and dew moisten the fertile soil,
> So that goats and cattle grow fat,
> And there are springs and thick-grown forests
> Such that the fame of Ithaca
> Is spoken of even in Troy,
> A city far from the land of the Achaians. . . ."

He paused in his recital and looked at me. "We couldn't possibly pass up an opportunity like this, could we?"
"No," I replied, "I suppose we couldn't. Only . . ."
"Only?"
"Only, if it's too steep for horses, what are we going to do with ours?"
Marcus lifted his head imperiously. "As Telemachos said to Menelaos, King of Argos: 'I will not take horses to Ithaca, but will leave them here for your own delight. . . .' "
"You're going to leave them here, on the *ship*?"
"I'm prepared to trust them to Captain Archimedes, along with a suf-

ficient sum of money to have them carried ashore when boats from Kyllene come out to meet him."

"Assuming, for the moment, that your trust is well placed, what's going to happen to our horses once the Kyllenians get their hands on them?"

"I'm sure that the Kyllenians will not want to incur the displeasure of anyone licensed to travel on an Imperial grain ship under the aegis of the *cursus publicus.*"

"Oh, fine. And how are we supposed to get from Ithaca to Kyllene ourselves?"

"Why, by boat of course. It can't be much more than thirty miles from here to the Peloponnesian coast—half a day's sail at most. What do you say?"

I thought about it, then gave a shrug. "I'm willing," I said, "but it seems to me that you're taking an awful lot on faith."

"And what better place to do it?" Marcus replied, slapping me on the back and gesturing once more toward the fabled Odyssean isle.

But Marcus's plans for a full-scale invasion of Odysseus's homeland almost immediately suffered a setback. The only boat that came out from the island to meet the *Isis* was a small weather-beaten dinghy with a small weather-beaten Ithacan at the tiller. Heron was the boatman's name, a ruddy-faced old fellow with a squinty smile and three or four days' growth of snow-white stubble on his chin. He and Captain Archimedes embraced each other with great enthusiasm when he came aboard, and nattered on for what seemed like an awfully long time in a species of vernacular Greek for which my studies of Plato and Sophocles had in no way prepared me. On the floorboards of Heron's boat were a dozen or so earthen pots full of dark brown honey, the quality of which—I had occasion to discover for myself—was little short of ambrosial. Its quality was so exceptional, in fact, that the captain regularly purchased all that Heron had for sale and delivered it into the keeping of the ship's cook. He'd been obliged to resort to this practice, he told us, because competition among his sailors for the opportunity to purchase some of Heron's limited supply had generated a great deal more discord and ill feeling than was compatible with ship's discipline. Now, however, under the new dispensation, every man was accorded an equal share—although the cook's ration and his own, the captain admitted, were sometimes more equal than those of the crew.

Once their business was transacted, the captain and the boatman shared a bowl of wine together and then bid each other farewell. It was at this point that Marcus raised the subject of our desire to visit the island.

"Who wants to visit?" the boatman asked, and Marcus indicated himself and the four of us.

"Too many people; not enough boat," said the Ithacan, vigorously shaking his head. "I can carry only two of you."

Given the size of his dinghy, this statement shouldn't have come as much of a surprise, but neither Marcus nor I had given a moment's thought to the possibility that Agricus, Hieronymous, and, above all, Dracena might not be able to accompany us to the island. That three of our party would have to forgo the experience of Ithaca was now a virtual certainty, and Dracena immediately asserted that, although he didn't much care whether he visited the island or not, he was duty bound to remain at Marcus's side under any and all circumstances.

At this moment the boatman further confused matters by announcing that his "little cockleshell" couldn't possibly carry even two people if one was as oversized as Dracena, and that meant that under no circumstances would Marcus be able to go ashore.

Marcus, of course, was having none of that, and took Dracena aside for a heated exchange of half-whispered views on the subject of where precisely the *singularis's* duty lay. Ithaca, meanwhile, was gradually slipping by some three or four miles to starboard—a primal-looking place of looming cliffs and Stygian shadows, whose timbered mountains gleamed pallid green in the mist-filtered light of the rising sun.

Marcus and Dracena kept on arguing, though it was clear after a while that the boy's facility with logic and words was steadily overcoming the man's recalcitrance and fixity of purpose. At one point Dracena made a valiant effort to reclaim some of the ground he'd lost to Marcus's reasoned arguments by declaring, loudly enough for all to hear, "Well, in that case I'll just swim alongside!" But Marcus simply brushed that assertion aside. Having attempted to match him forensically myself from time to time, I could well imagine how helpless Dracena was starting to feel as one impeccably logical proposition after another came crashing into the foundations of his resolve. In the end he was verbally bludgeoned into submission, but I could tell from his troubled expression that although he'd been confuted he hadn't been convinced.

The one question now remaining—in *my* mind, at any rate—was whether it would be Agricus or me who joined Marcus in Heron's boat. Ever since the incident of the brothel at Formiae I'd decided to take nothing for granted where my friend and my enemy were concerned. But as it turned out I needn't have worried. In the brief pause that followed Dracena's capitulation, Agricus's and Marcus's eyes met, and the two of them engaged in some sort of silent dialogue that resulted in Agricus saying, "I can see from your expression, Marco, that I'm still in your bad graces because of that little prank I played on our gladiatorial friend in Tarentum. But even if I could claim that I enjoyed your favor at the moment, I wouldn't dream of coming between you and your faithful idolator."

"That's very accommodating of you," Marcus responded, and in no more time than it took us to throw together a few of our belongings and arrange with our companions to rejoin them at the lighthouse in Kyllene at sundown the following day, he and I found ourselves waving good-bye to our friends aboard the *Isis* from the alarmingly porous confines of Heron's boat.

Porous or not, the boat managed to carry us to Ithaca, even though Heron had to tack repeatedly in order to make any headway against a north-by-northwest breeze, and even though Marcus and I had to row the last mile or so to shore after we came into the lee of the northern half of the island. As we rowed, we peppered Heron with questions about what he referred to as his "polis", struggling along as best we could in the Ionic dialect of the vulgar koine Greek that serves as the common tongue throughout the eastern provinces of the Empire. In his replies Heron evinced great pride in Ithaca's connection with Odysseus and Homer. But despite the fact that almost every one of the island's natural features had been named after the hero or the poet, there was virtually nothing in the way of ruins or inscriptions to substantiate the belief that anyone named Odysseus had ever reigned, or even lived, there. This lack of concrete evidence troubled Heron not at all, however, and he sat smiling at the tiller, secure in the knowledge of his homeland's undying fame.

After we'd rowed a half hour or so, he turned us to port just past a rocky headland and guided us into a large sheltered cove around which were scattered a few rude stone dwellings. "Phorkys!" he announced proudly, indicating with a sweep of his arm the all-but-deserted village. Marcus and I leaned on our oars and looked around us. Apart from the stone hovels, the only signs of human habitation were two tethered goats nibbling at some scraggly vegetation, an emaciated mongrel sniffing around the foundations of one of the houses, and a freshly washed cape and tunic that had been hung out on a line to dry. To the extent that the village itself was humble, so was its natural setting impressive. For scrub-encrusted cliffs soared skyward on all three sides of the cove—dark green palisades a good thousand feet high, bracketed by deep blue water and pale blue sky.

"Phorkys!" Marcus repeated excitedly. "The port of the Old Man of the Sea, Lucio—our first direct encounter with a Homeric reference.

Phorkys was the father of the sirens and the grandfather of the cannibal Cyclops Polyphemus."

"He must have had awfully simple tastes," I responded as I looked around at the primitive surroundings, whereupon Marcus reprimanded me for my irreverence with a playful whack on the head.

"He sleeps down there," said Heron pointing to the surface of the water.

"Who does?" I asked.

Heron responded, "Phorkys! The Old Man."

"Ye gods!" Marcus exclaimed. "We can't be much more than fifty feet from shore, and yet I still can't see the bottom."

"Well I see *something*," I said, feeling the hairs on the back of my neck start to bristle, "and I think that it may be moving."

"Where?" asked Marcus, leaning over the gunwale beside me.

"Right *there*!" I shouted, peering down through five or six fathoms of limpid turquoise and just barely making out a huge gray green object which, I realized later, could not have been anything but a boulder, but which, at the time, looked a great deal like some submerged monster that was starting to rise to the surface.

"That is Phorkys himself!" Heron declared, and almost before the words were out of his mouth both Marcus and I started pulling vigorously on our oars.

Heron found our behavior endlessly amusing and had to wipe away tears of laughter as we pulled his boat up onto the pebble-strewn beach.

"Is there any way up from here?" Marcus asked him in some embarrassment as we gathered up our belongings and surveyed the precipitous heights that closed us in.

"Many ways," Heron answered. "Which way do you want to go?"

Marcus and I exchanged blank looks. "Which way would you recommend?" Marcus inquired.

Heron shrugged. "That way," he said finally, pointing to his right, "takes you to the town, Alalkomenai, and the northern part of the island." Pointing to his left, he continued, "That way takes you to the Arethousa Spring and the Marathia farm." Last, he pointed behind us. "That way takes you to the village of ghosts and to the grotto of the bees, where I gather my honey."

"The grotto of the bees!" Marcus repeated in a voice alive with excitement. "That must be the cave of the nymphs that Homer describes. He says that bees deposit their honey there, and that it has two entrances, one for mortals and the other for gods."

"That's right!" said Heron, nodding emphatically. "If you go, you must use only the north entrance, or Poseidon will afflict you with running sores."

"You mentioned a village of ghosts," I said. "What is that?"

"Deserted since long before my great-grandfather was born," Heron replied with great solemnity. "It's said that the people went mad—very mad. Everyone died. We never say the name of the place, just call it the village of ghosts."

Marcus and I again exchanged a glance. "I guess we'll go have a look at it," Marcus said.

"The path begins behind that house there," said Heron in a fatalistic tone. "I will go now to my house, in Alalkomenai. Tomorrow we will meet here at sunrise and I will take you to Kyllene."

And with that he turned and headed off.

"I was hoping we might find a somewhat more seaworthy vessel to carry us to Kyllene," I said to Marcus as the two of us watched him walk away.

"I suspect that his vessel is as seaworthy as they come on this particular island," Marcus replied.

"Did you get the impression that he didn't think much of our plan to visit the village of ghosts?"

"Yes, in a way. But then I decided that if he really thought something bad was going to happen to us, he wouldn't have committed himself to meet us here tomorrow."

I pondered that idea, then shrugged off my misgivings and said, "Well, shall we get started?"

"We shall indeed," Marcus responded. "And, who knows, perhaps one of the wraiths haunting the village will turn out to be the ghost of Odysseus himself!"

# FROM THE
JOURNAL

90

[SEPTEMBER 19TH]

Please tell me, oh, ye gods, what have we erring mortals ever done to deserve the unfeeling arrogance of doctors? The fellow to whose care Portia and I have committed our son was nowhere to be found this morning. He'd left before dawn, his slave informed us, to assist a midwife with a "difficult" birth in some village five or six miles from here. Decius, meanwhile, had awoken in considerable pain, and the only remedy we could lay our hands on was some of the powdered mandrake root that Nestor carries around with him in his little box of sundries. When the doctor finally reappeared toward the middle of the afternoon, he not only failed to apologize for having gone off without so much as a word to us, but also went so far as to reprimand me for administering an analgesic without consulting him. Struggling to maintain control of my temper, I pointed out to him that he hadn't been available to consult with at the time of administration and, furthermore, hadn't bothered to advise us when he'd be likely to return from wherever it was he'd gone. To this the bleary-eyed fellow retorted that since babies adhere to no particular schedule when being coaxed from the womb, he had not been in a position when he departed to estimate how long he'd be away. I replied that I quite understood what he was saying and that it was precisely because I had no way of knowing when he'd reappear that I'd made the decision to ease Decius's pain on my own. He responded to this with a curt request that I "restrain the impulse to intervene" henceforth, and I answered that I'd be only too happy to oblige, unless, of course, I formed the opinion that my son was being neglected.

At that point I believe it was plain to both of us that further discussion would serve no useful purpose. The doctor, at all events, concluded our conversation by saying that he'd better go have a look at Decius's leg. And all he said once he completed his examination was, "I'll take another look after dinner."

I find it increasingly difficult to resist the conviction that his reticence with regard to Decius's condition is motivated at least in part by a perverse desire to torment us. And if I don't get any meaningful information out of him after this evening's examination, I'll find it all but impossible to resist the temptation to wring his neck.

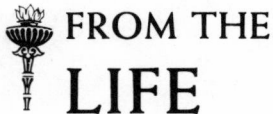
The trail scratched into the side of the cliff zigzagged upward through thick growths of scrub pine and thistle, and even though most of its course lay in shadow, both Marcus and I were pouring sweat long before we reached the top. The steady current of northerly wind that had impeded our progress shoreward from the *Isis* became audible in the nearby pine boughs, and as we forged our way up into the sunlight, the wind became palpable as well. Throwing ourselves down on a bare limestone outcropping, we let the sun's warmth and the air's flowing coolness dry the streams of perspiration on our skin. Then, having at last caught our breath, we stood up and surveyed our surroundings. To the west and slightly below us, no more than a mile away, was a village on the summit of a hill. This, we assumed, was Alalkomenai, where Heron lived, and running north from it was a narrow ridge leading to the broad boulder-strewn mountain meadows that comprised the other half of the island. A mile or two beyond Alalkomenai, and separated from Ithaca by a narrow channel, lay Cephalenia, stretching in a dusky green arc from north to south. Blocking our view of the southernmost reaches of this arc were the massive shoulders of the peak Heron had referred to—for no apparent reason—as Homer's Footstool, and roughly halfway between us and its summit was the mouth of a very large cave.

"The Cave of the Nymphs!" Marcus announced triumphantly. "That must be the north entrance, the one we mortals are permitted to use. Shall we investigate?"

"By all means," I responded, secretly thanking all the gods I didn't believe in that we hadn't spied the other entrance first and been tempted to commit an act of sacrilege.

And so we started up the mountainside, which was littered with rocks, bare of trees, and utterly deserted apart from a family of piebald goats who were browsing among the sun-bleached stones. All three of them lifted their heads and stared at us as we labored toward the cave, their jaws working steadily on the spear grass and wildflowers they'd uprooted and their faces reflecting that singular combination of blind impudence and bottomless stupidity on which the hircine fraternity—along with some of the *frumentarii* I've encountered—appears to have the monopoly.

When we arrived at last at the mouth of the cave, it quickly became apparent that all the energy we'd expended getting there was not going to be commensurately rewarded. The cave was little more than a large indentation in the mountainside, with no mysterious depths for nymphs to dart around in and a thoroughly un-Homeric collection of dried goat turds littering the floor. The Homeric bees had been totally domesticated, moreover, and lived not in hives but in squat little whitewashed boxes that had HPWN scratched into their wooden tops. As for the famous south-facing entrance of the immortals, it turned out to be nothing more than a large hole high up in the deepest part of the cave. Apparently the west face of the mountain resembled a sheer precipice, more or less, and rose almost straight up out of the sea. As the upward slope of the east face became progressively steeper toward the summit, therefore, the slopes running north and south from the crest became progressively narrower. Thus in the uppermost recesses of the cave, where its rear wall merged with its roof, there was comparatively little in the way of rock and earth separating its interior surfaces from the other side of the mountain; and it was precisely at the point where the cave's roof cut most deeply into the eastern slope of Homer's Footstool that the celebrated entrance of the immortals was situated.

No doubt a more enlightened pair of young men would have found the matter of the entrance's location endlessly fascinating, from a scientific point of view at the very least. But since Marcus and I had been anticipating a portal fit for Olympians, we could not repress a distinct sense of disenchantment. Feeling more than a bit disgruntled in consequence, we sat down on the lip of the cave and consumed the dry bread and green olives we'd brought along with us from the *Isis*.

"Well," Marcus said, chewing strenuously," I don't imagine the village of ghosts can be much more disappointing than this. Shall we go have a look at it?"

"Why not?" I responded with no great enthusiasm.

Although our comprehension of Heron's heavily inflected Ionian dialect was limited, we'd both gotten the impression from him that the village of ghosts was located just beyond the southern slopes of Homer's Footstool, and after half an hour's walk that was precisely where we found it. The so-called village occupied a rectangular stretch of level ground that was perhaps a half mile long on its east-west axis by a quarter mile north-south, and it shared the site with serried rows of ancient olive trees, whose squat old trunks looked more like stumps and whose trembly silver green leaves cast dappled patterns of sunlight and shadow on the crumbling foundations of what once had been people's houses. The village was bounded on the north by the mountain slopes we'd just traversed, on the east by a forest of pine and scrub oak, and on the west and south by steep brush-covered declivities that terminated after roughly a mile's steady descent in the dazzling blue waters of the Ionian Sea.

"It's pleasant here, isn't it?" Marcus said as we sat at the foot of an olive tree and surveyed the grove and its ruins.

"Yes," I agreed. "There's something very serene about this place, something . . . I don't know . . . *salubrious*."

"I know what you mean," said Marcus. "If there really are any ghosts here, I'll wager they're singularly benign."

We sat enjoying the rustic-archaic ambience and considered what part of the island to explore next. After all the walking and climbing we'd done, we were both feeling a little parched, and we decided, therefore, to head due eastward and try to find the spring called Arethousa that Heron had placed in the southeast corner of the island. Coming upon the overgrown remains of a pathway at the edge of the woods, we noted that it went in the right direction. We didn't follow it far, though. For after we'd gone a few score paces we were stopped in our tracks by the sound of a stentorian female voice adjuring us in aristocratically enunciated Greek to "*Halt!*"

Standing amid the trees to our right was a tall, beefy, middle-aged woman with coarse features and frizzy black hair. She was dressed in a plain homespun chiton that barely contained her mammoth bosom, but wore exquisitely wrought gold and silver jewelry that belied her peasant countenance and simple attire. A turquoise-studded gold tiara, white-gold-and-opal pendant earrings, and a chain-link silver necklace anchored by a hefty gold medallion proclaimed this substantial matron a woman of wealth, as did the small wide-eyed slave boy attending her, who peeked out at Marcus and me from behind the voluminous folds of his mistress's garment.

"I have waited long for your arrival," the lady said. "What message have you brought me?"

Marcus and I, bewildered, both realized that even though neither of us carried any message for the woman, one of us at least had better pretend that he did. Of course it was the nimble-minded Marcus who had wit enough to rise to the occasion.

"Forgive me, madam," he said, "but I am sworn to deliver my message to one particular person and no one else. If you believe yourself to be that person, you must confirm the fact by declaring both your own identity and that of the person at whose behest I have journeyed here."

The woman responded to this piece of pure invention as if it were precisely what she'd been hoping to hear. "I am the lady Penelope," she announced, "and the person who sent you to me is none other than my son, Odysseus!"

In response to this strange conflation of the *Odyssey* with the Oedipus tragedy, Marcus and I exchanged glances of incredulity, which, from the viewpoint of our interlocutrix, apparently bespoke a commendable desire to make sure that she was in fact the phantasm she claimed to be.

"Fear not!" she said, smiling. "For I can readily demonstrate that I am not an impostor."

"You can?" said Marcus in a tentative voice. "May I ask you to specify how."

"*What?*" said the lady indignantly. "Do you mean to tell me that my son never mentioned the fan-shaped mole I bear upon my breast?"

"Oh, no, madam. That is, he did mention it. In fact, he stated specifically that it was by that very mole that we would know you."

"And by it you shall!" the lady responded, starting abruptly to wriggle her right shoulder free of the collar of her garment.

"Oh, he didn't say we had actually to *see* the mole," Marcus said hurriedly. "He has far too much reverence for your modesty to insist on that. He said it would be sufficient if you simply made reference to it, as you have just now done."

"But unless you see it you won't be absolutely sure of me," the lady answered him, having by now worked free the better part of her formidable right bicep.

"Your son will be gravely displeased with us if he learns that we, uh, compromised you," Marcus pleaded.

"He need never find out," the lady replied decisively as her elbow, forearm, wrist, and fingers went the way of her shoulder and bicep.

"He warned us he'd interrogate your slaves in order to satisfy himself that we didn't abuse his trust," Marcus said, improvising frantically as the woman struggled to bare her ponderous udder.

"*You* won't tell anyone what transpires here today, will you, Hippolytus?" she said to the slave boy in a menacing tone. And he, in mortal terror, emphatically shook his head.

We were shown the mole.

"Now then," said the woman, leaving the proof of her identity exposed to general view, "what is the message my son has asked you to convey to me?"

"That he is returning here to Ithaca," Marcus responded with a little flourish of feigned enthusiasm.

"Oh, joyous tidings!" the woman sighed, clasping her hands to her bosom. "But *when* will he return? Did he say?"

"He will return on the rising of the next full moon," Marcus told her, and in a tone so histrionic that I thought for sure she would see that he was being insincere. But I needn't have fretted.

The woman almost swooned with happiness. "Why, that's barely a fortnight from now!" she exclaimed. "Come, both of you, to my house this very moment. I intend to accord you *all* the hospitality due you as emissaries of my beloved son."

And on that slightly suggestive note she turned and stomped off toward the southernmost reaches of the island, leaving Marcus and me to choose between running after her and running for our lives.

"That woman is deranged," I argued reasonably as we watched her slave boy scurry along in her wake.

"But quite harmless, to all appearances," Marcus replied.

"She didn't look so harmless to me."

"Aren't you the least bit curious about her?"

"I'm very curious about her. Let's go find Heron and have him tell us all he knows."

"Where's your sense of adventure?"

"I had it removed."

Marcus responded to this quip with an expression mingling amusement and exasperation. "You're not going to convince me that you're genuinely afraid of that bizarre creature."

"Perhaps not, but I'm certainly going to try."

Frowning but also smiling, Marcus paused to assess the strength of my feelings. "I'll make a bargain with you," he said finally. "If you'll go with me to that bizarre creature's house, I'll . . ."

"You'll what?" I interrupted. "You can't possibly be a better friend to me than you are already, and you can't possibly do anything more for me than you do right now."

"Well then," said Marcus slyly, after briefly considering the point I'd made, "suppose I promise that in return for going with me I will . . ."

"Yes?" I prompted him as he made a show of thinking deeply.

"I will . . ." he repeated, his face starting to light up with the excitement of inspiration, "I will prove to you someday that the statements you just made about me are wrong."

"Whatever in the world does that mean?" I asked.

His reply was prompt: "You said that I couldn't possibly be a better friend to you or do anything more for you than I do already. I am saying that if you'll go with me to the lady Penelope's house this afternoon I will one day prove myself a better and more helpful friend than you insist on believing I am at the present time."

"How do you propose to do that?"

"That's my affair. . . . Now, do we strike a bargain or not?"

"Oh, I suppose so," I responded grudgingly, thinking as the two of us shook hands that I wasn't any too sure that I even *wanted* Marcus to prove himself a better friend than he already was.

But the bargain had been struck, and off we went on the lady Penelope's track.

Her house was not much more than half a mile southeast of the village of ghosts—a large weather-beaten limestone affair with a primitive portico in front, the roof of which rested on rough-hewn, unfluted, and badly cracked marble columns. The masonry of the walls betrayed numerous jagged fissures, too, some with tufts of grass lodged in them and others with tendrils of vine snaking out. Taken as a whole, the building looked like it had been conceived with the most grandiose of intentions and constructed without the slightest trace of skill. We approached its front portal with an altogether appropriate degree of wariness. Since the double doors were standing wide open, however, we presumed so far as to step inside, but coming out of the bright afternoon sunshine into a cavernous unlit interior, we found it impossible to make out any but the most manifest features of the entrance hall. Beyond the hall, though, was a peristyle and garden court, in the center of which—with her identifying mole blessedly no longer on display—was the mistress of the house, seated at a brightly painted loom.

"She hasn't seen us yet," I whispered to Marcus. "We can still change our minds and get out of here."

He responded by calling out, "Gracious lady! We have arrived!" thereby rendering my earnest suggestion moot.

"Who are *you*?" she inquired haughtily as we stepped into the court, and even Marcus was somewhat taken aback.

"Why, the emissaries sent by your son, Odysseus."

Hearing this, the lady leaned forward and squinted at us. "Oh, yes," she said. "I believe I recognize you. What was the message you brought me again?"

"That your son will be here on the rising of the next full moon."

"But I know that already," she snapped. "My son wrote me."

Once again Marcus was equal to the occasion. "He feared his letter might go astray," he said, "so he sent us to tell you in person."

"Ahhhh," said the lady, "how like him to make provision for all contingencies. That is why they call him 'Odysseus of many wiles.'"

Though I wasn't at all sure that wiliness was entirely synonymous with attention to detail, neither was I about to chop logic with a madwoman. So I remained silent.

"You must be tired and dusty after your journey," the lady said, twice clapping her hands. Within moments a slave boy appeared from the shadows of the arcade behind her. He was about the same age as the one we'd seen her with earlier and proved to have the same name as well. "Show these young gallants to the baths, Hippolytus, and furnish them each with a clean chlamys. They shall dine with me this evening . . . and, of course, spend the night."

"Your hospitality is matched only by your beauty, lady," said Marcus in an access of recklessness, prompting our hostess to blush scarlet and reply with a sigh, "Ah, no one has spoken so sweetly to me since my beloved Odysseus embarked upon his travels."

"You're more demented than she is!" I hissed at Marcus in Latin as Hippolytus Number Two led us toward the rear of the house. "She can barely keep her hands off us as it is; it's irresponsible of you to lead her on."

"If I didn't know better, Lucio, I'd swear you were worried about being raped."

"I'm more worried about being squashed."

Marcus laughed. "But the woman's totally harmless, Lucio. I'm sure she's interested in nothing more sinister than a little flattery and flirtation."

"I wouldn't count on that," said Hippolytus Number Two in Latin every bit as colloquial as our own.

"I am Phrygian by birth," he explained in response to our flabbergasted stares, "but I was raised in a Roman household in Corinth."

"And you're telling us that your mistress is interested in more than mere flattery and flirtation?" I inquired.

"Yes."

"How do you know that?" asked Marcus.

"From experience," the boy responded grimly.

Marcus put the question that was foremost in both our minds: "Your mistress, is she as mad as she seems?"

"Madder," was the terse reply.

"Tell us what you know," I urged him.

"Though I'm only a slave," he answered, "may I ask you to do something for me in return?"

"What?" Marcus demanded.

"Take me away from this place; take me into your service."

"Why?" Marcus asked.

Because I can't bear being her catamite any longer."

"Her catamite?"

"Yes. We're all her catamites here, all five of us boys."

"And the other four, they're all your age?"

"Approximately. The oldest is fourteen, the youngest is twelve."

"And you're all named Hippolytus?"

"We're all *called* Hippolytus. Our true names are never spoken, on pain of flogging and . . . worse."

"Why Hippolytus?" I inquired, and then the obvious explanation struck me. "Of course! Phaedra, his stepmother, was in love with him. The Theseus legend."

The boy gave a somber nod.

"Are we in any danger here?" Marcus asked.

The boy shrugged. "I can't say. Our mistress is unpredictable."

"But how does one middle-aged woman manage to exercise power over five young fellows like you?"

The boy's eyes widened slightly as he replied, "The warder."

"The warder?"

"Her body slave," he explained, his upper lip curling, "a pig who'd turn the stomach of a goat."

"Perhaps it would be a good idea," I said to Marcus, "if we decided not to stay for dinner after all."

He ignored me and persisted with his interrogation of the boy. "Your mistress," he said, "is her name really Penelope?"

"No."

"What is her name?"

"I can't tell you that; I would be tortured and killed."

Marcus responded to this desperate-sounding assertion with an expression compounded of equal parts amusement and alarm. "Well, I'm certainly not so eager to have the information as to subject you to such an appalling risk as that. Are you permitted to say whether your mistress is a native of this island?"

"She isn't," the boy replied.

"Well then, can you tell me what she's doing here?"

After looking up and down the corridor to make sure no one was around to overhear him, the boy answered, "As I understand it, she's the wife of an extremely wealthy Athenian patrician, and she was sent here because she conceived an unwholesome passion for her son."

"And why are you and the others here?"

"She likes boys, so her husband keeps her supplied, through one of his estate agents."

"You've never seen her husband?"

"No."

"But you know his name."

"Yes."

"How do you know it?"

"The others told me, when I first came here two years ago."

"What became of those who were here before you?"

"When they got too old for the woman's tastes, she sent them back to the mainland, and her husband's agent provided replacements."

"How old is too old?"

"It isn't age that matters so much; it's looks."

"What about our looks?" I interjected anxiously. "Do we look young enough for her?"

"You don't, but your friend does."

"There, Lucio," said Marcus with a smirk, "I told you you had nothing to be concerned about."

"What does she make you do?" I asked the boy by way of retort.

"It isn't so much what she makes us do as it is what she does *to* us, or has the warder do."

"How long has all this been going on?" Marcus inquired in a tone of perfect equanimity.

"I don't know exactly. Ten years, at least."

"Do the islanders know?"

"Some of them may. I'm not sure. We're not allowed to speak to them. . . . Now please, will you help me? I miss my own mother so terribly, and if I have to remain here much longer I'll be too ashamed ever again to look her in the face."

"I can't promise anything," Marcus responded after ruminating a moment or two. "But if I can see any way of improving your situation before I leave here, I'll take action."

"Thank you," said the boy in a voice so freighted with gratitude and newly kindled hope that Marcus felt obliged to repeat his admonition. "Remember," he said, "there may be nothing I can do."

"I understand," the boy responded. "But I beg you to do everything you can."

Though the baths were rather dingy and far from clean, the cistern water in the vats was both plentiful and hot, and Marcus and I were long overdue for an ablution. After thoroughly washing ourselves, we sat swathed in towels and discussed the second Hippolytus's plea for help.

"I don't see that there's much we can do for him," I said. "Heron's boat is barely large enough to accommodate you and me, and I don't imagine there are any larger boats available, except possibly at the other end of the island."

"Which must be a good four hours' walk from here, at the least," Marcus added.

"At the very least," I agreed. "But we could probably reach Heron's village in under two hours. He might be willing to help us."

"And then again, he might not. Remember, he halfway warned us not to come to this part of the island in the first place."

"Do you think he has any idea what goes on here?"

"Since it's been going on for a good many years, I'd have to assume that he does. And if the lady Penelope's Athenian husband is anywhere near as rich as the boy says he is, then the last thing someone like Heron is going to want to do is cross him."

"We're stymied then. There's nothing we can do."

"With respect to taking the boy away with us, that's true. But there is another way of approaching the problem."

"To wit?"

"To wit: get rid of the warder."

"I don't follow you."

"It's very simple. One insane woman can't possibly control five catamites by herself. Five catamites can easily control one insane woman, however. Get rid of the woman's warder, accordingly, and the catamites are as good as free."

"By 'get rid of' you mean . . . ?"

"I don't see any other way. Do you?"

I thought about what he was saying and decided he couldn't possibly be in earnest. "You're not seriously proposing that we go so far as to *murder* our hostess's majordomo?"

"Oh, no? Why aren't I?"

"Because it's illegal, for one thing. People aren't even allowed to kill their own slaves nowadays, let alone someone else's."

"I'll grant you that there might be a legal objection of some sort, but would there be a moral one?"

"A fortiori there would."

Marcus shook his head. "No, Lucio. For there have always been immoral laws, and also moral ones immorally applied. I suggest to you that whenever there is a conflict between law and right conduct, right conduct should prevail."

"But to *kill* the fellow, Marco . . ."

"What are our alternatives? If we cripple or blind him, the boys will torture him to death. If we leave him unmolested, he will continue to torture them. By all rights the person we really ought to kill is the wealthy Athenian who's responsible for this infamous situation, but because he's out of reach, we must do the next best thing."

I listened to Marcus's words but could not shake off the eerie conviction that the Marcus I knew could not be uttering them. Yes, the indignities to which the slave boys were being subjected were infamous, and yes, Marcus and I were under some sort of moral obligation to help them. I could even concede that the action Marcus was advocating was the only feasible course open to us under the circumstances. And yet, even though logic seemed to compel the conclusion Marcus had come to, I knew that his plan was both anarchic and contrary to his nature.

What, then, was compelling him to espouse it?

No sooner had I asked myself the question than the answer hit me, and with a shock of understanding that was well-nigh concussive.

"This is all because Agricus can now say he's killed a man, and you can't," I blurted out.

And Marcus, looking me straight in the eye, responded, "Perhaps so, Lucio, but for better or worse my mind is made up."

FROM THE
JOURNAL

[UNDATED]

We drank wine with him, Portia and I, bowl after bowl. Except that the wine in our bowls was heavily mixed with water while the wine in his was neat.

He was frightened; his hands shook. It was terrible to see him so frightened.

He sat on the bench, his back against the wall, and Camilla stood beside him and rested her head on his bare shoulder, her small hands gripping his upper arm.

The wine seemed to take effect all at once. One moment he was sitting erect and speaking clearly, his fear causing his voice to quaver ever so slightly. The next moment his head was lolling and his speech was slurred.

Then he started to cry, and I had to leave the courtyard to keep from breaking down in his presence.

When I returned, Nestor was pouring him another bowl of wine. He wasn't crying any more; he just sat downcast, staring stuporously at the ground.

Before too much longer, he passed out.

The doctor and his slave attendant prepared him quickly, and this time I stayed, so someone would be with him if he came to while they were working.

I looked at his wound one last time before they started. I still couldn't detect any traces of gangrene. But the doctor said the signs were unmistakable. He even suggested that I smell the wound if I was in any doubt. I chose not to.

There's a great deal more flesh in the thigh than in the lower leg. Perhaps that's why I didn't recoil as much from the sight of this amputation as I did from the thought of the first one.

He came to when they reached bone and was immediately sick. I turned his head sideways so he wouldn't choke, but kept my hand cupped under his chin to make sure he couldn't look down toward his feet and see what they were doing.

I mean, of course, his foot.

His eyes were wild and staring when he finished being sick, and he struggled against me to lift his head. Then they started sawing through the bone, and he began to scream. I forced a fat plug of tow between his teeth and told him to bite down hard. Sweat ran off his brow in rivulets and tears streamed from his eyes.

"Easy, son," I said to him again and again. "It'll be over soon."

And after perhaps another quarter hour of horror it was.

The doctor washed the wound thoroughly with water and wine and then applied cauteries and salves. We removed Decius from the table and made him as comfortable as possible on a couch. He asked for his mother, I brought her in, and he sobbed himself to sleep in her arms.

Now we must wait and see if this wound goes septic like the first one. I haven't yet dared to ask the doctor what our choices are if it does.

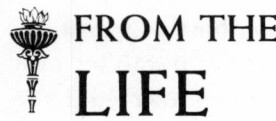
We met, or got our first look at, the warder at dinner that evening, and though the lady Penelope invariably addressed him as Adonis, he was a long way indeed from being the type of youthful beauty. Apart from his considerable height and sinewy arms, in fact, he was as sorry a specimen of humanity in his way as his mistress was in hers. Raw-boned and unkempt, his sallow skin festooned with warts and boils, the fellow seemed to me almost pathologically short-tempered, and he was not at all squeamish about laying the willow switch he carried with him hard across the necks and buttocks of the terrified boys who prepared and served our evening meal under his splenetic supervision. The five Hippolytuses were no more frightened of him, though, than he appeared to be of his mistress. Indeed, it became clear as the evening wore on that he stood in mortal terror of her, in part, I suppose, because she never ceased berating him for the poor quality of service his juvenile charges provided. Such meager advantages as his station in life afforded him were wholly contingent, it seemed, on his ability to cater to the whims of a madwoman, a task that would have taxed the ingenuity of the most obsequious and resourceful slave in the Empire, which the warder most decidedly was not. Despite his brutality, therefore, I felt a certain sympathy for him, and I could tell that Marcus, too, was not insensitive to his plight, a fact that gave me some grounds for hoping that he might reconsider his intention to make a trophy of the fellow's life.

I did not share Marcus's opinion that he was morally mandated to murder him. The penalty of death seemed to me wholly incommensurate with the wretch's crimes. He was merely an agent, after all; the true wickedness was chargeable to his principals—the wealthy Athenian and his demented wife. If the situation was really so infamous as to warrant immediate correction, then it was the madwoman who ought to die and not her slave. But when I made this point to Marcus while we were dressing, he refuted it with the assertion that the lady Penelope, being mad, was not responsible for her actions, while the warder, being sane, most assuredly was.

"True," I admitted, "but the actions for which he's responsible do not include the taking of life."

"No," Marcus responded, "but they do include the debasement of it, which in many ways is worse." I had no ready answer for this apart from the admonition that, in taking the power of life and death into his own hands, he might be arrogating to himself the prerogatives reserved to the gods. "And what else," he retorted, "do you suppose it is to be a man?"

Since there were only three of us dining that evening, we each had a couch to ourself, which was just as well, given our hostess's concupiscence and girth, not to mention her comparably huge appetite. Once she'd finished gorging herself and had temporarily exhausted her repertoire of lewd lisps and simpering leers, she announced that she would now entertain us with a recitation. And much to my surprise, entertain us she did.

"Now a year had passed since the Achaians, through their cunning, breached the walls of fabled Troy and brought low the people of Priam. And thus it was fully eleven years since Penelope, daughter of Icarios and wife of Odysseus, King of Ithaca, had admitted a man to her bedchamber. All over the kingdom women marveled at her virtue and sang her praises, for they well knew—better than their menfolk—how cold and dark a house can become if no logs are placed in the hearthfire. But Aphrodite, born of the foam, heard the praisesongs as she bellied with Ares, god of war, while her own husband, lame Hephaestus, lay snoring on the shoulders of cloud-crowned Olympus. 'This mortal seeks to shame me with her continence,' she said as Ares filled her body with his warrior seed; and so she sent forth Eros, father of desire, to Ithaca and Queen Penelope's bed. Once there, Eros appeared to the sleeping Queen in the guise of her beloved child Telemachos, and so filled her with desire for him that she awoke in terror and prayed aloud to the gray-eyed goddess Athene: 'Oh, daughter of Zeus, my loins burn and my breasts ache with a love I dare not acknowledge. Sooner than yield to it I would run a dagger through my womb. I pray you, save me from this choice between infamy and death.' And the wise goddess heard the unhappy woman and roused Telemachos from his sleep: 'Go now, son of Odysseus, and seek your father in the house of those who stood with him at Troy. Go first to Pylos and make inquiry of aged Nestor. He shall instruct you as to where your father may be sought. But go now, this moment, and do not stay to take leave of your mother. For with your father lost to her these eleven years, she will assail you with tears and lamentations and keep you from your rightful course, which Destiny forbid. For if she were to restrain you, a terrible fate would befall you all.' And thus Telemachos stole away from his father's house that very night and took ship for Pylos on the western shore of Pelops' isle.

"When Penelope awoke and learned that the gray-eyed goddess had answered her prayer she rejoiced and called all the noblest families of Ithaca to her house for a feast in homage to Athene. But though the goddess had removed the object of the Queen's desire from the kingdom, the flames that Eros had kindled in the unhappy woman's womb continued to heat her blood. And when she saw the beauteous sons of mountainous Ithaca arrayed before her with their mothers and sisters her fever of passion overcame her. 'The shade of my husband appeared to me last night in a dream,' she lied, 'and told me that the ship bearing our loved ones home from Troy had been driven by Poseidon onto the rocks of Mount Athos and wrecked. All on board perished, the shade said, so your sons are now fatherless and you wives widows.'

"Now when the people heard this news they set up a great cry of lamentation. But Penelope silenced them, saying, 'The shade of Odysseus commanded me, and all you other women widowed, to choose new husbands and resume our lives. All who aspire to take Odysseus's place in my bed, therefore, should attend me here and present their suits in a spirit of amicable competition. My son Telemachos, meanwhile, has embarked for Chalcidice to claim his father's body, and while he is gone I shall sit at my loom and weave a shroud. When my handiwork is finished and Telemachos has returned I will make known my choice of a stepfather for him.'

"And so it was that the noblest young men of Ithaca took up residence in the house of Odysseus. And so it was that Queen Penelope brought them each in turn again and again to her bed, trying to placate the fierce desires that boiled day and night within her loins. But every night, her womb flooded with adulterous seed, she would pray to Hera that the next man to enter her body might be her lord and husband, Odysseus. For despite her unremitting passions she remained in her heart his wife. And despite the supple sweetness of her suitors' bodies, she was sorely ashamed of her unquenchable desire for them.

"Nine years passed, and Odysseus, after many wanderings, set sail for Ithaca from the land of the Phaiakians. Telemachos, meanwhile, having searched the world over for his noble father, set off homeward from the Spartan court of Menelaus and Helen. For the goddess Athene had come to him in the guise of Odysseus and bidden him return to Ithaca and take shelter there in the house of Eumaios, the swineherd.

"Father and son were thus, and at last, reunited in Eumaios' presence, and the faithful servitor told them of the many suitors who now dwelt in the house of Odysseus and enjoyed the favors of Odysseus's Queen. Late that same night the three men entered the King's banquet hall and slaughtered the sleeping suitors where they lay. Then Odysseus climbed the stairs to his wife's bedchamber, where the youngest of the suitors, a mere boy named Peneleos, lay slumbering in Penelope's arms. Maddened by blood and wrath, Odysseus cut the heart out of Peneleos and then violently raped his unfaithful wife, to her great delight, amidst the flesh and gore of his youthful victim.

"Now the people of Ithaca, on discovering that their sons had been butchered, rose up in rebellion and drove Odysseus from the island. But he, calling on the comrades who had fought beside him at Troy, returned to Ithaca with a thousand men and laid waste the city where his people dwelt, selling those of the inhabitants he did not kill into slavery and parceling out their lands to his companions-in-arms. Their wasted city he left as a monument to his wrath, and it became what it is to this day— a village of ghosts.

"Nine months after the slaughter of the suitors, Queen Penelope gave birth to her second child, a girl. I am the great-great-great-great-great-granddaughter of that child, and I rule here in Ithaca today by right of birth."

Marcus and I exchanged a glance. The woman's madness had clearly failed to vitiate her powers of invention. Those powers, however, served also to magnify her insanity.

"I choose you," she said with great condescension to Marcus. "Tonight it shall be your privilege to lie with a direct descendant of the mighty Odysseus."

"I am most sorry, lady," Marcus equably replied, "but I have taken a vow of celibacy in anticipation of my initiation into the Eleusinian mysteries."

"Your vows have no meaning here," the woman responded in a magisterial voice. "You must come now to my bed and fill me with your manly seed."

"I cannot," said Marcus, shaking his head.

"I command you!" the woman shouted.

"I must be faithful to my vows, madam. As a descendant of Odysseus, I'm sure you can understand the importance of my doing so."

"*Adonis!*" the woman shrieked. "Make him obey!"

And with surprising agility the slave charged across the room and grabbed hold of Marcus's arm. "You'd best do as she says, young fellow," he half whispered to him as he jerked him up off the couch. "It'll go easier for you."

"Take your hand off me, slave," said Marcus in an ominously calm tone of voice, "unless you yearn for death."

"Yes, yes," said the warder, all but ignoring him. "Now you just come along."

Marcus's hand moved so quickly that I didn't see him strike. But all at once the hilt of his dagger was protruding from the base of the warder's throat, and the slave, eyes wide with horror, was reeling backward from him with streams of blood and the gargling sounds of strangulation issuing from his mouth.

"*My husband!*" the woman shrieked at Marcus. "You have returned at last and slain my poor Peneleos. Now punish me, my lord Odysseus, punish me as I deserve!"

This insane request was punctuated by the sound of Adonis crashing to the floor, at which point one of the Hippolytuses let out a cry of anguish and threw himself onto the warder's spastically jerking body. "NO! NO! NO!" he screamed. "Oh, Adonis, speak to me, I beg of you. Adonis, my beloved. Oh, please! Oh, please! *NOOOOOO!*"

The other four boys, having rushed into the room at the sound of the lady Penelope's shriek, now stood dumbfounded and staring. Seeing them, Marcus, his eyes wild but his voice calm, said, "As you value your lives, see that no harm comes to this woman. You are still her slaves, though you are no longer in her power."

Then, walking over to where the first boy lay sobbing on top of Adonis's body, he reached down and yanked his dagger clear. "I shall punish you in the morning, wife," he told the lady Penelope in ominous tones. And as she nodded submissively by way of reply, he turned to me and said in a muffled voice, "I'm going to end up madder than she is if we don't get out of here, Lucio. We should never have come to this accursed island!"

[SEPTEMBER 21ST]

We committed our son's body to the fire this morning; he lived fourteen years, seven months, and twenty-six days. His final words before he lost consciousness were: "Please don't despise me, Father. Please don't despise me." He believed, apparently, that I was disgusted with him for yielding to tears and crying out in pain during the endless hours of his ordeal. He went to his death convinced that I thought he was a weakling. He didn't give me time to explain that what I was feeling was not contempt but blame.

It is clear, therefore, that I am even more blameworthy than I'd thought. For he could not have so mistaken the anguish I was feeling for him unless I'd consistently denied him the opportunity to know me—unless, in other words, I'd utterly failed him as a father.

Oh, ye gods, ye cruel and capricious immortals, I call on you to condemn me, to flay me, to cut out my tongue and my eyes.

I have betrayed the trust and the love of my only son.

And I shall never be able to make amends.

[SEPTEMBER 30TH]

It is cold and wet here in Coriallum, and the northwest winds come whipping in angrily off the Channel.

Perhaps we are too late. Perhaps all of Nestor's efforts have been for naught.

Or perhaps he's just mad.

He's certainly been driving us like a madman—cursing, nagging, chiding, exhorting—forty, sometimes even fifty, miles a day. Had it been safe to travel at night, I'm sure he would have gotten us here in five days rather than nine. The horses are half dead with exhaustion because of him; not that it matters much, except to them.

He said he'd made some "tentative arrangements" with a ship captain here on his way south from Britannia to Italy, so he's gone off to find the fellow and try to persuade him to carry us across the Channel.

What a pointless exercise that whole endeavor now seems to me.

I haven't slept much since Decius died. I have no trouble falling alseep, but as soon as I do, I start to dream of him and wake. I dream that he's still alive, that the whole notion of his being dead is misguided somehow, a mistake, a misconception. I see him in these dreams, and sometimes he confirms my dreamer's suspicion that it was all a practical joke he and Portia and Camilla decided to play on me. The wagon wheel didn't actually injure him when it rolled over his leg, and the amputations weren't real, just cleverly faked.

If only I could never awaken from such dreams. But somehow, in the very midst of them, my sense of reprieve and salvation becomes so intense that I have to cry out, to proclaim my joy, to weep with gratitude and exult in my redemption.

And thus I am brought back to the intolerable reality.

I know that Portia must hate me for what I've done. She is deathly pale and hardly ever speaks. Her face is set—a mask of bereavement and rage. Yet she never weeps. She hasn't shed a tear since we left Iculisma.

She blames me; I can tell. And I don't for a moment blame her for doing so. It behooves me, therefore, not to impose myself on her or flaunt my grief in her presence. I must keep my sorrows to myself and do all of my weeping silently, while she sleeps.

Even Camilla shies away from me, as if she's afraid that I may kill her, too. She clings to her mother and shivers, from the cold perhaps, or, more probably, out of fear. I would approach her, attempt to comfort her, but the thought of her shrinking away from my outstretched hand is more painful than I can endure.

It seems I've destroyed not just my son, but also my family.

It only remains for me now to destroy the destroyer.

[OCTOBER 6TH]

It seems the gods never tire of sporting with us. After all Nestor's fretting
and agitation, our three-day crossing of the Channel was little short of
idyllic. We left Coriallum under overcast skies but made good progress,
thanks to a steady east-by-northeast breeze. The clouds then dissipated
during the night and the wind gradually shifted from east to south, so
that on the second day we fairly bounded over the placid seas. The breeze
flagged toward evening, though, and we encountered some fog during
the night. But not long after sunrise the fog burned off, and we covered
the forty-odd miles remaining between us and the Britannic coast with
the help of a few vagrant zephyrs and a favorable tide. Our landfall this
evening was on the southern shore of a crescent-shaped east-facing bay,
and we are now, according to Nestor, within three days' journey of our
final destination.

That's just as well, given that our passage cost us just about all the
money we had left. I counted eighteen denarii, twenty-odd sesterces, and
a handful of asses in my purse after paying off the ship captain. Nestor
says I needn't worry, though—that all will be provided for once we reach
our goal. He seems little short of ecstatic that we have finally arrived in
Britannia. He says we are quit of the Empire, that the last Roman settlement of any consequence is a good fifteen miles behind us on the river
Isca. Apparently much of the territory to the west is of such limited
military and economic value that it has been left in the hands of the
native inhabitants—a marginally civilized Celtic people called the Dumnonii. They mine tin, so Nestor tells me, and sell what they don't use
themselves to the Roman settlers in their tribal capital on the Isca. Apart
from that they simply farm, hunt, gather, and engage in occasional blood
feuds among themselves. They are so far out of the Roman orbit, in fact,
that one cannot hear Latin spoken anywhere west of where we are right
now. That means we are free, says Nestor elatedly: we've made good our
escape from the reach of the Emperor's writ.

I suppose he's right about that. But I can't honestly say that I care.

If we needed any confirmation of the fact that we have passed beyond
the Empire's bounds, the condition of the roads in this region has provided

it. They are not only unpaved, but also well-nigh impassable. At their best they are rutted and muddy, and at their worst they are indistinguishable from the bogs through which they pass. In two full days of travel we have covered fewer than fifty miles, and on no fewer than five separate occasions we have been hopelessly mired in the muck. Mired we would have remained, moreover, had not other travelers, native to this district, taken pity on us. We have yet to see anyone else traveling as we are, by wagon; and given the problems we've encountered, I can readily understand why. Most of the natives proceed from place to place on foot, though we've encountered one or two horsemen here and there. The Dumnonii are a dour, sallow-skinned, taciturn people who wear baggy ankle-length tunics and wrap themselves in voluminous black cloaks. The language they speak is utterly incomprehensible to me, but Nestor, fortunately, has a good ear for alien tongues and manages to sustain some form of communication.

Given our slow progress, we are still two days away from our destination, but the fairly constant drizzle we've had to contend with yielded to clear skies this evening. Given a little sunshine to dry out the roads, we may make better time tomorrow.

I've been giving considerable thought these last few days to the question of what I ought to do once we reach the end of our journey. I know that I have neither the desire nor the right to go on living, but I must wait to see what awaits us at our destination before making definite plans. Once I'm satisfied that Portia and Camilla are well provided for in their new circumstances, I'll slip off at my earliest opportunity and end my unprofitable existence.

It's odd, but every so often, while I've been pondering this particular matter, I've caught myself thinking that I'd do well to solicit Decius's advice, and it takes a real effort of will to grapple with the fact that his advice is no longer available. I'm sure he would applaud my intention to die, though. Not out of hatred, good-hearted as he was, but out of heartfelt pity.

[OCTOBER 8TH]

Here I sit, a scant ten miles—so I'm told—from Cape Belerium and the limitless expanse of the Western Ocean. Low clouds scud eastward above me: rolling, tumbling, dissolving, and re-forming each moment as they trace fugitive patterns of off-white and gray across the overcast plain of the sky. Before me to the east, a bay stretches away to a headland. It was from that direction we came here, to our journey's end.

I do not understand—indeed, I can hardly believe—the magical trick that Fate, with Nestor as accomplice, has played on me. Just at the moment when I'd lost all interest in living, when life from my standpoint had ceased to have any meaning, there came—or, rather, I came upon— this revelation, seated on a stool outside a rude stone, thatched-roof house here at the windswept western limit of the world, The man's eyes were closed, his hair white, and blustery zephyrs smelling of brine ruffled the fine gray filaments of his beard. Nestor bade me draw near the old fellow, whose face I thought I might know. And so, slowly, with an unaccountable feeling of trepidation, I approached the dozing figure to within a few dozen paces. With each step I took the figure's countenance became more familiar, but for the life of me I could not, or dared not, place it. I brought myself to a halt. I was afraid now, but of what, I had no idea. For a long while I stood there, my heart thudding, my mind unable to believe. And I'd be standing there still had not the seated figure all at once awakened.

I looked at him. He looked at me. And then, as of old, he graced me with a smile. With an arthritic expenditure of effort he raised himself to his feet and began to hobble in my direction, his arms outstretched. "Welcome to my afterlife, dear Lucio," he said to me. And the sound of his voice confirmed what I still can't quite credit as real.

It was Marcus.

[OCTOBER 9TH]

We are comfortably settled here. A house has been provided for us, a short walk from Marcus's and built, like his, of stone and thatch. It is clean inside, though spare, with one large room facing the hearth and two small bedrooms in the rear.

We used only one of the two last night. It will be some time, I think, before Camilla is ready to sleep by herself again, and some time longer before Portia and I are ready to resume sleeping with each other. There is a distance between us that I do not know how to bridge. And how could there not be? I am responsible, after all, for the death of her first-born child.

But still there abides the inconceivable yet incontestable fact of Marcus: alive although seven months dead. I talked with him for an hour or so last night and this afternoon, and he acquainted me with some of the details of his carefully prearranged "death." The fever he ostensibly died of came fairly close to killing him a few days before his official quietus, he said, and that fact had "lent an air of compelling authenticity" to his counterfeit demise. By the time he expired formally, all the soldiers in camp were aware that he'd been afflicted with one of the numerous forms of contagion that had claimed so many of their comrades, and this circumstance, among other things, constrained the members of his staff to take leave of his mortal remains from a medically prudent distance, a distance, not so incidentally, from which they were unable to detect such faint signs of respiration as Marcus was unable to suppress. And of course when the time came to transfer his remains from his tent to the funeral pyre, there was another man's body wrapped within the folds of his Imperial shroud, "one of the innumerable fresh cadavers recruited daily from the legions' ranks by war and winter."

Once he was satisfied that his subterfuge had served its intended purpose, Marcus had set off under cover of darkness for the obscure Danubian village to which, a few days before on some plausible pretext or other, he'd dispatched five picked soldiers of his personal guard. They, of course, were unaware that he had officially passed away, and continued in this condition of ignorance throughout the long journey north and west that they now undertook in the capacity of his escort. He'd acquainted them with the details of the ruse he'd perpetrated shortly after their arrival in this remote corner of western Britannia, and at the same time had released them from their vow of personal loyalty to him as Imperator Caesar. "Since the Emperor is an official personage," he'd said to them, "and I am officially dead, it follows that I am no longer Emperor." Having said this, he'd gone on to bestow a generous *donatio* upon the five *singulares*, which consisted not only of money but also of choice parcels of land he'd purchased on their behalf from the local clans; and he'd encouraged them, with the enthusiastic approval of the clans' elders, to reduce the surplus population of marriageable females in the district by taking Dumnonii women as their wives. All five of the soldiers, he told me, were now happily settled; and three of the Dumnonii maidens they'd chosen as brides were expecting babies come the new year.

As I listened to Marcus speak, question after question arose in my mind. How had he come to choose this particular region of the world as his place of postmortem exile, for example, and what part had old Nestor played in the conception and execution of the bizarre scheme that had brought him here? And who *was* old Nestor in actual fact, and why had he been chosen to serve as Marcus's intermediary with respect to me? Why, above all, had Marcus gone to so much trouble on my account after our bitter and angry reunion on the Danube last winter had finally put an end to a relationship that had in any case been virtually nonexistent for well over forty years?

All these questions occurred to me, and more, but I forbore asking them because I sense that Marcus has it in mind to get around to them unbidden before too much more time goes by. Then, too, he looks so terribly old and frail that I scruple to add to the drain on his wasting vitality. He begins to show signs of tiring after barely half an hour's conversation, but keeps on doggedly chatting with me till I fear he's nearly ready to collapse. He's been extremely sympathetic about Decius and keeps assuring me that I'll "recover from the loss." He's also expressed keen interest in my autobiography, and asked, with an almost comical degree of diffidence as I took leave of him today, whether I'd be "kind enough" to let him read "at least a part" of what I've written. I said I'd be glad to let him read as much of it as he wanted to, and added that I'd even make him a gift of the manuscript, if he liked, since I'd lost all interest in the work and had no wish even to look at it any more. "Oh, you mustn't lose interest in your "Life" just yet, dear Lucio," he said as he escorted me to the door. "There may, after all, be some pleasant surprises in store for you as you approach the final chapter."

[OCTOBER 12TH]

Marcus beamed at me when I made what I am coming to think of as my regular afternoon call on him today. "I've just finished reading what there is of your autobiography," he said, "and I must say that if I'd known how high an opinion you had of me when we were young I would have been tempted to take even more advantage of your good nature than I did."

"But you did know how high an opinion I had of you," I responded. "It just wasn't in *your* good nature to take advantage of mine."

"You still regard me as the Hercules of virtue, eh? Even after all the pain I've caused you."

"It's less a matter of regard than of affection," I countered. "And such pain as I suffered on your account was inflicted, I'm sure, out of deference to more important considerations."

"Ahhh. I caused you pain in the service of some higher purpose, in other words."

"Is that really so outlandish a conception?"

"I'd be more inclined to characterize it as ludicrous," Marcus retorted. "Unless, of course, you regard the singleminded pursuit of my own selfish interests as more in keeping with perfect virtue than your single-minded devotion to the person you believed me to be."

I had no ready answer to this, and responded with an irritated shrug.

"Well, it's clear that I'm not going to convert you to my way of thinking just yet," said Marcus. "But you might want to consider, these next few days, whether the real reason you always regarded my virtue as so impeccable was that there was no other way you could regard my behavior toward you as that of a friend."

"I'll mull that over," I said after finally wresting some meaning from his words.

"You do that," Marcus riposted. "And while you're at it, there's some of *my* writing that I'd like you to mull over as well."

Saying that, he rose and walked into his house, emerging a few moments later carrying one thick scroll in each hand.

Watching him move, I noticed that there was much more animation in his stride than there'd been when we first arrived here, and then it came to me that he'd been displaying much more vitality in general. "You seem to be feeling a bit stronger these past few days," I said, brushing aside some vague misgivings I had about the wisdom of making reference to his health.

"It's seeing you again, dear Lucio," he responded with an exuberant smile. "Your effect on me is downright tonic."

"It does me good to see you again, too," I answered with perfect sincerity. But even as I spoke, I was thinking, I wish I'd had as benign an effect on my son.

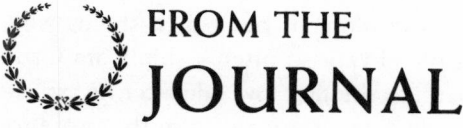
[OCTOBER 14TH]

Marcus paid an unexpected call on us this morning. He rode over to our house about the second hour and presented himself at our front door looking cheerful, vigorous, and fit. I greeted him and presented Portia and Camilla, both of whom were somewhat awestruck by his presence. He quickly put them at their ease, though, asking with all his practiced humility whether we could spare him a little food and drink after his "long journey" to our house. As the two of them bustled about preparing a plate of cheese and salt pork for him, he bent all his considerable charm and geniality to the task of drawing them out and making them smile. By the time he finished his breakfast, they both were utterly captivated, and I myself was beginning to feel the least bit jealous. My thoughts for some reason drifted back to the early days of our friendship, when Marcus used to make impromptu visits to Twopenny Street and the Hobnail. And all at once I remembered that I'd felt jealous then, too, every time I spied fresh evidence of his infatuation with my aunt Drusilla.

How sad it is that even after forty-five years I still can't feel love for anyone without fearing that someone else I love will steal my loved one away!

It was a fine autumn morning, bright, brisk, and blustery, with the wind whipping down clean and biting from the north. When Marcus offered to take me on a tour of our new Dumnonian domain I was quick, almost eager, to accept. He'd brought along a spare horse for me, a mare named Boudicea, who was, he assured me, "every bit as lazy as Incitatus." And so she turned out to be, as we slowly made our way up to the high ground that shelters our scattering of houses from the northerly gales. Once we gained the hilltop we had an unobstructed view in all directions: a green and dun-colored landscape of downs rolling away to the west and north, Britannia's slate and limestone coastline stretching away to the east, and the steely blue plain of the sea marching away toward its juncture with the sky at the southern horizon.

"See that little island there," said Marcus, pointing to a rocky citadel about a half mile off shore and roughly five miles to the east. "That's

Ictis, the Dumnonii's major tin depot. It's connected to the mainland by a causeway, which is submerged at the moment but which stands well clear of the water when the tide is out. Every so often a ship from Gaul or Hibernia will call at the island, and at the first low tide after its arrival you'll see Dumnonii men by the dozen carting ore out from the shore to be loaded aboard. They tell me that in the old days, before the big deposits were discovered in Tarraconensis, this region served as the primary source of tin for the entire western Empire. An average of two or three ships a day called here, whereas now there are no more than three or four a month." Marcus paused a moment and smiled a mirthless smile. "But the Dumnonii's loss is the Iberians' gain," he resumed at last, "and thus passes the glory of the world."

We rode along in a west-by-northwesterly direction, with Marcus pointing out various interesting features of the countryside. Then, on a rise, we caught sight of what appeared at first to be a monumental toadstool, but which proved as we drew nearer to be a rectangular slab of stone about fifteen feet square resting some six feet off the ground on three rough-hewn stone pillars.

"Exotic-looking, don't you think?" said Marcus as we brought our horses to a halt beside the strange apparition.

"What is it?" I asked.

"The Dumnonii call it a dolmen, which means 'table stone' in their language. They say it once stood at the core of a huge burial mound, built long before their tribe first settled here by warlike Celts, who were known as 'the People of the North,' and who practiced human sacrifice."

"Just like us Romans," I said, without consciously intending any irony. But Marcus burst out laughing all the same.

We rode on to the west and eventually came upon an upright circular stone, perhaps nine feet tall, that featured a circular hole some three feet wide in its center. "This was originally the entrance to a tomb, or so I'm reliably informed," Marcus commented. "And I have it on equally good authority that one can cure oneself of arthritis, scrofula, impetigo, impotence, and piles through the simple expedient of crawling through that hole three times against the sun."

And I thought: That, at least, would do you no more harm than consulting a doctor.

Half an hour's ride west of the circle stone was a Dumnonian settlement, huddled inside a twin-walled hill fort. Both the inner and outer walls were a good thirty feet high, with the latter some eight feet thick at the base and the former more than twice that. The ten-foot space between the walls was clearly designed as a death trap, since the outer gates faced north and south while the inner ones faced east and west. Having forced one of the exterior portals, a would-be marauder would find himself faced with an unenviable choice: he could either storm a fortified wall head-on or fight his way around to one of the interior portals under a doubly murderous hail of stones, arrows, and boiling pitch. The intimidating aspect of this formidable stronghold was only partly mitigated by the fact that both sets of gates were standing wide open on our arrival, and Marcus told me that as far as he knew they hadn't been closed for years. "Even here," he said in a voice commingling sarcasm and pride, "the Roman Peace prevails."

In the center of the fort's enclosure was a small marketplace and what passes in these parts for a tavern. Marcus and I, after purchasing some rock-hard bread, spent a quarter hour or so within the tavern's dingy confines enjoying a bowl of the local mead, which tastes like a happy mating of honey wine and cider but which is decidedly stronger than either.

"Did you read those scrolls I gave you the other day?" Marcus inquired as he gnawed on a granitic piece of bread.

"I read most of the first one," I replied, "and I would have read a great deal more if my Greek and your handwriting were a little better than they are."

Marcus smiled. "What do you think of what you've read so far?"

I paused to consider my reply. "I hope you won't be offended if I say that I found the work . . . rather austere."

At this Marcus laughed out loud, drawing to our table the concerted attention of the half-dozen dour Dumnonii in the tavern with us, none of whom appeared to have ever before encountered the phenomenon of laughter. "You're absolutely right, Lucio, and I'm not the least bit offended. I'd even go so far as to say that 'austere' is a charitable description."

"Did you intend it to be so . . . spare?"

Again Marcus laughed, though more quietly. "May the gods preserve your euphemistic soul," he said. "What I intended it to be was a sort of exercise in remedial morality, a highly edifying dialogue with myself on the subjects of Duty and Human Purpose. I wrote it to remind myself of all that I had once aspired to accomplish in my capacity as emperor, and to articulate for myself the values that I, as Caesar, was attempting to uphold."

"And you chose to express yourself in Greek because Greek is the native language of the Stoic creed."

"As always, Lucio, you give me too much credit," said Marcus, shaking his head. "I chose to express myself in Greek because Greek—especially written Greek—does not come as naturally to me as Latin, with the result that I was forced to concentrate much more intensely on what I was writing."

"I see. You used Greek as an aid to clear thinking."

"No, Lucio," Marcus responded, shaking his head once again. "I used Greek as a means of shutting out everything around me. I used it to exclude from my mind, for an hour or two every night, all traces of a world that no longer made sense and of a life that no longer held meaning."

I squinted at him in disbelief. "*You* felt that way?" I asked without bothering to mask my incredulity.

"Even I," Marcus affirmed with a cryptic smile.

"But it sounds like you were on the verge of despair," I objected.

"I wasn't on the verge, Lucio; I was over the edge."

"How terrible," I said. And then, "When did this happen?"

"The melancholy had been encroaching on my spirit for a decade or more, but it didn't begin to get the better of me until a year or so before your visit to my headquarters on the Danube."

"I see," I said again, thinking that what he'd just said made his behavior back in March a good deal easier to explain. "And when did you finally snap out of it?"

"Shortly after you set off on your return journey to Rome," Marcus replied, looking me straight in the eye.

"It would please me greatly to think that my visit had something to do with the revival of your spirits," I said.

"Then prepare to feel downright ecstatic, dear friend, for your visit had everything to do with my redemption."

"I don't understand," I said in all sincerity.

"I know," Marcus responded, rising to his feet. "Full explanations will be forthcoming as we proceed toward our various destinations."

The sun was west of the meridian as we rode out of the fort, and we headed west along with it for two or three miles until, arriving at the top of a bluff, we found ourselves gazing out at an endless expanse of dark blue white-capped water.

"Here we are!" said Marcus triumphantly.

"This is the Western Ocean!" I responded, my voice alive with excitement.

"Why so it is," was Marcus's reply. "The ocean that girdles the world . . . Well, what do you think of it?"

As I sat on my horse in the sunshine, with the wind off the water in my face, I thought of all the years that had passed since Marcus first showed me the sea, and of all the loved ones those years had swallowed up. "It's very impressive," I answered finally, with tears welling up in my eyes. "I wish I could have shown it to my son."

But this eloquent effusion of self-pity did not elicit from Marcus the expressions of heartfelt sympathy it was intended to. Instead, he frowned as though deep in thought and carefully dismounted.

"Forgive me, Lucio," he said as I followed his lead and lowered myself to the ground, "but I've been getting the impression, one way and another, that you feel responsible for your boy's death. Is my impression correct?"

"Yes," I answered. "I was responsible for both the fact of his passing and for the manner of it as well."

"I see," said Marcus, his expression still pensive. "If you don't mind talking about it, I'd be interested to know what it was you did, precisely, that resulted in his death."

"I made that journey up to Noricum to see you," I responded. "I foolishly allowed myself to become embroiled in the politics of choosing your successor, and thereby incurred the enmity of your son."

"Yes," said Marcus. "Go on."

"There's really not much more to say. It was your son's enmity I had to flee from, and it was my son who, in the process of facilitating my flight from yours, lost his life."

"I see," said Marcus, sitting down on the grass and gazing far out to sea. "So you're operating on the assumption that if you hadn't allowed yourself to become embroiled in Imperial politics, you would have lived out your life in peace and contentment on that little farm of yours near Lorium."

"Yes," I said sitting down beside him. "I don't think there's any question about it."

Marcus responded with a somber smile, "You were going to be a marked man when I died no matter what you did or didn't do beforehand."

"I don't understand."

"Don't be obtuse, Lucio. You know what kind of person Commodus is. You tutored him in athletics for—what was it?—three or four years."

"Yes," I acknowledged. "But I still don't see your point."

"Perhaps you don't want to see it," Marcus shot back.

"Perhaps. But I'm not aware of any such disinclination."

"Well, I'll make it as plain as possible. Given Commodus's character, and the character of those who serve him, it was inevitable that everyone who'd been closely connected to me and who failed on my death to make conspicuous demonstrations of their allegiance to him would be regarded as suspect at best and subversive by default. And as things have turned out even those who made the most profuse avowals of their loyalty and devotion are being persecuted and condemned to death simply because they were at one time or other closely associated with me. What I conclude from that, dear Lucio, is that you would have had to flee Italy eventually no matter what you did with regard to Commodus. So in that one respect at least you did nothing that contributed to your poor son's death."

"I could have opened my veins," I argued.

"What? And left your family at the mercy of Commodus's malice and caprice? No, Lucio; you served them best by taking them away."

"Perhaps," I responded in a sullen voice, still clinging tenaciously to my sense of guilt, "but that doesn't relieve me of the responsibility for letting that wheel roll over his leg."

"How could you have prevented that?" Marcus inquired blandly.

"By foreseeing the danger; that's how."

"Your son could have foreseen the danger, too, and your wife, and even your daughter."

"But I was the only one *responsible* for foreseeing it."

"How so? Is it the rule in your family that you alone are responsible for the safety of everyone else, that no one is responsible for himself except you, that no one except you cares about the welfare of the others? It was a freak chance, Lucio, from everything you've told me. One is always prone to discern portents of danger from hindsight after a calamity, but the fact is that only the most preternaturally overcautious among us take account of every conceivable hazard confronting those we love. What amount of money would you be prepared to wager on the proposition that a wagon standing on a downhill grade with its brake engaged and two horses motionless in its traces would all at once go a short distance backward at just the time when someone's limb was in a position to be run over? Not a large sum, I'm sure. The fact that something is foreseeable doesn't mean that one is bound to foresee it. The range of foreseeable contingencies is well-nigh infinite, and it is mere foolishness to suppose that you can guard against every hazard. You were unlucky, Lucio, tragically unlucky. And the concept of misfortune excludes the concept of blame."

I gave some thought to arguing the point further, but remembered what a futile exercise that was likely to be, so I quickly had resort to the one—as I thought—unanswerable argument that I'd been holding in reserve: "Whether I'm to blame for Decius's death is really beside the point, Marco. My real crime is that he went to his death believing that I despised him."

Marcus looked at me for a long while, his gaze intent but expressionless. "If by that you mean," he said at last, "that at precisely the time when you should have been making your son's last hours of life as free of suffering as possible you were indulging your passion for self-hate, then I agree that you are quite properly to be reproached. But to atone for the crime of self-absorption with an even greater concentration on yourself hardly seems sensible. The problem with you, dear Lucio, now as in our youth, is that you've always looked on self-loathing as a cardinal virtue, even on those occasions when it is nothing more than a refusal to face reality."

"What reality?" I demanded, even more sullen than before.

"The reality that your boy is *dead*, Lucio, and that all the self-loathing in the world won't bring him back to life."

For a moment I simply stared at Marcus, utterly—though unaccountably—astonished. "It won't?" I said finally, in a tone of childlike disillusion.

"Not even if you were to offer your own life in exchange."

"But you," I said, trying to stave off the agony of understanding, "you came back to life."

"Yes." Marcus nodded. "That is one of the few consolations we've been vouchsafed for our mortality—that we can die many times before death claims us, yet live on to experience rebirth. Alas, our power to effect a resurrection extends no further than ourselves; the power to resurrect another the gods have perpetually withheld."

I stared at him, still unbelieving, and he, with great compassion, gazed back at me. "He is dead, Lucio," he said at last, as the wind blew and the sun shone and the sea stretched away to the sky. And I, standing naked all at once before my grief, bowed my head with a sob and at last looked reality in the face.

 FROM THE
JOURNAL

[OCTOBER 18TH]

I've done a lot of thinking these past few days—about Decius and about myself. And one thing Marcus said to me as we looked out on the Western Ocean keeps returning to my thoughts: "You were indulging your passion for self-hate. . . ." How strange that sounded when he said it! And how strange it still sounds whenever I bring it to mind! But strange-sounding as it is, there continues to be something compelling about the idea. I spent most of yesterday looking over my Life, and the theme of self-disdain is unmistakable. If anyone—such as Agricus—had ever treated me with as much disrespect as I consistently treated myself, I would have erupted in self-righteous fury. Yet I read through what I've written without finding one instance of compassion for my sorrows or tolerance for my shortcomings. And Marcus was right—every time I blundered or misspoke I would revile myself with a veritable passion, as if I took deep visceral pleasure in doing so and was delighted to have the opportunity.

What kind of madness is this?

What possible purpose does it serve?

It occurred to me at one point that Nestor might be able to shed some light on such questions. Then I realized that I hadn't caught a glimpse of him for quite some while. I mentioned this to Marcus the next time we met, and he told me that Nestor had left for Hibernia a day or two after our arrival, but expected to return before the end of the month. I said that it struck me as odd that he'd departed so abruptly without even saying good-bye, but Marcus made excuses for him, saying that he'd been wanting to visit Hibernia for quite some time and that the opportunity to go there arose quite suddenly, necessitating a hurried departure. What, I inquired, was the appeal of such an obscure and out-of-the-way place. Marcus replied that he couldn't imagine but expected that "our mutual friend" would enlighten us when he got back. Then he asked me what I'd wanted to discuss with Nestor, and after a flicker of hesitation I told him.

"But Nestor has already talked to you about how to answer those kinds of questions," Marcus averred.

"He has?" I responded dim-wittedly. (Ah, ha! Self-hatred caught in the act.)

"Why, of course," said Marcus. "He told you to write your autobiography."

I gaped at him for several moments. "Are you suggesting that I resume writing it now?"

"Only if you want to understand your self-hate," he replied.

"But Nestor never said anything about my Life explaining my self-hate."

"Oh? And what did he say your Life was for?"

"He said that writing it would help me overcome my fear of death."

"Ahhh," said Marcus with a sly smile. "Could it be that understanding your hatred of yourself is in many respects equivalent to mastering your fear of death?"

"It's possible, I suppose," I acknowledged.

"Why not write another chapter or two and see," he suggested, affecting a certain artlessness.

"All right, I guess I will," I responded with no great enthusiasm.

And having delivered myself of that grudging affirmation, I suppose that now I must.

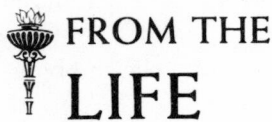
When I think back on Greece, I remember light—a shimmering crystalline radiance spilling from the sky and reflecting off the sea and the land. That spring and summer of my youth there was hardly any darkness at all, or so it seemed. I would awaken to the indigo stillness of dawn, pass the daylight hours bedazzled by dust and heat, and then savor the endlessly waning afterglow of evening until it yielded at last to a vision of stars and the brief inanition of sleep. If there are any consolations for the pain and confusion of adolescence, I believe they reside in such memories of earthly exhilaration and celestial light. For youth is no feast of joy, as some sentimental patriarchs maintain. It is an apprenticeship in sorrow, made bearable by an ignorance of time.

Heron's porous sailboat carried Marcus and me from Ithaca to Kyllene, where our three companions were awaiting us in various stages of anxiety, curiosity, and irritation. Once reunited, we traversed the northwest coast of the Peloponnesus, passing through Dyme and Patrai on successive days and coming eventually to Rion, where for half an hour or so we debated the question of whether we should proceed to Athens via Delphi and Thebes or continue along the coast road toward our objective, visiting Aigion, Sikyon, and Corinth along the way. Marcus argued strongly for the northern route, saying that Delphi rivaled, and in some respects surpassed, Athens as a place of pilgrimage, and adding that Corinth, as a Roman colony of relatively recent foundation, would hold no more interest for us than, say, Bovillae or Beneventum. Listening to him, I could not help wondering whether Marcus, in light of the unprecedented drinking, whoring, and, most recently, killing he'd engaged in since our departure from Rome, was feeling the need for an interlude of temperance and reflection. But if that was in fact the case, he was destined for disappointment. For Agricus registered a rare forensic triumph over him, pointing out that, Roman colony or not, Corinth was widely acknowledged to be the bawdiest city, not just in the Empire, but in the world, and adding that the best time for us to visit Delphi was clearly not now but in three months time, when the quadrennial Pythian Games were due

to be held, with me—he added glibly—as one of the principal participants. We continued, accordingly, along the Peloponnesian coast, and
if our reasons for choosing to travel to our destination by way of Corinth
were to some extent discreditable, we could always take comfort from
the thought that our zest for the fleshly pleasures was showing few signs
of satiation.

And, in fairness to our better natures, our minds as we made our way
toward Athens were for the most part taken up with a great many more
edifying concerns than those connected with the grosser appetites. The
district of Greece we were traveling through so bristled with historical
and legendary associations that we would no sooner put one behind us
than another would loom up ahead. On the shore at Aigion, for example,
was the Temple of Zeus of the Assembly, so named because it stands on
the site where Agamemnon gathered together all the kings of Homeric
Greece to fashion an alliance against Troy. And no sooner did we leave
Aigion than the slopes of Mount Helicon of the Muses became visible,
far away to the northeast across the waters of the Corinthian Gulf. Every
mile or so, it seemed, we would come upon another natural or man-made
reminder of some god or hero or monarch or tyrant who had worked out
a part of his destiny within the precincts of ancient Arcadia. Here, where
Artemis and Herakles had hunted, where Tyndareus and Leonidas had
marched, three boys, a soldier, and a trader rode along toward Athene's
city, our eyes wide and our ears closely attending as the shadows and
the whispers of the glory that was Hellas conjured eddies and faint echoes
in the light of Roman Greece.

As was more or less predictable—at least in retrospect—we did very little
in the brothels of Corinth that we hadn't done in the brothels of Capua
ten days before. We did a great deal more of it, however, largely because
there were so many more establishments where it could be done. The
entire city seemed to be one vast bordello, a consequence, I suppose, of
Corinth's unique location by the narrow isthmus where the sea routes
from Italy and the Ionian meet those from Asia and the Aegean. Aside
from port operations and prostitution, the economic life of the city and
its environs appeared to revolve around the transport of ships' cargoes,
and sometimes of ships themselves, across the three-mile-wide neck of
land that separates the Corinthian from the Saronic gulf. During one of
our infrequent respites from venery and drink we rode down to the high
ground overlooking the *diolkos*—the paved track that bisects the isthmus—
and watched a two-masted freighter make the transit from east to west.

It was an interesting spectacle to witness, as teams of slaves and oxen, with the aid of heavy winches, pulled the ship up onto a huge thick-wheeled platform at the water's edge and then slowly hauled it westward. In this task the vessel's sails were of considerable assistance, having been rigged so as to take advantage of the stiff northeasterly breeze that was blowing. "There you have the very essence of the Greeks' mentality," said Hieronymous as the platform and its burden approached the far end of the *diolkos*. "If there's money to be made in the enterprise, they'll undertake to sail a ship across dry land."

At Corinth we were within two days' ride of our ultimate destination, and as the third straight day of our isthmian debauch was dawning we decided that the time had come to conclude our revels and address the last leg of our journey. This was, in several pertinent respects, a thoroughly commendable decision. But it was also, in several other respects, catastrophically ill-advised. Decisions made toward the end of a long bout of carousal and fornication are seldom based on a careful assessment of all the benefits and disadvantages they may entail, a sad truth we had occasion to remember some ten or twelve miles down the Corinth-to-Megara road, when the dazzling Greek light about which we had all waxed so rhapsodic began to compound the effects of too much wine and too little sleep, thereby inducing in some of us pronounced feelings of vertigo, nausea, and suffocation. Happily, the road we were traveling on ran right alongside the sea, and moments after Hieronymous had shown us the way, Marcus and I half slid, half toppled off our horses and went staggering after him into the deliciously cool and salty water. Like him, we floated there, spread-eagled and face down, for as long as our lungs would sustain us. And we would have been quite content to take a nap in that undignified position had not the exigencies of respiration dictated otherwise.

Feeling moderately revived, we finally emerged from Poseidon's domain and resumed our eastward progress. And after a comatose night at an inn in Megara, we were ready at last to effect our journey's end.

Some five miles east of Megara we caught our first glimpse of the island of Salamis, where the people of Athens had fled after Thermopylae and from which they had witnessed the destruction of Xerxes' fleet by the "wooden walls" flotilla that Themistocles had persuaded them to build. Some ten miles down the road from that point we entered Eleusis of the Mysteries, and after an hour or so spent visiting the Telesterion and other famous sites we set off on the Sacred Way, craning our necks every quarter or eighth of a mile in the hopes of spying the rocky crown of Mount Lycabettus, at whose feet lay our Periclean goal.

There is nothing much new to be said about Athens, except, perhaps, that the extensive contributions made by the Emperor Hadrian and the Sophist senator Herodes Atticus to its inventory of architectural marvels has served to reiterate and reaffirm its inimitable splendor.

It was our fate to stay as guests in the latter's palace, an establishment unequaled in magnificence by anything I'd ever seen in Rome, even on the Palatine. We owed our welcome there to Herodes' close friendship with Hadrian, and, apart from Marcus, we quickly accustomed ourselves to levels of luxury that were in ludicrous contrast to the standards of discomfort we'd grown used to on our journey. For Agricus the palace was the consummation of a dream, and during the first several days we were in residence he was so exhilarated by his good fortune that he forgot to be disagreeable. Alas, enough of the novelty wore off in the days that followed for him to lapse into his old abrasive habits; but his beatitude, for as long as it lasted, was for me one of the highlights of our stay.

Marcus had decidedly mixed feelings about the lavish hospitality being showered on us, and even went so far as to petition Herodes' majordomo for a plank-and-skin pallet to replace his sleeping couch, alleging that he found it impossible to get a good night's rest on any piece of furniture that had been defiled by upholstery. Of course what he was really after was some cramped and airless cubicle within reasonable distance of where the rest of us were wallowing in excess. But the palace was simply too grand and too enormous to afford him the humble privations he hungered for. He had to make do with his pallet, and with the excitement of discovering Athens and its proverbially disputatious citizen body.

The most eminent among this population appeared, in a steady succession, night after night, around Herodes' table—politicians, philosophers, dramatists, rhetors, actors, great beauties (of both sexes), great ladies, and even an occasional famous athlete. For Hieronymous these dinners were a veritable, as well as literal, feast, and he vigorously expounded his philosophy of laughter to all who would listen to his arguments, delighting most when a Sophist or rhetor or some other sage would take issue with what he was saying and try to refute him. There was a tremendous volume of vehement give-and-take in these discussions, some of it amicable. But what impressed me most about them was that not once, after all the expatiations and interpositions, did anyone alter anyone else's opinion about anything.

Marcus would participate in portions of these symposia in an amiably Socratic capacity, posing nice questions and elucidating fine distinctions without in any way associating himself with the views of the disputants. As for myself, for once in my life I had the good sense to sit back and

enjoy the spectacle. Together with Dracena, who was equally removed
from all the intellectual ebullition, I simply listened and observed, silently
relishing all the extravagant luxuries and flamboyant entertainments that
I had no expectation of ever experiencing again. Yes, bizarre as the notion
sounds and much as it pains me to admit it, the time I spent in Herodes'
palace can only be reckoned as happy.

The idyll did not last long, however, for toward the middle of June the
great athlete Aelius Granianus of Sikyon paid a visit to Athens and accepted one of Herodes' invitations to dinner. Although only twenty-one
years old, Aelius had already established himself as one of the foremost athletes of his time. He'd won the boys' stade race at Olympia five
years earlier and had gone on to claim victories in that event at Nemea
the following year and at Corinth and Delphi the year after, completing
a sweep of the Panhellenic festivals and earning the title *periodonikes* at the
age of eighteen. He'd then graduated to the men's competitions, and at
the next Olympics had won not only the diaulos but also the race in
armor and the pentathlon as well—an unprecedented and, so far, unparalleled achievement. He was destined to become *periodonikes* in the
pentathlon a year after we met, and casting furtive glances at him while
dinner was being served, I could see why a boy who'd started as a mere
runner had risen to preeminence in an event that demanded not just speed
but also the strength and agility to jump, throw the javelin, hurl the
discus, and wrestle his fellow competitors to the ground. The one thing
that struck me most forcibly about him was his repose. I don't think I'd
ever before seen anyone so perfectly self-contained and at ease. He was
also, despite an incomparable physique and a fine-boned hawklike visage,
completely lacking in vanity, with regard to his athletic prowess no less
than his appearance.

When Marcus, to my great embarrassment, told him about the minor
victories I'd won at Venusia, Aelius, without the least trace of condescension, congratulated me and elicited details of the competition. "I
think that in many respects it's harder for a gifted athlete to win on the
Novice Circuit," he said with perfect sincerity, "than on the Circuit itself.
The judges tend to be much more biased in favor of local talent, and the
tactics employed by one's opponents tend to be far more unscrupulous
and injurious."

Hearing this, Marcus told him of my misadventure at the turning post
in the diaulos and went on to describe how Agricus had poured oil into
the starting grooves by way of retaliation.

"You went out and ran the long race after being knocked cold rounding the post?" Aelius asked me. And I, blushing violently, nodded yes.

"Clearly, you've been blessed with the gift of speed," said Aelius, "and from what Marcus Annius Verus has just told me and you yourself have just confirmed, it's equally clear that you've been endowed with a runner's heart. Given these two attributes, I suspect that it might be worth your while, here in Athens, to have a top-flight *gymnastes* observe your form and assess your prospects for a professional career."

"Did you have any particular *gymnastes* in mind?" asked Marcus, smiling broadly.

And the very next day I was introduced to Polyaenus.

[OCTOBER 21ST]

I found Marcus sitting on his stool by his front door when I paid my regular call on him this morning. He did not look well. His face was ashen, his eyes bleary, and his lips the color of mortifying flesh. I guess my surprise and dismay with regard to his appearance were visible on my face, because he gave me a wan smile on my arrival and said, "I had a bit of trouble falling asleep last night. Too little rest here in my dotage always makes me look like death."

I refrained from confirming that that was exactly what he looked like. "Perhaps you'd like to spend tonight with us," I said instead, thinking that he shouldn't be left alone in his condition.

"Gracious! Do I look that bad?" he responded with a little laugh.

"No, of course not," I replied. "It's just that Portia and Camilla enjoy your company so much, and we have this empty room."

"What about you, Lucio?" he asked me in a faintly sardonic tone. "Do you enjoy my company too?"

"What a question!" I exclaimed, feeling a little offended. "How on earth could you be in doubt about that?"

"Oh, I know you love me, Lucio," Marcus responded, his voice sounding weak with exhaustion all of a sudden as he leaned back on his stool and let his head rest against the wall of the cottage. "It's just that there are parts of me that I've never known you to acknowledge."

"What do you mean?" I asked.

He was silent a moment or two, then opened his eyes and looked at me. "In your Life, Lucio," he said, "there is a strange gap between your account of what transpired on Ithaca and your chronicle of our journey from Kyllene to Athens."

"A gap?" I said, trying to think what incident I'd neglected to include.

"Yes, Lucio, a gap."

I pondered before confessing, "I don't have any idea what you're referring to."

"No, I don't suppose you do," Marcus concurred resignedly, after assessing me.

"Well . . . ?" I said into a lengthening silence.

"You saw me kill a man, Lucio," Marcus responded in a tired monotone. "You saw me kill a man in order to stay one up on Agricus. You objected to the idea of my killing him before the murder took place, yet you never once raised the issue with me in the days and months that followed. And in your Life, moreover—the latest installment of which I read last night— you blithely proceeded from my murdering Adonis to an account of the last leg of our journey, with no more than one paltry passing reference to the crime you'd watched me commit."

As Marcus was speaking, his voice became steadily harsher, and by the time he'd said what he had to say, I could not help feeling that I was being rebuked. "You disappoint me, Lucio," he announced finally, thereby confirming my impression and causing me no little pain.

"But the slave was trying to make you submit to the madwoman," I argued, desperate to escape the agony of his disapproval. "And those poor boys—you were thinking of them when you . . ."

I never got to finish what I was saying, because Marcus, quivering with rage, rose to his feet with his face horribly discolored and bellowed at me, "Don't you *dare* make excuses for me, Lucius Aurelius Verus Celer, or for yourself on my behalf. Your love for me is worth *nothing* if it's based on a denial of what I am."

I stared at Marcus, appalled. And also frightened, knowing that such violent emotion would take its toll on him. And in fact he sank back down onto his stool after he'd spoken, visibly spent and despairing. "Forgive me, Lucio," he said in a voice so weak that I could hardly make out his words. "If I loved you less, I'd be far less prone to incivility."

It came to me when he said that, that all the trouble he'd gone to in order to save me from Commodus bespoke a great deal more than mere benevolence. I realized suddenly that there was something he wanted from me, something vitally important to him that I alone could provide. I hadn't the vaguest idea what that something was, but the fact that there was still some way I could be of service to him lifted my spirits and filled my heart. "For over forty years I bewailed your indifference," I said to him, paraphrasing the letter he'd written me on the occasion of Anto-ninus's death, "so I welcome your anger now. Only a friend could have spoken so honestly."

It took him a moment or two to identify the echo, but when he did he gave me a loving smile. "Am I still welcome in your house tonight, dear Lucio?" he asked.

"Of course you are," I answered.

"Thank you," he said, almost humbly. "There's no better refuge for a tired old man than the house of an honest friend."

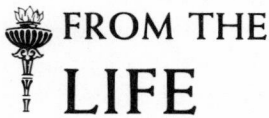
Polyaenus was the sweetest and most diffident man I'd ever met, and one whose achievements as a *gymnastes* rendered his diffidence incomprehensible. Small and wiry, with a shock of snow-white hair crowning a square-jawed, bright-eyed face, he had come to training after a moderately successful competitive career that had included dolichos victories at Olympia and Nemea. Those two victories, while by no means flukes, had each come as something of a surprise to the athletic fraternity and were tributes—if Polyaenus is to be believed—to what exhaustive preparation, polished form, and all-out effort can sometimes achieve despite "the handicap of mediocre talent." And in truth Polyaenus had managed only a few dozen victories in a career that had spanned fifteen years, which meant that he'd lost at least ten times as many races as he'd won. (A "great" runner like Kallistos, by contrast, could look back on a career of comparable length and count at least as many victories as defeats.) But as a *gymnastes* Polyaenus was without a peer. By combining his sharp eye for competitive ability with the most detailed understanding of the runner's art, he had turned out some fifteen or twenty athletes who among them had won well over twice as many races as they'd lost and who had accounted for no fewer than seventy victories in the last ninety Panhellenic races. Even I, who'd known little about athletics before coming to Greece, had heard of him and felt intimidated by his fame. I was totally unprepared, accordingly, for the shy, soft-spoken, and diminutive old fellow to whom Aelius introduced me.

Our first meeting took place in the middle of the great stadium Herodes had just had rebuilt to serve as the athletic focus of the annual Panathenaic festivals. Constructed entirely of gleaming Pentelic marble, the interior of the empty stadium was so deluged by direct and reflected sunlight that I found it necessary to shade my eyes and squint when I first entered the arena. Aelius and Polyaenus, on the other hand, having competed, and triumphed, in the molten summer heat that stadia such as Olympia's and Nemea's are notorious for compounding, seemed inured to the blinding brightness.

After the formalities of introduction were concluded, Polyaenus turned to me and in characteristic fashion said, "Perhaps you might be willing to run down to the turning post and back." It took me a few moments to realize that he was requesting me to display my form. "Three-quarter speed might serve on the way to the post," he said as I was about to start off, "and you might consider a sprint coming back." I complied with his suggestions and then waited, slightly winded, for his verdict. But all I got was, "It would be helpful if you'd run at three-quarter speed around the perimeter of the arena." Again I did as he suggested, eager to hear what he had to say about my prospects for an athletic career. He still wasn't ready to commit himself, however. "I'd be much obliged if you'd sprint diagonally from the northwest to the southeast corner of the arena, then jog a quarter of the way around the perimeter to your right, sprint the southwest-to-northeast diagonal, jog right again, sprint southeast-to-northwest, jog once more, sprint northeast-to-southwest, and then jog back to your northwest starting point." Only slightly daunted, I launched myself on this formidable exercise, which—I calculated a few hours later—involved about a mile's worth of running, more than half of it at a sprint. I was in a rather sorry state, accordingly, when I completed the undertaking and would have collapsed on the ground if I hadn't thought it would give an unfortunate impression.

Polyaenus chatted with Aelius briefly while I struggled to catch my breath, but finally turned to me and inquired, "Would you be interested in hearing my opinion?" Unable to speak, I simply nodded. "Well then," he said, "this is what I think: you are, as your body is now informing you, in something less than top competitive form. You haven't the musculature to be consistently successful in the stade race, and your slight build will hamper you in the diaulos as well. Your three-quarter stride is very compact and smooth, however. But you carry your head too far back, your feet tend to be splayed when they strike the ground, your arm motion is primitive, and you don't know how to breathe properly. Now, as to your athletic prospects, at your age intensive training should round you into reasonable competitive form inside of a month, but there's not much to be done about your physique. The defects in your running style can be remedied with sufficient application and instruction, though. So, in sum, I would say that, given a modicum of courage and determination, you could make quite a name for yourself in the long race and a fairly substantial living as well. For you can run, my boy, make no mistake about it; and once you smooth away the rougher aspects of your style, your three-quarter stride will be something quite exquisite to behold."

For several moments I just stood there gasping, not altogether certain that what he'd said had been what I'd been hoping to hear. But after due consideration I had to acknowledge that his assessment of my talent was not entirely uncomplimentary, and I had my wits sufficiently about me to say, "Thank you."

"It might make sense," he responded, "if we were to meet here at sunrise for the next few days and start preparing you for competition."

"It might indeed," said Aelius with a broad Apollonian smile.

And indeed it most certainly did.

I lived a very full life the next month or so, rising at first light and, at Polyaenus's "suggestion," jogging from Herodes' palace at the foot of the Pnyx past the Temple of Nike and the Theater of Dionysus on the southern slopes of the Acropolis down to the Itonian Gate and then east along the river Illisos to Hadrian's Bridge and the stadium. Polyaenus would be waiting for me there and would present me with my breakfast, which consisted of two large lemons, a handful of walnuts, a small piece of fresh bread soaked in Hymettus honey, and a *dikotylon* of fresh spring water. Then, for an hour or so, we would work on my form, which, in Polyaenus's system, was broken down into what he called the three "aspects" of running: the start, the sustaining stride, and the sprint. Toward the end of the second hour he would dismiss me, but not before providing me with uncharacteristically strict instructions as to what I was to eat for lunch and dinner—usually more in the way of nuts, fruits, bread, honey, and water. I would then set off on my return jog to Herodes' palace, where I would hurriedly bathe and strigil myself, emerging from the baths in time to join Marcus, Agricus, Hieronymous, and a dozen or so young Athenian scholars for Herodes' daily lecture on rhetoric, which, appropriately enough, was never less than a treat to listen to, despite the fact that he spoke in Greek. Lunch and an hour's sleep followed the lecture, and oh, how I relished them both! Naps concluded, we would set off to discover Athens, starting with the Acropolis on our first afternoon and proceeding day by day in ever-widening concentric circles until we reached the city walls. Toward the end of the ninth hour we would return to the palace for dinner with our host and yet another array of illustrious guests. I could seldom stay for the entire meal, since Polyaenus prescribed a full night's sleep, from dusk to dawn, for all athletes who had "respect for their vocation."

During the first few days of July, Polyaenus altered my schedule and ushered me into the next phase of my training. I still rose at dawn, but instead of jogging two miles to the stadium, I jogged seven miles around the city walls. Then, after Herodes' lecture, a light lunch, and a nap, I would run at my "sustaining stride" to the stadium and train there in the

heat of the day with the half-dozen other runners—Aelius among them—
who comprised what was colloquially referred to as our *gymnastes'* "stable."

"As a distance runner you must learn how to live with the sun," Polyaenus explained to me. "You must accustom yourself to the most terrible
heat and thirst, because all the most important games, apart from the
Isthmian, take place in high summer, and in all of those games the dolichos
is contested in midafternoon."

And so I learned the strategies for "living with the sun," from the most
obvious ones, like repeatedly dousing my body with water, to the more
esoteric, like anointing my shoulders and hair with an especially viscous
oil that reflected away some of Helios's heat.

By the middle of July, Polyaenus judged me far enough advanced to
try my legs in a race. I think he may have been rushing things a bit, but,
as always, he had his reasons. It wouldn't have been a good idea for me
to make my debut in a major competition, such as the Panathenaea,
which was to take place at the end of the month. So around about the
twelfth before the Kalends of August—or, in Greek parlance, the fifteenth
Hecatombaeon—I, along with Polyaenus and the rest of his stable, set
off for Hypata, in Thessaly, three days distant, to compete in that city's
biennial games in honor of Hermes, who, among his other attributes, is
the patron deity of all runners.

Polyaenus had a rule that all the athletes who trained under his supervision should not only compete in the same festivals but also travel
to and from the cities involved together. This policy permitted those of
us in his stable to continue our training en route to wherever we happened
to be going. In the middle of each day, two or three of us at a time
would run some five or six miles toward our destination while the others
followed along behind us with our horses. By the end of each afternoon
we'd all had a chance to extend ourselves a little without becoming too
fatigued, although there were stretches of road in the more mountainous
regions we passed through that taxed our energies to no mean extent.
None of us felt any inclination to complain, though, because by combining training with travel Polyaenus rendered both a good deal less
tedious. And the practice had the additional advantage of fostering ca-
maraderie among us, which was especially important for me, since, as a
"westerner" whose native tongue was Latin, I was patently out of place
in a profession peculiar to the Greek-speaking east; and if I hadn't had
the friendship of my stablemates to sustain me, I'd have been considerably
more distressed than I was by the hostility of the more xenophobic athletes
I encountered as opponents.

Our route to Hypata ran through the heart of mainland Greece: first

Eleusis of the Mysteries and then Plataea, where the natives of Hellas won their great victory over the Persian prince Mardonius. From Plataea we continued west to Thespiae, at the foot of Mount Helicon, where I was to compete four times, and win twice, in the games in honor of the Muses. From Thespiae we struck north for Orchomenus and Elatea, arriving at noon on the third day of our trip at the fabled pass of Thermopylae between Mount Callidromus and the sea. From Thermopylae it was only twenty-five miles up the Sperchius River valley to Hypata, a dusty town at the foot of Mount Oeta, where we were to compete the next day.

The biennial games at Hypata were a distinctly minor event on the calendar of Greek games, just as the host city was a decidedly undistinguished addition to the roster of Greek *poleis*. But the games' lack of distinction entailed advantages as well as disadvantages for the participants. Foremost among the former was the absence of qualifying heats, which was directly attributable to the fact that relatively few athletes took the trouble to show up. Foremost among the latter was the comparative meagerness of the prizes awaiting the victors, even though, to my impressionable eyes, they looked anything but insubstantial.

As at Venusia, the boys' events were contested first, and Polyaenus suggested that it might be a good idea for me to participate in all three of the foot races, even though I was expected to do well in only one of them. "You'll get a taste of the competition and a good look at your opponents," he said in reference to the stade and the diaulos. "Just run hard, learn what you can, and stay well clear of the herd at the turning post."

I did as instructed and made quite a respectable showing, finishing fifth out of nine in the stade and third out of eleven in the diaulos. "Now remember," said Polyaenus to me as the competitors in the dolichos were called to the line, "stay on the outside of the pack and no more than ten paces from the leader. Make your bid at the start of the final lap, so that you're not hemmed in the last time you round the post."

The dolichos at Hypata was only seven laps, or fourteen lengths of the stadium. I thought this might be to my advantage, since I would have more energy left at the end. I can't think why it didn't occur to me that all my opponents would have more energy left then, too.

I knew I was in trouble right from the start, because the lead runner set what seemed to me a blistering pace. I had not yet heard the time-honored runner's rhyme: "The shorter the race, the crueler the pace." But I could tell I was facing an altogether different level of competition from that which I'd encountered at Venusia.

Staying within ten paces of the leader proved to be no easy task, and by the time I came out of the turn at the end of the sixth lap I'd expended almost all the energy I'd expected to have left over. I wasn't totally spent, though, and so despite the murderous pain I was feeling, I lowered my head and lengthened my stride. Almost to my surprise, I immediately began to gain ground on the leader, and I caught and passed him coming out of the final turn. To my unalloyed shock, however, two other runners proceeded to sprint past *me*, and though I forced myself to the last inch of my endurance I couldn't catch up with them before they crossed the line.

But Polyaenus, to my everlasting astonishment, was not at all displeased with me. He felt I'd done quite well, in fact. "You see now," he said to me, "that winning on the Circuit demands great sacrifice, and that one must run with the mind as well as the legs."

To illustrate the point, he had me sit next to him the following day and watch Aelius compete in the men's diaulos. Even before the race began I could see that the great athlete's customary repose, which I'd always deemed so perfect, had been heightened to an almost spiritual level by the intensity of his involvement with the task at hand. "You see," said Polyaenus, "how he focuses himself and achieves communion with the god."

"Which god?" I asked.

"The god within him. The power that lifts him above the pain of effort and into the realm of ecstatic motion."

Then the race began, and at a pace that looked remarkably like a sprint. "Are they going to run that fast for the entire distance?" I asked Polyaenus.

Instead of answering me, he pointed at Aelius, who was gliding along, his beautiful body shining with oil, ten feet ahead of his closest pursuers. "Look at his head," Polyaenus instructed me. And when I did I felt emotion grip my throat. Aelius's noble visage was utterly still, except that it moved straight forward with his body. "You see," said Polyaenus, "it doesn't loll from side to side or bob up and down. That is the perfection of form—when the body becomes a moving pedestal for the all-commanding mind."

The two of us watched in silence as Aelius won the race.

"One day in the not-too-distant future," Polyaenus said to me as the victor took his lap of honor, "you will be running and in great pain. But all at once, because you have trained well, your body will align itself, and your mind will sense the alignment and rejoice."

He stopped talking and turned his gaze toward the vision of Aelius triumphant. "Then you will know what he knows," he continued softly, "and you will be ready to bear the terrible burden of winning."

[OCTOBER 24TH]

What a remarkable transformation we've all undergone since Marcus came to live with us three days ago. Of course it wasn't his intention to stay here permanently when he accepted my invitation, but he hasn't been well enough to be left unattended, and we, in any case, would be extremely reluctant to let him go. His presence has in some magical way lifted the pall we've all been under since Decius died. Even in his enfeebled condition he provides us with a focus for our existence that Decius's death somehow destroyed. His effect on Camilla has been especially dramatic, perhaps because of his uncanny ability to meet her on her own ground without in any way condescending or acting coy. He seems to take great and genuine pleasure in playing knucklebones with her and will read to her contentedly by the hour. Sometimes, when there's an interval of sunshine between the long spells of fog and rain, the two of them will sit outside together in perfect serenity, he dozing a little off and on and she doing her lessons or her sewing. They seem to be able to communicate without words or gestures much of the time, as if each has a special awareness of the other that renders normal give-and-take not only superfluous but distracting. Unquestionably they are kindred spirits, this tired old Emperor and my solemn little girl, but more than that, they are good friends.

The effect that Marcus has had on Camilla has served to lift Portia's and my spirits as well. But Portia seems to derive great additional satisfaction from having him in the house to take care of. And he does require her care, alas, for he is very frail. Yet in his frailty Portia appears to have discovered a new sense of purpose for herself. Perhaps she feels that in caring for him she can do for him all she was unable to do for our son and thereby ease the terrible pain of her thwarted solicitude. But she likes him, too; I can tell that. And how could she not? Frail as he is, he's lost none of his old self-effacing charm.

And although he constantly threatens to relieve us of his "burdensome presence," it is clear to me that he very much enjoys his new circumstances. He even went so far as to tell me the other day that he found his room in our house peculiarly congenial because, apart from his pallet and a stool, it is absolutely bare. "You can't imagine how much it means to me," he said, "to be able at last to indulge my ascetic passions to the full."

As for myself, I'm pleased beyond measure to have him so readily available for conversation at any time of day or night. For though it's true of close friends that they can often pick up where they left off even after the longest separations, it's also true that they will find each other changed by the passage of the years. So in a sense I am getting to know Marcus all over again, to recognize old traits that have withstood time's deformations—his sly sense of humor, for example—and to discover new traits, such as his heightened emotionality, that have emerged from his experience of life.

In one key respect, it seems to me, he hasn't changed much at all, because he continues to be reticent about himself. But I discovered this evening that this reticence itself has changed: it is no longer an impenetrable wall, proof against any and all would-be intruders, but has become merely an opaque curtain that he is quite prepared to pull aside upon request. I discovered this more or less by accident. As we sat chatting after dinner, reminiscing about this and that, he was seized by one of his terrible coughing spasms, and I could do nothing but stand there as he sat doubled over, his eyes running, his face scarlet, and fought what looked like a losing battle for breath. As always, the seizure left him shaken and exhausted, and as I helped him to his room I unthinkingly raised the question of whether I ought to alert the *singulares* who accompanied him here from Noricum to the fact that he desperately needed medical attention.

"There'd be no point to that," he wheezed as he sank down onto his pallet. "There's nothing any doctor can do."

"Are you quite certain?" I asked as I covered him with a blanket and placed his rolled-up cloak beneath his head.

"Quite," he whispered as he closed his eyes and folded his hands on top of his chest.

For several moments he just lay there, his mouth agape and his breathing labored. But then his eyes opened, and he nodded toward the stool at the foot of the bed. "Sit with me a while," he said in a breathy voice. And I gladly did as I was asked.

"Do you know what you're suffering from?" I inquired, leaning toward him.

"Too long life," he answered with a wheezy chuckle.

"No; seriously."

"I'm *being* serious," he replied. "Most men don't have your athlete's constitution, you know. As they get older, things start to go wrong."

"But usually there's something in particular," I objected.

"Not in my case," he said. "In my case there's been a generalized deterioration, or so competent medical authorities have repeatedly assured me."

"You're still being facetious, Marco," I said in a tone of mild reproach.

"Not really," he responded. "According to the doctors, I have a 'weak heart,' whatever that means, which is connected in some exotic way to an 'insufficiency of the lungs,' which has resulted, through the mediation of some mysterious process, in an 'enlargement of the liver,' which has precipitated, in some obscure manner, a 'weakness of the kidneys,' which has led—inevitably, or so I'm told—to an 'imbalance of the humors,' which means, as far as I can make out, that I have an excess of phlegm, a deficiency of bile, a thinness of the blood, and a superfluity of wax in the ears."

"That's quite a diagnosis," I conceded, and Marcus acknowledged the concession with a grave little bow of his head.

"It certainly is," he said. "But the doctors, in their wisdom, neglected to consider the one organ in my body that is most responsible, in my opinion, for the onset of my galloping decrepitude."

"And which organ is that?" I inquired.

"The one you know best, dear Lucio—my mind."

"I'm not sure I follow you," I said after considering his statement, "unless you're referring to the despair you mentioned the other day."

"That's precisely what I'm referring to, as it happens."

"So what you're saying, if I understand you correctly, is that your bodily deterioration was ultimately attributable to the condition of your mind."

"You understand me impeccably. And remember: it was your visit to my camp on the Danube that brought me out of that slough of despond."

"I do recall your saying that, believe me; and I'd like *you* to remember that you promised to tell me how my visit accomplished that remarkable feat of resurrection."

"And so I shall, in due time."

"That's fair enough. But I'd also be interested to know how you came to be in such a despairing condition in the first place."

"Ah, well, that, I believe, is relatively easy to explain. But I should warn you, out of deference to our friendship, that it's rather a long story."

"I have no pressing engagements that I'm aware of," I said.

"Very well," Marcus responded with a smile, "but I'll still make every effort to be concise."

Then, for a moment or two, his eyes closed, and I thought he might have dropped off to sleep. He hadn't, though, and in a slow contemplative voice he began to speak.

"Old Pius was lucky he died when he did. In his twenty-three years as Hadrian's successor the Empire languished in such a morass of peace and plenty that he was never once obliged to leave Italy. Within six months of Verus's and my accession, however, the Parthians started massing on the borders of Armenia, and within a year of Pius's death we were at war. In that same year, as you may remember, all Italy north of Rhegium was inundated by torrential late summer rains, which not only caused the Tiber, the Arnus, the Padus, and several other rivers to overflow their banks, wreaking great devastation, but also washed away more than half the crops awaiting harvest. The result, in just about every riverine municipality on the peninsula, was famine on top of flood, and these calamities were compounded by the wholesale contamination of many water sources, which led in turn to a spate of epidemics.

"For the next three years, Verus and I were totally immersed in waging war against Vologeses III, rebuilding Italy's cities, reclaiming Italy's land, and, above all, finding the money to sustain those three considerable undertakings. And no sooner had we won the war, rebuilt the cities, and reclaimed the land, than Verus's army returned from the east carrying plague, which proceeded, as you know, to ravage Italy and all the eastern provinces for the next two years and which carried off, among others, Commodus's twin brother, Antoninus. While the plague was still claiming its victims by the thousands, the German tribes along the Danube started threatening Noricum and Pannonia, and in the sixth year of my and Verus's conjoint reign barbarian armies swept southward toward the sea. We were able to push them back, but it took a good ten years to subdue them, and their subjugation, once accomplished, proved very temporary despite its enormous cost. Verus, as you know, was one of the earliest casualties, succumbing to an apoplectic seizure during the second year of the war, and within three months of his death my darling son Annius was carried off by a fever. I carried on, though, stiffening my resolve with heavy doses of Stoic introspection; and for the next five years I fought more battles than I can remember against an endless succession of Daci, Quadi, Vandali, Sarmatae, Iazyges, Macromanni, and what have you until their armies were so decimated that they had to retire across the Danube and regroup. Alas, just as the territorial integrity of Pannonia and Noricum was being restored, my great general Avidius Cassius raised the standard of rebellion in the east, and I was obliged to hasten southward to Syria to put down his treasonable revolt.

"Having now been Emperor for almost fifteen years, I was finally graced with a six-month interval of tranquillity, and it was during this brief hiatus between crises that I came to understand what one and a half decades of turmoil and strife were doing to the Empire I'd given all I had in me to preserve. That was when I began to despair, dear Lucio, for I discovered that the cost of defending Rome against her enemies and maintaining her frontiers intact was so exorbitant that the blessings of urban civilization she had bestowed upon her people had been undermined beyond all hope of restoration."

Here Marcus stopped speaking for several moments, and appeared to be lost in thought. But then, as abruptly as he'd gone silent, he started up again.

"All my life, Lucio, I'd clung to the belief that the Empire stood for something. It was on that belief, in fact, that my dedication to a life of service to the State was founded. And during my twenty-three years of tutelage under Pius, I managed to articulate, to my own satisfaction at least, what that something was. It had always been pretty clear to me what it wasn't. It wasn't Justice or Righteousness or Holiness or any of the other fictive virtues. It was a concept of civic life, rather, a specifically Roman concept based on the twin convictions that the greatest honor to which a man could aspire was the approbation of the people of his city, and that the greatest honor to which Rome could aspire was the approbation of the cities that paid her tribute. Until recently, Lucio, there had never been an instance of a city, once integrated into the Roman system, wishing to dissociate itself from the Empire. Indeed, one great irony of the wars we fought against the northern tribes was that the tribesmen weren't out to conquer Roman territory so much as they were attempting to make a place for themselves within the Empire. And the most terrible irony of all is that they, more than any other single factor, are rendering inclusion within the Empire a prize of well-nigh negligible value.

"In the old days we could finance our wars of conquest—and our civil wars as well—by plundering the peoples we conquered. Having plundered them, though, we incorporated their territories into the Empire and extended to these new provinces most, if not all, of the benefits of Roman citizenship. Now, however, there are no more territories worth conquering. The Empire has expanded to its natural boundaries—the ocean, the desert, and the trackless forest marshes north of the Danube and east of the Rhine. And so our wars can no longer be financed on the backs of the people we conquer; they must be paid for by us.

"And what has happened, and is happening, is that the cities that pay Rome tribute are ceasing to sing her praises and beginning to groan beneath her heel, while the Roman ideal of commonwealth is being supplanted by the primitive ethic of self-preservation. I have seen it with my own eyes, Lucio: men who'd endowed their native cities with magnificent public buildings and been honored by the people with seats in the curia or the prize of a municipal magistracy now avoid public office however they can, because they must collect the taxes that pay for Rome's wars and make up any deficits out of what's left of their own estates. And the people of their cities who once applauded them now live in fear of their exactions and curse their posterity with oaths born of penury and rage. The Empire's peasantry, meanwhile, find that their once-noble calling has degenerated into a form of servitude, because the State takes the lion's share of their crops in order to offset their tax arrears; and when they seek to flee their life of unprofitable toil they are compelled by Imperial mandate to return to their lands and grow food for the legions until they starve."

Again Marcus paused, as the gray October light began to wane. "You see, Lucio," he resumed finally, "I discovered as I approached old age that the resplendent Roman Empire to which I'd devoted my life was evolving irremediably toward petrifaction, and under my very own superintendence. Yet there was absolutely nothing I could do about it. You'll agree, I believe, that under such circumstances I had reason to despair."

"Yes," I said softly, "to that I will agree."

"But I think I could have endured it," Marcus continued in a contemplative tone, apparently oblivious of my words, "if only Annia had chosen some other time to die."

It was very quiet in the room then, as dusk approached.

"But I forgave her," said Marcus, exhaustion slightly slurring his words.

And as I sat there with my memories in the silence of his room, he breathed a tired sigh and gave himself up to the gentle consolations of sleep.

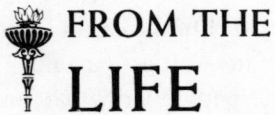# FROM THE
LIFE

By the time Polyaenus, Aelius, and the rest of us in the stable returned to Athens from Hypata, the Panathenaea was only nine days off. The preliminary heats in the boys' running events were to take place two days before the formal competitions began, moreover, so I had relatively little time to perfect my form and prepare my mind for my first great test in one of the most prestigious of the festivals on the calendar of Greek games. Worse still—from my point of view, at least—that summer's festival was not one of the "lesser" variety held three years out of every four, but was a Great Panathenaea, almost comparable in importance to the Big Four athletic meetings, which were held at Nemea, Corinth, Delphi, and Olympia. All the finest athletes in the Empire would be participating, and after my less than awe-inspiring performances at Hypata, I felt decidedly unequal to the challenge they represented. Polyaenus, sensing perhaps that my timorousness was eating away at my capacity for concentration, was wise enough to enter me in just one of the boys' foot races—the dolichos, of course—which at Athens was a murderous twelve laps. But the relief I felt when he informed me, in effect, that I'd have only one chance instead of four to embarrass myself in front of 50,000 people (the fourth event being the hippios, or double diaulos, which was contested at only a few of the Greek festivals) quickly became acute anxiety when the names drawn by lot for the seventh of the qualifying heats included my own and that of Didymos Klideus of Alexandria, who was known among those who followed Greek athletics as "the Comet."

Didymos was destined to succeed Aelius as the greatest runner of his time and had made his name in the boys' competitions. Fortunately for me, he chose eventually to concentrate his attention on the stade and the diaulos, and he was gracious enough to tell me one summer at Olympia that one of the main reasons he had made that decision was that I had always made him "work too hard" whenever we competed in the dolichos. And in truth the two of us did run some fiercely contested races against each other, in most of which I finished second. But I still count those few victories I wrested from him as among the proudest of my achievements as a runner. For when you ran well enough to defeat the Comet, you knew there was no other mortal in the world who could have matched you on that day at that distance.

The first race I ever ran against him was unquestionably one of the more memorable ones—not, alas, because I forced him to extend himself, but because he defeated me so soundly. It was a blistering-hot Athenian summer afternoon, and about five hundred spectators who had the leisure and inclination to devote a day to the Panathenaea's preliminary competitions were scattered around the vastness of the rebuilt stadium's forty-six tiers of seats. Marcus, Agricus, Hieronymous, and Dracena were among them, of course, so I couldn't delude myself, afterward, that I had lacked a strong incentive to do my best. Polyaenus warned me that Didymos would probably set a pretty fast pace, despite the fact that we would be running twenty-four lengths of the stadium's floor, but he advised me to run at my own tempo for the first nine laps and make up whatever ground I'd lost during the final three. He said that the other two runners in the heat would pose no significant challenge and that "all" I had to do in order to qualify for one of the sixteen starting positions was "outrun Didymos down the stretch."

As events transpired, he and I got to know each other a little before the race began, because the other two boys who'd been selected for our heat turned out, coincidentally, to be lovers, which perforce paired Didymos and me for the ritual of applying the oil.

"You're the new fellow from Rome; am I right?" he asked as he poured some "juice of the holy olives" onto my shoulders. And I acknowledged that that indeed was who I was.

"How I envy you," he said, which naturally led me to ask him why.

"Because you live in Rome, of course," he responded. "I've been burning to get there ever since I could walk, just like my father before me. He was on his way there for the first visit of his life when the boat he was on caught fire and he drowned."

"I'm sorry to hear that," I said.

"Oh, it's all in the past now; there's no need for condolences. The only truly sad thing about it is that he never did get to see the Urbs. Is it as magnificent as they say?"

"Yes, I suppose so," I replied. "But you know how it is when you live somewhere all your life. . . ."

"Yes?" Didymos prompted me, thereby demonstrating that he did not.

"Well, you get used to it. . . ."

"Even *Rome*?" he asked incredulously.

"Even Rome," I confirmed.

"Remarkable," he declared. And then, our mutual oiling accomplished, he gave me a slightly nettled frown and said, "Good luck."

I know now that one should always be very careful about deflating the enthusiasms of others. At the time, though, I was too blunt, and thus inadvertently gave my most formidable opponent an added incentive to run me off my feet.

This he proceeded quite efficiently to do, starting out like a sprinter and steadily widening his lead as the race wore on. By the end of the eighth lap he had at least fifty paces on me, and, Polyaenus's wise counsel notwithstanding, I decided I'd better start making up the lost ground then and there. Over the course of the next three laps I managed to cut his lead in half, and on the outbound leg of the final lap I closed to within nine or ten feet of him. Rounding the post for the last time, however, Didymos more or less took wing, and even if I'd had some energy left in reserve—which I most decidedly did not—I very much doubt that I could have caught him.

Polyaenus, as always, took a sanguine view of my defeat. "With a little more experience under your belt, you would have beaten him," he said. And I was far too exhausted to disabuse him of that fanciful notion.

I suppose it was much to Agricus's credit that he resisted the temptation to taunt me about my dismal lack of success at Hypata and in the Panathenaic heats. But it was fairly clear to me that his abnormally considerate silence was attributable more to Marcus's admonitions than to any concern he might have had for my feelings. And though I was grateful to Marcus for muzzling him, his action in doing so only added to my growing suspicion that the two of them had come to some sort of understanding during my absence from Athens, an understanding that touched on issues far more substantive than Agricus's genius for incivility. That suspicion had arisen initially because on my return from Hypata I'd found Agricus subtly changed. He seemed in some sinister way to be much more at ease with himself than before I'd left, as if some goal he'd long striven for was at last within his grasp. And though I had no concrete evidence on which to base this disquieting impression, I felt certain that it was no mere figment of my admittedly hyperactive imagination. Of course I gave some thought to the idea of mentioning these vague apprehensions to Marcus, but I could think of no way of raising the subject that wouldn't also give him the impression that I had doubts about his loyalty. So in the end I decided, wisely, to keep silent.

And so I took part in my first Great Panathenaea as a spectator, not a participant. But Didymos—may the gods exalt him—redeemed me somewhat for my failure to qualify by sweeping all four of the boys' foot races and becoming one of the most celebrated heroes of the games. Thanks to his brilliant achievement, I started taking a certain pride in having lost to him and was so eager to acknowledge my defeat that Marcus was moved to warn me against the gaucherie of dropping names.

Not many days were to pass before I raced against Didymos again. For no sooner was the celebration of the Great Panathenaea concluded than it came time to set off for Apollo's sanctuary at Delphi, where the Pythian Games—second in importance only to the contests at Olympia—were shortly to take place, on the slopes of Mount Parnassus. Marcus was planning to make the journey to Delphi, too, since the quadrennial festival in honor of Pythian Apollo was an event not to be missed. He had the choice, moreover, of riding to the games in great splendor and solid comfort with Herodes, who, as the sanctuary's greatest living benefactor, would also be its most honored guest, or of traveling along in Spartan simplicity with me and the other runners in our *gymnastes'* stable. To my great delight, but by no means my surprise, he chose the second option, asking for and readily obtaining Polyaenus's permission to join his small traveling party to ours.

The journey to Delphi is not a great deal shorter than the journey to Hypata, and at the beginning one follows the identical route. At Orchomenus, however, one leaves the northbound road and heads westward toward Chaeronea, where Plutarch lived his life and Philip of Macedon won his greatest battle. We spent the second night of our trip there, and the next day crossed into mountainous Phokis, leaving Boeotia and the Kephisos River valley behind us as we began our assault on the massive shoulders of the Parnassus range. Around midday we arrived at the famous "Split," or three-pronged fork in the Chaeronea-to-Delphi road, the northern branch of which goes toward Amphikleia, the southern toward Ambrossos, and the middle toward Delphi itself. I was riding rather than running at the time, and, with Marcus, Agricus, Hieronymous, and Dracena had reached the fork well ahead of Polyaenus and my stablemates. We stopped to wait for them, choosing as our halting place the twenty-foot-high mound of uncut stones that, according to legend, marks the spot where King Laius of Thebes was killed and buried by a young man he'd tried to bully off the road, unaware of the fact that he was the youthful stranger's father.

"If we'd been in old Laius's shoes," said Hieronymous, "it would have been just about here that we challenged the young ruffian who was coming toward us down the Delphi road."

"Poor Oedipus," sighed Marcus.

"Poor Laius," Hieronymous countered.

"I don't think he merits much sympathy," said Marcus sternly.

"Why not? Just because he exposed his infant son on Mount Cithaeron and drove an iron spike through the squawling baby's ankles?"

"Admittedly that doesn't speak well for him," Marcus said with a grim smile. "But what I find most objectionable about his behavior is the fact that he attempted infanticide in a craven effort to avoid his own fate."

"Well, how would you like it if the oracle of Apollo told *you* that your bouncing baby boy would grow up to be your executioner?"

"I wouldn't like it at all. But neither would I stoop to murder and mutilation."

"You'd calmly wait for the ax to fall, with true Stoic equanimity."

"Let's say that I'd play things by ear, as would you."

"As would *I?*" What makes you think so?"

"Well, first of all, you don't have any more confidence in the pronouncements of oracles than I do; second, you could never bring yourself to murder an innocent child, especially if it were your own; and third, you understand that the reason Laius and his son were so cruelly destroyed was that they impiously sought to escape their fates."

"What do you suppose would have happened if they had bowed to them instead?"

Marcus paused, his brow furrowed in thought. "The terrible prophecies of the Pythian oracle would still have been fulfilled," he said finally, "but in a much less terrible way."

"Elaborate, please."

"Gladly. And I'll begin by reminding you that the oracle speaks in metaphors, not only because a metaphor can accommodate many more ultimate outcomes than a specific prediction, but also because by metaphor an individual's fate may be made to stand for some aspect of our common lot as mortals. Thus when the oracle told Laius that if he had a son that son would usurp his crown and steal the heart of his wife, it was merely giving him a metaphorical description of the age-old process by which one generation reluctantly gives way to the next, as Laius refused to do at this very crossroads."

"I'm not aware that in the act of giving way to the next generation the presiding generation surrenders its wives, though a percentage no doubt would leap at the opportunity."

"No doubt," Marcus acknowledged. "Except that every man surrenders his wife to her newborn child the moment she first gives it suck."

"Ah," sighed Hieronymous, "the perfidy of mother love."

"There wasn't anything very metaphorical about what the oracle told Oedipus," Agricus remarked abruptly. "It told him he would *marry* his mother, after all."

"But that was just a child's version of the same metaphor the oracle had recited to Laius," Marcus responded. "What little boy doesn't secretly wish, sometimes, that he could rid himself of the imperious giant who comes between him and his mother each night and have her all to himself instead."

"Marcus! I'm surprised at you!" said Agricus, pretending to be shocked.

"You shouldn't be," Marcus answered him in a rueful tone. "My wish came true: my father died when I was three. But his death served only to make me aware of how much and how dearly I had loved him, in spite of all my shameful secret wishes."

"Oedipus didn't love Laius much," Agricus sneered.

"He didn't know Laius was his father. He'd just come from the oracle and, out of love for Polybus of Corinth, whom he believed to be his sire, had decided to exile himself from Polybus's kingdom forever."

"Sounds like a craven effort to avoid his fate," Agricus said with a nasty smirk.

"No!" declared Marcus. "It was Polybus's fate he wanted to ward off, even though he'd no doubt harbored many of the same secret wishes as I. He recoiled from the prospect of supplanting the man he believed to be his father and so renounced his kingly birthright."

"That, too, sounds like a craven effort to avoid his fate."

"And so it may have been," said Marcus. "But it was far less craven than the effort made by Laius. I feel sympathy for Oedipus because he was guilty only of trying to escape, which was a futile exercise but by no means abhorrent or infamous. For his father, on the other hand, I have nothing but contempt; because he would have made his escape over the body of an unoffending child. Both he and his son were weak, it's true. They both shrank from the hard truth that the shape of our fate is unalterable and that the only variable in our lives is how we meet it."

"Spoken like a true Stoic!" Hieronymous exclaimed with a laugh.

"Yes," Marcus acknowledged, smiling abashedly and going red around the ears. "But after all my Stoic sententiousness, the fact remains: those who attempt to escape their fate are merely human; those who attempt to destroy its embodiments are worse than beasts. Perhaps that's why

Laius lies here by the roadside beneath a pile of uncut stones while the promontory at Colonus where Oedipus met his fate is regarded as holy ground."

"Yet Oedipus is no less dead than Laius," Agricus languidly observed.

"But thanks to what we know of him, dear scoffer," Marcus replied, "we, his descendants, are more alive."

[OCTOBER 26TH]

I awoke at dawn this morning and shambled outside to stretch a bit and breathe in some salty fresh air. The sky above me and the arc of the sea to the south were a featureless gray, and a chill northeast wind warned that stormy weather was not far off. It was possible in the pale first light to see that the tide was out and that the causeway between Ictis and the shore was standing clear of the water. I didn't see the ship at first, because her sails were furled and her bows facing toward me. But as the light gained I was able to distinguish her presence at the seaward end of the causeway.

No one was stirring in the house, nor was anyone likely to be for quite some while. So after giving my stomach a little bread and hard cheese to work on I scratched a brief note on a tablet of wax, set it down gently on Portia's pillow, brushed her cheek with my lips (as I wouldn't have dared to do had she been waking), and set off on Boudicea's ample back to watch the Dumnonii load their tin.

When I arrived after less than an hour's ride at the landward end of the causeway I found the native tribesmen working at a furious pace, their sweaty faces grim with concentration. Five or six of them were responsible for shoveling ore as rapidly as possible into the succession of crude wooden carts that repeatedly traversed the five hundred or so feet of the causeway's length. These carts could hold perhaps thirty or forty cubic feet of cassiterite each and must have weighed many hundreds of pounds fully loaded. They were propelled by a dozen or more three-man teams, which pushed them out to the ship at something like a trot and back to the ore pile at a speed that can best be described as reckless. The shovelers, it was clear, were expected to have one team's cart filled before the next team brought theirs back empty, and great was the verbal abuse they were subjected to if they kept anybody waiting. The whole arrangement reminded me, for some reason, of the brick-stealing operations Agricus had organized when we were boys. Then, the impetus to work at breakneck speed had been provided by the danger of getting caught; but I could divine no such reason for the Dumnonii's frenzied exertions. Since it was clear that no one involved in the enterprise had the time or the inclination to enlighten me—much less the knowledge of Latin—I decided to walk out to the other end of the causeway and make inquiry of the sailors.

She was called the *Inskertcalduagh*, whatever that meant, and had come from some port in southern Hibernia. Her master was a diminutive middle-aged fellow with a curly red beard, an unpronounceable name, and a rudimentary command of Latin. As soon as he heard me speak it, though, his eyes widened and he declared, "You go here for some letter."

"I beg your pardon?" I responded.

"Wait," he commanded me, and disappeared into his cabin. "Here!" he said triumphantly when he reemerged, waving a slender scroll case. "From you! Old Roman!" he announced, pushing the leather cylinder into my chest.

Feeling more than a little bit astonished, I accepted the case and read the leather tag tied to its cover. "For the old Romans at Ictis," it said. The handwriting, unmistakably, was Nestor's.

It was clear that the captain was expecting me to open the case and read the enclosed communication then and there. I had to disappoint him, though, not just because the letter was addressed to Marcus as well as me, but also because rain had now begun to fall, and I dared not let the scroll get wet. As the rain started to come down harder, however, the captain's attention shifted from me to more important matters, and he began to shout orders at the ore loaders and his crew. All at once the loading process ceased, and a burly tribesman who'd been acting as the Dumnonii's foreman approached the captain with the crewman who'd been keeping a tally of the cartloads of ore the ship had taken on. The captain scrutinized the figures, unlocked his strongbox, and counted out thirty-seven silver denarii into the foreman's cupped hands. This business concluded, he shouted another series of orders to the sailors, who immediately started making preparations to hoist anchor and set sail.

The tribesmen's frantic exertions were now for the most part explained: they were being paid so much per cartload dumped in the hold, and the ship's captain wanted to be well clear of the land before the heavy weather brewing to the east got much closer. No one could blame him; the unprotected coastline hereabouts is no place to ride out a storm. But it saddened me to realize how desperate the Dumnonii must be for money, and I wondered for a fleeting moment what they would think of the farmers of Aquilonia. I wasn't about to tell them the farmers' story, nor could I have done so, given the barrier of language. Instead, I merely thanked the captain for carrying Nestor's letter here from Hibernia, then took leave of him and his ship and made my way back along the now deserted causeway to where Boudicea awaited me on the shore.

It was raining heavily by the time I started back, and an angry wind sent sheets of water pelting against my cloak. Deep beneath its woolen folds, the scroll case stayed tolerably dry, nestled against the skin of my stomach.

It took me the best part of two hours to cover the distance back to the house, and with the exception of my chest and abdomen I was thoroughly soaked by the time I got there. With my teeth chattering and violent shivers convulsing me, I rubbed Boudicea down and draped a blanket over her back. Then, tired and chilled to the bone, I made for the house, with memories of my arrival at Lorium in a comparably bedraggled condition long, long ago skittering unbidden through my mind.

All was quiet when I entered the house, and I found Camilla fast asleep on the sheepskin rug in front of the fire. On the far side of the room the door to Portia's and my bedchamber stood wide open, revealing that no one was inside. The door to Marcus's room, by contrast, was open only a crack, a fact that generated all sorts of unnamed suspicions in my mind. Anticipating I knew not what, I set the scroll case down on the table, walked silently over to Marcus's door, and gently pushed it open.

The two of them were seated together on the bed in an embrace. Portia's back was to me, her head resting on Marcus's shoulder. Stunned, I lifted my eyes to meet his, and in his expression read something that could have been either defiance or disapproval. I didn't know if he was saying: Yes, this is exactly what you think it is, and what are you going to do about it? or whether the message he meant to convey was, Why aren't *you* here comforting your wife instead of me?

Sensing my presence, Portia turned her head to look at me, with tears in her eyes and tear tracks running down her cheeks.

"You're *soaked!*" she said in genuine alarm, then rose from the bed without a word to Marcus and, wiping away her tears with her apron, commanded, "Take off those wet clothes this instant!" as she brushed by me and headed out the door. In the few moments that passed before she reappeared with a basin full of water Marcus and I stayed motionless and regarded each other in utter silence. But when she roused Camilla and hung the basin on a pivot over the fire, he smiled at me and said wistfully, "Ah, Lucio, if only I were healthy enough to be your rival, and if only your wife were fickle enough to be untrue."

"I have no quarrel with your first wish, at least," I told him.

He laughed a little by way of response, then admonished me. "You know you're on notice to get out of those clothes."

"So I am," I acknowledged. "I'm just glad that I found you wearing yours."

And this feeble attempt at humor cleared the air between us, for the moment, more or less.

Once the water had been heated, Portia swung the pivot around and put the basin on the floor in front of me. I'd been sitting for some time wrapped in a blanket, silently awaiting my ordeal. With the blanket still over my shoulders, I got up and gingerly tested the water with my big toe. "It's *scalding*," I observed.

"It just feels that way because you're so chilled," Portia answered me, sticking her arm into the water up to her elbow. "It's really more tepid than hot."

"Courage, Lucio," said Marcus, who was sitting on a stool by the fire and clearly relishing this climactic scene in the drama of My Bath.

Prodded by his malicious grin I screwed up my courage and stepped into the basin, resolved to deny him the satisfaction of seeing me wince, even though the water was so hot it stopped my breath.

"Stout fellow!" he exclaimed.

"Let me have the blanket," Portia instructed as she dipped an empty pitcher into the water, which was even then searing the flesh off my calves. She next handed the pitcher to Camilla, who was standing on the table behind me.

I did as I was instructed and prepared myself for the worst, which was prefaced by Camilla's altogether undaughterly giggle as she lifted the pitcher as high as she could above my head.

"YOW!" I exclaimed as the water came cascading over me.

And Marcus cried "Bravo!" by way of response.

But with that first terrible ablution out of the way, the worst was unquestionably over, and there were no further lapses of patriarchal dignity.

Feeling clean and warm in a freshly laundered tunic, I joined Marcus, Camilla, and Portia around the table for our midday meal. We hadn't been long at our food, though, when two of Marcus's *singulares*—or former *singulares*, I should say—knocked on our door to inquire after him. It seems they'd gone to his house (as they were in the habit of doing on a fairly regular basis) to make sure he was well and to pay their respects. Having found the house deserted, they'd come to ask us if we knew what had become of him. They were visibly relieved when they saw his frail figure seated at our table and raised their right fists to their hearts as a sign of their inextinguishable allegiance to him.

"Now none of that," he gently reprimanded them, and then invited them both to join us for lunch.

Of course no soldier ever declines the offer of a meal, so the two of them pulled stools up to the table and waded into the victuals with martial vigor. Marcus had apparently told them quite some time ago that friends of his from Italy might be coming here to visit him—without, of course, specifying why—and while consuming prodigious quantities of food the *singulares* demonstrated, with dozens of questions, a comparably voracious appetite for news of the Empire and the Urbs. I tried as best I could to satisfy their curiosity, even though I'd been almost as ignorant of events occurring in the world at large when I lived on my farm beside the Aro as they were now, living well outside the Empire's bounds. But I couldn't have done too badly, because they both leaped at Marcus's suggestion that Portia, Camilla, and I go back with them to the Dumnonian village where they live, and make the acquaintance of their neighbors and wives. Since rays of sunlight were now streaming groundward here and there through gaps in the westward-tumbling clouds, and since the village was not far away, we happily acceded to the proposal. For we—like the soldiers, I suspect—feel a sense of isolation here at the westernmost limit of the world; and the society of fellow Romans serves to ease the pain of loss we feel when we think back on all we knew and loved and left behind us.

Our visit to the village was a great success. We were warmly, almost enthusiastically, received and found the Dumnonii far less reserved and austere than our initial encounters with them had led us to believe. The wives of the five *singulares* were particularly hospitable toward us, and their husbands, it was clear, had given Romans a good name among the people of the tribe. This was only to be expected, I suppose, since the *singulares* are plainly formidable warriors, which earns them the respect of the men, and just as plainly men of means—by Dumnonian standards, at least—which gains them the esteem of the women. The women they married are thus the envy of all the others, not least because there are so many more of the others than there are men. This is a consequence of the fact that all the men are extremely touchy about slights, real or imagined, that reflect on their personal honor and regularly fight each other to the death with axes, swords, and a particularly nasty contrivance called a mace in order to avenge these unpardonable insults. Almost every man I saw working at the causeway this morning had killed at least one of his fellow tribesmen in order to maintain his honor inviolate. And yet not one of them ever gives a thought, to all appearances, to the indignity of toiling like a slave for a pittance many slaves wouldn't stoop to accept.

Prickly as they are with regard to one another, the Dumnonii were unfailingly cordial toward us. They made a big fuss over Camilla, who made friends with some of their children as if the language barrier didn't exist. Portia and I can stop worrying, it seems, about her having no contemporaries here to play and grow up with; though I confess that I'm still clinging to the hope that circumstances may yet permit her to live among and associate with Roman citizens by the time she's of marriageable age.

There was no question but that we'd be asked by the villagers to stay for supper, nor was there any doubt but that, having eaten it, we would be escorted back to our house by all five of Marcus's *singulares*. If we were his friends, then in their eyes we were unquestionably worthy of respect.

It was dark by the time we got home, but Marcus had left a lamp burning for us on the table. We took leave of the soldiers at the door, thanking them profusely for their hospitality and exchanging whispered good nights. While Portia put Camilla to bed, I went to check on Marcus and found him peacefully asleep. Reassured, I silently closed his door and then put some dry kindling on the embers glowing dully in the hearth. Before long I had a fire going, and after helping Portia tidy up I sat and stared self-consciously into the flames. The time had come to raise the subject that, I felt sure, had been on her mind no less than mine all day long.

When she was finished with her work, she came and sat down beside me on the rug. "Are you angry with me?" she asked.

"Should I be?" I answered her.

She was silent a moment, then murmured, "Yes."

"Why?" I wanted to know.

And she was silent again.

For a long time we were silent together, our eyes gazing intently into the fire. Finally she spoke.

"I don't know how it happened," she said in a voice so low I could hardly hear her. "I went in to bring him his breakfast. He asked me to keep him company while he ate. We started talking, about little things— the weather, how he was feeling, how he had slept. Then we began to talk about Camilla—how she liked it here, how she was reacting to . . . all the changes in her life. He asked me if she missed Decius very much, and I said I thought she did. Then he asked me if I thought about him often. I said I thought about him all the time. And then I started to cry. He asked me if I'd rather not talk about him. I said no, I didn't mind. Then he asked me, 'What was he like?' And I told him all about Decius—

about how solemn he'd been as a little boy, and about how we thought he might be mute because he didn't talk until he was four. And I told him he wanted to be a farmer, and how wonderful he was with animals, and how he worships you. . . ."

She lifted her hands to her face then and slowly bent forward beneath the weight of her grief.

"Portia . . ." I said softly, reaching out with trepidation and taking hold of her arm.

After several moments she sat up and let her hands fall into her lap. She looked desolated. "I know it was very wrong of me to talk to a stranger about such things. . . ."

I said, "No, no. Marcus isn't a stranger."

We were quiet for a little while, watching the fire.

"He asked me how you had taken it," she said at last.

"And what did you tell him?"

"I told him how strong and brave you'd been, and how your strength helped pull us through."

To this I responded with a laugh of self-contempt.

"He said you blame yourself for what happened. . . ."

I stared at the flames.

"Is that really true?"

Quivering, I turned to her and said, "It's not altogether false."

Tears welled up in Portia's eyes as she looked at me. "Oh, Lucio, you *fool!*" she said, forgetting for the first time in our marriage the duty owed to a husband by his wife. Then, seeing my tears, she reached out, took hold of my hand and pulled it up under her smock to her breast. "We've mourned him separately long enough," she whispered, and then pulled me to her with a strength I'd never known she possessed.

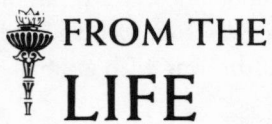
If the essence of Greece is light, the essence of light is Delphi. Nothing I'd ever heard or read about it had prepared me for that glorious aerie, and every time I competed there I had the sensation that I might at any moment take wing.

Perhaps that's why I never once lost a race at the Pythian Games.

I saw Delphi for the first time in the company of Aelius. We were running together at an easy pace up the steep, narrow road that debouches from the mountain passes at the level of the sanctuary, several hundred feet above the town. This approach was far less crowded than the almost-as-narrow main road, which had been so hopelessly congested that no one could move any faster than a slow walk. And although the higher road was by no means deserted, with only two days remaining before the festival, the two of us were able to proceed at a fairly steady trot, which was more than sufficient for training purposes given the steepness of the grade. About halfway into its fourth mile, the road began to level out, and we found ourselves traversing the broad mountain meadows of the high Parnassus. In some miraculous way, it seemed, we had left the dust and heat of summer far behind us; here, a cool west wind blew steadily toward the summit spiring above us into the sky, and the clarity of the air was so absolute that each breath I took felt like an inhalation of sunlight.

We ran on, with the west wind curling over our bodies like gossamer eddies in a river of silk, and after a mile or so the road began to ascend toward a treeless ridge line, beyond which was only the sky. Reluctant to let this interlude of Parnassian bliss come to an end, I slowed my pace a little as we came nearer the summit. But I arrived all too soon, nevertheless, only to discover that what had been awaiting me on that rise had been, not the end of the interlude, but its culmination.

I could see, I don't know how far—an arc of perhaps a hundred miles, with the sun dancing high on the meridian in the cloudless expanse of blue that crowned the scene. Below me the road zigzagged busily down the mountainside until it terminated at the Castalian Spring, a prodigious vertical drop from where I stood. Twice as far again below that lay the floor of the Plistus River valley, with the nearly dry riverbed snaking its way through miles upon miles of olive groves toward the Crisaean Plain (where the Pythian horse and chariot races would be run) and the far-away blue of the Corinthian Gulf, beyond which the gray brown mountains of Aetolia marched in austere procession from south to north. From either side of the valley's floor jagged rust and ocher cliffs rose toward mountaintops speckled with dark green pines, while at the southeast limit of the panorama, far away to my left, rose the imposing mass of Mount Helicon, from whose shoulders the Plistus began its twelve-league descent past Delphi to the sea. And perched far below me on the southern ramparts of Parnassus, in the very center of this sun-burnished vista, stood the sanctuary of Apollo at the base of the Shining Rocks, with the town of Delphi a little below it and to the west. Surrounding both *temenos* and *polis*, on every square foot of level ground, was a multicolored patchwork of lean-tos and tents, erected by the thousands of pilgrims who were gathering in this remote mountain vastness to honor Phoebus Apollo and his Pythian oracle, whose dwelling the god had founded here, suspended 'twixt earth and sky.

For a long while Aelius and I just stood at the precipice and drank in the view. And as we surveyed the terrible beauty so typical of Greece I understood at last what Pindar had meant when he wrote so long ago: "To see the sun shine on Delphi is just recompense for all our sorrows."

Walking slowly, the two of us made our way down the mountainside and slaked our thirst at the Castalian Spring, just to the north of the gymnasium and the athletes' barracks. Since we found ourselves so close to our lodging place, we decided to register then and there, and we were glad we did so, since there were only about a dozen pallets left. We would gladly have registered the other members of our stable if we'd been allowed to, but the rule requiring registration in person was subject to no exceptions. So our companions, not to mention about a hundred other athletes, were obliged to sleep on the sandy floor of the stadium, which was no great hardship at that time of year but which was an inconvenience, given the stadium's location a steep half mile or so from the athletes' mess and the training grounds.

Clutching the numbered bronze registration disks that would permit us entry to every one of the festival sites, we started down the crowded road in search of our stablemates and friends. We encountered them more than a mile east of town, and the first thing I did on greeting Marcus was tell him what I had seen a thousand feet higher up the mountain. After we'd located Herodes' pavilion and paid our respects, accordingly, the two of us set off on horseback for the heights, Agricus, Hieronymous, and Dracena having had their fill, for the moment, of traveling and looking at views. We were more than halfway up the zigzag cliffside road before I realized that in my eagerness to share with my beloved friend the experience I'd shared some hours earlier with Aelius, I had forgotten completely about visiting the Sanctuary of Apollo, which, then as now, was generally considered to be the eighth wonder of the world. I guess I got caught up in a feeling that at last I had an opportunity to repay Marcus—to some small extent at least—for all the acts of kindness and generosity he'd initiated on my behalf, his orchestration of my first encounter with the sea not least among them. (And it may have been, also, that I sensed even then that I was losing him to Agricus, and was trying to make up lost ground.) But alas, what he saw from the heights was not his first view of Delphi and the valley, as it had been mine, but merely the same view we'd both been looking at ever since the start of our ascent from Herodes' pavilion. Thus in my feverish haste to demonstrate my gratitude to him—or counter Agricus's encroachments on his affections—it seemed that I'd not only delayed his introduction to the *temenos* for no good reason, but had also dragged him up a mountainside after a tiring day of travel in order to let him share an experience whose impact was contingent on a state of affairs that quite obviously did not obtain. And though he went to great lengths to wax rhapsodic about the beauty of the view and expatiated endlessly on how glorious he found it, I knew that I'd stupidly inconvenienced him, and I felt like an out-and-out dolt.

My feelings of self-reproach soon gave way to wonder, though, for with the sun sinking low he and I and our three companions paid our first visit to Apollo's Sanctuary, which was an experience no whit less memorable than the one I'd had earlier in the day. It was a much different kind of experience, however, for instead of the aquiline sense of soaring high over all creation that I'd exulted in on the ramparts of Parnassus, what I felt as we trod the stones of the Sacred Way was a sort of inebriate giddiness brought on by the dense concentration of color and riches contained within the confines of the *temenos*. Though the enclosure could not have been more than half a stade wide by two-thirds of a stade long, it contained not only the awesome Temple of Apollo and a theater capable of seating some 5,000 people, but also well over two dozen smaller but no less magnificent buildings that included treasuries of the various *poleis*, temples of the various gods, and ex-voto structures such as colonnades and porches, all of them crowded with statuary and decorated in the most vivid shades of red and blue and gold. Added to this marble cornucopia were no fewer than fifteen commemorative columns of variegated design, several banquet halls–*cum*–council chambers, and innumerable painted statues of statesmen, generals, heroes, poets, tragedians, philosophers, sculptors, musicians, actors, and victors in the Pythian competitions. Rounding out the catalogue of sights were the three monuments that, with Apollo's Temple, form the heart of the ancient sanctuary, the Delphic Council House, or *bouleterion*, the Sanctuary of the Earth Mother Gaea, where the serpent Python lurks, and the Sibylline Rock, where men first came to hear oracles, even before Apollo's fire was brought to Parnassus.

Since it was nearly dark by the time our tour was concluded, I took leave of my friends and made my way back to the athletes' mess for a frugal meal. Then, after a brief conversation with Polyaenus regarding strategy for the next day's qualifying heats, I tiptoed into the dimly lit barracks, located my pallet, next to Aelius's, and within moments was as sound asleep as he.

The stadium at Delphi is situated about a hundred feet above and five hundred feet to the west of the sanctuary on a somewhat narrow natural terrace. Soaring skyward above it are the massive *Phaedriades*, the so-called Shining Rocks, which may have shone at one time but most decidedly shine no longer, owing to the thick growth of scrub pine and underbrush that now covers them. Because of the limitations imposed by the terrain, the running surface is about twenty feet narrower and fifty feet shorter than at Olympia. This is a good thing from a dolichos runner's point of view, because it means that a twelve-lap race is almost a quarter of a mile shorter than at many other places. It is a bad thing, however, in quite a few other respects: there is much less elbowroom on the straightaways (with a corresponding increase in elbows, and knees, given and received), much more mayhem at the turning posts (because the shorter straight-aways give the field less time to string itself out and undo the bunching that tends to occur at the turns), and three fewer starting positions than at Olympia (since even after two extra positions are, inadvisedly, squeezed in on the sides, the stadium still isn't wide enough to accommodate more than seventeen runners).

Given this last circumstance and the fact that hordes of athletes descend on Delphi in the hopes of competing in the Pythian Games, the qualifying heats in the running events are far more crowded, and more hotly con-tested, than at any other Panhellenic venue, including Olympia. In the boys' dolichos, for example, there were nearly two hundred candidates for the available starting positions, and that meant that there were no fewer than eleven runners in each of the seventeen heats. Which heat I would run in and which runners I would run against was determined by the number painted on the white pebble I drew out of the large black-figure amphora. Obeying some inner instinct, I waited till near the end of the drawing to take my turn, and my obedience was doubly rewarded when I pulled out a pebble numbered 4. For the fourth heat would be contested while the morning air was still cool, and by a field that consisted entirely of novices, nondescripts, and nonentities, like myself. Didymos, by contrast, drew number 13 and had to defeat a highly competitive field of opponents in the heat of the day in order to qualify.

Of course good fortune alone was not going to win me a starting position in the Pythian dolichos; I still had to outrun ten other athletes. And while there wasn't much question that I was faster than they were—in my trainer's mind, at least—an awful lot could happen on such a short and narrow track. Polyaenus decided, accordingly, that I should take the lead at the outset and run in front all the way. Given a faster field of opponents that might not have been such a good idea, but given the field I'd been blessed with, it was a more or less doltproof approach, and I won, without having to extend myself, by a margin of two dozen paces.

The next day, amid all the music and pageantry that marks the beginning of Apollo's games, I took my place, planted my toes in the concrete starting grooves, and prepared myself to compete for one of the two greatest honors to which a freeborn athlete can aspire—a Pythian victory. I was filled with excitement as I awaited the start of the race, but my excitation was due less to the importance of the race I was about to run than it was to an incident that had occurred perhaps a quarter of an hour before.

I'd been discussing race strategy with Aelius while casting my eyes in all directions in the hopes of espying my *gymnastes*, who for some reason was nowhere to be seen. He soon showed up, though, and with a look of keen elation on his face. "I just thought you'd like to know," he said, "that your sponsor has now entered you officially in the boys' dolichos."

"I should hope he has," I responded. As a "foreigner" who had yet to win a race on the Circuit, I had to have a Greek or patrician sponsor or I would not be allowed to compete.

Still looking elated, Polyaenus beamed at me and said, "Do you happen to know, by any chance, the name you'll be bearing in this competition, and henceforth?"

"I believe it's Lucius Celer," I replied, Marcus and I having decided some time before that "Lucius the Swift" was an altogether fitting name for an up-and-coming young runner.

"I'm afraid that's a bit abbreviated in comparison to what now appears in the Pythian Registry."

"What do you mean?" I asked, feeling both mystified and nettled.

Polyaenus, grinning gleefully, replied, "The name your sponsor entered in the register is not Lucius Celer, my dear fellow, but Lucius *Verus* Celer!"

For a long moment I gaped at him, unable to grasp the stupendous fact that Marcus had publicly professed himself my patron.

"Is that too long a name to run with, dear boy? Do you think it might slow you down?"

"No, no," I said, shaking my head. "Of course not."

"I'm glad to hear it," said Polyaenus, and then, without a trace of his customary diffidence, continued, "Now here's what I want you to do today. I want you to go out there with that shiny new name of yours and stick so close to Didymos for eleven laps that he'll be able to feel you exhaling into his earhole. Then, on the twelfth lap, I want you to forget about him, and about me, and about all the other runners as well, and seize the opportunity to show your friend Marcus how an athlete who bears his family's name can run."

I glanced over at Didymos as I bent forward in preparation for the start. He looked determined and composed, but not necessarily invincible. Then the command was given, and we took off.

The first three laps I did as instructed and galloped along no more than a stride or two behind him. But the pace he was setting was murderous— not very much slower than a sprint—and I knew that if I stayed with him for the next eight laps I'd be in no condition to overtake him on the last one. Risking a glance behind me, I saw that the two of us already had a good fifteen paces on the rest of the field. Didymos, it was clear, intended to break our spirits by opening up an insurmountable lead early on, and having accomplished that he hoped to coast through the final few laps to victory. It was equally clear, to me, at least, that if I tried to keep up with him I would be running *his* race, which was not the sort of race I could win. I had stayed with him throughout our Panathenaic heat and for my pains had been soundly defeated. The conclusion was thus inescapable: I would have to disregard Polyaenus's instructions, an action that would have been unthinkable had he not repeatedly exhorted me, and all the other runners he trained, to run with our minds as well as our legs.

So for the next three laps I let Didymos open up a lead on me and ran just hard enough to stay clear of the rest of the field. By the start of the seventh lap he'd put a good two dozen paces between us, but the gap was not any wider by the end of the eighth. Even Didymos, it seemed, could not run all-out forever.

As the ninth lap began, I picked up my tempo, and I was no more than twenty paces back going into the tenth. At the start of the eleventh, though, I was no closer.

The time, as they say, had come.

At first there was only the sun, and the sound of my breathing and my footfalls on the sand. I couldn't possibly sprint for two whole laps. So I would sprint for as long as I could.

Then there was the sound of the crowd's roar building as I swung around the far turning post and bore down on Didymos, now no more than a dozen paces ahead. I was breathing hard on every stride now, and the death pain was starting in my chest.

Then it was Didymos rounding the near post, his eyes meeting mine as we flashed by each other in opposite directions. In his gaze there was a fierceness, but also, perhaps, just a trace of consternation.

But now the death pain was building with the roar of the crowd, and the sun seemed to shine with redoubled heat. I could not continue like this for another lap. I could not breathe. I could not see. I could not . . . *stop!*

An instant after that staggering realization, came a flash of annihilating comprehension, and with it the clear recollection of Polyaenus's words: "One day you will be running and in great pain . . ."

What he had prophesied was now, miraculously, coming to pass. My every fiber and sinew all at once felt smoothly aligned; and as my mind rejoiced, as he had said it would, the sensation of effort utterly ceased.

Now there was only light and wind and a spirit in flight across the sand, a spirit that bore down on Didymos, bore down and bore down and bore down. I was close; we were abreast; I was by him. And the din of the crowd was like 10,000 bees all buzzing inside my skull. His spirit broke as we rounded the far post, and before me lay only an empty stretch of sand and the promise of glory.

Now came exaltation for Lucius Verus Celer—a sense of fruition, of vindication, and of love. High above me the mighty Parnassus looked down and acknowledged my ascendancy. And the sun flashed fire from a sky of ecstatic blue.

Even after I won I could not stop. I could not even slow down, or so it seemed. And the crowd's uproarious ovation gave way before long to a pious silence. For they, too, could sense the presence of the god.

Aelius was waiting for me when I finished my lap of honor, his eyes filled with compassion for my joy. "Hail, victor!" he said softly as I fell to my knees at his feet and burst into tears.

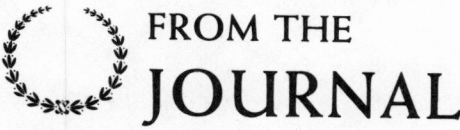
[OCTOBER 27TH]

Needless to say, I didn't get around to reading Nestor's letter until shortly after Portia and I awoke this morning, in each other's arms. Nor was I surprised to discover that Marcus had read it before retiring last night, the broken wax seal on the scroll plainly testifying to that effect.

Like most of Nestor's effusions, and indeed like Nestor himself, the letter is an odd amalgam of complacency, pomposity, and wisdom, in descending order of abundance. His concluding salutation, however, amounts to something of a revelation.

Tara, in the Kingdom of Meath
at the Court of the High King
On the twelfth (or thereabouts)
before the Kalends of November

My dear presenescent friends,

I am well established here in Hibernia, having been warmly received by the nobility and the people, who regard me as something of a phenomenon owing to my advanced age and itinerant disposition.

The Hibernians are a cheerful though somewhat disorganized lot, subdivided into "kingdoms" and tribes, the leaders of which profess a token allegiance to the High King, whose court is here, on top of the Hill of Tara. The High King (whose name must not be uttered, for some quasi-Judaic reason) is served by a priestly caste of Druids, who neither read nor write but who serve a twenty-year apprenticeship during which they are instructed in, and commit to memory, the entire liturgical canon of their creed. Some of them then go on to advise the High King on matters of State while others become bards and Druidic scholars, the most highly esteemed of all Hibernians (after his Highness himself).

Along with their disdain for literacy (an outgrowth of their not altogether fanciful belief that the meaning of words on parchment undergoes a process of degeneration over time) the people here evince an unquenchable curiosity about "the High King at Rome" and his far-flung "Southern Dominions." I've resisted the temptation thus far to refer them to you, my dear Marcus, but come spring, all being well, one or two of the Druids may join me on my return voyage to Ictis in the hopes of coming face to face with a real, live Roman.

I trust they won't find the experience too disillusioning.

But now I must close, for the sea captain who will shortly set sail for Ictis and Gaul—and who has most graciously agreed to carry this letter to you—is about to take leave of the High King's Court. In conclusion, therefore, I shall acquaint you with an old Hibernian saying that I think may have some relevance to the wider world we three have known. But let me say first, lest I forget, that I most earnestly hope that this finds both of you well, or at the very least healing.

*Until the spring, then, I remain
yours in eternal laughter,*

"Nestor"

Oh, yes; the old Hibernian saying I promised you.
Roughly translated, it is this: Things have never been better, and they're terrible.

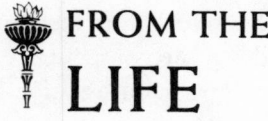
"What a perverse sort of fellow you are," said Marcus after jubilantly congratulating me on my victory. "No sooner do I bestow my family name upon you than you go out and so distinguish yourself as to have no further use for it."

And though I didn't fully understand what he meant at the time, it wasn't long before I was enlightened by events. For as a winner of the laurel crown I acquired a whole new degree of athletic and social legitimacy, in the Greek-speaking part of the Empire at least. And along with this newfound legitimacy I received not just the circlet of leaves that games as prestigious as the Pythian can get away with awarding, but also dozens of what might euphemistically be referred to as "inducements" to participate in other games on the calendar. A Pythian victor, it seemed, was in great demand as a competitor, and cities from Thrace to Alexandria thought nothing of including a meaningful bribe with the invitations to participate they showered on him.

Marcus's statement was, therefore, quite correct: I had no further need of his patronage. But I did not regard that fact as any great cause for celebration.

Nevertheless, I celebrated, and not just my one victory but Aelius's three (men's stade, diaulos, and pentathlon) and Herodes' two (four-horse and two-horse chariot). I celebrated so vigorously, in fact, that I can't recall being sober for more than two or three hours on any of the games' five days. I started drinking almost immediately after winning the dolichos and must confess to having been drunk even when, on receiving the laurel crown, I was granted the traditional victor's privilege of spending a few moments alone with Apollo in his temple. I remember standing there sodden and reading the sayings of the Seven Sages that had been chiseled on the base of the god's statue. For some reason "Nothing in excess" struck me as hilariously funny, and I feared I mightn't be able to stifle my impious giggles until the somber admonition to "Know thyself" struck home.

Needless to say, after five days of carousing I'd lost much of my competitive edge, a fact that quickly became apparent during the course of our stable's journey back to Athens. The first time it was my turn to do some running, I was able to cover no more than half a mile before feeling obliged to veer off the road and vomit out my insides. One consequence of this unedifying performance was that for the first time in our relationship Polyaenus became cross with me. And I myself felt sufficiently contrite—not to mention embarrassed—to promise him that I would never again so debauch myself after winning a race.

Neither Marcus nor I was destined to remain long in Athens once we got back, in my case because I had to depart soon for the late-summer games being staged by various cities (Ephesus not least among them) in Annia's father's province of Asia, and in Marcus's case because on his return he received a letter from Hadrian "suggesting" he spend the last month of his summer sojourn in Pannonia with the Emperor's adopted son and designated successor, who was serving as governor of that province. Since this gentleman was also my dear friend's prospective father-in-law, there was really no question but that the suggestion would have to be treated as a command.

Thus, on the Ides of August, Herodes gave a more than usually lavish dinner party in Marcus's honor, at the end of which he delivered a beautifully phrased speech exhorting him to "remember Hellas, and return before you grow old." As was often the case, Agricus, Hieronymous, and I found ourselves sharing the same couch, Herodes' majordomo being under the impression that the three of us, having traveled from Italy together, were bound to be fast friends. And we contrived to pass the evening quite enjoyably, with Agricus demonstrating once again that he could be remarkably good company when he put his mind to it, a fact that didn't surprise me so much as it made me feel more unequal to him than ever. Affable though he was being, the thought of him having Marcus all to himself for the next couple of months filled me with disquiet. I still believed that the day was coming when my patron would have to choose between us; and with Agricus acting so damnably amiable, what chance would I have against him, especially if I was a thousand miles away? It was possible, I conceded, that long years of hard experience had made me unduly wary of my nemesis. But it was no less likely, I felt certain, that my suspicions would be justified, to my sorrow, by events. What Marcus said to me after we shared a farewell embrace on the morning of his departure did nothing to allay my apprehensions. "Don't look so downcast, dear Lucio," was how he began. And his last words to me were, "It's not as though you really need me anymore."

I didn't argue with him, of course, but tried to console myself with the knowledge that our separation would be relatively brief. The Capitoline Games would be taking place in Rome in about two months, after all, so he and Dracena and Agricus and I could all look forward to being reunited at that time.

But, alas, though all of us could, by no means all of us did.

I was saved from feeling totally forlorn by Hieronymous, who decided it was time he paid a visit to his native city, Caesarea Palaestinae, which he hadn't seen since before the last Jewish revolt. With Polyaenus's permission, accordingly, he sailed with our stable to the site of our first Asian competition—the town of Perge, in Pamphilia. And it may well be that my trainer repented of his cordiality long before the voyage was over, because I clung to Hieronymous—or so it seems in retrospect—as the last fading link to my friendship with Marcus and almost totally ignored my *gymnastes* and brother athletes. None of them appeared to take my thoughtlessness amiss, however, and all warmly received me back into the fold when I returned, despondent, from the Pergaeans' port after Hieronymous, having found a ship bound for Judaea, had bid me farewell and sailed away.

Yet despite their friendliness and forbearance I felt lonelier than at any time since I set off from the Hobnail for Lorium. And my loneliness showed in my running. It was no easy thing, I discovered, to make contact with the god on a regular basis, though Didymos, to all appearances, managed to remain on reasonably intimate terms with him race after race. He trounced me at Perge and Heraclea, finished second to my third at Pergamum and Miletus, and pressed me hard at Sardes and Ephesus, though I managed to hold him off.

At Ephesus, of course, I had an added incentive to run well, given the possibility that the provincial Governor and his family might be in attendance. I scanned the crowd for some sign of Annia before, after, and even during the race, but in vain. To my great surprise and satisfaction, however, her father recognized me when I appeared before him to receive my victory wreath. As always he was most cordial and gracious; he even invited me to the palace for dinner. But we were leaving for Magnesia that very afternoon, so I had to decline. I would have accepted like a shot, even if we'd been leaving for Elysium, had he not advised me, in response to my halting inquiry after his family's health, that his wife and children had retreated to the country to escape the summer heat. With typical thickheadedness I came within a hair's breadth of asking him *where* precisely they had gone. But fortunately I caught myself, and asked instead that he be so kind as to convey to them my most sincere regards.

On the way to Magnesia I felt more heartsick and lonely than ever, as my love for Annia flared up anew. But, much as I mourned the fact, I knew she was irretrievably lost to me. So, with September nearly over, I blunted the pain of my thwarted affection by turning all my thoughts toward Rome.

[OCTOBER 31ST]

So much has happened these past few days. So much has changed—alas, not primarily for the better. Though Marcus appears to be out of danger now, he has had a serious setback, one that has left us all a little shaken.

I looked in on him the moment I finished reading Nestor's letter, not just to see how he was, but to find out from him if Nestor and Hieronymous were really one and the same. He was still sleeping—peacefully, to all appearances—so I had to swallow my impatience and wait till he awoke. But by midday he still wasn't stirring, and when I went in to check on him again I found him lying there with just his right eye open, the entire left side of his face looking calcified, and his mouth working soundlessly, like that of a half-dead fish. Keeping my voice as casual as possible, so as not to alarm Camilla, I called to Portia to come. She saw right away that Marcus had suffered some kind of stroke, and we agreed that I should go immediately to the Dumnonian village and notify his *singulares*. We also agreed that I should take Camilla with me and break the news to her on the way, which I did, presenting her with the least ominous interpretation of what had happened that still essentially comported with the facts. Inevitably, she asked me if Marcus was going to die; and I stooped to obfuscation to shield her from too much truth, replying that if the stroke had been bad enough to kill him, he would have passed away during the night. This half-truth seemed to reassure her that he was in no immediate danger of expiring. But it was clear to me that she was nevertheless distressed, poor mite, as well she might be—and as I still am.

Marcus had rallied a bit by the time we got back and had regained the power of speech sufficiently to inform the two *singulares* who'd accompanied us that the seizure he'd suffered was "a minor episode," from which he was making "a strong recovery." His entire left side was still paralyzed, however, and two or three of the *singulares* have turned up every morning and evening since that initial visit in order to be brought up to date on their revered former commander's condition. In general, I've been able to tell them, truthfully, that it is stable, but my demeanor is such that they must know I'm coloring the facts. Though he is holding his own for the most part, he is also much worse off than he was before the stroke. He has barely enough energy to sit up and take food, and his right hand and arm, which we believed were unaffected by the stroke, have become so weak and palsied that he has trouble using even a spoon. What's worse, he is now nearly blind, for his left eye, though its functioning appears unimpaired, has been rendered effectively useless by a paralysis of the muscles controlling the lid, while his right eye, though its lid functions normally, has so deteriorated over the years that he can't identify people's faces with it unless they're within three or four feet of his own. It lacerates me to watch him sometimes, for instance when the *singulares* come to pay a call. With his shaky right hand he will reach up to his left eye and lift the lid with his thumb. After he's seen who it is, he will thumb the lid down again and carry on as though nothing was wrong. In that one respect at least—his good humor and good courage—he has suffered no decline whatsoever. If anything, he seems even more cheerful now than he used to be; and when I made the mistake of asking him why, he said it was because he took his stroke as a sign that he hadn't "much farther to travel."

Of course he is no longer able to read by himself, so he spends many of his waking hours listening as Portia or I, or sometimes Camilla, reads to him. Fortunately, he brought even more scrolls here from Noricum than we did from Italy, so there's a wide range of authors for him to choose from. In general he still prefers the Greeks, though he never tires of hearing Horace's works recited and rather enjoys the contemporary Latin writers, such as Aulus Gellius and Apuleius, who take Greece as their setting and/or subject. Among the Hellenes, his favorites, apart from a predictable preference for Homer and the Stoics, are Hesiod, Plato, Heraclitus, Sappho, and Aesop.

On a somewhat less exalted level there is my own autobiography, the latest installments of which he's prevailed on me to read to him. He's been remarkably sparing of his comments, though, even when, as is more and more often the case of late, the narrative fairly cries out for an explanation of what was going on in his mind at the time in question. After reading him the most recent portion of my reminiscences yesterday evening I found myself provoked to the point of impatience by his reticence, and I had the temerity to raise the subject with him then and there. "I'm just waiting to hear your account of our final confrontation at the Capitoline Games before I say anything," he advised me blandly. "I believe it's the custom, after all, for the plaintiff to complete his arguments before the defendant undertakes to state his case."

I told him that it had never been my intention to write about him from an adversarial point of view. He said he understood that, but expected to stand indicted by my mere presentation of the facts.

Infirm though he is, he's lost none of his aptitude for paradox.

About Nestor, he's been considerably more forthcoming, and he readily confirmed that the old scoundrel is in fact our old friend from the Auriga Tavern. It seems that the two of them stayed in touch over the years, which I suppose is not so surprising, and that Marcus availed himself of his services from time to time, most particularly when he wanted something done unofficially, confidentially, and by someone who was in no way connected with the State. He had summoned him to his headquarters on the Danube right after I'd left to return to Rome, he said, and it was Nestor who helped him to perpetrate his fraudulent death. The two of them had calculated that, with all the pressing matters Commodus would have to deal with in connection with his assumption of power, it would be several months before he got around to persecuting such small fry as me. But when the new Emperor's summons to the Palatine was delivered to me a day or two after we encountered Nestor on the beach at Fregenae, it became clear that a little quick improvising was called for. Nestor, accordingly, planted in a few well-chosen ears the almost true rumor that I was writing Marcus's biography, and then hastened northward, back to the land of the Dumnonii, to make his report. Marcus by then was satisfied that the southwestern tip of Britannia would prove an acceptable place of refuge for all of us, and he dispatched Nestor back to Italy to assist in our escape. It was Nestor, in fact, who had suggested the Dumnonian domains to him while they were concerting plans for Marcus's "death", having actually visited them some twenty-five to thirty years before.

While Marcus was telling me this, I was asking myself how I could have spent so much time in such close association with Nestor these past few months without realizing who he really was. It seems strange to me that the passage of forty-five years should have so totally effaced all resemblance to the man I'd once known as Hieronymous. In retrospect, I can think of certain mannerisms and turns of phrase peculiar to Nestor that might have alerted me to his true identity. But as he himself is fond of saying, one cannot grow old if one keeps on changing. And I wouldn't be at all surprised if Hieronymous had kept on changing so relentlessly over the last four and a half decades as to preordain my failure to recognize him. Only with respect to laughter, it seems, has he proved immutable, assuming of course that his letter's concluding salutation can be taken to indicate a continued adherence to that idiosyncratic faith.

I wish he were here now to supplement my recollections with his own. I wish he were here so I could apologize to him for all the rudeness and mindless despondency I subjected him to. I wish he were here so I could thank him for everything he's done for us. And I wish he were here so I could tell him that, whatever names he goes by henceforth, I shall always think of him as a well-beloved and trusted friend.

In addition to all the things I want to say to him, I have one or two long-standing questions that I am impatient to have him answer. What the deuce, for example, had he been doing all alone on the beach at Fregenae on that morning in early July when I first encountered him? And what the devil had he meant by his assertion, at the time, that he was dying? Happily for me, he had touched on these matters when he reported to Marcus on his return here from Italy in August; and no sooner did I lament the fact that I would have to wait until spring to inquire about them than my frail old comrade provided some explanations.

Nestor's presence on the beach, he said, was a consequence of the fact that the ship he'd been on was attempting to reach the port of Ostia before nightfall and could not spare the time to call at Fregenae first to let him debark. So what the captain did instead, at Nestor's suggestion and expense, was have his crew fashion a raft out of half a dozen empty barrels and some canvas, load Nestor and his belongings on it, and run the ship as close inshore as possible, so that his passenger could paddle to the beach. This plan seemed like an excellent way to save Nestor a day's travel for about the same amount of money it would have cost him to go by land from Ostia to my farm. It proved less than economical in its execution, however, because Nestor neglected to pull the raft far enough out of the water to keep it from floating back out on the tide (with his clothing and personal effects still aboard) once he removed his tent and his seven carpets (which he'd gotten for practically nothing from a shifty-eyed publican in Massilia, who claimed he'd found them on the street). It was mere happy coincidence that Portia and I happened along the next morning, Marcus said. And Nestor's statement that he was dying was merely one of a number of ruses he'd developed over the years to discomfit such brigands as might regard an old man traveling alone as easy prey. By announcing that he is on the point of death he immediately raises the specter of disease or of madness in the mind of a potential predator, Marcus explained. And while the would-be robber is reassessing the situation, Nestor gains the time he needs to gauge the fellow's intentions and reach beneath his own robes for his dagger.

Hearing all this, I felt even greater admiration for the old fellow than I'd felt before. And Marcus agreed with me that if he is typical of those whose religion is laughter we should both undertake to convert.

Portia, too, was filled with admiration for him when I passed along Marcus's revelations, and she vowed to show him how grateful we are for all his efforts on our behalf when he returns from Hibernia. I said facetiously that I hoped she wouldn't show him *too* much gratitude, whereupon she laughed a little and began to kiss my chest.

What a change has come over *her* these past several days! And though I applaud it, I'm still somewhat troubled by the thought that it all seems to stem from the conversation she had with Marcus the morning I found her with him in his room. Ever since that day she's been a different woman—more cheerful, more self-confident, and infinitely more passionate. I wish I knew what it was that Marcus said to her. Or was it something *I* said that confirmed what she'd heard from him? I suppose that instead of just speculating about the matter I could ask her, or him, what transpired. But I'm loathe to run the risk involved in doing so. For once I ask the question, I'll be condemned to live with the answer.

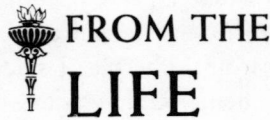
There was no letter from Marcus awaiting me when I returned to Athens at the end of September. Not that he'd promised to write to me. He hadn't. But I had sent letters to him: one with the First Centurion of Legion III Cyrenaica, whose path had crossed mine at Perge and who was on his way to Rome from Arabia to take charge of a Praetorian maniple, and the other with one of Annia's father's couriers who, under a warrant of the *cursus publicus,* was about to embark for Rome from Ephesus bearing dispatches from the Governor for the Emperor. Both letters should have reached Marcus quickly enough for him to get a reply to Athens by the time I got back from Byzantium. But then, one could never be sure about letters arriving where they'd been sent. So I proceeded, wishfully, on the assumption that either the centurion and the courier had been delayed on their way to Rome or else Marcus's putative reply had been delayed on its way to Athens. It was unthinkable that he had received my letters and simply neglected to answer them. Yet there were times when I entertained that very thought. He had said, after all, that I no longer really needed him. And that might reasonably be taken to mean that he no longer had much use for me. Of course I wouldn't have blamed him if he felt that way. But oh, how I prayed that he did not!

Polyaenus, my stablemates, and I sailed from Piraeus on the Nones of October and reached Brundisium after an uneventful four-day crossing. We then set off for Rome on the Via Traiana and made good time under dazzlingly clear autumn skies. At Beneventum we rejoined the Via Appia, and from that point on I kept tantalizing myself with the fantasy that Marcus, knowing full well from my letters when we'd be drawing near the City, had set off down the Queen of the Roads to meet us and was just around the next bend. We reached Rome without encountering him, however, and on our arrival went directly to the Synod of Hercules— the athletes' guild on the Esquiline—where we were allotted rooms and taken on a tour of the training grounds, baths, infirmary, and mess. Those of us who didn't already belong to the Roman chapter of the athletes' fraternity were assessed a whopping membership fee—fifty denarii for boys and a hundred for men—which was really not too exorbitant when you consider that, thanks in large part to a handsome Imperial subsidy, it entitled us to room, board, training facilities, baths, and medical attention whenever we came to Rome.

As a native of the Urbs, I was expected by my stablemates to lead them on a definitive tour of the City. But before we left the Synod's grounds I sent a slave to Marcus's house with a note saying that I'd arrived and was longing to see him. When we got back from our tour (which had *not* included a visit to Twopenny Street and my other boyhood haunts), the slave advised me that, having waited for a reply as I'd instructed, he'd been informed after a quarter hour or so that no reply would be forthcoming. Needless to say, this came as something of a shock. But still I clung to the fading hope that Marcus's apparent aloofness would turn out in the end to be the result of some sort of comedy of errors that he and I would have a good laugh about once we were finally reunited. Set against this hope was a growing sense that all my most terrible premonitions were about to be confirmed. And it didn't help matters any when, on consulting the competition schedule, I learned that the boys' foot races were to take place one year exactly from the day I discovered my aunt and my enemy in the cellar of the Hobnail engrossed in a carnal embrace.

But at least I wouldn't have to wait much longer to see Marcus. The date designated was not far off, and he'd been appointed honorary Prefect of the Games by the Emperor, who, though ailing, was still so enamored of things Greek that he was going to attend himself. If I won my race, therefore, I would receive my victor's crown from the hands of the icy-eyed Hadrian, who'd have Marcus in attendance close by.

The day dawned cool and cloudless, and by midmorning, when the Emperor's litter and retinue made their entrance, Domitian's Circus Agonalis in Campus Martius was flooded with October sunlight and thronged with over 20,000 spectators. Marcus, as expected, stood at his Princeps' right hand on the Imperial tribunal, and just to his right a few feet behind him stood Agricus, looking as sleek and self-satisfied as I'd ever seen him.

When the time came for me and the other runners who would contest the dolichos to appear before the tribunal and render a salute to our First Citizen I looked not at Hadrian but directly into Marcus's eyes. He returned my gaze impassively, letting me see that though he recognized me he was all but indifferent to my presence.

I discovered then that there is nothing more terrible than coldness in a pair of eyes that were once a source of warmth.

I felt numb as I made my final preparations for the race. What had happened? Had Agricus finally succeeded in turning him against me? Had I said something in one of my letters that had given offense? Or had he simply grown tired of my company and come to the conclusion during the course of our separation that he was well rid of me?

I didn't know. All I was sure of was that I had somehow proven unworthy of him, and been repudiated.

We lined up on the starting line, only eleven runners in all, because relatively few boys had good enough prospects of winning a Capitoline foot race to subject themselves to all the trouble and expense involved in journeying to Italy from the east. It was thus an elite field: Didymos, of course, his dream of seeing Rome having quickly come true; the Thracian Phobos, who'd beaten us both at Miletus; the Syrian Diodorus, who'd run brilliantly to victory at Pergamum; and the other seven runners, who, though they didn't specialize in the long race, had proven their speed by winning a fair number of the stade and diaulos events they'd contested.

For the first few laps I was barely in the race. Hobbled by despair, I plodded along at the back of the pack while Didymos, as was his custom, took the lead. It wasn't as much of a lead as he would have liked to take, though, because the field behind him was of too high caliber to let him get too far ahead. We all stayed pretty closely bunched, in consequence, so much so that even I, who was bringing up the rear, found myself less than a dozen paces behind Didymos with half the race already run.

On the seventh lap I finally looked up at the tribunal. The first six times I passed it I'd felt far too mortified to endure a second dose of Marcus's cold-eyed gaze. Now, curiosity or a vestige of hope impelled me to risk a glance in his direction. To my joy and amazement, I found him looking right at me, his involvement with my progress in the race far too blatant to be disguised.

That was all I needed to see.

He had *not* lost all interest in me. His apparent indifference was a function of something other than my unworthiness. What that something was I didn't know. Nor did I need to know. It was enough for me to be aware that it existed. And with the memory of how Annia, in a similar unguarded moment in the Theater of Marcellus, had revealed her true feelings with a look, I set out to overtake my ten opponents and win glory in my dearest friend's eyes.

I overtook eight of them with little difficulty, but Didymos and the Thracian, who were in the lead, saw me closing in on them and picked up their pace. We were well into the ninth lap by the time I caught up with them, and I was about to go to the outside to pass when Didymos for some reason landed wrong on his left foot and pitched sideways into the Thracian's path. In a futile effort to avoid him, the Thracian tried to stop himself while lurching to the right. I, in my turn, tried to stop and veer right, too, but as I began my maneuver the Syrian, who, unbeknownst to me, had been coming up on my outside shoulder, crashed into me from behind and got his legs entangled with my own.

All four of us went down hard, with our knees and elbows still pumping. I caught the back of someone's foot square in the mouth and the point of someone else's elbow flush on the nose. Though my head was on the ground for only a moment or two before I began to struggle to my feet, I remember seeing a little puddle of blood with fragments of broken teeth in it as I lifted myself off the sand. Once upright, I experienced a terrible dizziness and had to drop back down to my knees again or be sick. I noticed Diodorus writhing on the ground beside me as I sank down. Didymos and Phobos had started limping off in pursuit of the rest of the field. It occurred to me as I knelt there that, of the four of us, I seemed to be the only one whose legs, feet, and ankles had sustained no injury. All at once, I had my senses back, a renewed sense of purpose not least among them.

I got up, fought the dizziness, and began to run. Far ahead of me the seven boys who'd managed to avoid our pileup were already making their turn around the near post and commencing the tenth lap.

I would be needing the help of the god again, it seemed.

Spitting blood as I went, I picked up speed and soon overtook Didymos and Phobos. But as I rounded the near post ahead of them I saw that the rest of the field was now farther ahead of me than ever.

Naturally, I started to sprint.

I don't remember much about those last three laps except that the crowd, when it saw I was going to make an all-out effort to catch up, began to cheer me on, its roar of support for me swelling and swelling until I felt it was carrying me along, lifting me, and thrusting me forward at an ever-increasing speed. Only during the last lap did I realize that the words of encouragement they were shouting had reference to my status as a native-born son of the Urbs. *"Romanus! Romanus!"* was the cry. And at last it struck me that for the first time in my career I was competing before a crowd of my fellow Romans. I guess I'd come to think of Marcus as being more like my homeland than my native city; but the spectators' excitement was building to such a frenzy that it swept me along toward the finish line in a trance of exhaustion and pride.

I know I won but I have no memory of winning. I must have been somewhat out of my mind. I was nearly unconscious by the time the race was over and couldn't stand up without assistance for nearly a quarter of an hour afterward. I finally managed to make my way up to the tribunal, though, anticipating the love and approval I would see in Marcus's eyes. But he was no longer there. Having watched me run the race of my life, he had simply stood up and left. And as the Emperor awarded me my victory crown, it was my foe, not my friend, who witnessed the memorable event. But I think I could have borne Marcus's snub, and even what I believed to be Agricus's preferment, had it not been for the fact that in place of the malice and disdain I was expecting to see in my enemy's eyes, I saw there, instead, only pity.

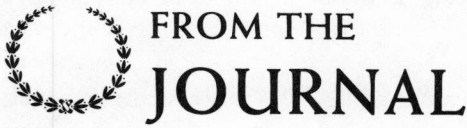 **FROM THE**
JOURNAL

[NOVEMBER 3D]

There was a silence in the room after I finished reading my account of the Capitoline dolichos. Then Marcus said, "You know, you really should take up running again. Nestor told me you used to run almost every morning while he was in residence on your farm."

"I'll consider it," I said tersely.

"That sounds so judicial, Lucio. I'd prefer you to say you'll think about it."

"Very well then. I'll think about it."

"Now you sound angry."

"I can't imagine why."

Responding to my sarcastic tone, Marcus thumbed open his left eye and subjected me to a moment's scrutiny. "You mustn't think," he said finally, thumbing his eyelid down again, "that my impromptu departure from Domitian's Stadium was occasioned merely by whimsy."

"I never have thought that," I answered him. "On the contrary, your action struck me right away as being thoroughly premeditated."

"I don't doubt it, my friend. But the premeditation involved wasn't at all as thorough as it should have been. You see, I hadn't anticipated that you might look up at me during the race. The gods alone know why I hadn't. In retrospect it seems like little less than a foregone conclusion. But at the time I thought that once you saw Agricus standing beside me on the tribunal and read the message of indifference in my eyes you would turn away from me forever. That little moment of recognition between us toward the middle of the race took me very much off my guard, in consequence, and nearly disrupted all my carefully premeditated plans."

"I hope you weren't unduly inconvenienced," I said in a less than genial tone.

Marcus noted my inflection and replied, "I wasn't, as a matter of fact, thanks to you."

"Thanks to *me?*"

"Yes. You see, I was at something of a loss after our eyes met, because our exchange of glances undid everything I'd managed to accomplish by not writing you, not receiving you, and not acknowledging you as a friend."

"How regrettable!"

"Yes," said Marcus with a forbearant smile. "But when you ran such a brilliant race after that terrible collision with the other runners, you saved the day for me. For by walking out on your victory ceremony I was able to repudiate our friendship far more dramatically than I'd been able to before. Whereas if you'd lost the race, I'd have been left with the consequences of that glance that passed between us, and all my efforts to push you away from me would have gone for naught."

"If only I'd known," I said.

"Not that the course of action I elected was without negative consequences of its own," Marcus continued, virtually ignoring my comment. "It was a serious breach of protocol, after all. The Emperor was extremely displeased with my behavior, and I don't think Annia ever fully forgave me."

I sat there, listening to this almost lighthearted account of the cruel rejection that had blighted much of my life and felt myself on the verge of ungovernable fury, and of tears. "What was my offense?" I managed, finally, to ask.

Marcus was quiet for several moments before replying.

"You were guilty of no offense, dear Lucio. You were as innocent of any wrongdoing as a newborn babe."

"Why did you repudiate me then?" I demanded, my voice breaking. "Because of Agricus?"

Again there was a long silence before Marcus spoke.

"You were meant to think it was because of Agricus," he said at last. "That's one of the reasons I made sure he was with me on the tribunal."

"But it wasn't because of Agricus in fact?"

"No."

"What was it because of then?"

"Can't you guess?"

"I haven't managed to up to this point."

"Well, if it wasn't because of you and it wasn't because of Agricus, who in the world is left who could have been the cause?"

"I don't want to play guessing games," I snapped at him. "Why don't you tell me straight out."

"Fair enough," Marcus sighed. "It was Annia."

I stared at him, incredulous. *"Annia?"*

"Yes, Annia."

"I don't understand."

"Well, you must admit, Lucio—I did see her first."

"But you were *engaged*," I protested, "to Ceionia."

"Yes. But I had just spent a month in Pannonia with Ceionia's father. And during the course of that month it became clear to me that the health of Hadrian's adoptive son and designated successor was even worse than that of Hadrian himself. In fact, the Emperor survived Ceionia's father by a good six months."

"So you had reason to believe your engagement to Ceionia would be canceled."

"I had reason to believe more than that, my friend. Because the most likely candidate to replace the heir apparent on his death was none other than my own maternal uncle, Annia's father!"

"Which meant that you and Annia were almost certain to be betrothed before long."

"Precisely. But it meant, also, that I could no longer be your friend."

"It didn't have to mean that," I objected. "I would never have gone within ten feet of Annia once you and she became engaged."

"Yes. But she might have gone within ten feet of *you*. And even if she wouldn't have, there was another serious problem that would have rendered our friendship untenable before long."

"What problem was that?" I asked.

For some time Marcus remained silent. Finally, he said, "I always loved her, Lucio, even as a little boy. I never fully understood why I loved her, but I most decidedly did. And unlike you, who'd been attracted to her initially because she bore a resemblance to your aunt Drusilla, I was never attracted to her for any other reason but that she was herself."

"But you never said anything," I wailed. "In fact, you led me to believe that you didn't care for her at all."

"That's true, Lucio," Marcus acknowledged in a sober tone. "But didn't it ever strike you as suspicious that every time the subject of you and Annia arose I would pull a long face, shake my head like a grieving grandparent, and mutter dire predictions of unutterable disaster?"

I thought back on all our conversations about Annia and, having reviewed them, was appalled to realize that Marcus was right.

"Are you telling me your predictions were false?" I forced myself to ask.

"Not entirely," Marcus replied. "But they were slanted, to make your relationship with Annia seem much more hopeless than it was."

"You mean that Annia and I could conceivably have had a chance together?"

"Not in the long run, Lucio. As Hieronymous pointed out, the two of you would not have worn well over the years. But in the short run, well, let's just say that liaisons such as yours had been 'regularized' from time to time in the not-too-distant past—with the help of friends in high places, of course."

I sat there, stunned to the point of tears by what Marcus was confessing. "So you deliberately misled me," I said.

"Yes," Marcus answered softly.

"Why didn't you tell me of your feelings for Annia? If you had, I swear, I would never have looked at her again."

"I know that, Lucio," said Marcus, smiling sadly. "But she was in love with you, you see. So I was ashamed."

"And what are you now?" I asked bitterly.

"Repentent," Marcus replied.

"Repentent!" I snorted. "I suppose you misled Annia, too."

"I let her believe that I wanted you all to myself." Marcus sighed. "That was unwise of me, of course. I was much too devious in those days."

"And you 'let' me believe that Agricus and I were in competition for your favor so that when the time came to drop me I would think it was because of him, and not Annia."

"I had to cover my tracks," Marcus admitted.

"And Agricus: what did you 'let' him believe?"

Marcus was silent a moment, then said, "I'm afraid the responsibility for Agricus's beliefs lies in good part with you."

"I don't follow you," I said.

"Well," Marcus began, "it's just that Agricus and I always understood each other perfectly. He was after a sinecure post in my service and made it clear to me that he was prepared to do absolutely anything to get it, even pretend that he was in competition with you for my friendship, which he never was."

"He wasn't?"

"Of course not. He wasn't even interested in my friendship. All he wanted from me was power and position. *Your* friendship was the only friendship he ever cared about. And you let *him* believe that, having met me, you had no further use for him."

"Ye gods!" I whispered to myself as the truth of Marcus's words struck home.

"But I was too devious, as I've said. Because Annia heard about what happened at the Capitoline Games and realized before long that she and I had never been in competition for you, but that you and I had been in competition for her. And it may please you to know that for the entire seven years of our engagement and the first eighteen months of our marriage she wouldn't let me touch her."

"What finally caused her to relent?" I asked.

And Marcus, with a wicked smile, responded, "Rut."

We sat in silence then as I tried to absorb the enormity of all I'd just been told. After a while, Marcus began to speak again, very softly, almost as if to himself. "But my deceit and my lack of scruple were punished, Lucio. Indeed, I punished them myself."

"How?" I inquired skeptically.

"By depriving myself of something I valued almost as highly as Annia's hand in marriage, something I'd come to rejoice in, depend on, and cherish."

"What was that?" I asked.

"Can't you guess?" Marcus responded.

"I told you; I don't want to play guessing games."

At this Marcus thumbed his left eye open again and looked at me long and hard. "You really don't know," he said in wonder, and, smiling, shook his head.

"No," I admitted, "I don't."

After looking at me a while longer, he thumbed his eye closed and told me. "It was your friendship, Lucio. But now I mean to win it back."

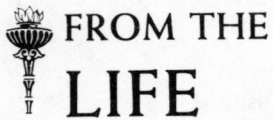
The collision I was involved in on the floor of Domitian's Stadium not only afforded me the opportunity to engage in some futile heroics, it also rendered me all but unrecognizable, thanks to a broken nose, a black eye, a swollen cheek, and badly cut lips. The dressings and salves Polyaenus had applied after the race added the finishing touches to my facial transformation, which I came to regard as no small blessing after Marcus bluntly demonstrated that our friendship was at an end. For once I realized that he'd turned his back on me and left the stadium, I wanted nothing so much as to run away and disappear myself. And since I was far too exhausted to do any serious running, I judged it providential that circumstances had so conspired as to provide me with an impenetrable disguise.

As soon as I decently could after the victory ceremony, therefore, I went off by myself to walk the streets of my native city and try to assimilate the calamitous repudiation I'd just suffered. As Marcus had intended, I was more than halfway convinced that Agricus was its cause, if not its author. Yet the utterly uncharacteristic expression of sympathy I'd seen on his face tended to belie such a conclusion. On the assumption, however, that Marcus, though prompted by Agricus, had gone a good deal farther in his rejection of me than Agricus had intended, my enemy's compassionate gaze was understandable. But it didn't change anything or negate his complicity in my humiliation. So I decided that I was as through with him as Marcus was through with me.

For a long while I wandered aimlessly, my mind oscillating between the pain I was feeling because of Marcus and the pain I'd felt as a child when, on returning to the Hobnail from the mud eaters' roost on the side of the Quirinal, I'd found my kitten gone and my aunt on the point of dismembering me. I guess it was the sense of hopelessness I felt back then, rather than just the pain, that corresponded to the way I was feeling that October afternoon. The day when Greffo hurled a stone at me and Aunt Drusilla slapped my face had marked the beginning of my . . . connection with Agricus. The day of my useless Capitoline triumph marked its end. So be it.

Tempus edax rerum.

As the afternoon waned I found myself walking through Trajan's Forum. There, all at once, I realized that my battered countenance afforded me a good prospect of safe passage through my old neighborhood. The very next instant I was on my way.

It felt strange indeed to stroll down Twopenny Street without being recognized by anyone I knew. And, emboldened by my apparently absolute anonymity, I nerved myself to walk into the Hobnail and order a bowl of wine from Glaubus, who served me with barely a look. He was unchanged, to all appearances, though rather less animated than I remembered him. The mostly familiar faces around the bar's interior seemed soddenly enervated as well, bereft of all the boisterous vitality I so vividly recollected. Or was it all the boisterous vitality with which I had so callowly invested them?

I was nearly finished with my wine when Drusilla came in from the kitchen with some food for a customer. She looked terrible—old, sallow, slatternly, and unclean. I could hardly believe that it was really my aunt. Yet there could be no doubt. Her eyes met mine as she made her way back to the kitchen, and for the briefest instant there was a flicker of recognition. Had I averted my gaze, I feel sure she would have known me. But I brazenly looked right back at her, and after a heartbeat or two an expression of sullen indifference appeared on her face as she turned away from me for the last time.

What had happened to her? What had happened to all of them?

Or was it what had happened to me?

When I lived at the Hobnail it had been an enchanted place inhabited by magical beings. Now it was a nondescript wineshop peopled with moribund slugs. I'd flattered myself in the months just past that I'd grown up quite a bit since quitting the haunts of my youth. Now I realized to my sorrow that my transition from dependence to autonomy had irretrievably diminished all the people on whom I'd once leaned for support, my erstwhile friend Marcus not least among them.

Feeling worn out and despondent, I left the Hobnail and made my way up to the rocky outcropping on the Quirinal, where I had foolishly kept faith with Agricus despite the threat of the mud eaters' stones. Here Fabia, at my enemy's prompting, had initiated me into the dark mysteries of a woman's body, and here he and I had presented two golden statues of

Friendship to our marveling fellow delinquents. The rocky ledge was empty now apart from a few tufts of dried-out grass, and I sat on its edge and looked down on the world that my emergence from boyhood had destroyed. All was the same, yet all had changed; the beholder's world had widened. There, far below me, what had once been my whole universe stood revealed as a backwater in time.

I sat there for hours as the October sun sank slowly westward. My thoughts were somber. My heart felt leaden in my chest. But all at once I felt a push against the small of my back, and for an instant thought that someone was trying to push me off the ledge. Turning sideways in alarm, I saw it was only a scruffy old cat, with one eye gone and most of the opposite ear. Again the unkempt creature rubbed against me, its orange coat matted and stained. And it was only when I heard the beast purring that I realized who it was.

Tears welled up in my eyes as I gathered my loyal old friend into my arms, and his purring rose in volume as of old. "It looks like you've seen some hard times too," I said to him, and held him close and wept as he thrummed blissfully away.

It was dark by the time I stopped weeping, and time for me to take my leave. "Farewell, my one faithful friend," I whispered to Romulus as I kissed the top of his head. Then I made my way down from the Quirinal's heights to embark on my life as a man in the lower regions.

As Marcus had foreseen, his fiancée's father died within a few months of my Capitoline triumph. Shortly thereafter, again as Marcus had anticipated, the Emperor adopted Annia's father as his successor, and Titus Aurelius in turn adopted Marcus and his fiancée's brother, to whom Annia was thereupon betrothed. When Hadrian died some five months later, though, that engagement was terminated, and it was Marcus who became the fiancé of the new Emperor's dark-eyed daughter.

When news of all these shifting alliances reached me in Athens roughly a year after my bitter victory in Rome, I innocently assumed that Marcus's engagement to Annia had been arranged for political and dynastic reasons. I even remember remarking to Polyaenus how ironic it was that the woman I loved had ended up betrothed to my one-time best friend despite the fact that neither of them cared much for the other!

Alas, my dear Polyaenus died of a fever the following winter, and from that point on I was very much on my own.

I enjoyed a moderately successful, though frequently lonely, career as a runner for the next eighteen years, traveling to just about every Roman province washed by the waters of Mare Nostrum. For companionship I sought out prostitutes, one of whom—whose sweet disposition belied her name, which was Xanthippe—kept house for me in the small villa I purchased on the western slopes of Mount Hymettus, a stone's throw from Athens' walls.

When, at the advanced age of thirty-four, I decided the time had come to retire from active competition, Aelius and I joined forces as trainers and soon had athletes winning prizes in almost every noncombat athletic event contested in the eastern Empire. In keeping with the best interests of our protégés, we made sure they competed in Italy as well as the Greek-speaking east.

Thus, after almost twenty years, I felt obliged to return to my home-land, shepherding my charges to the Augustalia in Naples and, of course, to the Capitolia in Rome. And no sooner did I arrive in the City than a slave arrived at the Synod of Hercules with a note from Agricus inviting me to dinner.

Marcus by then had been Consul twice and a father several times over, while Agricus, as his unofficial secretary without portfolio, had become an enormously powerful, although shadowy, factotum, who was spoken of in awed whispers by all those who did business on the Palatine. He had written me one or two letters every year since Marcus spurned me, not minding, to all appearances, that I never, even once, deigned to answer them. These letters were all languid, offhand affairs, with bits of news about Twopenny Street or morsels of political gossip of a somewhat more intimate variety than could be found in the *Acta Diurna*. There was never anything very personal in them, yet still they came. And so, when his invitation to dinner arrived, I accepted out of curiosity.

For the next six or seven years, until his death, we saw each other on a more or less annual basis. Our meals together were always very formal and correct. I would tell him about aspects of my life and he would reciprocate with aspects of his. Not once did he insult or demean or slight me in any way. He was the soul of good manners, and I never quite knew what to make of him.

He died less than a year after Annia's father so serenely passed away and Marcus became Emperor with Lucius Verus. Several months after his death I learned, to my amazement, that in his will he had left me a working farm near Fregenae and the not inconsiderable sum of 24,000 sesterces!

Had my professional life been less rewarding and my personal life less solitary I might have settled down as a gentleman farmer then and there. But it wasn't until several years after Agricus's death that I was introduced to the widowed daughter-in-law of the wealthy Neapolitan freedman in whose house my athletes and I were staying as guests during the Augustalia. I asked for her hand in marriage only five days after I met her and returned with her to Athens and my villa on Mount Hymettus (Xanthippe having died the previous year).

But Portia spoke little Greek and was homesick for Italy and her family. So I decided after a year or so to retire as a trainer and go back home myself.

We lived happily on our farm for the next decade and a half, with Portia bearing me first a son, named Decius after her father, and then a daughter, named Camilla after her mother. Life was as pleasant as it could be for a man of my melancholic disposition.

Then, in one of the series of letters he'd written me since becoming Emperor, Marcus requested me to tutor his son Commodus in athletics, a commission I decided not to refuse, even though it would oblige me to travel to the City and back every few days. But I certainly would have refused it had I known how idle, bad-tempered, and mean-spirited his son would prove to be, and it was with a feeling of great relief that I received the news, less than a month after Annia's death, that my tutelage was to be discontinued forthwith.

Apart from our correspondence, I had dealings with Marcus only one last time before his official demise. These dealings were the result of the visit two prominent senators paid to my farm less than a year ago, during which they urged me, as the Emperor's oldest friend—and one who knew Commodus well—to journey to the Danube and plead with Marcus not to abandon the adoptive principle honored by every one of his predecessors beginning with Nerva, in choosing who would succeed him. Commodus's well-known deficiencies of character did not go unmentioned in that connection, and since I found him every bit as unsavory as they did—and also because I wasn't about to let a good excuse to see Marcus again go to waste—I agreed to undertake the embassy they had proposed. When I presented myself to the Emperor in his camp, however, and stated the purpose of my visit, he advised me to mind my own business and peremptorily wished me a safe journey home. It had been the first time I'd seen him in almost forty-five years. But despite all the letters we had written back and forth since his accession, it was clear to me after the brief unfriendly audience I'd been granted that he in no way regretted having excluded me from his life.

[NOVEMBER 7TH]

I ran this morning, or hobbled, more precisely, covering two miles in a frosty fog without pulling any muscles or falling on my face. And I must admit that the experience wasn't far short of exhilarating. Running has been so central to my life, it seems, that my spirit wilts a little when I abstain. Of course in this instance I had reason to feel exhilarated even before I ran. For last night I finally summoned up the courage to ask Portia what had transpired between her and Marcus on that morning when I found them in an embrace. And the answer turned out to be not even remotely ominous. On the contrary.

He had merely told her that I blamed myself for Decius's death, she said. And when I asked her why she'd been crying she replied, "Because he had just explained how we could begin to heal the wound our son's death had inflicted."

"How can we?" I inquired.

With a sweetly lubricious smile Portia responded, "I think we may have already."

"What do you mean?" I asked her.

And her answer was: "He told me that the best remedy for our grief would be for us to have another child."

I pressed her right away to explain the reasons for her conjecture that she had already conceived. But the only response I got was: "It's just a feeling I have, Lucio. I can't give you any reasons for it." And almost before I knew it we were once again making love.

Now if only Marcus weren't becoming progressively weaker day by day, I would feel tolerably content with our lot here in Britannia. To be sure, the process of recollecting, and reliving, the cruel rejection I suffered at his hands has revived all the pain and rancor I had walled up inside my soul. But angry as I am at him, and have been all these years, I don't think I ever stopped loving him as a friend. On top of that, there's the fact that he has not only saved our lives, but undertaken to lift our spirits as well. Just being able to talk with him, no matter how painful the subject, is a pleasure I don't want to have to do without.

I returned from my "run" this morning to find him playing knucklebones with Camilla. Since he's too weak to sit up, let alone throw the tali, she makes his throws for him. And since it's too much effort for him to prop open his good eye on every throw, she calls out the names of all the four-bone combinations she rolls. Thus, when the two of them play together, it looks very much like Camilla is playing by herself. But that doesn't appear to detract one whit from the pleasure the two of them derive from the pastime. In fact, Camilla informs me that some of their games are very fiercely contested indeed.

When this morning's contests were over, Marcus slept, which is what he does almost all the time now. But he awoke toward evening and, after taking some food, asked me to sit with him for a little while so we could chat.

"You know, you mentioned that you never quite knew what to make of Agricus during the years just prior to his death," he said as our conversation turned to what I'd assumed was the final chapter of my autobiography. "Didn't it ever cross your mind that he loved you?"

"Agricus?" I responded.

"Yes. Agricus. You know, Lucio, sometimes your passion for self-hate badly obscures your view of other people. Did it *never* occur to you that you were the only person in the world he truly cared about and respected?"

"No," I replied straightforwardly. "I can't say that it ever did."

"Well, it should have."

"I don't see why. I never did anything to endear myself to him."

"Oh, no? What about that moment on the side of the Quirinal when you put your own life at risk rather than tell your fellow mud eaters what you knew about him?"

"Yes, there was that," I said after considering the matter. "But that's just about all there was."

"We could argue that point," said Marcus. "But even if you're right, even if that was the only thing you ever did for him, it was enough."

"Yes," I retorted. "He was so grateful he called me an idiot at his very first opportunity."

Marcus smiled at this. "Acts of great moral courage often seem idiotic to those who witness them, especially if they're among the beneficiaries. But the fact that Agricus regarded your behavior as less than intelligent is in no way incompatible with my contention that he was profoundly grateful. Look at the episode from his point of view. Because he'd panicked when he saw you hiding in the crevice next to his building, he'd falsely accused you of what amounted to a capital offense. When you were given the opportunity to take the noose from around your own neck and pull it tight around his, you kept silent instead, and kept faith. You not only declined to retaliate against him for a wrong he'd done you, in other words, but actually faced death in order to protect him. From the viewpoint of someone whose experience of life has led him to the conclusion that all human behavior can be accounted for in terms of selfishness, exploitation, or malice, your actions appear utterly incomprehensible. And after he thinks about them for a while, he realizes that his belief that the world is a place of unrelieved darkness must be radically revised. With one simple act of courage you forced him to reconsider all his most basic preconceptions. No one else, before or since, ever affected him so profoundly. Your actions not only saved his life but also changed it. So he was impressed with you, Lucio, very impressed indeed. And that's why he kept trying to repay you till the day he died."

"The way I see it," I said, "it wasn't until after his death that he did anything for me at all."

"That's because your perceptions are skewed," said Marcus. "May I point out to you just a few of the things he did for your benefit?"

"By all means."

"Thank you. Let's begin with the fact that he went back to that goldsmith's shop to get the statue of Friendship you left behind."

"I paid him for doing that," I announced defensively.

"Only after he'd done it," Marcus retorted. "He made you pay as an afterthought. And in your account of the episode I believe you wrote that you have never once doubted that the price he charged you was fair."

"That's true," I acknowledged. "But if he was out to repay me, as you're suggesting, then why did he charge me anything at all?"

"That's easy," said Marcus. "Because of your 'idiotic' behavior, you see, Agricus always felt that you had an advantage over him. He was grateful, but he didn't want you to know he was grateful. So he made it a practice either to charge you meaningless 'fees' for the services he rendered or else make it appear that they were merely a by-product of some other action he had taken just to please himself."

"As for instance?" I inquired.

"As for instance, your hillside tryst with Fabia," Marcus replied. "Could you ever have doubted that that entire scene had been staged for your benefit?"

"I never doubted it. But only because I never even considered the possibility."

"Well, you should have," said Marcus, "especially when Agricus, after putting Fabia in your way, so to speak, turned right around and renounced all interest in her."

"Yes," I said pensively. "There is something to that. But what he gave me in the form of Fabia he took away in the form of my aunt."

"Don't talk such drivel, Lucio. He and your aunt had a healthy animal appetite for one another; it wasn't his fault that you had some silly proprietary notions about her. And even though what went on between the two of them was none of your business, strictly speaking, he still had enough respect for your feelings—no matter how irrational he found them—to offer you the statue of Eurydice in exchange for ruffling your feathers."

"Soon you'll be telling me he was a better friend to me than you were," I said jokingly.

"I think that the facts as you now know them may well substantiate such a proposition," Marcus replied in a serious voice. "And it may even be the case that he was a better friend to you than you were to him."

"You can't be serious," I declared.

"Oh, no? I seem to recall that even after you'd been disgracefully rude to him in my mother's house he still made an effort to conclude a truce with you, despite the fact that he was the injured party."

"Yes," I admitted, "that's true."

"But you turned him down flat, if I remember right."

"Yes," I confessed, "I did."

"I will say in your favor," Marcus continued, his tone lightening, "that there were times when he disguised his good intentions so effectively as to mislead even me. When he intervened to save you from that 'gladiator' in Tarentum, for example, or the time he put oil in the starting grooves at Venusia. What he was doing on that latter occasion was avenging you. But he made it look like he was demeaning your victory in the dolichos, and even I was taken in."

"It seems I misjudged him all those years," I said.

"Yes, you did," Marcus replied. "But I don't think he ever took your antagonistic attitude too much to heart. In fact, the last thing I remember him saying to me, the night he died, was, 'Tell Lucio I knew he always liked me.' "

"He said *that*?" I asked incredulously.

"He did," Marcus affirmed.

"Perhaps that explains why he left me all that land and money in his will."

At this Marcus smiled slyly. "He left you all the money he had, dear

Lucio. As the years went by he came to understand that the exercise of power is far more satisfying then the accumulation of wealth, and though he had dozens of opportunities to enrich himself in my service, he refused ever to be bribed. The money he left you was all there was in his estate."

"What about the land?" I asked.

"I deeded that land to him a month or two before he died for the express purpose of conveying it to you. Didn't you ever wonder why Agricus, who had no use whatever for country life, should have died with a good-size farm in his estate? And didn't it ever strike you as odd that his farm happened to be directly adjacent to Lorium?"

"I guess I never gave those things much thought," I said. "But why didn't you just give me the farm yourself if you wanted me to have it?"

"Because it would have smacked too much of conscience money," Marcus responded, "and I doubted you would accept."

"Why did you want me to have it in the first place?"

Marcus propped open his good eye and looked at me. "Because it was time you returned home from exile," he said. "I wanted you back in Italy, near me."

There was silence for a while as I reviewed our conversation. I thought of all the unanswered letters Agricus had written me, and of the dinners we'd shared, and of his will. "So Agricus left me his entire estate," I said at last.

"Yes," Marcus replied. "And he performed one other signal service for you that I have yet to see mentioned in your autobiography."

"What service was that?"

"Why don't you write one final chapter about it. I'm sure you know what I'm referring to."

"No," I said uneasily, "I'm afraid I don't."

"You're afraid you *do*!" Marcus retorted. "So come now, do a dying old friend a favor and write the chapter you chose to leave out."

"*What* chapter?" I erupted. "I don't know what you're talking about."

"Just write it, Lucio," said Marcus, his tone unbending. "Write about the last time you and Agricus had dinner together, and write about what happened after dinner as well."

My heart sank when I heard him say that. And it is heavy now as I prepare to do as he has asked. It would seem that he knows about that night, and has known about it for over twenty years. I've never spoken or written of it myself, not even in this journal. Until today I would never have dared.

But now I must, so it seems.

And so, if I must, I will.

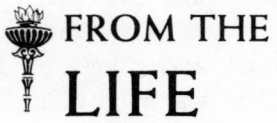
It was October of the year Annia's father died. Marcus had been Emperor for some six or seven months. I was in Rome for what proved to be my last Capitolia as a trainer. As usual, an invitation to join Agricus for dinner had arrived at the Synod of Hercules a few hours after I did, and as usual I told the slave who'd brought it that his master could expect me at the specified hour.

I sensed something was different the moment I entered Agricus's suite in the Tiberian Palace. For one thing, he didn't rise from his couch to greet me, as he had on previous occasions. And for another thing, he looked ghastly—gaunt, feverish, and emaciated.

"You look terrible," I commented by way of greeting.

And with a little bow of his head Agricus responded, "It's nice to see you again too." He gestured to the couch across from him and clapped his hands.

Even before I'd taken my place, two slaves appeared, bearing platters of ripe figs and roasted chestnuts. After setting the platters down in front of my couch, they mixed some wine for me and poured their master some water.

"You don't drink wine any more?" I asked once the slaves had left the room.

In lieu of a reply he tossed me a small pair of hinged wax tablets.

"What's this?" I asked.

"A communication from his Exalted Omnipotence, the Emperor Plenipotentiary."

"From Marcus?"

"We generally refer to him as Caesar in these precincts. I happened to mention to him that you'd be dining here this evening. So he seized the opportunity to transmit a few words from on high through me."

"Did he happen to mention what the few words were about?"

"No. But if you have any trouble comprehending his syntax after breaking the seal on those tablets, I'll be glad to help you parse out the syllables."

"Thanks very much," I responded with equivalent sarcasm as I broke the seal and read:

My dear Lucio,

Agricus has reminded me that I am now in a position to authorize certain of my friends to use my adoptive father's surname, "Aurelius," as well as my own, together with their personal praenomen and cognomen. Accordingly, you may style yourself henceforth "Lucius Aurelius Verus Celer." I know this is a matter of no great moment, but I wanted you to have it from me personally before the announcement appears in the Acta Diurna.

I have yours of the Ides last and will reply at length soon. Good luck with that Theban boy of yours in the Capitolia. People tell me that he's "faster than Celer at Delphi."

Did you ever in your wildest dreams imagine that your name would be incorporated into a popular epithet one day?

> *In haste, with all affection,*
> *Marcus*

I finished reading and looked up to find Agricus eying me with a certain condescending amusement. "He says I can use 'Aurelius' in my name now," I said.

"Ah."

"He says you reminded him to tell me."

"He's got me confused with his Secretary for Petitions," was my enemy's brusque reply.

There was a silence then as I sipped my wine and munched on some chestnuts.

"I understand he writes to you these days . . ." Agricus said eventually.

I responded with a noncommittal nod.

". . . and even receives replies," he added.

To my surprise I found myself feeling embarrassed, and stammered out, "Well . . . that is . . . it was our mutual understanding from the outset that we would write back and forth."

"I see," said Agricus with an eloquent absence of inflection in his voice.

"So!" I barked, shifting uncomfortably on my couch. "What news?"

Agricus's eyebrows rose. Then he shrugged and replied, "It's been a banner year for deaths since I saw you last."

"Oh?"

"Yes. My mother, for example."

"I'm sorry," I said automatically.

"Don't be. I wasn't."

"When did she die?"

"About six months ago. May, I think it was."

"Were you with her?"

"In body."

"What did she die of?"

"Lack of interest in living."

"Where was she when she died?"

"Why, here, of course, where she spent the last nineteen years of her life."

"Here? She lived here?"

"You sound surprised."

"Well, you said you weren't sorry when she died. Yet you brought her here to live with you on the Palatine."

"She was my mother, Lucio. I was responsible for her. But that doesn't mean I liked her. You, more than most people, should be able to understand that."

"Yes," I acknowledged, "I suppose I should. But if you really didn't like her, why did you bring her here where you'd have to deal with her every day?"

"I didn't have to deal with her every day. I hardly ever saw her, in fact."

"Why not?"

"I didn't care to."

"That must have been hard for her," I said.

"It was," said Agricus, and his smile was terrible to behold.

Slaves brought in a second course, roast flatfish cooked with lemon and herbs. It was delicious. Agricus barely tasted it.

"You mentioned deaths," I said finally. "Who died besides your mother?"

"The mother of our godlike First Citizen," Agricus replied.

"Domitia Lucilla?" I gasped.

"The very same."

"When did that happen?"

"A couple of months ago. Ye gods, Lucio, don't you get *any* news out there on the slopes of Mount Hymettus?"

"Not much, I'm happy to say. What did she die of? Not lack of interest, surely."

"A massive hemorrhage of some sort. It was very quick."

"The gods be thanked for that, at least."

"I'm sure they appreciate your gratitude. But I think you'll feel less grateful to them when I tell you who died just after she did, very quickly also, of a fall from a horse."

"Who?" I asked anxiously.

"Dracena," Agricus replied.

"Dracena!" I repeated in a stunned whisper.

"Yes," said Agricus.

"Of a fall from a horse?"

"Yes."

"But he was a superb horseman."

"Not at the age of sixty-two, he wasn't, nor with his horse at full gallop."

"But he died quickly, you say."

"Instantaneously—with his brains splattered all over the Via Flaminia."

"Ye gods!" I exclaimed.

"You mean they're no longer to be thanked?"

"No. Not as wholeheartedly anyway."

"They'll be crushed," Agricus smirked, as his slaves brought in the roast lamb and mixed vegetables.

Once again the food was delicious and once again Agricus all but ignored it.

"Any other demises to report?" I inquired as I finished off a spear of asparagus.

"Only one," Agricus responded.

"I'm glad we've finally reached the end of the list."

"So am I," said Agricus.

"Well, who is this final victim?"

"I am," Agricus responded coolly.

"You? What do you mean?"

"I'm not expected to live out the year."

"What? Why not?"

"Because I'm *dying*, Lucio. Can't you add two and two?"

"I'm sorry," I said in a voice full of contrition. "Truly I am."

"Your sympathies are appreciated."

"What's wrong? What are you suffering from?"

"Cancer. Of the bowel, poetically enough."

"I see," I said. "Are you in pain?"

"No; thanks to the dried gum of a certain kind of poppy plant that comes from east of the Indus."

"What's it called?"

"The elder Pliny called it *papaver somniferum*."

"How does it work?"

"Very effectively, thank you. Beyond that I don't know or care."

I reacted to this flip response with a moment or two of silence, and then said, "I'm glad you're not suffering."

And Agricus, after assessing me for a brief interval, responded, "You know, I believe you really are."

"So," I said, feeling somewhat embarrassed for no particular reason, "it's come down to a matter of months."

"Yes," Agricus acknowledged.

"Are you frightened?"

"Of what? Death?"

"Yes."

"It's only the end of my life, Lucio. I'm not frightened, just impatient."

"You look forward to dying?"

"I look forward to being dead."

"But *why*?"

At this Agricus favored me with a patronizing smile and ruefully shook his head. "Because I've never much enjoyed being alive."

"That's terrible," I objected.

"It's not uncommon, though," Agricus countered. Then, seeing the sorrow and the solicitude in my eyes, he said, "I've told you, Lucio; it's only my life that's ending. You really shouldn't take it so much to heart."

"It seems I can't help myself," I responded.

And Agricus, for the first and only time in his life, gave me a smile of unadulterated affection.

"You know, Lucio," he said, "I think you must be one of those demented creatures who believe, despite all the evidence to the contrary, that if we simply hold on long enough and don't lose heart, things will inevitably turn out all right."

"There are other dimensions besides the purely corporeal," I suggested.

"Not for a dead man, there aren't," was his retort.

And with that we both decided that any further discussion of our mortality would serve no useful purpose.

For the remainder of the evening the two of us reminisced—about Twopenny Street mostly, and our journey down the Appia with Marcus, and the summer we spent in Greece. Thinking back on those turbulent days of our youth, I found it difficult to remember the innumerable grudges I had for so long harbored against him. In retrospect, it seemed, we had been more like allies than enemies. And it saddened me to think that we had so often been at odds.

The night's second watch had already begun by the time we gave some thought to retiring. And given the lateness of the hour, Agricus pressed me to avail myself of one of his guest rooms rather than brave the maze of darkened streets between the Palatine and the Esquiline. I was tired, thus easily persuaded. Agricus conducted me to a spacious bedroom whose elegant furnishings included an enormous sleeping couch and whose wide south-facing windows framed an unobstructed view of the starry October sky. "I'll see you at breakfast" was the last thing he said to me after we bid each other good night. But when I got up the next morning he was nowhere to be found.

He died less than one month later. I had seen the last of him.

Tired though I was, I didn't feel much like sleeping after Agricus withdrew. So for the better part of an hour I sat by the window and contemplated the myriad pinpricks of light in the inky firmament. Having caught myself nodding off once or twice, I was about to make my way from the window to the couch when a soft knock on the door startled me into wakefulness. I assumed it was Agricus with an extra blanket or some such thing, or one of his slaves with some hot coals in a brazier. My assumption was incorrect.

Standing in front of me when I opened the door, looking even more beautiful than I remembered her, was the wife of the Emperor of Rome.

"Hello, Lucio," she said in a hushed excited voice.

And because I just stood and stared at her, she finally inquired, "May I come in?"

"Of course," I said, clumsily stepping aside. A delicious fragrance of jasmine and cinnamon filled my nostrils as she passed by.

Feeling both bewildered and aroused, I shut the door, bolted it, and turned to find Annia facing me only a few steps away, the light from the lamp near the sleeping couch reflected in the darkness of her eyes.

"You look fit," she said softly.

I replied, "You look . . . incomparable."

For a long time, we just gazed at each other.

"You haven't changed," she said finally, with the hint of a playful smile.

"You have," I said. "You've grown more beautiful."

She smiled outright. "It's one of the advantages of being the Augusta," she said. "One has the very finest hairdressers, cosmeticians, perfumers, and clothiers at one's command."

"But even they can't improve on perfection," I responded.

Still smiling, she slowly shook her head. "I'm a mother nine times over, Lucio. Perfection is the province of youth."

"Then you are still young," I said. And all at once we were in each other's arms.

"What are you *doing* here?" I asked when we paused for breath.

"What does it look like?" she responded with a salacious laugh.

"But why now? Why tonight?"

She looked deep into my eyes, and pretended to answer. "Because I swore twenty years ago by all that I believed in at the time that you and I would make love to each other at least once before we died."

"And this is the night?" I asked her.

"If you'll have me," she replied.

So we passed the next few hours in each other's arms, laughing sometimes and sometimes shedding tears. She told me that she never went to the Theater of Marcellus without suffering pangs of remembrance that seemed to grow ever sharper with the years. I said that I, too, would never forget the way our eyes had met that long-ago morning and revealed to each other the condition of our hearts. I said that I never saw anything new or inspiring in the course of my professional travels without thinking of her and wishing she were there beside me to share the moment. (And while that wasn't strictly true, the feeling that prompted it was genuine.) She asked me to tell her about my victory in the Capitoline dolichos, and when I finished, both of us wept, before losing ourselves again in each other's flesh.

"See what childbearing has done to me!" she wailed as we lay holding hands afterward.

And as I ran my eyes over her succulent curves I told her, "It has ripened you, dearest one, and burnished the luster of your beauty."

This response seemed to please her.

We made love again and talked some more, until the sky began to lighten. Neither one of us had yet made any reference to Marcus. But with our night together rapidly giving way to the dawn, I couldn't help asking her, "Did you come here to spend this time with me for reasons of vengeance or reasons of love?"

"I came here for reasons of vengeance," she answered without hesitation. "But I stayed for reasons of love."

And then, one last time, our bodies merged.

"We'll always have this to remember," she whispered to me as she nestled, fully clothed, in my arms by the door.

"Thanks to my so-called enemy," I said with a trace of remorse.

"And thanks to your so-called friend," Annia replied, her voice full of bitterness.

"I want more, so much more," I said.

"So do we all," she responded, unwittingly echoing what Marcus had said to me with regard to Drusilla as the two of us stood by the swimming bath at Lorium.

Then, after one last lingering kiss, she was gone.

I had seen the last of her as well.

[NOVEMBER 8TH]

I read Marcus the last chapter of my autobiography this morning, fearful of what his reaction would be. His first comment was equable in tone, however.

"That sounded like a remarkably faithful account of our beloved Annia's infidelity."

"But not entirely an unfamiliar one?" I suggested.

"No, my dear Lucio, not entirely."

"How long have you known about it?"

"Since the day after it happened."

"Who told you? Agricus?"

"Agricus!" Marcus snorted. "Why would Agricus have wanted to tell me? He was involved in the plot."

"Who, then?" I demanded.

"Why, Annia herself, of course."

"*Annia!*" I exclaimed. "Didn't she realize that telling you might be dangerous for all concerned?"

"You know how she was, Lucio. That kind of consideration seldom entered her mind. And besides, she had a pretty accurate idea after fifteen years of marriage of just how far she could push me."

"Why should she have wanted to tell you?"

"For the obvious reason—revenge."

"Revenge? For what?"

"For deceiving her, for repudiating you, for getting my way at her, and your, expense."

"She knew, then, why you repudiated me?"

"It became pretty clear when I asked her father to cancel my engagement to Ceionia so that I could marry her. I believe I mentioned how furious she was with me at the time."

"Why didn't she refuse to marry you?"

At this Marcus smiled indulgently and replied, "Because I was going to succeed her father as Emperor, Lucio."

"Oh," I said, my heart sinking a little. "So she told you about our night together the very next day."

"At her first opportunity, and in exquisite detail."

"That must have been hard for you."

"The fact that I more than halfway deserved it made it easier to bear."

"Then Annia wasn't being entirely truthful with me when she said she came for vengeance but stayed for love."

"It would have been more accurate if she'd put it the other way around," Marcus replied, with a wheezy laugh that threatened to develop into a coughing spasm. "You know," he resumed as the threat began to recede, "what I find most touching about you and Annia that night is the way the two of you lied to each other so convincingly."

"I only lied to her once, as far as I know," I protested.

"Oh? How about when you told her you wanted 'more, so much more'?"

"Well, that was in the nature of a mild exaggeration."

"Rubbish, Lucio. It was an arrant lie. Both of you were so desperate to recapture the feverish passion of your youth that your every caress was a falsehood. And I shudder to think what your night of bliss together would have been like if the two of you had been fools enough to tell each other the truth. There was Annia, after all, fast approaching forty and with nine full-term pregnancies under her belt, so to speak. What were you going to say to her as she lay beside you all pink and naked, with nearly four decades of wear and tear open to view? 'You're looking a little flabby this evening, my beloved'? Of course not. So you told her she had ripened to perfection, or some such extravagant rot. And she wasn't the least bit more honest with you. That business about the pangs of remembrance she experienced every time she entered the Theater of Marcellus—well, all I can tell you on the basis of my personal observation is that if she did suffer such pangs, she never once let them interfere with her enjoyment of a play. And you yourself were acute enough to notice how she evaded answering your questions about why she had chosen that particular visit of yours to Rome as the occasion for consummating a love you'd felt for each other since adolescence."

"Why did she choose that visit, then?" I asked, feeling more than a little aggrieved by Marcus's cynical dissection of an event that he, by his actions, had done as much as Annia to bring about.

"She waited until I was Emperor to cuckold me, Lucio. She bore that much of a grudge."

"You must have hated her for it," I said, wondering as I spoke how much he might hate me.

"It was my fate, dear comrade, to adore a woman who never stopped causing me irritation."

"But how did she get Agricus to act as her accomplice?" I asked, quickly changing the subject while I was ahead.

"That wasn't difficult. He was dying, for one thing, and, for another, he'd always felt that I'd treated you badly."

"Dying or not," I objected, not wishing to acknowledge the fact that my enemy had cared about me, "you could have made his last days pretty miserable for him if you'd been so inclined. Annia must have offered him *something* to make the risks he was running worth his while."

Marcus pondered a moment and then said, "Come to think of it, there was something she could have offered him."

"What?" I asked.

"The opportunity to bring you a little happiness."

I very nearly said, "Nonsense!" But I stopped myself when I realized how afraid I was that he might be right.

"And there was another question of yours that Annia never bothered to answer," Marcus went on, sounding an almost jaunty note as we continued to discuss my adultery with his wife.

"What question was that?"

"Why she chose that particular night?"

"It was my first night in Rome on that trip," I suggested.

"Plausible but incorrect," was Marcus's comment.

"Why did she choose that night then?"

"Because she calculated that she had the best chance of conceiving with you then."

I sat perfectly still, my heart pounding so violently that I felt my whole body reverberate with each beat. "Did she calculate correctly?" I finally managed to ask.

"Yes," Marcus replied.

"And she . . . ?"

"Yes," said Marcus. "She gave birth . . ."

I gaped at him.

". . . to twins, as a matter of fact."

"Ye gods!" I whispered.

"I hope it's not too late to offer you my congratulations."

"Were you . . ." I stammered. "That is, did you . . ."

"Did I consider doing away with them? Yes, I considered it. But if I'd tried, I would have had Annia to contend with. And given the friendship that you and I had once shared—and I had just recently revived—I doubt I could ever have brought myself to order that they be murdered."

"I'm dumbfounded," I said after a long silence.

"That's understandable," Marcus responded. "And I'm sure you'll understand when I say that this conversation has left me feeling a little tired."

"You'd like to rest for a while?" I asked.

"Yes," Marcus answered, his exhaustion all at once audible in his voice, "I'd like to rest."

So I left him and went for a long, long walk.

[NOVEMBER 9TH]

I returned from my walk yesterday afternoon with a number of questions about to burn holes in my skull, the most incendiary among them being almost too outlandish to ask. Any hopes I had of quickly subduing the firestorm of curiosity ignited by Marcus's most recent revelations were dashed, however, when I found him still asleep. He'd shown no signs of waking by the time Portia and I at last gave up and went to bed. But of course I was still so agitated that I couldn't even begin to emulate his somnolence. So Portia and I made love, and in the warm afterglow of our communion I finally managed to doze off.

We were awakened not long before first light by the sound of violent coughing, and having seized a lamp and rushed into Marcus's room, we found him struggling desperately to breathe, with blood spattered all over the front of his singlet. I was totally at a loss as to what to do, and stood there horrified as he wheezed and coughed up more blood. Portia was not as flustered. She hurried to Marcus's side and raised him to a sitting position. Within moments, as if by magic, his coughing began to subside. After a while, his breathing became less labored. But he looked ghastly— his face utterly white, his mouth hanging open, sweat running off his brow, and blood-flecked mucus trickling from one of his nostrils. After propping him up with some cushions, Portia turned to me, her eyes full of tears, and shook her head.

I took that to mean that my friend was dying.

Toward sunrise Marcus fell asleep, and Portia and I decided that, since he could die at any moment, it would be best if I stayed with him while she went with Camilla to notify the *singulares*. Our daughter, being a sound sleeper, mercifully enough, awoke when I kissed her good morning, unaware that anything was wrong. After she'd had her breakfast and rubbed all the sleep from her eyes, we broke the news. She took it well, apart from that same terrible expression of reproach and betrayal that I'd seen on her face when we told her about her brother. I know she doesn't blame us for Decius's death, or Marcus's dying, but there's something in

that look of hers that makes me feel I've failed her, that I've bungled the
task of seeing to it that all those she loves never die.

It must have been about midday when Marcus awoke. I was sitting by
his bed reading Martial's epigrams, of all things, and waiting for Portia
and Camilla to return when all at once he breathed my name.

"Yes, Marco," I said, taken by surprise. "I'm right here."

"That's more than I can say for myself," he quipped, and sat quiet again
for a while.

"What were you doing just now?" he asked me eventually.

"Reading Martial," I replied. "Though I can't think why."

"Because he's vulgar and full of life, Lucio. That's why."

"Yes," I said softly. "That must be it."

"Read me what you were reading."

"I'm afraid it's rather pertinent," I warned him.

"All the better," he said.

So I looked back down at the scroll and read: "Wealthy Paula wishes
to marry me/I don't want that old sow for a wife/But I may well decide
to propose to her/When she's nearer the end of her life."

Marcus wheezed at this, and nearly started coughing again. "I forgot,"
he said, "I mustn't laugh."

"What would Hieronymous say if he heard that?"

"He'd say I was guilty of blasphemy, and then punish me with a fatally
funny joke."

"No," I said. "I don't think so."

"Listen, Lucio," Marcus rasped, a note of urgency all at once audible
in his voice, "I can feel the life ebbing out of me—or out of my right
side, at any rate—and there are one or two points I want to clear up
with you before I embark on my . . . transition."

"Of course," I said.

"You see, until I saw you in my camp by the Danube last March I never
really understood the harm I'd done you. . . ."

"That's all in the past now, Marco. There's no need to . . ."

"I'm not apologizing, Lucio; I'm explaining."

"All right," I conceded. "Go on."

"I'd always told myself that it had been a simple matter of two men—
or two boys, if you like—wanting one woman that only one of them
could have. So of course I saw to it that the one who got her was me.
But when those two conniving senators with designs of their own on the
Principate sent you to me on that fool's errand, I realized it hadn't been
that simple at all."

He paused in an effort to catch his breath.

"You see, Lucio, you've always been a creature of your passions, and for that reason I guess I never took you as seriously as I should have. What have passions to do with running an Empire, after all? For most people, passions are little more than things that must be kept under control so that they can get on with the business of survival. But for people like you, the passions are everything. And when I saw you in my tent I realized at last that what I'd done to you was more catastrophic than death would have been for almost anyone else."

Again he paused for breath as I sat silent with my ever more turbulent passions churning away inside me.

"I fell ill after you left to return to Italy, Lucio. I may even have been falling ill when you saw me. And for several days my life hung in the balance. But as I lay there on my pallet, close to death, I had a flash of clarity. I understood why I'd been so ruthless in my quest for Annia, so much more ruthless than was necessary. To put it in Hieronymous's terms, Annia had been the one person in the world who made it possible for me to laugh. That was why I despaired after she died. And the moment I realized that, it came to me with a jolt that I had served the exact same purpose for you, just as you, parenthetically, had served the exact same purpose for Agricus.

"At that very instant, I understood what I had to do. I had to restore the laughter to your life so that I could laugh myself at the end of mine. And by a stroke of what I took to be the most supreme irony, I had at hand the means to do precisely that.

"So I sent for Hieronymous and set plans in motion for your escape, even though I knew that your escape, by itself, would do nothing to restore you to laughter, that it was merely a prerequisite, a terribly costly one, as it proved."

Marcus's breathing was shallow and labored by then, and I suggested he rest a while before completing his explanations. But he was bent on continuing.

"Ever since Nerva, Lucio, the Principate has passed by adoption. And I think Annia's father would have stood by me as his successor even if his own two boys hadn't predeceased him. But by the time it became clear that Commodus would be Annia's only surviving son, so many titles and honors had been heaped on him that to designate another to succeed me would have precipitated a civil war. You see, I *knew* Commodus was unfit to rule long before you journeyed to the Danube to tell me so. But there wasn't much that a fit ruler could accomplish in the face of the

Empire's inexorable decline, and a bad Emperor was far preferable to a war over the succession."

Marcus's voice was growing steadily weaker as he talked, but I willed him with all my might to finish his story.

"I imagine you understand me now, Lucio," he continued, "and have deduced why I was so short with you last March. But as I lay in my tent near death, I saw that my consistent refusal to do away with Commodus, despite his manifest deficiencies, had been motivated at least in part by my love for you. And I knew that I had to tell you that, so that you would understand. . . ."

"Understand what?" I asked in a tone of great urgency.

"That I didn't stop loving you when I expelled you from my life . . . that in my own way I kept faith."

"How, Marco? Tell me how?"

"By refusing to let the Oedipus tragedy be played out again by you and Commodus, and by letting the twin who lived succeed me."

Having said this, he sank back exhausted, while I sat beside him almost too stunned to think. I had remembered on my walk that in the course of his account of his Principate he'd told me that Commodus's twin brother had died. But until that moment I hadn't been able to admit to myself what that meant.

"I want your forgiveness, Lucio," he resumed in a fading voice, "in exchange for my own, for what it's worth. I wasn't much of a father to the children I had with Annia, but to the child she had with you I gave the world. Now, having never doubted your love for me, I ask you, do you still doubt mine for you?"

"No," I confessed in a quavery voice. "I no longer doubt it."

"Good," he said, and instantly fell asleep.

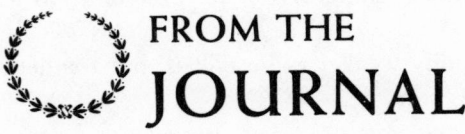
[NOVEMBER 11TH]

Surrounded by those who loved him, Marcus died about an hour after sunrise yesterday morning. Because his cubicle was far too small to accommodate all of us, two of the *singulares* had carried him, on his pallet, into our front room, and there, in front of the hearth, he passed his final hours.

He spoke only a few times after our last conversation. At some point during the night he said, "I feel so at peace, Lucio . . . so . . . complete."

Toward dawn, he asked me to raise the lid of his good eye so he could see everyone.

Finally, near the end, he said, "I tell you, Lucio, wholeness is as good as immortality . . . and a lot less protracted."

He was still smiling when he died.

Among his few effects was a small wooden chest. Inside it I found his signet ring, the scrolls containing his meditations, and a will witnessed by Hieronymous and the *singulares* leaving all the estate he'd brought with him from Noricum to me and requesting, first, that I build his pyre on a promontory overlooking the Western Ocean, and, second, that I leave his ashes "to be scattered by the winds."

There was one other item in the chest: a small tablet with his valedictory scratched into its waxy surface. He had called the poem "A Prayer for the Living," and beneath this title he had written:

> As we love
>   so do we transgress.
> As we transgress
>   so are we forgiven.
> As we forgive
>   so do we love.
> As we love
>   so are we redeemed.

Toward evening the *singulares'* wives and what appeared to be most of the Dumnonii from their village gathered in front of our house. They'd brought with them three cartloads of firewood for Marcus's pyre, and it was clear from their faces that they, too, were touched by the death of this man whom the Romans in their midst had so revered.

Holding Camilla around the waist with one hand and Boudicea's reins with the other, I rode at the head of the procession as we made our way through the twilight toward the sea. Beside me on another gentle mare rode Portia, and behind her came the phalanx of mounted *singulares* and the wagon bearing Marcus's remains. Behind the wagon were the carts bearing the wood for his pyre, and behind the carts marched the long line of solemn-faced Dumnonii.

The light was nearly gone by the time we reached the promontory, and it was dark when, with eyes averted, I ignited the fire.

What a glorious night it was—biting cold and crystal clear, with no wind, no moon, no clouds; only stars in bright splendor above the flames.

As the fire died down and the embers pulsed among the ashes, it came to me that something should be said.

And so, not forgetting the departed spirits of Annia and Agricus, I spoke the words that Marcus had left me about love and transgression and forgiveness and redemption, while my heart filled up with memories of the friend who'd been a father to me, and the son who'd been a friend.

And who knows but that my prayer was answered.

For there, far away to the west, two shooting stars traced a path of joyful fire across the night.

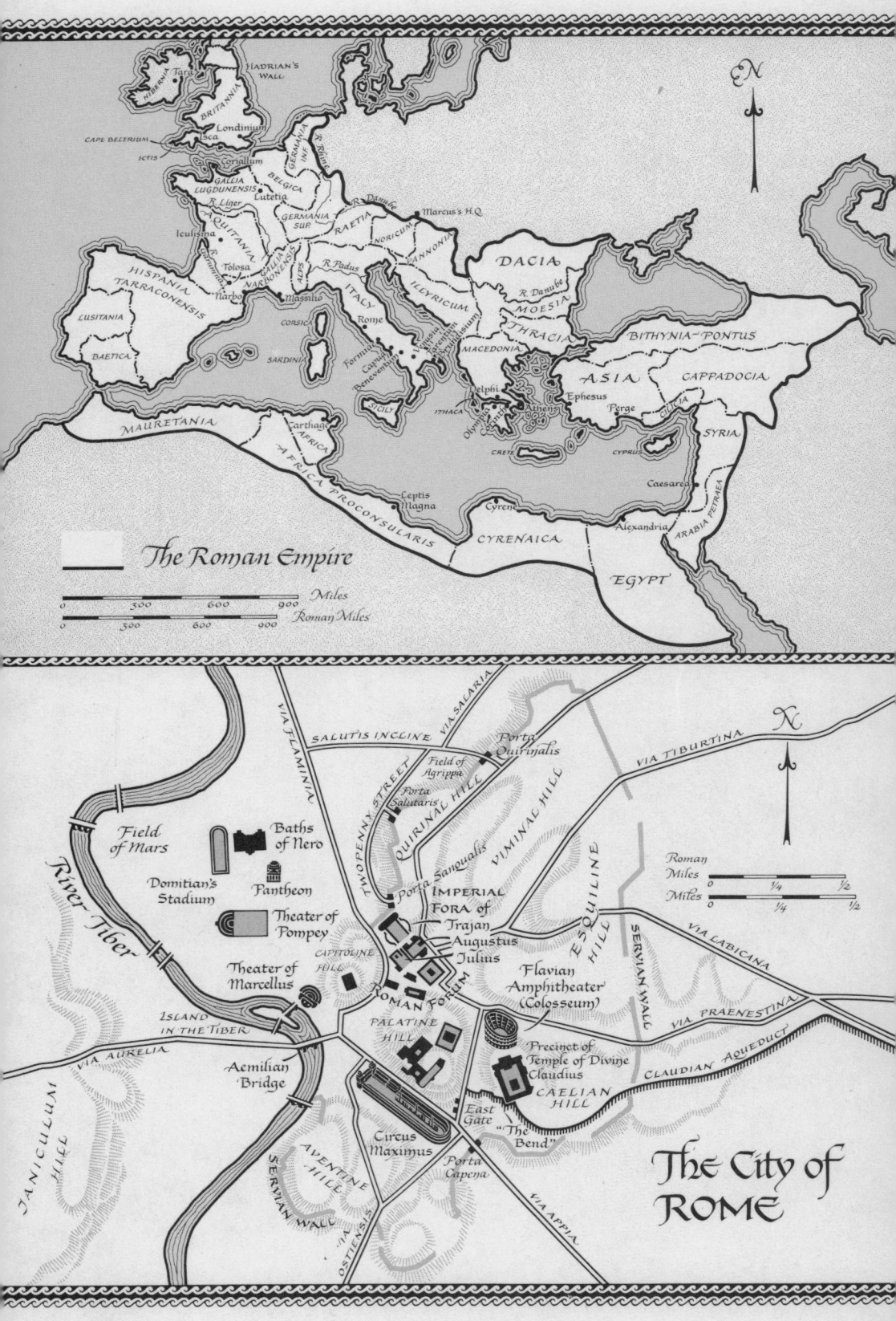

The Roman Empire

HADRIAN'S WALL
BRITANNIA
CAPE BELERIUM
HIBERNIA · Tara
Londinium · Isca
ICTIS
Coriallum
GALLIA LUGDUNENSIS
Lutetia
GERMANIA
BELGICA
GERMANIA SUP
R. RHINE
Danube
Marcus's H.Q
RAETIA
NORICUM
PANNONIA
DACIA
R Danube
AQUITANIA
Iculisma
Tolosa
R. Liger
ALPS
R. Padus
ILLYRICUM
MOESIA
THRACIA
HISPANIA TARRACONENSIS
GALLIA NARBONENSIS
Narbo
Massilia
ITALY
Rome
MACEDONIA
BITHYNIA – PONTUS
LUSITANIA
CORSICA
Delphi
Olympia
ITHACA
Athens
ASIA
CAPPADOCIA
Ephesus
Perge
CILICIA
SYRIA
BAETICA
SARDINIA
Formiae
Capua
Beneventum
SICILY
CRETE
CYPRUS
MAURETANIA
AFRICA
Carthage
AFRICA PROCONSULARIS
Leptis Magna
Cyrene
CYRENAICA
Caesarea
Alexandria
ARABIA PETRAEA
EGYPT

Miles
Roman Miles
0   300   600   900

The City of ROME

River Tiber
Field of Mars
Baths of Nero
VIA FLAMINIA
SALUTIS INCLINE
VIA SALARIA
Porta Quirinalis
VIA TIBURTINA
Field of Agrippa
Porta Salutaris
QUIRINAL HILL
VIMINAL HILL
Domitian's Stadium
Pantheon
TWO PENNY STREET
Porta Sangualis
VIMINAL HILL
ESQUILINE HILL
VIA LABICANA
Theater of Pompey
IMPERIAL FORA of
Trajan
Augustus
Julius
SERVIAN WALL
CAPITOLINE HILL
Theater of Marcellus
ROMAN FORUM
Flavian Amphitheater (Colosseum)
VIA PRAENESTINA
ISLAND IN THE TIBER
PALATINE HILL
Precinct of Temple of Divine Claudius
CLAUDIAN AQUEDUCT
VIA AURELIA
Aemilian Bridge
CAELIAN HILL
JANICULUM HILL
East Gate
"The Bend"
Circus Maximus
Porta Capena
AVENTINE HILL
SERVIAN WALL
VIA OSTIENSIS
VIA APPIA

Roman Miles
0   1/4   1/2
Miles
0   1/4   1/2